READER'S DIGEST CONDENSED BOOKS

READER'S DIGEST
CONDENSED BOOKS

Volume 4 • 1974

THE READER'S DIGEST ASSOCIATION

Pleasantville, New York

READER'S DIGEST CONDENSED BOOKS

Editor: John T. Beaudouin

Executive Editor: Joseph W. Hotchkiss

Managing Editor: Anthony Wethered

Senior Editors: Ann Berryman, Doris E. Dewey (Copy Desk), Noel Rae, Robert L. Reynolds, Jane Siepmann, Jean N. Willcox, John S. Zinsser, Jr.

Associate Editors: Istar H. Dole, Marcia Drennen, Barbara J. Morgan, Frances Travis, Patricia Nell Warren

Art Editor: William Gregory

Associate Art Editors: Marion Davis, Thomas Von Der Linn

Art Research: George Calas, Jr., Katherine Kelleher

Senior Copy Editors: Olive Farmer, Anna H. Warren

Associate Copy Editors: Jean E. Aptakin, Catherine T. Brown, Estelle T. Dashman, Alice Murtha

Assistant Copy Editors: Dorothy G. Flynn, Enid P. Leahy

Research Editor: Linn Carl

SPECIAL PROJECTS

Executive Editor: Stanley E. Chambers

Senior Editors: Marion C. Conger, Sherwood Harris, Herbert H. Lieberman

Associate Editors: Elizabeth Stille, John Walsh

Reader's Digest Condensed Books are published five times a year at Pleasantville, N.Y.

The original editions of the books in this volume are published and copyrighted as follows:

The Boy Who Invented the Bubble Gun, published at $6.95 by Delacorte Press
© 1974 by Paul Gallico and Mathemata Anstalt

The Good Shepherd, published at $7.95 by Doubleday & Company, Inc.
© 1974 by Thomas Fleming

The Property of a Gentleman, published at $7.95 by Doubleday & Company, Inc.
© 1974 by Catherine Gaskin Cornberg

His Majesty's U-Boat, published at $6.95 by G. P. Putnam's Sons
© 1973 by Douglas Reeman

© 1974 by The Reader's Digest Association, Inc.
Copyright © 1974 by The Reader's Digest Association (Canada) Ltd.

FIRST EDITION
100
All rights reserved, including the right to reproduce this book or parts thereof in any form. Library of Congress Catalog Card Number: 50-12721

Printed in the United States of America

CONTENTS

The Boy Who Invented the Bubble Gun

AN ODYSSEY OF INNOCENCE

A CONDENSATION OF THE BOOK BY Paul Gallico

ILLUSTRATED BY John McClelland

Red-haired, bespectacled nine-year-old Julian West believed what he read, that *anyone* could patent an invention. With courage, this stammering boy ran away from home and from a father who seemed always too busy to do anything but laugh at him. His father would care, perhaps even respect him, if he could just patent his invention and make his fortune.

So began a delirious adventure that reached from California to Washington, D.C., and catapulted the small boy into a deadly game between two great powers, across the path of an armed maniac and into the hearts of newfound friends who soon made his cause their own.

Paul Gallico, author of many books and screenplays, has written a new tale that is both suspenseful and heartwarming.

ONE

THE miracles of the moon walk had remained, in a sense, remote to Julian, as something taking place inside the big color television set and reflected on the glass screen. The visible, workable magic of the electric eye that operated the entrance doors to the San Diego Bus Terminal, however, was something so differently enthralling that it almost drove from Julian's head the enormity of the expedition which had brought him to the terminal at half past two in the morning.

A small carroty-haired boy peering through steel-rimmed spectacles, clad in jeans, Keds, a T-shirt and a leather jacket, he was carrying a cardboard suitcase containing two changes of underwear and socks, a clean shirt, pajamas, a toothbrush but no toothpaste, a hairbrush and, sealed in plastic containers or cellophane wrappings, the makings of tuna-fish sandwiches.

Aged nine and a half and a scientist himself, Julian was not unfamiliar with the principle of the electric eye, but the functioning of these doors coupled wonderfully the mixture of the practical and the dreamworld that animated him. For the doors turned him into a magician with powers over inert objects. He was enchanted the first time the portals swung open at his approach and he passed through in wonderment as they closed behind him. But then the scientific investigator came uppermost, and by edging forward and backward, he determined the exact spot to keep the doors open. However, the young and innocent scientist-wizard was not there to explore the mysteries of the electric eye. Instead he was bringing to life an imperative dream; he was on his way to Washington, D.C., to patent an invention, having stolen away from his sleeping household in a well-to-do section of San Diego with one hundred crisp bills in his pocket, his grandmother's birthday present to him. So he picked up his suitcase and trotted inside the terminal, whereby he was to influence the lives of a number of people there and cause repercussions affecting two powerful nations.

Julian had never before been inside a bus station and would have been terrified by the chaos of coming and going had he not been armored by the importance of his mission. He had been a tinkerer ever since he could remember. But now he had invented something. He had planned it, drawn it, machined some of the parts in the school shop, put them together and, except for one minor defect, it worked! His schoolmates had coveted it. And his father had laughed at him.

Julian thus moved into the midst of a world where the neon tube turned night into day. He went resolutely to the information booth, where a bored girl in uniform was manicuring her nails. Julian said, "I want to go to Washington, D.C., please."

The girl looked up from her manicuring. "Three ten from gate sixteen. It'll be announced. The ticket office will open in ten minutes." And she nodded in the direction of an unoccupied window.

Julian spotted a bench where he could keep the ticket window in view and sat down.

SAM WILKS was keeping a low profile off in a corner where he could watch the special policeman on duty in the terminal and keep an eye on the closed ticket window for the eastbound bus. He had not shaved or washed since he had fled from Carlsbad, near San Diego, two days before, after robbing and killing a gas-station attendant. His worn Levis, soiled shirt, leather jacket and ten-gallon hat were not likely to attract too much attention in that part of the country. Yet he had the kind of surly visage which led policemen almost automatically to stop him for interrogation. Once on the bus, with a certain two articles concealed about his person, he would be all right, but in the meantime he did not want to be jostled. He sat chewing a toothpick, his pale eyes never still, thinking hard about his plan.

Frank Marshall, with his square jaw, good brow, curly brown hair and clear blue eyes, looked like a movie actor or the all-American boy, except for the sardonic curl to his lips. He wore khaki trousers, a checked shirt and an army battle jacket from which all insignia had been removed.

The twist to Marshall's mouth was partially self-mockery; he looked upon the world with half-humorous derision. When he had returned from Vietnam fourteen months previously with some three thousand dollars in pay and crap-game winnings, he had thought it would be to pie in the sky, adulation and a job. Four months later he had removed the insignia which was to have proclaimed him a hero to his countrymen. He could not remove the scar that ran from his left wrist to above his elbow, but that did not show beneath his sleeve. As for jobs for veterans, that was a laugh. He had crisscrossed the West looking for any quick and easy money that was not criminal. His capital was depleted. He was twenty-five, too old to go back to school. Maybe he could get a break in the East. He knew a couple of fellows in Washington. He needed a stake.

With some time to kill, Marshall sauntered over to the newsstand and thumbed through the paperbacks. A man named Clyde Gresham was standing next to him, watching him furtively. Gresham was elegantly overdressed in a silk shirt, Givenchy tie, and a lightweight suit in matching pastels. He carried a panama hat in his beautifully manicured but pudgy hands.

When Marshall, fingering down an Agatha Christie from the rack, turned toward him, Gresham smiled warmly. "Going far?"

Marshall's cold eyes lingered on Gresham no longer than an instant before he turned, made his purchase and walked away.

THE hands of the clock moved so slowly that Julian wandered over to investigate a coin-operated machine next to the drugstore, one of those movable cranes in a glass case with various valuable prizes embedded in a morass of jelly beans. The deposit of a quarter activated the crane, which the player manipulated from without in hopes of latching on to a camera, radio or cigarette lighter. Julian had some change in his pocket. Twenty-five cents was a stiff tariff, but he coveted the camera.

He had his money in his fingers when his inquiring mechanical mind examined the affair more closely. Why all those jelly beans? Drag. Weight and surface against which the crane would have to pull. And all the prizes had either squared or rounded corners, nothing on which to get a solid grip. Julian put the coin back into his pocket and turned away, grinning at two high school students who were standing nearby, but they did not smile back. When he had gone the girl, whose name was Marge, whispered, "Oh, Bill, I'm frightened. Do you think he knew? I feel everybody is looking at us."

Bill, too, was nervous, about to explore the mystery which would make of him a man. But he said, "Don't be scared, Marge. He was only a kid." He fished a Woolworth's wedding ring from his pocket. "Here, put this on. Nobody'll think anything then." Marge did so gratefully.

They were not eloping, only slipping out of town. They liked one another, they were going together, and they had to do what all the other kids their age seemed to have done.

Marge was plain, but had a sweet expression, trusting eyes and a downfall of soft chestnut hair. She was sixteen. Bill, a year older, was tall, loosely put together, with the big hands and speed that had won him his position of wide end on the San Diego High football team. The coach was a square left over from the 1930s who preached that sex weakened your energies for the game. Elsewhere Bill was assailed by sex, sex, sex, and a certain shame that at his age he had not yet participated; also, opportunity had been a problem. The adventure upon which they were embarked was filled with excitement tempered by apprehension.

BACK on his bench Julian watched an olive-skinned, foreign-looking man whose name was Milo Balzare. He was carrying an extraordinarily shaped instrument case, which caused Julian to wonder what was inside.

Next his attention was attracted to the man sitting opposite him beside a fat, perspiring woman. A briefcase obviously belonging to the man was between them, and at this point Julian became witness to an international plot going awry. His participation in this fiasco would come later.

The man with the briefcase was Colonel John Sisson, an army ordnance officer temporarily attached to Military Intelligence in liaison with the CIA. Tall, his short hair graying, he was in civilian seersucker which could not conceal his commanding soldierly bearing. One knew he was "somebody."

The drama got under way with the loudspeaker bawling, "Attention, please. Will Colonel John Sisson please come to the dispatcher's office." At the repeat the colonel hurried off toward the terminal offices, apparently forgetting his briefcase.

And now the action speeded up. A man whose false papers identified him as Philip Barber, plywood salesman, arose, putting down the newspaper from behind which he had been watching the colonel. His real name was Nikolas Allon and he was a Russian spy connected with the KGB, a sleeper planted in the United States twelve years before for just this moment. He was small, with a toothbrush mustache, the type no one would look at twice. He was moving toward the vacated bench when the fat woman noticed the briefcase next to her, picked it up and hurried after the retreating colonel, calling, "Mister, hey mister, you forgot something." She was already ten feet away when Nikolas Allon arrived where the colonel had sat. To have walked off unobserved with the abandoned briefcase would have been one thing. To initiate an incident now by snatching it was unthinkable, in terms of the entire operation. Nikolas Allon just kept on going.

Julian saw the woman catch up with the colonel and thought, Haw! Grown-ups! If I ever forgot my school satchel like that . . . !

Puffing and panting, the woman caught the colonel by the sleeve and handed him his briefcase. He could do nothing but accept it with grace. She toddled off. The colonel, clutching his briefcase, turned away. Nobody saw the look of frustrated rage on his face or heard him grate to himself, "Damn busybody!"

The episode over, Julian reached into his pocket and pulled out an article torn from a popular science magazine and headlined ANYONE CAN PATENT AN INVENTION. Suddenly he became aware of a bustle and, looking up, saw that the ticket window was opening. Julian put away his article and got up.

WHEN JULIAN REACHED the window there was already a line. The two high school kids were at its head, and then came the colonel with his briefcase, the man with the toothbrush mustache and the dark foreigner with the strange instrument case. Julian got behind them and back of him were two men he'd not noticed before, then Frank Marshall and a dozen or so others.

The ticket seller asked Marge and Bill, "Where to?"

The phony wedding ring had given Marge confidence, but Bill, now faced with ultimate decision, lost his cool. He looked in panic at Marge, then gulped. "Two. El Paso. Round trip." The ticket seller stamped and handed out the tickets.

Colonel Sisson, next at the window, said, "Washington, one way, please." As he put his briefcase down to reach for his wallet, Allon, behind him, twitched, so close to giving way to his impulse that he broke into a cold sweat. He could have whipped up the case and been away in seconds, but that might have caused a hue and cry and that was not part of his assignment.

At the ticket window Allon had recovered sufficiently, once the colonel had departed, to say, "Washington, please. One way."

And then an incident occurred which did not surprise Julian, since he accepted grown-ups pushing kids about as a fact of life. Sam Wilks, the dirty-looking cowpuncher, suddenly appeared out of nowhere and thrust himself in front of Julian. The action irritated Frank Marshall, three passengers back. He stepped out of line, strolled forward, picked up Julian by the elbows and set him down in front of Wilks.

Bewildered, Julian looked up to see the young, tall, handsome man with bright blue eyes confronting the ugly-visaged cowboy. A veteran of television conditioning, Julian knew that here they were in real life, a goody and a baddy.

The goody had a smile on his face, behind which Julian was unable to read the hint of derision and challenge, but there was no mistaking the anger and truculence on the face of the baddy, though Julian had no inkling of how near the man was to a fatal explosion. Suddenly the special policeman appeared within corner-of-eye sight and the fury went out of the baddy's face.

"You're next, sonny." The goody winked at Julian.

The ticket seller, without looking up, intoned automatically, "Where to?"

"W-W-Washington, please. One way." Julian's stammer was another tribute to the overwhelming eminence and importance of his father, who, as sales manager of Dale Aircraft, president of the Rotary and co-owner of San Diego's pro football team, was always being interviewed and having his picture in the papers.

The ticket seller looked up and was startled to see no one there. Or so it seemed until he observed the top of Julian's head and half of his bespectacled eyes just over the counter. He said, "Half fare, fifty-three, seventy," whereupon Julian handed over three brand-new twenty-dollar bills. The ticket seller stamped the ticket and shoved it with the change onto the counter. Out of curiosity he inquired, "You all by yourself, sonny?"

Julian felt a cold surge of panic. Was this the end to the grand design? He managed to reply, "No, s-s-sir." He took his ticket and change and sauntered away. Satisfied, the ticket seller waited on Sam Wilks, impatient for a ticket to El Paso.

Marge and Bill were listening for the bus to be called when Marge asked, "Why did you say El Paso, Bill?"

"I had to say something. But we can get off anyplace." Then, after a moment's hesitation, "What did you tell your parents?"

"I said I was staying with Dottie. You?"

"I told mine I was going camping with Chuck."

All her doubts came back. "This isn't right, is it?"

Opposition was what Bill needed to bolster his own failing courage. He said, "Gosh, Marge, I thought we talked all that out. Today nobody really cares what you do. And it isn't like we just met."

Marge, relieved, whispered, "All right, Bill. If you say so."

The loudspeaker blared, "Bus three nine six for Tucson, El Paso, Dallas, Memphis, Nashville, Knoxville and Washington, D.C., immediate boarding, gate sixteen."

To the portals of gate sixteen went twenty-nine passengers, including those whose lives Julian was to alter.

The special policeman wandered over and stood casually by the gate. Sam Wilks, one hand tucked inside his jacket, was the first one through. The next few seconds would tell one way or the other. But the special merely glanced at him—obviously a cowpoke on the bum. Wilks passed through the gate and removed his hand from inside his coat. His description had not yet been broadcast. Once on the bus, he could still pull it off.

Allon had pushed to a position right behind the colonel. The colonel knew it and wondered how to accomplish his mission.

Marge and Bill played the honeymoon couple to perfection. Bill had his arm about her waist and Marge glanced shyly at her wedding ring. Frank Marshall went through with a jaunty swing of his shoulders. So long, California, hello, Washington. Here comes Marshall. Milo Balzare hugged his instrument case as though it were a baby.

Julian hung back. The special policeman and the gateman frightened him. At the back of his head was the worry that his mother might have gone into his room in the night to see whether he was all right, found him missing and given the alarm. His fears were unrealized. The big cop smiled at him, the gateman punched his ticket and said, "Watch your step. All aboard, please."

The bus was clean and shiny and smelled of plastic, metal and polish. Behind the driver was a well with eight seats, four on each side, with a view through the front windshield. These were already taken, as were the front seats three steps up, in the main body of the bus. The ill-smelling baddy was in one of them and a few seats behind was the man who had forgotten his briefcase. Farther back, absorbed in his paperback, the young man who had protected Julian's place in line was sitting on the aisle next to another passenger. But across from him there was an empty seat next to a well-dressed man by the window, and Julian asked politely if he might sit there.

Clyde Gresham examined Julian. "Why, sure, sonny, sit here by the window." He stepped into the aisle and stowed Julian's bag. "There, how's that?"

Julian replied, "G-g-great. Thanks."

Gresham smiled down at Julian with the warm fondness of one who seemed to like children, unaware that the man across the way had lowered his paperback and was giving him a look that was not exactly pleasant.

The driver was already at his wheel when a bus dispatcher appeared to make a last-minute passenger check. Was he being looked for? Alarmed, Julian slouched down in his seat, but the dispatcher's practiced eye had taken in the number of seats occupied, which tallied with the ticket count and he was satisfied. The only one who had noticed Julian's action was Frank Marshall, who wondered about it. But then he thought that nobody ever got hurt minding his own business and returned to his book.

The driver, working his lever, slid the doors shut. He picked up the microphone for communicating with the company headquarters. "Three nine six on time out of San Diego at three ten a.m."

In the dispatcher's office in Oklahoma City, where a constant check was kept on all their buses, an operator answered, "Take it away, Mike."

The bus driver picked up another microphone, the one for interior communication. "Okay, folks, we're off." He trod on his clutch, dropped into gear and moved his bus off into the night.

TWO

THE bus passed through the business district of San Diego and into the countryside lit by a waning moon which threw eerie patterns on the window through which Julian peered. Perhaps the most difficult part of his project had been realized. There was no way for his family to stop him now.

Thinking back about them he saw them, curiously, as actors in an old-fashioned silent film, moving jerkily and hysterically about in the wake of his defection. The recent spate of revivals of silent movies on television had become a cult among the young. Now the interplay of light and shade on the bus window turned it in Julian's mind into the picture tube onto which his movie flashed. The film began with Julian watching himself enter his father's study, where Aldrin West, in the striped trousers and cutaway coat worn by all important businessmen in the silent movies, was at his desk, speaking into two telephones at the same time. Julian was clutching the diagram of his invention, and he now filled the bus window with the first subtitle. *"Dad, can I speak to you?"*

Even at his desk his father loomed large and menacing. Aldrin West hung up the two receivers and glared. *"Well, what do you want?"*

Julian held out his diagram. *"Look, Dad, I have invented a bubble gun."*

Here Julian showed some technical knowledge of filmmaking for he now saw his father's face in close-up, looking angry and laughing sarcastically. *"Ha ha. What good is that?"*

Julian cut in on his own face, while the piano accompaniment hotted up. *"I'll make a million dollars with it."*

In the silents there was no mistaking emotions, so Julian's father clapped his brow, tore his hair and then, to a crashing of chords, arose and pointed dramatically to the door. *"Come back when you've got the million dollars and stop bothering me. I'm busy."*

Julian watched himself creep crestfallen from the room. He dissolved now to the title JULIAN'S BEDROOM—MORNING.

He listened with satisfaction to the music signifying excitement as his mother entered in her dressing gown and then, as she saw the bed unslept in and the note pinned to the pillow, registered anguish, fright and despair. Julian was not quite certain how to get the latter across so in addition to having her wave her arms about he used a subtitle, *Scream!*

As his pajamaed father rushed into the bedroom, his mother pointed to the note on the pillow, which Julian reproduced as best he could remember:

Dear Mom, Don't worry about me. I've gone to sell my invention. I will make a lot of money. Dad only laughed at me about it. I've taken the money Grandma gave me for my birthday.

Love, Julian.

P.S. Don't worry, I took some stuff for sandwishes.

His mother now pointed accusingly at his father. *"You've driven our child from his home."* She wrung her hands. *"What will happen to him? He will starve."*

His father pointed at the note. *"He said he took some stuff for sandwiches."*

His mother flung herself on the pillow. *"Julian, Julian. Oh, he's just a baby."*

At this juncture Julian took some liberties with his father's character. He went to his wife to comfort her. *"Don't worry, Mother. Our brave boy will be all right. How I have misjudged him!"* And as his father and mother fell sobbing into one another's arms Julian dissolved the scene to THE PATENT OFFICE, WASHINGTON.

He was standing there with several important-looking men in morning coats and top hats. One of them unrolled a large scroll decorated with seals and ribbons and reading *Patent for Bubble*

Gun Awarded to Julian West, and with a thrill he read his final sub-title, *"There you are, my boy. This will make you a fortune!"*

With a contented smile on his face, Julian leaned back and went to sleep.

THEY were driving dead east and the blinding yellow rays of the morning sun smote through the center of the bus and began to wake the passengers, who lifted their heads groggily in the stuffy atmosphere.

The bus was making time on a straight, uncluttered road when Julian awoke to a moment of overwhelming panic and loneliness. Why wasn't he in his bed in his room within reach of his ancient teddy bear, from which most of the stuffing had departed? Then he remembered and a little of his fright drained away. He was on his way to Washington to patent his invention, and show his father. To verify this he slapped the left pocket of his jacket, which returned a comforting crackle, and then he withdrew the paper, which he unfolded and studied lovingly.

There were two drawings. One was of the exterior, showing a compact, blunt-nosed automatic pistol, the kind sold in toy shops, which squirted a stream of water when the trigger was pulled. The other was of the internal mechanism, Julian's adaptation and invention, a gun that when the trigger was activated shot forth soap bubbles. All the parts had been numbered and labeled, and below appeared a careful account of its operation:

> Compressing the trigger, the soapy solution will be drawn to the bubble ring. The air bag will be compressed, releasing the air through the nozzle. This air will produce a bubble when going through the bubble-making ring.

In the lower right-hand corner was printed THE BUBBLE GUN, IN-VENTED BY JULIAN WEST, 137 EAST VIEW TERRACE, SAN DIEGO, CALI-FORNIA, APRIL 25, 1973.

He regarded it lovingly, remembering just how he had done this combining of a water pistol and his soap-bubble game. The latter had provided the ring that formed the soap bubbles at the muzzle. The tubing and rubber bulb of the air bag had come from the medicine chest at home. The compressor and plungers he had designed and manufactured in his school shop. He was still niggled by the bubble gun's occasional crankiness in operation, for instead of the one large bubble, a stream of smaller ones sometimes emerged, giving a machine-gun effect.

He thought back with delight to the day he had first shown it to his classmates and he heard again their impatient clamor.

"Hey, Julian, lemme shoot it."

"He said I could next."

"Can you make me one, Julian?"

When he had patented it millions of kids would want one. Then his father wouldn't laugh anymore.

"What have you got there, sonny?" The voice made Julian suddenly aware of the arid landscape whizzing by, the whine and rumble of the bus, and the passengers yawning, stretching, adjusting their clothing and chattering. He looked about and saw the grubby ten-gallon hat of the baddy where he sat up front; the short-cropped gray hair of the man who had forgotten his briefcase; the honeymoon couple not yet awake, their hands clasped and her head on his shoulder; the man with the strange instrument case, and all the rest of the passengers. Across the aisle the young man who had taken his part against the baddy still had his head thrown back in the sleeping position, but his eyes were open.

The question, of course, had come from the man next to Julian, who exuded a flowery fragrance like scented soap or toilet water. Julian's hand had dropped instinctively over his diagram so that no one could steal his invention before it was patented. But Gresham's dimpled face and pleasant smile boded no evil intentions. Julian replied, "My b-b-bubble gun," but he did not remove his hand.

Gresham said, "A bubble gun, eh? What does it do?"

Julian replied, "It shoots bubbles."

Gresham's smile grew even sweeter and he leaned closer. "You don't say. Did you draw that? What a clever little boy."

Julian studied the man again and saw no further cause to distrust him. Besides, the praise had pleased him. He said, "I'm g-g-going to Washington to p-p-patent it."

This extraordinary statement from the small, stammering boy across the aisle caused Frank Marshall to turn his head slightly to take in Julian and his scented companion, for the latter's flowery fragrance had reached Marshall and suddenly caused his hackles to rise. And what kind of a crazy deal was this, a kid going to Washington to patent a gun that shot bubbles? He sat up and sharpened his listening faculties.

Gresham asked, "What's your name, sonny?"

Julian returned the diagram to his jacket pocket. "Julian."

Gresham smiled indulgently. "And your last name?"

Julian did not reply, obeying the subconscious reflex of self-preservation. When his parents discovered he was gone they would call the police, and if Julian went around telling everybody his name they'd be able to find him.

His companion broke the silence. "My name is Clyde Gresham, but you can call me Clyde." Across the aisle Marshall shifted uneasily in response to the deep-seated instinct of an animal alerting to something repulsive in another. Gresham asked, "Where are your mommy and daddy?"

"Home. Back in San Diego."

"You mean you're going all the way to Washington by yourself?" Gresham asked.

Marshall looked across in time to see Julian nod.

Gresham succeeded in keeping the excitement out of his voice. "Well, now, it just happens I'm going a good part of the way. Would you like me to look after you?"

Julian saw nothing in the bland smile to intimidate him. What lay ahead was unfamiliar and being looked after might have its uses, particularly since this stranger would have no authority over him. He replied briefly, "Okay."

"Then we're friends," said Gresham, and he slid an arm around Julian's shoulder and squeezed it.

Julian reacted to this as he did to all adults who seemed unable to be in contact with children without patting them. He didn't like it and suffered it while planning to get away as quickly as possible. These thoughts led to an unconscious wriggle and Gresham removed his arm. Across from him Frank Marshall formed his hands into hard, tight fists.

Looking out the window Julian saw that the dun-colored lonely country had given way to a few green fields, some outlying barns, and then clapboard houses and adobe dwellings indicating the outskirts of a town. The driver's voice came over the loudspeaker.

"Folks, we're coming into Yuma, Arizona. Thirty-minute stop for breakfast."

The houses increased in number and soon the highway became the main street. Gresham slid his arm about Julian's shoulder again, saying, "We'll have a washup and breakfast together."

Although he knew it was none of his business Frank Marshall's anger was so intense that he got up and walked to the door as the bus halted at the station.

"This is Yuma." Bill looked questioningly at Marge. "Here?"

Marge had awakened with all the trust of a sleepy-eyed child. Her face had been burrowed in the boy's shoulder and his comforting arm had been about her, but now sitting up suddenly in the midst of a town and being asked again for a decision, she felt the panic that had beset her ever since leaving home. She searched for an excuse. "Someone might know us. Myra, a girl friend of mine, has an aunt in Yuma," and then it was her turn to inquire, "Are you sure you love me, Bill?"

The glib answer refused to come to the boy's lips. What *was* love? Was it thinking about Marge when he ought to be doing his homework, remembering the texture of her hair, her fingers on his hand, the feel and smell of her clothes? He was content when he was near her, but how could you tell whether that was love? If you said you loved someone, and didn't, that was unfair.

He looked at Marge again and there was something in the slightly pathetic curve of her lips, in the line of the young neck, that was moving. If one looked too long, tears could be dangerously close; unmanly tears. "I dunno, Marge. I guess I do because when I look at you I want to bust."

This satisfied her, for she snuggled closer to him. But Bill's own insecurity led him to say, "If Myra's aunt lives here, she might be around. We could have some breakfast and then go on to Tucson. Nobody knows us there."

The bus station at Yuma was classic, mingling diesel fumes with the aroma of frying eggs and bacon. There was a lunch counter on one side, a newsstand on the other, a few benches and, at the far end, lavatories. There was also a small Navajo trading post with blankets, baskets and turquoise jewelry.

Gresham, his arm still around Julian's shoulder, glanced about

23

him as they entered the waiting room. "Smell that bacon. I'll bet they've got pancakes too. Would you like some?"

Julian said, "Uh-huh, but I've got to . . ." Two of the passengers emerged from the door marked MEN.

"Sure," Gresham said, "we'll do that first," and they moved off toward the lavatories.

Frank Marshall now stepped out from behind the corner of the newsstand where he had been waiting and blocked their path. In a bland conversational tone he said to Gresham, "Take your arm off that kid."

Gresham's shock was total. The amazingly blue eyes of the young man who had ignored him so pointedly in San Diego seemed to take all of him in and at the same time not to see him at all. He loosed his grip upon Julian and huffed, "Who do you think you are? I'm looking after this little fellow."

Marshall said, "Get lost."

Julian moved a little away and gazed with curiosity from one face to the other. He watched Clyde's round, smooth cheeks collapsing, his lips trembling like a baby's. This was the second time that the man he had labeled as the goody had intervened in what was happening to him. It had seemed that Gresham had only been trying to be nice. True, he had been a bit icky, but then a lot of grown people were. What was it all about?

The two faces were close together, one smiling easily and the other suddenly disintegrating before Julian's eyes. The boy himself felt discomfort mingled with relief.

Gresham made a last attempt. "You can't . . ."

This time Marshall made no reply whatsoever. He simply stepped onto Gresham's foot, hard, and kept up the pressure as Gresham grimaced with pain.

Marshall said sweetly, "Sorry, dearie," and then allowed a grating note into his speech. "You're off the bus, too. If I see you again, you could really get hurt bad."

Julian felt a little frightened. What a strange way to fight. Violence on TV was fun, but so close by, it gave one a sickish feeling.

Gresham knew he was finished. He pleaded, "Listen, I've got to get to Memphis."

"There'll be another bus along. This is where we part company." Marshall removed the pressure from Gresham's foot and stood to one side. "Now get going," and without another word Gresham hurried out the exit.

Whatever it was, it was over, and Julian was no longer frightened. If he felt a moment of pity for the stranger who had been destroyed before him, it evaporated into admiration for the man who had accomplished it with such ease. He asked, "What happened? Was something wrong?"

Marshall said, "Never mind. If you got to go in there," and he nodded in the direction of the men's room, "get on with it."

Julian went in and Marshall waited for him, berating himself as he did so. "Marshall, why can't you learn to mind your own business? You could get stuck with the kid."

When Julian emerged from the men's room Marshall sauntered off. He did not turn around to see whether the boy was following him, for that was the surest way to make any stray come after you. Julian stood there watching him go, neither hurt nor puzzled. Children are not apt to linger over the curious behavior of adults.

He went over to the lunch counter and found a seat next to the dark-haired man with the instrument case, consulted the menu and ordered pancakes with little pork sausages. When they appeared he doused them with syrup and noticed that his neighbor had nothing before him, but was sitting there unhappily hugging the case. Julian asked, "What's your name?"

"Milo Balzare. You?"

"Julian. What have you got in there?"

"It is very ancient instrument. Am coming here to America to learn your popping music." He looked hungrily at Julian's plate. "How you say that, please? I like."

Julian told him, "Pancakes and sausages," and signaled the counterman. Balzare asked for the same.

The counterman yelled through the kitchen hatch, "Toss one. Porkers with."

The order appeared. The musician regarded the man and boy in amazement. "Is so difficult language. How you say—coffee?"

The counterman shouted through the hatch, "Draw one," and a cup of coffee was served. Julian laughed. He was having fun.

Far down the counter Marshall was drinking coffee and looking straight ahead. Julian thought that if Marshall glanced over, he might wave to him, but Marshall didn't.

THREE

BOARDING the bus after the break in Yuma, Colonel Sisson managed to stumble, drop his briefcase and spill the contents all over the aisle. Any film director watching this scene would have called for a retake, but the passengers behind him only casually glanced at the papers, mainly diagrams and blueprints. In obvious embarrassment the colonel attempted to cover up the nature of these papers as he scrabbled them up off the floor.

While they waited Marshall said to the driver, "The little fat guy who was going to Memphis ain't comin'. He changed his mind."

The bus driver shook his head in disgust. "He might have said something before. Passengers!" He picked up his shortwave microphone. "Three nine six on time out of Yuma."

When the aisle had cleared and the passengers settled, Julian found that his strange friend had moved across and preempted his window seat. But he didn't resent losing his view. Children were to be pushed around. He asked politely, "Can I sit next to you?"

Marshall only then realized that he had taken the boy's seat, felt guilty and replied, "Sure."

Julian slid down into the seat. Marshall looked out the window as the bus hit the highway again. Julian waited until Marshall got bored with the scenery and turned for his book. Then he asked, "What's your name?"

Well, he thought, I asked for it. "Frank Marshall," he said.

He looked down to find his place in his book when Julian said, "Mr. Marshall?"

The man gave up. He would have to cope with the kid. He said, "Just Marshall will do."

Julian then asked, "Why did you make that man go away?"

Marshall was aware that kids were a lot smarter than they used to be, but he had the feeling that this boy had a peculiar kind of innocence and trust. He therefore produced that completely phony voice used by adults when they are telling a thumping lie to the young. "Well, you see, kid, I recognized him as a—pickpocket."

Julian produced the folded bubble-gun diagram from his jacket and said with satisfaction, "He didn't get my invention. After I p-p-patent it I'm g-g-going to make a lot of m-m-money with it."

The word "money" startled Marshall and a slight change of expression came over his countenance. "Let's have a look."

Julian said, "I g-g-got to work on it some more."

Marshall said carelessly, "Okay, so don't," which produced an immediate unfolding of the diagram. He studied it, noting Julian's name and address, and then asked, "What's wrong with it?"

Julian replied, "Sometimes when you pull the trigger it shoots a lot of little b-b-bubbles instead of a b-b-big one."

"Why don't you ask the guy up front to help you, the one who spilled his papers? I had a look at 'em. That was ordnance."

"What's ordnance?"

"Guns and stuff. He's probably army in civvies." He studied Julian for a moment. "Do your folks know where you are?"

"No. But I left a note saying I was g-g-going."

Marshall's curiosity was past mild interest. "It doesn't make sense. What's the plot, kid? Come on, give."

"My d-d-dad thinks I'm a sissy and no g-g-good. When I showed him my invention and said I was going to m-m-make a million dollars he laughed and told me to come b-b-back after I had made it. That's why I'm g-g-going to Washington."

A million dollars had a sweet ring in Marshall's ears, but of course it was crazy. A kid going to Washington because his father had laughed at him. Marshall looked at the diagram more intently and then again at Julian. He said, "Well, your pop's probably having a fit right now. Did you say in your note where you were going?"

Julian said, "No. Anyway, he wouldn't care."

Marshall sat back for a moment and wondered just how true this was.

But, of course, Aldrin West did care, his concern intensified by a feeling of guilt and his wife's hysteria at the thought of her "baby" somewhere loose in the United States. She'd needed a doctor and sedation.

The repercussions of all this soon reached into a corner of the Missing Persons Bureau of the San Diego Police Department, where a bored sergeant in shirt sleeves took West's call. He repeated as he wrote, "Julian West, age nine and a half, red hair, wears glasses, has slight stammer . . . Didn't say where he was going." He listened. "Okay, Mr. West, that shouldn't be too difficult. We'll put it out on the radio and let you know as soon as we hear anything."

A short while later the police teleprinter was tapping out the alarm: MISSING FROM HOME, JULIAN WEST, AGE NINETEEN AND A HALF, RED HAIR, GLASSES, STAMMER. THOUGHT TO BE WEARING DENIMS AND T-SHIRT WITH LEATHER JACKET. ANYONE SEEING PLEASE CONTACT LOCAL POLICE.

BY MIDMORNING Bus 396 had metamorphosed from a transcontinental transporter to a cozy social center. Two men, chess fiends, had discovered one another and were engrossed in battle on a pocket set. Four other strangers were playing gin rummy. There was so much going on that any fears Julian might have had at being by himself vanished.

Three seats to the rear of him the dark-haired musician, Milo Balzare, withdrew an odd-looking instrument from its case and began to tune it. Julian went over to have a look. "What's that?"

Balzare said, "It is a fifteenth-century symphonia, also called a hurdy-gurdy."

The instrument resembled a mandolin, except that it had a handle at the bottom. Balzare turned the handle, thus producing a low drone against which he plucked out a gay melody with a pick. The person across the aisle said, "Say, that's great," and a group quickly gathered around.

Marshall had put his book aside and was listening with interest to a small transistor radio. The volume was turned down, so the broadcast was not generally audible in the racket of the bus.

Julian wandered away from the musician and climbed up onto his seat to take down his suitcase from the rack. "I'm hungry," he said to Marshall. "Are you?"

"Not yet. I want to listen to the news."

Julian took his suitcase, strolled down the aisle and addressed himself to Marge and Bill. "Hello."

Marge quickly withdrew her hand from Bill's and smiled at him. "Hello. What's your name?"

"Julian. Are you two on your honeymoon?"

Here Marge almost gave the show away by repeating "Honeymoon!" Then she recovered and said, "How did you know?"

Julian said, "Aw, I've been watching you. Would you like a tuna-fish sandwich?"

Marge exclaimed, "Would I!"

But small boys meant nuisance to Bill. He said, "Come on. Where are you gonna get a tuna-fish sandwich? Why don't you beat it?"

Julian said, "I'll make you both one." He knelt in the aisle, opened his suitcase. Curious now, Bill leaned over to look inside and saw a half loaf of white bread in cellophane, a plastic container of tuna fish, one of mayonnaise, some lettuce leaves in transparent wrapping and a knife. Julian expertly whipped up three tuna-fish sandwiches, handing two of them to Marge and Bill.

The latter had the grace to say, "Sorry, kid. These are great."

Julian said, "That's okay," reflected for a moment and then made a fourth sandwich, which he took to Marshall, saying as he handed it to him, "I'll bet you'd like this if you tried it." He sat down and chomped contentedly.

Marshall regarded him quizzically, bit into his sandwich and said, "Not bad." He ate silently, glancing every so often at Julian. When they were both close to their last bites and Julian was licking his fingers, Marshall said, "Did you know the cops were after you?" He indicated his now silent transistor. "I heard it after the news. General police alarm."

Wide-eyed with terror Julian asked, "Are you going to tell? I don't want them to catch me until I get my patent."

Marshall said, "Keep your hair on. How old are you? Nine, nine and a half?" Julian nodded.

Marshall said, "Cheer up, the fuzz added ten years. They'll be looking for some nineteen-and-a-half-year-old dropout." Only half meaning it he added, "If anybody asks you, you can say you're my kid brother."

Julian felt a sudden thrill. He looked up at the man next to him and was comforted by the mantle of his protection, and his last words repeated themselves delightfully in his mind: "You can say you're my kid brother." An only child, Julian had often longed for such a big brother. With him one could dare anything. He asked, "Were you in Vietnam?"

A curious expression which Julian was unable to interpret came over Marshall's handsome face. "What makes you think so?"

Julian pointed to the khaki jacket across his lap which now, folded inside out, showed Marshall's name followed by SGT.

Marshall was irritated. Behind those spectacles the kid had eyes. He was going to be even more of a nuisance than he had foreseen. "Forget it, will ya."

Julian was not put off. "Does S-G-T mean sergeant?"

Marshall turned on him angrily. "I said forget it. That's ancient history. I came out of school, they grabbed me, I went. Any more questions?"

Julian was not too upset by this sudden attack, for he had learned that adults only half meant what they said. He immediately inquired, "What are you doing n-n-now, sir?"

Marshall was forced to repress a smile. Kids *were* hard to beat. He replied, "Looking for a score. Make me some money."

Julian asked, "What d-d-do you do?"

Marshall laughed. "You name it. I'm lousy at it."

Julian laughed politely at the old joke.

Marshall said, "Okay, now I'll ask you one. That was a lot of baloney, wasn't it, about your old man not caring about you?"

The question drew back a curtain and allowed Julian a glimpse of his life at home, and with it came the perpetual pain of knowing that his father was disappointed in him. Julian quickly pulled the curtain shut again and merely shook his head. What was the point in trying to tell?

IN THE San Diego Police Department office of a Lieutenant King, the sergeant was holding delicately between thumb and forefinger a telephone receiver from which enraged sounds were emerging. He said, "You'd better handle this, Lieutenant. Aldrin West. He's boiling."

The lieutenant picked up his extension. "Lieutenant King speaking. . . . Yes, Mr. West, I know who you are. . . . What?" He covered the mouthpiece with a palm. "Phil, let's see that alarm on the West kid."

The sergeant shuffled through a sheaf of papers. "Here it is. Runaway. It's being broadcast every hour."

The lieutenant took one glance at the sheet, murmured, "Oh no," and then spoke into the telephone. "I'm sorry, Mr. West. We'll send out a correction immediately and notify all airports, terminals, state troopers' and sheriffs' offices in the vicinity. I'll give it my personal attention."

He hung up the receiver and said to the sergeant, "That lamebrain Cassidy sent out the wrong age on the kid. He's only nine and a half. Put out a correction right away."

JULIAN was happy. Traveling by bus was like watching two movies simultaneously. There was the ever-changing one outside the window and the other with the hurdy-gurdy music and friendly people inside the bus. The tires whined as they rolled through the wild, tumbled Arizona landscape of mesas, dry arroyos, and rock formations like cathedrals. Marshall was engrossed in his book.

Toward the front of the bus, Fate was preparing the first of the dramas she had decided to weave about the small boy with the red hair, the steel spectacles and the stammer.

Nikolas Allon, the Russian intelligence agent, was worried. He had had his instructions and, through bad luck which had led to an attack of nerves, he had blown two chances at the colonel's briefcase. A change of plan was called for.

The colonel was equally frustrated. Everything that had been so carefully worked out had gone wrong. Unless he could improvise he was in for a record-breaking chewing out in Washington. He put his briefcase on his lap, took out one of the blueprints and worked over it, aware that he was visible to Allon in the driver's rearview mirror.

The seat next to Colonel Sisson, who was by the window, was empty. So was the one in front, but it cut off Allon's view of him just below the shoulders. However, in standing up to take his satchel from the rack, Allon saw that the colonel was working on one of the blueprints in which the KGB was vitally interested. The Russians would prefer the entire contents of the briefcase, known to be details of a new type of weapon, but failing that, one clear picture of a significant part and the ordnance experts could reconstruct the rest. If Allon accomplished the latter without American knowledge he would surely be decorated. He therefore opened his satchel, made certain preparations, then replaced it and sat back to await his opportunity. In so doing he had missed the entrance of one of the principal members of the cast. Julian had

31

strolled up the aisle and, standing by the seat next to Sisson, had said timidly, "Sir, c-c-could I ask you something?"

Sisson, looking up at the boy, had replied, "Sure, sonny, sit down," and quietly slipped the blueprint marked TOP SECRET back into his briefcase. The height of the seat in front of him made Julian invisible through the rearview mirror and the racket inside the bus covered his and the colonel's conversation. As far as Allon knew, the colonel was doing exactly what he had been.

The colonel asked, "What's on your mind?"

Julian said, "My bubble-gun invention, sir. My friend back there said you'd know all about guns."

The colonel was startled. Then he remembered the ruse of his scattered papers. "What about your invention?"

Julian said, "S-s-something d-d-doesn't work right," and removed the diagram from his pocket to show him.

The colonel spread it out on his briefcase, his practiced eye taking it in at once. A smile of interest and admiration touched the corners of his mouth. "You dreamed this up yourself? Ingenious." He examined the sheet more carefully and reached for a pencil as Julian explained the problem.

Allon stole another glimpse into the rearview mirror. The colonel's shoulder movements and the angle of his head told him that his quarry was still working on the blueprint.

Over the loudspeaker the driver announced, "We'll be in Tucson in twenty minutes, folks."

Allon had accomplices in Tucson, El Paso and Dallas, but the farther the bus moved from the Mexican border the more difficult became the assignment. The time to move was now. Conditions were right. The bus was barreling along at some sixty-five miles per hour on a bumpy road. In walking to the lavatory he could clutch quite naturally at the seats to steady himself. As he made his final preparations he carefully dried sweat from his palms.

Toward the rear of the bus Marshall had seen Julian slip into the seat beside the colonel. With an inward smile he wondered what would be the reaction of an army ordnance big shot when confronted with a gat that shot soap bubbles instead of bullets.

The smile died away as something nagged at him. What kind of colonel spilled blueprints marked TOP SECRET all over the floor of a public conveyance? As he was reflecting he saw an unobtrusive little man several seats ahead of the colonel get up and march down the aisle of the swaying bus.

The colonel was telling Julian, "It's a matter of distance." He studied the diagram intently and then, tracing with his pencil, said, "The rubber air bag is too close to the muzzle to get the buildup for a large bubble every time you squeeze the trigger," and then he added, "Did you make a working model?"

Julian nodded and his hand stole to his right pocket. But he hesitated to take it out, for if he had made a serious mistake, he was ashamed to let the colonel see it. But Sisson had forgotten the model, so fascinated had he become with the diagram. He sketched over it, saying, "Move the rubber air bag back here, shorten your trigger action and lengthen your air hose."

Stark with admiration, Julian said, "Gee, I ought to have thought of that. Shouldn't I p-p-put another washer here?"

"Good for you. *I* should have thought of that." The colonel drew the washer in. "There, that ought to fix it. You're a pretty bright kid. What did you say you were going to do with this?"

Julian was exultant. "P-p-patent it in Washington."

The bus favored Allon, for just as he reached the colonel it lurched violently, enabling the agent to throw himself against the seat. His quick eye registered the small boy next to the colonel and at the same time the extraordinary ordnance design on which Sisson was working. The Japanese minicamera in his right palm took six pictures over the colonel's shoulder during the time Allon mumbled "Sorry," regained his balance and continued down the aisle.

Frank Marshall saw the splinter of light flashing from the unsteady passenger's hand, but it didn't register. His mind was on the amount of time the colonel was giving Julian. Wouldn't it be funny if his invention really worked?

As the passenger teetered along, Marshall saw that he was sweating violently and his right hand was clenched as though in a spasm. He thought, The poor bastard's going to be sick. I hope he makes it.

Suddenly the colonel glanced at Julian. How old could the kid be—nine, ten? "Are you really going to patent this?"

"Uh-huh." Julian fished forth the crumpled magazine article. The colonel glanced through it. "Sure," he said, "anybody *can* patent an original invention, but there's a lot more to it than what's mentioned here. Do your parents know about this?" Julian, suddenly close to panic, nodded.

"Have you got any money? Do you know anybody in D.C.?"

The word "money" led to "grandmother" because of the birthday present. Julian said, "My grandmother lives in Washington."

The colonel snorted. "Your grandmother will be a great help in the Patent Office."

Subliminally Marshall was aware of Allon emerging from the lavatory too soon to have been ill and marching past him up the aisle quite steadily, his hand no longer clenched. But, more interesting than that, Julian and the colonel were still chatting.

Marshall did not bother any more about Allon, except to note that he was taking his satchel from the rack again and the bus was entering the outskirts of Tucson.

The colonel returned Julian's diagram. He said, "This whole thing seems cockeyed to me, young man, but your engineering is sound and a lot crazier ideas have come off. If you need any help in Washington, get in touch." He took a card from his wallet, initialed it and handed it to Julian.

After an overwhelmed Julian had departed, Sisson glanced ahead at Allon, and could not think of a way to accomplish his mission short of going up to him and handing him the blueprints. That being ridiculous, the next move would have to be Allon's.

Julian dropped into the seat next to Marshall as the bus slowed down through Tucson and excitedly produced the diagram. "He showed me what to do. See?"

Marshall was not listening to him, but rather gazing toward the front of the bus. Julian asked, "What are you looking at?"

Marshall replied, "Nothing." Nevertheless he continued to watch the little man who had looked as if he were going to be sick. He was now standing, satchel in hand, obviously getting ready to leave the bus fast, and Marshall remembered Allon had bought a ticket to Washington.

"Tucson, folks." The driver drew up to the station and the bus doors hissed open.

At this moment the subliminal sense in Marshall came startlingly to life and brought what had happened into focus. And even as Allon was off the bus and running, Marshall was down the aisle saying to Sisson, "I may be wrong, sir, but I think the guy that just got off took a picture over your shoulder. When he passed you something flashed in his hand."

Fear settled in the colonel's stomach. He glanced at his briefcase, then gripped Marshall's arm. "*When?* Did you notice *when* he got the picture?"

Marshall said, "While you were talking to the kid."

The colonel yelled "Damn it all!" so loudly that it startled everyone in the vicinity, particularly the man named Wilks in the front seat. The latter's behavior had been subdued ever since he had gotten on the bus; he hardly moved at all, as though concerned with not attracting attention, and did not get out during stopovers. He sat hunched by the window, hat pulled over his eyes, moodily observing the scenery as it flashed by and occasionally studying a road map. The seat next to him was unoccupied. Two passengers had tried it and been driven away by his unwashed smell.

But now as the colonel rushed out the door while reaching inside his jacket for his shoulder holster, Wilks immediately arose, his hand movement duplicating the colonel's.

Marshall bumped Wilks as he dashed after the colonel, distracting him just long enough for him to see that the sudden furor had nothing to do with him. He removed his hand from his clothing, mopped his brow and sank back into his seat.

Colonel Sisson and Marshall saw Allon halting a taxi. The colonel produced his gun, a black army .45, his back to the bus so the passengers could not see it. There was a moment of frozen tableau as Allon, his face a mask of fright, glanced back at the colonel and Marshall. Then he jumped into the cab and was gone.

Marshall was unable to keep the contempt from his voice. "You could have had him, sir."

Sisson took in Marshall now, recognizing an ex-soldier. He reholstered his gun and said, "Thanks, but I didn't want him with holes in him." And suddenly he felt nine years old, like the kid with that diagram, and wanted to cry from sheer frustration. "What a foul-up!" he said bitterly. "They'll have my chicken feathers for this. That crazy kid! Tell the bus driver I'm not coming back."

Marshall said, "I don't get it," but Sisson was already running for a second taxi.

As Marshall climbed back into the bus he told the driver, "They won't be back."

35

The driver was beginning to feel a sense of injury. He said, "What's the matter with my bus? That's three guys."

Marshall laid a hand on his shoulder. "Weirdos. Forget it."

The driver looked up at Marshall. Smooth. Cool. If the guy knew something, that was nobody else's business. So what?

Marshall went back to his seat, passing Wilks, who remembered him from the bus station episode and whose thoughts were somewhat different. Dangerous! If he starts anything, he'll get it between the eyes.

As the bus moved off, Julian asked, "What happened?"

Realizing that the boy was too bright to be fobbed off, Marshall whispered, "Secret agents."

Wide-eyed, Julian said, "Gee, honest?"

Marshall made the motion of closing his lips with a zipper, and looking at the diagram in Julian's lap, thought, Now what did that scared little monkey want with a picture of that? Aloud he said, "Did the colonel say this would work?"

Julian nodded and explained the corrections. "Look, he gave me his address in W-W-Washington."

Marshall glanced at the card. The Pentagon building. He had been right about the colonel being in ordnance. If he said the thing would work, then the boy really had something. "When I was a kid," he said, "I was always tinkering too. I was gonna be an engineer."

Julian asked, "Did you invent anything?"

Marshall touched the battle jacket on his lap and a look of anger flashed across his face as he picked it up and irritably stuffed it down beside his seat. He replied, "Nothing," and then his countenance regained its usual bland expression as he added, "But you stay with your inventions, kid. You'll get somewhere." He glanced at the drawing again and leaned back, his eyes staring blankly in faraway thought.

FOUR

IT WAS dusk. Lights had begun to come on in the small community of Indian Falls, New Mexico, at the foot of the pass that led over the Black Range to the valley of the Rio Grande. No stop was scheduled there. Nevertheless, the bus had come to a halt at a road barrier where a sheriff's car and a confusion of people were gathered.

As the bus driver got out, two state troopers on motorcycles came roaring down the road posted INDIAN FALLS PASS, got off their cycles and talked to the sheriff, then briefly to the driver, who returned to his bus and spoke to the dispatcher's office. Then he said to his passengers, "Folks, there's been a washout twelve miles up the pass and they say we can't get through until morning. So we'll stay overnight here, motel and dinner on the company."

Marshall said, "A night in the sack suits me fine," and then he added hastily, "Can you look after yourself?"

If Julian was disappointed at the question, he did not show it. A motel room to himself was pretty exciting. There might even be a TV set and no one to tell him to turn it off and go to bed. He said, "Aw, sure. I got my case."

"Okay, kid, see you in the morning," and he was off the bus.

As people were pressing down the aisle, Bill looked at Marge, conscious of sudden excitement that the decision had been taken out of his hands. He put his arm about Marge's shoulder and whispered, "I guess here, maybe."

Marge nodded and leaned her head for a few minutes against Bill's cheek. Then they retrieved their bags and joined the line of passengers.

Julian, too, lagged behind, fascinated by the troopers' guns and shining cartridge belts and the single street of the small town that was almost like a movie set.

Behind the court, which was planted with flowers and cactus and yucca, the sign read INDIAN FALLS MOTEL, R. GRADY, PROP., and the motel's name was repeated in colored lights that blinked on and off. It was a fair-sized establishment since tourists coming through town at nightfall preferred to stay there and run the twisting roads of the pass in the morning.

R. Grady was known as Pop, his wife as Mom. Pop had been dried out by the sun until he was as stringy as a slab of jerked deer meat. Mom, on the other hand, was a rotund butterball with three chins. Behind the counter Pop booked the passengers in; Mom, billowing over a high stool, handed out the keys. At the end of the line Marge and Bill and Julian were waiting to be assigned rooms, Julian barely visible over the counter. Neither Mom nor Pop noticed him.

Pop looked queryingly at Marge and Bill, spotted Marge's ring and said, "Mr. and Mrs. . . ." and when neither of them said anything, chortled, "Newlyweds." He turned to his wife. "Number twenty-five for Mr. and Mrs. Newlywed, Mom."

"Welcome, folks. Now, where did that number twenty-five get to?" Mom began to search for the missing key.

Suddenly Pop saw carroty hair, a forehead and half of a pair of steel-rimmed glasses. Julian was on tiptoes to be noticed.

Pop said, "Well, hello, buster. Where did you come from?"

Julian replied, "The bus. C-c-can I have a room, p-p-please?"

"Ain't you with nobody?"

Julian shook his head.

Pop glanced at the key rack. "Looks like we're fresh out of rooms. What do we do about this shaver, Mom?"

She leaned over to look at Julian. "By hisself, is he?" Suddenly she looked sharply at Marge and Bill and an edge crept into her voice. "Say. You two are a young married couple. You're gonna have to get used to kids sometime. How about taking him in with you? Number twenty-five's got a foldaway bed in it." The boy and girl could only exchange one miserable glance before Mom said, "Well?"

"All right, you can put him in with us," Marge said.

Mom said, "Well, that's right nice of you. Oh, for land's sakes, here's the key right in my pocket." She handed it to Bill and said to Julian, "You go along with them, sonny."

Bill moved Marge off to one side and muttered fiercely, "What the hell did you say yes for?"

Marge was anguished. "What could I do? If I'd said . . ."

Julian moved over to them. "Is it all right for me to come?"

He looked so uncomfortable that Marge put her arm around him. "Of course."

Pop said, "Number twenty-five's right next to the office. I'll show you how to work the bed."

IN A photographic darkroom in a southwestern city in the early evening three men were examining developed negatives and wet prints. They were conversing in Russian.

The technician held up a print. "Excellent. You have done well, Comrade Allon."

The courier, clad in black leather for a night motorcycle ride, inquired, "What is it?"

Allon replied, "Secret weapon. You know where to find the plane. It will be waiting."

The technician studied the picture again. "What is this about soapy water and an air bag?"

Allon replied, "Code. The KGB will break it in a few hours."

The technician wrapped the finished work in plastic and then in waterproof linen. The courier stowed it inside his jacket and sealed the pocket with tape. Then all three men went out of the darkroom, the technician locked the door and they left a shabby building in the industrial part of town.

The courier straddled the latest model giant Honda and kicked it into life. He gunned his machine and shot off. When he reached the outskirts of the city he turned off his lights and became one with the darkness.

WITH the foldaway cot open beside the big double bed, and with a giant color television, the bureau and an overstuffed chair, there was hardly space to move in room 25. The foldaway joined the double bed so closely that the mattresses touched.

Supper in the motel dining room had been a success. Mom and Pop had been generous with their food and there were Mexican tidbits. Afterward, Julian, on his best behavior, had brushed his teeth and appeared in his pajamas. Bill slouched unhappily in the overstuffed chair, Marge sat on the arm. Julian gazed longingly at the big color set. "C-c-can we look at TV?"

Marge began doubtfully, "Well—"

Bill cut in curtly, "No, we can't," and then he added placatingly, "Look, Julian, it's been a long day and we're all tired. You better get to sleep."

Julian hadn't expected to be allowed to watch the box. That had gone down the drain along with the dream of the room to himself. And so he said amiably, "Okay," and studied the layout. There was no route to the foldaway except cross-country. He leaped onto the double bed, which turned out to be a kind of trampoline, and took three bounces, each one higher than the last, to land with a chortle of delight on his bed, where he cried, "Say, that's great," and settled himself between the sheets.

Marge could not look at Bill. Something deep inside of her wanted to laugh. She felt as though she ought to give Julian a good-night pat or kiss, but she was halted by a vision of herself bouncing across the bed to get to him. The deeply buried laugh pushed a little harder. Marge pushed back and told Julian, "Good night. Sleep tight."

Julian answered, "Good night," removed his glasses, which made him look extraordinarily young and vulnerable, put his head to the pillow and was off.

Bill got up and flipped the light switch and the room was illuminated only by the reflection of the motel sign. The two sat on the edge of the double bed, but with distance between them, and spoke in whispers. Marge looked over at the sleeping boy. "He's sweet."

Bill said, "He's a pest."

Julian had dropped off immediately, but now he stirred lightly and then was quiet. Bill looked inquiringly at Marge and reached for her hand, but she withdrew it, putting her finger to her lips. The two sat waiting and watching the sleeping child.

Two cars roared up to the shabby building in the southwestern city and disgorged Military Intelligence agents and three FBI men. Colonel Sisson was with them. They stormed up the stairs and down a corridor. An FBI man said, "This is it," and tried the door.

Sisson ordered, "Kick it in." They burst into the deserted darkroom, where the odor of chemicals had not yet evaporated.

One FBI man said, "We've had this place under surveillance."

Sisson remarked bitterly, "Some surveillance."

They went downstairs again and when they came out a third car was just drawing up. A young army lieutenant hailed them. "We think they've got a small plane on the Brubaker farm."

Sisson inquired, "Do you know where that is?"

The lieutenant said, "Sort of."

"Well, come on then," and they piled back into their cars. In the FBI vehicle the agents looked to their automatic weapons.

THE motel sign had been extinguished and the room was now in darkness except for a glimmer from a streetlight. Marge and Bill were standing facing one another tremulously uncertain, Marge in a pretty nightgown, Bill all buttoned up in pajamas.

41

"Gee, Marge, you look beautiful." The boy wasn't aware that he had opened his arms, nor Marge that she had moved into them. For a moment they clung to one another, experiencing a surge of tenderness they had not known or ever suspected was there.

Then they parted, shyly and with curiosity and wonder. Bill got into bed and moved over, near Julian. Hesitantly, and with a glance toward the sleeping child, Marge joined him. They pulled up the covers and, not touching, lay there side by side, afraid to move. Somehow the magic of the instant before was gone.

Bill was nervous again. How did one open this game? He whispered nervously, "I love you, Marge."

The girl replied dutifully, "I love you too." And each still remained rigid.

Something had to give. Bill reached for her. With a quick intake of breath she whispered, "Please. What if he wakes up?"

"He won't." Julian suddenly moved violently in his sleep, flung out an arm and hit Bill a resounding thwack across the ear. Bill, startled, yelled, "What the hell . . . ?" And Marge, in panic, shifted to the edge of the bed.

Bill sat up, rubbed his ear and turned Julian over so that his back was to them. The boy continued dead out. "It's okay." Bill moved toward Marge. "You couldn't wake him with a cannon."

Marge made a tentative move to abandon the sanctuary of the far side, but not a great one, wondering exactly what she was doing there in a strange place in bed with a boy.

Bill was furious with frustration. He had managed once to get over the hurdle of that first tremendous move, but did not know how to gather himself to do it again. He was spared.

"Mom?" Julian sat up and looked about him, confused.

Marge put her feet to the floor. "What is it, Julian?"

"I've g-g-got to go to the bathroom."

Bill said, "Oh, for Pete's sake, why didn't you go before? Hurry up, then."

Julian did his trampoline act across the double bed and disappeared. Bill suddenly felt that this exploratory voyage into the mysteries of sex was making him look foolish. What a mess!

Julian emerged from the bathroom and varied his act with a run, one bounce and a three-point landing on his own bed. He said, "Thanks," and was asleep immediately.

Bill made another halfhearted attempt, whispering, "It's all right now. C'mon back to bed, Marge."

She took her feet from the floor, but kept them curled under her. "Oh, Bill, can't you see this isn't the way we wanted it."

He sat up, suddenly relieved. He had not failed. She had let him off the hook. He looked at the unhappy girl. A ray from the street touched her brow and showed the shadow of her tumbled hair. She looked different by the dim light, and strange. He said, with a kind of half-grudging grace, "Okay."

"You're not angry?"

"No. Honest."

Marge leaned over to kiss him on his temple, but in the darkness missed and caught the side of his nose. He kissed back and got an eye. "Good night, Marge. Sleep well."

Marge whispered back, "Good night," and then barely audibly, "and thank you, Bill."

Sleep was upon Marge within minutes. She, too, had been let off from something she knew now that she had not really wanted, at least not on these terms. That self that, by the grace of one small boy, she had been given a few critical moments to reevaluate had been preserved in her.

Bill lay awake a moment longer and thought, Oh boy, if the gang ever finds out I went to bed with a girl and didn't do anything; and then quite suddenly he felt younger even than the child sleeping soundly next to him, and he was filled with the sense of something found and then lost. It would perhaps be a long time before he'd find it again. He was too old to shed tears. Instead he murmured bravely, "Oh, hell," rolled over and joined the other two in oblivion.

UNDER moonlight partially obscured by scudding clouds a light plane sat at one end of a long, neglected field bordered by trees. In flying suit and leather helmet the pilot sat on a wing, smoked and listened. When he heard the distant throbbing of a motorcycle he glanced at his wristwatch, stubbed out the butt, leaned into the cockpit and switched the machine into life. Right on time. Whoever they were, they were efficient as well as good-paying.

The racket of the approaching motorcycle grew louder, then it came leaping across the field to the plane, the rider pulling a package from his pocket even before he had dismounted. The pilot stowed it, climbed into the cockpit and said, "Pull those stones from under my wheels and get out of here quick. I see car lights."

The chocks removed, the pilot braked to give the courier time to duck out of the way, leap onto his cycle and drive off. Over the hum of his propeller he heard the grind of fast cars and saw the glare of headlights. He gave his ship full throttle.

The field was uneven and the little plane bounced and swayed. A stone fence at the end of the field rushed at him, but by then he was able to lift her off the ground. He flew level for a moment to pick up power just as three cars roared up to the side of the field and disgorged angry men. The pilot stayed even with the trees, using them for cover while he gained still more speed. Then he pulled her up, banked sharply and, as the clouds again cut down illumination, vanished into the night.

On the ground Colonel Sisson watched helplessly and one of the FBI men released a burst of useless machine-gun fire. The young lieutenant, who saw himself wearing a single bar for the rest of his life, said, "I'm sorry I took you to the wrong field first, Colonel, but there wasn't anything too definite."

Sisson felt sorry for him. This was obviously going to be the pattern: lousy intelligence, bad luck, rotten timing. He said, "Never mind. We've got to get in touch with the air force."

IN THE morning Marge was already dressed when Bill awoke and sheepishly climbed into his clothing. Julian was in the bathroom showering amid tremendous splashing. Distracted by the sound, Bill fell over Julian's suitcase, kicking it hard with his bare foot and yelling in pain.

He was hopping around hanging onto his big toe when he caught sight of Marge, who appeared to be in the grip of something extraordinary; it was the deep-down laugh of the night before which could no longer be controlled. At her first peal of laughter his own rage evaporated and they fell into one another's arms and laughed until they were weak.

When they had parted Marge regarded Bill with wry maturity. "Bill, do you mind? I want to go home."

Bill, too, had grown up. "Yeah, I guess you're right. We could get a bus back."

The bathroom door opened with dramatic suddenness and Julian, fresh and bright, shouted, "Hi, I'm ready!"

There was breakfast, and when the passengers emerged from the motel they saw the sheriff's men removing the road barriers, and a state trooper on a motorcycle appeared from the direction of the pass, followed by an Inter-State bus displaying its destination sign, SAN DIEGO. It pulled up alongside Bus 396 and the drivers exchanged a few words about the condition of the road. Then the passengers streamed back on board Bus 396. Marge, Bill and Julian were the last to appear, but only Julian climbed up on the step to the door. Marge came over, reached up and kissed him. "Good-by, Julian, and thank you."

Julian looked baffled. "What for?"

Bill held out his hand. "Good luck. Be seeing you sometime," and they turned toward the San Diego-bound bus.

The driver called after them, "Hey, aren't you two going on?"

Bill called back, "We changed our minds."

The driver used his fingers for counting. "That makes five. What's the matter with my bus? Of all the loony trips."

Marshall let Julian have the window seat as the bus moved off. "Sleep okay last night?"

Julian replied, "G-g-great. There weren't any more rooms and I had to g-g-go with Marge and Bill. There was a foldaway bed." He grinned in recollection. "I had to b-b-bounce over them."

Marshall studied Julian, half amused, wondering exactly what had happened and whether Julian suspected as he himself did that this was not a honeymoon pair at all. He thought probably not. It was this quality of innocence in Julian which had touched him. "What made them suddenly decide to go back to San Diego?"

"They didn't say."

"And you didn't ask?" Marshall laughed. "Kid, if you go on minding your own business like that, you'll go far."

FIVE

THE pilot of the light plane had just spotted the distant fringe of Pacific coast in the early-morning light when the two searching army jets picked up his blips on their radar and soon had him in eye range, flying at five thousand feet.

45

The first jet pilot tuned to the private commercial band. "Piper number VN four seven three, do you read me?" He received no reply. "Land before we shoot you down. Those are orders."

The man in the cockpit of the Piper took quick note of his position, the coastline and a stretch of flat beach vacated by the tide. He also saw something which he was convinced the pursuing jets might see, but would not think about. Their job was simply to get him out of the air. He picked up his microphone and tuned to the military frequency. "Okay, boys, I'm going down."

He kicked the right rudder, put his plane into a sideslip and dropped like an express elevator while the two jets descended to the level he had left. With the ground looming he kicked the rudder again, yanked the stick back and fishtailed onto the strip of beach. The Hovercraft that had been waiting in the shallows sent up a spume of spray as it darted inshore.

The man in the Piper climbed out of his cockpit, ran to the Hovercraft and handed his package to the man waiting at the open door. In exchange he received an envelope containing his pay. The door slammed and the Hovercraft roared off. It was several minutes before the jets realized what had happened. The second pilot, in a blaze of anger, put his ship into a dive, prepared his rockets for firing and at a thousand feet got the Hovercraft into his cross hairs.

The first pilot shouted into his mike, "Cool it, Johnny. We're over Mexico. You gonna declare war all by yourself?"

THUS far, luck had helped Julian evade capture, for although the dispatcher in Oklahoma City had warned all drivers to watch for a child traveling alone, the driver of Bus 396 was still mulling over the mystery of his defecting passengers. And furthermore, except during the boarding at San Diego, Julian had never actually appeared to be alone. It wasn't until shortly after two o'clock that Julian's incognito was to become violently destroyed.

There had been a short halt at Lordsburg, New Mexico, for a take-out lunch and Marshall had treated handsomely. They had changed seats again, with Marshall by the window. Julian had a hamburger in one hand, a Coke in the other, and on his lap a paper plate containing a cream puff and a Mars bar. Marshall was munching a ham and cheese on rye and washing it down with beer.

Julian finished his hamburger and got his nose into the cream puff. He said, "Say, this is great. I was all out of tuna fish."

As Julian got deeper into his cream puff and acquired a fetching white mustache, Marshall regarded him with curiosity and growing affection. He said, "Look here, Julian, this crazy caper of yours to Washington. How much money have you got?"

"Forty-four dollars."

Marshall snorted. "You know how far that will go? I've got my last five hundred on me, but in a town like Washington if I don't connect with a job right away, I'll be flat." He grinned suddenly at Julian. "I guess you and me are in the same boat." Here Marshall stopped, for suddenly looking up toward the front of the bus, he glimpsed something that was not as it should be.

SAM Wilks was a thief and a murderer, a psychopathic killer. By incredible luck he had avoided the police dragnet at San Diego, where he had abandoned his stolen getaway car. There had been no known witnesses to the crime and no accurate description of him available, and nobody had either expected or looked for him on an eastbound bus. He had expected to cross the border at Tijuana.

Hunched in the front seat of the upper level of Bus 396, a map of the area in front of him, Wilks was full of himself, knowing he was master of life and death. He had gotten away and would vanish into Mexico until the heat was off. He carried two articles which practically guaranted this, a .45 automatic pistol and an army hand grenade with the explosive force of a three-inch shell, from which Wilks always kept the pin half pulled.

They were approaching Deming, about an hour from El Paso and Ciudad Juárez, Mexico. He put away the map and mopped his brow for only the briefest moment of nerves, which he shed by thinking that he would enjoy killing that good-looking busybody who had been interfering with him. His right hand closed around the .45, his left around the grenade. He turned for a last look at the disposition of the passengers and then made his move.

JULIAN said, "What's going on up there?"

Marshall said, "I dunno." But he thought he did, for having half risen he had seen the character in the dirty clothes and ten-gallon hat go forward and lean over the bus driver. He was holding objects which Marshall had no difficulty recognizing. The bus driver momentarily took his eyes from the road to stare at Wilks with incredulity and then with a shaking hand pick up the microphone connecting him with headquarters.

THE main dispatcher's office in Oklahoma City was a vast, soundproof chamber filled with receiving and sending apparatus. At one end of the room there was a huge map of the United States into which boys stuck flags as messages were relayed, so that an overseer at a glimpse would know where every one of his vehicles might be within fifty miles. At the other end of the room the chief dispatcher sat with earphones at a plug-in switchboard which could connect him with any of the incoming or outgoing circuits.

At one of the receiving desks there was a bleep and then a muffled voice. "This is three nine six. Do you read me?"

The dispatcher yawned. "I read you, three nine six. What's up?"

His eyes popped as a tense voice said, "We're ten miles west of Deming. I've got a guy with a gun on me. He wants us to cross the border down at Juárez Oeste. And he says he wants half a million bucks or he'll blow us all up. He's got a bomb."

To the dispatcher it could be nothing more than a gag or maybe the driver had gotten loaded somewhere, but he pressed a button and said to the chief dispatcher, "Three nine six claims he's been hijacked," and then to the driver, "C'mon, cut out the clowning. Nobody hijacks a bus."

Fear distorted the driver's voice. "Listen, will you. He's letting me get through to tell you to keep the cops off and he ain't kidding. He says he wants the half a million in small bills and to have it waiting at the U.S. Immigration station at West El Paso."

The chief spoke into his microphone. "This is Chief Dispatcher Olson. Look here—"

The driver's voice rose to a near hysterical pitch. "I don't care who it is. He says a cop comes within twenty yards of us and the grenade goes bang. Says it'll kill everybody on board. I got twenty-one adults and three kids."

The chief said, "Okay, okay, we believe you. Keep cool. We'll do all we can to help you." Three nine six clicked off.

On the top step of the second level of the bus, the .45 in one hand, the grenade in the other, facing the rear but angled so that he could threaten the driver as well as the passengers below him, Wilks was in complete control. He said to the driver, "Okay, bud, speak to these folks."

One by one, in unbelieving horror, the passengers had become aware of the man with the gun and the grenade. The driver picked up his microphone. "Our friend here would like to jump the border at Juárez and if you'll stay in your seats and keep calm, he says nobody ought to get hurt. We should be there in about an hour."

Speaking loudly so as to be heard over the roar of the big wheels on the highway, Wilks said, "That's about the straight of it. Stay where you are and don't nobody try to get brave. See this here pin?" He held up the grenade so they could all see the pin at the side partly withdrawn from the ring holding it. "If this comes out the rest of the way, we all go." He laughed. "That's okay with me, so don't get any ideas that I ain't got the guts to do it," and he flipped the grenade in his hand.

The bus erupted into cries of alarm and incredulity. Wilks laughed again. "Just keep nice and quiet on account of these here things are kind of nervous like."

One passenger rose from his seat. "You can't get away with—"

Wilks leveled the .45. "Shut up."

His admonishment was unexpectedly followed by Marshall's sharp cry to the passenger, "Sit down! You don't argue with a hand grenade."

Wilks caught Marshall's eye and called out sarcastically, "Well, now, one of them *he*-roes. Tell the folks what happens when one of these things goes off."

Marshall arose and said placatingly, "Listen, fella, you got a gun on us. What about getting rid of that grenade. There are women and children on this . . ." His voice trailed off, for a sour expression had come to Wilks's mouth and the .45 was now leveled at Marshall's head.

The hijacker said, "Shut up and sit down. Don't try no *he*-ro stuff with me. You been in my hair before and I'm figurin' on putting a bullet through your skull before I get off this bus. Maybe I'll do it right now."

Marshall went white and sweat appeared on his brow. He remained standing, but Julian, looking at him with surprise, saw that he was holding on to the sides of the seat in front of him. Wilks laughed loudly. "Yer scared, ain't you?"

Marshall did not reply and Julian regarded him with overwhelming disappointment, unaware that Marshall was within seconds of being killed by a psychopath as dangerous as his bomb.

As Wilks's trigger finger began to tighten, the bus flashed by a crossroads and two state troopers on motorcycles roared out and onto the highway in pursuit. Wilks, relinquishing the bead he had drawn on Marshall, now concentrated on the discharge mechanism of the grenade and ordered the driver, "Tell your company if them cops come any closer, this thing goes off."

A four-year-old girl sensed danger and began to cry. Her mother hugged the child to her and called out, "Oh, you beast!"

At once Wilks became transformed, replying with exaggerated courtesy, "Why, ma'am, I ain't no beast. I got kiddies of my own at home I wouldn't want to see no harm come to any more'n you would yours. I like kiddies and kiddies like me. You got nuthin' to be afraid of as long as nobody don't try nuthin' funny."

The bus had gone silent inside. Marshall, still pale and staring straight in front of him, had sat down. The appearance of the law, he knew, could make matters worse. One could smell the fear in him. Julian threw him an anguished look. That wasn't the way goodies behaved on TV.

Back in the dispatcher's office, the bus driver's circuit had been switched on to a loudspeaker. The chief dispatcher was connected with the police by telephone.

The driver's voice now came booming from the speaker. "Listen, will you. There are cops following us. Tell 'em to lay off. And no roadblocks. He was gonna kill a passenger a minute ago because he didn't like his face." The dispatcher repeated the message into his telephone.

Again from the loudspeaker the bus driver's voice: "He's asking what about the money."

The dispatcher said into the mike, "Tell him we're rounding it up and we'll get it to him on this side of the border."

Number 396 was approaching a crossroads. Two more motorcycle policemen, a sheriff's car and two state troopers' vehicles were at the side of the road, but they made no move. Wilks waved his gun to the right, and reluctantly the driver tugged at his heavy wheel and headed south. The troopers and police joined the cortege.

At police headquarters a captain was snapping orders into the telephone. "I want outriders no closer than fifty yards in front to clear the road. We've contacted the Mexicans at Juárez Oeste that they'll be crossing the border. And there'll be a man in West El Paso with the money. . . . No, no, don't try anything! And tell the FBI if there's a shoot-out, they'll have the blood of those passengers on their hands."

By this time some thirty motorcycles and state troopers' cars were following 396. Ahead troopers were waving trucks and cars to the side of the road. Above three helicopters clattered.

Wilks could not keep from smirking at the size of the escort and its helplessness in the face of his power. The bus entered the town of Morellos. Nothing moved in the streets. As they emerged from the other side of town he said, "Them cops sure had that town fixed up nice. That's the way it's got to be all the way." He tossed the grenade into the air again. Then, grinning, he looked at Marshall and said, "That's what got you scared, ain't it? Some *he*-ro. Yer nuthin' but a yellowbelly."

Wilks's satisfaction with the way things were going had made him forget his intention to kill Marshall, but Marshall, still visibly shaken, did not know this. With a sidelong glance he became aware of Julian's reproachful eyes, magnified by his spectacles, questioning him and waiting for him to do something, increasing Marshall's frustration to the point where it almost overcame his fear. But the man with the grenade was in command. Marshall had noted that when he flipped it he caught it so that one finger was at the loop of the pin already half pulled out. One twitch and the bomb would be armed.

IN THE fantasy that was now being entertained by Julian, the bubble gun became the classic long-barreled Colt. He would beat the baddy to the draw and save Marshall and all the rest.

Julian had no way to compare the dreamworld of television, in which puffs of smoke issued from six-shooters but somehow the good guys never got hit, with the cruelty of reality, in which bad and good people could suddenly be shot down. He had no inkling of the speed with which a tragic situation could explode, or of the

51

mind of Wilks, who, ill-favored though he seemed, had spoken to the woman in the language of reasonableness: "Why, ma'am, I like kiddies and kiddies like me." Nobody had been hurt, there had been no violence, and within that context Julian's scenario—*Boy Hero Saves Hijacked Bus*—would work.

To realize this beautiful dream Julian arose and stood in the aisle. Automatically, the .45 followed him, the muzzle at one end of an imaginary line and the boy's forehead at the other. Wilks said, "Where do you think yer goin', sonny?"

Stiff with horror, Marshall hissed, "Sit down."

This frightened man was not the friend who had been looking after Julian and offered to be his big brother.

Julian said, "B-b-but I'm thirsty."

The fear Marshall had known for himself was nothing to what gripped him now for the child. Out of the corner of his mouth, careful not to move, he said, "You'll get killed! Sit down." There was no telling what could light the fuse of that filthy human explosive up front.

Wilks sneered. "Well now, mister, that ain't no way to talk to the little feller."

Blind anger suddenly replaced Marshall's fear. "You're just looking for an excuse to kill someone, aren't you?"

It did seem that the more one accused Wilks of villainy, the more eager he became to exhibit the sweet moderation that lay behind the deadly weapons he wielded. He whined, "Now, now, you folks got me all wrong," and then to Julian, "Pay no mind to that yellow-belly. You just get yourself a drink."

Politely Julian said, "Thanks," and marched down to the water cooler, where he pulled a paper cup out of the dispenser, filled it and took a long sip. The water cooler was just outside the lavatory. He asked, "Can I g-g-go in here a minute?"

Wilks laughed. "Sure, kid. When you gotta go, you gotta go."

Julian carried his cup of water into the lavatory and shut the door. Inside, using a piece of soap from the washbowl, Julian did what was necessary to implement the glorious dream.

And all the while the bus was rolling down to Mexico with its helpless outriders front and rear and helicopters overhead; in city rooms far and near, news wires were humming about the first hijacking of a transcontinental bus.

In the grip of euphoria, Wilks shouted to Milo Balzare, the foreign musician, "Play something to cheer the folks up," and he waved the .45 in his direction. Music was indeed all that was lacking in that weird scene. Balzare took up his hurdy-gurdy and a melancholy melody rang through the bus as the door to the lavatory opened and Julian emerged, no longer carrying his paper cup, but with his right hand in his jacket pocket.

Wilks turned his attention to him. "Feel better, kid?"

The way Wilks talked made it somehow simpler to go on. "Uh-huh. Thanks. Say, would you like to see my bubble gun I invented?"

Julian was level with Marshall, who, noting the hand in his pocket, had a frightful prevision of what was coming and the results, and breathed in anguish, "Oh, Julian, don't."

But there was no Marshall for Julian then, only his own line to follow, and he moved past him and produced his bubble gun, a replica in miniature of the .45 which now stiffened in Wilks's hand and was again leveled at Julian's freckled forehead. Wilks shouted, "Hey!" and the smell of death filled the bus, though Julian was unaware of it as he pulled the trigger of the only existing model of the bubble gun. A large soapy sphere blossomed from the muzzle, floated away, caught a splinter of reflected light which turned it first gold, then blue and pink, after which it vanished in midair, leaving a single drop to fall into the aisle.

That anticlimax was as much a shock to the passengers as it was to the terrorist. Somebody laughed hysterically and Wilks, lowering his gun, said, "Whaddya know. You invented that? Lemme have a look at it," and Julian continued down the aisle.

Wilks was enjoying the kindly figure he was cutting behind the ever present threat of his weapons. They could all see that Sam Wilks loved children. He let the .45 hang from his trigger finger and held out his hand for the bubble gun. Close to him now, Julian pointed it into Wilks's face and pulled the trigger for the second time. Here Julian's fantasy was fulfilled. And reality of an unexpected nature took over.

Instead of the fat, soapy sphere, from the muzzle streamed small bubbles which enveloped Wilks's face, momentarily blinding him. He yelled, "My eyes. I'll kill . . ." but that was as far as he got. The bus driver, ready with the big wrench he had managed to sneak to his side, leaped up and with a backhand stroke hit Wilks on the

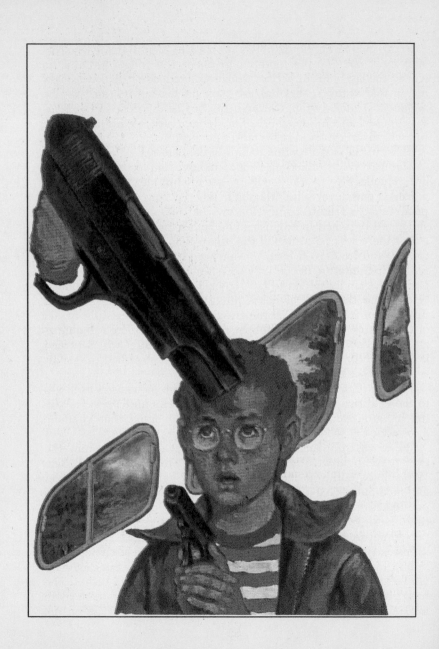

head and, even as the hijacker was falling, trod on the brake and jerked the bus to a halt.

And then, as Julian saw it, Marshall was the one who really saved the situation, for as Wilks toppled forward, the ex-soldier saw that the finger looped in the grenade pin had pulled it loose. He had ten seconds. He needed only seven to whip down the aisle, knocking Julian out of the way, dive frantically under the unconscious Wilks and come up with the grenade, which he flung out the driver's open window and into a cabbage patch, where, with a shattering roar, it sent up a geyser of earth, knocking two troopers off their motorcycles. Pieces of metal rattled against the bus, starring one of the shatterproof windows. A shower of dirt and cabbage leaves descended. And then it was over.

There was hysteria within the bus, blows, the screaming of the women, and a swirl of dust invading the interior from the landing helicopters. Passengers piled up, blindly and insanely trying to hammer at the unconscious hijacker until, minutes later, rangers and state troopers crowded through the narrow doorway, weapons cocked. "Okay, okay, break it up. . . . Where is he?"

One by one they dragged off the passengers trying to get at Wilks. At the bottom of the heap Marshall was protecting Julian with his body. Now he climbed slowly to his knees and the boy stirred, his glasses knocked awry, his expression dazed.

The driver pointed to the prone figure of Wilks. "That's the guy and his gun is under the seat. The kid squirted something in his face and I hit him with a wrench."

One of the troopers snapped cuffs onto Wilks's wrists, two more dragged him erect, and another, peering into his face, said, "Say, he's wanted! They just sent over a description of the guy who shot that filling-station attendant at Carlsbad. A woman saw him from a window, but was scared to report it."

In the pandemonium of everyone trying to tell how it had happened, Marshall and Julian were unnoticed. Marshall helped Julian up, brushed him off and put the bubble gun back in the boy's pocket. Then to his surprise he found himself saying, "If anybody asks, say it was a water pistol. You want to keep it secret until it's patented, don't you?"

Julian shook himself like a dog just out of water. "You got the grenade, didn't you?" His fantasies had evaporated. Reality was big brother Marshall, who in the nick of time had grabbed the grenade and saved them all.

Suddenly Julian seemed to levitate. A passenger had seized him by the elbows and hoisted him up shoulder-high, shouting, "Hey, everybody! Here's the hero!"

A reporter who had landed moments earlier in a press helicopter squeezed into the bus and queried, "Who? What did he do?"

Julian looked down to Marshall for help, but the latter only grinned at him. "You're gonna be a hero, kid. Don't forget it was a water pistol."

The troopers called for an emptying of the bus, herding the passengers into a field in an attempt to sort out what had happened. On the road, a king-size traffic jam had built up, drivers leaning on their horns or abandoning their vehicles to see what the excitement was about. Photographers and reporters cornered Julian in one group, the driver and his wrench, which he had never let go, in another.

Marshall hovered about, keeping an eye on Julian. Nobody but the boy seemed to connect him with the crucial episode of the grenade, which suited Marshall, who did not like cops or newspapermen. He was still considerably shaken by what he had been through, but what was taking precedence in his thoughts was the boy's gun, which, in obedience to Marshall's instruction, he was describing as a water pistol. The damn thing had worked.

"What's your name, sonny?" a reporter was asking Julian.

Marshall had meant to warn him not to give his right name. Within him was the heartbreaking certainty that here was the finish of the boy's odyssey.

Julian did not see Marshall's frantic signals. "Julian West."

"Where do you live?"

"S-S-San Diego, C-C-California."

"Where were you going?"

Marshall spoke up quickly. "To Washington to visit his grandmother."

"Tell us how it happened!"

During the interview two state troopers emerged from their patrol car and stood watching and listening. One finally nodded to the other. "That's the boy," and they pushed forward to tower over Julian. A sickish feeling gripped Marshall. There goes Julian.

One of the troopers bent down and said gently, "I think your daddy would like to know where you are."

Julian looked up at him miserably. Marshall walked away.

ONE would have said that Aldrin and Ellen West had been turned to stone there by the telephone, waiting in anguish for it to ring. When at last it delivered its signal it took West three rings before he could unfreeze to face the news.

"West speaking . . . Thank God!" He turned to his wife. "They've found him, Mother." The lieutenant's voice was still coming from the receiver. "Where did you say? Near Mexico? On a bus . . . ?"

It was unbelievable, but the voice at the other end was firm. West shouted to Ellen, "He's a hero. Shot a hijacker or something. And he's okay."

She began to cry. "Aldrin, tell them to send him back. . . ."

The excited words tumbled from West. "Please have him sent home. The fastest way . . . Thank you, Lieutenant. And keep us posted. We'll be right here."

He hung up, nearly sick with relief, but when he turned to his wife again there was a puzzled frown. "What did they mean, he shot him with a water pistol? Good grief, Ellen, it must have been his bubble gun."

JULIAN and the two troopers were over by the radio car. Within, the operator removed an earphone and spoke to one of the troopers, who told Julian, "They've just been on to your home in San Diego, and your ma was plenty worried about you. We'll get the road cleared and start you home in a jiffy."

The trooper had unwittingly edited the message of West's concern. Thus Julian's vivid imagination could picture his mother, but not his father. He supposed he would laugh at him again when he got home and probably take away his bubble gun as punishment.

A tall sheriff came up to the car and drawled, "We have to get this road opened up. You two fellers better take charge."

One of the troopers said, "Okay," and to the operator, "Keep an eye on the boy till we get back."

In the field, troopers, sheriffs and FBI men were arguing over jurisdiction of the prisoner, now conscious and sullen. The press, eager to get to wire services and photo labs, had retired to their heli-

57

copter, as had the army, and their helicopters rose, beating up dust that for a few moments shut off all visibility.

When it cleared Julian was no longer beside the radio car. The operator wondered whether to notify the troopers, but just then a bleep from his set called him. He figured the kid wouldn't have gotten far anyway.

Julian hadn't. He was just down the road, fighting back tears and kicking viciously at weeds at the side of the highway, when Marshall appeared out of the settling dust and saw him. "Hey kid, you all right? What's the matter? Don't you know you're a hero—picture in the papers? Don't fold up now."

Julian kicked savagely at a tumbleweed. "The p-p-police phoned my home. I've got to go back. I d-d-don't w-w-want to. I want to patent my bubble gun."

Marshall patted Julian absently. "Let's see that thing again."

Julian handed him the bubble gun. Reflectively Marshall pressed the trigger. A single bubble emerged, turned to pure gold and, borne aloft on a wave of hot air, twinkled for an instant and then, *plop*, was gone.

He looked down at the unhappy boy. "You wanna get to Washington?" Julian nodded, not wanting to burst into tears.

Marshall said, "Okay. Keep your mouth shut and do as I say." He stowed the bubble gun back in the boy's pocket, took Julian by the hand and they strolled unnoticed through the hubbub, past assorted lawmen, past the bus, the radio car and the line of stalled northbound traffic. Marshall glanced up at the drivers of transport vehicles and walked on until they came to a huge canvas-covered truck with a young, bored-looking, short-haired driver. Marshall said, "How 'bout a lift, Mac? Our old lady's took sick and me and my kid brother got to get to Albuquerque."

The driver looked them over lazily and said, "What's goin' on up front there?"

Marshall replied, "They caught some crook hijacking a bus. Big deal. You been over to Vietnam?"

The driver looked more interested and replied, "Ben Hoa. Thirty-first Carriers. And you?"

Marshall replied, "An Loc. But you guys really caught it."

"You said it. Okay, get in. I go through Albuquerque."

They quickly climbed into the cab, Julian between the two men.

He was in a state of pure bliss to be with Marshall and on a new adventure. Police whistles shrilled and traffic started up.

The truck began to crawl. Marshall winked at Julian. "Your shoe-lace is untied." Julian got his meaning, bent down, carefully untied both laces and then tied them again.

Meanwhile traffic had speeded up and they were passing the scene of the action. Marshall saw the bus ready to take to the road again and the radio car now surrounded by troopers arguing agitatedly. Marshall turned to the driver. "That musta been where it happened. They sure got a lot of law around."

The driver said, "I don't go much for cops." Then they were rolling up the road, and every turn of the wheels was putting distance between them and those left behind.

BACK in San Diego, Lieutenant King of the Missing Persons Bureau was going through one of the most uncomfortable moments of his life, trying to explain to a man with a thundering temper and a woman on the verge of screaming hysterics that Julian and his bubble gun had vanished again.

THE truck drew up at an intersection in the heart of Albuquerque. A policeman was directing traffic, and passersby were stopping at a corner newsstand for papers. The driver said, "Okay, bud, Albuquerque, and watch out for the cops."

"What cops?"

The driver snorted. "While you were sacked out last night I heard on the radio that there's a five-state alarm out for your kid brother. Look here, feller, I can see this is some kind of caper."

Marshall said, "I swear it isn't. Just hang on to that kid a sec." He jumped down from the cab, bought a morning paper and was back in again, handing it to the driver. "Here, read this."

The man stared at the headlines about the bus hijacking and photographs of Julian. "Well, for Pete's sake. This the kid?"

Marshall said to Julian, "Show him," and Julian produced the bubble gun and squeezed off a whole flight of colored bubbles.

The driver goggled. "Well, whaddya know?" then to Marshall, "So, where do you come in?"

Julian said, "He's my friend. He's helping me. I'm g-g-going to Washington to patent it and they're t-t-trying to stop me."

The driver grinned. "Okay then, good luck. Get out on this side and the cop won't notice."

They shook hands and Marshall and Julian slipped from the cab. The driver wheeled his truck around the corner and left them feeling naked, conspicuous. Marshall had to take a chance. He said to the news vendor, "Excuse me, Mac, where's the bus station?"

The man didn't even look up. "Straight ahead, four blocks."

Marshall looked in the direction indicated. There was the cop at the intersection and, two blocks down, a prowl car at the curb. There were now several reasons why Marshall wanted to finish what he had started. If they picked up the kid, he would, of course, be sent home immediately, but Marshall was uncertain as to what charges would be brought against himself.

They were opposite a J. C. Penney store. Marshall suddenly said, "C'mon, kid," and entered the store.

When they emerged from J. C. Penney's, Marshall's battle jacket had been stowed away and was replaced by a leather windbreaker, and on his head he wore a ten-gallon hat.

But the greater transformation had been worked upon Julian. He was practically unrecognizable in a shirt with BUFFALO BILL lettered across it, and fringed buckskin trousers and coat. Covering his carroty hair was a Buffalo Bill stetson, and glued to his chin and upper lip were a mustache and goatee. He was carrying a toy rifle, and around his middle was a leather belt with a holster into which the bubble gun had been thrust. They were now prepared to make the test.

They passed the cop at the intersection and approached the corner. Farther along, the policemen in the prowl car smiled at Julian's costume as they went by. Marshall was satisfied.

Julian said, "Is this what Buffalo B-B-Bill really looked like?"

Marshall stopped so abruptly that Julian, who was holding his hand, was almost yanked off his feet. "Listen, kid, that stammer of yours. If anybody got suspicious that's the first thing they'd nail you on. Do you have to do it?"

"I g-g-guess not—if you say so." He was already half hypnotized by his worship for Marshall.

Marshall said, "Right. So, from now on cut out the stammer. Let's hear you say bubble gun."

"Bubble gun."

"That's great. Now say ding, dong, bell, pussy's in the goddamn well."

Julian repeated, "Ding, dong, bell, pussy's in—"

Marshall stopped him. "See, there you are."

Julian said, "Okay," and then, utterly finished with that subject, went on to the next. "What do we do now?"

Marshall said, "We find the bus station. Our through tickets to Washington are still good. Let's go."

SIX

In a secret engineering laboratory somewhere in Moscow a Russian arms expert completed the object on which he had been working under heavy guard. He hefted it in his hand and laid it on the workbench before him. A red light flashed on a wall panel. Someone had begun the long routine of penetrating the laboratory. It would be someone properly identified. Nevertheless, the expert, as a precaution, threw a cloth over the object and waited.

The visitor wore the insignia of an army colonel, but he held even higher rank in the branch of Soviet counterespionage. He said, "Have you completed it, Comrade Vosnevsky?"

"Yes, Comrade Veznin." He removed the cloth.

The colonel examined the object, then gave Vosnevsky a long, hard stare. The latter, who was valuable enough and sufficiently high in the Party to do so, returned the look.

As their bus droned on toward Washington, Marshall explained the distant peaks of the Sangre de Cristo Mountains to Julian as a knife-edge sharply dividing rainfall, so that drops falling on one side ran eastward while those dropping a few inches away headed west and wound up in the Pacific Ocean. At least that was the way Marshall saw it, and Julian, who took it as gospel, thought of himself perched on the topmost spine of the ridge with a sled in the wintertime, trying to make up his mind whether he would slide down to the east or to the west.

Marshall illuminated the boredom of the endless plains and wheat fields of Kansas with the saga of the convulsions that had shaken that state, which Marshall remembered from his high school history days. Through his eyes, Julian saw Northerners,

61

Southerners, soldiers, rebels, pioneers in covered wagons, outlaws and gunslingers.

They crossed the Mississippi at its confluence with the Missouri at St. Louis, and Marshall, who had once made a short trip on its broad, yellow waters in an old stern-wheeler, pictured for Julian the days of the river gamblers and the derringers fired under tables when an ace too many made its appearance. Marshall never talked down to Julian or attempted to impress him, probably because he was talking more to himself than the boy and trying to revive some of his own lost faith in his country and countrymen.

To Julian, those days and nights of rolling across the country were as close to heaven as any boy had the right to expect. He had earned the friendship of an adult and had lived through the maddest kind of storybook adventure in which he had played a real-life hero, though curiously that incident left less impression on him than the joy of the trip with Marshall. For they lived during that time as men on the loose, washing when it was convenient, and abusing their stomachs at all hours with dubious frankfurters, burgers, greasy fries, candy bars and ice-cream cones.

And yet all the time what he knew he would do was at the back of Marshall's mind, though he despised himself for it. Julian appealed to him because he was a dreamer with the courage to attempt to grasp the dream. He had few of the irritating traits of the small boy. He wasn't a smart aleck or a know-it-all, he didn't pry and could take no for an answer. Besides, he showed complete faith in Marshall, as evinced by the instantaneous cure of his stammer. This worship, this love—they were painful for Marshall to contemplate, and he had to disconnect them from what he intended to do.

So, when at last the opportunity did present itself, the intention which had lain dormant in Marshall's mind took over. It was one thirty in the morning. A difference in the music of the tires caused by a change in the roadbed awakened Marshall and through the window he saw the orange glow of Pittsburgh's furnaces. When he looked on Julian curled up asleep with his head on his Buffalo Bill jacket, it induced his affection, until he saw an edge of the diagram of the bubble gun showing from the pocket of his coat.

The bus driver's voice boomed over the intercom, "Coming into Pittsburgh, folks. Forty-five-minute refreshment break."

Through the announcement Julian didn't move. Marshall saw

that no one was observing him. Then, with infinite care not to rustle it, he transferred the diagram from Julian's pocket to his own. What he needed would surely be available at the terminal.

But he had to slip out of his seat without waking Julian. He let all the others disembark first, to see whether their bustle and the noises from without would disturb him. But the boy only shifted position and thereafter was dead to the world.

Marshall found the coin-operated photocopier next to a stamp-vending machine. He flattened out the diagram, then tore a square from an envelope, wrote on it and drew a heavy border around it. He placed it on the diagram and made his photocopy. He examined it with satisfaction, made two additional copies, then retrieved the original diagram and removed the piece of envelope, which he shredded and dropped into a refuse basket. He pocketed Julian's drawing and once more carefully examined a photocopy. Where in the lower right-hand corner it had read BUBBLE GUN, INVENTED BY JULIAN WEST, 137 EAST VIEW TERRACE, SAN DIEGO, CALIFORNIA, APRIL 25, 1973, it now read TOY BUBBLE GUN, INVENTED BY FRANK MARSHALL, 39 ORCHARD ST., ABILENE, TEXAS, APRIL 3, 1973. The border he had drawn had completely concealed the fact that a new address and inventor had been superimposed.

The photocopies he stowed in an inside pocket—but how to get the paper into Julian's pocket unobserved? The sooner he returned to the bus, the better. Marshall hurried back and tiptoed to his seat, to find Julian still asleep and almost in the same position. The bus was half empty and it was no problem at all to restore the diagram to his pocket exactly as it had been before. This done, he settled back and was actually asleep when they pulled away from the terminal.

THE SHAFT of the Washington Monument poked into the haze of the hot morning air heavy with traffic fumes. Marshall and Julian stood on the sidewalk transfixed by a strangeness which separated them from the camaraderie of their trip.

It had been ten o'clock when they had emerged from the bus and marched unchallenged through the humming Washington, D.C., bus station. Marshall had changed into his battle jacket, carried his Western hat and had attracted no notice with the small boy in the Buffalo Bill outfit.

Now, with no more than a taxi ride separating him from the Patent Office and the realization of his dream, Julian did not know how to show his gratitude or to say good-by. Fingering his mustache and goatee, he asked, "Should I keep these on?"

The question yanked Marshall's scattered thoughts back onto an orderly track. What he didn't want for at least twelve hours was a hullabaloo over Julian West and his invention and so he replied, "Yeah, you better. It got us past the cops, didn't it?"

Julian made a tentative trial at parting. "Well . . . thanks for everything . . . If you hadn't thrown the grenade, we . . ."

"That's okay. If you hadn't distracted that loony cowpuncher, I could be lying in a mortuary parlor. I was scared."

Julian looked at him and pulled at his lower lip. "For real?"

Marshall said, "Look, kid, after you've been around awhile you learn that there are times to be scared and others not to be. But you can't always pick 'em. See?"

Julian was satisfied and Marshall now had to try to prepare the boy for what he was about to do to him. "Listen, kid, do you know anything at all about how the Patent Office operates?"

Julian reached for the diagram. "Well, I show them these." He patted the bubble gun in its absurd Western holster.

Marshall said, "It isn't all that simple. They've got to make a search and maybe somebody else thought of it first."

Julian refused even to consider this, but Marshall was insistent on conditioning the boy for the catastrophe he was preparing for him. "A lot of people get ideas which are almost the same."

Julian said, "That's why I better hurry. I gotta get mine in first." And his gaze into Marshall's face was so straightforwardly innocent that the deviousness of Marshall's own mind at that moment forced him to wonder whether Julian actually suspected what he was up to, but the moment passed and he realized there was no guile in the purely practical statement.

He said, "Look, Julian, you haven't got a grandmother here, have you?"

Julian shook his head. "No. She lives in Olympia, but that's Washington too, isn't it? So it wasn't really a lie."

"Where are you gonna stay tonight?"

Julian shrugged. "Somewhere. I've got some money left."

Marshall tried again. "Oughtn't we to phone your old man?"

Julian shook his head emphatically. "He wouldn't care. He's too busy." Then he added, "I've got to go to the Patent Office."

Marshall's good impulses faded. He, too, had to get to the Patent Office and what was more, with a head start. And he had to stop worrying about Julian. Sooner or later the cops would pick him up and send him home. He would come to no harm.

He said, "Okay, we'll get a cab and I'll drop you off there." Then Marshall began the perpetration of his black deed. "Hey, wait a minute. I gotta make a phone call. I'll be back in a sec," and he was off, leaving Julian standing on the sidewalk.

Marshall wasted no time. He reentered the station and exited the other side, where he told an arriving cab, "The Patent Office," got in and was driven away.

After some twenty minutes of standing, a solitary and slightly absurd figure, outside the bus station, Julian realized that something had perhaps gone amiss, though the suspicion that he had been ditched never entered his mind. He decided to wait another five minutes and then go back. Now, more uncertain, he gave it ten and then went back inside, where he found the public telephone booths, but none of them contained Marshall and he then fell prey to the sudden panic that he might have missed him in the crowd or that Marshall had now returned to their rendezvous. He ran to the door and looked out at where he had been standing, but there was no sign of his friend.

He wandered back into the terminal, hoping to catch a glimpse of him, but as he threaded through the passing throng Julian suddenly became aware that people were turning to look at him. Intuition, plus some of Marshall's hard practical wisdom that had rubbed off on him during the voyage, caught him up. As long as he had been in the company of his "big brother" no one had paid him any attention, but now by himself, in this outfit, he was highly conspicuous.

Julian drifted out of the maelstrom of passengers and ducked into a corner, where he quickly stripped off his mustache, goatee and the Buffalo Bill outfit, stuffed them into his suitcase and resumed his leather jacket. He took off the cartridge belt and holster and restored the bubble gun to his right-hand jacket pocket. Then he emerged the same small boy who had boarded Bus 396 in San Diego, California, so many ages ago. Well, not exactly the same.

He found himself missing Marshall dreadfully, to the point where he was close to being frightened.

If there had never been a Marshall, he would have wandered through his dreamworld untouched, following the line of least resistance toward his objective. But there had been Marshall, tall, handsome, laughing, with those funny eyes that lit up as though there was a battery behind them. There had been the Marshall

who had fed him, looked after him, treated him like a man and taken him seriously. Now he was gone, leaving nothing but a memory, and Julian realized a void such as he had never felt before. He thought of going to the information desk and having Marshall paged, but then he said to himself, Boy, would that be a great idea! Tell everybody where we are.

It wouldn't do to linger in that terminal with the police on the lookout. He pulled himself together, strode purposefully through the exit and to the head of the cab line, where the driver was reading the morning paper, and asked, "Are you free?"

The driver, who was a young, pleasant-looking black man with an amused quirk to his lips, looked up. The face of the small boy at his window gave him a shock, as though he had seen him before and ought to be saying, "Why, hello there," instead of, as he did, "Sure. Where to?"

Julian replied, "The Patent Office, please. The place where I can patent my invention."

Startled, and not sure if the kid was just stringing him along, the man said, "That's about a three-dollar trip across the river. Don't get me wrong, but have you got that much money?"

Julian reached into his pocket and produced what he had left, some twenty-seven dollars. The driver smiled and said exaggeratedly, "Excuse me, *sir*. Get in. You got yourself a ride."

Julian said, "Thanks. Do you want it now or later?"

"Later will be fine," the driver said as he moved off.

Julian sat back and studied the driver's license framed behind cellophane. It showed his photograph, name—Meech Morrow—and a number. He asked, "Is it far, Mr. Morrow?"

The driver replied, "About ten minutes," and then chuckled at the kid's formal "Mr. Morrow." Warming to him, he asked, "What's your name?"

Julian had been on the verge of blurting it out, but remembered that this might be unwise and replied, "Herman."

"Well, Mr. Herman," Morrow said, "you'll be there in a jiffy."

Julian nestled into a corner and gave himself up to the golden dream in which every child would be wanting a bubble gun invented and patented by Julian West. As Meech Morrow's cab edged through downtown Washington's midmorning traffic in the direction of the Potomac Bridge, other events that were to affect the life and times of that same Julian West, inventor, were taking place.

AT CRYSTAL Plaza in Arlington, Virginia, across the river from Washington, Frank Marshall emerged from the building where the Patent Office was located with a number of forms and booklets in his hand and an expression of brisk satisfaction on his face. He glanced at his wristwatch, which registered eleven o'clock, consulted an address on a sheet of paper and walked quickly to a neighboring building, where he studied the lobby directory board, which was three-quarters filled with the names of patent attorneys. Others listed on it were engineering, drafting and research firms concerned with assisting would-be inventors in meeting all the requirements of the Patent Office. He noted down the name of a drafting firm as well as that of a patent attorney and then headed for an elevator. With any luck and the investment of the last of his cash, he might file at the Patent Office before closing time.

IN THE vast complex of the Pentagon building, the photograph of the President was looking down from the wall of the conference room where Major General Thomas H. Horgan was meeting with two generals, three colonels, several CIA men and a pair from the FBI. Horgan was chewing out Colonel John Sisson. "You sure screwed this one up. What was it that was photographed, anyway?"

Sisson was not easily cowed, but the absurdity of his situation, together with the battery of angry looks being fired at him, caused him to reply inanely, "Well, er, a pistol that shot bubbles."

Horgan's voice rose. "That shot *what?* What the hell are you talking about? You said there was a diagram? What kind?"

Sisson could not have reproduced it at that moment if his life had depended on it. He blurted out, "Well, sir, I never really paid much attention to it. It was just a kid bothering me for help—something about a washer in the wrong place—and before I knew it—"

General Horgan completed the sentence for him. "—the stupid Russian photographed it and made the American army look like one big pack of fools."

A general with one star less, but from a different department, came to the rescue of the unhappy Sisson. "Now wait a minute, Tom. Maybe it's not so bad. The Russians put a set of phony rocket plans in our hands and you were smart enough to spot them. So we organize our own phony plans for them to get the message and cut out the kidding. Now we can both stop wasting our time."

Horgan, still furious, snarled, "With this foul-up we don't know where we're at. Besides which, we've been saving up that Russian pigeon, Allon, for years and now we've gotten him to blow his cover for nothing." He pointed at Sisson. "Listen, I don't care how you do it or where you get it, but I want that diagram before tomorrow. I want to know just what they've got."

The general who had spoken up asked, "What became of the kid, John?"

Sisson replied miserably, "He just disappeared. Haven't you been reading the papers?" He needed a scapegoat, and turned to the FBI men. "Listen, can't you guys find a boy whose description has been broadcast all over the country? And I thought you were supposed to stop what Allon got from leaving the country."

One of the FBI men said, "The hell we were. That was a CIA job. And the child is for the local fuzz."

The second general said, "Look, let's go back and get the whole thing from the beginning and maybe we can see some daylight. John, could this kid have been in cahoots with Allon?"

"A ten-year-old? No." And Sisson again launched into his story, racking his brain for every scrap that might provide a clue. The men around the table listened silently. A glance of one of the CIA men drifted to the portrait of the President and a stab of light on the glass over it gave him the impression momentarily of an eyebrow having gone up.

The steel and glass of the Patent Office building jolted Julian into reality. Anyone Can Patent an Invention had been the headline which had seduced him into attaining that goal. But he wasn't "anyone." He was Julian West, age nine and a half, fifth grader, with a messy diagram in one pocket and a dubiously performing bubble gun in the other. San Diego, where he had read the headline, was a million miles away.

Julian got out of the cab and stood on the sidewalk, facing the building. How was anyone to understand the feelings of a small boy confronted with his first plunge into a world far removed from every security he had ever known?

But in a curious way Meech Morrow did, not so much because he had children of his own, but because of the figure Julian cut. Not quite four feet tall from the soles of his Keds to the top of his carroty hair, suitcase in hand, steel-rimmed glasses on his nose and head tilted to look at the top of the building, he penetrated to Morrow's heart. Besides, something bothered Morrow. Where had he seen the boy before? Whatever, to abandon him was unthinkable and so he said, "I'll wait for you."

Julian, startled, plunged his hand into his pocket. "Gee, I forgot for a minute, but I wasn't going without paying, honest."

Morrow said, "You can pay me when you come out. Maybe you'll be needing another ride somewhere. I'll stop the clock."

Julian said, "Aw, you got work to do," but some of the fear had been drained out of him. He wasn't completely alone. Somebody was standing by.

Morrow laughed. "That's all right, kid. Go ahead and tell 'em about your invention."

Julian said, "Thanks. I'll hurry." And he marched across the sidewalk and was whirled within by the revolving door.

Meech Morrow watched him go and scrabbled in the well at the side of his seat until he found a two-day-old newspaper. He read the story again, looked at the photograph and began to laugh. Well, he said to himself, ain't that Mr. Herman some kid.

IN THE OFFICE of Peabody and Wilson, Drafting Engineers and Patent Consultants, a young man, using a pen as a pointer, was smiling at the photocopy. He said, "That's amusing. Have you got a model?"

Marshall asked anxiously, "Do I have to have one?"

"Not really. You could put it in later."

Marshall asked, "How long will it take?"

"Not too long. The Patent Office closes at five. We could do it by four. In the meantime you could be filling out the forms. The filing fee is sixty-five bucks and my drawing's fifty."

Marshall said, "Okay. But couldn't you make it by three thirty?"

The draftsman said, "I'll try." They were always in a hurry, these inventors, even with the craziest ideas, always terrified that someone might get in ahead of them.

SEVEN

AFTER some twenty minutes Julian emerged, clutching pamphlets and forms, and as he approached the cab Morrow said, "Well, Mr. Julian, how did you make out?" He was immediately sorry that he had called him by his right name, for to the dazed expression on Julian's face now was added terror.

For an instant he thought the boy was going to run, and Julian, his false identity pierced, had actually been minded to do so. Then he remembered that he had not paid the man and remained on the sidewalk, a picture of abject misery.

The driver said, "You got nothing to be afraid of with Meech Morrow." Julian got in the cab. "You're the boy I read about in the paper, but we'll forget about that. What happened in there with your invention? They give you the runaround?"

Julian shook his head slowly. "They were busy. A man asked if I'd researched it and said if I hadn't, I ought to." He said unhappily, "It's gotta be in India ink on special paper, drawn with drafting instruments, and I have to take it to a patent attorney."

Morrow said with a note of contempt, "Brother, they don't make it easy." He looked back. "What do we do now?"

As Julian drew his diagram from his pocket a card fluttered to the floor. With a sudden change of expression he handed it to Morrow and said, "Could we go there?"

Morrow looked at the name and Pentagon address and whistled with astonishment. He asked, "You know him, boy?"

Julian nodded. "On the bus he helped me with my invention and said if I got into any kind of trouble . . ."

Morrow whistled. "Kid, you got some muscle there. Want to go see him?"

"Yes, please."

Morrow said, "No charge for waiting time, but that's a four-dollar trip. Okay?" Julian nodded, and the cab was off.

JULIAN's invasion of the Pentagon was classic. The two marine guards didn't see him, because they weren't looking for a small boy to march unquestioningly between them into the main entrance. He had left his suitcase in the cab, for when he had tried to pay, Morrow had said simply, "Skip it, kid. I'll be here when you come out." Morrow had figured the boy would be ejected in minutes, with nothing but the initialed card of a colonel in ordnance.

The lobby of the Pentagon presented the most efficient and complicated security check—barriers, sergeants behind desks, marines and military police.

Julian approached a naval petty officer and showing him the card said, "Please, sir, where can I find Colonel Sisson?"

The petty officer said, "Ask him, sonny," and indicated a corner of the lobby where everyone was khaki-clad.

Julian took his card to a sergeant. "Please, sir, where can I find Colonel Sisson?"

Like a shuttlecock the name of Sisson was batted to and fro until it reached a corporal in front of a huge directory. He called back, "Southwest wing, corridor G, second floor, room nine three four." But by the time the answer wafted back to the sergeant, Julian was no longer there. An important piece of brass with an overloaded briefcase had approached the sergeant, making him forget about the boy. The two guards at the inner entrance, seeing him leave the desk with the sergeant apparently satisfied, made no attempt to stop him. And thereafter Julian, with the wing, the corridor, the floor and the room number firmly in mind, proceeded to penetrate the recesses of the most protected building in the world.

A guard asked, "Have you got a pass?" Julian showed him the colonel's card. The guard said, "Okay."

Another asked the same question. Julian showed the card and said, "The sergeant at the desk said it was okay."

"Billings? A fat guy?"

"Uh-huh."

"Okay, go ahead."

The third was more adamant. "Nix, sonny. Nobody gets through here without a badge."

Julian said, "But Colonel Sisson's my—"

He was going to say "friend," but the marine finished it for him, grouching, "Oh, for Pete's sake. I wish the brass would let us know when their kids are coming. Go ahead and see your daddy, but don't say I let you through."

The farther he went, the easier it seemed. Julian walked past two guards who never even questioned him and a third who seemed satisfied with his credential. He said, "Hey, you got yourself in the wrong corridor, sonny," and he led the way to the outer office of Colonel John Sisson, from whence Julian was ushered to the portals of Major General Thomas Horgan's office.

The arguments around the conference table were still raging and had increased in scope, for Horgan had called in a member of the President's Advisory Committee, in case the matter should call for diplomatic intervention and attention, and a pair of experts on Russian matters. The newcomers had not only solved nothing but had raised General Horgan's temperature to the point where he blew off at them all. "And you can think only about your own jobs. Don't you ever give a thought to your country? Sisson, you're gonna find yourself on the retired list so fast—"

At this point the general's sergeant, whose length of service entitled him to take liberties, entered and saluted. "I beg your pardon, General." He handed Colonel Sisson a card. "Colonel," he said, "excuse me for busting in, but there's a kid outside who knows you and says he has to see you on something important. He got right through to your office without a pass and I thought . . ."

Sisson took the card and mechanically turned it over. When he saw his initials in his own handwriting a chill slid down his back as he remembered the boy and his diagram. He thought, That's impossible. It's only in the movies that the marines arrive in the nick of time. Then he asked, "He wouldn't be a four-eyed kid with red hair and a stammer, would he?"

The sergeant said, "He didn't have no stammer. . . ."

Julian entered as though on cue, looking about him anxiously at the beribboned officers and grim civilians around the long table, until he located Colonel Sisson. He went directly to him and said, "Excuse me, sir, I thought this was your office and you said, sir, that if I—"

Sisson leaped out of his chair and seized him by the shoulders. "Julian! Have you still got that diagram?"

"Is it all right, sir? I mean, you said if I was in trouble I should—"

The words came tumbling from Sisson. "That's just exactly what I said and you were perfectly right to come. You see, they'd all like to look at your invention."

It bewildered Julian, but he took out the grubby drawing; Sisson placed it dramatically on the center of the table.

General Horgan managed to get out, "What the hell is that?"

Sisson announced, "This, sir, is the kid, and that's his diagram," and then to Julian, "Have you got the gun too?" Julian produced the gun and Sisson put it on the table.

The articles lay there, hypnotizing the entire assemblage, until General Tom Horgan arose to scrutinize the diagram. There was silence while the general picked up the bubble gun, weighed it in his palm and then fitted it to his grip. He held it up, examined it closely. Finally, holding it at arm's length, he squeezed the trigger.

Before the eyes of the experts a soap bubble began to form at the muzzle, expanding until it was the size of a grapefruit, at which point it detached itself, became exquisitely iridescent and drifted straight for the portrait of the President, where it burst silently, leaving a tiny damp stain on the glass in the frame.

"Ha!" None of them knew whether this was the beginning of another bellow until it was followed by similar explosions. "Ha ha ha ha ha!" The general was laughing! He squeezed the trigger again and a whole stream of bubbles emerged.

And now the hypnotic spell was broken. They all raised the roof with their merriment as the general pounded the table with his fist in hysteric guffaws and began to find words. "Wait until those Russian brains try to figure this one out. This is the funniest damn thing that ever happened. John, you're a hero. I'll get you a medal for this if it's the last thing I do. Oh, brother, I'd give my retirement pay if I could be over there when they get a load of this."

73

The conference disintegrated, the general slapping Sisson on the back. The marines sometimes did arrive in the nick of time. Julian thought they were all crazy.

IN A conference room in Moscow there was high tension as General Barzovsky, his staff and experts from the KGB, the MVD and allied intelligence, espionage and counterespionage units awaited the revelation of America's newest and most secret weapon. The spy planted in the United States twelve years before to be available for that one moment had succeeded in photographing it; a Soviet technician had succeeded in making a model.

The conference room was extraordinarily like the one in the Pentagon. General Barzovsky appeared just as massive and formidable as General Horgan. He looked up as there was a stir at the door, murmurs, heel clicks, the sound of passwords. Then a major in his greatcoat and epaulets entered with Comrade Vosnevsky, still in his laboratory overalls, and behind him Comrade Allon, flanked by two members of the counterespionage group.

"Well?" rumbled General Barzovsky.

"Proceed," ordered the major.

Comrade Vosnevsky, the ordnance engineer, was not entirely happy, but he produced an enlarged photocopy of a diagram of the interior construction of a pistol and a model of the gun. These he laid in the center of the conference table.

General Barzovsky arose, leaned forward and examined both articles. "And what, may I ask, is that?" indicating the diagram.

The major clicked off the reply. "It is a photograph of the diagram of the latest secret weapon of the United States Army obtained by Comrade Allon."

"And that?" inquired the general.

"That," replied the major, "is a working model of the secret weapon itself, achieved by the skill of Comrade Vosnevsky."

General Barzovsky regarded the diagram again, looked over the silent assemblage, then held the gun at arm's length and squeezed the trigger. A grapefruit-sized bubble formed at the nozzle, detached itself and floated away, and then another and another as the general kept squeezing. They were all the same size, for the engineer had constructed the model from the corrections made by Colonel Sisson. They were even more beautiful than those that had entertained the Pentagon group, for the bubbles caught up the colors of the room's magnificent crystal chandelier, and floated away to burst here and there before the horrified gaze of the on-lookers.

It was as though the general was hypnotized, for he could not seem to stop squeezing the trigger until one of the bubbles which had settled on his hand, where it reflected himself expanded five-fold, blew up quietly and broke the spell. He then put the gun back onto the table, sat down and thundered one ham of a fist on the wood, while from his massive chest there burst a tremendous "Ho!"

Comrade Allon slid to the floor in a dead faint, for there was nothing for him but the firing squad, and thus he missed the gen-eral's second and third "Ho's!" and the tears streaming from his eyes. General Barzovsky was laughing his head off. Then it was per-mitted for everyone to laugh, and yells and bellows went up from the gathering to join the hilarity of a Russian general with a sense of humor—until the last of the bubbles exploded into nothingness.

In Sisson's office Julian asked, "What happened?"

The sergeant, at his desk, was still grinning, and the colonel, in his swivel chair, the diagram and bubble gun before him, likewise smiled. "It's too complicated, Julian." And then, feeling that this was on the short side, he said, "Often when men get into a panic they do something silly in the hope that what is worrying them will go away."

Julian, in a straight-backed chair, the soles of his Keds barely meeting the carpeting, stared, and the colonel continued. "Thanks to you, something sillier than usual happened and everybody is pleased with me, and I shall be eternally grateful to you."

"Me?" Julian cried. "What did I do?"

The colonel said gravely, "As I told you, it's difficult to explain, but I want you to promise me to keep your lip buttoned about any-thing you saw or heard in that room." Here the colonel extracted from his desk a rubber stamp and carefully pressed the stamp first on Julian's diagram and then on the back of the boy's hand. In glorious purple ink it read TOP SECRET.

Julian looked at the mark on his hand as though it were the Con-gressional Medal. Then he whispered, "I won't say anything to anyone, ever." Once again he felt the sweet thrill of having participated in the important, even dangerous, world of grown-ups. This time it was too tremendous even to be talked about.

The colonel asked, "How did you make out at the Patent Office?" The exquisite feeling drained from Julian's breast and he was back once more in the world of trouble. He simply shook his head and produced a pamphlet from the Patent Office entitled *Patents and Inventions, An Information Aid For Inventors.*

The colonel sighed. "I know it practically by heart," and opening the booklet at random, began to mutter the long extract of instructions. When he had finished he looked over at Julian, who was regarding him miserably. "Did they tell you about researching and recommend that you acquire a patent attorney?" Julian nodded. "Did you see an examiner?" But the colonel answered his own question. "No, you wouldn't until you'd filed your drawing and claim and paid the fee." The boy's lips were trembling now and Sisson said, "Look, Julian, it isn't as bad as it sounds. Anyway, we can fix you up with your first step, the drawing. I'll have one of my draftsmen get on it right away and you can file it tomorrow morning and see what happens."

"Gee, sir, would you?" But immediately his face clouded. "I haven't got the filing fee. I spent almost all my money getting here."

Sisson nodded gravely, "I see. Would you let me give—"

Julian was positive and immediate. "I couldn't, sir."

The colonel reflected a moment. "Here, I'll fix up a note," and he took a pen and a sheet of paper, speaking as he wrote, "I, Julian West, of— What was your address again?" Julian gave it to him. "Promise to pay Colonel John Sisson, on demand, the sum of sixty-five dollars." He counted out the money from a billfold and handed it over, along with the bubble gun. "Now sign this and it's legal."

"That's terrific, sir. Thank you very much. What time do you think the drawing will be ready tomorrow?"

"Say ten o'clock."

Julian said, "I'll be here for it, sir."

The colonel looked up. "You've got a place to stay?"

Julian nodded. He didn't wish to burden the colonel any further. The cabdriver could help him find a cheap room.

"Hang on a sec while I have a word with my assistant about the changes." He left the office and returned minutes later to find his sergeant alone. He asked, "Where's the boy?"

77

The sergeant replied, "He said he'd be back in the morning."

The colonel looked puzzled, then glanced at the note that Julian had signed and said, "Get me a Mr. West at 137 East View Terrace, San Diego, California, on the phone."

The sergeant balked. "You ain't gonna give him away, are you, sir? That's the kid who was in the papers with the hijacker on the bus. I recognized him."

The colonel said, "His parents must be frantic. By the time his father gets here the kid will have his mission accomplished."

It HAD been a good hour since Julian had vanished into the Pentagon. Meech Morrow had slumped into his seat and was talking to himself. "You're sure one smart cabdriver. They must be holding the kid to send him home and you got about nine dollars' worth of nothing on the clock, besides wasting half the day. Meech Morrow, the great philanthropist." At this point Julian emerged from the doorway ten feet tall and beaming.

Morrow sat up blinking. "What happened?"

Julian said, "The colonel was okay. They're gonna make me the design. I gotta be back for it at ten in the morning."

Meech Morrow liked things to make sense. This did not. But then nothing had since he had encountered Julian, including his own behavior. He said, "Come on now, quit kidding."

Julian began, "The colonel said . . ." whereupon he remembered. "I'm not allowed to say," and he exhibited the back of his hand.

The cabdriver grinned. "Top secret, are you? Well, you won't be for long with every cop in town looking for you. What are you going to do now?"

Julian stared at Morrow without replying.

Morrow said, "You better come home with me or you won't be making it to any Patent Office in the morning. To keep it strictly business let's say you pay me off now. That'll be nine and a half."

Julian handed him a ten. Morrow asked, "Okay if I keep the tip?" Julian nodded. Morrow said, "Right! Now get up front here with me. From now on, Julian, you're my guest."

At TWO thirty that afternoon Julian was finishing lunch with the Morrows and, at the same hour, Frank Marshall was entering the offices of the drafting firm of Peabody and Wilson.

The draftsman, who was waiting with his drawing, asked, "You getting a patent attorney?"

Marshall said, "Can't afford to. I'm down to my last five hundred."

"You can't afford not to. They'll run you ragged over there if you try to push this through yourself. Go to Williams and Burdett on the eighth floor and ask for Jim Williams. They're reasonable." He scribbled on a card and gave it to Marshall.

Jim Williams was a fat, brisk little man with alert eyes.

"I'm in a hurry," Marshall began.

Williams said, "Yes, yes, I know," and glanced at his watch. "Two-hundred-buck retainer. If the patent is denied, it won't cost you any more. If it's granted, another three hundred. You'll want to get this in before closing." And he was on his way out of the office, with Marshall trooping after him.

Two hundred dollars was steep, but at least Williams was a hustler. At twenty past four they were in the office of an examiner and Frank Marshall's papers had been dated, time-stamped and given a registry number, and Marshall had been relieved of his sixty-five-dollar filing fee. Williams told Marshall, "There's some more processing before we start the search, but it's too late this afternoon. We can get it done tomorrow morning. Anyway, you're registered now, so you can sleep tonight."

Walking to the exit, Frank Marshall wondered if he could.

At ten fifteen the following morning Julian emerged from the Pentagon accompanied by Colonel Sisson. Meech Morrow's cab was faithfully drawn up at the curb behind a black limousine in which a sergeant was sitting at the driver's wheel. Sisson said, "There you are, young man. The driver will look after you."

In his cab Meech Morrow grinned and wondered whether Julian would remember him. He did. Julian cried, "Excuse me," and ran to the cab. "Look, Mr. Morrow, I'm going in a general's car."

Morrow nodded. "You're in good hands. I guess you won't be needing me anymore."

Julian held out his hand. "Thanks, Mr. Morrow, and thank Mrs. Morrow again too, please."

Morrow held the small hand for a moment, then eased into gear. "Good luck, kid. Let me know how things turn out."

Julian said, "I will." And it wasn't until the car turned the corner that he realized he had not asked Morrow for his address.

An hour later Julian sat in a straight-backed chair in the office of an examiner in the United States Patent Office. On the desk lay an expert drawing of the bubble gun, plus the filled-out forms and the receipt for the filing fee. Julian was at the end of his quest, the patenting of his invention.

The examiner leafed through the papers, picked them up and laid them once more on his desk. He looked at Julian sharply. "You did say this was original?"

Julian replied, "Yes sir. It's my invention, but the drawings were made by Colonel Sisson, a friend of mine in the Pentagon." He reached into his pocket. "Here's *my* diagram."

The official compared it with the work done by the draftsman. He asked, "What's this top secret stamp on it?"

Julian had a moment of alarm. "I'm not allowed to say."

For a moment the examiner found himself bewildered. This certainly seemed to be some kind of nonsense, but he decided to treat it strictly as business. He therefore said to Julian, "Actually, young fellow, a duplicate set of these drawings passed through my office late yesterday. They're probably being processed right now. Let me have a look." He got up and went into the corridor. Julian followed, his heart thumping violently.

As they emerged from the office a door about three down from them opened, and to his astonishment Julian saw Marshall, accompanied by a fat little man and an official who was saying, "That's all okay. Now go to the third floor, second office on the right. They'll look after you."

Julian's lips formed the word "Marshall," but no sound issued and he was suddenly horribly frightened. His examiner was saying to the other official, "Wait a minute, Fred. I've got an identical set of plans for that invention presented by this kid as his own. Can we have a look?"

The official said, "Sure." The two groups moved closer.

It *was* Frank Marshall, Julian's pal. There was the handsome figure, the worn battle jacket and those unforgettable eyes. The boy was suddenly flooded with relief. Of course. They had lost one another in the terminal and Marshall knew that he, Julian, would be at the Patent Office and had come to find him. He said, "We got lost, didn't we? I couldn't find you in the station."

Frank Marshall did not reply. Now Julian noticed that those bright blue eyes were stony cold.

Julian's examiner said to Marshall, "Do you know this boy?"

Marshall replied, "Never saw him before."

A stricken cry emerged from Julian. "But, Marshall!"

Marshall turned his back. The examiner glanced at the papers and said, "That's right, they're duplicates."

The official said, "We processed them this morning."

The fat man took back the papers. Marshall said, "Okay?"

The official nodded and Julian watched them go off down the corridor. He felt sick. Distantly he heard the examiner say, "Suppose we go back to my office for a chat, sonny."

Numbly, Julian followed him and then he was once more in the straight-backed chair, where he sat paralyzed, his thoughts ranging far in search of the answer to the impossible. How could Marshall, his friend, have done this? Why? The diagram had never left his pocket until he handed it over to Colonel Sisson. Where? When? How? He half remembered then. Pittsburgh. He had been asleep and a shadow had fallen across him and a touch, and then he had slept more peacefully because it would have been Frank Marshall's hand.

The distant voice was saying, "I'll accept this application if you like, but the one you saw go down the hall is time-stamped yesterday and it will have priority. If there was any funny business with that young man, I suppose you could sue."

Julian was unable to reply. The chill at his feet moved up, gripping his middle.

The examiner said, "Wait a minute. Did you ever make a model of your invention?" Julian nodded.

"Well, that's something. Where is it?"

"I gave it to the cabdriver's baby. The one where I stayed last night."

It seemed to Julian that he had turned to ice, yet in his mind he heard again the baby's gurgle of delight as the stream of bubbles emerged from the gun and sailed around the Morrow apartment, sticking on bits of furniture, even on the baby's nose.

The baby's name was Matthew, he was a year and a half old and sat in a high chair. There was Della, aged twelve, and Tom, the boy of fifteen, and Abbie—Mrs. Morrow—who had the most beau-

81

tiful face of anyone Julian had ever seen, and who, when she looked at him, made him feel good all the way through, and happy.

After a fabulous ham-steak dinner Julian had had to reenact the shooting of the hijacker, with Meech Morrow as the hijacker and Tom as the driver. Matthew screamed with delight, Della and Abbie Morrow had applauded and looked upon Julian with wonder and admiration.

Afterward, Julian had been bedded down on the living-room couch and Mrs. Morrow had covered him with a blanket and dropped a featherlike kiss on his cheek. Morrow had looked in and ordered, "Now, you go to sleep. Don't worry, I'll get you to the Pentagon at ten."

And in the morning Julian had filled the soapy solution compartment of the bubble gun for the last time and presented it to the baby as the only thank-you gift he could leave behind. And as he went out the door he saw a bubble floating across the room and heard Matthew's laughter.

The examiner, suddenly on the verge of losing his temper, said, "What are you talking about, boy? What cabdriver?" But then he looked at Julian and he recovered his temper, for something of the boy's state of mind had managed to penetrate to him. There was more behind this curious mix-up and the strange encounter in the hall. But, whatever it was, the official wanted to be quit of it. He sighed. "I'm afraid I can't help you. It's up to you now, my boy. Do you want to take the drawings or leave them?"

Julian, feeling that something inside him had died, arose from the chair and without taking the papers turned and went out. He found his way down the corridor and a flight of steps to the lobby, where he sat on a bench, his back against a pillar, dry-eyed and staring at nothing, in his hand the grubby original diagram of the bubble gun which the examiner had returned to him.

He did not see Frank Marshall as he emerged from the elevators, but Marshall caught sight of the small figure dwarfed even more by the pillar, and kept on going. He had snatched no more than a glimpse of the child's face and did not wish to be reminded of Julian's look in the corridor just a while ago when he had denied him. It was necessary to be tough. In today's jungle you had to look out for number one!

As he made for the revolving door, and his exit forever from the life and times of Julian West, inventor, Marshall felt himself yanked to a stop as though someone had flung a lasso around his shoulders. He slowly turned for one last look. He had not thought that it would be so shattering. He had expected tears or abject misery, but not the look of one whom disillusionment had robbed of every aspect of childhood.

To his surprise his feet turned away from the door and brought him standing, towering, before Julian. The child did not look up. The two legs that had come to a halt before him meant nothing.

Marshall squatted down, his face level with that of the boy. He heard himself say "Julian," and realized that he was still under the spell that had seized him at the door. Now Marshall was confronted with the full force of the white, stricken face.

Marshall said in a voice he hardly recognized, "Okay, kid, so I'm a rat."

Julian stared at him, a flicker of life returning to his eyes, but he remained silent.

Frank Marshall had to explain and drive that terrible look of a beaten man from the face of the boy. He said, "Look, I guess you won't understand and it's tough when you get a kick in the pants, but you're young, sort of a genius. You're gonna invent a lot of things besides the bubble gun." He paused and his voice dropped as he added, "But right now, Julian, I need the patent more than you do."

Their eyes, on a level, were caught up. Julian said nothing.

Marshall continued. "See, I put my last buck down for that patent. I'm flat on my—" He stopped quickly. "I'm flat broke, but I can get some sort of job to keep myself going and when the patent goes through, I'll have a stake. I could get a real start."

If only the boy would burst into tears or lash out at him instead of this uncomprehending stare. Yet, though Marshall was too guilt-ridden to see it, something was awakening behind the lenses of the spectacles.

He pleaded, "Look, kid, we had a great time together. And I kept the cops off your back. You got your picture in the papers, you're a hero and back at school all the kids will be envious."

The boy's face was no longer dead, but perplexed and questioning. Marshall didn't know which was worse. He got in quickly with, "You know you had plenty of guts going off like you did—and you weren't scared like me of that hijacker." This last brought up something that had been missing, and after a moment's hesitation he said, "Do you want to let me have the gun? You won't be needing it now and they asked me about it upstairs."

Automatically, Julian's hand went to the pocket where the bubble gun used to live. Marshall's eyes followed the gesture. Julian's hand came out of his pocket empty, pulling a part of the lining with it. Then Marshall knew that for whatever reason he no longer had the bubble gun, but that if he had, he would have given it to him. And it was Marshall, not Julian, who fought back tears.

He said, "What else can I say, kid? Maybe it's a good lesson. Never trust anybody, especially a guy like me." He rose, saying, "I'll let you know how things come out," and then after another hesitation, "No hard feelings, eh, Julian?"

Julian looked dumbly into Marshall's eyes and slowly shook his head to show that there were none. He felt nothing but the deep and unappeasable sorrow of disillusionment and the shattering of trust.

Marshall held out his hand. "Will you shake?"

Slowly Julian put a limp hand into Marshall's and they shook. Marshall strode quickly away and plunged through the door.

As Marshall went out through one side of the door, Aldrin West came in the other. West almost immediately spied his son and hurried over to him. "Julian! Thank God I've found you."

The meeting was like nothing he had imagined. He had seen himself throwing his arms around the boy and hugging him hard and Julian returning the embrace. He was not prepared for the diffident person who, his face almost expressionless, greeted him with "Hello, Dad."

His father sat down beside him. "Julian, I've just seen the colonel. He told me all about you and I'm proud of you. You're the greatest son a man ever had and I've been a rotten father."

Julian looked surprised at this and shook his head. Parents were as they were and that was that. He said, "No, you aren't. . . ." But then suddenly his voice trailed off. He stopped and the faraway look with which West was to become familiar passed into his eyes.

West said, "Your idea is great. The colonel said it'll work."

But the look on Julian's face was so remote that West became alarmed. "Has something gone wrong? Have you filed the papers? Now that I'm here I can help you."

Julian had been comforted by seeing his father and having him there, but now all the sadness within him forced him to shake his head again. He began, "They were stol—somebody got there ahead of me. I was too late."

EIGHT

They were on the jet, homeward bound. Julian had told his father the story piecemeal, except for the top secret part, interrupted by long silences puzzling to Aldrin West, but which because of his new respect for his son he did not attempt to penetrate. West felt that there was more than a generation gap between himself and his son. There was a mystery connected with what had really happened to Julian.

It seemed to Julian that every part of the story he told his father was in some way attached to the pain of an unhealed wound—Marshall, Marshall, Marshall.

Childhood was over. Julian stood on the threshold of young man, with all the pangs of adolescence still to be suffered. He was unable to put into words his emotions of love and pain. Most difficult of all for him to understand was the nature of his hurt, stemming

85

not only from what had been done to him but from what Marshall had done to himself. But speak of these things to his father? Impossible.

The view from the window of the aircraft showed the green striations of the Appalachian Range. Julian was concluding the most difficult part of his narration. "I guess he took it and copied it while I was asleep." And then almost immediately he felt the need to defend. "It didn't get into the paper, but he was the one who threw the grenade out the window." Then as his thoughts turned back to more recent events, he murmured half to himself, "He said he needed it more than I did." And again Aldrin West was aware of change and that it was no longer a child speaking when Julian said briefly and quietly, "I guess maybe he did."

West, however, mistook it for the helplessness of the young and supplied some adult belligerence. "Look here, Julian, we can fight it in court. I'm a witness as to when you made it. He wouldn't dare stand up to it. We can beat him."

Julian, once more lost in thought, was looking out of the window at midwestern farmlands. Then he became aware that his father had spoken to him and he replied simply, "I don't want to."

Here again was the shell Aldrin West was unable to penetrate. What dark shadows had fallen upon this boy? He tried another tack. "Well, then it doesn't really matter. What's important is that you set out to do something and you did it by yourself. You've shown that you're a man. . . ." West had wanted to go on with this speech of fulsome praise, but it dried up against the barrier of the child's inattention once more.

Julian's mind had been turning back to the trip and all the times that Marshall had been there when he needed him, and he saw once more the gay, half-amused expression on Marshall's face. He suddenly laughed aloud, and when his father looked at him, he said, "He got the truck driver to take us and then he changed me into Buffalo Bill."

West was seized by jealousy. He was Julian's father. He ought to come first with him. And yet someone else had managed to take his place. But this was ridiculous too. The boy had had an exciting adventure, a momentary relationship with an apparently attractive ex-soldier type who would be a hero to any child. He loved his son and wanted to hold him hard to himself and shelter him. Instead he felt himself pushed into flat sentences such as, "There's the Mississippi down there. Old Man River."

Julian said, "I know. We came over it on a bridge. Marshall said he went down it on a riverboat once."

A little later something which had been at the back of West's head ever since he had reunited with his son surfaced into an exclamation of surprise. "Hey, what happened to your stammer?"

Without looking up he replied, "Marshall said to cut it out."

The plane was over the Rockies and West observed, "The Great Divide."

Julian said, "Uh-huh. Marshall said when it's raining, half the drops go into the Pacific and the other half into the Atlantic."

West regarded his son with a sense of helplessness. He hadn't been getting through to him at all. But he had one more card to play. They would be arriving home soon. He said, "I'll tell you what we could do. Next to the trunk room we could make a kind of lab and fix up a lathe, a drawing board or anything you need."

Julian's attention was riveted to the window and the wild moonscape of the badlands of the West, the tumbled country akin to that which carried the deepest memories for him.

". . . and we could work it out together."

His father's voice broke in on Julian's vision. He turned from the window and gave his father a half smile. "Okay, thanks. That would be great."

Aldrin West and his son had yet to touch one another since their meeting. Julian hadn't even taken his proffered hand when they had made their way through the airport in Washington. Now to cover his disappointment he himself looked down out of the window over Julian's shoulder. The landscape had changed again.

West said, "We ought to be home in about an hour. Your mother will be so happy."

Julian made no reply.

JULIAN had changed. There was a slight difference in the way he wore his clothes, in the sound of his footsteps, and yet he remained remote, which enabled him to survive the spate of publicity that attended his return.

His father tried daily. He tried hard. His eyes had been opened to the insensitivity of his own past behavior. He had been badly frightened by Julian's escapade, which might have ended in disaster. His problem was that he did not know what to do. His avenues of approach to Julian consisted of showing an exaggerated interest in his extracurricular activities and Julian accepted this gratefully and responded. Yet Aldrin West was aware that he never penetrated the curious reserve which had fallen upon the boy since he had found him in Washington.

Although West did not know it, he *had* achieved something important. He had shown Julian that he cared, by his concern over Julian's trip and above all by his crossing the continent to bring him home.

Although West was a businessman, not a psychiatrist or even a person with much understanding, he thought it strange that Julian had never broken down. One would have expected a child of his age to shed tears at being robbed of the most important thing he had ever achieved. West, during the ensuing days, was often to wonder at Julian's stony-faced acceptance of things as they were. Outwardly he was a normal schoolboy. The laboratory in the basement had to be accounted a huge success, for when his homework was done Julian was always down there tinkering. But the barrier between his father and himself stayed. As for his mother, she remained blissfully unaware. She had her son back. She was pleased with her husband's efforts, and the manifestations of Julian's independence were realized without too much regret.

It was several months later that Julian came home from school, entered the vestibule noisily and heard his mother's voice from upstairs. "That you, Julian? How was school?"

"Fine. I'm going down to my shop, Mom." He slung his satchel over his shoulder and went down the steps. He hurried through his lessons and thereafter became engrossed in a mechanical problem.

Due to his youth and inexperience Julian's scientific bent was still imitative and adaptive, like his transformation of a water pistol into a bubble gun. Now he was trying to convert a flight toy he had acquired into a toy helicopter.

One of the best things about his lab was its aloneness. His mother never came down. There, with the cellar door closed and lights blazing and the stillness, except for the occasional whine of his drill, his thoughts would sometimes wander far afield and old sadnesses would be revived.

AT SIX ALDRIN WEST came home, set his briefcase down and looked casually through the letters of the late-afternoon delivery. One of them brought a look of curiosity to his face and he examined both sides of it. He called out, "Julian?"

The reply came from below. "I'm down here, Dad."

West descended into Julian's laboratory and asked, "Who do you know in Sheridan, Alabama?" and handed him the letter.

Julian examined it. "Julian West, 137 East View Terrace, San Diego, California," it read in a wandering handwriting that gave him a strange feeling. He finally opened the letter, and his father, looking over his shoulder, saw that it was written on the letterhead of Collins Garage, 43 Main Street, Sheridan, Alabama. Directly beneath this had been pasted a two-inch-square advertisement from a mail-order toy company with a picture of a gun with soap bubbles emerging from the muzzle that looked very much like the one Julian had invented. The text boasted:

Bubblegat! Looks like the real thing. But shoots bubbles. Amaze your friends. Every boy should have a Bubblegat. Order now while they last. Fill out the coupon and send $1.65 to include the cost of mailing to Bubblegat, P.O. Box 37, Fort Lauderdale, Florida.

The man and the boy stared at this advertisement, uncomprehending, then their attention was drawn to the scrawl beneath it. Julian read out loud:

"Dear Julian, I guess somebody beat us both to it. So I was a rat for nothing. Like I said, I blew all my dough so I am down here in Sheridan working in a garage. Hope you are OK.
Your old pal, Frank Marshall."

As Julian finished reading his chin and lower lip began to tremble and his face screwed up curiously. He placed the letter on his workbench, put his face down on his arms and gave way to crying. For the first time since Washington the emotional dam had burst, drawing out the agony that had so long lived in his heart.

Aldrin West looked at his son with amazement. "What are you crying about, son? It serves him right."

Julian raised his head only long enough to shake his head before he was seized by a fresh paroxysm of sobs.

His father groped. "Is it because somebody else thought of the bubble gun first? Look, it can happen to anyone. It shows you your invention was okay."

Punctuated by sobs came the muffled reply, "Who cares about an old bubble gun. It's Marshall."

West picked up the letter and read through it again and for the first time had one of those moments of clarity that are able to sweep away stupidities and demolish all barriers. He let the letter fall to the workbench and put a comforting arm around Julian. He said, "Julian, I guess perhaps I understand. We'll write. Maybe we can give him a hand."

Julian lifted his head from his arms and looked up at his father standing close beside him, and in his ears rang the simple phrase that West had used in all sincerity, "Maybe we can give him a hand." Julian put his arms about his father's waist and his face against the rough material of his jacket and hugged him hard.

Paul Gallico was a well-known sports columnist when, in 1936, he left the New York *Daily News* to freelance. Today, at seventy-seven, he is an immensely popular writer of fiction and nonfiction and the author of a score of motion picture and television scripts, including the recent international film hit, *The Poseidon Adventure,* and an award-winning television production of his great best seller, *The Snow Goose.*

Paul Gallico

Ideas for his stories come from many and sometimes unexpected sources. When Princess Grace of Monaco sent the author a ceramic mouse, he wrote and dedicated to her a children's book, *Manx Mouse.*

For *The Boy Who Invented the Bubble Gun,* the idea originated with a stepson of film producer Elliott Kastner. The boy, the owner of a water pistol, said one day, "Wouldn't it be fun if a pistol were to shoot bubbles instead of bullets?" Intrigued, Kastner had an engineer design such a gun, submitted the diagram with a working model to the Patent Office and was granted a patent pending. Then in 1971, Gallico recalls, Kastner approached him about a possible screenplay based on "a little boy who invented a bubble gun and ran away to Washington to have it patented. He wanted the boy to make the trip via a transcontinental bus on which there would be some amusing characters." Gallico's imagination supplied the rest.

Three of his twenty-four novels have appeared as Condensed Books selections: *Mrs. 'Arris Goes to Paris, Mrs. 'Arris Goes to New York* and *The Hand of Mary Constable.* The irrepressible Mrs. 'Arris will be off on another surprising journey in a forthcoming volume.

When not writing, the author enjoys fencing, cooking and fishing at his home in Antibes on the southern coast of France.

The struggle of an American cardinal to fulfill his calling as

THE GOOD
SHEPHERD

A CONDENSATION OF THE BOOK BY
Thomas Fleming

ILLUSTRATED BY
Jim Sharpe

"*Frater noster taciturnus*"—our silent brother—whispered the Pope of Rome. And the new American cardinal kneeling before him knew why he had been chosen to receive the red biretta. Archbishop Matthew Mahan, kindly smooth talker, master fund raiser, war hero, had been accommodatingly silent on *Humanae Vitae*, Rome's birth control encyclical. Cardinal Mahan would also be expected to be silent on divorce, on celibacy, on all controversial issues with which a rebellious clergy was plaguing the Vatican. But Father Matthew Mahan had known and cherished the late Pope John XXIII, who had seen that the Church could not stand still, who had not feared to change its age-old ways. Now, in Rome, memories of John came flooding back to Matthew Mahan.

Set against a crowded tapestry that encompasses both the grandeur of Rome and the politico-religious life of a middle-sized American city, this is the story of a cardinal's arduous struggle to be a true priest—a good shepherd—in the Church he serves and loves.

I

THE silver-haired woman walked to the window of her penthouse
and gazed down at the city. It was twilight, and for a moment
Rome was magic, a gigantic festival of light being staged for her
benefit. All because of this piece of paper in her hand, a letter that
began, "Your friend will be one of five Americans. The news will
be announced tomorrow. . . ."

Beyond the dark hollow of the Tiber, the dome of St. Peter's
Basilica suddenly rose from the shadows of Trastevere as the floodlights came on. The woman's eyes recoiled from a sight that not so
many years ago had soothed and strengthened her. Now it only
seemed to arouse enormous sadness—or, occasionally, a sickening
panic. But tonight she turned her back on St. Peter's dome and took
the creaking elevator down to the street floor. She wore a white
linen suit and almost no makeup. Her purse, her shoes were also
white. She paused before the wrought-iron doors of the apartment
house and took a deep breath of the soft air of Roman spring.

Behind her, the *portiere* of the apartment sat at his window.
"There she goes to her lover again," he grunted.

From the kitchen his wife unleashed a stream of vituperation
on Italian men. The American madonna was beautiful, she swore,
in a spiritual way beyond his animal understanding.

He barely listened to his wife's insults. "I still say she has a lover.
There is something about the way a woman carries herself, once
she has awakened a man's desire."

95

Unaware of the controversy she was generating, the woman in white strode swiftly along the Via Margutta past the antique stores and art galleries, acknowledging the greetings called out from doorways. She turned into an alley and thence into the Piazza di Spagna. A half hundred young people from a dozen nations, sexually indistinguishable, lounged on the ancient yellow Spanish Steps, some singing, most simply staring. She was glad it was too dark to see their faces. The vacuous boredom on so many of them, especially the American faces, always pained her.

She stepped into a small black cab at the head of the taxi rank and said in perfect Italian, "The Church of St. Peter in Chains, please." The driver made a couple of turns and then he was roaring down the Via del Corso. Here his Italian fondness for combat with other drivers flowered as he charged between buses and taxis.

The woman in white sat in the back seat scarcely noticing that her life was in danger. She had survived many similar rides. They swept past the Piazza Colonna, a favorite arena for Rome's increasingly violent political demonstrations, and on past the imperial forums, where fragments of ancient Rome's power and glory gleamed in a battery of floodlights. Just beyond was the Colosseum, a living monument to ancient Rome's other heritage, her incredible bestiality. Exultantly shifting gears, the driver hurtled into the shabby Via Cavour, past strolling prostitutes in gold miniskirts and past fifth-rate hotels. Opposite a glossily modern hotel the cabdriver stopped. The woman in white paid him and got out.

Walking once more with that stride of hers, she entered a dark, narrow passageway, at the end of which she emerged into a small cobblestone square. On her left was an old church, originally built in the fifth century. A man in a white shirt stood in the doorway. The woman took a black veil from her purse and draped it over her hair. At the doorway, she slipped money into the man's hand, murmuring, "Thank you, Mario."

She entered the church and stood for a moment gazing at the marble statue on the right. It was by Michelangelo, and it depicted Moses after he had received the Ten Commandments on Mount Sinai. But tonight the woman had not come to admire this massive masterpiece. Nor to pray. She had come to commune with two men who had brought her to this church ten years ago, two men whom she loved in ways that she herself sometimes found hard to understand. Especially the love that she felt for the man who was still alive. He was almost four thousand miles away, across the vast Atlantic, but standing here she felt his presence, could almost hear his voice, see him smile. She could relive for a fierce moment the days and weeks and months when her love for him had been a constant torment. Yet she found strength, even a bittersweet happiness, in this memory. Now this man meant something more profound, more immense, than that old lost passionate wish to touch him, to hold him, and be held by him. He had acquired a meaning that pervaded her soul.

The woman in white came here often for this communion. It had sustained her when she thought her heart was about to wither. Tonight she had not come seeking his strength but rather to share his joy.

For five minutes she stood there, her mind, even her body radiant. Then she thought of the other man, the one who was dead, and a shadow seemed to fall upon her joy. On the altar the candlelight flickered weirdly. She raised her eyes into the darkness beneath the roof of the Church of St. Peter in Chains and whispered, "Watch over us, Don Angelo, watch over us, *please.*"

II

AT THAT very moment the man for whom the woman in Rome was praying emerged from his limousine and paused, almost blinded by the eleven-a.m. American sunshine. With the seven-passenger black Cadillac behind him, he looked like a creature from another planet. On his head he wore a tall, purple and gold miter, in his hand was a bronze shepherd's crosier. A purple and gold cope covered his shoulders and was fastened across his chest by a gold clasp. On his feet were square-toed purple shoes with large silver buckles.

The sun was warm on the man's back. Only a faint breath of March's chilly wind stirred the air. Archbishop Matthew Mahan was not disturbed by the humdrum architecture of the church confronting him. Holy Angels was little more than a big, slant-roofed red brick rectangle with a touch of pseudo Georgian in its white doors and trim. Instead, he noted with approval the freshness of the white paint. Beside the church the massive red brick rectory showed the same meticulous maintenance. Across the parking lot, now half full of gleaming new station wagons and sleek sedans, the one-story red brick school, an equally trim cluster of buildings, occupied the entire north side of the block. Up and down the surrounding streets spread the homes and grounds of affluent Catholics. Younger priests called this suburb the Golden Ghetto.

That sarcasm might have disturbed some churchmen in the year of our Lord 1969. But not Matthew Mahan, who prided himself on being a realist. The Church had to serve both the affluent and the poor. If the sight of Holy Angels stirred any emotion in him, it was pride. His energy, his vision had planned this center of Catholic life when the Golden Ghetto was still on the drawing boards of the real estate men. Even more of his energy had raised the money to pay for the huge Catholic high school. It was this kind of foresight, this kind of alert awareness of the modern family's compulsion to flee ever farther from the smoggy city, that had won Matthew Mahan the admiration—and cooperation—of the real estate entrepreneurs.

There was also nothing disturbing about the three priests and that crowd of smiling, smartly dressed parents who waited for him at the church doors. From square jaw to bulging belly, Monsignor Paul O'Reilly looked like the personification of the Irish pastor, stern but kind. Flanking him, Fathers Emil Novak and Charles Cannon seemed model curates, earnest and humble. No, Matthew Mahan thought ironically, nothing here to disturb an archbishop.

But something was disturbing this archbishop. Beneath his purple and gold vestments prowled a malevolent pain. It seemed to open and close with every breath he took, like some exotic tropical flower. This morning at four another metaphor had suggested itself: a rotating medieval mailed fist with jagged spears on its knuckles. The bread and wine he had consumed at his morning Mass, followed by bacon and eggs and home-fried potatoes, had temporarily stilled it. But it had returned in this flowering guise as his Cadillac rolled off the expressway into the Golden Ghetto.

Matthew Mahan had never had a serious illness. And he would not admit that any aspect of his job troubled him. Whatever was happening in his innards had nothing to do with the knowledge that behind Monsignor O'Reilly's smile lay treachery and hatred;

that behind the timidity of Fathers Novak and Cannon lay fear and loathing and rebellion. Nor would the archbishop admit, as he got out of the car, that the pain had anything to do with the weariness that he felt seeping through his body.

He glanced at his wristwatch. They were only ten minutes late—not disastrous if what was to come inside the church ran on time. With abrupt irritation he peered into the limousine. "Come on, Dennis," he said. "We've got a schedule to keep."

The pale, freckled face of Father Dennis McLaughlin responded with a nod. He was frantically clipping notes to pieces of paper scattered on the seat beside him and on the car floor. They had gotten through half the day's mail en route from the city.

"I don't want to forget—anything," Dennis said, the hiatus an unspoken apology for the numerous things he had forgotten in the past two weeks. Dennis McLaughlin emerged into the sunshine and stood by the archbishop. He was as wiry, bony, sinewy as Matthew Mahan was solid. Shaggy red hair rioted around the back edge of his round white collar. Matthew Mahan consciously suppressed the additional flicker of irritation caused by his new secretary's haircut, or lack of one, and strode up the walk.

Dennis found himself marveling at the broad smile on Matthew Mahan's face as he shook hands with Monsignor O'Reilly and the curates. Did it prove that the archbishop was what he liked to consider himself—the thorough politician—or what Dennis suspected: the compleat hypocrite? Fathers Novak and Cannon looked like frightened birds.

"I'm sorry we're a little behind schedule," Matthew Mahan said, smiling at the group of parents as he spoke.

"The children have been very patient," said Monsignor O'Reilly in a superbly neutral tone.

"Joe, how are you?" The archbishop had spotted Joe O'Boyle, local captain of the annual archbishop's fund drive. Insurance man. Father of eight. "One of your gang in here?"

"My daughter Morrin."

"Good. Good." Matthew Mahan turned back to Monsignor O'Reilly, whose stolid face might have been chiseled from marble. The whole man was marble—or some cheaper stone—a statue by some third-rate sculptor. The statue moved, stalked into the church, his curates hurrying after him. Matthew Mahan followed.

Going up the aisle, he found himself wondering why he did not appoint another auxiliary bishop—a young man—to handle these chores. Was it the memory of his own career as auxiliary bishop—the way he had quietly absorbed control of the archdiocese from old Hogan? Or was it simply the pleasure he got out of fulfilling all the duties of his office, especially this one—administering the sacrament of confirmation, conferring the gifts of the Holy Spirit, which only a bishop was empowered to bestow?

It was more than the sacrament, he decided, as he nodded and smiled at the curious, expectant faces in the first ten pews. The girls were all in white, the boys in blue blazers and gray pants (in his day it had been dark blue suits). In the city, where so many of the parishes were now filled with the poor, the nuns had abandoned a strict dress code. It was somehow comforting to see the tradition continued here—although he was sure that Dennis McLaughlin would argue that these parents should instead donate the price of the blazers and dresses to the poor.

Monsignor O'Reilly and his curates entered the sanctuary and took seats to the right of the altar table. Matthew Mahan remained in the center aisle, waiting for the organ music to end. As the last notes died away he opened his arms and said, "Peace be with you, my dear friends, and especially with you, my dear young people who are going to receive your confirmation today. First, though, I'm supposed to find out if you're ready to receive it. Let's see. Do you know why I am here? Why couldn't Monsignor O'Reilly or Father Novak give you this sacrament? Can you tell me?" He pointed to a towhead. "What's your name, son?"

The boy stood up. "Thomas Maloney, your Excellency."

"Now, now, don't call me that. The popes don't want us to use all these titles anymore. Pope John asked us to call him Don Angelo. Don is an Italian title of respect. But I couldn't manage that one. I called him Santo Padre. That's Italian for Holy Father. Somehow it sounds better. Anyway, I want you to call me Father. I want to start you people off right. You're the ones who will really change the Church. Now, why am I here, Thomas?"

"Because only a bishop can administer this sacrament."

"Right. Now let me find another victim." He eyed a boy with blazing red hair. "Don't you think this getup I am wearing is pretty ridiculous?"

The boy shook his head.

"You don't? Come up and take a closer look."

The boy timidly approached him. Matthew Mahan took off his miter and put it on his head. Everyone roared. "Now, you would feel silly walking around with that on your head. Tell me, then, why do you think I wear it?"

"Well—because other bishops did, a long time ago."

"Right! I'm wearing this outfit," Matthew Mahan said, speaking to all the children now, "to remind us that the sacrament of confirmation goes all the way back—almost two thousand years—to the Apostles, who were the first bishops. What does this mean?" He pointed to the crosier and chose a girl.

"It means you're the shepherd of the people."

"Like who?"

"Like Jesus."

"Right. He was the Good Shepherd. I'm only mediocre."

It was amazing, thought Dennis McLaughlin, watching from the sacristy. The total transformation of the man from the moment he began talking to the children. He emanated radiance, a kind of excitement and joy. Was he basically an actor? Was this an act? Or was the smooth reserve that you saw most of the time an act?

"You're doing awfully well," Matthew Mahan was saying. "I think I may tell Pope Paul the next time I go to Rome that we all ought to resign and let you people start running the Church when you're eighteen or so. . . . You, young lady." He pointed to a girl in the first pew. "Who received the first confirmation?"

"The Apostles," she said.

"Right. Where?"

"In the same room where Jesus had the Last Supper with them."

"Right again. And what did they see?"

"Tongues of fire above their heads."

"Do you think you'll see tongues of fire today?" Whirling, he picked a boy in the second pew. "What do you think?"

"I—I don't know," he said.

"Well, you won't. The only tongue you'll see is mine. Here it is, wagging away." He stuck his tongue out and walked down the aisle while everyone burst into laughter again. "Just a poor old bishop's tongue," he said as the laughter died away. "Not much good for anything but trying to persuade people to do what they

101

should be doing without being told. Those tongues of fire the Apostles saw—that was to help them *believe* that they were receiving the Holy Spirit. No one had ever received it before, you see, and Jesus knew how hard it was to create *faith* in people, faith that inspires people to *do* things. But when the Apostles went out and started converting people, right in the Temple at Jerusalem before the eyes of the men who had killed Jesus, then people began to see what the Holy Spirit really meant. How many did they convert in the first few days, does anybody know?"

A hand shot up. "Eight thousand," said a deep voice.

"Eight thousand people. Can you imagine that? And the Apostles laid hands on them, and the Holy Spirit entered into these converts. Then what did they do?"

"They went out and converted more people."

"Well, some of them did that. But they *all* did something even more important. What? What are Christians supposed to do? This is the most important question I've asked yet."

"Love one another," said a clear, sweet voice after a pause.

"Right. From the very start of the Church, this was what made the Christians stand out. That's how I hope you'll show everyone what it means to receive the Holy Spirit. We don't have time here to discuss what it means to love each other. It's not easy. It's easy to say, but not easy to do. I hope you'll discuss it in class this week and each write me a letter about it. Give me at least one example of how you loved someone and did something about it."

In the sacristy, Dennis McLaughlin almost groaned aloud. He would have to answer all those letters. He fumed at himself for being an incurable idiot. This man did not talk you into becoming his secretary. You talked yourself into it with your absurd illusions about penetrating the power structure.

"Now I think we're ready," Matthew Mahan said. He entered the sanctuary and took the bishop's chair.

Monsignor O'Reilly said the Mass. After the Gospel, Matthew Mahan gave a brief sermon. He talked about his own confirmation, how he had gone home, convinced that he possessed the Holy Spirit, and attempted to convert his younger brother, Charlie. "I didn't think he was a very good Christian," he said. "I told him he had to stop calling me names, had to loan me his baseball glove whenever I wanted it, and give me the last extra helping of dessert.

I had it all backward. I thought I had to convert everyone else, since I was more or less perfect. It took me years to know better. "Now I know that the most important gift of the Holy Spirit is the *power* to love. That may sound strange to you. Of course, you love your families. Love seems easy at your age. But when you grow older it's more challenging. Especially the kind of love that Jesus urges us to practice. The love for the lost sheep, for sinners, for people who are in trouble. He tells us that it is better to go looking for one lost sheep and let the ninety-nine obedient, faithful sheep stay on the hills. That's risky, hard. Not many Catholics—not many people of any religion—practice that kind of love. It's the kind I hope you'll practice when you grow up."

The children then streamed up to the altar. Matthew Mahan anointed each with the holy chrism and laid his hand against their cheeks. Watching, Dennis McLaughlin remembered his own confirmation. It had left him bewildered, wondering why he had spent four weeks memorizing catechism questions that had never been asked. That night he had lain awake trying to detect some sign of the Holy Spirit in him. But he did not feel braver, stronger, or happier. The next day in school the bullies were tormenting "Brains" McLaughlin, Sister was screaming imprecations and whaling away with her ruler, and the standard topic of male discussion was still Mary McNamara, who would, it was rumored strongly, hold up her skirts for a nickel.

After Mass, helping Matthew Mahan take off his vestments, Dennis noticed that the archbishop was soaked with perspiration. "Whenever I speak in public, I sweat like a steer," he remarked. "It makes me wonder about my vocation sometimes."

"I thought you were having a good time," Dennis said.

"I was. I hope the kids were, too. How do you think it went?"

"I thought you were great," Dennis said.

Matthew Mahan looked almost angry. "You're not joking?"

"No—why—no," Dennis said. "I—I mean it."

The pain flowered in Matthew Mahan's stomach. Would you ever be able to talk naturally with this enigmatic young man? "Take my things out to the car, will you?" he said, trying to sound friendly. "I have that little call to pay on Monsignor O'Reilly."

Dennis was tempted to say good luck. But having collected one rebuke for candor, he decided silence was safer.

DENNIS WAITED IN THE CAR with rotund Eddie Johnson, the archbishop's black chauffeur. While Eddie listened to a ball game on the radio, Dennis revised a draft of a speech that Matthew Mahan would be making next week. The subject was the renewal of the Church since Vatican II. Like so many statements that emanated from bishops, from the Vatican itself, he thought sourly, it had everything but passion. It committed the archdiocese to the idea of renewal, but scarcely a single specific issue was discussed, and it was full of cautionary maxims against going too far too fast.

On the radio now, a voice was somberly announcing that Dwight D. Eisenhower had just died in Washington, D.C. "My my," Eddie Johnson said. "Poor old Ike." Dennis, unmoved, finished his revision and took from his coat pocket two letters he had received in the morning mail. One was from his mother in Florida, the other from his friend Andrew Goggin, S.J., in Rome. He would read Mother's first. Then, like the old glass of cherry soda after the milk of magnesia, he would read Gog's.

Dear Dennis:

I thought you promised to write once a week. It's been three weeks now. I had to find out from your brother Leo about your wonderful promotion. I'm not surprised, really. I knew they'd soon realize they had one of the most brilliant young priests in America. God would not disappoint me twice. You know how upset I was when you left the Jesuits.

I can't tell you how pleased I was to hear that you were out of that dreadful slum neighborhood. I was sure one of those people was going to stick a knife in you while you were busy trying to save their souls. That's the only kind of gratitude they've ever shown since the day we freed them from slavery.

Now that you are promoted, I guess you won't be getting a vacation for a while. That's too bad, because I was hoping you might spend a week or two down here with me, like you did last year. Leo sounds like he's working awfully hard, and I can't see why the editor of the paper won't give him a raise. Can't you speak to the archbishop about it?

I hear a horn outside. My neighbor is taking me for a drive down to Miami. This is a short letter, and they'll get shorter until you write me a *good long one*.

Love,
Mother

Good old Mom. The memory of those two weeks last year made him shudder. He had been trying to decide whether to leave the Jesuits or the priesthood or both, and he had made the mistake of talking it over with her. How strange it had been to discover at twenty-nine that this woman who had always seemed spritely and courageous was also trite and querulous, that her little maxims about praying together and keeping the heart pure were the fifth-rate philosophy of the world, culled from cheap magazines. Why, why hadn't you seen this before, Dennis?

Because you had spent ten years of your life in an intellectual balloon, smiling grandly on Mother and the other lilliputians, seeing their shortcomings as mildly amusing. But when the desolation came, when the balloon ran out of hot air, you found yourself surrounded by leering faces, asking why, why this intellectual young Jesuit had to go to the roots of his life. He'd been appalled to discover that the intelligence he'd always assumed he inherited from Mother must have come from nonexistent Father, the man with the smiling face and the pilot's cocky hat, that bodiless being who grinned so confidently from Mother's dresser. But how could a man draw sustenance of the sort he was seeking from a ghost? Perhaps this hunger explained your capitulation to Matthew Mahan. If you were looking for a father, Dennis, you've found one in the classic mold. A combination slave driver and SOB.

No, he was not *that* bad. Balance, Dennis, what has happened to the beautiful balance, the discrimination that was your pride? Has it withered in the glare of the burning cities, crunching bombs, bullet-crumpled leaders, the ghastly symbols of the 1960s? Was it also—that balance—your curse, the cause of your collapse? Wasn't lack of passion, the very thing for which you taunted the Church, your own tragicomic flaw?

He had sat through endless discussions of spiritual dryness with his Jesuit superiors. He had wondered if the Ph.D. in history he was getting from Yale had something to do with his inner emptiness. He had decided there was some central flaw in his personality that forced him relentlessly to see the fly in every ointment. By temperament he was a spectator who liked to smile down at the groundlings and the actors in the modern theater of the absurd.

It was his mounting dread of this fate, this hollowness, that had driven him out of the Jesuit order, where he was highly esteemed as one of their most promising young scholars. He was becoming, he had decided, a papier-mâché priest, fluttering in windy emptiness. One thing relieved this dry emptiness while deepening his despair: his lust. Like one of the creatures from the apocalypse, lust stalked him. Neither prayer nor mortification helped in the least. He had once toyed with extremes of penitence, wondering if it were time to fashion a whip of razor blades, favored by some Irish Jesuits in the early years of the century. But the idiocy of the idea made him laugh.

So he resigned from the Jesuits and sought a career in the city's slums, hoping that pity would replace conviction. But there, too, he saw all the wrong things. He was appalled by the stupidity of the poor, by their self-hate, their degradation, and anguished by the pitiful formulas he had to offer them as solace.

When the archbishop had summoned him to the chancery, he had been close to walking out on the whole show. Give up a role you were never meant to play, he had told himself. Take your Ph.D., pay the Jesuits for your expensive education, and retire to some university faculty where you can devote your life to turning out dry and disillusioned students like yourself.

"Jee-sus," gasped Eddie Johnson. "You hear *that?* Two out in the ninth, two men on, and they pitched to Willie. . . ."

"Terrible," Dennis murmured. "Terrible."

Hurriedly he opened Goggin's letter. A few laughs is what you need, Dennis. Old Gog never fails.

Dear Mag,

Your latest depressing letter lies on my desk while Roman rain patters on the Villa Stritch's tiles. I don't know how the First Person permits it to rain so much on the very bosom of Mater Ecclesia. Proof perhaps of your dubious speculation that God is a woman and jealous of other females, including her own daughter. Ho-hum.

The Villa Stritch is where the American employees at the Vatican hang their birettas. A drafty old barn, but we do our best to warm the atmosphere with laughter. God knows it isn't easy in this sixth year in the reign of Pope Paul, who has quietly crucified the best hopes of the best people.

As for yours truly—well, once a week I wander over to the Jesuit GHQ, just around the square from the Vatican, and help translate the latest bad news from English into Italian so that Father General's Italian secretary can condense them (no doubt leaving out the cries of despair) for our Maximum Leader.

Two days a week I go for a delightful ride in the country in one of our Fiats. Except that every mile involves at least one duel to the death with an Italian driver, it is a pleasant run. My destination is the Vatican Radio transmitting station, whence I broadcast the Divine Line in English to South Africa. While I babble my message of racial equality, I always have the image of huge electronic ears jamming every word I say.

Two more days a week I play linguistics at the Biblical Institute, where I listen to a lot of people hint at things that they're afraid to say openly about the Gospels. The more I ponder it, the more it becomes for me the Church's only hope—the creation of a new Gospel, in which His various sayings are arranged in reasonably chronological order and He himself is placed in the social context of first-century Palestine. We should be able to see Him as He was, and nevertheless have the spiritual miracle remain—His *acceptance* of the crucifixion, His awareness that only by His death could the victory He sought become possible. This to me is so much more poignant, so much more beautiful, than the picture so often given, of God taking on human form to do the beings He created the favor of redemption.

This is burn-at-the-stake thinking, and every one of us over at the Biblical Institute knows it. What we need, Mag, is a writer with power, grace, and courage. To wit, you. I curse the day that you blundered into American history in search of your so-called mystery of freedom. The world doesn't want to be free, old boy, and it never did. My idea is totally different. The Church is necessary to the stability of mankind. She must proclaim the New Gospel, out of the fullness of her wisdom and the depths of her delving into the mystery of God's dialogue with creation; we must present the world with a coherent account of one of the greatest acts of love in human history. Wouldn't you want to be remembered as the writer of that book? You could do it, Mag, if you could only get your carcass over here to the Vatican Library.

Seriously, something has to be done. Or at least begun. I have no intention of spending my life aboard a drifting ship. As for you, all your yakking about lust and emptiness would vanish if you could find a purpose for your priesthood. Come over here and get to work before some swinging nun retires you to humdrum domesticity forever.

Gog

Dennis stared numbly at Goggin's letter, wondering why he thought it would cure his depression. A "swinging nun" might indeed cure it. And maybe there was another cure: tearing off this round white yoke around his neck once and for all, and breathing the sweet air of American freedom. He suddenly found it unbearably close in the limousine. He flung open the door and got out, taking long, deep breaths. Here in the suburbs the air was still sweet. But in the city? Twenty miles away he could see the gray pall of smog. The air of American freedom was anything but sweet these days. Which made Father McLaughlin worse than a man without a country—he was a man without a cause.

INSIDE Holy Angels rectory, Archbishop Mahan sat at a table with Monsignor Paul O'Reilly and Fathers Emil Novak and Charles Cannon. "Gentlemen," he said. "Can't I help resolve this distressing situation?"

The curates stared stonily at him. "Only if you state in writing that nothing we say will be held against us—by you or by him," Father Cannon said. Only just ordained, he could have passed for a teenager with his freckled face and drifting hair.

"Have you ever heard anything betray a bad conscience more clearly?" Monsignor O'Reilly growled.

"Perhaps it would be better if we discussed things separately," Father Novak said. Though he was thirty-five, he had a boyish look. Last year he had been reported to the chancery for paying too much attention to a woman in his parish. He had denied it vehemently, but possibly this brawl with his new pastor was part of a plan to justify his departure from his priesthood.

"I hate to, but it may be the best way to begin communicating. You two go on upstairs. I'll talk with the monsignor first."

"Would you like something to drink, your Excellency?" Monsignor O'Reilly said. "Scotch? Bourbon? Sherry?"

"Sherry would be nice," Matthew Mahan said, and in the same moment knew it was futile to pretend friendship with this man.

O'Reilly took an Irish crystal decanter and two small gold goblets from the antique French sideboard. He had obviously inherited the expensive tastes of his mentor, Archbishop Hogan. "Tio Pepe," he said. "I hope you like it."

Archbishop Mahan nodded, and sipped the wine. "You realize

we're dealing with a problem that could tear the diocese apart."

"Naturally we each have our own point of view," O'Reilly said. "I'm concerned about the damage to the souls of my parishioners. I was trained by the Jesuits, you know, in Rome. At the Gregorian. That tends to make me much more sensitive to the importance of moral theology."

The old Roman ploy. Matthew Mahan carefully controlled his temper. How many times had he heard this lofty reminder during the 1950s, when O'Reilly had been Archbishop Hogan's vicar-general and considered his probable successor. O'Reilly had taken a very dim view of Matthew Mahan, fund raiser and public relations monsignor extraordinary, appearing from nowhere to shunt him aside.

"No one is more sensitive to moral theology than I, Monsignor. But I am also sensitive to what happened in Washington, D.C."

"You mean Cardinal O'Boyle's stand against those priests who thought they could defy the teaching of the Holy Father?"

"I mean the headlines, the exchange of insults—what that did to the faith of the people."

"It helps to know where the Church stands. Where would we be if the popes hadn't struck down heresy every time it arose?"

"Monsignor," said Matthew Mahan abruptly. "I came here to restore peace to this parish, this rectory. Have you any suggestions?"

"Only one, your Excellency. Do your duty. Settle this issue, as other bishops have, by a firm, clear, unequivocal statement."

"You cannot involve the diocese in this personality clash—"

"This is not a personality clash. It is a theological conflict. Direct my curates, your Excellency, to acknowledge the Holy Father's teaching, or suspend them. That would satisfy your desire to keep our dispute as secret as possible."

Matthew Mahan shoved aside his sherry. "Do you think it's an accident, Monsignor, that you've had eight assistants in ten years? Why do you think men keep asking for transfers? I'm going upstairs. When I come down, I hope you have something more realistic to suggest."

In Father Novak's third-floor room, Matthew Mahan was appalled by the unmade bed, the unwashed clothing, the plates with yesterday's supper on them. "He's refused to let the housekeeper come upstairs to clean, or even to take the dishes down," Father

Novak said. "He said it wasn't safe for her. Would you put up with that sort of innuendo, your Excellency?" He lit a cigarette. His hands were trembling.

"Sit down, sit down, Emil," said Matthew Mahan. "Tell me . . ."

For a half hour both curates told him. Monsignor O'Reilly had started waging the war of petty slights against them when he discovered that they did not accept the teaching of *Humanae Vitae,* the Pope's encyclical on birth control. "Whether we're right or wrong doctrinally, he hasn't got the authority to tell me to be in by ten o'clock," Father Cannon said, his voice thick with outrage. One night he actually had been locked out of the rectory.

Matthew Mahan accepted a cigarette from Father Novak and assured both priests that the harassment would end, today. "But to settle this situation, you'll have to agree that under no circumstances will either of you speak publicly against *Humanae Vitae.* This, I might add, is something on which *I* insist. Monsignor O'Reilly would want a good deal more."

"How can we be pastors to people if—" Father Cannon began.

"You're free to deal with *individuals* as your conscience sees fit. But when you are up in that pulpit you are not pastors, you're teachers, and I, your bishop, will tell you what to teach."

For a moment Matthew Mahan was dismayed by the words he had just spoken. Never had he imagined himself saying such a thing. "Let me explain," he said. "I am trying to keep peace— Christian peace—in this archdiocese. That is the paramount thing. I am ready to do anything—including the suspension of all three of you—to prevent this situation from exploding into a scandal."

He saw a vaguely resentful look on Father Cannon's face. Plus a little fear. The beginning of wisdom, he hoped. But Father Novak was the one who needed delicate handling.

"This must be hard for you, Emil. You had a taste of injustice at your last parish. I'm not telling you to swallow your anger. Admit it exists. Then ask yourself, All right—but what's the best thing for the Church, for the people—all of them?"

Father Novak was silent. Like most liberals, Matthew Mahan thought, he was not satisfied with an archbishop who merely allowed him freedom of conscience on this agonizing birth control issue. He wanted the archbishop's power on *his* side. His own opinion, he assumed, should be the official position of the Church.

"Try to see it from my point of view," Matthew Mahan went on. "From the point of view of Catholics who have made tremendous sacrifices to have big families. . . ." A voice suddenly howled in his mind, the cry of a lost soul. He could see his own brother's sneering, twisted mouth: You tell 'em, Bishop. A pulse throbbed in Matthew Mahan's forehead. He looked out the window at the spring sunshine and wished he were far away.

"What's your personal opinion of the Pope's encyclical, your Excellency?" Father Novak asked, his manner suddenly open. Matthew Mahan sensed a trap. Emil was active in the Archdiocesan Association of Priests, which had rebellious tendencies.

"My opinion isn't the issue, Emil. Let's just say I agree with Cardinal Cushing. You can't put a cop under every bed."

From the sudden pleasure in Father Novak's eyes, Matthew Mahan suspected he had said too much. Cushing could hold all sorts of far-out opinions without upsetting anyone. He recalled a morning at the Second Vatican Council, when Cardinals Cushing and Spellman were conversing animatedly in a coffee bar. "There they are, the roughie and the smoothie," someone had said. And Matthew Mahan had realized that he preferred the smoothie style— without Spellman's conservative politics.

"Well," said Father Cannon. "I'd like to resolve it. This is no way to live. I'll agree to keep silent publicly."

Matthew Mahan suspected that he had been wanting to say this for some time. "Emil?" he asked.

Father Novak, clearly disappointed in Father Cannon, nodded.

"Good," said Matthew Mahan with a heartiness he did not feel. "Now let me talk with Monsignor O'Reilly."

Monsignor O'Reilly was watching television. He turned off the sound, but left the color picture on. "No doubt you've heard me thoroughly reviled," he said.

"On the contrary. I got the impression that you had two very contented curates until this business came up. This *is* one of the two or three best-run parishes in the diocese. Now, have you given this thing more thought?"

The monsignor kept looking at the screen. "I can live with my conscience only with the solution I have already proposed."

Rage boiled in Matthew Mahan's brain. Part of it was anger at himself for the conciliatory tone he had just taken. He switched off the television and roared at O'Reilly. "I may not have a Roman education, Monsignor. But I am not stupid when it comes to motivation. I consider this entire charade an oblique attack on me, and you are very close to arousing my enmity. Do you wish to continue as pastor of this parish? Answer me."

A triumphant hatred gleamed in O'Reilly's eyes. In this moment of the naked display of his own power Matthew Mahan felt a twist of defeat. He had said what O'Reilly would have said to him if their positions had been reversed.

"You know the answer to that question, your *Excellency*."

"Then listen." He described the promise he had extracted from the curates. "They agree to make no statement of their views on *Humanae Vitae* in public. You can't ask more than that."

"I say they should interrogate every woman in the confessional on what she is doing about the Holy Father's encyclical."

"I absolutely forbid such a thing. The confessional is not a witness stand in a law court. A priest is not a district attorney. The care of souls, Monsignor, does not involve forcing them to reveal their guilt. Now, will you accept my compromise?"

"If you order me to accept it, I will accept it."

"I order you. I also order you to restore civil discourse to this rectory, to give Fathers Cannon and Novak the housekeeping services they require and their seats at your table. I must also insist that you give them keys to the front door, so that they can go and come as they please."

"I trust you will also take responsibility for the gross misconduct that may arise from this freedom on Father Novak's part?"

"He will take responsibility for his own actions."

A contemptuous nod. "Is there anything else?"

"A little advice. I think it was Cardinal Mercier who said that the besetting sin of priests was not liquor or women. But jealousy. I urge you to think about that, Monsignor."

Matthew Mahan trudged up to the third floor again. There he urged the two curates to do or say nothing that would further aggravate the situation. He looked hard at Father Novak. Did he get the message? One could only hope.

As he left the rectory, Matthew Mahan was again engulfed by a tremendous rage. He saw O'Reilly's face contemptuously staring past him at the television set. Should he go back? No. He struggled to calm himself. Would it have been better to capitulate, to take the hard, heartless line that the Pope—apparently without realizing its heartlessness—had laid down? Had *he*—Matthew Mahan—won anything in this compromise? He rubbed his twinging stomach. He had tried to meet them as a brother in Christ. But how do you maintain that stance when you have to deal with resentful double-talkers like Novak and SOBs like Paul O'Reilly?

MATTHEW Mahan eased himself into the back seat of the car. "God help us, what a mess," he said to Dennis McLaughlin. "I feel like a member of a United Nations truce team."

"How did it go?"

"It's solved, temporarily."

Dennis, who knew only that it was an argument about birth control, ached to hear some details. Matthew Mahan had no intention of giving him any. Though, as they rolled through the Golden Ghetto, he did have to fight an impulse—a need to share with someone the agonizing loneliness of the role he was playing. Perhaps more important still, a need to really communicate with the priests of Dennis's generation. He could endure the hostility and contempt of the O'Reillys. But this subtle, impersonal hostility of the young disturbed him enormously. The averted eyes, the downturned mouths of Fathers Novak and Cannon rose before him in memory. To his dismay, as he turned to Dennis, he saw the same patina of negation on his somber face.

Abruptly, he began talking about the death of President Eisenhower, telling some of his favorite stories of Ike in Europe—one in particular that had never failed to draw uproarious laughter. Dennis managed the merest ghost of a smile. Matthew Mahan sighed. "We're getting pretty old, all of us World War II types. Is it true what they say, that for people your age it's just a lot of history like the First World War and the Civil War?"

"For a lot of them it is. Then there are some, like me, who'd like to forget the whole thing for personal reasons."

"What are they?"

"My father was killed in it."

"Dennis—I had no idea—"

The young eyes flashed almost wickedly at him for the hollowness of his automatic sympathy.

"Where—was he killed?"

"I don't know."

"What outfit was he with?"

"I don't know. My mother never talked to us about it."

The sad implication of those words was instantly clear to Matthew Mahan. But now, he sensed, was not the time to try to do anything about it.

Dennis talked on. "It's your enthusiasm that turns today's kids off. They just can't understand how you could be enthusiastic about any war, even if Hitler *was* a total monster."

"I don't think we were enthusiastic," Matthew Mahan said warily. "Not the people I was with, the ones who were getting shot at. The enthusiasm came later, after we won."

"Nobody over thirty seems able to understand why we don't have the same attitude toward Vietnam."

"I see," Matthew Mahan said. "I see."

He did not see. Everything about the young had been growing more and more opaque. With a sigh he let the conversation lapse and began worrying about his appointment for lunch with Monsignor Gargan, rector of Rosewood Seminary. They were a half hour late going to pick him up.

Eddie Johnson made good time on the road, and ten minutes later Matthew Mahan sat in a booth in the Red Coach Grill listening to Monsignor Harold Gargan. It was like a visit to the Wailing Wall. Almost everything at Rosewood was bad and getting worse, he was moaning. They had caught another three seminarians saying an unorthodox Mass in the locker room of the gymnasium. Total enrollment had fallen below a hundred for the first time in twenty-five years. . . .

"What do I do with these amateur liturgists?"

"Discipline them—mildly. Cut weekend privileges, something like that. We don't want to throw out half the senior class."

"I get this desperate feeling when I wake up in the morning. We've got to do something—to reverse the slide."

"I get the same feeling most mornings, multiplied by ten, Hal. But just because a lot of people are losing confidence in the country and the Church doesn't mean we have to do the same thing. The one thing we've got to avoid is public humiliation."

Gargan nodded glumly. Matthew Mahan had to remind himself

that this man had graduated only a year ahead of him. He could not be more than fifty-six or so. But he looked very tired.

"I think you should get away from the place for a while. When did you take your last vacation?"

"I went to the shore for a couple of weeks last summer."

Matthew Mahan took out his checkbook and wrote a check for a thousand dollars. "How about trying two weeks in Florida?"

"Thanks, Matt," Gargan said, his voice charged with emotion. "It might do me a lot of good. I haven't slept more than three hours a night for a month."

"I'm not doing much better. Patience, Hal." He peeled bills off a roll of cash to take care of lunch.

All the way back to the seminary in the car, Gargan complained about the students' lack of interest in athletics. As they drove through the grounds where his priesthood had begun, where he had spent six of the happiest years of his life, Matthew Mahan saw what Gargan meant. At this time on a Friday afternoon there would have been at least two softball games going strong. Today three seminarians played with a Frisbee. They weren't even doing a good job of catching it.

They left Harold Gargan at the administration building. The car was swinging out through Rosewood's gates when the archbishop reminded himself with a pang of guilt that he had been to the seminary and had not gone to see Davey Cronin. "I didn't have time," he said out loud.

Dennis McLaughlin looked at him questioningly. "To see the bishop," Matthew Mahan answered the look. "Bishop David Cronin, my one and only auxiliary. One of my sentimental mistakes, I'm afraid. He taught dogmatic theology when I was here. He sort of became—my mentor. To be honest, he got me through this place. I wouldn't have graduated without the tutoring he gave me, and not just in dogmatics. But my mentor is eighty-one now. . . . I took him along as an expert at Vatican II. That was another mistake. The old boy went from moderate to radical overnight. He scares the life out of me."

"I'd like to meet him," Dennis McLaughlin said, brightening.

"You will, you will," Matthew Mahan said. "I have him in for a Sunday night supper every so often."

But not so often lately, a nasty voice reminded him. He shook it off and pointed out that they were now in the world of the really rich. The houses sat among rolling hills or acres of meadow in which saddle horses gamboled. The archbishop amazed Dennis with his knowledge of each property owner. "Here's one of the richest," he said as they swept into the driveway of a Spanish-looking villa. "Here we're due to call on rather an unusual lady."

A serving girl with a pugnacious Irish face opened the door. In the huge entrance hall a woman with a cane came toward them. She was a spooky old lady, extremely tall, with a gaunt face and deep-socketed, intense eyes.

"Miss Childers," said the archbishop with a literally beaming smile. "It's so nice to see you." Father McLaughlin was introduced, and they adjourned to tea in a Victorian sitting room with a pro-fusion of overstuffed chairs and bric-a-brac. But Miss Childers was remarkably contemporary. What did the archbishop think of the Vietnam war, now that President Nixon was committed to fighting on? Dennis concealed a smile as his Excellency tried to talk out of both sides of his mouth. And the liturgy? What did he think of these floating parishes? Jazzmen and modern dancers performing at the altar? Miss Childers had gone to a guitar Mass in the city and loved it. Once more his Excellency seemed both with it and against it. And what about priests marrying? His Excellency temporized. There was nothing inherently wrong with it.

"I see a good deal right with it," Miss Childers said. "*Better to marry than to burn,* as Saint Paul said. Unsatisfied yearning is what burn means, as much as the fires of hell. Sometimes when I think of what my father did to me, I hate him, I really do."

The archbishop seemed unduly upset by these words. "It's—almost impossible—to judge the previous generation."

"My father was a selfish old bastard. I think it's healthier to say that sort of thing, don't you, Father McLaughlin?"

"Yes. . . ." Dennis saw the archbishop eyeing him. "If it's true."

"Oh, it's *true.*" She offered the archbishop a second cup of tea, but he rose, murmuring about appointments in the city.

"I suppose that bored you stiff," he said in the car.

"Not at all," Dennis said. "She's a swinger."

"She is an amazing old girl. Her father was governor in the 1920s. A ruthless crook. Her mother died when she was quite young, and the old man turned her into his companion. The terrible things people do to each other." Matthew Mahan shook his head. You should know, your Excellency, whispered the nasty voice.

And suddenly the pain was ripping his body while those seemingly innocent words tore his mind from the moving car to a suffering woman's face thousands of miles away in Rome. In counterpoint another voice whispered, Forgive me, Mary, forgive me.

"I suppose there's a big bequest there," Dennis was saying.

"What?" Matthew Mahan said dazedly. "Oh. Around a million, she's intimated." He glanced at the somehow accusing young face. "I suppose you don't think much of the way a bishop has to hustle around buttering up the rich."

Dennis decided a simple shrug was the best answer to this. The archbishop did not spend his time chasing bequests. But why say that when he seemed about to make an interesting confession?

"We get twenty percent of our income—about the same as most dioceses—from bequests. Over two million last year."

A nod this time, Dennis. Now a nice neutral question: "Would you like to do the rest of the mail?"

"Good idea."

First came requests for help from obscure missionaries. "Give them the usual," Matthew Mahan said, which meant a letter full of blessings and a check for twenty-five dollars. Next, the priests who were in Brazil in response to Pope John's request for volunteers from any U.S. diocese for service in South America: Father Tom O'Hara reported the collapse of his car. What he really needed was a jeep. "Send him thirty-five hundred." Father Jerome Lang had a bright boy who wanted to be a priest, but could not afford the education he should get first. "Send him three thousand," Matthew Mahan said. Father Edward McMullen wanted to build a chapel for an outlying village. "Send him five thousand."

Matthew Mahan could almost hear the groans of his iron-jawed money manager and chancellor, Monsignor Terence Malone. He knew he was too generous with these young priests. But it made him feel better—and not many things did these days. A letter from Father Peter Foley, chaplain of the state prison, introduced one of his model prisoners who was about to be released after serving ten years for armed robbery. Would the archbishop help get him a job? "Write to Mike Furia. He manages to hire a lot of these poor guys for his overseas companies." Matthew Mahan twisted his episcopal ring, a habit that Dennis already knew as a sign of uneasiness. "I wish I could get Foley away from the prison. He's the only guy in my seminary class I haven't settled in a good parish. But he insists he *likes* being chaplain. What's next?"

One pastor wanted advice about handling his parish council, which was so conservative it barely tolerated the use of English in the Mass. A parent complained of lack of heat in the parochial school. A woman accused a priest of improper advances. A sociologist wanted to know how many priests the diocese had lost in the last five years, with case histories, please.

Suddenly, Matthew Mahan found himself wishing he could stop the frantic daily treadmill on which he and Dennis were running. If somehow, somewhere, they had time to sit down and talk in a relaxed, man-to-man way, he was sure they'd find common ground. Dennis would be surprised to discover that the archbishop had been something of a rebel in his youth, that he tried to understand the impatience of young priests and laymen. They might even enjoy a mutual laugh or two. But there seemed to be no way to turn off the treadmill. In the end, Dennis was sitting with at least a pound of papers in his lap. "That takes care of that," the archbishop said.

Dennis was inclined to remind the archbishop that hours of labor were needed before "that" was taken care of. But he found it more satisfying to say nothing, to contain his bitterness.

III

THE fading light was softening the landscape on both sides of the freeway now, making the factories and gas tanks and power grids capable of being welcomed in spite of their ugliness. They were, unchangeably, part of his city. "You probably won't believe this," Matthew Mahan said, "but the city air smells good to me."

"The university chemistry department has entered a class-action suit against these factories," Dennis said. "There's no reason why they should release those fumes so close to the city."

The city. Yes, there it was ahead of them, looming up on its long, narrow hill. As Matthew Mahan looked meditatively at it, the pain flickered menacingly. He suddenly remembered that it had begun yesterday evening on his flight back from Washington,

D.C., where he had pleaded in vain for the apostolic delegate's help in controlling his rebellious nuns. Looking down on the city as the plane landed, he had found himself murmuring, "Would that you might know the things that would make for your peace."

No lamentations now. There is work to be done. "Have you checked the chancery switchboard to see what calls we have?"

"No." Dennis twitched. A tendency to forget or fail to record telephone messages was his worst failing. Typical intellectual, off on cloud nine, was Matthew Mahan's not always patient excuse for him. He watched Dennis pluck the white telephone from its cradle in the armrest and jot down names as the chancery switchboard answered his questions. Dennis read the list of callers. Mike Furia, chairman of the archbishop's fund committee. Herb Winstock, the vice-chairman. Mrs. O'Connor, the mayor's wife, another potent fund raiser. "A man named Fogarty."

"Bill Fogarty?"

"I think it's Bill. He's at the Garden Square Hotel."

"Eddie," said Matthew Mahan. "The Garden Square, fast." He explained the abrupt about-face to Dennis. "Bill and I were in the same class at the seminary. We lost him about fifteen years ago. Woman trouble. Lately I heard they'd split up and he was drinking the bars dry. I wrote asking if I could help."

At the hotel, a long-haired desk clerk ran his finger down a list of names, and said there was a Fogarty in room 1515.

"Give me the key to that room," Matthew Mahan said.

The clerk stared in astonishment.

"I am Archbishop Mahan, and that man is a priest. A sick priest. Give me the key."

The archbishop and his secretary were soon striding down the upstairs hall. There was no answer to Matthew Mahan's knock on the door of 1515. He inserted the key and stepped into the room. The hot-air heat had turned it into a sauna. The drapes were drawn. Matthew Mahan fumbled for the light switch. Bill Fogarty was sprawled on the bed, a two-day stubble of gray beard on his face. The archbishop took a deep breath and stood there remembering seminary days, hearing Bill Fogarty sing his outrageous parody of "Mother Machree." *"Sure we'll love the dear surplice that drags on the ground . . ."* Wait, it had been a duet, you and Bill had sung it as a duet. There but for the grace of God go I.

A handsome black-Irish buck, that's what he had been, Matthew Mahan thought mournfully, looking down at the ruin of the man on the bed. What wreaked such havoc—spiritual failure—whatever that meant? Matthew Mahan knew only that it had something to do with pride and the way pride so slowly slides into arrogance and too often ends in despair. No one had been prouder than Bill Fogarty, prouder of being a priest, prouder of his unique ability to hold an audience, to make them laugh, and to make them cry.

The pride had seemed innocent enough, even justifiable to his friends and admirers in Rosewood's class of 1939. It had seemed perfectly understandable when Bill became the darling of the uptown Catholics, always invited to parties and on trips to Florida's poshest beaches. And what harm was there riding back and forth on these outings with a very attractive and very divorced woman?

Alas, Archbishop Hogan thought there was a good deal of harm. Bill suddenly found himself exiled to what Matthew Mahan's generation called Siberia—the dreary downstate boondocks where Catholics were a timid, unaffluent minority. When Bill balked, he was publicly excoriated as a disgrace to the priesthood. He had crept to his assignment a cowed, embittered man. His divorced friend was horrified by what she had inadvertently done, and deeply sympathetic. Result: clandestine romance. Bill applied to be laicized. He waited two years in vain for the permission to come through, then left the Church and married the lady. Matthew Mahan, when he became archbishop, had looked up Fogarty's case in the files. Hogan had never sent the papers to Rome.

Like so many ex-priests' marriages, Bill's was doomed from the start. He never resolved the conflict between the woman and his priesthood. He loved both. Now he was ending his life probably hating both.

Matthew Mahan gently shook him. "Bill. Bill."

Fogarty awoke and lay there staring numbly. Tears trickled out of his eyes and down the unshaved cheeks. "O Jesus," he said. "O Jesus, Mary, and Joseph, what's going to become of me? Sally left me, Matt, she walked out on me."

"I know, Bill. I heard about it. I wrote you a letter."

"Yes. I wouldn't have had the guts to call you otherwise. Matt, I'm finished." Fogarty was sobbing.

"Bill. Would you want to return to the priesthood?"

"Would you—even consider it?" The voice was choked.

"I would, Bill. But you'd have to get yourself back in shape. Join Alcoholics Anonymous. And spend some time at a monastery down in Kentucky. When you're well, we'll talk."

"I don't deserve it, Matt." But the offer got his feet over the side of the bed. "You're wasting your money, Matt."

"It's my money. If I feel like wasting it, I will."

No. That was too arrogant, Dennis McLaughlin thought, as he saw Fogarty flinch from these words. But Archbishop Mahan either didn't notice or didn't care. As usual, Dennis told himself.

"See if he's got any clothes, Dennis."

A search revealed only empty whiskey bottles and a stink in the closet that made Dennis struggle for breath. Anxiously he wondered if he were getting an attack of the claustrophobia that had sent him fleeing off elevators and avoiding planes for the past two years. Combined with his asthma, it could come close to killing him. "Can I wait in the hall?" he asked. "I feel a little—sick."

Matthew Mahan, irritated, sent him out with a curt wave. From the hall, Dennis heard him arrange things on the phone with the hotel office. So crisp, so businesslike, the perfect spiritual executive, he thought sourly.

A few minutes later a bellboy stared curiously as two priests helped a man out the rear door into the night. Eddie had the car running, and they were on their way to St. Peter's Hospital.

There was work to do. Matthew Mahan used his car phone to call Mother Margaret Canavan, the head nun at St. Peter's. She was rather stiff about the short notice, but she agreed to have a private room ready and a psychiatrist to get Bill Fogarty through the night.

"It will be rough, Bill," Matthew Mahan said. "But trust them. They're on your side." And after ten minutes of soothing reassurance they left him giving his vital statistics to the nurse.

"You sound like you've done that before," Dennis said.

"In a way. Most of the time it's a priest in good standing who's on the sauce." He sighed and lit a cigarette. "You can't believe what a fantastic priest Bill was. He could—he had this kind of holy power to make people do things. I never had the gift. I always had to make my mark the hard way."

"I'm amazed to hear you say that."

"Why?"

"Because you seem—seem to handle people so effortlessly."

"Ah," said Matthew Mahan, pleased by the compliment. "It's just practice. And this bishop's ring," he added.

"What happened to the woman Fogarty married?"

"A familiar story. Her husband drank, she had a mental breakdown. They split up, and we say she can't get married again. Result, we've created a tragedy that's very likely to involve a half dozen more people before it's over. It takes superhuman effort to keep these women in the Church without destroying themselves—and other people. I know that from experience." As Matthew Mahan said this, his mind again leaped to that penthouse apartment in Rome, and he stood there looking out at St. Peter's dome, then turned to a heartbreakingly beautiful woman and said, *Are you all right, Mary? You're sure?*

"Don't pastors do anything for these women?" Dennis asked.

"Pastors?" Matthew Mahan struggled to return to the reality of time and place. "Most of them are scared to death of a divorced woman. Afraid of going the Fogarty route."

"What about these good-conscience divorce programs that bishops are operating in Louisiana and Oregon?"

"There's good reason to take a very dim view of them. When you tell people that all they need to return to the sacraments is their own judgment that there was no way to avoid the breakup, you create a nightmare for canon lawyers."

"Maybe it would be better if we all went the Fogarty route." Dennis added hastily, "I mean—get married."

"Sometimes I think that's all guys your age think about."

"It's pretty hard *not* to think about it."

"I know, I know. There've been nights . . ."

And days, days under budding branches, sunlight on glossy dark hair, turning to search the direct green eyes. The face too perfect to tolerate sadness on it. *Are you all right, Mary?*

Dennis was brooding over the impossibility of discussing celibacy with any priest over forty. It meant revolution to them. There his Excellency was, practically strangling with rage. Or was it embarrassment at admitting he had been frustrated in his time? The episcopal dignity had been compromised. Quick, change the subject. "Do you always deal—with alcoholic priests yourself?"

"I try to, for several reasons," Matthew Mahan said. "My brother was an alcoholic. I made a mess of helping him. And it's one of the few chances I have to do some real pastoral work. As we said at Vatican II—it's part of a bishop's job to be a father to his priests. It sounds great, but priests are grown men. Most of them don't want a father. . . ."

Dennis nodded. "Like the laity—they don't want shepherds anymore. They're not sheep."

The implication made Matthew Mahan recoil. "People still need care, help. I'm not quite ready to give up that image."

"Most people my age have given it up."

The cold arrogance disturbed Matthew Mahan enormously. It was not the first time he had caught this undertone of contempt. But for the first time he could locate one source of his uneasiness with Dennis's generation. Their contempt for people of his generation who tolerated imperfection translated itself into contempt for the whole idea of tolerance. "I wonder if you'll feel the same way in twenty years?" he said.

"Who knows where I'll be in twenty years?" Dennis said.

Again the tone was icy. Matthew Mahan felt poised between anger and sadness. The past two days flickered behind his eyes in disconnected images—the Jefferson Memorial serenely Greek beside the water as the plane landed in Washington; the suave Roman courtesy of the apostolic delegate, subtly refusing his agitated plea for assistance in words of empty reassurance; Monsignor Paul O'Reilly's stony hatred; the unspoiled faces of the confirmation class; the tormented face of Bill Fogarty; and now this stiff-necked rebuke from thirty-year-old Dennis McLaughlin.

To lose his temper would only widen the gulf, Matthew Mahan realized with some regret. Letting go of his anger, he succumbed to muddy, stagnant sadness. Was there any hope of escaping this insistent sense of bafflement, of failure? It seemed to infest the very fabric of faith, to defy every effort, every prayer.

"The trouble with that attitude, Dennis," he said, "is you may give up caring about people completely. Like that young priest in Pittsburgh—Ross or something—who recently announced that the real reason for the priest shortage is the Catholic laity. They're not worth bothering about. That's what he actually said."

"Yes," said Dennis.

The response could not have been more inert.

The car stopped. Eddie Johnson was opening the door, lifting out the briefcase with its daily burden of problems. Matthew Mahan stared at the cathedral illuminated by floodlights that cost as much to maintain each year as a grammar school teacher. The product of his predecessor, the huge white Romanesque-style structure was unique—uniquely expensive. Sandblasting its limestone exterior to prevent the city's polluted air from turning it gray cost another five grammar school teachers. The same Archbishop Hogan had built the twin stone buildings, complete with turrets and parapet, that comprised the archbishop's residence and the diocesan offices. Wryly, Matthew Mahan remembered that the pastor in his first parish assignment used to call the cathedral the White Elephant and the residence Castle Rackrent. What did they call it these days? He must ask Dennis McLaughlin sometime.

In the front hall of the residence they were met by the housekeeper, Mrs. Norton, who had kept their supper warm for two hours. At the long table, Matthew Mahan hurriedly ate a single slice of the overdone roast. His stomach felt too uneasy for more. Dennis McLaughlin ate in silence, as usual. The archbishop resorted to the most obvious conversation starter of them all and asked Dennis what sport he had preferred at college. Track. Cross-country running. It was logical. The wiry, almost skeletonic frame. "What do you think about while you run?"

"Nothing. That's what I liked about it."

Another enigma. Matthew Mahan said good night and trudged wearily upstairs to his bedroom. He had barely taken off his coat when the red light on his telephone glowed. He answered it.

"Excellency." It was the apostolic delegate in Washington. "I am calling you because of a message I received from Rome scarcely an hour ago. I would not want you to think that I concealed such happy information from you because of the delicate nature of the subject we were discussing yesterday."

"There is no need to worry. I understand your position."

"Yes, of course. But now may I tell you what you will hear officially by telegram tomorrow? The Holy Father has seen fit to add your name to the distinguished fathers of the College of Cardinals. May I extend my heartfelt congratulations."

"You're sure?" Matthew Mahan said dazedly.

"Beyond all doubt. There are four others—Archbishops Cooke, Dearden, Carberry, and Bishop Wright. May I say that for the first three, the honor is perhaps a perquisite of their sees, whereas for you—I do not believe your see has ever had a cardinal. So it is a signal mark of the Holy Father's affection for you."

"I—I can hardly believe that. I mean I can hardly believe—I can't believe—that I am worthy of it."

"Of course, of course," said the sibilant Italian voice. "As for the problem we discussed yesterday. You may be sure that I will do my utmost to place your views before the proper persons in Rome. Cardinal Antoniutti, one of my dearest friends, is now head of the Sacred Congregation for Religious and Secular Institutes. I can't understand why this did not occur to me before."

When Matthew Mahan had said good-by to the apostolic delegate, he caught sight of himself in the mirror above his bureau. This glum-faced man with the square fighter's jaw darkened by five-o'clock shadow, this potbellied fifty-five-year-old, who had mounted the stairs wondering if he were a walking, talking mistake—*this* was a cardinal? A prince of the Church?

Matthew Mahan sank to his knees beside his bed and gazed up at the crucifix: You are not worthy, he said to himself. There is no comparison between your doubts and discouragements and disappointments and that suffering figure, taking upon Himself the incomprehensible burden of the whole world's pain.

To his lips came the words from the Mass, words that were always deeply meaningful to him although he never completely understood why: "Lord, I am not worthy . . . but only say the word, and my soul shall be healed."

UPSTAIRS in his third-floor bedroom, Dennis McLaughlin was communicating with Rome.

Dear Gog:
   I am glad to see that your determination to save my soul has not lapsed along with most of your theology. But it may be too late. Instead of being picked off by a swinging nun, I've been plucked by an archbishop. As of two weeks ago I have become secretary to Archbishop Matthew Mahan. Yes. I, the depreciator of all authority, have been catapulted into the highest councils of the Establishment. Before many more moons I will know pre-

cisely where to place my intellectual dynamite to bring the whole power structure crashing around our ears.

So much for rhetoric. Now for reality. I am so tired I can hardly keep my eyes open past nine p.m. Working for this man is like trying to run the mile against an express train. 1) I write his Excellency's speeches. 2) I scour the papers and magazines for bits and pieces that will keep him "in touch" with the latest in theology, modern morals, student behavior, ecumenical dialogue, and contemporary politics. 3) Draft replies to his correspondence with everyone from the manager of our inglorious baseball team to The Apostolic Delegate. 4) Accompany him everywhere to take notes on what is said and decided. He has a horror of being misquoted. 5) Deal with the newshawks who are always trying to get him to say something for or against contraception, abortion, divorce, the war, student riots, clerical dropouts, President Nixon, Pope Paul, and whether or not he is ever going to let Catholics receive Communion with Episcopalians.

Sounds alarming? The most unnerving part is yet to come, old friend. *I seem to be enjoying it.* What this reveals about my character, or lack of it, you can imagine, after having spent your youth listening to me dissect myself. What do I think of his Excellency? I don't even know. Some of the things he does and says appall me, others confuse me, and a few I find strangely moving. But there is one thing I can't forgive him: his colossal self-confidence. He never betrays the slightest hint of doubt as he moves from one situation to another, full of good humor and sententious remarks.

Meanwhile, beyond the episcopal residence the city is smoldering and our once docile Romans are as combustible as the rest of the populace. The blacks hint that they'll make us another Watts. The students are rancid over the war, and Papa Paolo's ruling on birth control has three-quarters of the women seething. I doubt if there is a priest our age who can follow Il Papa's logic or accept his conclusions. If his Excellency gets tough and orders conformity to *Humanae Vitae* in the confessional, we may have many suspended priests on our hands.

Let me try to describe his Exc. He is about 6'2", beefy, with long arms and big hands. He has an interesting face—square jaw, high cheekbones, an extremely mobile mouth, breaking easily into a cocky don't-kid-me Gaelic smile and the next moment becoming a hard, harsh line. Only in the nose have his mother's Italian ancestors made their contribution—no Irishman ever wore Mahan's nose. It comes straight from some old senator who strode the Forum no doubt with an arrogance that equaled Caesar's.

I am fascinated by how everything about his Exc. is so beautifully interwoven to create the appearance of an effortless exercise of authority. I used to think of power as crude as well as cruel. But watching him in action—has it really been for only two weeks?—I realize how beautifully the good ones disguise the cruelty and modulate the arrogance.

Even when he gets mad it is part calculation, I think. Whether it is or not, when the episcopal temperature rises he is *très formidable*. The large head lowers and begins shaking back and forth like a bull about to charge. He is prone to unleash this temper on yours truly. One of my more menial tasks is keeping the battery of six pens on his desk full. Nothing drives him into a frenzy more than an empty pen. Remembering such details is not one of my strong points, as you well know, and I've had to rescue several empty pens from far corners of the office, where they have been unceremoniously flung. I think he fancies himself as Jehovah hurling thunderbolts. He is also snappish when I forget to give him messages, or to cancel or change an appointment. Most of the time, though, he *tries* to be polite to me. He has sensed he is on the wrong side of the generation gap with his younger priests, and sort of practices on me. You can imagine how cooperative I am. In spite of all his efforts to be republican, there is something inescapably *royal* about him. Maybe it's the setting in which we labor.

This episcopal residence from the outside is just another fake medieval mélange. But inside, you, the antiquary, would spend hours silently drooling. Even I am reluctantly impressed. Hogan, the previous archbishop, apparently had expensive inclinations. Start with the chapel, which is in a little wing that connects the house with the chancery office. It's a baroque jewel, imported in toto from a French château. The altar is mahogany, carved from a single piece of wood, with intricate filigree around and above the tabernacle. The stained glass is all purple and blue, in imitation of Sainte-Chapelle in Paris.

Then move through the rooms the archbishop lives in. You never saw such treasures: Sèvres porcelain, Beauvais tapestries, paintings by a Zurburán, a Correggio, a Pisanello, all worth a bundle. His Exc. sleeps in a Chippendale four-poster. In his office, which he enters from his bedroom, he sits at a lovely Louis XVI *table d'anglaise* designed by Dugourc. On either side of the door are two seventeenth-century mahogany Spanish folding desks, the fronts inlaid with velvet panels. His Exc. uses them to store and partially display his collection of seashells, which is apparently one of the best anywhere around. But apart from the seashells, everything else he has added to these two magnificent rooms is unmentionable. He has plonked a big leather swivel chair behind the desk, and covered the walls with pictures and plaques of the sort local politicians accumulate. And beside that beautiful bed he has a recliner chair. But his Exc. doesn't seem to *see* any of the expensive stuff. I have yet to hear him so much as comment on a single piece of furniture or a painting. But in the files I've seen the data on each and also the insurance figures. The joint is worth a million if it goes up in smoke.

Not bad for the son of an Irish saloonkeeper, or whatever he was. The question is how long can he remain ensconced in all this splendor while the archdiocese smolders around him? What kind of smoldering? Well, take the Sisters of the Divine Heart, who run Mount St. Monica's College and a couple of high schools. These girls have really flipped out. They have abandoned our lily-white parochial schools and dispatched half of their nuns into the ghettos. The archbishop grew so agitated he betook himself to Washington yesterday to see what sort of whammy he could concoct with the apostolic delegate. The nuns are not under diocesan jurisdiction, which makes them difficult to control. From the way he's acted since he got off the plane, I don't think the A.D. gave him much help.

Simultaneously, he is trying to bank a fire glowing in the breast of one Father Vincent Disalvo, who is trying to forge an alliance between university students and the blacks in his downtown parish to break the color line both in the city and that all-white nirvana known as suburbia. His Exc.'s big worry is that Disalvo will turn off a lot of the diocese's heavy contributors. What if he can't raise money enough to keep the schools open? Wouldn't it be terrible if the parochial school system fell apart and the R.C.s had to join the United States of America?

Mahan is a kind of symbolic figure in this parochial school thing. Practically single-handed, he raised the umpteen million bucks that built a lot of the schools that are now going broke. I guess he's also kind of symbolic in regard to the blacks. During the 1950s he was their biggest advocate, defender, what have you, here in town. Now they're starting to give him the same kind of headaches they're giving everyone else. If I had an ounce of human kindness in my crab-apple soul, I'd feel sorry for him. But we

I stopped writing this to answer a summons from downstairs. I found the archbishop being saluted by the Right Reverend Monsignor Terence Malone, our iron chancellor, and Monsignor George

Petrie, our suave pseudoliberal vicar-general, plus sundry other highly placed chancery trolls, all with glasses in hand. Even our housekeeper, Mrs. Norton, was tippling. The reason for this revelry was swiftly explained to me: our noble lord has landed a red hat. He stood there exuding his all-American vitality, his face beatific. I hereby order you, as my agent in the Imperial City, to find out why and how this happened.

It was a hideously charming little party and I was flattered to find myself on the inside of the Big Story. See how I succumb to the lure of power and influence? You will have to set my feet once more upon the straight and narrow. I don't know whether I'll be coming to Rome for the consistory or if I'll be left here to mind the telephones. But I would say we have a fair chance of a reunion on Ye Olde Aurelian Way.

As ever,
Mag

IV

MATTHEW Mahan woke up to the cathedral bell softly tolling five a.m. He sighed and tried to go back to sleep. Impossible. Words and images churned in his mind. His Eminence. A prince of the Church. No longer one of twenty-five hundred bishops, but one of a select hundred and thirty or so cardinals. Why him, the swimmer against the Vatican tide? What did they want from him?

Then the pain began slowly, and built remorselessly to an explosion that sent slivers of anguish up, down, and around the center of his body. The pain of the day before was a caress compared with this agony. Was it cancer? Matthew Mahan remembered his father in the hospital, teeth clenched, jaw muscles bunched, refusing to cry out against the probing pincers of the crab. No, cancer did not come and go like this. Or did it? Medically he was an ignoramus. Soon the pain was almost a separate thing with a personality of its own, a small, ferocious animal. By six, when his alarm went off, it was almost unbearable. But he managed to shave and dress and walk down to his chapel. He nodded to Dennis McLaughlin, who was just finishing his Mass, and knelt before the altar. He studied the writhing Christ on the crucifix. Baroque ecstasy, blending pain and beauty.

Dennis helped him vest and then served his Mass for him. The

Host and wine that were transmuted into Christ's body and blood seemed to have a soothing effect. Breakfast was even more helpful, and by the time he finished, the pain had vanished. He tried some unsuccessful small talk with Dennis McLaughlin over the coffee, and then said briskly, "You'd better call Monsignor Cohane over at the paper and tell him the news. Let him set up a press conference. See how many copies of my standard biography we have in our files. We'll need a couple of dozen pictures, too."

Dennis McLaughlin nodded and reminded him, "We're scheduled to be at Mount St. Monica's at ten forty-five."

"I know," said the cardinal designate, and retired to his room to stretch out in his recliner chair and read his breviary. After completing half the day's reading, he got up and went into his office. On his desk, in small gold frames, were three pictures. On the right was one of his father on the beach. The barest hint of a smile was on his tough, handsome face. In the middle was a much earlier picture of his mother, taken in a city garden. She was a pretty, smiling young woman. A mass of dark hair fell to her shoulders à la Mary Pickford. On the left was a portrait of his brother Charlie and his wife and their seven children, taken four years ago. They looked marvelously happy, as if they had just been named Catholic family of the year.

Around the walls of the office were many more pictures, almost all of them commemorating a sports event. A smiling Matthew Mahan was presenting a trophy to the winning baseball team, basketball team, football team, track team—everything, he had once remarked, except a winning horse.

Above the door hung the archbishop's coat of arms. On the right side of a green shield was a golden griffin standing on its hind legs, all but embracing a golden halberd, symbol of the martyrdom of Saint Matthew. On the left was the symbol of the archdiocese, a lamb feeding before a church spire. Beneath was Matthew Mahan's motto, *Dominus in corde*—May the Lord be in my heart. Above the shield was a Maltese cross, and surmounting this was a green broad-brimmed pontifical hat with five gold tassels running from it down each side of the shield.

By now it was eight o'clock. He spent the next hour reading reports from the committees of the National Conference of Bishops. The one on diocesan financial reporting was the most important

131

and the least comprehensible. Every subdivision of every diocese seemed to use different accounting methods to keep track of its money—the result, a haphazard jumble that drove businessmen berserk. It made him grateful for Chancellor Terence Malone, who was considered a financial genius.

Malone was one of the few chancery officials he had held over from Hogan's regime, and his right-wing politics did create problems. The building committee, which he dominated, recommended construction of three new churches and schools in the city's ever-growing suburbs. Fierce protests from the National Association of Laymen that the archdiocese was ignoring the needs of the decaying inner city were dismissed by Chancellor Malone.

"Your Eminence," Dennis said from the doorway. "The car is here. Monsignor Cohane wants to know if two o'clock would be a good time for a press conference."

"Perfect," Matthew Mahan said. "Get your hat and coat. I want you to come and take notes on what is really said at Mount St. Monica's. Sometimes nuns hear only what they want to hear."

The Saturday morning traffic on Kennedy Parkway was light. Without warning the pain began stirring again beneath Matthew Mahan's belt buckle, but he tried to disregard the agony of it. He picked up the phone beside him and gave the operator a number. In seconds there was Mike Furia's rugged voice.

"Padre. How goes it?"

"Fine. Look, Mike, I'm calling from the car. I have some news I wanted you to hear from me rather than from the TV."

"What's happened? Has Father Disalvo decided to improve the liturgy by saying Mass in the nude?"

Matthew Mahan laughed briefly. "No. Somebody in Rome has gone crazy. They're making me a cardinal."

"Well I'll be damned," roared Furia, almost shattering Matthew Mahan's eardrum. "When I knocked out that German tank only twenty feet from your foxhole, I never thought it was a prince of the Church I'd be saving. Is this one of those deals where you go to Rome and throw yourself at Il Papa's feet?"

"More or less."

"Listen, we'll charter a plane and go with you. We'll sell the seats for a thousand bucks apiece."

"Mike—that sounds a little steep—"

"If it goes the way I think it'll go, we'll need two planes. It's time they recognized the best damn archbishop in the country."

Matthew Mahan slipped the phone back into its cradle and cast a slightly uneasy glance at Dennis McLaughlin. Why, he asked himself irritably, did he worry about what Dennis would think of Furia's suggestion? Organizing a group to go to Europe with a new cardinal was not unusual. It was undoubtedly being done in New York and St. Louis and Pittsburgh at this very moment. Maybe frankness was the best way to face it. These young people had to accept the fact that, in the modern Church, money and the sacred—if that was not too grandiose a word for his elevation—were inextricably mixed.

"Mike wants to charter a plane and organize a cheering section for our trip to Europe. He says he can get a thousand dollars a seat." His eyes rested on the dark red hair that vanished unwillingly beneath Dennis's round collar. "Mike's a wonderful guy. But a little too enthusiastic. I have to rein him in a lot. He's been having trouble with his son, Tony. Mike and his wife are separated, which is probably the root of the problem. Tony dropped out of Georgetown, and Mike had him located—in a commune." Matthew Mahan fiddled with his episcopal ring. "Well," he said, "you've been on the job two weeks now. How do you like it?"

"A lot more than I thought I would," Dennis said with a slightly strained smile.

"Good. I thought you'd like to know that I'm satisfied."

There was no evidence of pleasure, much less warmth, on Father McLaughlin's face. He ran his hand through his unruly hair and nodded. "Good—good. I'm—glad," he said.

"Now," Matthew Mahan said. "Who else did I decide to call?"

Dennis looked at a list. "Your sister-in-law, Bishop Cronin at the seminary, the mayor, the president of the City Council."

"You take care of the last two," Matthew Mahan said, picking up his phone again.

A querulous voice answered. "Rosewood?" It must be Mary Malone's fiftieth year at the seminary switchboard.

"This is Archbishop Mahan, Mary," he said. "Ring Bishop Cronin's room, will you please? If he isn't there, try the library."

He could hear Dennis on the other phone. "Yes, your Honor. His Eminence thought—no—he just thought a statement . . ."

133

"Cronin here," a dry voice rasped.

"Mahan here. I thought you'd like to hear some interesting news I just got from the apostolic delegate."

"Now what could that be?" said Auxiliary Bishop Cronin in his ripest Irish brogue. "Is he bringing over his sister and her twenty kids, and wants you to get the pack of them city jobs?"

"No, nothing like that." Matthew Mahan caught a glimpse of his own smiling face in the rearview mirror.

"Then it's got something to do with unused miraculous powers of the papacy. From now on, me boy, you'll be able to ban books before they're written. Let's get to the point."

"From now on I've a new name, but I won't let you use it."

"*Eminence?* By God, that's the best news I've heard since Vatican II."

"I'd like you to come to Rome with me for the consistory."

"Out of the question, Matthew me boy. Aside from the fact that a man of eighty-one has no time to waste, I don't trust myself to stand up to the triumphal pretensions of that accursed city."

"Nonsense. Don't make me pull rank on you."

"I dare you," said Cronin, laughter breaking through. "Well, it's glorious news, lad. You're always in my prayers. This shows how much pull I've got with His Infinity upstairs."

"Stay in contact with Him for my sake, will you please?"

"You know I will. God love you now."

Matthew Mahan dropped the phone back into its cradle. He began to think about their destination, the College of Mount St. Monica. "I'm trying to prove my good faith in this thing," he told Dennis McLaughlin. "But if I don't make any more progress than I did last time I talked to Sister Agnes Marie— The truth is," he said with a quick smile, "I think I'm still afraid of Agnes. I sat next to her for a year in St. Patrick's School. She gave me a permanent inferiority complex."

EDDIE eased the limousine past massive iron gates. A plaque on some iron fretwork above them read:

COLLEGE OF MOUNT ST. MONICA
FOUNDED 1910
SISTERS OF THE DIVINE HEART

They rolled up a curving drive through a half mile of open woods to a wide lawn. The six-story main building, Sacré Coeur, was topped with three weird cupolas, like something from a fairy tale. "Every time I come here," Matthew Mahan said, "I wonder how in God's name they managed to create such ugly buildings."

As Eddie slowed to a stop, the chapel bell began clanging mightily. Instantly a horde of young women came racing out of the building to swarm around the car. Many of them were wearing shirts and blue jeans. More than a few were in miniskirts that drew a pleased "Wow" from Dennis McLaughlin. Now the doorway of the main building was filled with a swirl of women headed by plump, placid-faced Sister Agnes Marie. Most of them, including Sister Agnes Marie, were wearing tailored suits.

Matthew Mahan was stunned. "What the devil—"

"Maybe they're going to burn us at the stake," Dennis said.

The pain stirred greedily in Matthew Mahan's stomach. Summoning calm by an act of the will, he said, "I suppose it was on the eleven-o'clock news." He climbed out of the car, forcing a smile. "What's all this?" he asked Sister Agnes Marie.

Sister Agnes Marie raised her hand and five hundred feminine voices cried, "Congratulations, your Eminence!"

"Now, now," he said. "You shouldn't call me that until I get down on my knees before the Holy Father."

"We like to be a few steps ahead of the Church," Sister Agnes Marie said. "Will you say a few words, your Eminence?"

There was no escape. Matthew Mahan walked up the steps and turned to look down on the crescent of smiling young faces. For some reason the innocence he had grown used to seeing in his visits here was no longer visible to him. To these faces, somehow slyly knowing, how could he communicate his desire to reach into their hearts with the healing power of grace?

"This is—a delightful surprise," he began. "I don't feel I deserve those congratulations. I don't feel the honor that the Holy Father has offered me is a personal tribute. It is a recognition of the steady growth of this archdiocese in loyalty to the Church and the word of God that she preaches. And that heartens me—heartens me tremendously. Without the support of young Catholic women like yourselves, all the titles in the world will not do me or the Church any good. Without you, I am nothing."

There was a scattering of applause, not very enthusiastic, he thought. Then out of the crowd stepped two girls with guitars. They strummed a few bars and everyone began to sing a modern folk hymn about Christian unity and love. The voices rose and fell in a melody that seemed both mournful and joyful. Matthew Mahan began to feel better. When the song ended he said, "Thank you from the bottom of my heart. I will always remember this day. I'd like to give you my blessing now."

Two girls in the front knelt, but most of them did not even bow their heads as he raised his hand to form the cross. "May the blessing of Almighty God, the Father, the Son, and the Holy Spirit, descend upon you and remain with you always."

He turned to Sister Agnes Marie and said, "That was very nice of you, Mother Agnes—I mean Sister Agnes."

Why couldn't he just call her Agnes? When they'd sat side by side in school he had called her Aggie. Sometimes, when in the company of those who hated her for her astronomical marks, he'd called her Baggy Aggie. He decided it made him feel better— or safer?—to use a title, even if her refusal to accept the traditional Mother which went with her position confused him.

She turned aside his thanks. "It was the girls' idea. They decided you deserved a royal welcome."

"It was royal. Most definitely royal." He then introduced Father McLaughlin to her, and together they moved past the rapidly dispersing faculty into the lofty, domed rotunda. Casually, Sister Agnes Marie caught the arm of a young woman whose dark hair was long and flowing. She, too, was wearing a suit, but her skirt was inches shorter than Sister Agnes Marie's. There was no doubt that her legs were shapely, and equally little doubt that Dennis McLaughlin was noticing them.

"Sister Helen," said Sister Agnes Marie. "Would you join us in my office to take some notes? This," she said to Matthew Mahan, "is Sister Helen Reed."

"Reed," said Matthew Mahan. "Is this Dr. Bill Reed's daughter?"

"Yes."

"Well, my goodness. I haven't seen you since you entered the novitiate—"

"Five years ago."

"I thought between us we'd have your father converted by now."

"You can't convert a stone."

Matthew Mahan recalled that, at his last annual checkup, Bill Reed had been furiously exercised about the way "left wing" Catholics were turning his daughter into a radical.

Sister Agnes Marie's office had been transformed by her into a light-filled model of modern decor. The chairs, onto one of which Matthew Mahan now lowered himself, were light, attractive, and spare in design, but clearly unsuited to a six-foot-two-inch archbishop who weighed a hundred and ninety-five pounds. Even Dennis seemed to sit down with extra care. Sister Helen Reed, as petite as Matthew Mahan was bulky, was perfectly at ease in her chair, crossing her legs with no heed to the way her skirt rode up her thigh.

Sister Agnes Marie sat behind her desk and pushed a buzzer to order some coffee. "Now," she said. "What have you heard from our esteemed apostolic delegate?"

The question was asked in the mildest tone. Diffidence was Sister Agnes Marie's style now. But her words, in spite of their aura of humility and submission, so often suggested the opposite of those virtues.

"Mother—I mean, Sister Agnes," he said. "I have no desire to decide this matter purely on the basis of higher authority. I would hope to reach a consensus with you and the other sisters—one that would preserve the peace of the archdiocese and yet permit you the discretionary freedom you want, to some extent at least."

"Perhaps you might begin by giving us some idea of what this discretionary freedom entails," Sister Agnes Marie said.

Did that semi-smile on her face mean that she knew he hadn't answered her question about the A.D.?

More mockery? "I approved your decision to abandon nuns' habits. I went out of my way to find you a chaplain that *you* approve. I have never kept you out of civil rights protests or anti-war rallies."

Her expression seemed to imply that these were hardly liberal gestures. His temper flickering, Matthew Mahan abandoned the positive approach. "Now, I prefer to tell you what I will *not* tolerate. Not for one more day. I will not tolerate sisters moving into a parish unannounced and starting a guerrilla war against the pastor. Which you're doing in St. Thomas's."

"We wrote the pastor that we intended to open a clinic in his parish. We never heard from him."

"Of course you didn't. He forwarded the letter to me and I asked the vicar-general of the diocese to investigate it."

"He wrote us a very intemperate letter," Sister Agnes Marie said. "So intemperate that we did not feel we could receive it in the spirit of holy freedom, so we—I decided to ignore it."

"And that is why two hundred and fifty people showed up in front of St. Thomas's rectory last week demanding free access to the parish bowling alleys, social hall, and gymnasium?"

"The real reason for that protest was the situation in Farrelley's parish. How long must people wait for pastors like him to die?"

Matthew Mahan's temper began to flame. Because of Sister Agnes Marie's bluntness. Because he was about to defend the indefensible. Jack Farrelley did run his parish to suit his own convenience, with a month in Europe each summer, a month in Florida each winter. There were a half dozen like him in downtown parishes, all inclined to the sumptuous life-style of the former archbishop. "He has been there for thirty-five years—"

"About thirty years too long, I'd say," Sister Agnes Marie said.

"And there has never been a single criticism leveled against him, even when the parish became heavily Italian."

"It is now heavily Puerto Rican."

"We know that, we know that. We have demographic maps."

"A pity you don't send them to your pastors, your Eminence. Please don't regard what I am saying as impertinence or, worse, disobedience. We are only responding to the summons of the Gospel, seeking out, in our Lord's image, the lost sheep—"

"Let me go on, Sister Agnes," Matthew Mahan said. "At least one of your clinics is soliciting funds from people in the parish and from well-to-do people outside it. The average man is soon disenchanted with a church that bombards him with pleas three hundred and sixty-five days a year. When I became coadjutor bishop, we had dozens of Catholic organizations competing for funds. I brought order out of chaos by insisting that all appeals be authorized by the chancery office. We soon found we could include most of them in our annual fund drive."

"We asked for a grant from Catholic Charities. Monsignor O'Callahan turned us down."

"I saw your application. Your program was vague and goals undefined. It didn't meet the tests of professional social work."

"But we are not doing social work. We see ourselves as translating the Gospel into acts, making it flesh once more."

"Isn't that what the Church is doing and has been doing since the Resurrection?" Matthew Mahan snapped. He lowered his head and began to shake it back and forth, and Dennis braced for the explosion. "Sister Agnes. I am giving you an *order*. You will not raise another cent without my permission. Do you understand?"

Her expression betrayed no emotion. "Yes, your Eminence. But I reserve the right to appeal your decision to Rome."

"You have that right. I intend to talk there with Cardinal Antoniutti of the Sacred Congregation for the Religious." Maybe this red hat will serve a purpose after all, he thought grimly.

"I'm afraid we have no hope of winning an argument with you, your Eminence, but we feel conscience-bound to try."

Matthew Mahan saw clearly that Sister Agnes Marie was one-upping him. But there wasn't time to play psychological warfare. "Now, on the matter of St. Clare's Hospital . . ." St. Clare's was over a hundred years old. Its clientele was now almost totally black and non-Catholic. After much soul-searching, Matthew Mahan had decided to close it. "You know how many thousands of dollars we are losing there. Yet you let your nuns join a demonstration, demanding in the name of the community—whatever that means—that the hospital stay open."

"Your eminence, I led that demonstration," said Sister Helen. "Those people have nowhere to go. As you may recall, I'm a nurse by profession, and I've seen what comes into that clinic."

"I know, I know. I've read the studies," Matthew Mahan said testily. "But where are we going to get the money, Sister? If you can raise it, the hospital can stay open."

"If *you* can't raise the money, how can we hope to, your Eminence?" said Sister Agnes Marie.

"I sent a plan to Catholic Charities," Sister Helen was saying, "to convert the whole hospital into an outpatient clinic. I never had a reply."

"I'm sure it was impractical, or I'd have heard of it."

"Are you sure you didn't hear of it because Monsignor O'Callahan disapproved of our counseling women to use the pill?"

139

"I—haven't heard that, either," Matthew Mahan snapped. There was nothing in this world he disliked more than being caught off guard. "But if that was his reason, I would support Monsignor O'Callahan a thousand percent. Really, Sister, don't you see that I have no alternative?"

"As women, I'm afraid *we* have no alternative, your Eminence," said Sister Helen. "We find the Pope's position intolerable."

So do I, he wanted to say. But he could never say that. Especially to anyone as antagonistic as this young woman.

"I'm afraid I must issue another order. You will cease this sort of counseling forthwith. The most you are permitted to do is tell a woman—if *she* raises the question—that there are two points of view on the subject. Such counseling entails great delicacy. I must avoid engulfing the diocese in controversy."

There was no trace of sympathy on Sister Agnes Marie's face. Sister Helen was patently hostile. He glanced at his watch. "Sister Agnes. With this news from Rome, my time will be devoured for the next month or two. Perhaps it would be best if you worked out guidelines for marital counseling—and discussed them with Father McLaughlin. He's worked in those downtown parishes. Just remember this. I don't want anything happening that I haven't approved in advance."

Sister Agnes Marie nodded. Meaning yes, or merely that she had heard him? "I'm afraid my time is going to be limited, too. Sister Helen here may act as my deputy. She's serving as my vicar for our inner-city missionaries."

The word missionaries came close to making Matthew Mahan explode again. Only huge exercise of willpower got him out of the office without a farewell exchange of insults. "Did you hear what she said?" he asked Dennis in the car. "She's sending *missionaries?* To *my* diocese?"

Dennis McLaughlin somewhat desperately tried to make light of it. "Who knows? They might work."

The cardinal missed the humor—totally. "I just gave you a serious responsibility. If anything else goes wrong with those screwball women, it will be your fault. Is that clear?"

"Yes."

That was the last word spoken by either the cardinal or his secretary on the ride back to the city.

V

THIS isn't real, Father Dennis McLaughlin told himself. Standing in the center of Matthew Mahan's office, facing the white glare of the television camera lights, his eyelids felt as if they might peel off like grape skins. Out in the hall, he could hear the cardinal designate answering questions from the press. The honor belonged not to him but to the people, he was saying.

A busty blonde in a pantsuit rushed up to Dennis. "Have you got another bio?" she asked in a voice that struck him as exceptionally sultry. But he decided on second glance that it was only his perpetually lusting imagination. He gave her a handout on Matthew Mahan that had been produced by some previous secretary. Great writing it wasn't, but it told more than he'd known himself when he wrote to Gog only yesterday.

Older son of devout Catholic parents, father a professional baseball player, then minor league umpire, who put his savings into a local restaurant that failed to survive the crash. Thereafter a Parks Department official. Matt ordained at Rosewood in 1939, one of the first to volunteer for the chaplain service in 1940 when war loomed, a local hero by the time the war ended, numerous letters to the papers praising "Father Matt's" courage and compassion. Ultimate accolade, a column by Ernie Pyle.

Home again, Father Matt quickly proved that he also had what it took to succeed as a civilian. He transformed the Catholic Youth Organization into a social dynamo. Gymnasiums sprouted like magic throughout the diocese. As monsignor in charge of diocesan education he repeated the performance with new parochial schools, winning praise from that master apostle of bricks and mortar, Francis Cardinal Spellman. Known as a forthright spokesman for the rights of labor and minorities, particularly blacks. Injudicious remarks in this area placed him under a cloud with the then archbishop. But thanks to money-raising talents, aging Archbishop Hogan made no protest when John XXIII appointed his friend Mahan (they had met in France during World War II) coadjutor bishop, making him, in 1960, heir to the archbishopric.

Now the cardinal was standing in the doorway. Dennis suddenly found that he wanted to see Matthew Mahan less penetratingly and to think more about what was happening to himself.

What gave this man such power to disturb him? As usual, there was no time to do more than record the question inside his head and then stand there smiling vapidly as the cardinal designate, with swift sure strides, stepped into the center of the lights. The way he walked and the way he talked were part of it—that enormous self-assurance, the vitality, the charisma (ugh) that wove a circle of charm around everyone near him. Was it simply envy, envy from a man who had neither bulk nor charisma?

"Are we ready, Dennis?" Matthew Mahan said in a low voice. "I can't take much more of this." He was looking unusually pale.

"They're ready, but I couldn't persuade them to limit it to just one interview," Dennis said, hating the plea in his voice.

Matthew Mahan sighed. "Oh, well. I guess another five minutes won't kill me."

"Hello, your Eminence." The anchorman of KTGM's news team made a lunge for the episcopal ring. His foot caught on a television cable, and he had to cling to the cardinal's hand to keep from falling on his face. Raucous laughter from the technicians.

"Now, Jack," said Matthew Mahan. "That isn't necessary."

"I like to do it," said Jack Murphy. "It gives me the feeling that everything's kind of in place, you know?"

The moment they had returned from Mount St. Monica's, Matthew Mahan had ordered Dennis McLaughlin to locate a folder marked NEWSMEN and had checked salient facts about all the men he would be meeting at two o'clock. Now, therefore, he could joshingly smooth Jack Murphy's dented self-esteem. "How's Jack Junior these days? Is he having a good season? I haven't had much time to follow sports lately."

"He's averaging twenty points a game." Dennis would almost swear he saw Murphy grow taller. You had to admire it, Dennis thought ruefully. Within Jack Murphy there glowed a gratitude which guaranteed that there was not the faintest possibility of his asking his Eminence a single difficult question.

"I thought I'd ask you a couple of quick ones about Pope Paul," Jack was saying now. "Is there anything you'd like to talk about?"

"Well," said Matthew Mahan. "It mightn't hurt to mention the annual fund drive. You could ask me what we hope to do with the extra million we're trying to raise. We want to expand our psychiatric services, old-age centers, marital counseling. . . ."

"Fantastic, your Eminence," Murphy said, scribbling notes.

"It'd be nice, too, if you gave me a chance to talk a little about what we've been doing in the spirit of Pope John's *aggiornamento*— you know, updating the Church here in the archdiocese. We have parish councils now, and a functioning priests' synod, and we're doing wonderful things at the cathedral with the new liturgy. It isn't just a case of saying the Mass in English, Jack, as you know. It's getting the people to participate in the act of worship. To get them involved with the government of the Church, too. We've got five laymen and five laywomen on our diocesan board of education. Participation, Jack, that's what the life of the spirit is about, a sense of being part of a genuinely loving community."

Dennis had to admit that his Eminence was a magnificent salesman, even that some of these things were actually happening.

A technician thrust a microphone into Jack Murphy's hand. "Quiet, everybody," somebody yelled. The red light on the TV camera announced that its omnipotent eye was now open.

"First of all, your Eminence, let me say that this is the best news this city has heard for a long time. . . ."

A hand seized Dennis McLaughlin's arm. He turned and stared into a face distinctly like his own—freckled, bony, with unruly red hair. The one difference was that the other face was eight or nine inches above his. "Hello, Big Brother," the newcomer said, his grin making it clear that he enjoyed the phrase.

"Where've you been?" snapped Dennis. "The press conference is over. TV now—"

Leo McLaughlin groaned. "Oh, hell, my watch stopped."

Three years younger than Dennis, Leo was managing editor of the diocesan newspaper, the *Beacon*. How much longer he would be was a question. To hear him tell it, he was locked in ideological combat with the editor in chief, Monsignor Joseph Cohane, day and night. Most of his attempts to report on liturgical experiments by young priests, the ferment in Catholic colleges, or the Vietnam war went into Cohane's wastebasket.

"How am I going to explain missing this one?" Leo asked. "It's like missing God's birthday."

"Calm down. I'll give you the standard press release. Maybe you can pick up a few things from the vidiots."

They stepped to the door of the television room. The cardinal

143

was now handling a non-Catholic reporter, famous for explosive questions, as easily as he had Jack Murphy. "Do you approve the idea of a married priesthood?" the reporter was asking.

"For an old man like me, the question is irrelevant. If married priests can make the Church more effective, I'm for it. But I'd like to see some real evidence before I make that judgment. The tradition of a celibate clergy is a thousand years old. You don't throw that sort of thing away like a wrapper on a candy bar."

"Yes, I see what you mean," said the reporter feebly.

Why, Dennis wondered, did they all put him on a pedestal? Why not talk to him as one human being to another?

"The whole thing bores me," Leo said, collapsing into a chair beside Dennis's desk. He waved a copy of the *Hard Times Herald* at his brother. "Here's what I really should be writing for. They want some more stuff from me." Under the transparent pseudonym Leo the Great, Leo had done a number of articles for the *Herald,* diatribes on the Church's failure to condemn the war and join the revolution. The sort of journalistic trash that was ruining the underground press, in Dennis's opinion.

"I hope you put some facts into your next effort," Dennis said.

"I thought you were going to stop playing Big Brother–Ph.D.–Jesuit–Junior Jesus," Leo said.

Last year they had had a bitter argument about Dennis's fondness for giving Leo large amounts of unwanted advice. Leo's tendency to attack his older brother did not make it easy for Dennis to abandon the role. Nevertheless, Dennis tried. "Sorry," he said.

Leo laughed. "Poor old brother. He quits the Jesuits, turns his back on all that intellectual prestige to become a priest of the people. Two months later he's handing out episcopal press releases. The tragedy of a would-be saint. Guys start out like you, determined to make the organization go straight. Next thing they get you running the show. Bye-bye idealism."

"I'm interested in finding out where idealism ends and realism begins. Maybe you ought to get interested in the same thing."

"Now, now, Big Brother." Leo pulled out a pad. "I'll interview *you.* An off-the-record with one of the cardinal's intimates. What was *he* doing when *he* heard the news?"

"He was about to have a Scotch-and-soda nightcap and go to bed," said Matthew Mahan. He was standing in the doorway, a not quite believable smile on his face. "The phone rang. It was the apostolic delegate. He sounded as surprised as I was."

Dennis, feeling painfully foolish, said, "Your Eminence. This is my brother, Leo."

"I know him. I know him," said Matthew Mahan. "I like what he writes in the *Beacon*, too, most of the time."

"I skipped your press conference, your Eminence," said Leo. "I thought I'd rely on nepotism to get some personal details."

"Let's see," said Matthew Mahan with pseudo solemnity. "I drank my whisky, intending to keep the news a secret until morning. Then about ten o'clock I reconsidered and decided to celebrate with the people who work their heads off for me, day in, day out. So I called in Chancellor Malone and Vicar-General Petrie and the rest of the chancery crowd, and we hoisted a few." He wagged a finger under Leo's nose. "That's off the record, you understand?" He turned to Dennis. "Would you be a good fellow and call Dr. Reed for me? Tell him I'd like to stop by his office tonight. I'm going to lie down. I'm not feeling very well."

"I'm sorry, terribly sorry. Can we—I do anything?"

"No. Just tell Bill I've got a pain in my belly."

Dennis watched the cardinal designate walk away with the plodding step of a very tired man. Why was he continually noticing details that seemed to lure sympathy out of the recesses of his mind, no matter how harshly he ordered it to keep its distance?

Leo's eyes reflected only mockery as he watched the same exit. "It's five o'clock. *Saturday*," he said. "Let's go out for a beer."

"I'll have to get out of uniform. Give me ten minutes."

Dennis called Dr. Reed, then trotted up to the third floor. Quickly he changed into a blue turtleneck, gabardine slacks, and a tweed sports coat. He stood before the mirror transformed from cleric to layman. If only it were as easy to change the inside as it was the outside of your persona, Father McLaughlin.

"Does that hurt?"

Bill Reed's stubby fingers pressed down on Matthew Mahan's abdomen. The pain leaped into angry life. "Yes," he said.

It seemed to hurt everywhere Dr. Reed probed. Lying on the examination table, Matthew Mahan thought perhaps by this pain God was warning him against the most obvious sin that might tempt him now—pride, self-satisfaction. But did he need the warning? Every day of his life seemed to send him this message. Still, he would watch himself. *Thy will be done*, he prayed.

"Okay, sit up," Bill said. "What's eating you?"

From this dour, sallow-faced man the question almost seemed an accusation. But Cardinal Mahan and Dr. Reed had too much in common to be troubled by that. For eleven months—June 6, 1944, to May 8, 1945—they had shared a special agony. Young Dr. Reed had been in charge of the forward aid station where the 409th Regiment's wounded were brought. When Matthew Mahan was not in the lines, this was where he spent most of his time. How many awful nights and days had he watched Dr. Reed's face while he systematically separated the wounded, to work first on the slightly injured and last, when he had time, on the men who were almost certainly going to die.

With his fondness for sardonic remarks, Bill had called the mortally wounded men Matthew Mahan's patients. "Three more for you out there, Padre," he would say, and Chaplain Mahan would stumble out and kneel beside the dying men, give them his blessing, and, if they were Catholics, absolve their sins.

Dr. Reed called himself "a scathing atheist," but Matt and the Protestant chaplain, Steve Murchison, used to tell him that when they saw him talking to the wounded they knew he was no atheist. This inevitably made him splutter about the "God stuff" they were "selling."

After the war, at Matthew Mahan's urging, Dr. Reed had migrated from his hometown to the city. He had married a devout Catholic who raised their only child, Helen, as if afraid her unbelieving husband would steal the girl's soul. Otherwise, the marriage had been extraordinarily happy. Four years ago Shelagh had died of cancer. The effect on Bill had been catastrophic. Each time Matthew Mahan saw him he seemed more drawn.

"Are you afraid to tell me what's eating you?" Bill asked now.

"How about giving me your diagnosis first?"

"You've got an ulcer, I'm certain. I want you to go into the hospital Monday for a gastrointestinal series and X rays."

"I can't, Bill. It's the beginning of Holy Week. The fund drive comes in two weeks. I've got speaking appointments straight through, three and four a day."

"When was the last time you took a vacation?"

"I went to Brazil last year. Visited our missions down there. And back in 1967 I went to Rome. Every five years or so a bishop has to go report on his diocese."

"Neither trip was exactly a vacation."

"I took it easy in Rome. Hit all the best restaurants."

"And between meals worried your ass off about what the Pope was going to say about your report."

No, Matthew Mahan thought. I worried about a woman. A woman with haunted eyes who responded bravely, always bravely, to my perpetually fatuous question: *Are you all right, Mary?*

Bill Reed sighed. "A lamebrain atheist like me can't win this kind of an argument. But I can say that you probably got the ulcer because you are working too hard. Frankly, Padre, if I had a choice of diseases for you, I'd pick this one. It's safer than a coronary." And he went on to explain how an ulcer worked. The new cardinal only half listened. His eyes were on the furrows in Bill Reed's haggard face. The man looked like he was dying of some mysterious disease that dried out the flesh and the spirit.

"Titrilac comes in liquid form and in pills," Bill was saying. "Carry the pills in your pocket, and take one if you need it. Take the liquid a half hour before eating. This second prescription"— Bill scribbled as he talked—"is for some pills that reduce the amount of acid secreted by your stomach." Next Bill handed him two mimeographed pages listing foods he was forbidden to eat and sample meals of what he was permitted to enjoy—if that word still meant anything when all his favorite foods were on the wrong list. "Booze is out, and so is smoking," Bill said.

"*Smoking,*" Matthew Mahan said. "Come on, Bill. You remember when I tried to give it up. I didn't sleep for a month."

"How much are you smoking now?"

"Oh, about a pack a day."

"Cut in half this week, half again next week."

"If the condemned man can make an observation, I think you're taking entirely too much pleasure in giving these orders."

Bill almost smiled. "How often does anybody get a chance to order a cardinal around?"

Bill was trying to cheer him up, and it *was* a consolation, Matthew Mahan thought as he rubbed his aching stomach, to know how many men like Bill, men of all faiths or none, were his friends, on a deep, unshakable level reached a quarter of a century ago in that fiery trial they had all endured in Europe.

"How are things with you, Bill? *You* look tired."

"What the hell is this? Are you trying to play witch doctor on me in my own office?"

"So when is the last time *you* took a vacation?"

"Oh, I go up to my shack on weekends and putter around."

"Alone?"

Bill's eyes were on a pen that he kept turning in his hands. "Yeah. It guarantees you a rest."

"Nobody ever sees you anymore—not since Shelagh died."

A nerve twitched in Bill Reed's drawn cheek. "I know, Matt. I just don't have the heart for going out."

"Bill, you're a young man. Why don't you marry again?"

A dry sound. "I'm a hard man to please, Matt."

It was hopeless. Matthew Mahan groped for a new approach. "I saw your daughter today. Sister Helen."

A mistake. Bill's face became a mask of fury. The Catholic Church had destroyed his daughter's mind, he said angrily. She was now living in a rat-infested slum, and totally rejected her intensely conservative father and everything she had enjoyed in her girlhood—the baronial house on the parkway, the beach house, the country clubs, sports cars, and chic clothes that Daddy's money had munificently supplied. He was hurt, confused, outraged.

"Bill. If it makes you feel any better, I can't figure them out either. People her age. I've got a secretary, a very bright kid. At least four times a day he says things that are incomprehensible to me. The links we assumed were there, connecting us to the next generation, have snapped, Bill."

Gruffly, Bill changed the subject and demanded a firm date for the gastrointestinal series. Matthew Mahan told him he'd consult his appointment book, shook hands, and departed. Walking back to his residence, he felt dogged by a sense of personal defeat. There was nothing he could *do* to solve his problem except take the pills and stay on the diet. Beyond that, the solutions seemed to lie in not doing, not working so hard, not caring so much. Lord, Lord. *Thy will be done,* he prayed. But why this, why now? When he needed all his resources to hold back the waters of chaos?

Mrs. Norton appeared in the hall seconds after the big iron front door clanged shut. He gave her the doctor's diet sheets. "I'm afraid this is going to be an awful nuisance for you."

"Oh dear, dear," she said. "I was saying only the other day that you didn't look well to me, for all the flesh on you. No, this won't be any trouble. Not a bit at all."

Calling Dennis McLaughlin on the telephone intercom, he asked him to come down and take the prescriptions to the drugstore. When his secretary appeared, he was still clad in turtleneck and tweed jacket. He gave Dennis the prescriptions and said, "I seem to have an ulcer. At least that's what the doctor says, based on an educated guess."

"Oh. Oh. I'm—sorry."

"So am I. I'm afraid you'll have to do more and I less."

Dennis nodded and started down the stairs. Suddenly, Matthew Mahan felt compelled to say something about his outfit. "Dennis. Would you, as a personal favor to me, only wear those clothes when you are off duty? It's what I've asked all our priests to do."

Dennis looked more wistful than angry at the rebuke. "I went out with my brother for a drink. Do you want me to change now?"

"No, no."

"Oh, I almost forgot. Again." Dennis smiled guiltily. "Father Reagan called. He'd like to speak to you about a demonstration that Father Disalvo is planning at St. Francis tomorrow."

"All right. I'll call him. As soon as I've finished the cream of wheat I'm condemned to eat for supper." Wrong. You must handle this illness without any pleas for pity.

In his bedroom, he switched on the television news. "As of last Sunday 33,063 Americans have died in Vietnam fighting. . . ." Then the local news began. He was watching himself answer nice harmless questions from Jack Murphy when the telephone rang. It was the president of St. Francis Xavier University again. Matthew Mahan turned off the sound on the TV and settled into his recliner chair for a long session.

"I want to extend my personal congratulations, and the best wishes of every member of our faculty," Father Reagan said.

Father Philip Reagan had been one of those almost too handsome boy geniuses in which the Jesuits seemed to specialize during Matthew Mahan's two student years at St. Francis. In fact, Reagan had taught him freshman Latin. He had been considered a brilliant classical scholar then, but had never fulfilled his promise.

"Thanks," said Matthew Mahan. "I gather you have a problem?"

"It's this rally," said Father Reagan. "Solidarity Day, they're calling it. Father Disalvo is planning to lead ten thousand blacks out here. He estimates there'll be five thousand students to greet them. Campus security can't possibly handle a crowd that size."

"But Father Disalvo promised to clear all plans for demonstrations with me. I haven't heard a word of this."

"I only know what my security people tell me."

"Don't you know by now that cops and lawyers love to anticipate the worst? Add mayors and university presidents to the list." Mayor O'Connor's rugged Irish good looks at that moment filled the silent television screen, no doubt mouthing hypocritical praise for Cardinal Mahan. "What am I supposed to do about this demonstration, presuming it exists?"

"I was hoping—that you'd forbid it. Or forbid Father Disalvo to participate, which would pretty much defuse it."

"Meanwhile, you independent Jesuits can go on pretending to be in favor of free speech and free association, while poor slobs like me get pilloried in every underground newspaper."

"I don't think we ever . . ."

On the television, the mayor had been replaced by Father Reagan himself. Matthew Mahan felt a little conscience-stricken. "Calm down, Phil," he said. "I'll get hold of Disalvo tonight."

Grateful murmurs from Father President. Matthew Mahan hung up and turned on the sound in time to hear his old friend Steve Murchison, the city's Methodist bishop, telling the people how pleased Protestants were by Pope Paul's choice. "His Eminence and I were chaplains together, you know. The 409th. He saved my life. I've seen Father Matt do things under fire that only a man in—"

Without waiting to hear the rest, Matthew Mahan turned off the sound again and called Steve. "What are you trying to do to me," he said, "making me sound like Batman? The next time I get on television, I'm going to tell them a few things you did—"

Murchison chuckled. "How are you, Matt?"

"I could be better. . . ."

"Remember what I used to say about you Romans being too *visible* with all your schools and colleges and what have you?

You're a target for nuts of all kinds. Learn to travel light, Matt."

"You may have something there, Steve. Anyway, I do appreciate all you said just now on the tube, even if it wasn't true."

"I don't need absolution, you Irish faker."

"Good night, Steve. God bless you."

Matthew Mahan next dialed the mayor's private wire. "Jake," he said. "I just wanted to thank you for the nice things you said on television. I wish you meant them."

"Well, we politicians have to stick together."

"I wish you'd stick a little closer to me when it comes to getting that parochial aid bill through."

"I told you before, Matt. Your schools have wrecked the public school system in this city. Would the blacks be able to scream de facto segregation if we had your kids in the public schools? Why don't you make yourself a real hero, Matt, and get out of the education business before you tear the city and state apart?"

Matthew Mahan felt his temperature rising in five-degree leaps to the boiling point. In public his Honor pretended to be a model Catholic. In private he talked to his archbishop as if he were an uncooperative ward leader. In any case, arguing with him on the school topic was futile. "Jake," he said. "I called to find out what you know about a parade being planned by Father Disalvo tomorrow. From downtown out to the university."

The mayor knew nothing. "It sounds like a lovely way to burn down half the city. I'll call the police commissioner."

"Don't get excited, Jake. I've got Disalvo on a tight leash."

"I wish you'd shut him up. If you don't, I may arrange to do it with a couple of nightsticks."

"Now, now, Jake, don't revert to the old style."

"When it comes to Disalvo, I wish you'd revert. On parochial schools, I wish you'd stop reverting."

Cardinal Mahan hung up, seething, just as his secretary appeared at the door with the medicines. "Do you know Father Vincent Disalvo, Dennis?"

"I've heard of him, of course. But not met him."

"You will soon. I want you to put on your clericals and go down to St. Sebastian's parish right now. Bring him back—whatever he's doing. If you're wondering why I don't telephone him, he's never in the rectory, and he never returns calls."

As the door closed, the telephone rang again. With uneasy prescience, Matthew Mahan knew who was calling.

"Matt?" said the tired familiar voice. "I didn't want the whole day to go by without at least calling to tell you—"

"I meant to call you, Eileen," Matthew Mahan said guiltily, "but I've been up to my ears in reporters."

"I know. I keep thinkin' how proud Charlie'd be."

Would he really? Matthew Mahan could only remember hate-filled diatribes flung at him over the telephone by his brother at three in the morning. The ruined political career: They didn't see me, they saw my big brother the bishop. I never had a real friend. They were all your friends. "I wish he was here. With all my heart and soul, I do, Eileen. How are you?"

"Oh. Pretty well. The job's boring, ya know." Thanks to her brother-in-law and Mike Furia, she was a receptionist at the Furia Brothers Construction Company.

"How's Timmy?"

"Matt, I don't want to spoil your big day. But—"

"Don't be silly. Tell me."

"Oh, Matt. He won't—he won't talk to me. He seems to be in another world. I found some pills. . . ."

"How's he doing at the university?" Timmy had done well at school, and Matthew Mahan had twisted a few Jesuit arms to get him a scholarship at St. Francis Xavier University.

"I don't know. I never see him study. He's never home. Sometimes I get so worried I—I just sit and cry."

Matthew Mahan pictured his nephew as he last saw him, six months ago. The urchin face, the half-wise, half-mocking smile—the same smile he'd seen on the girls at Mount St. Monica's.

"We'll have a good talk soon. Look, tell your boss you want a leave of absence to take a trip to Rome."

"Rome? You mean for your—"

"Of course. I want you and Timmy to come. We'll get someone to take care of the younger kids."

"Oh gee, I can't wait—he'll be so excited—"

"Good night, Eileen. I'll remember Timmy in my morning Mass."

"Oh yes, Matt, I know you will. Thank you. . . ."

It would be better, he thought as he hung up, if she hated you. Hate could be conquered by love. But what can love do with a defeated blob? No, that was too harsh. Eileen was doing her best to bear a burden she was too weak to carry.

He went to his bedroom to finish the day's reading. He saw that he was on the last page.

Come let us return to the Lord,
For it is He who has rent, but He will heal us.
He has struck us, but He will bind our wounds.

For a moment Matthew Mahan's eyes blurred. He wiped away the tears and read the final prayer of the day.

We want to be strong enough, Father,
to love You above all
and our brothers and sisters because of You.

DENNIS McLaughlin called Eddie Johnson and asked him to bring the car around. Eddie had been on his way to bed. "That man we work for don't know the dark from the light."

"I could take a cab."

"Oh no. He say take the car, we take the car."

At last, Dennis thought, he was to meet Vincent Disalvo. He had marched in one or two protests led by this radical priest, but had never become a member of his Council for Peace and Freedom. In fact, Dennis admitted gloomily, his activist career was pretty much over when he returned to the city from Yale last year. In vain he reminded himself that his reasons for giving up that heady way of life were good and sufficient: he was thirty years old, and the egotism, the superficial thinking, the neurotic hatreds of so many radicals had chilled his fervor.

It did not work, this dutiful reminder. He did not like playing observer, but he could not play that other game again. At Yale he had been the clerical civilian, reveling in his chance to show the WASPs and Jews that a Catholic priest could not only think, he could feel. Now, thinking, feeling were verboten, except as directed by Cardinal Designate Mahan. He, like Father Vincent Disalvo, Fathers Novak and Cannon and all the rest of them, the lesser shepherds, were men under obedience. Stop, Dennis told himself, stop. It was not *that* bad. His brother Leo had gotten to him. He was making up for those years when Dennis had been

Mother's darling, the model to be emulated. Now Leo was the man of action, the mover and the shaker, while poor old Big Brother—Father Dennis was the pathetic captive of the Establishment. Leo's condescension was blatant. But the gambit Dennis found it hardest to forgive was the celibacy probe. Last year, in a careless moment, Dennis had confessed to his anguish. And Leo had never let him forget it. He made a point of giving certain girls more than a casual fondle and then suggesting that at his request they were ready to solve Dennis's problem. And all Dennis could do was wanly smile—No thank you, I prefer—what?

What do you prefer, Dennis? That is the unanswered question.

"This here's St. Sebastian's," Eddie Johnson said.

It had started to rain. Dennis rang the rectory bell. A short priest with a large paunch opened the door. Dennis introduced himself, asked for Father Disalvo, and was told that he was at a meeting over in the school.

St. Sebastian's school was separated from the church and rectory by a large playground. The building was dark now except for the windows on the top floor. Dennis trudged up six flights of stairs. On the final landing he heard voices passionately arguing.

Disalvo was sitting on top of a desk. Some of his lieutenants were sideways in their seats with their feet up. Back of him, surrounded by blacks, was Sister Helen Reed. She glared at Dennis with intense dislike—the same expression he had seen on her face at Mount St. Monica's earlier in the day.

"What can we do for you, friend?" Disalvo asked. His high-pitched voice was disconcerting. He had wavy dark hair and a round face. He wore a blue work shirt and dirty chinos.

"I'm Dennis McLaughlin, the cardinal's secretary," he said. "His Eminence wants to see you immediately. The car is outside."

Disalvo glowered. "What does he want to see me about? I would like to finish this meeting."

"His Eminence is not well. He'd like to get to bed early."

"Oh my, now would he?" mocked a tall, thin black.

"Okay," Disalvo said. "If you cats don't mind waiting. This shouldn't take more than a half hour, an hour at the outside."

Dismay was evident, but they murmured that they'd wait. On the stairs Disalvo said, "I'd better get into clericals."

"It wouldn't be a bad idea," Dennis said.

"What's on the great man's mind?"

"Something about your march tomorrow."

"It's not a march," Disalvo said. "I guess you could call it a patrol. I don't know how much longer I'm going to take this. Getting dragged up to the palace in this goddamn car like a tribune summoned by the emperor."

"Time to become a tribune of the people?"

"You're damn right it is. Time and past time."

The cardinal awaited them in his office, his feet up on his Louis XVI desk. "Hello, Vinny," he said in a hearty voice that struck Dennis's ear as totally phony. "*Buona sera, caro.*"

Defiance, ferocity vanished. "Hello, your Eminence," Disalvo said, holding out his hand. "Congratulations."

Matthew Mahan shook hands without bothering to take his feet off his desk. "Sit down, Vinny. Would you like a drink?"

"No, nothing," Disalvo said, his eyes roving nervously.

"I hope I didn't get you out of bed, Vinny."

"No, no. As a matter of fact, I was having a meeting. Of the Peace and Freedom Council."

"Oh. Sorry to interrupt it, but maybe you could tell me what it's about and save yourself the trouble of a report."

"Well—we were discussing this trip—that we're going to take out to the university tomorrow. Talking about how we could break through the apathy out there."

"Trip?" Matthew Mahan said. "Are you going by bus?"

"No. We thought we'd go on foot."

"A march?" His voice was still cordial, but there was a threat in it. "Remember, Vinny, what I told you about marches."

"We think of this as—well, a patrol, your Eminence. No more than a few dozen people. You don't have to get a parade permit unless you have more than fifty."

"Are you going to carry placards?"

"Well—we thought we might carry one or two."

"No. You won't. How many students do you expect?"

"I have no idea," Disalvo said. "Maybe two hundred."

Matthew Mahan roared with unfeigned laughter. Dennis was enraged. He had no great love for rhetorical terrorists of Father Disalvo's sort, but the man was sincere. It was bad enough to cow him. Laughing at him was detestable.

"Vinny, I'm not laughing at *you*," Matthew Mahan said. "I'm just thinking of old Flappy Reagan, as we call him around here. Always in a flap about something. He told me you were coming with ten thousand screaming blacks to join five thousand inflamed students. Do you see what I have to put up with?" The cardinal took a deep drag on his cigarette and looked at it ruefully. "I'm not supposed to be smoking these things." He stubbed it out. "Okay. Let's settle this right now. What do you want to do?"

"I want to lead a delegation from the Peace and Freedom Council. Twenty blacks and sixteen whites. From St. Sebastian's to the campus, where I'm scheduled to speak at three."

"Take a bus to the campus. No march."

"Your Eminence," Father Disalvo said desperately. "I can't withdraw this proposal. I'd lose every bit of influence I have. The blacks are getting more militant every day."

"You know how much I care about those people, Vinny. I stood up for them when there weren't a half dozen other Catholics in the country saying a word. I'm one of the founders of the Catholic Interracial Council."

"Yes, your Eminence. But the situation has *changed*—"

"I know, and you're meeting change realistically. That's why I've given you all the freedom I think you can handle. It's a lot more than plenty of people think you should have. You don't realize how much time I spend defending you. I'm on your *side*, Vinny. But never forget what I told you about that collar you're wearing. If I ever took it off you, you'd be a has-been in two weeks. You get attention because you're a priest. And because you're a priest, you've got to demonstrate responsibility. Now look me in the eye and tell me you really believe your effectiveness would be hurt if you canceled this patrol." His tone reduced the idea to idiocy.

"It would, your Eminence, I swear it."

"Then you can do it. But limit the number to *twenty*."

"All right, your Eminence."

"Dennis, get Father Reagan on the phone for me."

Dennis dialed the university. "Phil," Matthew Mahan boomed into the phone. "I've got Father Disalvo here. He is coming out to visit you tomorrow. Do you know how many people he's bringing? Twenty! That's right. He originally intended to bring thirty-six, but when he heard how nervous you were, as a gesture of Christian

157

charity he reduced it to twenty. He also says that he expects about two hundred students. All right, Phil? So sleep tight. No one's going to tear up your office tomorrow."

Matthew Mahan hung up and sighed. "Well, Vinny. What are you going to talk about tomorrow?"

"Mostly I'm going to attack Nixon. The war. Try to get more students to see the connection between the war and black poverty."

"I don't agree with it, but—okay. Just remember, no talk about violence, not even a hint that this city might burn."

"I got that message the last time, your Eminence."

"I just want to make sure you've still got it." He held out his hand. "Thanks for coming up, *amico mio.*"

As Father Disalvo went out to the waiting car, Dennis looked at his watch. It was eleven thirty. Disalvo's followers, including Sister Helen Reed, would have waited an hour and a half—if they waited. Not exactly the sort of experience that builds charisma. Did his Eminence understand this? Dennis wondered. Did he apply the negative nuances of power that subtly?

"Tell me frankly, Dennis, how do you think he feels about the deal we just worked out?"

Dennis was too surprised by the question to look for a diplomatic answer. "I think he's mad as hell," he said.

"Really?" To Dennis's amazement, there was dismay, genuine dismay, on Cardinal Mahan's face.

VI

"AND the money—you just can't believe the way he handles money. He's a corporation sole, you know, which means he literally *owns* everything. The archdiocese levies a tax of five percent on each parish. That adds up to around four million dollars—without the annual fund drive."

"Wow. This is fascinating stuff," said Leo McLaughlin as he thrust another bourbon and ginger ale into his brother's hand.

You are talking too much, a drowsy voice whispered in Dennis's skull. But he did not care. He was not talking to Leo and his wife, Grace, who sat openmouthed on the couch. No. His audience was a young woman in a pale pink suit with a skirt that stopped a foot above her knees. He was talking to the dark hair that fell in a glossy fountain down her back, to the curve of those nylon legs, to the breasts that created a lovely hollow within which a gold cross rested. If Sister Helen Reed was impressed by his revelations, she did not show it. A small Mona Lisa smile was all she deigned to bestow on Father Dennis McLaughlin. So he talked on.

"He's got the style of a Renaissance prince. I think it's a reaction to the Depression, when his father lost his life's savings. He's paying me six hundred dollars a month. I couldn't believe it. That's three times what a curate gets. He just laughed and said I was working three times as hard."

"You like it," said Leo. "You don't have to think."

"Is he going to publish a financial report?" Helen asked.

"Not if he can help it. The chancellor, Terry Malone, is against it, and Matt goes along. There are figures in the draft report I saw that he wouldn't like to make public. The cost of running the episcopal residence, for instance: $32,567.80. And something called travel expenses that came to $26,896.50."

"And he won't give us twenty-five thousand for our inner-city project," said Helen Reed.

"Careful," Dennis said. "No revolutionary statements, please. Didn't I tell you that my head is on the block if you girls try anything drastic? Let Father Disalvo play local radical."

"He's a jerk," Sister Helen said.

That had a satisfying sound. Dennis had assumed that Sister Helen was enamored of Disalvo, the city's leading militant. Her attitude inspired more revelations, beginning with an account of the way the cardinal cowed Father Disalvo. Then the worries over the fund drive, which did not seem to be going well. Next, the failure of the state senate even to report out of committee the bill to subsidize parochial schools. On and on Dennis talked, while Leo stuck another bourbon into his hand. Sister Helen was smiling now, even laughing at Father McLaughlin's snide cracks, at his description of the wreckage of the Jesuit order.

They were at the table now, dining on veal parmigiana as only Grace née Conti cooked it. The wine was flowing. "Leo," said Dennis, raising his glass. "Allow me to toast you as a diplomat." It had been Leo's idea, this "Easter truce session," as he called it, between Father Dennis and Sister Helen. Dennis had summoned her to his office for a conference earlier in the month, and she had icily told him she was too busy. Mentioning it to Leo on the phone, he learned that Helen and Grace were old schoolmates at Mount St. Monica's. It was easy for Leo to discover that Helen had no place to dine on Easter Day, thanks to her feud with her reactionary father. So the banquet had been arranged.

But Father Dennis had been unprepared for the chic, beautiful girl who greeted him in his brother's living room. He had murmured idiotic things. Only after the first drink did he regain some shreds of his savoir faire. Now, smiling at Leo through the alcoholic haze, he felt wonderful. And Leo's fondness for sneering at Mother's Jesuit genius had strangely diminished.

"What are we going to do about the Church?" Leo said in a harsh tone as he raised his glass in response to Dennis.

"Little Brother, you are speaking to an intellectual. We don't do anything. We just talk about it."

"Maybe it's time you started doing something," Sister Helen said, her voice amazingly seductive.

"Don't you realize, Big Brother," Leo said, "that you are in a position to blow up the whole crummy show? You are on the inside of one of the most important archdioceses in the United States. Do you get a look at his checkbook?"

"I draw the checks."

"Fantastic. Then you see him in action. Absolute master of a ten-million-dollar-a-year operation with no accountability to anyone. Has he spent any of it—questionably?"

A shrug from ossified Father McLaughlin. "All his sister-in-law's bills come to us. She's a widow."

Leo began asking questions like a parody of a CIA section chief. Was there a copying machine in the office? Did he have access to all Mahan's correspondence? How far back? What about tapping his telephone? Now wait a minute. It's simple, all you need is a tape recorder and a jack with a suction cup. If he catches you, he can't put you in jail. That would ruin the episcopal image.

"You'd be back in the ghetto, working with people you really care about," Sister Helen said.

Somehow, through the alcoholic blur, a cry almost sprang to Dennis's lips: My priesthood, my priesthood, don't any of you understand? But obviously no one did.

So Dennis's words remained unspoken, and over a glass of port they listened to Leo expound the "theology of action." *The way, the truth, and the life* were all one thing—action—and without it nothing existed.

It was sickening, Dennis thought, gripping his refilled port glass as if it could hold him upright. He was listening to the same revolutionary ideas he himself had spouted two years ago and since discarded. But suddenly Leo was in new, exciting territory. The Catholic Church in this country was one of the few institutions in which the expectations of the people were rising faster than the Establishment could meet them. That was the moment when revolutionaries must strike. The sentimentalists will cry out, Give them time, they are doing their best. Nonsense, no Establishment ever voluntarily surrendered its power.

Sister Helen turned to smile admiringly at Dennis. "It makes so much sense."

She was paying *him* a compliment, regarding *him* as the source of this wisdom. Suddenly, the several possibilities of the situation coalesced in Father McLaughlin's double vision. In the glow of Sister Helen's smile he coolly agreed to supply Leo with enough material from Matthew Mahan's files for a book that would rock the archdiocese—perhaps the entire American Catholic Church. Not that Leo would ever write the book, or that Dennis thought it was worth writing. Leo was much too disorganized, and the realities of Matthew Mahan's day-to-day activities weren't worthy of righteous condemnation. No, Father McLaughlin had another motive. Remembering his brusque exchange with the cardinal about celibacy, he saw how he could resolve that question.

The evening ended with a long, cold cab ride downtown. Dashing Father Dennis insisting on taking Helen to the ghetto, joking as they went about negotiating a truce between Cardinal Mahan and Sister Agnes Marie. Then in the semidarkness of the tenement hall outside her door he felt her eyes upon him before she took out her key and slid it into the lock. She turned to him, and he said, "Would you be shocked if I kissed you?"

"A kiss of peace?"

"You might call it that."

He kissed her firmly on the lips. Incredible sensations occurred in his body. When was the last time you had kissed a woman? Seventeen, the night of your senior prom, with your arranged-by-

Mother date. The kiss had come from her, inexplicably, as they had said good night. So the answer to your question is: Never. The realization brought Father McLaughlin close to weeping.

On this same Easter Sunday evening, Matthew Mahan sat alone in his study writing a letter.

Dear Mary,

Thanks for your cable and for the letter that followed it. The whole thing is still dreamlike. It's hard to believe that in three weeks I'll be in Rome kneeling before the Pope.

This has been the worst week in the year for me, as usual. I try to preside at all the Holy Week ceremonies in the cathedral and keep up a normal work schedule. It has left me and my secretary frazzled. As he trudged out of here a few hours ago, the poor fellow looked like a fugitive from a concentration camp.

He's new. Have I told you his name—Dennis McLaughlin? I can't remember when I last wrote. He's an escapee from the Jesuits who got tired of playing intellectual Ping-Pong and decided to see what it was like in the trenches. I snatched him out of our downtown parishes, and I'm not sure I can hang on to him. Like so many of the young, he's practically tongue-tied when it comes to talking to someone my age. But he's exactly the sort of help I need—he's in touch with the young, and a hard worker.

We'll be in Rome from April 27 until May 6. That should give us more than enough time to pay a few visits to the Tre Scalini. I could write you a sermon on patience in response to a lot you've said recently about the way things are going in the Church. But we'll have lots more fun arguing face-to-face.

With much affection as always,
Matt

The cardinal addressed and stamped the envelope, then stood up, sighing. It was time to head for the Downtown Athletic Club, where he was taking his brother's family for Easter dinner. He gazed wistfully at his shell collection. He had several thousand more shells stored in the cellar, carefully catalogued. He used to spend at least one relaxing evening a month changing the display, cataloguing new purchases, deciding what he was prepared to trade. But for months he had not had a single night to spare.

They were waiting, Eileen and the seven children, in the lobby.

All but Timmy were dressed in new clothes charged to Matthew Mahan. The cardinal kept no track of how much he gave Eileen, but it never seemed to be enough. She was not a good money manager. But this was not the moment for negative thoughts. He threw himself into greeting the children.

"Timmy, how are you?" Long-haired Timmy, wearing an army fatigue jacket with a dozen or so buttons on it in favor of peace and power to the people, responded only with a limp handshake.

He turned to the five girls, greeting each by name and telling her how pretty she looked. Alas, untrue—they all had their mother's buckteeth and narrow jaw. Then he turned to his favorite, little Matt, a beautiful child, with his father's jet black hair and a face that exuded Irish pugnacity. He took the small outstretched hand. "How are you, young fellow?"

"I'm fine, your Eminent."

"Your what?"

The girls started giggling and even Timmy smiled.

"Your Eminence," his mother said.

"Your Eminent," Matt said, unbothered.

"Now listen," Matthew Mahan said. "No one in this family is to call me that. I'm Father Matt, as always. You don't call a baseball player by a different name when he gets traded to another team, do you? Well, I've just been traded to the cardinals."

Matt II grinned. "What position are you going to play?"

"What position do you think I ought to play?"

"Center field. That's where sluggers play." Everyone laughed.

In spite of this amusing start, Matthew Mahan found the dinner depressing. The girls giggled and quarreled among themselves. To converse with Eileen was hard going. With Timmy he got nowhere. He had hopes of Timmy's becoming a priest. But as he turned seventeen the boy had undergone a transformation from true believer to defiant cynic. Now he responded to his uncle's invitation to Rome with a sullen shrug. "Sure, I'll come. Why not?"

Matthew Mahan welcomed the appearance of the waiter with the check. In another five minutes he was shoveling his nieces and nephews into a taxi. He slipped two fifty-dollar bills into Eileen's hand. "If you want to buy a couple of dresses for the trip."

Depression wrapped itself around Matthew Mahan like a huge serpent. Riding home in a taxi—he would not let Eddie work on

Easter—this new sense of helplessness tormented him again as he thought how little, in fact, he did for his brother's wife and children. If Charlie were only alive . . .

But if Charlie were alive, Charlie would still be a drunk and drunks do not make good fathers. You know, too, that those seven children were what destroyed him. Especially the five girls. His last two years had been pure nightmare. Again and again he had poured out his defeat and self-hatred to Matthew on the telephone: What's your opinion on birth control, Bishop? After number seven, why, my wife said no more. My good Roman Catholic wife, Eileen. And what did she do to make sure? She kicked me out of bed. You and I, dear brother, excuse me, dear bishop, are now fellow celibates. How does that grab you?

Please, Charlie, be quiet, he prayed. When it came to tormenting his elder brother, Charlie Mahan might as well have been beside him in this taxicab instead of silent beneath a gravestone. But it was understandable, Matthew Mahan told himself, struggling to regain control of his mind. There on the next corner was the Kit Kat Lounge. Four years ago Charlie had stumbled through its doors at three a.m., into the path of a parkway bus.

"Three twenny, ya Eminence," said the cabdriver.

As Matthew Mahan entered the residence a wave of total gloom engulfed him. And at once a strange sound reached his ears. Laughter, filtering through the closed doors of the sitting room. Was Dennis giving a party? Had the revolution reached his residence? Then he heard an unmistakable Irish brogue. "He may send us into the night with a volley of anathemas."

Matthew Mahan opened the door and found an aged cleric with a long beak of a nose cheerfully demolishing the archdiocese's supply of Irish whiskey. Near him sat a large, dark-haired man in a very expensive shirt with his tie askew. "Don't worry, I'll write him a check," he said in a cheerful rasp.

"The hell with anathemas. I may just call the cops."

"Matthew me boy!" said Auxiliary Bishop David Cronin, raising his glass high.

"Padre," said Mike Furia, rising from his chair to extend a ham-size hand.

"I told him, your Eminence," Bishop Cronin said, "that a man who hobnobs with the Pope has no time for the likes of us."

"I decided I'd take the bishop out for Easter dinner and give him one more chance to turn wop," Mike Furia said. "It's his only chance of getting past Saint Peter."

Matthew Mahan absorbed all the nuances of these remarks with a smile. The three of them had spent many a cheerful Sunday evening with their feet up on old Hogan's antiques, insulting each other and solving the problems of the archdiocese. But lately the parties had dwindled to a stop. Old Davey Cronin's radical rage at the way things were going in the Church had become an embarrassment, even in private. Since last July, when Pope Paul had issued *Humanae Vitae,* his birth control encyclical, Davey had become totally obstreperous. Mike Furia knew how Cronin was hurt by Matthew Mahan's avoidance, and was now simultaneously rebuking him and trying to restore the old camaraderie. Fortunately, they had come at a moment when he was desperately in need of remembering better, happier days. A need that did not escape the sharp Irish eyes of the old bishop.

"By God, he's got the glooms for sure. Has Rome withdrawn your red hat? Saying it was all a clerical error? You could get worse news than that, lad. The more I think of it, the more I dread the thought of you associating so closely with the present occupier of the Chair of Peter."

"There we disagree. He's doing the best he can."

"The best he can what? Turn a mess into a catastrophe? The man knows no more about leadership than I do about atomic physics. Much as I disliked what old Pius Pacelli stood for, such as business as usual while the Jews were getting cooked, the man was a leader. He knew you couldn't prance six paces forward and tiptoe five back. He went straight at the objective, and carried the whole Church behind him."

Old Davey was tireless in his determination to turn Matthew Mahan into the nation's leading liberal Catholic spokesman. It saddened him to realize that his refusal to cooperate had become a threat to their friendship. The front door clanged at that moment, rescuing him from an awkward pause. He peered into the hall. It was Dennis McLaughlin. "Back so soon? I thought it would be an all-night party."

"Leo ran out of booze."

"Why don't you come in and have a drink with us?"

"I really—I think I've had enough—your Eminence."

"You can have some strong coffee and a sandwich, then. I need someone to give me some scholarly answers to this terrible old heretic." Dennis walked cautiously into the room with the step of a man who had pillows tied to his feet. "Here's a refugee from the Jesuits," the cardinal said as he introduced Dennis.

"Oh?" said Davey. "A man with sense enough to depart the company of those intellectual egotists may be just the sort of fellow you need around here."

"Sit down," said Matthew Mahan. "I'll raid the icebox." Mrs. Norton had made sandwiches, and the coffee was in the percolator, needing only to be plugged in. He put everything on a tray and carried it back to the sitting room.

Davey was crowing with delight. "Matthew," he said. "You didn't tell me your secretary was a historian. Listen to him. He's trying to cast aspersions on the grand project of my old age."

"What would that be?" said Dennis, smiling in a relaxed way that Matthew Mahan had never seen before.

"To bring down and pin in the mud where it belongs the whole cursed doctrine of infallibility."

"You see?" Matthew Mahan said. "He comes and drinks my whiskey, insults me for not running things his way, and then he tries to blow up the cornerstone of the Church."

"The cornerstone, my foot," said Cronin. "It's the millstone around your neck, your Eminence. Since the day that prince of fools, Pio Nono, His Holiness Pius IX, proclaimed that insufferable doctrine on July 18, 1870, the Church has been reeling toward destruction like a man drunk on absinthe. Infallibility has infected every part of the mystical body of Christ, like a cancer that destroys freedom everywhere it crawls."

"How do you explain Pope John?" asked Dennis.

"Even the most terrible drunkards have moments of shining sanity. Their friends rejoice, the members of the family cheer and praise God. But unless you blow up the still where the noxious stuff is being cooked, the mania soon reappears. Do you think the next pope will be any better than the one they have in there now? Don't be silly. They aren't going to allow this power to pass from their hands. Someone must strike it from their grip."

"But how?" asked Dennis, interested, but puzzled.

"By writing the true history of Vatican Council I. By proving that there was no more holy freedom in St. Peter's in 1870 than there is any day in the Kremlin. That Pio Nono used everything from bribery to physical force to whip a majority out of those poor sods, trapped there with half of Rome dying of the plague. A council without holy liberty, engineered by the one man who stood to gain by its decision—that was no more a council than the battle of the Boyne."

"And do you think you can prove this?"

"I *know* I can. At the very least, I'll make enough of a noise to scare the spaghetti out of them over there and maybe interest some real historian like yourself to tackle the job. Do you read German?" Bishop Cronin asked. "Because Germany's where the gold is. The best Germans broke away from Vatican I, you know, and formed the Old Catholic Church. They said the New Church Pio Nono had created was a monstrosity. Give this lad a day off," Cronin said to the cardinal, "and let him come out to the seminary and look over what I've written."

"Do you expect to get my imprimatur for this book?"

"I should say not. But if you'd like to give it to me for friendship's sake, I won't refuse it."

"How can you be so brazen with one foot in the grave?"

"That's what makes me brazen, Matthew me boy. I wish I'd had the courage to be brazen twenty years ago when I had something to lose. That's the real test, and I flunked it."

"I'll admit this much," Matthew Mahan said. "What you say explains what happened at Vatican II."

"What do you mean?" Dennis asked.

"The Germans ran Vatican II. They organized all of Europe except Spain. And they knocked the Curia's control of the council into the Adriatic. If John hadn't died in the middle of it, I'm almost afraid to think of what that council might have decided. They were fully capable of kicking infallibility even farther than they kicked the Curia. But Montini was Pope in time to intervene, and the Germans had to settle for what they could get."

"Which was not enough," said Bishop Cronin. "They should have nailed an annually elected assembly of bishops to the Chair of Peter like James Madison glued the Congress to the presidency."

"Now you're being ridiculous," Matthew Mahan said. "If all the things you say about the Curia are true, why are we about to go to Rome to watch me stagger around in my cappa magna?"

The old Irish eyes bored into him. "*Romanita*," he said.

"I hate to sound like a dummy," Dennis said, "but what's *that?*"

"*Romanita* is the Roman way of doing things. Now this fellow here, who's midway between being his Excellency and his Eminence, is marked by the boys in the Curia as undependable."

"I don't believe a word of it," said Matthew Mahan. "This ancient revolutionary is trying to picture me as a church burner, because I took a very strong stand on the birth control issue. I collected a lot of cases in this diocese."

"One of them your own brother," Mike Furia said.

"Yes, one of them my own brother—cases where attempts to follow the Church's teaching of rhythm or abstinence led to tragedy. Drunkenness, mental illness, complete family breakdowns. I sent them to the Papal Commission on Birth Control with the strongest letter I could write, telling them that in my opinion the Church had to change its position. I did local surveys to back up the national surveys. I thought that this city was particularly significant, because you can't say we're succumbing to the dominant secular culture when two-thirds of our population are Catholic. Believe it or not, our surveys showed a higher pro-birth control position here than in the country at large."

Cronin chuckled. The look with which he was regarding Matthew Mahan struck Dennis as remarkably affectionate. It was the first time he had ever thought of anyone feeling affection for Cardinal Mahan. He began wishing he were not quite so drunk.

"*Romanita* surely didn't come into those surveys," said Matthew Mahan.

"True. But it was *Romanita* governing you when seventy-eight American theologians published a paper calling the Pope a fool. Think what it would have meant to them to have included a bishop in that statement—an archbishop, in fact! But you held your peace. You could have made one devil of a rumpus over here. You shut your trap—and now you have your reward. That's *Romanita*."

Matthew Mahan sipped his milk and shrugged. "You might be right. It's the best explanation I've heard yet."

"*Romanita*," said Bishop Cronin, turning to Dennis, "really has only one principle." He ran his hand along the gilt edge of the antique table. "Smooth, keep everything smooth. No bumps, no shouts. But the business gets done their way."

"That happens to be an attitude I share," said Matthew Mahan.

"So stop wondering why you're getting a red hat. What they're saying is, 'Welcome to the club.'"

Matthew Mahan was not amused, but Cronin did not pause to notice. "If you'd only take my advice, Matt, you could exercise real leadership. Now, here's a lad with a good head and, if he's as Irish as he looks and sounds, a good pen, no doubt. Let him write a book for you. There's an intellectual vacuum in the American Church right now. Fill it with bold brave words."

"No. I've told you a half dozen times, that's not my style. And will you get it through your head, once and for all, that I'm a pastor, not an intellectual? I'll not embroil this diocese in any more turmoil than it's in already."

Cronin was serious now, too serious. "Matt, when will you get it through *your* head that you can't be the pastor you dream of being unless you stand up to those bureaucrats in Rome? Do they let you say what you really believe, what people are desperate to hear? Can you speak to your younger priests honestly about celibacy? Can you lift your hand to help the divorced and separated? Even your good friend Mike sitting beside you?"

Matthew Mahan shook his head ominously, and Dennis braced himself for the explosion. But the words were still Bishop Cronin's. "Ah! When it comes to taking good advice, there's nothing worse than an archbishop. Hearts of stone and heads of oak."

Mike Furia roared with laughter. Dennis saw with frank astonishment that the cardinal was smiling. It was somewhat tense, but it was a smile. Matthew Mahan, reading Dennis's face, thought, Maybe this will convince you that I'm human.

"Well," said Bishop Cronin. "Perhaps we'll find new answers to our dilemmas—or new dilemmas for our answers—in Rome."

VII

FROM a window seat in the forward section, Matthew Mahan looked out at the airport lights flickering in the dark. With him on the plane were a hundred and thirty of his well-wishers. When Joe Cohane headlined the pilgrimage in the *Beacon,* the grandiosity made Matthew Mahan slightly uncomfortable. Now, back of them on the runway was a second 707, also loaded with pilgrims. He was on his way to the greatest moment of his life, with a full week of celebration ahead of him. Why, then, this sagging, soggy sadness?

The cardinal sighed. He knew part of the answer. So did Mike Furia, who sat beside him. As chairman of the cardinal's fund, Mike had had to impart the bad news. The big givers simply weren't coming through. The stock market was currently a disaster area. How many usually dependable donors had said these last few days, "If the market goes up even twenty points, I swear . . ."? The computer whiz kids in the marketing department of Furia Brothers Construction Company were predicting a fifty-percent drop in the big contributions.

Outbursts of rioting on the anniversary of the assassination of Dr. Martin Luther King, Jr., and a new rash of campus disorders added to public uneasiness and an inclination to "take care of number one," Mike morosely pointed out. He also maintained that Pope Paul VI had not helped by saying on Maundy Thursday that the Church was in a "practically schismatic ferment." Was the Church, too, about to come apart? "People don't like to put their money on a loser," Mike had growled.

Stop it, stop brooding, Matthew Mahan told himself. Think of Rome, now only hours away, a city where you will regain your spiritual balance by visiting churches that echo with Pope John's husky voice. You will feel once more his heavy peasant hands consecrating you a bishop, see the serenity in his dark brown eyes, hear the words: To help you hold fast to the hope and faith I see on your face, Matthew, let me make you a promise. I will be in paradise long before you. Think of me as your friend there. When you join us at last, I will be the first to greet you.

How little he had thought about Pope John in recent years. Matthew Mahan, the nonscholar, the old smoothie, the whirlwind organizer, the Irish charm boy, had been too busy to manage enough meditation.

And Mary. Mary Shea would be waiting in Rome.

He began feeling better. He started kidding Mike Furia, who was cheerfully pouring airline bourbon into one of several silver flasks in his five-hundred-dollar attaché case. Mike always filled his flasks when he traveled by air to Europe. The absurd price the airline charged made him determined to gouge them. "Once a mafioso always a mafioso," the cardinal said.

"Don't knock it, it's in your blood, too," Mike replied. "The assistant chaplain thinks it's a good idea."

Red-haired Jim McAvoy, as slim as he had been during his wartime year as Chaplain Mahan's assistant, was doing the same with the Scotch. Beside Jim sat his chic blond wife, Madeline, whose stunning looks belied her remarkable personality. She ran her six children—and to some extent her husband—and was simultaneously one of the most active and prominent Catholic women in the city. With so many Catholic couples taking the divorce route, it always reassured him to see Jim and Madeline together.

"I was hoping you'd tick them off, your Eminence," Madeline said. "They're acting like a couple of six-year-olds. Maybe it's going back to Europe with you. They think they're in the army again and are planning on raising hell."

"That was my department," Mike Furia said. "Jim had to behave. He was exhibit A for the padre's sermons."

In the first row of the second section, Dennis McLaughlin tried to rest. For the past week he had worked every night until three a.m. But it was the alarming emotions churning through his body that really wore him out. It was his first flight across the Atlantic, and the thought of hurtling out across those miles of empty ocean chilled him. Would the claustrophobia be worse? What was it, after all, but the fear of sudden death, extinction, when life, love, had been barely touched? Now, Dennis thought, you have a double reason for terror. Death may include damnation.

He could hear Bishop Cronin proclaiming the need for Vatican Council III. What was the source of that old man's fire? Did he draw something from that primary ancestral soil, something that you can never touch? But now, now you have touched a different kind of fire, and what has it done for you? Mordantly he let his mind re-create the recent scene in Matthew Mahan's office when his Eminence asked him for a report on what was happening between Dennis and Sister Helen Reed. Would you be on this plane now, Dennis, if you had blurted out the truth? No. Nor would you still be wearing this tight, white round collar.

What was it you had said to her that first night, when you picked up your collar and flipped it off the bed? You know what I always think when I see a priest in one of these collars? I think it's a kind of spiritual chastity belt that divorces his head from his body. That's why only abstractions come out of his mouth. No gut thoughts or heart thoughts. No man thoughts.

I want to love you, she had said. Do you love me?

Of course. Just let me look at you. And touch you.

Who *are* you, Dennis, now that she has given you her body to explore, to hunt buried pleasure?

You were sitting in the easy chair, she on the couch. Green eyes glowing with expectation. She knew. She awaited you, ripe with rebellious love. And what happened next? Fear—the fear of the celibate, the unmanning fear. For a moment the shame had been unbearable.

Then came the miracle. Her understanding. Perhaps it was better for them, this almost love; perhaps it was all God permitted them. For three weeks now it had been enough to touch. But how long could the hero conceal his humiliation?

The jet engines roared and the acceleration pressed him back against his seat. His pulses pounded, his guilt-charged brain seemed to vanish in a flash of fire. Death, damnation waited at the end of the runway. . . . They were airborne. Like a huge animal, the jet groaned as it devoured altitude. Slowly the terror ebbed from his body. In a few moments the aisle was full of people with drinks in their hands. He cheerfully accepted a glass from a purring stewardess. "Hey, that cardinal's a doll," she said, rolling her eyes. "How did the girls let him get away?"

Did he get away, or did he get away with it? Dennis mused, thinking of blue letters from Rome and replies addressed to Mrs. Mary Shea, 41 Via Margutta. Revealing that the cardinal had a love in Rome—that would win eternal admiration from Leo.

It shocked him to see how callously aware he was of his real motive for playing his brother's silly espionage game. He took morbid pleasure in following the twists and turns of his conscience. After that Easter night when his Eminence had invited Dennis to join the gathering in the sitting room, when he had felt "a man among men," he had adopted a selective approach in deciding which secrets of Matthew Mahan's episcopacy he'd betray. Only decisions, habits, policies, that in your intellectual majesty you saw fit to disapprove, were communicated to Leo.

You gave Leo a xerox of the proposed diocesan financial report, which his Eminence had decided not to issue this year. It was thirty-five pages of laborious reading and almost totally unrewarding from Leo's point of view. It was almost malicious to torment him with this sort of thing, but his extremism deserved it. There were, of course, those two rather large items identified as the cardinal's living and travel expenses, but Matthew Mahan had demolished any questions these might raise in an attached memo explaining that the living expenses concealed numerous gifts to priests who needed money for one reason or another, salaries for the housekeeper and assistant housekeeper, and gifts of cash to his dead brother's family. The travel item included bishops' meetings, conferences in Washington, and a tour of South American missions. This didn't add up to much ammunition.

Anyway, Dennis's whole purpose in going along with the "plot" had been to gain him unlimited opportunities with Sister Helen. It was amazing how she made the thrown pens, the snappish orders, the outrageous working hours so much more bearable. He had a consolation which made him indifferent to his Eminence, impervious to his Eminence, superior to his Eminence.

How brave you are, Father McLaughlin, he mockingly congratulated himself. Now that we are stabilized at thirty-five thousand feet and the booze is flowing, you can enjoy yourself, accept friendly greetings from the titans of the city's power structure. Now here came Mike Furia to clap him on the back. "Hey, Dennis, how's it going?" The man exuded a warmth that was hard to resist. And it was somehow flattering to find him treating you as an equal. A man among men. Dennis knew him to be a shrewd, sophisticated man. Furia Brothers was one of the big construction companies of the world. They had gotten their start building parochial schools, with the help of some arm-twisting by Monsignor Matthew Mahan. By now they were building dams, skyscrapers, airfields, and shopping centers from Vietnam to London, from Rio to Rome. Mike had spent most of his time on planes during the years it took to build this empire. His wife had a pathological fear of flying and never traveled with him. When his marriage broke up he had settled, at Matthew Mahan's urging, for separation rather than divorce.

"Looking forward to kissing Il Papa's ring?" Furia asked.

173

"Not really."

Mike exchanged cheerful insults with Herb Winstock; chatted with Kenneth Banks of the City Council and the NAACP; greeted Mrs. Dwight Slocum, wife of the city's richest Protestant. All of these people—devout Jew, black Baptist, idealistic WASP—served on the executive committee of the cardinal's fund. Ecumenical? You bet. There is nothing more ecumenical than money. That was his Eminence's (unspoken) motto. And there was something else besides riches that almost every man on this plane had in common: they had served with Matthew Mahan in the 409th regiment. No wonder, Dennis thought, that the cardinal waxed sentimental about GI Joe at the annual division reunion dinner and refused to speak out against the Vietnam war.

"Your boss ever talk to you about the war, Dennis?" Mike asked. Dennis shook his head.

"He's so afraid of bragging, he won't tell anybody anything. You ought to write a book about him, Dennis. You really should. The things we saw him do. We're in the Hürtgen Forest, see? Goddamn Germans dug in ten feet deep everywhere. We're coming down this ravine when they open up with machine guns. . . ." He was bringing a formidable fist down on the back of Winstock's seat.

You are going to spend the night listening to these stories, yards and yards of them, Dennis told himself. Look interested.

"Hell," said Herb Winstock. "He walked right into the teeth of those guns to get to our dying guys, wearing his Mass vestments, walking slow like he was in the cathedral. He earned a DSC damn near every day we were in action."

"The guy just wasn't afraid of *anything*," said Jim McAvoy. "Following him made a man out of me. I mean, I was the original callow kid. I was sure I was going to fink out under fire. I forgot all about it after watching him in action for ten minutes." The stories multiplied, conspiring to make Matthew Mahan out as a cross between a saint and Superman.

Dennis was grateful when the lights were turned out. His mind yearned for sleep. His body refused it. First his back ached, then his eyes, then his neck. His mind drifted to the day he had sat on Davey Cronin's sagging daybed at the seminary, reading the bishop's manuscript. The immense effort that the old man was making staggered him. The text was too emotional to be history and too burdened with abstruse arguments to be successful. Cronin seemed to read his mind. "I know I'll never finish it," he said. "All I hope is to get enough on paper to catch the nose of a bright young dog like yourself who likes to feed on red meat."

Then Dennis's own sudden outburst: "I'm afraid you've got the wrong dog. I don't believe this fanatic first-century Jewish revisionist named Jesus is the Son of God. I'd better tell that to Cardinal Mahan, and be on my way."

And then the old man, with a very serious face, talked about history, and about his own belief: "And I believe—I do—in the Holy Event. Exactly what the devil that means I don't pretend to know. But it changed the course of human history, and you can't walk out on history. . . . Out of it came the Church—and for all its terrible blunders, there's something grand about it, soaring as it has above history. It's the one thing around that puts poetry in the mouths of common people, lad, and gives them someplace to look for consolation and hope. Only the Church can change men's hearts. But the truth is—and it must be told by someone—that the Church has been seduced by the lust for power.

"But listen, now. What disturbs me most in that bit of foolishness you just bespoke is the idea of talking to Mahan about it. Don't do that. The likes of Matt were not made to deal with problems that torment types like you and me. He was born to lead the common people, to fill their hearts with hope and faith of the sort that they must have to live at all. Shackled though he is by subservience to Rome and the canon law, it's toward freedom that he leads them, true shepherd that he is at heart. He loves too much, too readily. He has a heart that's too full, too good to free himself from those shackles. If God is willing, the likes of you and me may yet strike them off him."

Still no sleep. The night flight to Europe, Dennis concluded, was one of the most exquisite forms of torture devised by man. Another two hours and he would confess to any sin.

In the forward section, Matthew Mahan was reminiscing with Mike Furia about their first trip to Europe. Mike brooded into a silver cup half full of bourbon. "So we didn't get our heads blown off like we thought we would. Here we are, twenty-five years later, and when I ask myself why, what difference it made, I don't have an answer."

"Mike. Remember what I told you about four-a.m. thinking?"

"You told me. But you didn't convince me."

"You put together a big business, Mike. You give jobs to thousands of people. Good jobs, and you treat them fair and square."

"Three cheers," said Mike. "I happened to find out that's the best way to do business. But that's not what I'm talking about. I'm talking about the people who mean something to a paisano like me. A man without a wife, a father without a son. What the hell is he? In ten, twenty years I'll be dead. The rest of the clowns in the family will either sell out or run the company into the ground."

"Mike, isn't there a hope that Betty will calm down and help you and Tony get back together some one of these days?"

The contempt on Furia's face made Matthew Mahan wonder how well he really knew the Furias. Did marriages break up over things like Betty's resentment of Mike's traveling?

"Her revenge is making sure my son hates his old man's guts. He's a lost boy taking refuge in a commune, where they publish that radical *Hard Times Herald* trash."

"The answer is prayer, Mike. Nothing else but prayer."

"Padre, you've got a hell of a lot more faith than I."

"You've got faith all right. I'll do the praying. You'll feel better after some sleep, Mike. Look, the sun's coming up."

Racing toward dawn at six hundred miles an hour, they were soon winging through midmorning brightness. A light breakfast, and then the pilot was saying, "In a few minutes we'll be landing at Rome's Fiumicino airport. Temperature, fifty-eight degrees. Light rain and some fog. I regret to inform you there has been a wildcat strike of baggage handlers. It may mean delays. . . ."

How right he was. They sat in a leaden stupor in the three-story glass terminal, waiting for the plane to unload while Mike Furia gave them a lecture on the history of the building and the airport, which Matthew found very unpleasant listening. "They paid twenty-one million dollars for this hunk of marshland that they knew was fogged in half the time. Why? It was owned by the Torlonia family, very big in the Vatican. The runways were built by Manfredi Construction, and Castelli Construction put up the hangars. Guess who owns both companies? The Vatican. Another Vatican outfit put up this abortion of a building. We bid against them. Their low bid had to be a lie. A year later they went back for as much again to finish the job. And what have they got? An airport built on shifting sand. A terminal that stinks, literally, because of this stupid rubber floor."

As the minutes ticked on, the cardinal decided to take charge of the situation. "Let's go get our own bags."

"I'm with you," Mike said.

"Round up a squad, Sarge." Mike soon had a dozen volunteers.

It was one p.m. when they reached the Hotel Hassler. Matthew Mahan, exhausted, was not surprised to discover alarming pains in his stomach. But he waited in the lobby until everyone was checked in. With Dennis and Mike Furia expediting the job, this took another hour. Finally they felt free to stagger to the elevator and down the hall to their fifth-floor rooms. "You will be bunking with Bishop Cronin, Dennis," Matthew Mahan said.

"What's the program, Matt?" Mike Furia said. "Three hours' sleep and then tie on the feedbag?"

"That sounds sensible. I'm afraid I can't join you. I've got a date with a lady. Mary Shea. Do you remember her?"

"Sure. I thought she lived in Venice."

"She did. But she's lived here for years. I promised to have dinner my first night. . . ." He had thought that by being frank he would escape embarrassment. But he felt strange. Or was it Dennis McLaughlin and Mike Furia who were feeling strange? "I'm afraid she still thinks of me as her spiritual adviser," he went on. "Though I don't think I ever gave her a word of good advice."

Mike Furia nodded. "Perhaps we can have a nightcap later. I'll tag along with Dennis here and old Davey, and maybe Bill Reed."

When Mike's door was safely shut, Matthew Mahan and Dennis walked across the hall to the cardinal's suite. He paused at the door. "Let's see, you're right next door, Dennis."

"I'm afraid the porter had my bags on your truck."

"Oh. Come in then, come in." He walked in, followed by Dennis. On a table was a huge spray of red roses with a white envelope. He ripped open the envelope and read, "To the best cardinal they've found yet. With much love, Mary."

Dennis looked at the roses curiously. "From Mary Shea," Matthew Mahan said. "This looks suspicious, doesn't it?" But his attempt at humor made no impression. "Someday I'll tell you more about her. It's an amazing story. Now let's get some sleep. . . .

177

If you go out tonight, Dennis, do your best to slow old Davey down. He's got a heart condition, which he consistently ignores."

Dennis McLaughlin nodded as he lugged his bags out to the hall and closed the door behind him. Matthew Mahan gulped down a handful of Titrilac pills to quiet his complaining stomach, and stripped off his clothes. For the next ten minutes he soaked in the hottest bathwater he could endure, with a washcloth over his face. Shaved and in clean pajamas, he felt almost human and lay down on the bed, thinking about himself, his mother, Rome.

He remembered the first time he had come here, leading a group of pilgrims for the Holy Year in 1950. He had been filled with awe, vibrant with emotion. He was visiting his mother's city, the place where his priesthood had been born. It was his mother who had created—but never forced—his vocation, who told him on her deathbed, "Someday you will go to Rome a bishop. When you do, think of me, pray for me at the Church of St. Peter in Chains. It was our family church. There . . . I received my First Communion." He had visited the church on that first trip. And on the second trip, a second visit that still seemed half dream, half miracle.

Throughout his ten years as a bishop, he realized now, he had been moving slowly away from his mother. More and more his spirit turned to that stolid, silent man, his father, who never said a word of approval—or of disapproval—about his priesthood. That man who had died stoically of cancer of the stomach, with never a sign of fear—or of faith. No, Bart Mahan had perfunctorily accepted the Host that his son placed on his tongue, and there was no hint that he prayed. Only silence broken by small talk about baseball, city politics. More than once Matthew Mahan had puzzled over the mystery of that mortal silence. Today, for some reason he did not completely understand, he said a prayer: O Lord, help me to understand.

What was there about his father that attracted his mind, his spirit, *now?* The calm, almost emotionless way that he accepted disappointment, the loss of lifetime savings? You could use some of that calm. Too much of your mother's violent emotionalism has always surged around inside you, controlled only with enormous effort and, to quote Bill Reed, at the expense of your stomach.

Matthew Mahan moved restlessly in the strange bed, trying to find comfort. It was more than calm, more than steadiness that turned his mind and spirit toward his father. It was—it had to be—his independence. Not something flaunted, argumentatively proclaimed, but a quiet, incontestable fact. Bart Mahan had always been his own man. And a bishop: Didn't a bishop have to be his own man, too, except . . . when he was the Pope's man?

A low, gentle snore filled the room. Cardinal Designate Matthew Mahan was asleep.

HE AWOKE to late afternoon sunlight and the telephone ringing. A woman's voice. "It's suppertime, your Eminence."

"Mary," he said, struggling up. "How are you?"

"Mildly ravenous, but I thought first you'd like to make a visit. I go there quite often in the evening. For a thousand lire the sacristan keeps the church open an extra half hour. When I told him I was bringing a *neo porporato* . . . I'll pick you up. You're on the way."

"No, I'll pick you up."

There was a tiny pause, which told him she understood exactly why he said it. "All right," she said in a voice strained too much to be offhand. "We'll have a drink here first."

The penthouse was only a five-minute walk from the Hassler. She welcomed him at the door, wearing a dark red linen suit. She had warned him her hair had turned gray. It stunned him to find that it made her more beautiful than ever. There was scarcely a line in her face. Her figure was as slim as when he had first seen her in 1949. She had been twenty-six that year.

He took both her hands, and for a moment Mary Shea and Matthew Mahan simply faced each other. "This was the right place to meet," she said. "I should have known I was going to kiss you and cause a scandal." She touched his cheek with her lips and stepped back again, their hands still joined.

"You look—as wonderful as ever, Mary."

"Stop it, you clerical flatterer."

"I don't flatter people I care about."

"You look tired. And you've gained weight."

"Good God, you sound like my doctor," he said with a grin, releasing her hands and patting his waistline. "Only ten pounds in three years. That's not a mortal sin."

Mary studied him for another moment, and tossed her head in that feminine way that made her hair swing around her neck.

Twenty years ago the sight of her flowing black hair had turned his brain to jelly. He wanted terribly to share his feelings with her as he had shared them in the past. To confess his ulcer, his troubles with liberals and conservatives, his weariness. But her recent letters, lamenting the failure of renewal in the Church and the betrayal of the spirit of Pope John, forced him to assume another role. He must be the consoler now. Perhaps he had even passed beyond that role; perhaps he was now the defender of the Way Things Are Done. He thought guiltily of Dennis McLaughlin. That was unquestionably the part you played for him.

"The way you talked about your hair—you made it sound like you were turning into a grandmother."

She smiled and gave it a pleased pat. "My hairdresser deserves the real credit. It was his idea to silver it."

"What have you been doing besides writing me those—those gossipy letters?"

The pause gave him away, and once more it was clear she caught the meaning he had tried to avoid. "Oh, I keep on painting. And I've done another translation—a marvelous young poet."

"I wish you'd publish your own poetry, Mary."

"Oh, stop flattering me, you big Irish lug. I've told you there are too many minor poets around already."

Matthew Mahan sighed. "I give up. What's the latest gossip?"

"They're giving Wright the Congregation for the Clergy."

"Good. He's a good man."

"Oh, how you people stick together. You're worse than politicians. He's a standpatter with liberal window dressing."

"They say the same thing about me, Mary."

"I know. But I know your heart is in the right place."

Matthew Mahan strolled over to the window and studied the illuminated dome of St. Peter's. "It's wonderful that you, of all people, can say that, Mary. But don't expect too much. The situation is—so delicate. So very delicate."

"You sound like Pope Paul. Fix me a drink."

"The usual?"

"Of course."

He found the full bottle of Cinzano Bianco beside a silver ice bucket. Cinzano was certainly on Bill Reed's forbidden list, but Matthew Mahan flinched from refusing to join Mary in a drink that had become almost a ritual. She had ordered it for them before their first dinner in Rome. This situation was delicate, too.

In a moment they were clinking glasses. They drank in reflective silence for a minute or so. Then Mary made a visible effort to brighten their mood. "Let's see. What else have I heard? Oh. You're going to be required to take a CIA-style oath."

"There's nothing CIAish about the oath we take."

"This is a new one—an oath of secrecy. Under pain of excommunication, you'll have to promise right there before Il Papa never to disclose a word of anything he says or writes to you."

"That—that's incredible."

"I know. It gives you an idea of the prevailing psychology. They act as if they were a fortress under siege."

"God help us all."

Too frank, too frank, Matthew Mahan warned himself. You are here to sustain this woman, to give her the hope and faith and love she needs to survive. "I've brought your old friend Cronin along. In the mood you're in, I'm not sure you should see him. The two of you may try to depose poor Paul with a coup d'état."

"I know. I've sent him a lot of material for his book."

"You have?" Matthew did not like to be taken by surprise. What in the devil's name did Mary think she was doing, playing games with Cronin behind his back? Then the realization that he almost asked her that question shocked him. He concealed it by hastily draining his drink. "What time are we due at the Tre Scalini?"

"Eight thirty. If we want to make our visit, we ought to leave now. I don't like to keep the sacristan waiting."

Squeezed into a tiny Fiat cab, they drove to the Via Cavour and climbed together up the tunnel beneath the slope of the Borgias to the Piazza of St. Peter in Chains.

Matthew Mahan paused at the piazza and looked across at the building where his mother had been born. The windows were open to the warm April night, and voices and bits of music drifted toward them. A man in his undershirt with a glass of wine in his hand paused at a window, threw back his head, and laughed. A little girl ran to him and threw her arms around his waist. Matthew Mahan's throat tightened. Life, love is truly indestructible, it empties and fills and empties, year by year. . . .

"Remember the first time we came, Matt?" Mary said softly.

"Could I ever forget it?" . . .

You must go, said the old man with the huge nose and the sagging cheeks, to this church at twilight, my favorite time to visit it. I wish I could go with you, but trust me, I will be there in spirit. You must do two things. You must stop before the statue of Moses and try to see it above an immense tomb with thirty-nine other statues of similar magnificence. See it for what it was intended to be, the very essence of the old law; all that Christianity must never become, all the terror, the agony of the law, and the majesty of it. I have always found in Moses' gaze which is fixed on infinite distance a sadness, a longing, even, that is I think only visible because the work is on our level. If it had been raised to where it was intended to be—at the summit of the tomb of Julius II—it might have become imperial. Think of the way God has of teaching even popes a lesson. This Julius was a tyrant, more an antipope than a pope. He died the most hated man in Italy, and his successor immediately canceled Michelangelo's work on his magnificent tomb. In the end, they shoveled his bones into the grave of his uncle. And Michelangelo's *Moses* is here in this humble church.

Now go down to the reliquary under the high altar and look at the chains which supposedly bound Peter. I used always to think, Alas, Saint Peter is still in chains, and to reproach myself for that thought. I used to wonder if I was a secret heretic. Now I know I was only telling the truth.

Go now, and when we meet again, let us talk of some thoughts I have to free Saint Peter from his chains once and for all. . . .

All this spoken with a magic combination of sadness and vivacity. Overcome with emotion, they had fallen to their knees, ignoring the old man's protests, and kissed his ring. Then they had left Pope John XXIII smiling after them, an ugly yet beautiful old man, bulky in his white robes, as the peasant he was. They had driven directly to this church, fifteen hundred years old, entered its dark interior, and approached the magnificent *Moses*.

At first, Matthew Mahan recalled, he had been seized by a kind of panicky humility. He knew nothing about art. What was this amazing old man in the Vatican trying to tell him? Why couldn't he *say* it, instead of sending him on this strange errand? Then he had looked around the church and remembered that his mother had knelt here as a girl. He remembered, too, the incomprehensible coincidence that had brought him to the attention of John not once, but twice, and made him archbishop of one of the largest dioceses in America. A remarkable calm had descended upon him, and he became totally involved with the statue, giving himself to every twist and fold of the marble, to the incredible arms and hands, the curve of the muscles, the ridges of the veins, the massive reality of shoulders and chest. Finally, the face, abstracted, somber. There was not a hint of triumphant power in it, not a sign that the prophet was even aware that beneath his right arm he held the tablets of the Law. Then suddenly he saw the immense sadness on his face. A weariness born of living and knowing the children of men. Is this all, is this all I have to give them? he seemed to be saying. Is there no choice but to lay this burden upon their backs? He mused, listening, perhaps silently praying, for a voice that would say: *My yoke is sweet . . . my burden light.*

Was all that in the statue? Matthew Mahan had dazedly asked himself. Or was it infused by that radiant old man in the Vatican?

Beside him he had heard Mary Shea saying in a low voice, *"Come to me, all you that labour, and are burdened, and I will refresh you. Take up my yoke upon you, and learn of me, because I am meek, and humble of heart: and you shall find rest to your souls. For my yoke is sweet and my burden light."*

He had glanced down at her in astonishment. She smiled at him. "That's Don Angelo's favorite passage from the Gospels. He told me that he first realized what it meant, standing here."

All that had happened ten years ago. It was impossible to believe it was a mere ten years since he had first heard Pope John's cryptic words of hope and radical faith. Now the years coalesced and it was only yesterday: Saint Peter is still in chains. Then, you had wondered what the old man meant. The Pope was still a prisoner of the Vatican, as the President of the United States was a prisoner of the White House, in the sense that neither could leave without elaborate protection. But that was too trivial a sense of "chains" to make Angelo Roncalli fear he was a secret heretic. Moreover, why was it juxtaposed to this statue of Moses?

"Remember how baffled I was by what he said about Saint Peter being in chains?"

Mary nodded. "The whole world found out about it in the next two or three years." She sighed. "If only he hadn't died so soon."

"I don't feel that way, Mary," Matthew Mahan said. "Remember what he told that fellow who said he should abolish the College of Cardinals and fire the whole Curia?"

" 'It's not for me to do everything,' is what he said."

"What he wanted done," Matthew Mahan said slowly, because the thought was coming to him as he spoke, "involved all of us. It was part of the thing itself—*all of us doing it.*"

"Yes," Mary said. "But if he were still here, there wouldn't be—a perpetual spirit of obstruction."

Matthew Mahan had an almost physical sensation that she'd thrown something at him. It caused him to move his head abruptly in what seemed like a shake of disagreement. "Let's go inside."

Mary exchanged a *buona sera* with the sacristan, and they entered the church and went to stand before the *Moses*. Would he again be able to feel what Don Angelo had created for him here? A wave of emotion—regret, perhaps fear—flooded him.

Then an extraordinary thing began to happen. He found himself *within* the statue: he could feel the folds of Moses' robes around his legs, the weight of the stone tablets beneath his right arm, the almost unbearable tension in the left arm. He was not watching a prophet gazing into history's distance; he himself was there, yearning for a glimpse of the face, the sound of the voice he had heard ten years ago. That was what his straining body needed—to find peace; peace that the lawgiver can never know in his perpetual struggle with rebellious men. The realization that he had become this lawgiver, this wielder of authority, in spite of all his inward wish to escape the role, struck him like a blow from one of those huge marble hands.

His eyes filled with tears. It was so natural: a leader—a bishop—has to give orders; he has to see that those orders are enforced; and he has to enforce laws not of his own making. "Father, forgive us," he whispered, "for we know not what we do."

"Every time I come here," Mary said, "I feel that either he or you—sometimes both—are here with me."

"Yes," Matthew Mahan murmured. "Yes." How could he explain his own desolating loss of peace to her? For Mary this was a church of fulfillment, of happiness. But now he almost expected that massive left hand to rise and point accusingly at him. He felt his heart pounding as he turned away. There was no sense in this church

of his mother now. He was utterly alone, unable to share his grief with anyone. He could only reach out to the lost image of the old man in the Vatican and say, with extravagant hope that he was listening, Now I really understand.

Mary walked ahead of him into the reliquary, saying, "The old chain is still there, Matt, and over at the Vatican they're reforging the few links Don Angelo managed to break. Why can't they see that they're destroying themselves?"

"I don't know," he said. "I don't know."

The banks of votive candles before the altar flickered eerily on the bronze doors on either side of the chains. Matthew Mahan stared numbly at them, thinking, Not just Peter's chains but yours, too. He had no idea how long he stood there. Mary finally touched his arm. "Matt, it's time to go."

"Oh, yes, yes," he said. "Of course."

Outside it was totally dark. He felt incredibly exhausted. Maybe the whole experience had been nothing more than exhaustion, he told himself, an unparalleled seizure of nerves. But he knew this was an evasion, that what had just happened to him was a truth he could never deny without risking his soul. Walking away from the church, they passed an outdoor café. "How about an aperitif?" he said. "It's a long way to the Piazza Navona."

Agreeable as always, Mary sat with him at one of the green and yellow tables. While they waited for their Cinzanos, off to the left a strange glow fell across a field from searchlights playing on a massive hunk of rock. "What's that?" he asked, knowing that Mary's knowledge of the city was practically encyclopedic by now.

"Probably part of Trajan's Baths. They were the first ones to admit women."

"And right after that," he said, "Rome started collapsing?"

"Don't be such an *obvious* male chauvinist!"

She began asking him about people they both knew. He gave her the little information he had, mostly a list of divorces—divorces for the most part in which the permission of the Church had not been sought. Mary was amazed. "I can't believe it," she said. "I thought I'd still be a pariah if I came home. Now I realize I wouldn't even be noticed. What's the explanation for it, Matt?"

"I don't know. I've always been wary of attributing personal decisions like divorce to some sort of national trend, but an awful lot of middle-aged people are getting divorced, people of all religions. I think they're seduced by this myth of experience, the great enricher. But it's their children it breaks your heart to think about. . . . Speaking of children, how's Jimmy?"

"Oh, just great, from a distance," Mary said, fingering the stem of her glass. "I've tried hard to take your advice and not smother-love him. He enjoys his job. All those languages he learned spending summers over here with me are paying off. No other young editor can match his publishing contacts in Europe. But I suspect his moral life leaves something to be desired."

Matthew Mahan sighed. "I'm afraid there's not much you can do about that, even less that I could. His letters got pretty perfunctory after he graduated from college. I could see that he'd had just about all the clerical advice he could swallow."

She touched the back of his hand lightly with the tips of her fingers. "What you've given him, Matt—what we've both tried to give him—will come through eventually, I'm sure of that."

"I am, too," he said, trying to sound convinced. "How is our friend Monsignor den Doolard?"

"Gone home. There's nothing for him to do in Rome these days."

Den Doolard was a brilliant Dutch theologian, one of the hardest working *periti*—experts—at Vatican Council II, a constantly cheerful, undiscouraged man. "Did he request a transfer?"

Mary nodded. "It's just as well. He might have ended up like Father Giulio."

"What's wrong with him?" Giulio Mirante had been a council *perito*, too, appointed by John himself. He was in the Jesuit order but not of it, serving as chaplain of an orphanage to which Matthew Mahan had contributed handsomely.

Mary glanced at her watch. "He'd better tell you himself. If I try, I may spoil our evening—and we'll be late for dinner."

In uneasy silence they strolled through Trajan's Park to steps that led down to the Colosseum. They found a cabstand on the Via dei Fori Imperiali, and a taxi whisked them to the entrance of the Piazza Navona, beyond which no cars were allowed. With Mary's hand resting lightly on his arm, they walked into their favorite Roman enclave. The palazzos, the church, and the other buildings along each side and at each rounded end composed a perfect harmony of architecture and space. Three fountains in the center of the oval added their own contrasts. At this hour of the evening there were strollers everywhere, the very old hobbling on canes, the very young pushed in carriages.

When they'd completed their circuit of the beautiful piazza they turned back to where the restaurants glowed busily between the darkened façades of church and palazzos, and were soon sitting at a choice window table inside the Tre Scalini, sipping another round of Cinzanos. The food was superb, as usual, and Mary entertained him for a while with funny stories about her landlady. "She keeps telling me I should marry. 'It is never too late,' she says."

A temporarily forgotten sense of guilt assailed Matthew Mahan. There was something he had wanted to say to Mary Shea for years. Prudence had held his tongue, but tonight he knew he would say it. He would shuck off once and for all this role of protector that had been half hypocrisy for too long. But he did not want to interrupt her gaiety with a solemn outburst.

They finished a bottle of Valpolicella with their main course, and Matthew Mahan surreptitiously swallowed two or three Titrilacs to calm his ulcer. "Why don't we have our coffee and *gelato* on the terrace?" he said, and they moved outdoors to sit there watching as the Romans and the tourists slowly vanished. They sat on, lulled by the splash of the fountains and the magical mingling of light and water and marble.

"What a wonderful reunion, Mary," he said at last. "I can't tell you what it means to me to see you so well, so lovely. . . . I hope what I'm going to say won't upset you, but for years there's been something I wanted to tell you, something on my part that has been less than honest, and has, well, troubled me. Back in the early 1950s, when I was the hustling young monsignor, ready to take on anything the bishop assigned to me, I—I wasn't ready for you, Mary, for a woman with such depth, such sweetness, my spiritual superior in so many ways. I thought it was just a matter of giving you the standard consolations. But all the time a voice inside me was saying, 'Not for her, she deserves something better. She wasn't born to live a mutilated life just because she had the bad luck to marry a drunkard.' The more I saw you, Mary, the more panicky I became. I disguised it. I played comedian.

"I did all I could to make you happy—and to avoid telling you the truth. I knew there was no hope of your getting an annulment, but I told you to come to Rome, because if you'd stayed in the city I didn't know what was going to happen to me."

The *gelato,* the best ice cream in Rome, was untouched on the plates before them. As he talked, Mary had slowly leaned back in her chair, as though to see him in perspective.

"I never thought you'd *stay* here," he went on. "I thought a year, maybe two, would give me a chance to get a grip on myself."

A small smile played across Mary's lips. Now, in the same deliberate way, she leaned forward and took his right hand, which was closed in a fist on the table, in both of hers.

"Oh, Matt, Matt. To think I've let this trouble you."

"You let—"

"Do you think I didn't know, Matt? It's the rare woman who doesn't know when a man is in love with her." She slowly unbent his contorted fingers. "Or when she's in love with a man. Matt, I was the one who decided to come over here, knowing that there wasn't any hope of annulment. I came because I saw that you were a great priest. That no matter what you felt about me, your priesthood was the center of your life. I didn't want to be guilty of destroying that part of you, Matt. When I came over here I knew I was going to stay a long time."

A chaotic mixture of joy and sadness surged in his body. "My God, what an egotistic ignoramus I am."

Mary threw back her head and laughed heartily, the way she used to laugh. "No," she said. "You're just a man. And like all men, you naturally assume you're running things."

Now a question he had always been afraid of rose to his lips. "How has it really been, Mary? All those years I asked you, are you all right, I always took the answer you gave me—too easily. It was what I wanted to hear."

"I know, Matt. That's why I gave it to you."

She ran her finger around the rim of her wineglass. "It was terrible at first. I—I drank and—there were men. I was bitter. Empty. Giving you up—seemed to take all I had left. This isn't a good country for a woman in that frame of mind. It's so easy to be exploited, and Italian men are artists at it. That's why I moved to Venice, with a businessman I met in Rome. I also wanted to be someplace where you wouldn't visit me. There was always too much of a chance you'd show up in Rome. Well, the thing went sour—for the most banal reasons. But *he* was in Venice. I met him. And everything began to change."

"Roncalli?"

Mary nodded. "Don Angelo told me we all had to spend time in the desert—forty days, forty months, in his case thirty years. Thanks to him I was able to come back to Rome, back to you, without the old fear."

They began to eat their *gelato,* savoring the dark sweetness of the chocolate in silence. In the shadows of the piazza the fountains splashed. Matthew Mahan sat with the woman he loved and slowly realized that there was one more question.

"And now, Mary. How are you now?"

For the first time she avoided his eyes. "Not good, Matt. Oh, I know you'll say what my psychiatrist says: Don't be so involved with the Church. Let the clerical politicians play their games."

"Don't put words in my mouth, Mary. What's this about a psychiatrist?"

"Depression, Matt. For the past year or so. Insomnia. Sick thoughts. Even my digestion—I was living like an ulcer patient."

"And your psychiatrist blames the Church?"

"No. My morbid interest in the Church. In where it seems to be going. Or not going. It's really a sense of loss, Matt. Loss of him, Don Angelo. Every day they seem to do something else that drives his spirit out of the Church."

Something close to panic seized him. Was *he* part of this betrayal? Wasn't that the conclusion to be drawn from what he had just experienced in the Church of St. Peter in Chains? But to say that would be devastating to this anguished woman.

"Mary, try to be—a little understanding. Toward Paul. The men around him. Maybe it would help if I suggested including me. We're all victims of the same incredible explosion of problems. And we're just ordinary men, Mary. Not saints or geniuses like John. You do the best you can. But the situation sort of engulfs you."

"But *charity,* Matt. Charity and love. I'm sure you make them your first principles. And reasonable freedom. You're not browbeating your priests over that unspeakable encyclical on birth control. You fought that."

"I'm trying to handle it—another way." A wave of weariness washed over him. "Mary, popes make mistakes, just like everyone else. But we shouldn't let anything shake our confidence in the *Church*. Christ himself told us that the gates of hell wouldn't prevail against it."

"What about the gates of heaven? Why don't we look in that direction? Matt, hope is being destroyed, and that's what people want and need. I can't tell you how much your becoming cardinal meant to me this way. Now you're in a position to be heard. You've got to speak out, Matt. Somebody has to raise his voice."

He sat there paralyzed. Mary, too? Where did all of them—Cronin, Mike Furia, Dennis McLaughlin—get these incredible expectations? Hers was the most impossible summons. "Mary, I'm not that important—to start lecturing the whole Church."

"One of eleven American cardinals. Of a hundred and thirty in the whole world? If you speak forcefully, they've got to listen."

"But it's not my style. I try to avoid brawls, not start them."

"You fought old Hogan. You spoke out for Negro rights. The liturgy. Psychiatric help for Catholics. Honest labor unions."

The causes of the 1950s. How simple they sounded. How could he tell her the difference, explain how threatened the Church seemed to him now, why he must *defend* it, preserve it rather than try to change it? He saw from the anguish on her face that there was no way to explain. And then he saw what he could never endure: tears.

For a dazed moment he was on the verge of snarling a decree. No. Somehow, no matter what it cost him, no matter how soft, how vulnerable it made him, he would be a man of love. He took Mary's hand and held it between his two big hands. "Don't, Mary, don't," he whispered. "We'll do it. We'll find a way."

VIII

EARLY the next morning, Dennis wrote to his brother, bringing him up to date on the highlights and revelations of the trip.

Dear Leo:
    It's the beginning of our first full day in Rome, and I'm so tired I'm seeing double. The flight over was sheer barbarism. We all staggered into bed yesterday afternoon and napped a few hours before dinner. The cardinal went off with the mysterious Mary Shea. I met her today, and I must say I congratulate his Eminence on his

191

good taste. She's a real beauty, svelte, sexy, and mature. I had dinner with our millionaire godfather, Mike Furia, and Bishop Cronin. What a combination—but it was interesting. Mike F. said that he'd probably be what he calls a hit man in the Mafia today if he hadn't met Padre Matt in W.W. II. Incidentally, if you think you're cynical about the Church, you should talk to Furia. What he knows about the Vatican's business dealings!

Furia and Cronin got talking about the odd way that Mahan became a bishop in the first place. It's a series of coincidences, built around Pope John XXIII. It seems that Roncalli, who was an Italian army chaplain during World War I, decided to give a dinner for American army chaplains just after W.W. II ended in 1945. (He was the papal nuncio in France by this time.) Since Roncalli's English wasn't very good, Captain Matt, with his decorations and his mother's good Italian, was tapped to be interpreter; the two of them got along like father and son. Father Matt suggested inviting Protestant and Jewish chaplains as well as Catholics to the dinner. Roncalli loved the idea and it was a big success. Thereafter he kept Matt on his staff practically full time until the division sailed for home.

Back in the States, Big Matt corresponded with him sporadically. Then Mary Shea came into the picture. She is the very rich niece-in-law of our fair city's old boss, and Matt was assigned to soothe her spiritually when her marriage collapsed. Since money was no problem, he told her that her best chance for an annulment was a direct appeal in Rome. It didn't work. But Mary decided to stay in Europe, and she settled in Venice. And guess who was the patriarch of Venice? Naturally, Patriarch Roncalli got to know the rich American lady. In that respect, good Pope J. was, I gather, no different from any other prelate. She was soon invited to dinner at the patriarchal palazzo, and guess who she talked about? Who else but that wonderful monsignor who was charging about our archdiocese, building schools and gymnasiums by the dozen and raising money by the ton. Good old Matt. Imagine her surprise when Roncalli brightened instantly and began agreeing with her paeans.

When the miracle occurred in 1958 and the old man became Pope, he was better informed on our archdiocese than he was on any other in the United States. So he promptly made Matt an auxiliary bishop to old Hogan, and soon thereafter coadjutor with a guarantee of succession. Talk about casting your bread upon the waters—or in this case, upon grass widows. There are some curious questions unanswered, of course. Since Big Matt's suggestion had failed to get her an annulment, wouldn't Mary Shea have looked upon him without much warmth? What has been the source of her continuing allegiance? The Renaissance possibilities are obvious. If they should be fact, he is a real fraud and deserves all the opprobrium you plan to heap on him. But you keep that diabolical pen of yours in your pocket until we find out *what the truth is*. I know you liberals aren't much interested in that these days, but I'm old-fashioned enough to believe it's important.

Best,
Dennis

He had just addressed the envelope when there was a knock, and in came Andy Goggin escorted by Bishop Cronin in a tam o'shanter. "I found this innocent wandering about the lobby," he said, poking Goggin with his blackthorn cane, "and thought he was one of those clerical panhandlers. But he gave me the password, McLaughlin, and I agreed to deposit him at your door."

Goggin was skinnier than ever, which drew appropriate comment from the bishop. "I asked him if they were using the rack over here, for I couldn't imagine how else he'd been stretched to such a length."

"He says you're writing a history of Vatican I with him," Goggin said.

"He's liable to say anything," Dennis said.

"We're on our own, lads," said Bishop Cronin. "His Eminence is guiding his millionaires about the city in a bus. I offered to supplement his comments with a few of me own, and he insulted me by saying he couldn't afford to have the big givers scandalized."

"I'm in the hands of you two experts," Dennis said. "Before the day is over, I expect to know the essential Rome."

At this point there was another knock on the door, and Jim McAvoy came in. "We missed the bus," he said. "Do you think we could join you fellows for the morning? We can pick up the cardinal and his crowd at the Cavalieri Hilton for lunch."

Bishop Cronin looked annoyed. But Dennis could see no way of saying no to one of the biggest givers in the diocese. He introduced Goggin and they descended to the lobby. Madeline McAvoy looked pleased at her new prospects. "We may learn more from a tour with three clerics," she said to Dennis. "I'm sure the cardinal is going to give the standard lecture, which we've heard before."

"Well now," said Bishop Cronin briskly. "There's only one place that means Rome to the likes of us. St. Peter's."

They found a large taxi, crossed the Tiber on the Ponte Cavour, and headed for Vatican City along the Via della Conciliazione, which, Cronin told them, Mussolini had built, thereby destroying the Borgo, one of the most charming sections of old Rome. Next he pointed out the ancient Castel Sant'Angelo, the tomb of the emperor Hadrian, and the Ponte Sant'Angelo. "I never cross on that bridge," he said. "I don't trust the damn thing. In 1450 it collapsed and drowned a hundred and seventy-two Christmas pilgrims."

Soon they walked into St. Peter's Square and stood for a moment, feeling minuscule within the immense embrace of the circling columns. "When I was here the last time," Mrs. McAvoy said, "a guide told us that those columns represented the Holy Father's arms reaching out to the whole world."

"There's something *to* that," said Cronin with a wicked glance toward Dennis and Goggin. "The columns were designed by Bernini, who was educated by the Jesuits, creators of the doctrine that the way to salvation was blind obedience to the Pope."

"Yea, verily," said Goggin. "As our sacred founder, Saint Ignatius, wrote, 'If we wish to be sure that we are right in all things, we should always be ready to accept this principle: I will believe that the white that I see is black, if the hierarchical Church so defines it.'"

They strolled toward the basilica until they reached the obelisk in the middle of the square. "Now stand a moment, if you will," Cronin said, "and send your imagination way back, long before this place was built. Saint Peter was crucified somewhere along the route we have just come, in or near the Roman Circus of Caligula. No one knows where the devil he was buried, though the popes would like mightily to believe it was beneath that great mass of stone facing us. But the best evidence tells us it's more likely to have been under a little shrine to Saint Peter that stood here on Vatican Hill. It was in the corner of a cemetery, that shrine, and it was not much more than two niches in the side of the hill. There was a bit of an altar table in front of it, and under the altar was a movable slab of stone, behind which the old fisherman's body may have lain for a time. The whole thing was no bigger than an ordinary house door.

"This is what that pseudo Roman, the emperor Constantine—that wonderful example of Christianity, who put his wife into a steam bath and raised the temperature until she was boiled alive—found. After he'd slaughtered all his enemies and become the boss of bosses, he decided to build around the humble shrine a church big enough to hold an army. For it was armies and not religion that old Constantine was thinking about, you may be sure. He was the first imperialist to discover that Christians made good soldiers."

Madeline McAvoy was obviously enjoying the bishop's unorthodox approach to church history, but Jim was wary. "If it wasn't for Constantine," he said, "the Romans would have kept on persecuting the Christians. They'd have remained a minority."

"Best damn thing that could have happened," Bishop Cronin said. He led them across the piazza. About a hundred yards from the portico he raised his hand like a traffic cop, pointed at the façade, and rapidly read the inscriptions—titles of the Pope in Latin. "Pontifex Maximus, that's the key phrase, children. It was borrowed straight from the empire, one of the many titles of the emperor. You see," he said, speaking directly to Dennis, "this marriage of the Church and the state is no joke, lad."

"Where did you find *him?*" Goggin whispered to Dennis.

"Ex-professor of theology at Rosewood."

"Now here," said Cronin as they entered the church, "we see the beginning of the great conspiracy. . . ." He was launched now on an architectural tour in which history and theology were so intertwined that the McAvoys found their heads reeling. And their bewilderment was in no way eased by the two young Jesuit-educated priests, who plunged enthusiastically into an involved discussion of the history of papal power and the shaky foundations of the doctrine of the Pope's infallibility.

Cronin led them up the nave. "Magnificent as this altar and canopy is above Saint Peter's tomb, the eye is not drawn to it but to that." He pointed to the western apse. "There is where Bernini, the Jesuits' favorite architect, wanted your eye to go. To Peter's Chair. The story is that the Apostle sat in it while taking his ease in the house of Pudens, a good Christian who gave him room and board. But there's not a word in writing about this holy chair until the year 1217. At any rate, 'twas a perfectly ordinary wooden chair, which even Constantine did not see fit to meddle with. It sat in the

195

baptistry of the old cathedral. See what the Jesuits' boy did with it."

They gazed up at its baroque splendor encased in black and gilt bronze, at its feet four huge statues. These, Cronin explained, were the great doctors of the Church: Saints Augustine and Ambrose in front; and behind, two fathers of the Eastern Church, Saints John Chrysostom and Athanasius. "You will notice that the Greek saints have no miters. The implication is that whatever they say has no authority. But here, my children, here you see what the popes aimed at by heaping up so much marble and brass and gold. At this, a throne. A simple chair, sat upon by a fisherman, has become a veritable explosion of spiritual arrogance."

By now Jim McAvoy was frowning severely. "Are you trying to tell us that the whole idea of a pope as the successor to Saint Peter is a mistake? A lie?"

"Let's call it an exaggeration. An exaggeration that became first a distortion and then a disaster." Without warning he about-faced and led them back down the nave to the Chapel of the Presentation. Here, he told Dennis, was what he had come this morning to see. He pointed to a large bronze relief of Pope John XXIII on the chapel wall. While a squadron of angels descended from above, the Pope in his tiara and robes blessed a humanity that struggled to reach him from behind bars. To Dennis's amazement, Bishop Cronin knelt. Glancing up over his shoulder he said, "Come now, all of you. Say a prayer with me here." They knelt beside him. Dennis made no effort to pray. He was a spectator here, nothing but a spectator.

"It's good," Cronin said. "Very good and very fitting. He visited the jail here in Rome, you know, his first year as Pope. Right into the maximum-security section he went, surrounded by killers and rapists. A murderer fell on his knees before him and asked if there was any hope of forgiveness for him. The old boy simply lifted him up and held him in his arms."

Dennis felt frighteningly tired. Last night's sleep had not been much more restful than the night on the plane. Mike Furia, he remembered, said that jet lag always ruined his sleep for a week. With the exhaustion came an unbearable tightness in his chest. The doctor who had treated his last asthma attack had carefully explained the psychological connections, noting how often his attacks coincided with seeing his mother. But what did mother love

have to do with the terrible things old Davey was saying about this gigantic parade of marble and bronze and gold?

The doctor had also warned him not to get overtired, Dennis numbly recalled, as Cronin led them out of the church at a brisk trot to look at two great bronze doors. "These," said Bishop Cronin, "are *The Doors of Death*. A mutual friend had brought the artist who did them, a fellow named Manzù, to John, and something flowed out of the old man that stirred the man's soul. He locked himself in his studio for days and nights on end, and this was the result, a protest against death in all its shapes and forms. See here, the death of Saint Stephen. Can't you all but feel that mighty rock smashing his skull? Next the death of Pope Gregory VII, who finished his days as a starving beggar on the side of the road. Here we have death on earth, a mother dying while her child weeps. This is the worst of them, in my opinion, death in space. Have you ever seen anything more terrifying than that fellow's silent scream as he chokes for breath?"

Dennis stared at the falling man, the outstretched hands, the terrified, sucking mouth. He heard Goggin say something about how universal it all was, but his eyes remained riveted on the man in space. The void. He found it more and more difficult to breathe. He walked away from them and found himself staring down at the shield of John XXIII in the portico pavement, which suddenly seemed to grow enormously large. Dennis realized he was falling.

Several hours later he awoke in his hotel room with Bishop Cronin sitting beside the bed, looking worried. Matthew Mahan was standing behind him, looking even more concerned. "How are you feeling, lad?" Cronin asked.

"Not good," Dennis croaked. "I'm afraid I've ruined your day."

"The devil with the day."

"I'm having an asthma attack."

"We know that. We've had Bill Reed in to look at you. We've been clapping this oxygen mask here on your face."

"I haven't had an attack in two years," Dennis gasped.

"Stop talking," Matthew Mahan said. "I've just been examining my conscience. I've been working you like a galley slave."

"I was doing all right until last week. Three-a.m. nights."

"Why didn't you tell me?"

"Who can tell you anything?" asked old Davey.

"Why don't *you* go down and get something to eat?" the cardinal said. "I'll take over here."

With a wink at Dennis, Cronin departed. Matthew Mahan took his seat beside the bed. "How did things go on your . . ." Dennis began, but he ran out of air.

Matthew Mahan handed him a bottle. "Bill Reed left these antihistamines for you to take."

Dennis gulped down a pill and lay back on the pillows again. "I'm really sorry—" he started to say.

"I ordered you to shut up," Matthew Mahan said.

Dennis smiled, in no shape to disagree.

"I was supposed to go over to the Vatican this afternoon to see Cardinal Antoniutti about our nuns," Matthew Mahan said. "But while I was saying Mass this morning, I decided not to go."

Dennis conveyed surprise without saying anything.

"If we can't solve that problem on our own, I don't deserve a red hat. The whole thing boils down to me doing a better job of explaining myself to those ladies. Instead of playing the authority game, as I have. It's my fault if I haven't shown them that I want the same things they want for those poor people downtown."

Dennis was glad he was forbidden to say anything. What could he do but agree? He noted the cardinal's hand moving back and forth across his stomach. "I'd better take some of my own medicine," Matthew Mahan said. "They're giving a reception for us at the embassy tonight. The four other new American cardinals arrived today. They all headed for the North American College. They're all graduates but Cooke, and he would have been, except for the war." He smiled wryly. "One of the many clubs I don't belong to. I'm afraid I got awfully tired of their inside remarks during the council. Personally, I think more college in America and less in Rome would make better bishops in the long run."

Dennis again found difficulty breathing. Matthew Mahan was still talking. "It's one thing to be loyal to the Pope on a spiritual basis. Letting the Curia run the American Church is another matter. On that I agree with old Davey. But I don't feel we have to wreck the papacy to get our freedom." He patted Dennis's arm. "Go to sleep now."

Dennis fell asleep at once. His dreams were bizarre. Helen Reed was in almost all of them, always just beyond the reach of his fingers, the touch of his lips. He awoke to find the oxygen mask over his nose and mouth and Matthew Mahan's face so close to his own that it was a visual collision. The cardinal's steady blue eyes seemed to penetrate to the depths of his soul.

"It's all right, Dennis, it's all right," he said gently. "You must be getting better. You haven't had any trouble for a couple of hours. Were you dreaming?"

Dennis nodded, the oxygen hissing coolly down his throat.

Matthew Mahan glanced at his watch. "There, that's two minutes." He took the mask off and hung it over the bedpost.

"Haven't you gone to dinner yet?" Dennis asked. He was pleasantly surprised to hear his voice so clear.

"Hours ago. I also put the world's oldest heretic to bed. I don't want him dropping dead on me in the middle of Rome. How could we ever explain the odor of sanctity arising from the likes of him?"

Bewildered, Dennis looked at the empty twin bed.

"I put him in my room."

"Really—*you* shouldn't be losing all this sleep."

"I can afford to lose sleep a lot more than I can afford to lose a good secretary."

If emotion were the real cause of his asthma attack, Dennis thought gloomily, he should be strangling to death now. How does the young snot who is betraying his benefactor respond? "I feel fine," he said desperately. "Why don't you try to get some sleep?"

"I'll nap later. It's five thirty. I'd better be off to say Mass." He picked up the oxygen mask. "Need a whiff before I go?"

Dennis shook his head. "Your Eminence," he said as the big man strode to the door. "Thank you—for—for staying up with me."

Matthew Mahan's lips curved into the cocky Irish grin. "The least I could do. After almost killing you."

Five minutes later Bishop Cronin was in the room, telephoning for two continental breakfasts. "By God," he said. "You're cured. It's a miracle. I think we'll give credit for it to old Pope John. You fell on your kisser square across his coat of arms, a gesture of devotion which is typically Italian to say the least."

Breakfast arrived and Dennis decided he was hungry. He smeared a piece of fresh Italian bread with butter and marmalade. "I can't get over the nursing care I've gotten," he said. "The cardinal sitting up all night with me—"

"I've had two heart attacks now, each of which carried me to within a handshake of Saint Peter. And both times who do I find sitting beside my bed at three or four a.m. but himself. How can you help but love a man like that?"

Yes, Dennis thought. How, how?

MATTHEW Mahan took a quick shower and shaved. Freshened, though a little light-headed, he started toward the elevator. He was going to say Mass at the Church of St. Peter in Chains. To combine this with what he had experienced there two nights ago might bring stronger, clearer insight.

He had not taken more than ten steps when a woman appeared in the hall. She had a sensual, arrogant mouth and dark hair elaborately done. A white evening dress fell from beneath her cloak to silver sandals. She stared coolly at him, a mocking smile playing across her lips, and walked ahead to the elevator. She had come from Mike Furia's room. Matthew Mahan was shaken. Was there anyone he could trust? A brutal loneliness assailed him, bitter, like the isolation Jesus must have felt. All through his Mass he struggled to accept the pain of it, as Jesus had.

After Mass, he met the somber gaze of Moses with a new understanding. He said a silent prayer to Pope John, asking for guidance. Slowly he became convinced that he must do something. Mike Furia was more than a soul whose shepherd he was ordained to be. Mike was a personal friend, a man with whom he had shared his life. To be silent now would be betrayal of Mike's soul.

By the time he reached the Hassler it was eight o'clock. With nothing to reassure him but grim determination, he was about to risk friendship, episcopal dignity, even self-esteem.

"Hey," Mike said as he opened his door. "I just had breakfast delivered. Will you join me? I'll call for another order."

"No thanks, Mike. But I'll drink your leftover milk."

"Okay," said Mike, returning to the table where his coffee steamed in his cup. Matthew Mahan took a glass from the bathroom and poured some warm milk into it. He sipped it gratefully.

"What's up?" Mike said. "How's Dennis?"

"Fine, thank God. Listen, Mike, you're not going to like what I'm about to say, but I've got to say it. I couldn't face myself in the mirror or consider myself a priest if I didn't."

Mike Furia stared at him, baffled. He hunched his huge shoulders and leaned forward in his chair. "I'm listening," he said.

"On my way out to say Mass, I almost bumped into a woman who—obviously spent the night in this room."

"Well I'll be a son of a bitch." Mike jumped to his feet. "Matt," he said, "it's none of your damn business."

"Mike. What kind of a friend—or priest—would I be if I let you lose your soul in front of my eyes without saying a word?"

Mike's eyes could not have been more contemptuous.

"What possible—value—what good can a woman like that do you? Do you even know her name?"

"Of course I know her name. She's a dress designer. One of the best in Rome. She's separated, like me, and can't marry again because it's against the law here in Italy."

"I'm sorry," Matthew Mahan said humbly. "I thought—I thought she looked a little like a call girl."

"Matt, I haven't taken a vow of celibacy. I thought you understood that."

"Mike, you've got a wife, a son. Spiritually, this takes you further away from them."

"You want to know the last time I had sex with my wife, Matt? That's all I ever did with her, have sex. I've never made love to her—at least, not since Tony was born. The last time was ten years ago. We were separated long before we made it legal."

"Mike," said Matthew Mahan. "How could we be friends for so many years, close friends, and you never told me this?"

"I hinted around it often enough. But what did we usually talk about? How to get a gymnasium built, a million raised. You didn't want to hear my story. What the hell, you're no parish priest."

Nothing could compare with the pain of those words. "I was a priest first, Mike. I still am."

"Well, if you expect me to get down on my knees and beg your pardon—or God's—forget it."

"I didn't—I don't. I'm— What can I do to help?"

Mike seemed to sway in the middle of the room. Then he spun away and sat down. "I guess it's about time we had it out, Matt. I don't believe any of it, the whole schmeer."

"You mean the Church—being Catholic?"

"You got it."

"And this has been going on—for a long time?"

"A hell of a long time."

"But how do you explain the help you've given me? You've raised millions for the Church."

"I raised millions for *you*. For our friendship. I believe in that—even if it's in the past tense now."

"Why do you believe in that?"

"Because you saved my life. You have a hand on me, Matt, as we used to say in the family. You've got it for the rest of your life, whether I like it or not."

And all the time you thought it had been sanctifying grace, a triumph of your priesthood. Instead it was the code of the mafiosi. Swallow the humiliation, Matthew. Here is a soul in torment.

"Mike," said Matthew Mahan. "It's true I took tremendous satisfaction from your career. You were one of my saved souls. The fact that you were my good friend—well, I assumed that was God's pat on the back. But I see how I let my self-satisfaction deceive me. It's my worst fault. A form of pride. I'm sorry, Mike."

"Sorry for *what*?"

"For failing you—as a priest."

"You didn't. I never gave you a chance to fail me."

"I never looked for the opportunity, either."

He got up and walked leadenly to the door.

THAT night, after the reception for the American cardinals at the embassy, Matthew Mahan gave a private dinner for the closest members of his party. Monsignors Petrie and Malone, Davey Cronin, and Dennis McLaughlin; Mary Shea, Mike Furia, the McAvoys, and Bill Reed. There was a great deal of kidding about Bill Reed's stubborn unaffiliation with any church. Bishop Cronin, to Terry Malone's outrage, maintained that this proved Bill had more sense than anyone else at the table. To confuse matters, Bishop Cronin defended himself by quoting Pope John. "I do not fear the habits, the politics, or the religion of any man . . . as long as he lives with an awe of God." Bill Reed declared himself ready to subscribe to that article of faith. Without it, he said, anyone who practiced medicine would soon lose his mind.

George Petrie and Terry Malone left early. This troubled Matthew Mahan a little—but not as much as Mike's hostile mood.

Throughout dinner he had talked only to Dennis and Mary Shea, and from what Matthew Mahan could hear, it was largely a cynical diatribe against the Church in Italy. He had been pained to see both Dennis and Mary smiling in approval. Jim McAvoy was the only one within earshot to disagree with Mike, and poor Jim was promptly buried by a barrage of negative statistics.

Matthew Mahan ordered a round of Asti Spumante. Avoiding Bill Reed's glare as he took a swallow, he smiled at Mike and asked, "What did I hear you saying about the Church in Italy?"

Mike was not even looking at Matthew Mahan. "Have you ever heard of the Società Generale Immobiliare?" He was talking directly to Mary, challenging his Eminence, preaching a contrary gospel. "It's the biggest real estate and construction company in Italy. In fact, one of the biggest in the world. The Vatican owns twenty-five percent of the shares and about ninety-eight percent of the control. I've worked with them on a couple of dozen jobs, including the Watergate apartments down in Washington, D.C. That complex is running about sixty-seven million. Seventy percent of the common stock and fifty percent of the preferred is owned by Immobiliare. Then there's Immobiliare Canada. They own the Stock Exchange Tower in Montreal. When you go into a deal with those guys, you need the best lawyers in the world behind you."

"You mean they're crooked?"

"Oh no. They just press the contract to the outer limits. They're working for the Pope. It's their duty to get everything they can in every deal—and a little extra." Mike Furia grinned. "We'd be here until dawn if I started listing what SGI has built since the war—apartment houses, office buildings, luxury homes, and a couple of suburban developments. In 1967 they showed a profit of six point two million. Not bad when you consider that they only paid one point five million to get control in 1949. They also own the biggest cement and construction-material maker in Italy. And then there's Pantanella, just about the biggest pasta manufacturer—"

"And the banks. What about the banks?" said Cronin.

"Well, they own one big one outright, the Banco Santo Spirito, and they're tied into three others. The four handle about fifty percent of all the foreign trade transactions. Then there's a couple of thousand small banks all over Italy that are owned outright either by the Vatican or the local parish."

"And they all charge interest, do they not?" asked Cronin. "Which all the Church fathers, numerous councils, and a half dozen popes have denounced as usury—a serious sin. All of them cited Scripture. But when it became clear that all Europe was ignoring their pronouncements, they got into the business themselves. Some of these are the same heroes—I mean Pius XI and XII—who refused to allow the Catholic couple with eleven children to touch a contraceptive, even though there's not a single line of Scripture to support them, and only two vague pronouncements by previous popes before 1930."

All eyes in the room turned to Matthew Mahan. For a moment he felt only outrage. Why did they expect him to answer every charge that anyone made against the Church? But then he sighed, seeing something else on Mary Shea's face. The assumption that no real answer was possible.

"Before we burn down St. Peter's," he said, "remember that the Church is more than an investment company or an enemy of contraception. No matter how wrong she is on some things, each day she brings into the world enormous amounts of God's grace."

"But if the vessel in which the grace comes is polluted, the grace itself may be of no avail," said Cronin.

"I don't believe that," Matthew Mahan said. "I don't think you do either." But the anguish on Cronin's face was all too real.

"That's—that's almost a loss of faith you're describing, Davey."

"Call it what you will," said the old man.

"Is it you or the Asti Spumante talking? I can't believe we'd ever part company on this point."

"No, no, of course not, Matt."

His automatic answer was more painful than defiance. Wasn't he saying, You're not worth arguing with, your Eminence?

"Dennis, I think Bishop Cronin's overtired. Why don't—"

"I am not in the least overtired. But I do think it's time for me to shut up and go to bed." He got up and strode out of the room.

Bill Reed announced that it was bedtime for him, too.

"Well, I'm a bottle finisher myself," said Mike Furia, holding up his glass for the waiter to fill.

"Likewise," said Mary with defiant gaiety. Matthew Mahan wondered if he should try to explain what had just happened between him and Davey Cronin. He decided to try. "He's a little like a

205

father who can't realize his son has grown up. But I can't just spout his opinions automatically anymore."

Jim McAvoy said, "He's practically a Protestant."

"Not really, Jim. Underneath that scathing language there's a tremendous faith, a tremendous love for the Church."

"I sense it," Madeline McAvoy said. "I sense it very much."

Matthew Mahan felt a surge of affection for the McAvoys. These were the kind of people he was trying to save from the rising waters of chaos. He turned to Mike Furia with new determination. "That stuff about the Church in business, Mike. It costs about twenty million dollars a year to run the Vatican. You've got to generate income from somewhere besides contributions."

"Maybe it wouldn't cost twenty million, Matt," Mary said, "if they didn't have apostolic delegates all over the world, and the Curia with its perpetually growing bureaucracy."

"Or the Vatican Radio," Mike Furia said. "Or their own newspaper. *L'Osservatore Romano* loses two million a year."

"No free world government publishes a newspaper," Mary said.

It was incredible, the defiance in her voice, in her eyes. Was he losing Mary, too? For twenty minutes he tried to explain the origin of the Vatican's involvement with the business world, but his audience was unimpressed. The party broke up with lackluster goodnights, an off-key ending to what should have been a very happy evening. Mary Shea sensed his emotion and said softly, "Don't let it upset you so much, Matt. You can't change the facts."

Alone in his room, Matthew Mahan gulped a half dozen Titrilacs to defend his stomach and decided Mary had given him good advice. Tomorrow was Sunday. He had reserved it, thank God, as a day to relax, think, pray. A miniretreat that would, he hoped, recall memories of the five-day retreat he made before his consecration as bishop. Pope John had sent his own personal confessor, Monsignor Alfred Cavagna, to see him each day to give him subjects for meditation. Matthew Mahan had asked for and received profound advice in dealing with his chief failing, the sin of pride. With beautiful simplicity the old priest had spoken to him of the necessity of letting go of every wish, every personal desire; handing them over to God, so that whenever one was fulfilled the victory belonged to God, and if it was unfulfilled, it was a chance to learn God's true intentions through suffering. How hard it had been to keep this wisdom in mind while sitting on an archdiocesan powder keg.

Fortunately, Matthew Mahan had brought with him to Rome Pope John's book, *Journal of a Soul;* he had it now to console him. There were more than a few sentences underlined. He turned to an entry for January 24, 1904. It lifted his spirits a little. "My pride in particular has given me a great deal of trouble. . . . I have yet to learn my A.B.C. in the practice of true humility and scorn of self. I feel a restless longing for I know not what—it is as if I were trying to fill a bottomless bag."

From his hotel window Matthew Mahan could see the illuminated dome of St. Peter's. Suddenly he remembered sitting in the papal library and listening as the bulky old man recited his favorite passage from the ritual for the consecration of bishops. He remembered the flash of humor in John's brown eyes as he came to the last sentence: "Let him learn from wise men and from fools, so that he may profit from all." "That," he had said, "is perhaps most important, when it comes to running a diocese."

Now Matthew Mahan turned to another page in the book. Two maxims immediately caused him pain.

Always to be engaged in the work of God and free from worldly affairs and the love of filthy lucre.

To cherish humility and patience in myself, and teach these virtues to others.

How often he had failed to live up to these ideals. Where, how, had he lost touch with them? Meekness and humility did not come easily to his nature, he thought moodily. Not by accident was his nickname in high school "the Mouth." He was always monopolizing the limelight, and loving it. But now it was past time for the movement toward a new self to be completed.

It was also past time to let go, once and for all, those dreams of glory that he had cherished for the first years after his consecration. He had seen himself succeeding Cardinal Spellman as de facto leader of the American Church. John's death had turned those pipe dreams into the ashes they deserved to become. Reality had been the order of the day for the past six years. Five months after cancer killed John XXIII, John Kennedy died and America reeled off course like a rudderless ship. It was hard to say whether the Church had merely succumbed to the madness or had contributed to it. Perhaps that was another reason why he had lost touch with the memory of John XXIII. Tomorrow—

The telephone rang. "Your Eminence, a cablegram . . ." Five minutes later it was handed to him by a bellboy. He read it and slipped it into his wallet. Then, wistfully, he fingered the pages of *Journal of a Soul*. He would not be reading it tomorrow after all. The cable gave him one of those rare opportunities to reach out as a priest to a fellow priest. He could not pass it up for his own spiritual gratification. John would understand. Santo Padre, he prayed, stand beside me now and in the years to come.

IX

At TEN the next morning, Dennis McLaughlin and Matthew Mahan rolled out of Rome in a Mercedes, with a picnic basket in the trunk and a talkative young man named Tullio as their chauffeur. Dennis was puzzled but pleased that Matthew Mahan apparently worried enough about his health to be taking him off for a quick rest cure. Tullio assured them he would have no difficulty finding Nettuno. It was one of Rome's favorite bathing resorts.

Soon the white buildings of Nettuno were visible, and Matthew Mahan watched until he spotted a sign: SICILY ROME AMERICAN CEMETERY. "That's what we want," he told Tullio.

The cemetery rose in a gentle slope from a broad pool. In the center of the pool was an island with a cenotaph on it, flanked by rows of cypress trees. They left the car and walked down a wide, grassy mall toward a white-pillared memorial at the end. The thousands of crosses were in precise rows on either side of the mall beneath rows of Roman pines. It was a brilliantly sunny day, and the crosses were bright under the dark, brooding trees. On one side of the memorial was a chapel, on the other was a museum room with maps of the American operations in Italy.

A pudgy gray-haired man emerged from the museum and introduced himself. "Would you like to look at the grave now, your Eminence? I'll be glad to lead the way."

"Thank you," Matthew Mahan said. "We'll find our way by ourselves, if you don't mind. Just give us the directions."

The man gave them a map marked in red. Halfway down the mall, they turned into a shadowed lane flanked by white crosses. Dennis looked bored, obviously thinking of this as an aberration born of World War II combat neurosis. Matthew Mahan was counting the rows. At the thirteenth he stopped, and Dennis McLaughlin stood frozen in astonishment. On the horizontal arm of the cross in front of him he saw the name:

RICHARD MCLAUGHLIN
LIEUTENANT, USAAF

"He's here," he whispered. "Here?"

"Yes," said Matthew Mahan. "I contacted the American Battle Monuments Commission in Washington. I still hadn't heard from them when we left home. Their cable arrived last night."

Dennis nodded automatically. He was in the void now, falling like that figure on the Manzù doors of St. Peter's, dying in space. "I never knew him," he heard himself saying. "I was three years old when he—went in the army."

"Yes, you told me," Matthew Mahan said. "But I thought—you should at least know where he died. He was copilot on a B-26. The plane was hit by German antiaircraft fire only a couple of miles from here. He was badly wounded and the pilot was killed. He held the plane on course long enough for the rest of the crew to get out. He got the Distinguished Flying Cross for it."

"I never knew him. And my mother hated him, couldn't forgive him, for dying."

Tears were strangling his throat. Suddenly there was a big hand on his arm wrenching him up like a drowning victim toward sunlight, air. "It's all right, Dennis," said Cardinal Mahan in a voice he had never heard before. "Don't be afraid to cry. Everyone should cry for their dead. I cried almost every day during the war. So did other men, even tough mugs like Mike Furia."

He opened his arms—yes, Dennis, the sardonic, who faced the world with arms crossed on his chest like a shield—opened them and flung them around the solid, bulky blackness that confronted him. He was weeping, yet he was breathing, miraculously breathing. "I never knew him," he repeated. "Sometimes—I try to be him. But you can't be—something you don't know. Every time you reach out—all you get is emptiness."

"Now you know where he is, Dennis. Here with his friends."
Softly, gently, the big hand patted his back. He was being held,
caressed, like a child, yet he felt no resentment. "The older I get,
the less I grieve for those who died in battle. There's a poet who
said they remain forever young. It's true, especially if you've loved
them before they died. You loved him, Dennis. Someday in heaven
you'll know him—and love him even more."

But how do we know he didn't die in mortal sin? What if you
go to heaven and find out he's in hell, what would you say to God?
Out of my way I'm going to hell with my father. That had been
the favorite fantasy of teenage Dennis McLaughlin. Through his
tears he tried to tell this to Matthew Mahan, interlacing it with
sardonic laughter. Was he collapsing into hysteria?

"This is a dangerous thing for a bishop to say, Dennis, but I
believe that every man who dies fighting for a good cause goes to
heaven. The Muhammadans say he does. Courage is a better absolution than any priest can give."

Ten minutes ago, Dennis would have laughed this idea into
oblivion. Now he accepted it in silence broken only by his sobs.

"I'd like to say a prayer for him, Dennis." The cardinal knelt.

Dennis knelt beside him, no words in his numbed brain, staring
down the rows of crosses, trying to comprehend the immensity of
death's grasp. "I can't pray," he whispered.

"Would you let me pray for both of us, Dennis?"

He nodded his head.

Matthew Mahan was swept back to the blasted landscape of
war, when he prayed for the men he had joked with only hours
before. He let his mind empty, as he had done in those awful days.
Anguish made formal prayers meaningless. "O God," he said at last,
"we kneel here in search of comradeship. Two lonely men, dedicated to your service, in search of comradeship with this brave
man, Richard McLaughlin, and his friends. Help us to see them
as they were before they died, Lord, young and full of laughter.
Help us to remember their courage. We know they weren't heroes
twenty-four hours a day. Sometimes they were afraid, and cried
out to you. You came, especially to those who died trying to help
their friends. Greater love than this, no man has, Lord. No one
knows this better than you."

For a full minute there were no words. But the prayer was not

210

over: "O Lord, we believe that no sacrifice is in vain, that its graces are stored in heaven to be used for the works of love. Pour into our hearts, O Lord, especially into the heart of Richard's son Dennis, the grace he needs, as we all need it, to love himself, his fellowmen, his priesthood. Thank you, O Lord, for giving us this day. Your ways are a mystery to us, but we shall always believe in your justice and your love."

Silence again for another full minute. The prayer was over. Dennis raised his head and smiled wanly. "Thank you. Thank you."

The superintendent was waiting for them at the museum with a package containing photographs of the cemetery and of Richard McLaughlin's cross. He gave it to Dennis and launched into a diatribe against the generals who fouled up the Anzio beachhead operation. Dennis McLaughlin listened, slowly letting this dumpy, earnest man return him to the world with its idiotic fascination with violence.

Something had happened to him kneeling before that cross. He did not understand it, did not understand why that intense emotion had not crushed his chest, stopped his breath. What do you feel, Dennis? He tried to let the words come into his mind unhindered by preconceived ideas . . . more free, more real.

Matthew Mahan told Tullio to drive them to a good beach. "We'll eat our lunch down there and take a walk." As they rolled past villas, hotels, restaurants (most of them closed until late May) Dennis found it hard to believe that thousands of men had died along these roads. He began asking Matthew Mahan about his experience as a chaplain. "Before the plane trip I hadn't realized you were such a hero," he said half jokingly.

"Oh, those stories. The fact is, Dennis, if you really don't care about dying, almost anybody can be a hero." But he talked as for twenty-five years he had never talked to anyone about what those experiences meant to him as a priest. He had never before shared his doubts about his faith. "The terrible part of it was the way it kept happening. Again and again you'd think, This time God will listen, this time my prayers will do something. But at the end of every day there was a new batch of bodies. After a while I went a little crazy. It wasn't enough, not to care whether you lived or died. I started trying to get myself killed. I was saying to God, Take me and let the others go. I'd be dead by now if it wasn't for the Protestant chaplain, Steve Murchison. One day, just before we crossed the Rhine, he took me aside. We'd been under heavy artillery fire all day and taken terrible casualties. I'd walked around in it and never got a scratch. 'Matt,' he said, 'you're not Jesus.'"

Matthew Mahan leaned back and stared up at the car's gray roof. He was back in that shattered French town, staring into Steve Murchison's rawboned Yankee face, hearing his voice: "I saw you out there today waltzing through the shrapnel. And I thought to myself, That guy *wants* to get killed. . . . Think a minute, Matt. What are you saying to the men when you stroll around out there like an umpire on a baseball diamond? You're saying, If you were as holy and as brave as me, you'd be doing this, too. You make them feel like dirt, because they've got their heads down in their holes and are saying prayers to God to give them the guts to stay there. And if they do come out of a hole to help a buddy, they squirm along on their bellies like snakes and they look up and see Father God Almighty Mahan walking toward them looking about ten feet tall, his Irish grin saying, *O ye of little faith.*"

It was dusk. The burial teams were loading the shrouded bodies on the trucks while Steve was talking. Up ahead, the Germans started shelling again, and the shells made a crunching sound like bones breaking. More than anything Matthew had wanted to grab this man by his battle jacket and scream with anger. But he could say nothing. All he could feel was emptiness.

"You think that doesn't break everybody's heart, Matt? Day after day?" Steve was pointing at the bodies with a shaking finger. "Getting yourself killed won't solve a damn thing, and it has nothing to do with faith. Faith means going on, no matter how bad it gets, and still trying to serve. Dead priests don't serve, Matt." He stepped back. "You're going to hate my guts for saying this, Matt, but so help me God, it's spoken out of love."

"That was the worst night of my life," Matthew Mahan told Dennis. "The worst. I had to face the fact that everything Steve had said was true. Where did he get the grace to know that much about faith? Why did I know so little? That was the night I joined the ecumenical movement."

"It's the difference between Protestant faith and Catholic faith," Dennis said. "One ventures. The other tries to apply a set of formulas, and when they don't work, hysteria sets in."

"It's not quite so neat, Dennis. It's the difference between real faith and false faith, between caring and grandstanding. There are plenty of formula boys in both churches."

Silence. He hadn't intended his answer as a rebuke. But it was disconcerting the way Dennis and his generation could draw such different conclusions from the same experience. "Anyway," he said, trying to restore their mood, "I never got up off my belly for the rest of the war, and I was better able to bear the dying. Steve and I kid about it sometimes. He says that at one point he grabbed me by the shoulders and this was a laying on of hands that gave me the consolation of the Holy Spirit. I told that story to Pope John. Would you believe it, he took it seriously?"

"Why not?" Dennis McLaughlin said.

Ahead of them the Tyrrhenian Sea glistened in the sunlight. At a wide swatch of white sand Tullio stopped the car. He took a blanket from the trunk and spread it on the beach, and Dennis lugged the picnic hamper. There was a bottle of Soave Bolla packed in dry ice, a chicken, olives, celery. They drank the cool wine, which went beautifully with the chicken. The air was hot and still.

"Too hot for a couple of guys in clericals," Matthew Mahan said. He stripped off his collar and rabat, and, to Dennis's surprise, also his shoes and socks, and rolled up his trousers. "I can never go near a beach without shell hunting. Want to join me?"

"How did you get interested in shells?" Dennis asked, as small icy waves lapped over their bare feet.

"When I was about ten, we spent summers at the shore. When my father had time off and joined us, he and I would get up early and walk the beach. I loved those walks." How much, how much. Matthew Mahan was astonished to find his eyes blurring. "My father never talked much. We'd just tramp along. Every so often we'd pick up a shell. If we found one that was especially interesting, he'd say keep it, and presto, I was a collector."

"What's this one?" Dennis picked up a tiny brown and white and gold shell that rose from a narrow stem to a bulging middle and then narrowed to a point at the top.

"That's a *Fusinus syracusanus*. Like a piece of architecture, isn't it? Look at this one." The cardinal picked up a brown and white speckled shell. It was almost round, with an opening at the top and a tiny knob at the bottom from which spiral lines ran out. "This is a Mediterranean version of the New England moon shell. You can see here what I find so fascinating about shells. They illustrate a principle of growth that not many people understand—the dynamic spiral. To produce a spiral you need three things. Growth has to follow a continuous course—it can't backtrack. It also must proceed freely, without interference. And it must never lose touch with the beginning of the spiral—that little knob at the bottom. You know, that part hardens, for all practical purposes it's dead. But the lip of the spiral stays alive, keeps growing. One of the best examples of this is the American chambered nautilus."

"A principle of growth," Dennis said, staring at the shell. The idea stirred a vague excitement in his mind. "Can I keep this?"

"Of course. I've got an interesting one from Mauritius—almost the entire shell consists of the whorl. Spiral growth needn't follow a lockstep rhythm. There are great leaps forward."

"Do they all curve in the same direction?"

"Practically all. All but the left-handed whelk."

Dennis felt strangely exhilarated. The cardinal began talking about the importance of shells in various parts of the world—for dyes, for jewelry, for currency. In Japan, Shinto priests sound the call to worship on triton's trumpets. In India, left-handed spirals are sacred. In the Fiji Islands, the golden cowrie is worn by chiefs as a symbol of sovereignty.

"Do you have one?" Dennis asked.

"Sure. It cost me a fortune. Do you think I ought to wear it when I do battle with Sister Agnes Marie?" He grinned.

The cardinal was enjoying himself tremendously. It was the only time Dennis had seen him relaxed except for the confirmation ceremony at Holy Angels. Again he felt awe at the natural radiance of the man. But this time it was untinged by envy. Because this time it was being given to him alone? No, Dennis, he told himself. Accept the human reality, the *happiness* that this man is sharing with you—and something deeper that lay just outside his mind's reach. He fingered the moon shell in his pocket.

For an hour they walked and talked, rambling reminiscently. Matthew Mahan told him the story of Mary Shea—the whole story, including what they had told each other three nights ago at the Tre Scalini. Dennis thought of the sneering suggestion in his letter to Leo and writhed. That, of course, was only a small part of his

betrayal of this man. But he would atone for it, he told himself
feverishly. He would swear Leo to silence, force him to return
every document, convert him to Matthew Mahan.

The cardinal also talked freely about his early life, and about
that day at the end of his freshman year at the university, when he
had known with finality that he would be a priest.

"I went into the Jesuits right after high school," Dennis said.
"I should have waited longer to decide, finished college first, as
you did. Maybe by then I'd have had a chance to meet a few intelligent women. I don't mean I would have married," he added
hastily, seeing the look on the cardinal's face. He explained his
belief that physical celibacy was not the heart of the problem: it
was rather that most priests never had a chance to know or understand women as mature, equally human beings. "I mean really appreciate them. We just see them as temptations."

"I know, I know," Matthew Mahan said. "But it wasn't much
different for me, Dennis. I scraped up dates for proms, that sort of
thing. But most of the time I hung around with a bunch of guys my
own age. It was the Depression, you know. Everybody was leery of
getting involved with a girl. There wasn't much hope of finding a
job to support a family. I was pretty unprepared to deal with
women—in a mature way." Totally unprepared, whispered a cor-
rective voice in Matthew Mahan's mind. "When I met Mary Shea, I
couldn't believe she was real at first."

The cardinal picked up another moon shell and reminded himself that he was here to help Dennis, not to lament his own now
ancient travails. He asked him what he planned to do, after perhaps a year or two as his secretary. Did he want to write? Teach
at the seminary? Be a parish priest? Dennis didn't know.

"It'll come, it'll come," Matthew Mahan said. They were back
at the car now and soon were racing toward Rome. Matthew
Mahan talked to Tullio about the social unrest that was tormenting
Italy. Scarcely a day went by without a strike. Tullio admitted that
he was a Communist and firmly believed that the time had come
to get rid of capitalism. And the Church, too? Oh, no, not the
Church. He was a good Catholic. He saw no conflict—but the
Vatican would have to stop being capitalistic.

Dennis said nothing. He was abstracted, staring out the window,
until St. Peter's dome was visible, looming above the city.

Then he said, "Old Davey claims that Rome will never be able to stand up until we get that thing off its back."

Matthew Mahan sighed. They were in the real world again. As they sped through the empty Sunday streets, Dennis gave an account of old Davey's tour of St. Peter's, doing his utmost to shock him with the outrageous sayings of their eighty-one-year-old heretic. But as they parted at the Hassler, Dennis grew solemn. "That was quite a trip. I can't tell you which I appreciate more—what happened at the grave or our time on the beach."

"It was good for me, too, Dennis," Matthew Mahan said. And in his room he knelt and thanked God for His guidance, for giving him words that might heal. How strange the life of the spirit was. By letting go, by giving up the old guardians, by venturing forth fearful and alone, you discovered that new communions awaited you. *My yoke is sweet and my burden light.*

THE next morning, Dennis McLaughlin joined Bishop Cronin, Monsignors Malone and Petrie, Matthew Mahan's sister-in-law and nephew, Eileen and Timmy, and two busloads of pilgrims at the Church of St. Peter in Chains, where the priests celebrated Mass with their cardinal-to-be. Then they returned to the hotel, had breakfast, and Dennis helped Matthew Mahan put on his robes. The outfit was simpler than the traditional one, thanks to a directive that Pope Paul had issued. Matthew Mahan had been delighted to forgo most of the archaic ornaments. But the loss of the *galèro*—the flat hat with thirty tassels—caused a pang. He remembered his first visit to New York's St. Patrick's Cathedral, gazing up at the ceiling above the high altar where the *galèri* of dead cardinals dangled. It had pleased him to think that his hat would be the first to hang in his cathedral. But *Roma locuta est; causa finita est.* Rome has spoken; the case is concluded.

Earnestly, Dennis helped him into his red rabat—the sleeveless, backless garment worn beneath the red wool cassock—then the cassock itself, with trimmings, lining, and buttons of red silk; then the mozzetta, the small cape worn over his shoulders. Around his waist went the red watered-silk ribbon sash with silk fringes at both ends. On his head he put the red watered-silk zucchetto—the skullcap. "Well, that does it. How do I look?" he asked.

"Fine," said Dennis. "Have you got your red socks on?"

He hadn't. He quickly changed socks, put on his shoes, and checked himself in the full-length mirror.

"Dennis," he said. "I'm ready now. I'd like to have five minutes alone to pray. I'll see you downstairs."

The lobby was jammed with pilgrims, all eager to get a first look at their cardinal in his red robes. When he emerged from the elevator they cheered like rock fans. He had no time to do more than wave. The Vatican representative, Monsignor Tonti, was hurrying him. "We have only five minutes," he said.

"Baloney," said Matthew Mahan as he, Dennis, and Bishop Cronin got into the limousine. "The Vatican's just like the army, hurry up and wait. I bet we stand around for at least a half hour."

"My bet," Cronin said, "is that we'll rue this day. Wait till you hear the oath you have to take, Matt. They've added a vow of silence as total as any Carthusian monk's. . . ."

After a few detours forced by traffic around the Piazza Campo dei Fiori, and accompanied by a running commentary from the old bishop, they arrived at the apostolic chancery, or *cancelleria,* on the Corso Vittorio Emanuele. Around them in the courtyard rose forty-four superb granite columns, supposedly taken from the ruins of Pompeii. The façade of the building, which occupied one whole side of the piazza, was unbelievably delicate.

"I remember some writer," said Bishop Cronin, "who said it reminded him of an ancient casket of mellowed ivory."

"Does it look familiar, Dennis?" Matthew Mahan asked. "The chancery office in New York is a copy."

"This is the chancery for the diocese of Rome. And the Sacred Rota," Monsignor Tonti said.

Matthew Mahan twisted away from the thought that he was receiving his official nomination as a cardinal in the building where Mary Shea had sought in vain the annulment of her marriage.

Inside, they were led to a large, crowded hall that was known as the Riaria Hall. There were cheers and claps from some of their pilgrims as they pushed their way to the far end, where the other new cardinals were waiting. Matthew Mahan exchanged handshakes with his four fellow Americans, Cooke of New York, Dearden of Detroit, Carberry of St. Louis, and Wright of Pittsburgh. Standing a few feet away were cardinals-to-be from other parts of the world. Cronin ticked some of them off for Dennis. An impressive-looking black man was archbishop of Tananarive, Madagascar. "And that's Cardinal Derrieux, Jesuit theologian of no place in particular. There, the boss is talking to him now. Old Matt's a great fan of his. Fussed over him like he was the Holy Spirit incarnate during the council. They met during the war."

"A little professional jealousy in those remarks?"

"No, no. I acknowledge his superiority. He's got a mind of pure crystal, while mine is Irish peat. But he's too cold for my taste."

Dennis studied Derrieux's face—the deep-socketed eyes, thin, bloodless mouth, weak chin, sharp, somewhat feminine nose. He was smiling at Matthew Mahan now, an empty smile compared with Mahan's warm grin. But Derrieux's name stirred Dennis's mind. He had been one of the lonely intellectual heroes of the 1950s, calling again and again for more freedom in the Church.

Bishop Cronin was telling him how his dislike for Derrieux had begun in the days of Vatican II, but Dennis's attention flagged. He felt a tightness in his chest as more and more people were crushing into the hall. He urgently wished for the papal messenger to arrive. In the Sistine Chapel, Pope Paul was meeting in a secret consistory with the present cardinals. To get his mind off his breathing difficulties, Dennis asked Bishop Cronin what happened at that ceremony.

"Nothing much," said Cronin. "The great man sits on his throne and reads out the names of the new boys. The assembled yes-men in red raise their zucchettos and give him a little bow of assent. Il Papa also often uses the occasion to announce some new appointments. They tell me there's a new Secretary of State in the wind."

"Who is it?" Dennis asked.

"Jean Villot, so they say. He's a mere lad, sixty-three."

But Dennis had stopped listening. Suddenly he thought he saw a face that could not be here. Hallucination. There it was again. Disembodied, peering over the shoulders of short monsignors: Helen, Sister Helen Reed. She had that solemn look that had stirred him the first time he saw her. But here? No. She was four thousand miles away in the scabby streets of St. Sebastian's parish. Then his eyes caught hers and her mouth became a radiant smile. She was real. He squirmed and elbowed through the crowd to end his disbelief by taking her hand.

"What are you doing here?"

"I talked Sister Agnes Marie into it. Somebody had to defend our position against your friend with the red hat."

Dennis laughed. "You've come a long way for nothing. I don't know what happened to him, but he told me he'd dropped the idea. In fact, he turned down lunch with Cardinal Antoniutti."

Helen was clearly astonished that the great intellectual revolutionary could be so naïve. "You're sure he isn't lying? Maybe he's found out your—arrangement with Leo."

Dennis looked nervously around them. In the semicircle of cardinals, Matthew Mahan was now chatting amiably with John Dearden. "I don't think so." Jammed against Helen as if they were in a subway rush hour, he could feel her breast against his arm. The temperature rose, the oxygen supply fell. Panic and anger mingled in his chest. It was impossible. He was always being pushed one way or another, forced to feel when he did not want to feel. It was absurd, his entire life was a charade.

"I'm staying at the Pensione Christina. There's a beautiful terrace overlooking the Tiber," Helen was saying.

The choice his father had made, the simple act of bravery, life like an arrow's trajectory from the happiness of home and marriage to the hero's grave. To silence beneath that white cross. Wasn't that better than this daily travesty?

"I've got an appointment at the Congregation for the Religious this afternoon," Helen said.

None of these composed men, these princes of the Church, showed the slightest sign of inner anguish. What was their secret? Was it simply being born at the right time? Was it that simple?

His thoughts were interrupted by a voice calling orders in Italian. Since there were very few Italians in the hall, nothing happened. Then an American voice began bawling, "Make way, make way. Please make room here." Then came a small, solemn-faced man in the red robes of a cardinal, with parchmentlike papers in his hand—the *biglietti*. The official letters from the Pope, making them cardinals. Standing in the center of the semicircle, the cardinal read the notification from the Pope and summoned each man to receive his *biglietto*.

Cardinal Derrieux stepped forward to reply—in Latin—to the Vatican messenger on behalf of all the cardinals designate. Dennis could pick up enough of the flowery phrases issuing from the prim mouth to find himself sharing some of Cronin's dislike.

"What's he saying?" asked Madeline McAvoy, who'd joined them, looking very stylish in a blue suit.

"That all Catholic mothers with six or more children are going to get hand-illuminated copies of *Humanae Vitae.*"

"You're terrible," Mrs. McAvoy said. But she loved it.

Cardinal Derrieux finished his speech and stepped back into the ranks. Now the photographers took over, and then the radio reporters with tape recorders, thrusting their microphones into the faces of some new cardinals and ignoring others. Only one accosted Matthew Mahan.

"Is it all over?" asked Mrs. McAvoy with evident dismay.

"No," said Dennis. "This afternoon they come back here to the chancery for visits from other cardinals and officials. Then, in St. Peter's, they get their red birettas from the Pope on Wednesday, and on Thursday they concelebrate Mass and get their rings."

People were moving toward the door. Madeline McAvoy wasn't the only one who was baffled and a little annoyed by the undramatic ceremony, as Dennis heard in the snatches of conversation swirling around him. He seized Helen's hand and edged her into the stream, where Andy Goggin suddenly turned up beside them. Dennis introduced him to Sister Helen.

She made a great fuss over him. "I've heard Dennis talk *so much* about you, the great Biblical scholar." Dennis shrugged wryly.

"It makes me lose my appetite just thinking about the next event on our schedule," said Goggin. It was a luncheon at the North American College for the five American cardinals. The rector, and perhaps the cardinals themselves, would orate.

Sister Helen suggested lunch at her pensione, and Goggin instantly accepted for both of them. Half an hour later they were enjoying an aperitif on a terrace above the Tiber.

As Dennis looked across the river at St. Peter's dome, something stirred in his mind that carried him back to the beach at Nettuno. His hand went to the moon shell in his pocket. Was a dome the same as a spiral? A dome pretended to infinity, but achieved only immensity. It was not a natural, it was even an unnatural symbol.

While he brooded, Helen was interrogating Goggin. He fielded her questions about Biblical studies and his Vatican Radio work with deft irony. A little puzzled, she asked him if he agreed with the revolutionary vision of the once and future church, as foretold by Dennis McLaughlin.

"I stopped smoking that stuff about a year ago," Goggin said. "I thought he had, too." He leered at Dennis.

With humiliating, almost maternal approval, Helen began telling him what Dennis was doing to bore from within Matthew Mahan's regime. Their food arrived, but Dennis had lost his appetite. The whole thing sounded so incredibly childish compared with the reality of Matthew Mahan, the memories that were now indelible. The weary bedside watcher at five a.m. with the oxygen mask in his hand, the comforter among the graves at Nettuno.

With almost diabolical directness, Goggin proceeded to insert a needle in this exposed nerve. "All this destruction your friend Dennis talks about. Don't you think it breaks the first law of Christianity, *love one another?*"

"I think—" Helen looked at Dennis, but help was not forthcoming. "We're interested in destroying phony titles, misused power."

"What if you can't destroy an idea without destroying the man who believes it? Or the titles and power without the men who possess them?"

"A certain amount of suffering is inevitable." Sister Helen glanced at her watch. "It's time for my date at the Vatican." She jumped up. "Dennis. Do what you can to change this great man's mind, please," she said. She strode away from them, those lovely scissoring legs tormenting Dennis's eyes. The quintessential American girl, exuding health, vitality, self-confidence.

Goggin asked, "Do you take her seriously?"

"That's asking for a one-hour disquisition on the nature of love."

"I wasn't trying to undo the romance. I was only talking to hear myself." Goggin's laugh was forced.

"You can be so damn cruel, do you know that? We both have a talent for it. So far we haven't used it on each other."

Goggin leaned forward. "Do I have to spill my guts, too? Do you want me to say I'm in love with you, not queerly but sacredly? I'm in love with you as a priest and, finally, with the idea of the Church. With Mother Church eventually creating the mystical body of Christ that embraces the entire human race. And until now that's what I thought you were in love with, too."

He strode off, leaving Dennis alone on the terrace. He sat

there for a long time staring at the vile-looking Tiber. It was ocher-colored, a river of foul sludge. He sighed, finished his coffee, and asked the waitress for the bill. She smiled politely and told him his American sister had already paid it.

X

"YOUR Eminences—if you'd just stand over here so that we get St. Peter's in the background."

The new American cardinals were in the garden of the North American College. The luncheon and the speeches were over.

Cardinal Carberry of St. Louis, the oldest of the five—he was sixty-four—murmured as they lined up for the insatiable photographers that he was beginning to feel like the victim of a firing squad that couldn't shoot straight. Watching Cardinal Krol, of Philadelphia, who would probably be the next president of the American Bishops' Conference, Matthew Mahan felt uneasy. Krol was an outspoken conservative who hailed the birth control encyclical with trumpetings about the sacredness of human life. But at the same time he was a genial man, essentially likable. Was the Pauline line veering toward public relations to sell its judgment and theology? Stop, Matthew Mahan. That is almost heretical.

On the way back to the chancery for the afternoon visits he bought several newspapers, including the Communist daily L'Unità. All of them had extensive coverage of the papal consistory with profiles of the new cardinals and much speculation about the promotion of Jean Cardinal Villot of France, a moderate progressive, to the key post of Secretary of State. L'Unità summed up the Villot appointment as a piece of Vatican window dressing, a sop thrown to the liberals.

The afternoon passed in a blur of faces and handshakes with dozens of diplomats, cardinals, monsignors. Most were strangers to him, all were ill at ease in his presence. It was Wright and Cooke and Dearden that they came to see, each of whom had power—actual or potential, it amounted to the same thing. He, Mahan, was an oddity, the American friend of John. He could see the puzzlement in their eyes as they extended suave congratulations. He found himself wishing he had Davey Cronin with him to give them his outrageous explanation of why Mahan was here.

223

The visit of Cardinal Villot was the only one that caused Matthew Mahan to grow tense. Villot was soon to be the second most powerful official in the Vatican. If Davey Cronin was right, and *Romanita* was the answer to Matthew Mahan's own elevation to the cardinalate, here was the man who might tell him. But there was no hint of such a possibility in Villot's conversation. His thin face seemed animated by nothing but good humor. *Romanita,* however, included the art of making the remark politic at precisely the right moment. Perhaps this was not it.

Matthew Mahan rode back to his hotel through the Roman dusk. In the lobby, he saw Bill Reed sitting in a chair and was tempted to sneak past him. But he looked so forlorn, it would have been a sin against charity.

"Hello, Bill," he said. "Giving your feet a rest?"

"More or less," the doctor said, good humor returning to his face. "Do you think maybe an atheist's feet get tired quicker than a Christian's tramping around all these churches?"

Before Matthew Mahan could answer, a desk clerk touched him on the elbow. "Eminence," he said, "this cable arrived an hour ago."

Matthew Mahan nodded his thanks and ripped it open: WE HAVE SENT SISTER HELEN REED TO ROME TO DEFEND OUR POINT OF VIEW AT SACRED CONGREGATION FOR RELIGIOUS. SHE IS AT PENSIONE CHRISTINA. SISTER AGNES MARIE. "Look at this," he said, handing the cable to Reed. "That spitfire of a daughter of yours is here."

"Really?" said Bill in a stricken voice. "Well, I'm the last person she'd get in touch with."

"Now, that's absolutely absurd," said Matthew Mahan. "Let's get in a cab right now and go see her."

"No, Matt. I don't want to waste your time. And as your doctor, I'm telling you to go to bed. You look exhausted."

"Baloney," he scoffed. "I'm operating on sanctifying grace."

"Rest, not grace, will heal that ulcer." He shook his head as the cardinal started to argue. "I'd like to see Helen—but I know what I'd hear, and I'm not in the mood to hear it. Shelagh and I spent our honeymoon in Rome—I'm afraid it's got me down."

"All the more reason to see Helen. You used to say she was a carbon copy of her mother. Come on. Let's take a chance." What could a girl, especially one who was a nun, say to her father that would be so terrible?

Bill let himself be hoisted out of his chair and led to a taxi. The affable lady at the desk of the Pensione Christina assured them that the American sister was in her room on the second floor.

"Who's that?" asked a young voice in response to the knock.

"A surprise," said Matthew Mahan.

Sister Helen opened the door. She was wearing a dark blue bathrobe and her hair was encased in a towel. Her face looked hard in the shadowy light. "I thought you might want to have dinner with me and this fellow," Matthew Mahan said quickly.

"I'm sorry," she said. "I have a dinner date."

"Do you have time for an aperitif?"

"Not really. I'm getting dressed, as you can see. I have nothing to say to him," she said, staring stonily at her father.

"Sister, this is no place for me to give you a lecture. But common politeness, not to mention Christian charity—"

"Have nothing to do with it. You must think you can work miracles with a wave of your episcopal hand. The difference between him and me is fundamental. It goes back to the Gospel. Didn't Christ say He would turn son against father and daughter against mother and so forth? That's what happened here." And she stepped back and slammed the door.

Bill Reed took a deep breath. When he exhaled it was almost a groan. "I told you, Matt. I told you." In the taxi he went on. "She always quotes the Gospel at me, Matt. I can't figure that out. I thought raising a daughter in the Catholic Church was safe."

"It isn't the same Catholic Church anymore. . . . Tell me, Bill. Why haven't you married again? With a wife—"

"Yes, she wouldn't be able to hurt me quite so much. I know." He sighed and looked out the window. "Maybe because I'm a doctor, it was a special kind of defeat for me to have my own wife die of cancer. To realize I'd been hearing the symptoms at the breakfast table—and not paying any attention to them."

"Bill, that could happen to anyone. Any doctor."

"Sure. Which doesn't mean I can forgive myself."

"God forgives you, Bill."

"Well, I can't talk to Him, so I'm stuck with doing the job for myself. We atheists—whatever you call us—have to play a double role, sinner and judge. We're pretty hard on ourselves."

"Can't you let a friend get into the act?" Matthew Mahan asked softly. "We'll go up to my room and sit around drinking beer the way we used to in the aid station. And when you're telling me one of those dirty stories you loved to shock me with, I'll put my hand on your arm . . ." He reached out as he spoke.

"Thanks, Matt," Bill Reed said in a choked voice. "But it wouldn't do any good. I don't have the guts to risk more pain."

"My stomach would feel better, Bill, if I made you a convert—not so much to Catholicism as to—to the presence of God."

"Matt, it's enough for me to know I stir so much concern in you," Bill said. "It makes me believe that somehow, in spite of all the evidence to the contrary, I am doing something important." They were at the hotel. Matthew Mahan paid the taxi driver and they walked into the lobby together.

Upstairs, Matthew Mahan sat down and wrote a letter.

Dear Sister Agnes Marie,
    I have just encountered something so spiritually saddening that I must speak to you about it. I don't know whether you are aware that Sister Helen Reed is bitterly alienated from her father. He is a lonely man, deeply wounded by his wife's death. This evening, with my usual overconfidence, I thought I could be the instrument of reconciliation. Instead, I was a fool. I heard her say things to her father that only worsened his loneliness.
    I don't know where this revolution which is racking the Church will take us, but I am reminded of a saying attributed to the liberator of Ireland, Daniel O'Connell, that no political revolution was worth the loss of a single life. I believe that no revolution in the Church is worth the loss of a single soul. Tonight I saw a soul in torment, in grave danger of being lost. Dr. Reed is not a Catholic. But other sheep I have which are not of this fold.
                                            Sincerely yours in Christ,
                                            Matthew Mahan
PS: I've decided not to see Cardinal Antoniutti. If you and I can't settle our differences between ourselves, we don't deserve to be called Christians. In next year's budget, your sisters will have $25,000 from the archdiocese to help pay their expenses downtown. I will also try to keep St. Clare's Hospital open.

Letter in hand, Matthew Mahan knocked on Dennis's door. He found him with his Jesuit friend Andy Goggin and Davey Cronin, poring over a road map. They were driving up to Florence tomorrow to visit the suburb of Isolotto, which was apparently involved in a nasty clash with the Vatican. Matthew Mahan shook his head. "Don't you ever quit looking for ammunition?"

"Now, Matt, you can't deny this is rare stuff," said Cronin. "A revolution practically in Il Papa's backyard. You might be glad to know a bit about it yourself the next time you get one of those stop-everything letters from some Curia cardinal. You can fire back a comment about the beam in his own eye."

Matthew Mahan yawned and gave Dennis the letter to mail. "If anybody is looking for me, I've gone to bed."

"Oh! A priest named Mirante was here."

"He's an old friend. I meant to tell you I wanted to see him."

"Here's his telephone number. He seemed awfully anxious."

Matthew Mahan sighed. All he wanted to do was sleep. But a half hour later, Father Mirante was sipping Cinzano with him in his suite, talking about their mutual friend Mary Shea.

"She is depressed," Mirante said. "I have sent her to the best psychiatrist in Rome. One who understands the reality of the religious factor. The situation as he explains it is really quite simple. She has invested her emotional capital in, shall we say, Vatican futures. And finds herself in a declining market."

"Are things really that bad in the Church, Giulio?"

Mirante's mouth drooped. "You ask a prejudiced observer."

"You're in trouble, Giulio. Mary told me. Why?"

"You have perhaps heard of Isolotto?"

"The parish that's having a brawl with the bishop? My secretary and auxiliary bishop are going up to take a look."

"Eminence," Mirante said. "Do you think that wise? This dispute has become a test of Roman authority. That is why I am no longer a Jesuit." Swiftly he sketched the case. Some militants had occupied Parma Cathedral to protest the links between diocesan authorities and local banks. The parishioners of Isolotto wrote a letter backing the protesters. Their priest, Don Inzo Mazzi, signed it. The cardinal archbishop of Florence suspended the priest and closed the church. Months of guerrilla warfare followed. When a neighboring priest expressed sympathy for Don Mazzi, his church, too, was closed. Currently, about three hundred people were holding a Bible service each Sunday in front of the Isolotto church.

"They sent me up to mediate," Mirante continued. "I was totally converted to the parishioners' side. These people are good Catholics who ask nothing more than the holy freedom proclaimed for the Church by John. I decided they needed support, not discipline, and I made a statement on their behalf. I was ordered back to Rome immediately and told to say nothing more on the case under pain of excommunication. A week later I was expelled from the Jesuit order. My papers and books were confiscated, my orphanage was taken away from me, and I was told to report to the archbishop of Reggio di Calabria if I wished to continue to serve God as a priest. I am staying now with friends in Rome."

"I'm appalled," Matthew Mahan said. "That's all I can say. But what—what else can I say—or do?"

"I will learn by your example. I can never forget you were—"

Tautly, Matthew Mahan finished his sentence. "Consecrated by John. But don't expect to see a saint like him in these shoes."

"I know, I know," Mirante said. "And tomorrow you will take an oath of fealty to the new Pope."

What, Matthew Mahan asked himself, should he do with this unhappy man? He took out his checkbook. "You will need some money. Here's five hundred dollars to keep body and soul together for a month or so while you decide what to do."

"Let me assure you, Eminence, the loyalty of the beggar is to the man who lifts him from the gutter. So it will be with this one."

"I'm sure it will. Just so you don't see me as another John. I have no pretensions to that kind of holiness. A bishop has to run his diocese with the greater good of the greater number in mind."

He stopped, distressed at the implications of what he had just said. But wasn't it true? Did all the emotion of the last two days wither in the cold light of this premise? No, both realities must be sustained. He stood up. "I'm afraid I'm tired, Giulio."

Mirante knelt and tried to kiss Matthew Mahan's ring.

"Oh, no, please, Giulio. . . ." He helped the fragile man to his feet and threw his right arm around him. Where have you seen someone do that? As he closed the door he remembered. It was John. The way John had greeted him in the Vatican on his first visit.

THEY were driving through Rome's darkening streets. Beside Dennis, Bishop Cronin was strangely silent. Beyond the bishop was Matthew Mahan's somber profile. You would think we were going to a funeral, Dennis mused. But a cardinal was the Pope's man, and old Davey did not want to see Matthew Mahan become anybody's man. Why? There was something mysterious between those two, an understanding they shared about the Church.

It had surfaced last night when the cardinal came into their room and told them to forget about going to Isolotto. He and Goggin had been outraged, but Cronin was amazingly mild about it. I couldn't agree with you more, Matt, he had said. They had talked for a few moments. Then Matthew Mahan had urged Dennis to go see Sister Helen Reed. "Talk to her about her father. I've never seen anything so cruel. . . ." He told them about the visit to her pensione.

Go see Sister Helen Reed. An episcopal command. Why had he tried to make excuses, while Goggin eyed him mordantly? Was he afraid of what might happen? Torn between sex and your priest-hood? But there was no conflict in the church of tomorrow, where every act of love would be equally valued. Dennis squirmed in his seat. He did not believe it. The mind mocked hope.

But he had gone to see Sister Helen, and they had another lunch on the terrace. Helen was furious. There were only *two* women employed in the entire Vatican. And she had not even seen Cardinal Antoniutti. Yes, she was assured, the matter would be brought to the cardinal's attention. An answer before she left Rome? Impossible. . . . The cardinal's duties, my dear sister . . .

Dennis tried to joke her into a better humor. He told her why Matthew Mahan had sent him. With money enough for the best lunch on the menu. They would start with champagne, then discuss their parent problems. His mother, her father. But seriously, her father was a charming man. Why?

Yes, through it all there *was* a priest's concern. What was it, exactly? Perhaps you are about to discover something essential. You are the enemy of cruelty and hate, the apostle of compassion, forgiveness. Marvelous. So is Mother. So is Il Papa. What if that's all there was to it?

Then there were her hands. Leading you up the stairs. Today what would it be? Celibate caressing? No, no, no. Today would be the love of the man for the woman. Sunlight and darkness. Suddenly, a tearful woman in your arms: Hold me hold me hold me please hold me. Dennis can we really love each other?

"Is THERE A RECEPTION after this?" Matthew Mahan asked now, in the car on the way to St. Peter's.

"A brief one, our monsignor says. No drinks."

"Good. My stomach is killing me. Did you get anywhere with Sister Helen?"

For a minute Dennis thought he would strangle. "No. She is—convinced that her father is the personification of racist reaction."

"What nonsense. Where do people her age get these ideas?"

A half hour later Matthew Mahan sat in the Hall of Benedictions, directly above the entrance to St. Peter's Basilica. There were about two thousand people in the huge room, and at least a thousand of them were Americans. The thirty-four new cardinals sat on the right, the hundred or so senior cardinals on the left, all dressed in ceremonial red with their white lace rochets. Before them, in his throne on a platform, sat Paul VI in white robes and a red cape fringed with ermine.

The huge chair in which Paul sat made him look almost ludicrously small. He spoke, in Latin, of the importance of cardinals in the structure of the Church. The task, he said, was to build up the Church. He called on them to serve, to witness, to sacrifice for the truth. Above all, he depended on them for their unswerving support of the Prince of the Apostles. He hoped he would always be able to say, "You continued with me in my trials."

As in the last consistory, in 1967, Paul was making his point that the College of Cardinals was no anachronism, as many leading churchmen had been saying. Cardinal Suenens of Belgium had recently suggested that an assembly of bishops should replace the cardinals as electors of the Pope.

It was easy enough to explain. Whether the explanation was sweet or sour depended on your point of view. Sour: The Curia had no intention of surrendering control of the Church to a bunch of unknowns. As long as they handpicked the cardinals, they were almost certain to have one of their own in the Chair of Peter. True, the system wasn't perfect. A secret saint like John XXIII might slip by them once in a century. Sweet: When you have inherited a system that has worked for four hundred years, you are not inclined to surrender it to possibly unstable critics. Mater Ecclesia endures forever; the critics disappear.

Pope Paul was again making it clear that the Chair of Peter had

no intention of abandoning its claim to absolute authority over the entire Church. Wasn't it the only note he could sound? The responsibility for abandoning authority might be more agonizing than the results of wielding it. Was there a place between these alternatives? Was that where Michelangelo's *Moses* was looking with such hunger? Was that where John XXIII lived? O Lord, tell us what we are doing wrong, Matthew Mahan prayed.

Now the Pope asked each of them to take his vow. There was, he explained, a short addition to the oath, designed to ensure his access to the counsel of all the cardinals.

The priest standing to the right of the papal throne began to read the vow, and the cardinals repeated it after him, each inserting his own name in the first sentence:

> "I, Matthew Mahan, Cardinal of the Holy Roman Church, promise and swear that from this hour on, for as long as I live, I shall be firmly faithful to Christ and His Gospel and obedient to Saint Peter and the Holy Apostolic Roman Church and to the Supreme Pontiff Paul VI and his successors lawfully and canonically elected: furthermore that I shall never divulge to anyone the deliberations entrusted to me by them either directly or indirectly to their damage or dishonor unless with the consent of the apostolic see.
> "May the all-powerful God so help me."

While he repeated these words, Matthew Mahan kept his eyes on the Pope's face. He felt an intense desire to locate this man in his own soul. He was vowing personal loyalty, personal obedience to this man—a huge step beyond the loyalty and obedience he owed him as head of the Church, and he was prepared, truly prepared, to say these words. But not the last added passage. With the vow of silence a worm of nasty distrust entered. The hallmark of authoritarianism, Cronin would say. It always goes too far because it thinks in terms of power first and people second.

But he did not see this in Paul's face. He saw only sadness. Was it the sadness of defeat or of the ultimately lonely?

One by one now, as his name was called each cardinal mounted the platform and knelt while Paul solemnly placed the red biretta on his head, repeating in Latin the ancient exhortation "to be fearless, even to the shedding of blood, for the exaltation of the Holy Faith, for the peace and tranquillity of the Christian people, and for the liberty and expansion of the Holy Roman Church."

Finally, Matthew Mahan heard his own name. As he knelt before the Pope, their eyes met. The tiniest hint of a smile appeared on Paul's lips. *"Frater noster taciturnus,"* he whispered as he placed the red biretta on Matthew Mahan's head.

Our silent brother. Back in his seat, Matthew Mahan pondered the words. *Frater noster taciturnus,* our silent brother. Old Davey was right. They were aware of his silence on the birth control encyclical, the great issue of Paul's pontificate. The words were not a rebuke, but a plea, a somber, heartbreaking plea.

Then that insidious word *Romanita* flowered in his mind. The most cruelly effective moment had been selected to deliver the essential message: This honor we bestow on you, Cardinal Mahan, has nothing whatever to do with your three decades of labor on behalf of Holy Mother Church, even less with any spiritual pretensions. You have been bought, Cardinal Mahan, as part of a worldwide political campaign. When we dangled the bait you snapped at it, and now we are pulling on the hook.

No, he told himself desperately. *Frater noster taciturnus.* It was natural for Paul to think of him as a silent brother; couldn't he have placed the red hat on his brother's head as proof of his willingness to tolerate reasonable dissent, loyal freedom within the Church? Yes, yes. Matthew Mahan could not accept the cynical explanation. *Romanita.* The word quivered down his nerves like fingernails scratching a blackboard.

Cardinal Yu Pin, the archbishop of Nanking, China, was now replying on behalf of the new cardinals. Pope Paul announced that Jean Cardinal Villot was indeed to become his Secretary of State. And then the consistory was over. Paul left the Hall of Benedictions, and laymen and priests swarmed around their cardinals. Matthew Mahan smiled, nodded, and shook hands while the words echoed in his mind. *Frater noster taciturnus.*

They drove directly to the Hotel Excelsior, where all of the Mahanites, as Dennis called them, were giving a dinner for their hero. Speaker after speaker heaped praise on him until he began to wonder if they were talking about somebody else. He stood up, finally, to cries of "Speech, speech," and good-humoredly denied it all. Informally, then, he rambled from memory to humorous memory, speaking to individuals in the audience.

Dennis sat in the back of the hall listening to the adulatory laughter. Why aren't you laughing? he asked himself. Was it this afternoon's lovemaking in the Pensione Christina that made you unable to tolerate Mahan's sentimentality? He stood up. The cardinal was still talking. There was only the slightest break as their eyes met. "I don't want you to think of me as Cardinal Mahan. I hope I'll always be Father Matt to every one of you. There's only one way in which I want to be a cardinal. In Latin the word means hinge. I want to be a man who opens doors, doors to hope, to faith in God; doors to love for every person in the city."

Tremendous applause. Dennis turned his back on those noble words and rushed to the door. Out in the corridor, the pain in his chest was like the thrust of a dagger. It was freedom he was fighting to preserve. Freedom from that complex man who combined roars and smiles, power and guile, fear and love. Summed up in one unbearable word. Father.

MATTHEW Mahan's miter pressed painfully on his throbbing temples as the procession of white- and gold-robed cardinals left the Chapel of the Pietà and began the long walk to St. Peter's main altar. They could hear through the open front doors the distant sounds of bands playing and crowds cheering. It was May 1, and Rome's Communists were filling the city's streets with pageantry and protest. Out there, some might say, was the voice of the future. Here they were about to reenact a ceremony that was two thousand years old.

Rome's streets had echoed to the march of many legions. It was easy to say that the Communists out there were another false answer to man's perpetual search for worldly happiness; to say simply that here within these sacred walls was the true answer. But the hostility of the young had sharpened Matthew Mahan's eyes to incongruities. Ahead of him marched thirty-three men like himself, princes of the Church, dressed in white and gold. Should a church created by a man who said *Blessed are the poor in spirit* have princes? His eyes rested on monuments to other popes, egotistical Renaissance princes. What did *they* have to do with the simple men in dusty robes who trudged the roads of Palestine? *The foxes have holes, and the birds of the air nests: but the son of man hath not where to lay his head.*

Who was sending him these thoughts? Was it the voice of John XXIII? His mind drifted back to last night. The party had ended in his suite with a dozen or so close friends killing off some good champagne, which was why his head was aching and his stomach twinging. They had spent the last half hour discussing the difference between Popes John and Paul, and he had surprised himself by strenuously defending Paul: Turning the Church in a new direction was an immense responsibility; it had to be done slowly. But inevitably, he found himself talking more about John. . . .

John loved to walk. The first time I met him, in Paris, he walked my legs off. And I was a chaplain in an infantry regiment. So he had been, come to think of it. I never could figure out what we had in common. He was really an intellectual, you know. He used to call me his American education. He must have asked me a couple of hundred questions about America, that first day. We were the future, he said. Later, he called me his American son. It sounds better in Italian. More playful. *Mio figlio Americano* . . .

A roar of acclaim filled the cathedral. The crowd was greeting Pope Paul. He moved on to the high altar, and there, with the thirty-four new cardinals, he began celebrating Mass.

Matthew Mahan raised his eyes above the blaze of light that engulfed them and glimpsed familiar faces in the stands. His eyes sought the face of Pope Paul, whose hands were outstretched, reading in Latin the prayer of the Mass. The Gospel was from Saint Matthew and told the story of Jesus' failure in the synagogue of his native Nazareth. "The people asked, *Is not this the carpenter's son? . . . Jesus said to them: A prophet is not without honour, save in his own country, and in his own house.*"

Matthew Mahan thought of Pope John. To these Romans he had been the peasant from Bergamo, and now they were doing their best to keep him in the grave by calling him Good Pope John, the people's Pope. Good for an illustration on a holy card, but it would take a hundred years to repair the damage to the Church. So said the realist, the wielder of power. Was this the voice that had whispered to Matthew Mahan yesterday? The voice of the modern power broker, coolly rounding up the lost sheep by tempting him with trinkets of red and gold? No, he still refused to believe it. The sadness of Paul bespoke his innocence.

After the sermon, the Pope descended to a simple chair at the foot of the altar. Again the names of the new cardinals were read out, and each advanced to kneel while the Pope placed a plain gold ring on the fourth finger of his right hand. "Receive the ring from the hand of Peter and may the love of the Prince of the Apostles strengthen ever more your love of the Church."

Again Matthew Mahan was one of the last called. As he knelt before the Pope and their eyes met, he again searched desperately for the truth he was seeking on Paul's face. Concern and sadness were there, gentleness and resignation. The contrast between this man's delicate personality and John's earthy reality so overwhelmed him that he almost repeated to this visibly suffering man John's unforgettable greeting at the opening session of Vatican II: "*I am Joseph your brother.*" What was the full quotation? . . . *whom you sold into Egypt. Be not afraid, and let it not seem a hard case that you sold me into these countries; for God sent me before you into Egypt for your preservation.* Yes, those words would proclaim his fraternity. They would also declare his forgiveness of one who had sold *him* into bondage. As the Pope slipped the ring onto his finger, Matthew Mahan found himself compressing his lips, as if he feared he might actually say the words.

To his dismay, with those unspoken words came a surge of anguish—the very opposite of the peaceful humility he had longed for—and this Pope suddenly seemed to personify the fragility and weariness of the old world, struggling to come to terms with the new. It was Matthew Mahan's country, with its vision of freedom as a spiritual necessity, that was creating this travail. Trust us, he wanted to whisper. Have faith in us and we will make you free.

He started back to his seat, voices shouting inside him. Who do you think you are, Mahan? The accidental archbishop lecturing the successor of Saint Peter. You are a fool. He did not know where he was. Cardinal Dearden reached out and gently guided him. As he sat down, his body was shaken by an unbelievable pain. The rest of the Mass was a blur. Going down the aisle, smiling and nodding, his head afloat on a rubber neck. If Dennis had not been just outside, he would never have found the limousine. At the Hassler, the driver bade him an extravagant good-by. He leaned against the car and pulled a thousand-lira note from his pocket. "Give that to him," he said to Dennis. Slowly, carefully, he reached the lobby without attracting any attention.

"What's the rest of today's schedule?" he asked Dennis.

"Lunch here with your seminary class."

"Oh, yes. Yes. I should go, but—" A spasm hit him, the worst one yet. He stumbled out of the elevator. "Dear Jesus—Dennis, put your arm around me." They walked to his room like a three-legged man. "I'm afraid—the ulcer's kicking up." He retched and suddenly his mouth was full of blood. He stumbled to the bathroom. Coming back, wiping his mouth, he said, "You'll have to go down and apologize to them, Dennis. Say I've got a virus."

Dennis nodded and departed. Matthew Mahan lay in bed, shuddering with anticipation before every spasm and almost crying out in agony when it hit. Here is the real teacher of humility, my dear prince of the Church. Should he call Bill Reed? No, he knew what was wrong. He had brought this on himself by ignoring his diet. He had no desire to be lectured like a naughty boy.

Downstairs, Dennis McLaughlin listened through a long lunch to the class of '39 uninhibitedly recalling their seminary days. To hear them tell it, they were a bunch of rowdies. There was Eddie ("the Mug") McGuire; next to him George Petrie of cultured voice and elegant phrase; then nervous, reticent prison chaplain Peter Foley, the only man who did not have a parish. Fifteen of them in all sat here paying homage to the man who had been their leader "from the foist day inside the wall," as Eddie the Mug put it. "Remember Matt's imitation of the Old Man?"

Just then from the doorway a voice droned: "I want you young men to know how lucky you are to be here at Rosewood."

The room exploded into shouts of joy. "It's the big cheese himself," rasped Eddie McGuire, raising his well-filled brandy glass.

Matthew Mahan stood there smiling. He looked terrible. His face had a deathly pallor. In spite of his protests, Dennis vacated his seat at the table and sat in another against the wall. A waiter came in and Matthew Mahan asked for a glass of milk.

They were boys again, Dennis thought, listening to the guffaws, watching them pound their fists on the table with glee. Maybe they were always boys, condemned forever to cavort in the boys' playground behind chastity's barbed-wire fence.

Was that true? Did they act any differently from any other random group of alumni thirty years out? Probably not. No matter how excluded you feel by the generation gap, there is a link between you and these men. No. That word suggests chains. What held you was a living thing, a sense of something shared. They had kidded him about being a runaway Jesuit, wanted to know how he survived working for the "eminent slave driver." It had been a strange, exhilarating experience. What they really shared was this big, smiling man sitting in the seat of honor.

The milk had dampened Matthew Mahan's pain. Eddie McGuire was making a speech. He vowed that they had debated for weeks over what to give their new cardinal to commemorate his elevation. He didn't seem to have any needs. So they decided to give him something personal. A certificate proving that he was a cardinal, written by George Petrie, the best Latinist in the class, and surrounded by their pictures, proving that they weren't fictitious witnesses. "But when we got here," Eddie went on, "we went slightly nuts. We decided to get you a real present." Bending while he talked, Eddie fished from under the table a sleek-looking multiband radio in a walnut case. "The guy we bought it from guaranteed us you could get the Vatican on it. We couldn't think of anything a cardinal needed more these days."

For an appalling moment Matthew Mahan did not know whether he was going to laugh or weep—or snarl. *I am Joseph, your brother.* The infinite sadness in Paul's eyes. Did they *know* what his elevation really meant? Were they mocking him, too, this little circle, his old reliables? The truth, how often it comes hurtling at us unexpectedly, the truth on the lips of poor old Eddie McGuire, the class joker. It was too much, too much to bear.

What could he say to these old friends without destroying this happy occasion? Weren't they a mirror image of what had gone wrong? Hadn't they settled for something safer—doing the job? No, that was unfair. Unjust to Peter Foley, to Eddie, who gave tirelessly to his parishioners, to a half dozen others. Don't, the new cardinal told himself, let your own sense of personal failure ruin your appreciation of these good men.

But too many of his priests were satisfied with just "doing the job." And he was guiltier than all of them—he had been too busy doing *his* job to lead them in the right direction.

"Matt—are you okay?"

Eddie McGuire's familiar croak returned him to reality. "What? Sure . . . I'm all right, Eddie." He was on his feet now. "I'm just a little stunned. I couldn't help thinking just now, there isn't a man in this room who isn't doing a good job. And that includes me. But is that good enough for us?" What better place to start changing their complacent mediocrity? But the last thing they wanted was a pep talk. Yet this was no pep talk. This was from his soul to their souls. How could he make them see it? Only by sharing his failures.

"The other night I met a woman here in Rome, a woman from our diocese. I sent her here fifteen years ago to get an annulment. But that wasn't the real reason I sent her. I sent her because I didn't have the spiritual strength to cope with her agony. She never got her annulment. She knew she never would. She remained here to spare me. Yes, even to save me from my guilt, my failure. We're all doing our jobs. But our jobs don't seem to include going out, searching for these people. *The lost sheep.* Yet we know how important our Lord thought they were. When I get home, I'm going to dedicate myself, and if possible our archdiocese, to this mission. I'm depending on you for support."

The smiles had faded into bafflement now. They didn't even know what he was talking about.

His eyes blurred with tears. He picked up his radio and walked dazedly away from them, his head down. In the silence he heard Peter Foley say softly, "God bless you, Matt."

Then Eddie McGuire began to roar out "Auld Lang Syne," and in a moment everyone was singing it. Matthew Mahan stood in the doorway smiling at them and then walked unsteadily to the elevator. He did not realize Dennis McLaughlin was beside him until he heard him murmur anxiously, "Are you all right?"

He nodded. "They didn't know what I was talking about."

"Maybe some of them did. I did." Dennis's voice trembled slightly. The burdens, the pain vanished from Matthew Mahan's body and mind. There had been a beginning, a new beginning, after all.

CARDINAL Mahan sat with Mary Shea on the terrace of her penthouse sipping the sweet wine known as Lacrima Christi. Moonlight glistened on her silver hair. "I'm so glad you could give me this last night, Matt."

"You would have had that anyway. I'm glad I was able to give you—the rest of it, Mary. What we said."

"What *you* said."

They had eaten in her apartment. Savory fettuccine, delicately herbed roast lamb, cool red Valpolicella, endive salad. Most of it was off his diet, but two days of living on mush had soothed his stomach. It was not his stomach that worried him anyway; it was his spirit, and in some profound, mysterious way it was linked with this woman's spirit. To heal himself he must heal her.

So he had reached out, clumsily confessing everything. He began with his physical wound, the ulcer; went on to what had so shaken him in the Church of St. Peter in Chains. He had concealed nothing, not even the Pope's tormenting words, *Frater noster taciturnus,* Paul's sadness, and the insane temptation to reassure him; but above all, the desolating sense of guilt, of remorse, that involved her and the Church and his priesthood.

Mary had listened, deeply moved. When he began to tell her about his floundering speech to his seminary classmates, she cried out, "Oh, Matt, don't be so hard on yourself, don't." But she had let him silence her with a wave of his hand. She knew—she was too sensitive not to know—what he was doing. He was stripping away the Roman collar, the sacerdotal robes, coming down from the altar in a nakedness more real, more meaningful than flesh.

Were they two in one spirit now, truly one? Otherwise what he was about to say would be rejected with scorn or rage or perhaps despair. "You know what grieves me most, Mary? I've been afraid to say it to you, afraid for—all the reasons you can imagine. I think you should marry again. I think you should have married again four or five years ago."

"Why, Matt?"

"Because you're a loving person."

"I have my son. You. The Church—"

"Your son doesn't need your love anymore. I can't return your love in the way—the only way—it deserves to be returned. And the Church—you can't love the Church, Mary, the way you're trying to love it, without being wounded."

"You're speaking from experience?"

"I suppose I am. But I can bear it—because it's my choice."

"I made some choices, too, Matt, fifteen years ago."

"You can love someone else, if you open your heart to it."

"Are you telling me to walk out of the Church?"

"No. I'm telling you that if you marry and come home, I'll receive you into the Church with my blessing. I'm going to begin a program in the diocese, Mary, for people who have divorced and remarried in good conscience. It's within my power as a bishop to do this; there are bishops doing it now. I didn't have the courage before. I thought of what the conservatives would say. And of people like yourself who had spent fifteen, twenty desolate years. I didn't know how I could face you. But now—I'm facing you."

"I don't know whether I can ever love anyone but you, Matt. And tonight makes the possibility even more dubious."

"That saddens me terribly, Mary. Promise me this much. You'll try. You'll at least consider offers."

"Now you sound like a marriage broker. What are you going to do, raffle me off to the highest bidder?"

"If I could, it would solve my fund-raising problems overnight."

"Don't. I don't want to joke about it."

"Why not? We celibates live paradoxically. We laugh and cry at the same time."

Mary inclined her head toward St. Peter's dome riding on the floodlight's glow. "Have they approved this program, Matt?"

"No. That's another reason why I hesitated."

"What if they say no?"

For the first time all night his stomach throbbed ominously. "Let's face it when—and if—it happens."

"I'm not worrying about myself, Matt, it's you."

"I know."

XI

THE big jet poised at the head of the long runway like a sprinter waiting for the gun. They were off, racing down the concrete for a nerve-twisting sixty or seventy seconds, and into a forty-degree climb. At three thousand feet the plane leveled off. Matthew Mahan unbuckled his seat belt, stretched his legs, and thought about the past three days. The anticipation of his evening with Mary had given him a curious feeling of freedom, a euphoria that had carried him through the concluding ceremonies. On the day after the Mass in St. Peter's, Pope Paul had held a special audience for the friends and families of the new cardinals.

This had been pleasant but perfunctory. The Pope had obviously selected in advance something nice to say about each new cardinal. He called Matthew Mahan the "master builder," to which in an irreverent moment he had almost replied, Yes, they used to call me the patron saint of the contractors. Instead, he disavowed the compliment and, looking at Mike Furia and the rest of his moneyed circle, said it was these dedicated people who had made possible the miraculous multiplication of parish buildings.

The next day Cardinal Mahan had taken possession of his titular church—a new church in a new Roman working-class district that had been donated by a wealthy Italian American and named for America's first saint, Mother Cabrini. He was unbothered by being given this church instead of one of the historic Roman churches, such as SS. John and Paul, which Cardinal Cooke had received as an inheritance from the late Cardinal Spellman. He recalled that Spellman had spent a million on SS. John and Paul, and said to Terry Malone that they might get off without spending a cent. This hope had swiftly withered, and he'd found himself underwriting a new building that eventually could cost them two hundred thousand dollars. But American cardinals were supposed to be rich. How could he disappoint his adopted parishioners? He had yet to hear the lecture that would certainly emanate from Terry Malone's disapproving iron jaw as soon as they got home and faced the diocesan deficit.

The more Matthew Mahan thought about returning home, the more uneasy he became. Resuming the old way of life, playing the smoothie, was out of the question. But the alternative? That remained a mystery. If the cardinalate was the culmination of his clerical career, what he felt now was not culmination but collapse.

Mike Furia was sitting beside him reading *Business Week.* They had had very little to say to each other since their unpleasant exchange. "Are we still friends?" Matthew Mahan asked.

"I hope so," Mike said, holding out his hand.

A crunching handshake and the air was cleared. But Matthew Mahan knew that the old camaraderie could never come back. They began discussing the deficit.

"Have you ever thought of the obvious solution?" Mike said. "To get those parochial schools off your back?"

"It's been suggested most often by our friend Mayor O'Connor."

Mike was undeterred. "I haven't had the nerve to say this before, Matt. You're into too many things. You're like a company that's putting out too many products. When a corporation realizes this, it cuts back. Concentrates on what it does best. Now this may make you mad as hell, but you don't do education best. Yet you're spending ninety percent of your income on it. It makes no sense."

Matthew Mahan stubbornly shook his head. Here Mike was, asking him to turn his back on Matthew the master builder, on the very part of himself that the Pope had saluted. Those were *his* schools. "There are too many people involved, Mike. Too many people who've made sacrifices—"

"Of course, you couldn't junk everything overnight. You'd throw the city into chaos. But start phasing them out . . ."

Another shake of his head, and the conversation ended. "Mike," Matthew Mahan said after a minute or two. "Would you consider taking some advice from me—even if I won't take any from you?"

"Try me," he said.

"Get a divorce. And get married again."

"After the way you worked on me to make it a separation?"

"We were both being men of the world, Mike. I wanted to keep you around as a fund raiser. You wanted to keep on building schools and hospitals for me." Mike nodded, acknowledging that the truth was now being exchanged. "When we get back, Mike, I'm starting a new program—receiving divorced Catholics back into the Church if their divorce is in good conscience."

Mike stared at his hands. "Funny you should tell me this. I was— I thought of getting married again—just the other night. That disaster with Betty—it hurt me more than I admitted. . . ."

"To prove that I mean this for your sake, and only for your sake, I'm accepting your resignation as chairman of the cardinal's fund."

"Go to hell," Mike growled. "You're not getting it."

"I want it."

Mike managed a smile. "You missed a punch in the mouth the last time you gave me advice, your Eminence."

Matthew Mahan met the smile. "That's a risk us brainless clerics take every so often."

He left Mike alone to think and wandered through the plane. Many of the pilgrims were dozing. It made him feel better to discover that they were as weary as he felt. Dennis McLaughlin and

243

Davey Cronin were asleep side by side. He felt a rush of affection for both of them. "It looks like they'll stay out of trouble for the rest of the trip," he said to Bill Reed across the aisle.

Davey opened one eye and said, "The hell we will. I was just dreaming that you were crowned Pope."

"That's not a dream, that's a nightmare."

"Ah!" Cronin said, sitting up. "Pope of the reformed Church. Rome, you see, was destroyed, buried under tons of spaghetti—"

"Another word and you'll be anathema."

"I've been that for years. It's a grand feeling, Matt."

Back in his seat, Matthew Mahan took from his briefcase the Pope's latest statement on the liturgy. Immediately he found a phrase that made him grind his teeth: "We wish to give the force of law to all that we have set forth concerning the new Roman missal." Why that obnoxious phrase, "the force of law," to something associated with worship, an experience that had value only when it was free? He reminded himself of his vow of fidelity and obedience. But soon his jaw was clenching again. The Pope hoped that this new Mass meant the end of experimentation. The order of the Second Vatican Council to leave room for "legitimate variations and adaptations" must, of course, be obeyed. However, all variations and adaptations must be submitted to the Holy See.

Roman law, Roman legalism; couldn't Paul see how much damage it had already done to the Church? Didn't he realize this was not the way to run a church that only a few years before had gathered her bishops from all corners of the world to proclaim themselves in favor of holy freedom? Cronin was right. Brick by brick, the Curia was entombing Vatican II in traditional architecture that proclaimed business as usual.

Matthew Mahan snapped his briefcase shut. Forget it, forget it, he told himself. Such thoughts are useless.

Back in the second section, Dennis McLaughlin and Bishop Cronin were looking through a diary that their now mutual friend Goggin had smuggled out of the Vatican Library and photocopied for them. It was the private journal for the year 1870 of Cardinal Antonelli, the Secretary of State during Vatican Council I. He had opposed the council and deplored the idea of infallibility, but had had to swallow his objections under the imperious commands of Pio Nono. In revenge, he had kept a scrupulous record of the

Pope's constant efforts to control the council. Cronin was wildly excited. But the more Dennis read the more uneasy he became.

Did the evidence prove what Cronin was hoping to prove? Just because Pio Nono wanted his own way—infallibility at all costs—did that really invalidate the First Vatican Council? There was not as much freedom as there should have been. But still the opponents of infallibility had fought ferociously. There seemed to have been freedom of debate, as much as in the U.S. Congress. If infallibility were to be denied on scholarly grounds, the challenge had to go beyond merely the history of Vatican I—it had to stress the often ignored fact that Vatican I had been disrupted by the outbreak of war between France and Prussia. It had never really had a chance to address itself to the relationship between the bishops and the infallible Pope. And Vatican II, as Matthew Mahan had recently told him, was repeatedly frustrated by maneuvers of the Curia in *its* attempts to tackle this same fundamental problem. Perhaps the fathers of Vatican I had never intended the doctrine of infallibility to enhance the Pope's administrative and legal powers. And it was these powers to which the fathers of Vatican II had so clearly demonstrated their hostility.

Dennis turned to discuss this with Cronin. The old man's head nodded toward his chest. Rome had worn Davey out. For a moment Dennis was amused. Then an odd droop at the corner of the mouth suddenly troubled him. "Bishop, are you all right?"

Instead of answering, Cronin fell forward and was sliding off the seat when Dennis caught him and lifted him back. He was shocked by how little the old man weighed, "Dr. Reed—" But Bill Reed was nowhere in sight.

Frantically Dennis bolted into the forward section and found the doctor chatting with Matthew Mahan. "Bishop Cronin—he's fainted," Dennis whispered. The two men rushed back ahead of him. Cronin's breath was coming in noisy gasps. Jim and Madeline McAvoy hovered over him with exclamations of dismay.

Cronin gasped as Reed ripped away his collar. "I sound—worse than you, Dennis. Maybe it's one of your pills I need."

"Take it easy. Take it easy," said Bill Reed in a voice that struck Dennis as surprisingly gentle. He was taking the pulse.

"If 'twas easy," said Cronin, "it wouldn't be—so hard." His head flopped to one side and his eyes rolled back.

245

"Get a stewardess," said Bill Reed. "Pull up the arms of these seats." A stewardess was already there. She quickly turned three seats into a narrow bed. Bill Reed knelt beside the old man, his fingers still on his pulse.

"Is there anything you can do, Bill?" Matthew Mahan asked in a choked voice.

Reed shook his head. "You'd better pray."

Matthew Mahan stood in the doorway between the two sections and said, "Bishop Cronin, our old and dear friend, is gravely ill. Please join me in prayers for him." Dennis stared at the cardinal's rosary. "Our Father . . ." Matthew Mahan began.

"Give us this day our daily bread . . ." responded the voices of the pilgrims, Dennis's among them.

"Hail, Mary . . ." said the cardinal.

The response came from more than a hundred voices. "Holy Mary, Mother of God, pray for us sinners, now and at the hour of our death. Amen."

"Hail, Mary, full of grace . . ." said Matthew Mahan again.

Once more the response. In the tiny interval before it began, Dennis heard the harsh, painful sound of Cronin's breathing.

Five more times the Hail Mary was said. Bill Reed stood up. "You'd better give him the last rites, Matt."

"Get my briefcase, Dennis."

Numbly he obeyed. By the time he returned they had finished another Hail Mary. Matthew Mahan handed him the rosary. "Father McLaughlin will continue," he said. "I am going to give Bishop Cronin Extreme Unction."

Slowly, in the silence that was not really a silence, filled as it was by the jet engines' throb, Matthew Mahan removed Cronin's shoes and socks. There was a hole in the sole of the right sock. Dennis's eyes blurred when he saw it. He fingered the rosary dazedly for a moment, then pressed his thumb and forefinger on the ninth bead and began, "Hail, Mary . . ."

Matthew Mahan had the holy oil out now. Solemnly he anointed Bishop Cronin's eyes, ears, nose, mouth, hands, and feet, saying each time he placed his thumb on the old man's body, "Through this holy unction, and of His most tender mercy, may the Lord pardon thee whatsoever sins thou hast committed . . ." Dennis could not hear him. He only saw his lips moving.

246

As the cardinal finished anointing the feet, Dennis saw Cronin's eyes flutter. The rest of the plane responded to the tenth and final Hail Mary of the decade. Dennis paused, and he heard Cronin whisper hoarsely. "The Church, Matt. The poor dear suffering Church. You must speak out—save her from them—"

Matthew Mahan's response was so extraordinary that Dennis's lips were paralyzed on the word "Our" as he began the second decade of the Rosary. The big man bent his head low and lifted the small, frail old man up into his arms. Dennis had no idea how long he held him close. Time seemed to stop. As the cardinal slowly lowered his friend back on the seats, Dennis managed to continue. "Our Father, who art in heaven, hallowed be Thy name . . ."

Matthew Mahan asked Bill Reed a question. The doctor shook his head. Cronin saw, and understood. He was holding a cross— the cardinal's pectoral cross. With both hands Cronin raised it to his lips and then rested it on his chest.

For the next hour Dennis continued the Rosary, while Matthew Mahan knelt beside his old friend. The shadows deepened as the sun dwindled below the western horizon. For a while, death and darkness seemed synonymous. Only the plane, the thing of metal and wire that felt nothing, seemed alive. The cardinal was holding Cronin's right hand now. The bishop's other hand still clutched the gold cross. As Dennis reached the final Hail Mary of the fifth decade, the cardinal stood up and signaled him to stop. He turned to Bill Reed. "I think he's gone," he said.

Dr. Reed pressed his fingertips against Father Cronin's throat and nodded. He began to cover his face with a blanket. Matthew Mahan stopped him. "No, please don't cover him, Bill. Somehow that makes death seem shameful—"

"I'm sorry, but he has to be covered. We have the other passengers to consider. This could create hysteria."

It was the stewardess. The cardinal did not explode, as Dennis feared. "Of course, of course," he said, patting her shoulder. "But first we'd like to say a few prayers. There's nothing against that in the regulations, is there?"

"No—of course not, your Eminence. I guess—I'm more upset than anyone. I—I've never seen anyone die before."

Matthew Mahan took both her hands in his. "It's all right, it's all right. Sit down now and let me say a few words."

He stationed himself once more in the doorway between the two sections. "What has been a joyous experience has become a time of sorrow, and for no one more than me. I have lost one of my best, my oldest friends. But even in this sorrow I hope you can join me in finding a different kind of joy. David Cronin lived and died a priest. His thoughts were forever turned to others, offering them advice, help, love. Everyone who knew him came away richer in spirit. He brought the same selfless love to the Church. He never stopped thinking of ways to make it more holy, more responsive to the needs and the hopes of men and women everywhere. God grant us all the grace to follow his example.

"In a way, we have all been privileged to be present at his death. He met God's summons with a faith that abolished fear. I would like you to come from your seats one or two at a time and kneel beside him with me, and say a personal prayer."

One by one they came, and many of them wept. By the time the last one—Mike Furia—knelt beside the cardinal and whispered, "I know how you feel, Matt," it was totally dark outside. Matthew Mahan remained on his knees, gazing at the silent, shadowed face until the pilot announced that they were beginning their descent.

THEY landed smoothly. As they taxied to the terminal, Dennis saw an ambulance waiting, its lights flashing. Bill Reed joined two airport policemen who took Bishop Cronin's body off the plane.

In the terminal the pilgrims clustered around Matthew Mahan for a subdued farewell. Photographers and reporters crowded in. Jack Murphy invited the cardinal to a VIP lounge where TV cameras were set up. Reporters fired questions at him as he walked. What had he discussed with the Pope? The state of the Church? Was the Pope critical of the American role in the Vietnam war? Any hint that Rome might abolish clerical celibacy? The cardinal parried these queries lightly. Then Tom Sweeney of the *Garden Square Journal* asked him, "Do you have any comment on the recent revelations about your finances and personal life?"

"What are you talking about?"

"There was a series of articles published about you during the past week in the *Hard Times Herald*—the underground paper, quoting a lot of confidential information leaked by someone in the chancery office."

Already dazed by Bishop Cronin's death, Dennis McLaughlin now found himself paralyzed. Leo, his own brother, had not waited to find out the truth. The truth was not important. In the VIP lounge, he saw Leo slumped in a chair just beyond the glare of the television lights. There was something disturbing about his smile—it was so brainlessly mocking. Almost immediately Dennis saw himself arguing in a new, more serious way with Leo. Something very important had happened to him in Rome.

Questions flew from unidentified reporters. The joy in their eyes was blatantly sadistic as they dealt with an exhausted, emotionally battered man.

Before the battery of microphones, Cardinal Mahan was telling Jack Murphy about Bishop Cronin's death, and about his own renewed dedication to the people of the archdiocese. Mayor O'Connor came on to welcome him home and say some effusive things about his importance to the "spiritual progress" of the city. The cardinal replied warmly, and the ceremony was over. Dennis was ridiculously grateful for television's superficial approach to news.

"What the devil were they talking about?" the cardinal asked Dennis in the limousine. "These articles about my finances?"

Confess now? Dennis asked himself. No, it would embarrass the cardinal in the presence of Mike Furia, the McAvoys, and Bill Reed. You can admit the truth in private and disappear quietly. No need to tell the world that his Eminence had naïvely employed a betrayer in his own office.

Matthew Mahan headed for that office the moment they reached the residence. "Call Joe Cohane at the *Beacon*," he said. "Ask him what he knows about these articles."

"You don't have to do that," Dennis said in a leaden voice. "I can tell you. My brother wrote them—under the by-line Leo the Great. Here are the clips. He gave them to me at the airport."

Matthew Mahan sat down and began to read. The columns were sneering attacks on the way he ran the archdiocese. When it came to money, Leo the Great had written, Cardinal Mahan "behaved like a Renaissance pope." Leo described the "outrageous sums" he gave to "favorites" who were working as missionaries—really colonialist emissaries of American power—in Brazil. His Eminence's personal finances were "a smelly mystery." No accounting was ever made of them. But the cost of running the episcopal residence came to $32,567.30 last year, and "travel expenses" for his Eminence came to $26,896.50. "Staggering sums" were obviously funneled to his seven nieces and nephews, who had charge accounts at all the city's department stores, payable by the chancery office. In fact, tongues often wagged in the chancery about the cardinal's long and frequent visits to his widowed sister-in-law, "an attractive matron in her forties." Then there was the svelte divorcee, Mary Shea, whom the cardinal visited regularly in Rome. As for Matthew Mahan's rating as a pastor, he was "a conscienceless careerist," in secret disagreement with the Pope on birth control, but greedy enough to sell his convictions for the price of a red hat. At heart he was an authoritarian of the worst kind—interested only in maintaining his personal power.

In Matthew Mahan's mind one part of the man he had been until he went to Rome ten days ago filled the room with roaring rage. Then another self, a vision not yet real, faced Leo with tears on his cheeks and asked him why he inflicted these wounds. No, he could never do that. He looked up at Dennis's stricken face. Anguish like that which had erupted when he knelt before Paul to accept the ring vibrated in his flesh. "Dennis. Do many people know who Leo the Great is?"

Dennis nodded. "Can I sit down?" He slumped into a chair. "I—I want to confess something that will—probably end our relationship. Those columns are my fault. I knew how he felt about you. I—encouraged it. I mean—I was the older brother. I was the one who filled him with bitterness about the Church."

Matthew Mahan saw pain, essential pain, on Dennis's face. "Maybe I was changing when I came here. Or it started here. I don't know. But I didn't understand what was happening. I didn't know what I felt about you until—until Rome. I had visions of this scene—of your firing me—with an exchange of mutual insults. And now . . ." His eyes were wet. "All I can say is I'm sorry."

"Firing you? I'm not firing you." Matthew Mahan's voice was quiet. Maybe that roaring, raging primary self could be conquered yet. "You and your brother are not the same person, Dennis, no matter how much you love him. A man is not condemned for what his brother does. He shouldn't condemn himself either."

The truth, now is the time for the *whole* truth, Dennis murmured to himself. Even if by telling it you destroy your chance to prove

251

that you love this man. "It's worse than that," he said. "I leaked information. From your files. I suggested things. . . ."

Too late, thought Matthew Mahan, too late. You had sensed a chasm between you. But was it really too late? There was what had happened at the cemetery. There was the moment in the elevator after the class of '39 lunch; his old friends hadn't understood, but Dennis had. Matthew Mahan lit a cigarette. The match trembled slightly. Dennis McLaughlin found it easier to watch the trembling flame than to look the cardinal in the face.

"Give me ten minutes to think," Matthew Mahan said.

Dennis nodded and silently departed. Matthew Mahan stared at the smoking cigarette between his fingers. He started to stub it out, then suddenly crumpled it into a ripped, broken little pile. Rage came storming up through his body into his arms, his hands. He raised his big clenched fists and brought them down on his antique table desk with a tremendous crash.

Call him back, flay him alive, whispered a voice.

Desperately he prayed. Lord, give me wisdom, give me the grace. He paced the office, struggling for control, and slowly the rage ebbed from his body. He sat down and called Dennis back.

"I think what hurts me most," he said, picking up the sheaf of articles and letting it flop back on his desk like a dead snake, "is the stuff about me giving money to my sister-in-law. It can't be more than three or four thousand a year. Old Hogan, now, had only one relative, a niece, a single girl who had a very good job. One Christmas he gave her a mink coat that was worth ten thousand all by itself. Year in, year out, he spent at least thirty thousand on her. And she didn't need it!" Matthew Mahan sighed. He was sounding silly. He was too hurt, too tired to think straight. "I guess it's an old story. You tell yourself you're doing better than the previous regime. You never stop to think how you look to the next generation." He tried to smile, and failed. "Cohane *will* want to fire Leo," he said.

"He's already quit. I'm glad he's out of it. He's too involved with the Church. It's almost—sick."

"For a layman, you mean," Matthew Mahan said with a tired smile. "It's interesting that an apostle of the younger generation like yourself should reach that conclusion. We're always begging laymen to get more involved. But I'm afraid there's a limit. It has something to do with priesthood, I think. A layman can't understand that idea, really, not the depths of it. No matter how much we priests try to get in step with the twentieth century, we're still men apart. There's a terrible loneliness in that truth, Dennis, but a little glory, too. Our kind of glory. . . . How are you feeling?"

"Terrible."

"I mean physically. Why don't we do a little work before we go to bed? At least organize this mess. Disasters we can't do anything about we'll put at that end." He pointed to the right. "The trivia at the other end. And the crises in the middle."

For a moment Dennis thought surely he was going to weep. He was being forgiven, without even the humiliation of hearing the words spoken. "I'm ready whenever you are," he said.

ALTHOUGH Matthew Mahan had been able to control his anger over Leo McLaughlin's vicious attack, he found it difficult to deal with its impact. Everywhere he looked it seemed to leer at him. At Holy Angels, Father Novak announced from the pulpit that he was leaving the priesthood. He denounced reactionary pastors and standpat archbishops who, he said, played the Vatican game and were rewarded with red hats. And even Monsignor O'Reilly managed to refer to Leo the Great's articles when he told his parishioners how lucky they were to be rid of Father Novak.

Father Vincent Disalvo was demanding a hundred thousand dollars in the name of the black community for his Council for Peace and Freedom. "Black people," he said, "are at least as important as Cardinal Mahan's relatives, clerical favorites, and great and good friends, who are reportedly devouring twice this figure each year from the chancery trough."

Even in the chancery office the slander was doing its deadly work. Chancellor Terry Malone asked for "an hour alone—I mean without Father McLaughlin around." He sounded so absurdly conspiratorial, Matthew Mahan almost laughed. "The vicar-general will be with me," Malone added.

The burly chancellor and the suave vicar-general arrived, solemn as men on the way to a grave. It soon became clear that they hoped they were digging one. "Your Eminence," Malone said. "At the risk of upsetting you, it is our considered advice that you should discharge Father McLaughlin."

253

"Why?"

"Are you going to issue a denial to those articles his brother wrote? Every priest in the archdiocese has read them. Joe Cohane says you could sue for libel and run Leo the Great and that hippie rag out of the state."

"I know. I prefer silence, Terry. Silence is the best answer."

"Then you must get rid of Father McLaughlin."

"*Why?*"

"We strongly suspect he leaked a lot of that information to his brother. A thorough investigation—by me personally—exonerates the chancery office. Who else could have done it?"

Be calm, Matthew Mahan. You are not dealing with stupid men. "Now, Terry," he said. "Those articles were such a mess of wild exaggerations, rumors, absurd charges. The fellow worked for the diocesan paper. He could easily have picked up most of his ideas just talking to priests who have no great love for me."

"There were facts that could only have come from our files. Financial facts that will upset a lot of younger priests. For the good of the archdiocese you should discharge him."

"I have absolute confidence in Father McLaughlin's loyalty to me," Matthew Mahan said. "What do you think, George?"

"Let me put it this way, Matt," Vicar-General Petrie said smoothly. "Even if he's innocent—which I am inclined to doubt—I think you have to make a show of cleaning house. A gesture of authority. Those articles were cleverly aimed at making you look not only corrupt but ridiculous. To keep the brother of the man who wrote them on your staff—in the most intimate of all jobs—suggests you may really be as foolish as they make you sound. I can't think of a better way to demolish your authority."

The vicar-general was crushingly right, and the voice in which he spoke—whose voice but Old Smoothie Mahan's?—gave the very advice he'd have given himself if he had never gone to the Church of St. Peter in Chains, never visited a cemetery in Nettuno, never walked a beach discussing moon shells and spirals and John XXIII with a young priest—

Terry Malone cleared his throat. He knew when to press an advantage. "George is speaking of the impact on your priests. Keeping McLaughlin around will have even a worse effect on the laity. The big givers. You know how conservative they are."

Yes, I know. Haven't I sold them carefully calibrated sections of my soul for twenty years? "Yes," he murmured. "This is sound advice. But there are other considerations—spiritual ones." The look of incomprehension on their faces stopped him. How could he explain to these men? He had never in all the years they had worked together had a personal conversation with either of them. "He's—he's fighting for his vocation, you see. I think I can—help."

It was hopeless. He was contradicting the argument he himself had used to hold the diocese together: The good of the majority was more important than the troubled individual. Somehow, he got the two men out of the office with promises to think the matter over very carefully.

Several days later he called Terry Malone in to tell him he wanted a million dollars to keep St. Clare's Hospital open, and twenty-five thousand to fund projects for inner-city nuns. The cardinal listened to forty-five minutes of protests. The chancellor left, assuring him that Monsignor O'Callahan, head of Catholic Charities, would be even more upset by these decisions.

He would wrestle with O'Callahan later. More urgent business was a conference with lean, intense Monsignor Tom Barker, head of his diocesan Rota. Barker, who had a doctorate in canon law from Rome, was aghast at the idea of receiving good-conscience divorced Catholics back into the Church. Every Vatican department concerned was sure to disapprove it. Matthew Mahan told Barker that he would take complete responsibility. Only then did the anxious canonist agree to write to the rotas where similar programs were already operating. After a long-faced Barker departed, Matthew Mahan dictated a letter to all his pastors, urging them to seek out divorced Catholics and advise them to petition the marriage tribunal.

The next day, Vicar-General Petrie reported that the Archdiocesan Association of Priests was about to move for a full report on the archdiocese's finances. Some militant members were planning a motion to demand that the cardinal explain his policies in person. In other words, defend himself against the accusations of Leo the Great. In the past, Matthew Mahan would have testily told George Petrie to make sure neither motion passed. But the cardinal could sense in the vicar-general's helplessness now a certain I-told-you-so satisfaction.

255

Matthew Mahan decided, however, that the best response was prompt publication of a full report, whether the Association of Priests' motion passed or not. "When can I get it, Terry?" he asked.

Chancellor Malone was appalled. "I have no idea. It's not something to rush into. I'll discuss it with our accountants and find out how long it would take to prepare judiciously." After getting buried in an hour-long lecture on thirty-two different "generally accepted accounting principles," Matthew Mahan realized he would be lucky to see a first draft in September.

The next day came a report that Monsignor O'Reilly was organizing suburban pastors to ask the cardinal to repudiate Leo's allegations with a ringing affirmation of *Humanae Vitae*. And then came Mike Furia and Chancellor Malone to hold a wake for the fund drive, which they estimated would fall two and a half million dollars short of the goal. It was especially disappointing to find that contributions had declined during this past week, despite the news coverage of his Eminence's triumphs in Rome.

"Maybe the answer is psychological," Matthew Mahan mused. "What does the average guy think when he sees pictures of his archbishop being dined at the best hotels in Rome, marching around in gold vestments? Maybe he thinks about his mortgage and decides the fund doesn't need him."

Terry Malone growled that at least they needn't debate building those new churches and schools in the suburbs.

"Do me a favor, will you, Terry?" Matthew Mahan asked. "Run a financial study of what our parochial schools will be costing us by 1976? Based on reasonable estimates of rising costs."

"I bet it will knock your head off," Mike Furia said.

Mike lingered after Terry Malone departed to tell Matthew Mahan that he was leaving for a long trip to check out his overseas companies. Mike had not resigned as chairman of the cardinal's fund, but this trip was the nearest thing to it. Even though Matthew Mahan had asked for the resignation, he felt as if his old friend were deserting him. Get used to it, a voice whispered.

Mike was absorbed in his own problems. "I thought you'd like to know I'm getting a divorce. My wife can't believe it. The animal is finally standing on his hind legs and fighting back."

The bitterness in these words pained Matthew Mahan. "Mike," he said. "Try to bring some charity—"

"Charity I'm trying. Five million bucks in stock."

"I mean charity—from the heart, Mike."

"I haven't got it, Matt. Not for her."

"All right, all right. At least you're not looking for revenge. I hope you get married again—soon."

"As a matter of fact, I've got someone in mind. But I haven't asked her, so I'm not telling you her name. It's probably a pipe dream anyway."

"I'll be praying for you, Mike, whether you like it or not."

No comment, only a brief smile from Mike.

The day's blows were not over. A call from Father Reagan at the university announced that nephew Timmy's scholarship had been discontinued. It seemed that the students demanded to know why a boy whose marks were slipping badly, and who was on drugs half the time, should have a scholarship. Father Reagan had been at a loss for a satisfactory explanation.

"Do you people *run* schools anymore?" Matthew Mahan asked crisply. "Lately I get the impression that they're running you."

"We're doing the best we can," Father Reagan said in a strangled voice. "I think your Eminence should know that Timmy is not exactly one of your admirers. He supplied a lot of material for those vicious articles on you."

"I hope you have evidence for that statement."

"We have a rather effective intelligence system, your Eminence. You could talk with the priest who runs it."

"No. I'll take your word for it," Matthew Mahan said.

He called his sister-in-law to tell her the bad news, and that he was being forced to cancel her charge accounts. Perhaps she had heard about the articles accusing him? No, she had heard nothing. He told her not to panic. He would ask Mike Furia to raise her salary. But cash would have to stop slipping through her fingers.

"I'll try, Matt," she promised. "But I just think it's terrible that anyone should attack you. . . ."

He agreed, no question about it, it was terrible that anyone should attack such a paragon of sanctity as Matthew Mahan. He hung up and stared out the window at the vanishing sunlight. Except for twenty minutes at lunch, he had been behind this desk all day. Dennis McLaughlin appeared in the doorway. "Why don't you take a nap before dinner, your Eminence?" he said.

257

"Didn't I tell you to call me Father?"

"I'm sorry—everyone else—"

"I can't do anything about the rest of them. But I've got you right under my thumb. It's Father or else."

"Or else you won't take a nap?" Dennis smiled.

For one moment Matthew Mahan felt almost good. A month ago Dennis would have retreated from the apparent rebuke. Did it mean anything? Was it worth the loss of respect and loyalty it might cost him—was already costing him—in his chancery, worth the possible wreck of his authority as bishop? Yes, he thought. Let the ninety-nine stay on the hills.

"All right. All right. I'll take a nap. For a man who's supposed to be an authoritarian, I spend an awful lot of my time around here taking orders."

XII

DENNIS McLaughlin stared gloomily at the letter from Monsignor Barker of the marriage tribunal. It was the fourth or fifth jittery letter from him in three months. Again he complained about the cardinal's good-conscience program. This time he wanted him to know that at a regional conference, all of the canon lawyers agreed that Matthew Mahan was breaking too sharply with tradition. "It was felt that any decision to undertake this practice should be a decision of the whole Church and not of one bishop or a group of bishops," Monsignor Barker wrote.

Dennis hated to give the letter to the weary man in the next room. It meant another hour of his time and energy consumed in cajoling Monsignor Barker from overt hostility to sullen docility again. These days there didn't seem to be a single thing the cardinal tried to do that wasn't met with a barrage of obstacles. Even his decision to keep St. Clare's Hospital open as an outpatient clinic had earned him nothing but brickbats. It would cost a million dollars. Too much, said Terry Malone. Too little, said Father Disalvo. The cardinal's announcement that the clinic would be set up and supervised without fee by one of the best doctors in the city—Dr. William Reed—fared no better. Totally unacceptable, said Disalvo. Reed was a rich folk's doctor, and Reed was white. The head of the hospital should be black—

Dennis's telephone rang. "Hello," Helen Reed said. "Are you busy?" This was one thing Matthew Mahan had accomplished, Dennis told himself. Through St. Clare's he had effected a reconciliation between Helen and her father. She had now moved back home.

"No more than the usual," Dennis said.

"Why don't you come over for dinner, then? Dad's meeting with the hospital's trustees. I'm eating alone."

Alone. The word tolled like an ominous bell in Dennis's mind. "I'd—love to come. But the cardinal may need me. He had another bad night."

"If he'd do what his doctor tells him—"

"I know, I know. Look, I'll call you back."

"Call by five. So I can cook something *decent*."

Dennis sat for a long moment moodily contemplating his mess of a life. A little therapy was in order. A letter to Goggin.

Dear Gog,

I told you in my midsummer communication about the horrible impact of the articles that my brother with my unholy help wrote on the cardinal. The explosion of disaffection goes right up to the chancellor and vicar-general. You can't conceive of the outrageous scenes at the deanery meetings, with the vicar-general (now also our most reverend auxiliary bishop) entertaining every kind of insulting motion from both conservatives and liberals, practically encouraging them to tear each other and Matthew Mahan apart. Although the cardinal does not credit Leo's articles as the cause of the chaos, I know that they inflicted a near-fatal wound on his authority, particularly among the younger priests. They'll never respect the great man again, says Leo proudly.

The cardinal's reaction drives me to distraction. He absolutely refuses to fight. Six months ago he would have taken on all these birdbrains and eaten them alive, feathers and all. A few bellows, a few twisted arms, maybe a few secret flourishes of the checkbook, and peace would have been restored. But now he is trying to be a different kind of bishop—one who really practices Pope John's holy freedom. The tragedy is, Leo's devious slanders have shrouded the effort in a miasma of meanness and distrust.

His Em. has sold off all those beautiful antiques that filled our residence, and replaced them with junk. Even our chapel went to the auctioneers and the money to the archdiocese. He traded his

259

Cadillac for a Ford. He sold his shell collection for a whopping one hundred and fifty thousand dollars. All without a peep of publicity, so that his enemies cannot see what is happening.

The personal money issue is complicated by the reality of the diocese's financial structure, which may be one thing you ivory tower scholars don't know about. Unlike the Protestant churches, where the laity are the legal owners, our bishops own it all. They have no board of laymen to whom they must present an audited report each year. An R.C. bishop has absolute control of diocesan cash and property. When you own it all, there's not much point in paying yourself a salary. If Mahan did get a salary in line with his responsibilities, he could afford to give his sister-in-law twice as much as he has been giving her. But this is impossible to explain in public. In a very ironic way he is a victim of the system. Anyway, the cardinal would never try to explain it because it would only embarrass his sister-in-law.

As for the effect of all this on me? My hours have improved considerably. The cardinal no longer hurtles about the archdiocese. He has almost become a recluse. So I've had time to plow through most of Bishop Cronin's anti-Vatican I stuff. I'm afraid the old boy's "evidence" of lack of freedom doesn't knock out the council, but it has whetted my appetite to write a serious history of the Church from a whole new point of view. Unfortunately I haven't found this new needle in my historical haystack yet.

But the hell with me intellectually. I am concerned about the state of my soul—which is rotten. I find myself yearning for a scourging. In a way, I am getting one. You know what was happening between me and Helen Reed. It stopped when I got back from Rome. I know it was something to do with the cardinal—my new respect for him. But this doesn't mean I've stopped loving Helen. Throughout the last three agonizing months I can honestly say there's not been a day or a night when I did not want her in my arms. To make my torment more exquisite, I see her constantly.

The cardinal had asked Bill Reed to reorganize and expand the outpatient services at St. Clare's Hospital. He warned him that this would involve working with his difficult daughter, who had been appointed head of nursing services there by her mother superior, Sister Agnes Marie. Reed succumbed to his Em.'s blandishments. I was told to work on Helen, to reconcile her to her father. You may marvel, but I was genuinely concerned for her, as a priest. And as a lover, I knew how she needed to love her father, too.

Dr. Reed deserves a lot of credit for the reconciliation. He threw himself into working at St. Clare's, and watching him deal with patients and staff, Helen realized he was neither a Protestant ogre nor the reactionary that her New Left friends painted. In a month she went from raging antagonism to guilty adoration. Soon she was talking about leaving the convent to become a doctor. She is currently on leave from the order, and her ecstatic father is inundating her with biology and chemistry books.

For us, Helen has constructed a fantasy future. She gets her M.D., and I get a quiet country parish from my friend the cardinal. By this time marriage will be a licit option for padres. I will minister to my congregation and write while she practices medicine. A lovely dream in which I consistently point out one large flaw. The chances of my becoming one of the first married priests in a thousand years are very slim. If you hear anything whispered around the Vatican that would alter this dour prophecy, for God's sake rush the news. Because if it weren't for the cardinal, I think I'd have walked out of the priesthood. But I couldn't do that to him now.

Best,
Mag

Dennis addressed the letter and went to mail it. In the distance thunder rumbled. Suddenly he could feel Helen's trembling body in his arms in the Pensione Christina. Hold me, hold me, please hold me, she had said. Yes, you had said, we can really love each other. But now, back home, this other love, somehow more real, certainly more terrible, stood between them, his love for this bulky man whose task was the orchestration of love, the movement of love beyond the personal toward some unspoken immensity.

He made it back from the corner postbox just as the first huge raindrops began to fall. On the second floor he heard a squawk of static. The cardinal was listening to his shortwave radio again. It had become an obsession. Dennis peered in at him and he looked up with a tired smile. "I just had a phone call."

"Who?"

"Father—ex-Father Novak. He wanted to know if there was any chance of his getting permission from Rome to come back to us."

"What did you tell him?"

"What *could* I tell him? No."

"You don't think there's the faintest possibility?"

Matthew Mahan gave Dennis a curious look. "Why so intense?"

"I think everybody my age lives in hopes," he said evasively.

"I know. I just got some confidential material from the Catholic Conference Office in Washington. They made a secret survey which shows something like seventy-five percent of the clergy thirty-five and under would like the option to marry. Nobody in the hierarchy seems to realize this. We're sitting on a land mine."

Could he tell him what he had just written to Goggin? No, he could not add another burden. He looked appallingly ill—cheeks hollow, vitality gone from his eyes. Yet there was also the need to be honest with this man. It was time to speak the truth.

"Father—could you spare me another five minutes?"

"The rest of the afternoon, if you need it."

Dennis sat down in one of the leather armchairs that had replaced the French antiques. "I think you should know—really why I'm intense on this subject of our hopes and options. I'm in love with Helen Reed. I want to marry her. But I don't want to leave the priesthood. I can't—let Helen go on thinking—it only gets worse, for both of us. Do you think there's *any* chance of a married priesthood? In, say, five years?"

Matthew Mahan sat behind his desk like a statue. Not of marble, but of wax. Another of his failures. Another humiliation. He heard himself telling Terry Malone and George Petrie that he was prepared to risk his prestige, his authority, for the sake of this priest. This young lost sheep. Let the ninety-nine stay on the hills.

But wait. What is he really saying? Isn't he trying to tell you how much he cares about his priesthood? Remember the cold-voiced young man a few months ago: Who knows where I'll be in twenty years? How different from this open, troubled young face.

"Dennis, you've read those drafts of the committee that's studying the subject for the National Conference of Bishops. You can see the direction they're taking."

"But if seventy-five percent of priests under thirty-five expect the rule to be changed—if you spoke out, that could start a trend—"

"Dennis, don't you think I'm in enough trouble?"

"I didn't mean to put pressure on you. I just—had to tell you. Helen invited me to supper tonight. Do you need me?"

"No. No, of course not."

In his own office, Dennis found his hand shaking as he dialed Helen's number. "About six thirty," she said cheerfully. "Would you pick up a bottle of wine at Sweeney's?"

He hung up, telling himself, Tonight you will be faithful to your vow. For the sake of that man in there.

Except for his morning Mass, Dennis McLaughlin had avoided the chapel for months. As he entered the now drab room, only a single votive candle glowed before the tabernacle, on a plain oak table that replaced the magnificent hand-carved altar. Above it was a cheap new crucifix. He knelt to pray: Lord, I am not worthy of him. Say but the word and my soul shall be healed.

Bong, bong, bong. Three a.m. Pain gnawed in Cardinal Mahan's stomach. There would be no more sleep now. With a sigh he heaved his legs over the side of his bed. A draft of cold air filtered through his sweat-soaked pajamas, but his body burned as if he were running a fever. The dry heat of desolation.

He trudged downstairs to the chapel. Although he had seemed not to notice the priceless works he had lived with, he found he missed particularly the anguished baroque Christ, the purple glow from the stained-glass windows. The sale of old Hogan's total collection had brought close to a million dollars. And the money, where was the money? Matthew Mahan asked the figure on the cheap gold cross as he knelt on the prie-dieu. Spent, Cardinal Mahan, like yourself. The fund drive had ended in catastrophe. They were borrowing their operating expenses from the banks for the first time in his ten years of episcopacy.

For the thousandth time, Matthew Mahan prayed that he could accept this humiliation. He almost laughed. There were so many humiliations.What tortured him most was his ineptitude. It was incredible how badly he was handling crises that he had once smiled or growled or bellowed through. Why? Because he could not scour the old smoothie from his soul. He still loved the flattery, the deference, the little perquisites of power. When he tried to avoid them the result was confusion. More terrible was the other answer—that his elevation to the cardinalate was a fraud. Not only was his Eminence unworthy. He was a purchased man, a pawn on the chessboard of international power. And to know that was to be paralyzed. The prayers dwindled away. Now you cannot levitate the simplest cry: My Jesus, mercy. There it goes, spinning to the ground like a dead bug. Prayers without wings. Some apocalyptic penance—like the trials of Job—was needed.

With the loss of the power to pray had come other losses. He read his speeches with leaden automation. The ability to persuade, to control a single man or a small group of men in private talks, had lapsed. Gulfs yawned between him and other people. Old friends couldn't talk to him.

You should get away, really you should, Dennis, young and earnest, had pleaded with him yesterday.

It was indeed imperative for the cardinal to get away, but only to get away from Mahan, and that was easier said than done. But the love on Dennis's face. Can't I accept that, Lord?

No. Because Dennis's love is for something that doesn't exist, this cardinal-cum-saint that he imagines, this defier of Vatican decrees. On July 1 a letter had arrived from Cardinal Confalonieri, prefect of the Sacred Congregation for the Bishops. July 29, 1969, would be the first anniversary of the encyclical *Humanae Vitae.* Nothing would make the Holy Father happier than to hear a statement from Matthew Mahan on that day supporting the Pope's stand on birth control. It was, of course, only a confirmation of everything he had understood when he heard *Frater noster taciturnus* from Paul's lips.

The following day Dennis had laid a clipping on his desk. An interview with Cardinal Suenens, the primate of Belgium, on the failure of the reform movement in the Church. "What is wanted," Suenens had said, "is to liberate everyone, even the Holy Father himself, from the system—which [has us in] its grip. . . . For while popes come and go, the Curia remains." He called for the election of the Pope in future by "representatives of the universal Church," including the laity.

"That's exactly how it should be," Matthew Mahan had said to Dennis. "Thank God someone important is saying it. This could matter."

"Then why don't you agree with him—in public?"

He had tried to explain how he felt about the oath of personal loyalty he had taken to Pope Paul.

"Aren't your convictions more important than that damn red biretta?"

Old Davey's spirit obviously infested this boy's soul. Reacting to it, the old smoothie had almost turned on his shouting act. "Dennis," he'd said instead. "*I'm* not important enough. And my convictions aren't the point. The question is, should I attack the man who made me a cardinal four months after I took that vow."

"You wouldn't be attacking him," Dennis sputtered in indignation. "That red hat is part of a carefully calculated carrot-and-stick operation. They honor you, and turn it into a weapon."

"Don't be naïve," he had said, and had seen hope turn to anguish on that young face.

Matthew Mahan sighed and arose from the prie-dieu. Back in his room, he began fiddling with his shortwave radio. Before dawn the Vatican came in with remarkable clarity. A voice began speaking in Italian. Coincidence. An attack on Cardinal Suenens by Jean Derrieux, Matthew Mahan's old friend, castigating him for undermining the papacy. The propaganda tactics were superb—liberal attacking liberal.

Matthew Mahan snapped off the speaker in midsentence. Everything he heard on this radio depressed him.

Was there any consolation? He picked up one of a dozen letters he had received from divorced couples who had been accepted as good-conscience cases. This one, from an Irene Tracy, told him "from a heart bursting with joy how grateful my husband and I are for the way you have reached out to us." She went on at length about her disastrous first marriage, the strains on her children, her love for her second husband. "And now I feel so much at peace—with God, with the Church, and with my husband."

But the diocesan Rota had processed almost a hundred cases, and you had only a dozen letters like this. There's no sense meditating on failure. Think instead about your visit to Sister Agnes Marie. You had healed your differences, supported her programs, yielded on the counseling of poor women on birth control. You had called her Agnes, and she (shyly at first) called you Matthew. You had told her what you were doing in the inner city, appointing your best black priest to the parish, opening parish facilities to the neighborhood.

"That," she had said, "should shut up Father Disalvo."

He had been hurt. "I didn't do it for that."

"I know. . . . Matthew, I know what you're going through. I went through it myself many years ago."

"You?" he said incredulously.

"God hasn't abandoned you, Matthew. It's his way of purifying us. Once you take the risk, rely on nothing but Him, He has to make us truly worthy before He enters the heart."

"Do you think that's happening to me? I didn't *ask* for this."

Sister Agnes laughed briefly. "Who would? But somewhere you made a fundamental decision to go beyond where you were. Most people stop at some safe point. There are all sorts of places to stop. Preacher, politician, man for all seasons. You were a very good bishop for the other Church. The one that is passing away."

He forced a smile, not to hurt her feelings. Perhaps he had made a decision. But he was not accepting the loss of power, prestige, popularity that it involved. If God was turning His face away, it was because he, Matthew Mahan, was a spiritual failure.

"I can only promise you what I know," she said. "Someday it will end. Then the joy begins. A sweetness beyond words, beyond everything. Then perhaps you will go further, into the very darkest night, walking not toward joy, but light. Pure light."

He took her hand and was shocked by how warm it was. Her utter calm was not cold. "Thank you, Agnes."

"Perhaps it would help"—her voice rose slightly—"perhaps it would help to know that *you* are part of *my* joy."

A knock on his door halted the recollection. Dennis peered anxiously in. "I saw your light. I thought—you might be sick."

"Just the usual insomnia."

Dennis pointed to the radio. "Any news from there?"

He summed up what had just been said about Cardinal Suenens.

"That wraps it up, doesn't it? If you open your mouth, you're a heretic—disrespectful and inopportune."

"Dennis. . . ." Matthew Mahan sensed he had to reach out to him, for his own soul's sake as well as for Dennis's. "I've been thinking about you and Helen Reed. Praying, too. I've decided to speak out about the celibacy statement. Not in public. But on the floor when the bishops meet in Washington in January."

Dennis nodded glumly, the old dissatisfaction on his face. Didn't you hear what I said? Matthew Mahan almost cried.

"I wish I understood what you are really trying to do."

Now was the moment for the grandiose spiritual remark: I'm trying to save my soul, Dennis, I'm trying to save the soul of this archdiocese. He could hear his father's growl: No grandstanding in this family. "I'm doing—the best I can, Dennis."

266

THE LONG PARTING KISS Helen Reed had given him last night was still on Dennis McLaughlin's lips as he came downstairs to begin his day's work. Not even the taste of the bread and wine at his morning Mass had diminished (no, it had intensified) the sadness, the anguish of that kiss. Another failure spewed into his confessor's ear, he thought wearily. The monsignor had been amazingly gentle about Helen. "You won't be the first priest who's had this problem, nor the last," he had said. But Dennis could not forgive himself. His depression was compounded by that three-a.m. encounter with the cardinal. Matthew Mahan had invited him to the kitchen for an "insomniac's lunch." The cardinal looked ghastly. And the sadness . . .

Dennis found himself fingering the moon shell on his desk, his souvenir of that walk along the beach at Nettuno. As always when he held the shell in his hand, he was aware of something that eluded him—an idea, an insight, even a reality lurking in those delicate brown swirls. He put the shell down. A knock—one of the chancery typists delivering the mail. Quickly Dennis looked through it and opened the obvious leading contender for attention. The papal seal and the Washington, D.C., postmark meant the apostolic delegate. As he read, he began cursing softly.

Your Eminence:
    It pains me to be under the necessity to write this letter. Our Holy Father has been extremely distressed to learn of the programs you and some others have initiated in regard to divorced persons who have entered into second, canonically invalid marriages. He has directed me to order you to suspend these programs immediately. The value (or scandal—here I add a personal comment) of such programs will be weighed by the proper authorities in Rome, and a decision issued which will be binding for the universal Church. Please communicate to me your compliance.
                                    Sincerely yours in Christ,

Dennis McLaughlin walked into the cardinal's office. "Excuse me. I thought you should see this immediately."

A little of the old Matthew Mahan reappeared as he read the apostolic delegate's letter. For a moment Dennis expected the roar of rage he would have welcomed. But the moment passed. Matthew Mahan's face seemed to crumble.

Spiritually he was no longer in the room with Dennis. He was in Rome, facing the anguished woman whose soul he had so confidently promised to save. Confessing to her this final humiliation. What would she do now? What would you say to the others who were waiting? Trust in God but not in the Church? No, that was unthinkable, unsayable. If the Church was not God's voice, your whole life was a sham, not just your cardinalate.

"Why, Dennis, *why?*" he murmured.

"Do you want to—reply to this?"

"Write that we will suspend the program. Send a copy to Barker at the Rota telling him to process all cases now on the docket, but not to accept any more. Tell him to see me about counseling for those we turn away. Call Cohane. There should be a story in the paper. Say something about my being pleased that Rome has decided to give this matter serious attention. Make it clear that the premature raising of so many couples' hopes is my fault."

"I won't write that," Dennis cried. "Why don't you fight?"

"Dennis—I love the Church more than your good opinion of me. And I love and want that very much." A ghost of a smile played across his lips. "God seems determined to deprive me of everything I love."

Dennis strode back to his desk fuming. Suddenly with the force of a physical blow he realized how utterly he had lost contact with the spiritual life. Stupid, stupid! *O ye of little faith.* He picked up the moon shell and stared at the lines that spiraled up wider and wider. The dynamic spiral—the image of the Church's growth. The holy spiral, unpredictable; moving upward toward infinity; each spiral both a new beginning and a continuation of the past. This man, this suffering cardinal next door, impossibly trying to combine obedience and peace, must be the spokesman for a Church that would proclaim a new beginning. John's living voice, consecrated by John's own hands—

The phone was ringing. Dennis snatched it and heard Mike Furia's ebullient rasp. "Is the boss around?"

The children of this world perpetually distract the children of light, Dennis thought as he called the cardinal.

Matthew Mahan picked up the phone with a sudden sense of dread. "Hello, stranger, how's the world treating you?"

"Australia's treating me pretty good. Japan lousy. Italy very,

very good. The rest of Europe stinko. I got in the day before yesterday. I gather our collection plate isn't improving. Did you ever get the report on the school costs?"

"I got it last week. It indicates that we'll be in the red for ten million dollars by 1976. I'm going to take your advice, send out a memo telling all pastors to face up to the necessity of phasing out parochial grammar schools."

"That takes guts, Matt. Listen, I've got something I want to talk about. Can you lunch? At the athletic club at twelve?"

IN THE lobby of the athletic club, Mike crushed his hand and then refused to let it go. "Hey, what's wrong? You look awful."

"Just not sleeping too well. You look great, Mike."

Mike had lost ten or fifteen pounds. He was tanned. He exuded vitality. Or was he just nervous? He was into a second Scotch before Matthew Mahan had taken more than two sips of milk.

"What's on your mind?" Matthew Mahan asked finally.

Mike hesitated, his glass in midair. "I spent the last three weeks of my trip persuading someone to marry me."

"That's great, Mike. Who's the lucky woman?"

Slowly Mike put the glass down on the table, his eyes on Matthew Mahan's face. "Mary Shea," he said.

Blackness engulfed Matthew Mahan. He thought he was fainting. Then Mike's anxious face reappeared. A blurred version. "That's—that's the most wonderful news, Mike."

"Really?" Mike was plainly worried that the cardinal was lying.

"Really. Why don't you believe me?"

"She told me, Matt. I know what she's been to you. I'm not sure you want to see her married to a lug like me."

"Don't be ridiculous." With an enormous effort Matthew Mahan stifled an urge to weep. "Tell me about it."

Mike smiled. "It started last May, the week of your elevation. I remember asking myself why the hell I never had the brains or luck to find someone like her. We had dinner together one night. When I got home, I telephoned her every other day."

"Where is she, where's Mary now?"

"Right here in the city."

"Why didn't you bring her along?"

"She was as nervous about what you'd think as I was."

"No," Matthew Mahan said. "No, Mike. I'm the one who's nervous. I'm the one who has something—shameful to tell you."

"What?" Mike was utterly baffled.

"You want me to receive you and Mary into the Church."

"More than that. Mary wants you to marry us."

"I can't do either one, Mike." He told him about this morning's letter from the apostolic delegate.

Mike's face twisted with an emotion that was hard to identify—contempt, anger. "Matt; I told you—I've got my own arrangement with whoever the hell is running this crazy world. But I don't know what this is going to do to Mary."

"I don't either. But we must tell her. And hope for the best."

It was an unpleasant lunch. Mike's mood was sour. "That ex-Jesuit, Father Mirante, tracked us down and gave us an earful. He said the Dutch bishops are going to maneuver Il Papa into a corner on the celibacy question. Where do you stand on it, Matt?"

Was Mike being sarcastic? He decided it didn't matter. "It's a question the whole Church should debate openly. I'm inclined for optional marriage myself."

"Good thing. According to Bill Reed, you may be hearing wedding bells in your residence before long. Doc says his daughter and your Father McLaughlin can't keep hands off each other."

Matthew Mahan nodded, although the words suggested a more painful reality than Dennis had admitted. Mike, only marginally interested, launched into every vicious Vatican story he had heard. Matthew Mahan winced at the thought of this man saying these things to Mary, destroying her faith day by relentless day.

They went uptown in the cardinal's Ford. Mary greeted them at the door of Mike's apartment with her warmest smile, but with no pretense that Matthew Mahan was unexpected. He watched her as she kissed Mike and entwined her fingers in his thick, tanned hand. Did it hurt to see this? No, old wounds no longer counted. On the contrary, for the first time in months his heart stirred with a tremor of hope. They were in love.

"Let Matt tell you about his good-conscience divorce program," Mike said.

He told her, humbly pleading behind the neutral words for a pardon he did not deserve and could not receive.

Mary sat in strangely composed silence. "Oh, Matt," she said after a moment. "I feel so awful—for you. But it isn't as terrible as you think—assuming one's as much in love as I am." She slipped her arm around Mike. "I'll be all right now. I needed someone, Matt, and I inflicted myself on you. It was so unfair. Then when I turned to the Church as a whole, it was like trying to embrace a cloud. I needed a whole person, and I've found him."

Matthew Mahan detected a warning note. Though everything she was saying was true, she was talking too intensely. "It would have made everything perfect to have you marry us, Matt," she was saying. "And it would be more—more complete, if I were at peace with the Church. But we can't have everything—"

"You are at peace with the Church, Mary. As long as you know in your heart that you're doing the right thing. I have a definite feeling that God has played a part in this."

"I do, too, Matt. Of course, this pseudo agnostic here scoffs at that kind of thinking. But I scoff right back." She pushed a small fist against Mike's big chin.

Again the cardinal sensed a false note, gaiety concealing a conflict. He tried to gloss it over. "Well," he said, standing up. "Even if I can't do much for you legally, there's nothing to prevent me from giving you my blessing, for what it's worth."

"It's worth a lot to me."

"And me, too," Mike Furia said.

Quickly Matthew Mahan made the familiar cross in the air above them with his right hand and murmured his blessing. Mary looked up at him, her face solemn. Then she was full of frowning concern. "Matt, you look so tired. What have you been doing?"

"Oh—worries. Work. Old age. And problems, problems."

"Yes—but you—"

You used to thrive on work and problems? How could he explain to her his overwhelming sense of failure?

"Bill Reed told me you should take a month off," Mike said.

"I know. I know. Maybe I will, after Christmas."

"I was hoping you could marry us just before Christmas." He heard an ominous falling note in Mary's voice. "We wanted to spend our honeymoon in Hawaii. Mike says it's marvelous—"

"We'll still do it," Mike said. "Just because Il Papa's eliminated this guy . . ."

Wrong, Matthew Mahan thought. Too abrasive, Mike.

"When we get back," Mary said, ignoring Mike, "I'll make you take a vacation."

Riding home, Matthew Mahan suddenly remembered the expression on Dennis McLaughlin's face when he had told him to extinguish all hope of a married priesthood. It was alarmingly similar to the sadness he had glimpsed on Mary's face when he had given her his blessing.

XIII

ON DECEMBER 21, Matthew Mahan read in the evening paper that Michael J. Furia and Mary Shea had been married at a private ceremony in the mayor's office, with the chief justice of the state's supreme court, an old friend of the brides father, officiating. It was no surprise. . . . He had had dinner with them only a week earlier. Mary was defiantly gay, Mike exultant. But again there had been a sense of strain.

While Mike was pouring after-dinner cordials, the cardinal found Mary looking somberly at him, as if she wanted to say something but was forbidden. He could only hope and pray that this would pass, that she would be sustained by Mike's obvious devotion to her. The danger he sensed was Mike's tendency to consider the man as arbiter of all opinion in the family. He obviously assumed that Mary agreed with him when he unleashed another round of wisecracks on the financial games the Vatican capitalists played. Last May this tone had been in accord with her own bitter feelings. But Mike seemed to have no awareness that the institution he was talking about was also the Church of John XXIII, which had reawakened hope in her heart.

He had called Mike the next day and tried to explain this.

"Listen, Padre," Mike had said. "She's out of your hands now. I think the best thing you can do is stay away from her. Frankly, you're bad medicine. She was really depressed this morning."

"All right, Mike. I'll keep out. Depend on it."

Nothing more was heard from the Furias, and Matthew Mahan was engrossed with Christmas activities. In his limited spare time he worked on the drafts of the American bishops' statement on priestly celibacy that were sent to him as a member of the committee. He did his utmost to urge an undogmatic point of view.

But the final draft of the twenty-seven-page statement that arrived from the head of the committee was an all-out defense of celibacy, an unwavering affirmation of the prevailing rule.

Ten days after it came, Dennis went with Matthew Mahan to the airport for the trip to Washington and the semiannual meeting of the American bishops. Matthew Mahan did not say a word about his promise to speak out on celibacy at this gathering. Was there any point to it now? Never had he been more aware of his outsider's role in the American hierarchy.

On the plane, he found the celibacy statement on top of the load of papers in his briefcase. He leafed through it listlessly, until on the last page he came to a note in Dennis's scrawl.

"The more I think of it the more I see the Church's policy as interference with the most essential human freedom—the freedom to love. *Humanae Vitae* threatens this freedom within marriage itself. Archaic canon laws cripple those who attempt to recover from a failed first marriage. A meaningless celibacy prevents priests—supposedly men dedicated to love—from realizing it on the deepest level of their lives."

The passion in those words made Matthew Mahan wince.

THE next morning, three hundred men in somber black gathered in the ballroom of the Statler Hilton. The president, Cardinal Dearden, began with a rhapsodic report on the recent Synod of Bishops in Rome. He quoted the Pope, with special emphasis on the "love which bishops must nourish between themselves," and closed with a call to his fellow American prelates to cooperate in attacking the nation's spiritual and social problems. The applause was warm. It was hard to argue with such sentiments.

They turned to the agenda. The establishment of a national office for Black Catholicism was overwhelmingly endorsed. The English translations for the new order of the Mass were also approved. Then finally, after the committee reports, came the discussion of the celibacy statement. Matthew Mahan declared that he admired the document as a comprehensive survey, but he could see no point in America's bishops making the statement now. He had heard that the Dutch bishops were going to suggest that the entire Church debate the question. Why not wait and see what the response was before making a definite statement?

One bishop asked with heavy sarcasm if Cardinal Mahan was implying that majority rule should decide this issue.

"Of course not. I am only suggesting that new light may be shed on it by bishops from other countries."

"You just said this was a comprehensive survey. You were a member of the committee that drafted it. If any aspect of the subject was omitted, why don't you enlighten us now?"

Bishop Cassidy, from a California diocese, stood up. "It seems to me, your Eminence, that you miss the point. We know where the Holy Father stands on this subject. He has asked us for our support."

"I would like to think he has asked us for advice."

A murmur of shocked disapproval ran through the room. "I think it is clear that he wants no advice on this issue," said Cassidy.

"He may need it, whether he wants it or not."

Cassidy glowered. "When you knelt before him, did you feel he was a man who needed advice?"

The sadness in Paul's eyes burned into Matthew Mahan's soul once more as they forced him to make these arrogant statements. "I felt he was a deeply troubled man." More shock and dismay. "Gentlemen, please—I am saying to you here what I would not dream of saying for publication. My feeling, our feeling, is not the issue. I am not suggesting a repudiation of this statement, only a delay. The haste with which we are rushing to get this on record will strike many young priests as disheartening. We seem to be more interested in supporting the Pope—who after all does not *need* support—than we are concerned for their priesthoods."

The bishop of—was it Wilmington?—now arose to accuse Matthew Mahan of gross sentimentalism. What the younger clergy needed was leadership. This was what Pope Paul was trying to give them. Give way on this question, the speaker predicted in a voice that quivered with rage, and there will be a union of priests telling the bishops what to do.

Matthew Mahan looked around the ballroom. Was anyone on his side? *Thy will be done,* Lord. Cardinal Dearden recognized a new man, not more than forty. In a southwestern twang he declared himself very much on Matthew Mahan's side. A bishop from Minnesota agreed, adding that Minnesota Catholics would not be upset in the least by a married clergy. Matthew Mahan was tempted to add a few more persuasive words of his own. But the mere thought of getting to his feet again sent a shudder of exhaustion through him. Silent brother, he told himself wryly.

The opposition had the last word. A New Jersey bishop made a ferocious attack on the Dutch Church, and on Cardinal Mahan for suggesting that the bishops should consider anything that came out of Holland. Perhaps Cardinal Mahan was misled by the difficulties in his own diocese into imagining that there was a similar revolt against authority across the United States.

Who would have thought eight months ago, Matthew Mahan, that you would have been accused of incompetence, cowardice, and disloyalty before your fellow bishops?

Cardinal Dearden called for a vote. Did the bishops approve the substance of the document? Only two no votes were recorded. Should the document be released? A two-thirds majority was required. To Matthew Mahan's amazement, the vote on release was a hundred and forty-five in favor and sixty-eight opposed. If only a few more bishops had voted no, he would have won the debate he thought he had so humiliatingly lost. In agony he asked himself why he had not risen to reply to the New Jersey assault. As he stood up and felt his legs trembling under him, he knew the answer. He was simply too exhausted.

Up in his room, he flung himself on the bed and wept. He wept for the death of that old self, the smoothie whom he still loved in spite of all his attempts to evade him. He wept for Dennis. He wept for the Church.

DENNIS met him at the airport. The celibacy statement had already been released. "I tried to talk them out of it," Matthew Mahan said, and told him of the close vote.

"If you'd won, I'd start believing in miracles."

At two in the morning Matthew Mahan was still awake, listening to the Vatican Radio and wrestling with his thoughts, when the telephone rang. It was a person-to-person call from Mike Furia.

"Mike. Where are you?"

"San Francisco. Have you seen Mary?"

"No. Why should I? Isn't she with you?"

"I thought she might stop— She left me, Matt. To go back to Rome." There was anguish in his voice. "We got into an argument

275

about the Church, and all of a sudden she burst into tears. I didn't know what was happening. She left a note—saying she loved me— but she didn't have the strength—to be worthy of me. *Her* worthy of *me?* What the hell should I do, Matt?"

"First, cable Father Giulio Mirante. Ask him to find her. The second thing . . ." He hesitated. "This will make you sore, Mike."

"Tell me, the hell with that."

"Whether you believe in it or not, start taking the Church seriously, Mike. Stop talking as if the Pope and the bishops were just another bunch of businessmen. Our business is caring for souls. Now it's yours, too—for one soul."

"I get the message. Say a prayer for her, Matt, and me?"

"I'm praying right now, Mike."

Matthew Mahan knelt in his chapel for the rest of the night.

Coming out of the chapel, he almost collided with Dennis. "A cable from Rome. Just arrived."

He opened the envelope. It was from Cardinal Confalonieri, of the Sacred Congregation for the Bishops. "WE WISH TO INFORM YOU THAT HIS HOLINESS PLANS TO RESPOND TO THE DEFIANT STATEMENT OF THE DUTCH BISHOPS ON OR ABOUT FEBRUARY FIRST. WE URGE YOU TO PREPARE FOR PUBLICATION IN YOUR DIOCESE AN ENTHUSIASTIC STATEMENT SUPPORTING HIS HOLINESS. THE HEIR OF PETER INTENDS TO MAKE NO COMPROMISE ON THE GREAT PRINCIPLE AT STAKE. . . ."

Something had to be done. Something had to be done. Anguish throbbed in Matthew Mahan's mind and body. Dennis's sad face. Mary's suffering in Rome. She and Dennis had to *know,* they had to *see,* that love existed for them, love unto the limits of risk. "Dennis," he said. "Make arrangements for us to go to Rome."

Give me strength, Matthew Mahan prayed as the jet thundered skyward. Whom was he talking to? He sensed it was Pope John. But would he approve of this trip? He who chose the motto "Obedience and Peace"?

It was insane. Was it a reaction to Davey Cronin's lectures, and months of patient brainwashing by Davey's spiritual heir, young Dennis? The humble disciple of Pope John was appalled at the arrogance of what he was doing. Who was he to come hurtling into Rome to lecture the Prince of the Apostles? And with whose support, Cardinal Mahan? Only the voiceless generation, your Holi-

ness. The younger priests, the legions of the divorced, the multitude of unwanted, unloved children, their mothers and fathers broken in health and spirit.

Again he reread the letter he had written to the Pope.

Your Holiness:

A brother bishop, a brother in Christ, writes to you out of the fullness of a heart that shares a shepherd's concern for the flock of the people of God. I must tell you, your Holiness, speaking with a directness that I like to think is American, that our Church is in grave danger. Never before have we, the shepherds, set ourselves against the great mass of the faithful. But now, your Holiness, we are alienating the many. Your encyclical on birth control has for the first time turned the women of the Church against us. This is truly new. Even in nations where great numbers of men have turned against the Church for political reasons, most of the women remained faithful. However, in their deepest hearts our women no longer feel that you have the right or power to tell them how many children they should have.

As for the divorced, there is scarcely a family in America that has not suffered this tragedy. Why do we treat these unfortunate people like pariahs, while other Christian churches embrace them when they seek forgiveness? Now you may also lose your priests, by insisting they adhere to a rule that no longer makes sense to them. They have been taught to regard their fellow ministers as brothers. They see their lives supported and enriched by happy marriages, their congregations uplifted by the example of genuine love in their midst. Why, they ask, can we not experience such love and shine it forth to others?

True to the vow of secrecy I took to your Holiness, I have spoken to no one about this. I only wish a chance to sit down with you as I was privileged to sit with your beloved predecessor and open my heart to you, to tell you what I do not believe you hear within the walls of the Vatican, to warn you that the Church we both love, the vessel in which the spirit of God voyages among the children of men, is in danger of catastrophe. Hear me, I beg you, before you speak against the Dutch bishops.

Sincerely yours in Christ,
Matthew Cardinal Mahan

It said too much. But it told the truth, the spiritual and the emotional truth, which was what he now had to do.

Beside Matthew Mahan, Dennis McLaughlin tried to make up his mind whether he was more frightened than exultant. This was a living challenge to the papal monarchy. How could he not exult? Then fright would take charge. Fear for Matthew Mahan, whose torment was tearing him apart, who was appalled by what he was doing; the loyal man was shuddering at this implied threat to betray the Pope who had made him a prince of the Church.

Dennis saw that Matthew Mahan was fiddling with his cardinal's ring. This symptom of disturbance had become acute in the past three days. He was tempted to say, Why don't you take it off and put it in your pocket? Instead he said, "Why don't you take a pill and try to sleep?"

"I never sleep on planes, I'm afraid." But five minutes later he was dozing.

As he spread the light airline blanket across Matthew Mahan's chest Dennis found himself praying: Dear God, watch over him, please. Give him the strength, give him the strength. He stared moodily out at the stars. What were their chances, really? Weren't you more interested in the attempt than in the possibility of success? He had poured out a lot of his guilt to Helen last night. Calmly, she had told him to endure it. He *was* guilty. It was marvelous the way women accepted reality. He had been unable to tell her the next thought that had singed his brain. If they failed, and if he left the Church to marry her, would his book be worth writing? Wouldn't he be dismissed instantly as a failed priest trying to justify his weakness?

He fell asleep. When he awoke, the overhead lights came on. The stewardesses began passing out orange juice and coffee. They would be landing in a half hour.

"At least we won't have to worry about four hundred pieces of luggage this time." Matthew Mahan shook out some pills and swallowed them with his orange juice.

"Hey, that isn't on your diet," Dennis said.

"I know. But I'm thirsty." There was a reckless glint in his eyes. "Did you wire Father Mirante to meet us at the pensione?"

"Yes. But if they find out you're talking to him—"

"We have to talk to him. He knows where Mary is."

They taxied to the Pensione Christina. It was inexpensive and they could be anonymous there. Father Mirante was waiting in

279

the lobby. Upstairs, Matthew Mahan showed Mirante his letter to Paul. He read it and said something in Italian. Matthew Mahan laughed. "He says I've been seized by heroic inspiration. A polite way of saying I'm out of my mind."

Mirante smiled nervously. "No, your Eminence," he protested.

"Never mind, never mind," Matthew Mahan said. "What do you think our next move should be?"

"To call Confalonieri. You sent him this letter?"

"Of course. Is there a chance of getting to see his Holiness?"

"There's always a chance. What will happen if you see him and he tells you to go home and keep your mouth shut?"

"I'll go home and keep my mouth shut."

"Are you sure? Or is it possible that your young friend here will persuade you to do something more daring?"

Suddenly Dennis did not trust Father Mirante.

Matthew Mahan asked him if he had located Mary Shea. Mirante nodded. "She is staying at a little convent on the outskirts of Rome. One to which she has contributed a great deal of money."

"Take me there, now."

MARY met him in a small, bare sitting room. She looked ill. "I'm not sleeping," she said with a wan smile. "I'm trying to make it this time on prayer. No pills."

He told her why he was here—the clerical reason. "But you're the real reason, Mary. I'm here to tell you something. Something I never thought I'd have to tell you. You've committed a sin."

She shook her head, wide-eyed. "How—"

"A sin against the Christian ideal of love. You can't let a man start to love you the way Mike loves you, and then walk out."

"I thought it was better now than later."

"That's another sin, Mary. A sin against faith."

Her lovely face crumpled. "Matt, if you could have married us. If I felt I had your—your real blessing—"

He seized her arms and gave her one fierce shake. "Mary! You have it." Behind those words he was saying, Receive ye the Holy Spirit. "As a bishop of the Holy Roman Catholic Church, I absolve you of all stain of sin in the love of this man. I affirm before God that it is a true, good, holy marriage."

"Oh, Matt." He took her in his arms and prayed once more: Receive ye the Holy Spirit. He let go, totally, absolutely forever, the wish to hold her in any other way. Suddenly in his soul there was a soaring joy, like light-filled water leaping from a fountain in a deserted square. He searched her face for similar joy. It was not there. "Mary, Mike wants to come here. To you."

"Yes." Her voice was calm. But there was no joy in it.

"Are you—all right, Mary?" Those old familiar words.

She smiled. "Yes, Matt, I'm all right. Are you?"

"Only if you are."

The convent bell tolled, summoning the nuns to chapel. Lord, say but the word and her soul shall be healed.

DENNIS McLaughlin was spending the afternoon telephoning around Rome in search of Goggin. He found him at last in the office of the Jesuit general near the Vatican. Goggin was naturally astonished. "I'll meet you at the foot of the Spanish Steps." And in twenty minutes they were drinking *caffè doppio* in an old marble-floored restaurant. Dennis told him why they were there.

Goggin's eyes widened. "Old pal, don't get grandiose on me." And he told Dennis how Paolo and everyone around him were steaming about the Dutch moves on celibacy. "I spent this morning translating a thing for tomorrow's radio—how the Church is prepared to use its coercive powers to ensure the unity of the faith."

"Nice," said Dennis. "Now tell me what you know about our ex-Jesuit Father Mirante. Is he working for the Vatican?"

"I don't know," said Goggin. "Leave it to me to find out."

At the pensione, Dennis found his boss on the telephone. "Cardinal Confalonieri will be on retreat for the next two weeks? May I speak to Monsignor Draghi? On retreat, too. Odd they'd go at the same time. Well, I may still be here when they get back. I intend to stay until his Holiness sees me."

He hung up and nodded to Dennis with a grim half smile. "The freeze is on. Everybody's out of town. Including the Pope. I haven't called him directly. I tried Villot. I got Bellini, the Substitute Secretary of State, who said he didn't know what I was talking about and that there was no hope of a break in his Holiness's schedule for a month. I asked him to see what he could do to change that, and he got a little unpleasant."

Dennis nodded. "Goggin says they're all breathing fire."

"Well, we knew it was probably a fool's errand. But let's just sit for a day or two and see what happens."

Father Mirante returned after supper. He could not have been more negative. His Vatican friends were appalled by what Cardinal Mahan was doing. Archbishop Bellini would take charge of his letter.

"How do we get around him?" Matthew Mahan asked.

"There is no way around him. He bestrides the Vatican. No one speaks to his Holiness without his permission."

"Did you tell your friends how serious I was?"

"Of course. And their advice is to go home."

Soon after Mirante left, Goggin called. "Our friend went sour a year ago. When his superiors tried to straighten him out, he trotted up to Isolotto. He misjudged the temper of the times, oh, grievously. By now I'm sure he's ready to perform any service."

Dennis told Matthew Mahan what he had just heard. "It's really a little like war, isn't it?" the cardinal said slowly.

That night Dennis was awakened by Matthew Mahan stumbling around in the dark. He turned on the light and saw blood on the rug. "Are you—all right?" he asked.

"Yes, yes. Nothing unusual. I'm sorry—let's clean up this mess." And together they scrubbed with cold water and towels.

It must have been close to dawn when Dennis finally fell asleep. He awoke to find Matthew Mahan quietly saying Mass at the dresser. Dennis stared out the window at the ocher Tiber. People scurried along in a drizzling rain with their coat collars turned up against a wolfish wind. "Sunny Italy," he said.

After breakfast the cardinal settled down to read *L'Osservatore Romano,* and asked Dennis to go out and buy a copy of Pope John's *Journal of a Soul.* Father Mirante was just arriving as he came back. "What do you think you'll get if you talk him into going home?" Dennis asked. "A professorship at the Gregorian?"

Mirante glared at him. "Would you believe me if I said it is to his advantage as well as mine that he goes home? Do you think it's impossible for a man to act in his own interests and out of love and concern for a friend at the same time?" The pain on the middle-aged face was exquisite.

"I'm beginning to think anything is possible," Dennis said.

"Why do you torment him? You are the evil genius here."

"Evil?" Dennis said. "Compared to you, Father Mirante, I don't think I understand the meaning of the word."

They went upstairs in silence. Dennis gave the book to the cardinal as Mirante launched a feverish monologue in Italian. Matthew Mahan listened somberly. "He says they are preparing to disgrace me, Dennis, accusing me of misuse of archdiocese funds. Apparently Leo the Great's columns have traveled far."

"They wouldn't dare. They'd lose more than you."

"Yes. I think so, too," Matthew Mahan said. "I should have expected this. But it still hurts."

"They can be petty as well as stupendous," Father Mirante said. "Your Eminence, I see only the futility of this. The danger both to your reputation and your health."

"I know, I know, Giulio. But when it's something your soul summons you to do . . . It's seldom—too seldom—that we let our own souls speak. Don't you think so?"

Tears suddenly streamed down Mirante's face. He fell on his knees and clutched Matthew Mahan's hand to kiss his ring. "Forgive me," he said. "I am not worthy of your friendship."

"I don't know what you're talking about, Giulio. But God's forgiveness is always yours for the asking. You know that." Matthew Mahan just stood there letting Mirante cling to his hand. Dennis thought, I must never forget this moment.

Mirante lurched to his feet. "I will tell them that I am on your side." The door slammed after him.

At lunch, Dennis noticed that Matthew Mahan barely touched his food. "Are you planning a hunger strike?" he asked.

"Actually I—I feel a little nauseated. Maybe it's a virus."

After supper the telephone rang, and Dennis answered. It was Mirante. "This is not the conspirator, it's the friend," he said in English. "Tonight you will be visited by Cardinal Derrieux. Prevent him if possible, my young friend, from seeing your cardinal."

"Why? They're friends. He's—"

"He *was* a great liberal. Now a week scarcely passes without his denouncing one of the Pope's enemies. He sees Villot on the throne. A French pope. For that he will do anything."

Dennis hung up and reported the conversation. "Derrieux? I can't believe it," the cardinal said. "I'll certainly see him. Giulio's a pendulum, swinging from one extreme to another."

At eight thirty Cardinal Derrieux's secretary called. The cardinal wished to see his Eminence. Would nine p.m. be convenient?

Precisely at nine there was a knock on the door. Dennis opened it and Jean Cardinal Derrieux stepped in. His pinched cheeks, small narrow mouth, dominating high-crowned nose, and intense dark eyes had the impact of a knife blade. He wore a red cassock, and a jeweled pectoral cross glittered on his chest. He held out his hand, ring turned upward. Dennis brushed his lips against the thin, feminine fingers, then stepped back and let Matthew Mahan, in clerical black, shake hands. "Jean," he said. "I'm glad to see you. If they had to send anyone, I'm glad—"

"I wish I could agree," said Derrieux as they sat down in the room's two wing chairs. "I think it would be best if he left," he said with a nod toward Dennis.

"I see no reason for that. Father McLaughlin is completely aware of why I am here."

"Too aware, from what I hear. Time is too short for niceties; I am told by many who know you that you are this man's dupe."

"I am no man's dupe," Matthew Mahan said.

Derrieux reached inside his cassock and took out a piece of paper. "Cardinal Villot has given me this letter which you wrote to his Holiness. He is, of course, horrified by it. So am I."

"Has his Holiness seen it?"

"His Holiness is an old man. Not a well man. It is our task to protect him from this sort of aberration."

There was pain on Matthew Mahan's face. Dennis felt it in his own body, along with anger: Get mad, get mad. Tell him off.

"Aberration?" Matthew Mahan said. "You—would say such a thing? One of the great spokesmen for freedom in the Church?"

"This is what you do with your freedom," Derrieux said with an almost animal bark. "You and your friends in Holland."

"I have no friends in Holland."

"You are prepared to lie as well as threaten?"

"That's a very serious thing to say to me."

"I say it with evidence in hand," Derrieux snarled, shaking the letter in his face. "Do you take us for fools? The Dutch bishops betray the Pope one day, you join the assault the next."

"There was no collusion. I will swear to that," Matthew Mahan said, picking up his pectoral cross from the table between them.

Derrieux gave no sign that he had heard. "You presume to lecture the Holy Father!" he shouted, shaking the letter again.

"I presume to tell him what's in my heart and head."

"Nonsense, vile nonsense is in your heart and head. You are the captive of this young mountebank and his generation."

"I will not allow you to insult Father McLaughlin, a fellow priest, a dedicated fellow priest."

"We have evidence that suggests otherwise. He has a carnal relationship with an ex-nun. He connived with his brother to disrupt your diocese. Yet when your chancellor and vicar-general urged you to dismiss him, you refused."

"Is that—is that true?" Dennis asked Matthew Mahan.

The cardinal avoided his eyes. "Derrieux, my friend," he said with a tremor. "This has nothing to do with my letter."

"It has everything to do with it. What could produce this monstrosity but evil? A web of evil in which you have been trapped, my friend, with your tragic innocence." He pointed at Dennis. "I see it in his eyes. Hatred of the Church, of the priesthood."

Just hatred of you, your Eminence. With a mighty effort Dennis did not say it. He hoped his face was expressionless.

"This is vicious," Matthew Mahan said.

"Evil. The kind of evil he represents deserves no mercy."

"Please!" Matthew Mahan brought his fist down on the table. "Let us discuss what is in that letter. What is happening to the Church. While we sit here reviling each other, people are dying spiritually. Priests are watching their vocations die. This young man is a priest. Deeply, profoundly a priest. If he falls away, anyone can fall away, anyone will."

No, no, I am not worthy, Dennis thought. Forget me, forget this absurd love that has happened between us.

"Your infatuation with this heretic is truly alarming, your Eminence," Derrieux said. "It suggests the most frightening thoughts." He stood up and flipped the letter onto the table. "The Church, which you see as crumbling, is undergoing a transformation that will carry it triumphantly into a new era." He snatched up *Journal of a Soul*. "We are purging ourselves of this infection. I'm told you are a disciple. Perhaps that explains this act of idiocy."

He dropped the book on the table with a thud and walked to the door, where he turned with a royal sweep of his cassock. "I am told by the Cardinal Secretary of State to order you to go home. Write another letter, asking the Holy Father's forgiveness. The cardinal will try to obtain it for you. But he guarantees nothing."

He opened the door and strode off without bothering to close it. Dennis kicked it shut and whirled to face Matthew Mahan, eager to explode. But the hot words were strangled in his throat. Matthew Mahan sat leaning back in the chair as if he had been battered by a hundred punches. "He was my friend."

The sadness in Matthew Mahan's eyes was unbearable. "Did you refuse to fire me?" Dennis asked, and knew the answer. He stumbled in another direction. "I—how would he know?"

"Petrie," Matthew Mahan said wryly. The room was charged with defeat, disaster.

"You're not going to let that man discourage you?"

"No. I said we'd stay here until the Pope saw us. We will."

"I'm sure the Pope hasn't even seen your letter," Dennis said.

"He saw it," Matthew Mahan said. "Why else would I be told to ask his forgiveness? He saw it. Let's go to bed, Dennis. I feel terribly tired. We can talk in the morning."

Dennis lay rigid. For hours sleep was out of the question. At last he dozed. Half in, half out of sleep, he heard bells tolling distantly. Then a voice, "Dennis. . . ." Faint, unrecognizable. *"Dennis. . . ."* He woke up to the harsh, unmistakable sound of a man fighting for air.

He turned on the light and cried out with anguish. Matthew Mahan was slumped against the back of his bed, his pajama shirt soaked with blood. Dennis stumbled to his feet.

"A hemorrhage," Matthew Mahan whispered. "Bill Reed warned me— Get me to the bathroom. . . ."

"No. Lie still," Dennis cried and snatched up the phone. A sleepy clerk answered. The pensione had no doctor.

"Ambulanza, ambulanza!" Dennis shouted. *"Presto! Subito!"*

"Get me a towel. I'm making such a mess," Matthew Mahan said as Dennis hung up. Within minutes the towel was soaked red. A knock on the door. The room clerk stood there wide-eyed.

"Ambulanza?" Dennis asked. The fellow turned and ran downstairs. Dennis realized that he had not called yet. He had come to see if these crazy Americans were drunk or something.

He put another towel in Matthew Mahan's clutching fists. Then the spasm was over. No more blood. Over. "Thank God. Here, let me get this off you." Dennis stripped off the pajama shirt with trembling fingers. "Can you move to my bed?"

Matthew Mahan nodded. Dennis draped the cardinal's arm around his shoulders and pivoted his feet over the edge of the bed. His flesh was incredibly cold. When Dennis stood up, his knees buckled under the deadweight. The two of them lunged forward and fell onto the other bed. Dennis lay crushed beneath the heavy body, pure terror swallowing him. He struggled free and with an enormous effort straightened Matthew Mahan in the bed. Tenderly, tears streaming down his face, he cleaned the blood from the cardinal's face and hands. Matthew Mahan smiled faintly and whispered, "Anoint me, Dennis."

"What— No."

"Anoint me, please."

He took the silver vials from the briefcase and knelt beside the bed, struggling for self-control. Then he dipped a finger in the oil and made the sign of the cross on Matthew Mahan's eyes, ears, nose, mouth, hands, and feet, repeating the formula, "Through this holy unction and of His most tender mercy, may the Lord pardon thee whatsoever sins thou hast committed. . . ."

"Thank you. I'd like to confess and receive Communion."

No, I can't hear your confession. The guilty cannot forgive the innocent. He stifled the words, took a stole from the cardinal's briefcase, draped it around his neck, and knelt by the bed again.

"My deepest and most inveterate sin has been pride," Matthew Mahan said. "I struggled against it. But it has a thousand disguises. As soon as I thought I had expelled it from my soul, it was back again with a new demand. I've also struggled, usually in vain, to forgive those who hurt or attacked me. I loved the power and privileges of my office too much. I thank God for having made me aware of this—but it was almost too late. I ask His forgiveness for those years of self-indulgence."

At first, when Dennis tried to speak the words of absolution, they froze in his throat. Sobs racked his body. Then he heard a voice which did not belong to him but to his priesthood. "I absolve you from your sins, in the name of the Father and of the Son and of the Holy Spirit."

From a small, watch-shaped silver pyx he took a white Host.

287

He filled a glass with water and put it on the night table beside the bed and then placed the Host on the cardinal's tongue. He began to choke. The water saved him. He whispered, "Thank you, Dennis. Now we have nothing to fear."

"Where is that ambulance?" Dennis cried.

The room clerk was back in the open door babbling in Italian. "*Sciopero, sciopero, sciopero.*"

"What does it mean?" Dennis asked Matthew Mahan.

"Strike. The ambulances are probably on strike."

"Call Father Goggin. . . ." He scribbled the name and phone number on a piece of paper. The clerk fled once more.

"I don't think it matters, Dennis," Matthew Mahan said. "That's too much blood for even a fat man like me to lose."

"No. You're going to be all right. I know it."

"Dennis. We came a long way—together. I knew the risk—"

The phone rang. It was Goggin. "I'll get a taxi," he said. "I've never been sick here. But someone must know a doctor. . . ."

Dawn turned the sky to furtive gray. Traffic moved in the street.

"Pope John said, the day he consecrated me," Matthew Mahan whispered, "he'd be the first to greet me in heaven. Is there anything to worry about—when you have such a promise?"

"The Church—the Church needs you. I need you."

"Don't be—too anxious about the Church, Dennis. Take your time. We have our Lord's promise. Tell them the truth in your book—but be patient if they don't hear you."

"The hell with the Church! No—I don't mean that." He struggled to control himself. "Are you in pain?"

"No. No pain at all."

The words struck Dennis like the tolling of a funeral bell. Incredibly, his mind leaped beyond this room where death was strangling his naïve vision of the future. He saw himself telling Helen that he was choosing his priesthood instead of her. He knew that he alone was the sufferer, that Helen no longer needed him. He knew, too, that thanks to this dying man beside him, even he might approach that inner circle of healing love.

Matthew Mahan had closed his eyes. Within the darkness, he seemed to be voyaging across a vast sea. There was a sense of flowing, as if he were riding a current that carried him toward a blurred horizon. At times the sea was turbulent. He was carried up toward an angry sky on great waves of regret. One after another, his failures surged up through his soul. And he thought of the divorced, the lonely, the poor in spirit—the lost sheep whom he had failed to seek strenuously enough. So many failures. Why was there at the same time this peace?

He opened his eyes and saw Dennis McLaughlin's tear-stained face. Behind him, although he knew they were not there, he saw Mary, Mike Furia, Bill Reed, and Helen, the last two not sad at all, but smiling, for they already knew the miracle of love achieved. There were other faces beside the bed now. Dennis's friend Goggin looking frightened, and a swarthy man with a black bag. He felt a hand on his wrist, the disk of a stethoscope pressed to his chest. "*Ambulanza. Subito. Subito.*" Goggin was telephoning.

"It's all right, Dennis, it's all right," Matthew Mahan whispered. "Just hold my hand."

He tried to close his fingers, but there was no strength left. No strength, no pain. He closed his eyes again and saw a wide white beach. The air seemed full of bells ringing out a song of praise. The beach vanished. A ghostly fog rolled in. The air was still full of bells. He heard a soldier's voice, "Padre, hey Padre," and an Irish brogue, "Matthew me boy." Finally a voice that came to meet him in the mist: "*Mio figlio Americano.*" Strong peasant hands seized him, rough familiar arms crushed him to an unseen chest. He was safe in the land of his fathers.

"Too late," the doctor was saying. Goggin had found a private ambulance service. Too late.

It was six a.m., and the bells of Rome were ringing. Dennis looked down at Matthew Mahan. They had been defeated, utterly. But, strangely, he felt no grief.

He spent the day filling out endless government forms, sending cables, fending off reporters, haggling bookings for himself and the cardinal's coffin on the first available flight.

The grimmest task was telling Mary Furia. "Oh, God, it's my fault, my fault," she sobbed.

"No. Mine," Dennis said. Then he spoke as a priest. "Really—it was neither one of us. He knew. He knew what he was doing."

It was midafternoon by the time he and Goggin returned to the pensione. On the corner they picked up a newspaper that had a large headline about Il Papa. Goggin rapidly translated. Paul had refused to consult the Church on clerical celibacy, as the Dutch bishops had requested. Celibacy "cannot be abandoned or subjected to argument," the Pope said.

"But the case is not closed," Dennis said.

Upstairs, Mary Furia knelt beside Matthew Mahan's body. The undertaker had dressed him in his red cassock and cape. "I trust you are satisfied, Father," said the undertaker.

"Yes," said Dennis.

"I feel the need for a ceremony," said Goggin. He took from his pocket a small looseleaf book that Dennis realized was a draft of the New Gospel. Goggin stood at the foot of the bed. Mary Furia stood on the right, Dennis on the left. Matthew Mahan's face was empty. Death was truly a thief, Dennis thought.

Goggin began to read. " 'What is this talk of being a shepherd?' the people asked Jesus. 'We are not sheep, to be led to the trough or to slaughter as you choose.'

" 'You are sheep in your needs,' said Jesus. 'In the hunger of your hearts for my peace. You are sheep in your blind worship of lust and money. You are sheep in your hatreds. You are sheep in your endless fears for tomorrow. You are sheep in your loneliness. This is why I say that I am the good shepherd, who sees that he must lay down his life to feed his sheep with the truth of his love. My father loves me because I lay down my life that you may take it up again more abundantly. No man takes my life away from me. I am laying it down of my own will. . . .'

"A dispute rose among the people over these words.

"Many of them said, 'He is possessed by the devil, he is mad. Why do you listen to him?' But others said, 'These are not the words of the devil. Can the devil open the eyes of the blind?' "

Dennis looked out the window at St. Peter's dome. In his pocket, his index finger slowly circled the outer spiral of his moon shell. "Amen," he said. "Amen."

When Thomas Fleming set about writing *The Good Shepherd* he kept remembering, without quite knowing why, the Michelangelo statue of Moses he had seen two years before when in Rome with his wife and four children. Sitting in his study in New York, staring at a photograph of the statue, for untold moments he was lost in its strength and sadness, unconscious of his own identity; when he came back to himself, he knew he had the core of his book.

Thomas Fleming

In 1927, Thomas Fleming was born into an Irish-Catholic family; he was reared in the Church and educated in its schools. It was not until 1945, fresh from St. Peter's Prep, that he edged out of its sheltering arms by enlisting in the United States Navy. He saw no action on the USS *Topeka* (the war was nearly over), but through his friendship with a remarkable Protestant chaplain he was exposed to the unorthodox ideas of religious philosophers. His deep involvement with the Church that would always be an integral part of his life could never again be unquestioning.

After the war, two other extraordinary men influenced young Tom Fleming's life and attitudes. The first was a free-thinking Irish Jesuit under whom he studied at Fordham University and on whom the character of Bishop Cronin is so affectionately modeled. The second was the famous editor, writer, and Catholic convert, Fulton Oursler, who convinced his brilliant assistant, Fleming, that his future lay in writing.

At first, Fleming could write only in spare time. But with the success of his first novel, *All Good Men,* he gave up his job (by then he was executive editor of *Cosmopolitan*) and has never found it necessary to hold another.

Thomas Fleming is also a distinguished historian. A condensation of *The Man Who Dared Lightning,* about Benjamin Franklin, appeared in The Reader's Digest in 1970; his biography of Thomas Jefferson, *The Man from Monticello,* was a Condensed Books selection.

THE
PROPERTY
OF A
GENTLEMAN

·

A condensation of the book by
Catherine Gaskin

·

Illustrated by
Ben Wohlberg

Joanna Roswell was young, beautiful, and had a promising career as an antiques expert in one of the world's great auction houses. Yet something was missing from her life. Then comes the invitation to accompany Gerald Stanton to Thirlbeck, ancestral home of the earls of Askew. They hope they'll be asked to arrange a discreet sale of whatever antiques might be housed in the decaying old manor. Once there, Joanna finds priceless treasures. She also discovers that it is easy to believe in ghosts.

Against her will, Joanna becomes deeply enmeshed in the lives of the two men who stand in the path of Thirlbeck's rich but deadly legacy—Robert Birkett, the present earl, and his reluctant heir, the disturbingly intent Nat Birkett.

In this, her finest novel, Catherine Gaskin weaves a rich tapestry of romance and mystery. A gripping tale from the author of *Edge of Glass, Fiona,* and *A Falcon for a Queen.*

PROLOGUE

ABOUT half of the ninety-three passengers, those in the tail section, on the flight out of Zurich bound for Paris and London survived when the plane plowed into a mountainside shortly after takeoff. Among those killed were an antique dealer from London by the name of Vanessa Roswell, and a man, presumed to be Dutch, whose body no one claimed and whose passport the authorities, after close examination, found to be forged.

Within hours of the crash, Joanna, the daughter of Vanessa Roswell, and a friend, Gerald Stanton, were on their way to Zurich, with the desperate unspoken hope that Vanessa might be among the survivors. Before he left London, Gerald Stanton managed the difficult feat of reaching by telephone a remote hacienda in the mountains of Mexico, to summon Vanessa Roswell's husband to Zurich. He arrived the day after the crash. Her body had already been identified, so he went to a hotel to which the police directed him. There he found, sitting in silence before a fire in a private sitting room, Gerald Stanton and a young woman. A beautiful young woman, he thought, gauging her with his painter's eye, although her face now wore the numbed expression of shock and grief. She looked at him without recognition. That was not surprising; she hadn't seen him for twenty-seven years.

"Joanna," he said quietly. "I'm Jonathan—your father, Jonathan Roswell."

CHAPTER ONE

BUT IT was not my father, Jonathan Roswell, whom Gerald and I discussed at lunch one day more than two weeks after the Zurich crash. It was, rather, the man we were going to visit, Robert Birkett. "When a year in jail, Joanna, is for manslaughter of one's wife and son—as it was for Robert—it must be a particular sort of hell."

Gerald drew slowly on his cigarette, not at all hurried by the thought that we still had a long way to travel that afternoon. He had deliberately sought out this well-recommended restaurant far off the motorway, had had his martini to the exact degree of dryness and chill his cultivated palate demanded, had had his wine with lunch. Because I was driving I restricted myself to a glass of sherry.

"Robert's father and grandfather were typical English eccentrics," Gerald continued. "They were recluses and autocrats; their estate, Thirlbeck, must have seemed like their own kingdom, so isolated and remote. Robert quarreled with his father. Then he committed the heresy of joining the International Brigade during the Spanish Civil War. While in Spain he married an aristocratic girl whose family, of course, fought on the other side—with Franco. She was a Catholic, naturally. Robert returned to Thirlbeck only for his father's funeral. He was actually on his way back there when the accident happened. So he attended his father's funeral and then the funeral of his wife and son. Afterward they charged him with manslaughter—said he'd been drinking and lost control of the car. A year's sentence."

"And I suppose he's kept to the pattern himself—a recluse in his own isolated world ever since." I said it absently, thinking of the journey ahead.

Gerald stubbed out his cigarette and added to my impatience by pausing to light another. I realized I was fussing, worrying about small things. After all, this was a restaurant, not Hardy's, the auction house that was the center of both our lives. In Hardy's one was not permitted to smoke in the public rooms. But Gerald smoked incessantly at other times; he was in his late sixties, and a lifelong devotion to good wine and food had produced only a pleasing roundness of face and the slightest thickening at the waist.

I suppose if I had to name my closest friend, I would have named him. I was twenty-seven. It was nice to have a friend who had never even remotely threatened to become a lover.

"Quite the contrary," Gerald answered. "Robert got out of jail just after the war started in 1939 and immediately enlisted. He was antiestablishment before anyone heard the word. Nothing would persuade him to take a commission. Perhaps he intended to serve out the war anonymously. But he wasn't born to be anonymous. He won a Military Cross at Dunkirk and a Victoria Cross in the Western Desert. When it was all over he made an effort to disappear. But people like Robert find it difficult to disappear."

"What happened?"

Gerald frowned a little. "I know he went back to Thirlbeck, and I think he stuck it out there for perhaps six months. Then he left, and so far as I know he's never been back. He began to travel. I'd known him at school—at Eton. Whenever I encountered him in later years he always was just back from some odd spot like Yucatán—or sailing round Cape Horn. I don't think he ever had a permanent home—always rented villas. He never married again. That might have been too permanent also. But he probably has had a dozen-odd mistresses—some rich, some famous, some both. All of them beautiful, those that I've seen. He could always attract women, could Robert. He has style as well as charm. You'll see."

Outside, the bright April morning had darkened to a rain-threatened afternoon. "Odd," I said. "I don't remember ever hearing of him. And I'm not too stodgy to look at gossip columns."

Gerald shrugged. "Well, he's in his early sixties now—he's not one of the *young* beautiful people. And in the last few years it's been common knowledge that he's short of money, probably broke. He doesn't buy jewelry for the beautiful ladies any longer, nor give parties. He may yet become a recluse. By necessity, not by choice."

"Unless he decides on a sale and then lives off the proceeds."

Gerald's lips tightened just a trifle. "My dear Joanna, I really am surprised that by now you do not display more discretion. There is not yet even the whisper of a sale. All we know is that he is financially embarrassed, that he returned, hardly a week ago, to a house he has not seen since 1945, and that he has invited me to visit. In this business we go anywhere we're invited socially—and keep our eyes open. And then, perhaps I'm wrong, but Robert gave me the impression of a fearful man needing . . . help. I believe that is why he asked me to come." He gave me his smile of restrained affection. "And that is why I asked you to come with me. We all have need of our friends, Jo."

Gerald paid the bill and then wandered off to the gents' in a leisurely fashion. I went out to the car, emptied the ashtray, studied the map, and cursed myself for being a fool. Was I going to spend my life emptying ashtrays, because that was what they had taught me at Hardy's? But they'd also taught me a reverence for people like Gerald, who seemed to know far more than I could ever hope to. So I was willing to empty ashtrays and chauffeur his stately Daimler just for the experience of being with him, of going over a house and seeing his discerning eye scan a library or a ceramics collection, while I made notes. I was privileged, and I knew it.

As I waited I swung the driving mirror down and combed my hair. The face I saw always seemed to belong to a stranger. Was it because I tried to please too many people too often, never letting my own personality come through? Twenty-seven. Not old, but not so young either. I worked more determinedly at my hair. Was all my passion, were all my young years to be spent authenticating pieces of ceramics, my specialty at Hardy's? Then I saw Gerald strolling toward the car, and like a dutiful girl guide I rushed to open the door for him. I did it before I could stop myself. Damn it! Hadn't I any blood in my veins besides what Hardy's put there?

But Hardy's was in my blood, whether I liked it or not. There had not been the slightest thought of refusal when Gerald had suggested that I join him on this visit to Thirlbeck, home of Robert Birkett, eighteenth earl of Askew, where we might find treasures or perhaps—in Gerald's favorite phrase—a load of old rubbish.

GERALD had told me to take the turnoff from the motorway at Penrith. I thought there might be a stream of cars heading for the Lake District this Friday afternoon, but it was spring, still cold, and the traffic was thin. A slashing rain closed the horizons; Gerald dozed, and I was left to my thoughts.

Gerald probably had been my mother's closest and oldest friend. They had met soon after I was born, when she was trying to set up in business in Kensington; he had taught her much of what she came to know about antiques, introduced her to other dealers, and kept a friendly eye on her rather chaotic business methods. He had watched her indulgently through a series of love affairs and comforted her when they inevitably ended. He'd never lectured or tried to change her. She had been a beautiful, passionate woman, and in a world that too often contains dull, safe people, Gerald had prized her. For what he had done for Vanessa I loved Gerald. Now it seemed almost as if I had, with her death, slipped into her place, though I was unlike her in so many ways.

Gerald had, of course, been my introduction to Hardy's—that and the fact that Vanessa had been there every week, viewing, attending the sales, bidding when something interested her. Some of her buys had been inspired, some good, some bordered on mad extravagance. This quality in my mother had been well known and, I thought, hadn't helped when I went for my interview with the directors of Hardy's. My chances hinged on whether they believed I might have Vanessa's brilliance without her hasty excesses. Other things did help; I was the right age then—eighteen. Better, in their eyes, to have too little education than too much of the wrong kind. They would teach me what I needed to know.

I had come through the interview, Gerald carefully absenting himself, and had taken my place on the front counter, as everyone who worked for Hardy's did for some period. Except for the beginner's salary it was wonderful. I had everything going for me— my beautiful, flamboyant mother giving me an airy little wave as she ascended the great staircase to the salerooms; there was Gerald, who was my friend and mentor; and there was also the fact that I was the daughter of Jonathan Roswell, some of whose paintings were even then beginning to bring very respectable prices in the salerooms. After a year on the front counter someone decided that my aptitude might lie in ceramics. For the next few years I saw less of Vanessa because I had taken a flat on my own. I went on working, growing up, and somehow waiting for something to happen—perhaps waiting to become identifiably my own self.

The rain was drifting off into mist. I enjoyed the power and smoothness in the big car. Smoothness was Gerald's whole life-style, and on it he spent what was necessary of his considerable fortune.

He had money for a way of life that had thrown him into the company of people who trusted Hardy's with the sale of their most valued possessions, people who didn't want publicity for such sales. At Hardy's their treasures would be discreetly marked with the obscure designation THE PROPERTY OF A GENTLEMAN, or some other kindly shield. Of course, all was recorded—the price, the owner's name, the buyer, and if the object had ever passed through Hardy's before—all of it there in the leather-bound daybooks kept since Hardy's had opened in St. James's two hundred years ago. And how much of the information in those books— and more—Gerald literally carried in his head!

This venture today had been brought about by Gerald's long-reaching contacts. And I was along because he had wanted me with him, and because I was only two days back from Mexico, and the shock of my mother's death and the spell of the man who was my father were still upon me.

When, in Switzerland, Jonathan had turned to me after the funeral and said, "Will you come back to Mexico with me—for a few weeks of sun and quiet, Jo?" it had been Gerald who pushed me toward the decision. "You should go, Jo. I'll make it all right with Hardy's."

I looked at the stranger who was my father, who was proposing that I learn to know him after twenty-seven years, and I answered with a nod. I had not regretted the decision.

It had been what he promised—quiet, remote, an almost peasant style of life lived by the numerous descendants of a family who had been granted huge acreage and licensed to mine its silver by Spanish kings. Their sprawling hacienda was nearly in ruins. Jonathan had stumbled across it twenty years ago and had asked to rent one of the dilapidated outbuildings as a studio and living quarters. He had lived as a member of the family ever since, paying for expensive items like electricity, transport, and the food they couldn't grow themselves. They didn't consider his paintings true pictures at all, and so they didn't take his work seriously. What they did take seriously was his concern for them, his efforts to keep their way of life going, even though the silver mines had long since passed from their control. As his daughter I was regarded with curiosity and veneration. At first I found it uncomfortable, and in the end succumbed—to the place, to the gentle people, to the atmosphere of life centuries ago.

I could remember standing beside him, staring up at the great stone sixteenth-century aqueduct which still fed the hacienda its water. "How clear the air is—and the light's so harsh."

"A painter's light, Jo. I see all I need in it—bright, fierce colors and black shadows. This landscape says everything I want to say." And it was there that he had become one of the foremost abstractionist painters in the world. "I'll never leave here," he added. "They'll bury me with their family, Jo—there beside the chapel."

Somehow, in that short time, I knew at last why he and Vanessa had parted. Impossible to imagine her in this setting. Impossible to imagine him anywhere else. He had been right to ask me to come; now I had a father whom I'd begun to understand.

Then back to London and, with my bags hardly unpacked, Gerald's phone call; he wanted me to come with him to visit Thirlbeck and had gotten the permission of my director. I visited Hardy's, and everyone was kind and said nice things about Vanessa. I wandered upstairs to the largest of the salerooms, where they were auctioning English pictures. The room was packed, and the prices were running high; dealers murmured deprecating remarks about what other dealers bought. It was very far from the clear, calm silence of Mexico. I was back to my old world, but something in it had changed.

Afterward I went and gave my routine donation of blood at St. Giles Hospital. Then at home I cooked some chops for supper, and sat and willed the telephone to ring with a call from Harry Peers, but no call came. Harry had sent three long, extravagant cables to Mexico, but no message waited for me here. I began to repack for this trip with Gerald, a kind of hurting ache in my throat at the thought of Harry Peers. Gerald said Harry had flown unannounced to Switzerland on the day I left with my father for Mexico and had just missed me. That was Harry. In the end I finally telephoned his flat, and his manservant told me that Mr. Peers was out of the country; he didn't know when he would be back. So I would wait, and sometime he would phone. I wished I could feel angry with him, but I couldn't. I could either accept him as he was or do without him. I didn't want to do without him.

GERALD's voice came to me over the soft clicking of the windscreen wipers. I had thought he was asleep.

"It's wonderful how the excitement comes back. I was beginning

301

to think I was too old for this business." Because of his age Gerald now worked only in an advisory capacity, and he was, therefore, free to indulge his passion—the quiet search for what was still unknown and undocumented. As if he knew I would bridge his thoughts he continued. "I can't find a record of Thirlbeck's contents anywhere. It must be the only house of any size in England which hasn't been photographed and written up. They must have been eccentrics with a vengeance, those Birketts." Then he added, "Robert won't be expecting you, but he will accept you. He is charming, always, with women."

Gerald continued in a low tone, as if his words were almost for himself. "All those years—and a house unvisited, unrecorded. What shall we find, I wonder? Of course, there *is* something—something so superlative that even the Birketts haven't been able to hide its existence. But who would ever buy it? No one in his right mind. Still, what an auction La Española would make. . . ." His voice trailed off into a sigh. I kept the pace, driving steadily at seventy, and asked no questions. "I hope the place isn't too run down," he said a minute or so later. "I hope there's ice for the drinks."

We edged toward Thirlbeck by miles of those tortuous, magical roads of the Lake Country; the mountains humped about us, fantastic shapes, like a strung-out menagerie of child-drawn animals marching along the skyline—not high mountains, really, but the rises and descents so sheer that they seemed to tower above us.

"Theatrical," was Gerald's comment. "We'll have to remember to call them fells," he said, nodding at the mountains. "And the small lakes are tarns. Well, we shall make mistakes, but then, here all visitors are contemptible tourists. I know an art dealer—odd sort—who comes up here every year for fell walking. I took the trouble to telephone him before we left. He's heard of Thirlbeck, of course, but he doesn't *know* anything about it. It's just a name on a map, in a valley that's almost completely bounded by the national park. My friend once wrote and asked to come onto the estate. He got a less than polite letter warning him of legal action if he tried it. When they say trespassers will be prosecuted they *mean* it. Oh, Jo, I wish we'd *get* there; it's been a long day. I've never much cared for the Lake District. Too violent. Too much rain."

"And this is my first time here. Funny, I really don't know England at all. It's shameful, but on holidays I always shot off to

Paris and Rome and Madrid to look at museums and churches." The thought came sharply, unexpectedly. "Gerald, have I spent too much of my life with my nose pasted against the display cases in museums? I'm twenty-seven—don't laugh! It sounds young to you. But quite suddenly I'm beginning to feel that I've missed out on something. And I haven't really any idea what it is."

"Why don't you marry Harry Peers? You could have the Metropolitan Museum *and* a suite at the top of the Hotel Pierre. You could *buy* those little pieces of Chinese porcelain, instead of just looking at them. Perhaps Harry can give you all the worlds you think you might have missed."

"What's wrong about that idea, Gerald, is that Harry hasn't asked me to marry him. But yes, I think I would if he finally decided that I was right. Because he'd want it to be for good—and forever. His values are still working-class. He'd never gamble on marriage the way he does in the property market."

"Well, then, he's a bit of a fool, something I didn't think I'd ever say of Harry Peers. If he won't gamble on you, Jo, he *is* a fool."

I smiled. "Gerald, you're kind. That will make reading his doings in the gossip columns a little easier."

Perhaps I was thinking too much of Harry, but then the bend in the road at that particular point was very sharp. I was almost on top of the other car before I saw it and applied the brakes sharply. "Sorry," I said to Gerald. "But he's absolutely crawling along."

"Yes. . . . It would have been a pity."

"What would have been a pity?"

"If you'd run into the back of a . . . well, I'd guess it could be about a 1931 Bentley. Beautiful condition, isn't it?"

I dropped back. We were within ten miles of Kesmere, the town closest to Thirlbeck, and for all I knew, there wouldn't be a stretch of road on which it would be safe to pass before then. The bends were sharp and numerous. I sighed; it would soon be dusk.

Then the Bentley, a convertible with the top down, pulled over to the side and stopped. I saw the driver signaling me to pass with an impatient gesture. I had the impression of a youngish man with careless, tow-colored hair. I saluted to thank him, and drove on.

We went about two miles farther, dropping down almost to the floor of the valley, and once again I had to touch the brakes quickly. Both of us had almost missed it—a break in the high stone wall we had been following for about half a mile and, between crumbling stone pillars unpleasantly topped by barbed wire, a strong pair of galvanized iron-mesh gates. Behind the wall, which was also spiked with barbed wire, were the ruins of a gatehouse. A bleak, rather crudely lettered sign hung on the gates.

THIRLBECK
STRICTLY PRIVATE
TRESPASSERS WILL BE PROSECUTED

I looked at Gerald. "This is it?" The road beyond the gatehouse seemed barely more than a half-overgrown track, rising at an impossibly steep angle between hand-cut stone walls.

"Has to be." Gerald drew a deep breath. "Good grief—do you suppose this is the *main* entrance?" He was fumbling in his jacket pocket. "Must say his directions weren't very explicit. . . . Where's that letter?"

I was out of the car by now, and Gerald had wound down his window. "This has to be his back door," I said. I was rattling the chain and lock that secured the gates and looking beyond them to the ruined lodge, which must once have been quite beautiful. Then I saw, propped against its side wall, the rusted remains of heavy wrought-iron gates, a tracery of design through them, and what might be part of a crest. "I hope his front door is more welcoming. We'll have to go on, Gerald. I'm sorry."

He had found the letter. "Yes—he says go through Kesmere and take the right. . . . Oh, well, we'll ask when we get there."

I took one last look at the road and saw that its paving had been hand laid, as were the walls. There was a kind of lordliness in that, a memory, even, of the days when labor had been so cheap; and now the weeds grew through the stones, and the noble emblem on the great gates had rusted into anonymity.

FOR all its splendor, the Bentley had a noisy engine; I heard it coming before it rounded the last bend. It stopped in front of the big gates, and the man got out. He looked less young, less sporty now. He wasn't old or even middle-aged, but it was a tired face, a thin, straight-cut mouth, and weather wrinkles about the gray eyes. He had heavy brows, darker than his tow-colored hair. He was wearing a thick sweater and stained corduroy pants.

304

"Do you need help?" It was said rather brusquely, as if he didn't want to waste any time on pleasantries.

Gerald answered. "Lord Askew is expecting us. We—"

"Lord Askew is *expecting* you." He didn't attempt to disguise his sarcasm. "Lord Askew hasn't been here since who knows when."

"You're misinformed." Gerald's tone grew terse. "Lord Askew is in residence, and we are expected this evening. His note says 'go through Kesmere,' but we thought this might be a shorter way."

Now the man rounded the car to speak, and I saw a strange softening of that strained face as he looked at Gerald. They were such an odd contrast: the one with the whiff of the farmyard about him and yet driving that elegant Bentley, and Gerald in his London suit. Still, they recognized the basic honesty in each other.

"You know he's here, then? It's hardly been a week."

"He asked me here. I might presume to say I am a friend."

"A friend. I'm surprised to hear he has a friend in England. Well, no matter. I might be able to help you. This road isn't easy, but it is the shorter way by about twelve miles. Saves you going into Kesmere and looping back."

"But the place is padlocked," Gerald said.

"I rent a piece of land from Askew. I need access and have a key."

Gerald brightened. "Well, then, let's get on."

The man turned to me. "You used to driving steepish inclines?"

"I've driven mountain roads—I take it all carefully."

"Better watch it up there. It's slippery in places. I wouldn't want the responsibility of sending you over the side of a fell." With this, he brought out a bunch of keys.

I was back in the car, the engine turning over. I didn't want the man to change his mind. "Thank you," I said as he swung the gates open for us and we drew level with him. "How far?"

"About three miles. Over the rise and down again."

We went on, and the dim green beauty would have forced silence on us even if we had not been so tired. There were moss-covered rocks within a grove of larch trees, and everywhere the sound of rushing water, as though a stream accompanied us all the way. The rain had stopped, and a flash of the last of the sun came through the trees. It was a scene from an oriental watercolor—the mossy, green stillness; the rocks, each seemingly placed with its own significance. A thousand men could have taken a thousand years to create it. And it had grown here, naturally, in this remotest part of England.

The shock was all the harsher when we emerged from the larch grove and topped the rise. Here was the roof of heaven. We were almost among the clouds. The fells slipped down into a green pasture, then to the dark beauty of a long, slender tarn. And those unbelievable stone walls marched relentlessly up the sides, into the heights—put there time out of mind to mark one man's land from another's, to keep sheep from straying. How could men have built such straight lines over the roughness of a mountainside, with nothing to guide them but their eyes?

In all this secret place there was only the intensity of the terrain, the sheep grazing by the tarn, and the narrow, stone-lined road winding on forever. I was taking the pace very gently on the steep grade. About a mile down beyond the crest a copse of white birches straddled the road. As we descended into the copse we were in the shadow cast by the opposite fells. Suddenly, in spite of the car heater, it was cold.

Then I saw it—a tall white wraith of a dog who stood for an instant beneath the birches and then took flight straight across our path. I slammed on the brakes. Whether it was weeds beneath our wheels or just the suddenness of the braking, the car slipped sickeningly sideways, sliding too fast down the slope toward the next bend, the wheels locked in a skid. I corrected as much as I could, easing my foot off the brake, doing a kind of manic steering. We grazed the wall with the back fender, and I heard stones topple. Then we were straight again; I put my foot very gently on the brake, and we came to a halt. Without a word to Gerald I turned and looked back; the dog had crossed the road and was almost lost among the birches, the long, high stride like a deer in flight.

It was a time before Gerald spoke. "Jo! What possessed you? Is there something wrong with the car?"

I turned to face him. "You didn't see it—the dog? It took off from the trees straight in front of us! I would have crashed right into it!"

"The dog? *What* dog? I didn't see a dog."

"Gerald, it was a very large dog, a whitish dog with long legs. You had to have seen it!"

He took a cigarette from his case and lit it. The trembling of his

hands told me that he did not believe me; he had seen nothing. "I must have nodded off, Jo, dear. No, I missed the dog. Let's get on, then, shall we? It's getting dark. It can't be much farther."

. The words were spoken with infinite kindness. He was prepared to give me the benefit of the doubt or at least not question me further. But it was impossible to believe that so close to the end of the journey, in such a place as this, he had nodded off in sleep. My eyes had seen what his had not. That also was hard to believe.

We went on, and very soon the house became visible about another mile away. As the mist reached us and moved before us the house kept appearing, vanishing, and reappearing—a stone pile, a formidable and strangely beautiful outline in the settling dusk. I wished Gerald would speak; I thought perhaps I was imagining this also.

He did, and his words reflected my own sense of unease, but at least he saw what I did. "I would feel better if there was even a light," he said. "I suppose they *do* have electricity."

"It isn't quite dark yet."

"It feels dark."

The valley floor widened as we drew nearer the house; here were meadows where cattle grazed. Around the house itself was a parkland of ancient trees flushed with the first green of spring. The tarn drifted off into a slim, dark finger close to the walls of a dark and tangled outer garden. Farther on, in what was meant to be the formal garden, daffodils now held sway, thousands of them, rampant, wild, thin little things, growing weaker with the years. Quite abruptly we reached a wide graveled area, weed infested, in front of the house. Half-obliterated paths led off toward the lake and a forest of untamed rhododendrons. "Well," Gerald said, "this has to be Thirlbeck. And . . . yes, it *is* worth seeing!"

It was a magnificent piece of domestic Tudor architecture, loosely wedded to a rough stone peel tower that must have been some centuries older. The house would have been built in Elizabeth's reign, I guessed, when the noblemen, beginning to feel some security, no longer enclosed themselves in castles and fortresses. It was a house of windows, in those times a sign of wealth—tall, mullioned windows, thrusting out in square bays and rising a full two stories. It was beautifully proportioned; its builder had borne in mind that its origins were firmly rooted in that crumbling stone tower which must have been the refuge of the whole manor at the times of the border raiders. There was still a strong sense of the wildness of Scotland even in this graceful structure.

"And to think it's been here so long, and no one seems to know about it—or care," I said softly.

As we sat, feasting our eyes, a door opened. A light shone on the steps, and suddenly what seemed like a dozen enormous shapes came bounding toward the car with a silent, deadly kind of speed. Within seconds the great white hounds were all about us—not really more than eight, I thought, though they seemed more. They were the largest dogs I had ever seen—at least three feet high at their shoulders; they stared at us—huge heads on long necks, deeply whiskered brows, with hairy, bristly faces and little beards. Long, thin tails curled over those powerful but slender backs.

Gerald said faintly, "One might have expected it. These, without doubt, are the hounds of the Birketts."

We didn't move, and the dogs stood motionless, their eyes fixed intently on us. It seemed an interminable time before a tall lean man with faintly hunched shoulders started down the steps. As he drew near, Gerald rolled down the window a few inches.

"Is it safe, Robert?"

The man bent to our level. "The dogs? My dear Gerald, they're gamboling puppies. I'm glad you made it before dark. I saw your lights up on the edge of the fell. The drive over Brantwick in the dark is not for the timid. How are you, Gerald? Good of you to come. Come in—come in! No, really, the dogs are all right. Here, let me help you with the bags. You're both staying, of course."

He was, as Gerald had promised, completely charming. I slid from the car, and even in the fading light I was aware of his curious combination of silver hair, which must once have been very blond, with a rather dark complexion and brows. An incredibly handsome face. The eyes were light—gray or green—I couldn't tell.

"Gerald seems not about to introduce us. I'm Robert Birkett."

"Joanna Roswell, Lord Askew," I answered. "I work at Hardy's, and I often drive Mr. Stanton—"

I stopped because he had put the suitcases down and was staring at me with strange intentness. "You said Roswell? Are you related to the artist Jonathan Roswell?"

"His daughter. You know him, Lord Askew?"

"I used to. But—well, it must be close to thirty years since I last saw him. Of course, he's become famous since then." I smiled now, pleased. So few people seemed to have met my father. He answered my smile. "And your mother—" He stopped abruptly. "How clumsy of me. Please forgive me. She died in that plane crash. I was shocked to read her name in the list. Forgive me," he repeated.

He bent to pick up the cases, and I sensed real distress at what he thought was his blunder. "Well, then," he said quickly, "welcome to Thirlbeck." As Gerald emerged warily from the car Lord Askew called to the hounds. "Ulf, Eldir, Thor, Odin—mind yourselves now!" They moved back obediently.

We followed him toward the house. The double doors had now been opened wide and more lights turned on. I knew, without being able to see her face, that the woman standing in the doorway was beautiful. She carried the assurance of beauty. A sharp wind blowing from the tarn molded her long, thin pale dress about her body. Her long hair was dark, with a sheen of blue. She was like something from those birch woods, a creature of black and white, with hands whose incredible grace and form I could already see and marvel at.

We had mounted the steps, and Lord Askew paused. "Carlota, may I introduce Miss Joanna Roswell. Miss Roswell, this is the Condesa de Ávila. And this, Carlota, is my friend, Gerald Stanton."

Gerald was gazing at her, enchanted. She smiled, familiar with the effect she had had on him. "Please . . . you must both be tired after that fierce drive." Her speech was almost accentless, with but a trace of Spanish. She moved before us into the great hall. Her dress, high-waisted and long-sleeved, low-cut on a beautiful bosom, was pale champagne in color. Several of the dogs flanked her silently, seeming for these moments like creatures from a medieval tapestry.

The hall was splendid, almost bare of furnishings, but warm with the richness of the intricately carved paneling which reached the full two stories. The staircase, which split at a landing, went off on two arms to an upper gallery. There was the scent of flowers from a large jar filled with daffodils on a long oak table. There was the brightness of two fires burning in opposite chimneys. There was little else—a few tall, carved oak chairs, one silken rug. And this graceful creature gesturing toward an open door. "Here is a fire and the drinks. Roberto remembers that you like martinis, Mr. Stanton."

I was conscious of two things as I followed: that Gerald had said all Robert Birkett's mistresses had been beautiful, and that the great white dog that had appeared like a phantom in front of the car at the birch copse, the dog that Gerald had not seen, belonged to the family of these great hounds.

CHAPTER TWO

IT WAS grandeur, and the beginning of decay. We sat in the library, and Gerald had his martini exactly as he liked it; the condesa was expert at that. But my heart ached over the ominous stain of damp in the plaster over one corner of the huge room. Save for the fireplace wall and the great oblong windowed alcove, the room was lined with mahogany bookcases with faceted glass fronts, behind which was the dull gleam of gold-stamped bindings. Under the windows were ugly iron radiators, which gave out a faint heat. The chintz covers of the chairs and sofas were thin to the point of shredding, the flowered patterns of fifty years ago badly faded.

I was not part of the conversation; I roamed the room, glass in hand. There was a single tall prunus jar on top of one section of the bookcases, and I was trying to get a closer look at the plum-blossom design, but it was lost high in shadows. I moved slowly around the perimeter of the room and saw, with a sense of sickening disappointment, that in the damp corner the pale vellum bindings of the books were horribly stained. I wondered if they would survive handling. Lord Askew must have watched my progress. "They're all locked, I'm afraid. I must ask where the keys are." He shrugged. "Perhaps no one knows anymore."

A lifting of Gerald's eyebrows told me to mind my own business. But, of course, this *was* our business. The library held more than books. Crowded between the decaying sofas and armchairs, arranged with no eye to displaying them to advantage, were some of the most beautiful pieces of furniture I had ever seen. Mainly French, I thought—Louis XIV and Louis XV—marquetry tables, writing tables, two magnificent bowfront commodes placed awkwardly back to back, some carved gilt chairs with rough string tied across the fronts so that no one would inadvertently sit on them. They stood about like pieces in some fantasy furniture shop, unrelated, a collector's dream, but a guardian's nightmare when one remembered the fatal combination of the invading damp, and the heat from the big iron radiators. The sale of almost any single piece, I guessed, would have brought the money to find and fix the place where the moisture seeped through the wall. Under our feet, as a cushion for the great dogs who lay about, were rugs, most of them Persian. But the big main one before the fire, the one in imminent danger from the spluttering sparks, was surely Aubusson.

I began to be impatient. What else was in this house? And why had no one known that these pieces—a superb collection—were here? But then, given Gerald's story of the Askew family and the isolation of this valley, what might not have come to it unknown and unmarked? I began to realize more fully the implications of Askew's invitation to Gerald, and the thought was enough to drive out all fatigue. I returned now to my seat near the fire, more anxious to listen to the talk.

The firelight lovingly played over the carved wood of the mantel and reached to the outstretched forms of the dogs on each side of Lord Askew's chair. They seemed extraordinarily content, as if in the presence of their master. Yet Askew had returned only a week ago, and surely this great pack could not have traveled the world with him. I mused on them as the talk went on about me. I still wasn't included, but suddenly, like the dogs, I felt content just to be here.

It was strange, then, to see the condesa shiver and lean further toward the fire. Askew also noticed the gesture and was on his feet at once, laying more split logs on the fire. He smiled. "My poor Carlota, it seems a long way from the sun, doesn't it?"

He said nothing more, but she seemed warmed by his words. The look which passed between them was its own communication. She had to love him to be here with him, this far from the sun. She was about forty, I guessed, but she had the smooth grooming of the international beauty whose age is difficult to tell.

The door opened then, and a man said, "Mrs. Tolson wishes to tell you, my lord, that the rooms are ready. She's put the young lady in the Spanish Woman's room."

I glanced at the condesa, wondering if this was some kind of insolent gibe offered to her. But neither she nor Askew reacted with any sign of outrage. Evidently the Spanish Woman referred to was not she, and all of them understood that.

"Has she, indeed?" Askew said. "Not the coziest place, is it?"

"Can't be helped, my lord," the man answered. "It's the driest—at short notice." He didn't look in the least like a servant, with his flannel trousers and a tweed jacket. He was tall, with stooped shoulders, and very powerfully built. He had a mass of dark hair thickly frosted with gray. It was difficult to see his eyes behind his heavy pebble glasses, and his long, dark, rather melancholy face seemed closed against the coming of strangers. I judged him to be a few years older than the earl, but he seemed rocklike and monumental by contrast. "I've got the fires going," the man continued, "and there's three hot-water bottles in the bed. Be comfortable enough, I should say. I've put the young lady's bag there, and Mr. Stanton's is in his room. Anything else, my lord?"

It was the most curious mixture of familiarity and deference. That he was the man in charge of this establishment there was no doubt; that he respected the titular owner was not open to question either.

Lord Askew gestured with his glass. "Nothing, Tolson, nothing. You've managed very well, as always. Thank you."

The man stepped back, closing the door without another word.

"That was George Tolson. You'll get used to him—Cumberland independence and all. The place couldn't have held together without him all these years. He's been steward and handyman and bookkeeper all in one. He believes I never should have left, but my coming back makes problems. More fires, more hot water. He's never been a butler, though he's trying his best now. . . ." Askew paused, and in that instant his eyes seemed to go beyond the house, to the lake and the surrounding fells and dales.

"There must have been Tolsons here as long as there have been Birketts. Two of his sons have tenancies of land within this valley, two more have farms at Thirldale, just beyond the gates. That's about the area of the original estate. We've sold off a lot of other land. . . . I wish the entail would allow me to sell to the Tolsons; they deserve to own the land they farm." He nodded, as if reinforcing his own words. "The Tolsons are strong men, all of them, intelligent and competent. Tough, as farmers here have to be. George Tolson and his brother, Edward, were just a few years ahead of me.

My father sensed the good material he had, and he saw that they both got to the grammar school in Kesmere. Edward went on to become a solicitor—my father got him articled to a London firm. He was more than a success. Handled all the estate business until he died about two years ago. But George Tolson never had any idea of leaving Thirlbeck. He's become quite a patriarch over the years— I swear he must have chosen all the wives for his sons. If he did, he showed eminently good sense. They're a clannish lot; they've kept this valley just about totally closed off. That's the way my father wanted it, that's the way he trained Tolson. I've sometimes thought how much better it would have been for my father and Thirlbeck if Tolson had been his son. . . ." He brought his lips together in a wry smile, switching the subject off.

And then the noises began—a heavy metallic clanging. Gerald and I straightened and glanced at Askew. He gestured to dismiss the sound. "That will be Tolson closing the metal shutters he's had put on the windows on this floor. Part of his idea of security. One of his sons, Ted, fitted them. He is a very handy mechanic as well as a farmer. The Tolsons are almost self-sufficient. One of the granddaughters lives here in the house, and others have come in to help since we arrived. Carlota thinks—"

Suddenly Askew rose, and the dogs all scrambled to their feet. It was like seeing an army come alive. He had evidently decided against telling us what the condesa thought about Tolson and his family. "Shall we go up, then? Give you a chance to get settled before dinner." Then he looked down at the condesa. "You stay, my love. No need to leave the fire. I won't be long."

She stretched her slender body in the big chair, and the shining black hair fell forward, an incredibly sensuous movement. "Will you pour me a whisky before you go, Roberto—please?"

She accepted it from him with a charming smile, and then her eyes were drawn back to the fire, as if it were a substitute sun.

GERALD and Askew went ahead into the hall. At the landing, where the two arms of the staircase branched, they waited for me. "Mostly sixteenth century—except for the peel tower, which might go back to the twelfth," Askew was explaining. "The townspeople used to come out here to the tower for protection from the border raiders. Very feudal. The Birketts exploited their power in every way possible, I'm afraid. The title dates from Elizabeth's time, and the first earl built this house. Modern conveniences were introduced about fifty years ago—electricity, bathrooms, and the heating, which never really has worked. But it's better than outright freezing. I'm afraid the whole place needs a complete overhaul, but it won't be done in my time. If it is *ever* done. . . ."

"What will happen to it?" I couldn't bear Askew's detached tone. He shrugged. "I expect it will fall down when there isn't money to keep it together and when the Tolsons' ingenuity and energy is exhausted. Perhaps the National Trust will want to preserve it. I haven't offered it, and I don't know if there's enough money to endow it or that I care to spend that much on it. Perhaps you can end up giving too much to a mere building. Well, it doesn't concern me greatly. Shall we go on?"

He had treasure all about him, a truly great inheritance, and he didn't care. For this, I felt myself almost hating him as he led the way up to the gallery, then to Gerald's room. It was comfortable—in its masculine, red-plush Victorian style—rather than imposing; and it was stuffy. The fire must have burned there all day. "I thought you'd find it warmer than most we have to offer, Gerald. Bathroom's through here. Miss Roswell, I think Tolson means you to use this bathroom, too—there's a door from the passage."

Gerald waved airily. "Jo will manage, Robert. At Hardy's we bring them up to manage. And she's been *very* well brought up."

I felt my anger at Askew extend to Gerald also. He didn't have to make me appear such an earnest child. And yet, I supposed that was how I often did appear. When Askew gestured to show me to my own room I followed silently.

We came out on the gallery above the hall again. Askew paused. "Let me see. . . . Yes, this is it. I haven't had time since we returned to see all the rooms." He opened the door and waited for me to precede him. But the involuntary stiffening of his body warned me that something had disturbed him. "I hadn't remembered it quite like this," he said, as if he were talking to himself.

It seemed an immense room, its size increased by the fact that only one light burned there—an absurdly modern lamp perched on a stool by the bed. The shadows, therefore, were black and deep, and the glow from the leaping flames of two opposite fireplaces didn't bridge the darkness between them.

315

"Can you stand it? Perhaps I should ask Tolson . . ."

"Please, don't." I moved past him, fascinated by the room's somber magnificence. A huge four-poster bed, hung with dark blue velvet curtains, hardly impinged on its space. There was a long oak stretcher table in the big rectangle of bay windows, and a straight-backed chair at one end. A tapestry-covered chair stood before one of the fireplaces, with a footstool beside it, and a carved oak chest flanked the second fireplace. A few pieces of blue delftware were the room's only ornaments; the biggest piece, a deep bowl, had been placed in the middle of the table. I moved toward it, and quite distinctly came the sad-sweet smell of last summer's roses. The bowl was full of petals, and I couldn't stop myself from running my hand through them.

It did not seem like a place just disturbed from a period of long neglect. The wax polish on the table shone lustrously, and the delft pieces had been recently dusted.

"I suppose Tolson's right. It's dry enough. The chimney probably has a common flue with one of the chimneys in the hall, and Tolson keeps fires there all year round. There are some closets. . . ." He was opening wide doors in the paneling on each side of one of the fireplaces. In the dimness I hadn't noticed the carved wooden knobs indicating the doors. "Shelves this side—hanging on this side." He shrugged. "Well, it will have to do, though I wish Tolson could have managed something a bit less forbidding."

"I like it, Lord Askew."

He glanced at me curiously. "Do you? Shall I draw the curtains? It would make it cozier."

"No, thank you. One gets enough of drawn curtains in London." We moved toward the windows at the same time. I realized now that this room was directly over the library and shared the same oblong bay of leaded glass windows that faced out across the lake. The rain had cleared, and an icy moonlight struck obliquely through. "Look," I said, "there's snow on the mountain."

"That's Great Birkeld—the highest around here. It catches all the weather. Quite often you can't see it for days at a time because of clouds. The word changeable must have been invented for this country—mist, bright sun, pelting rain, snow, clear moonlight. Heaven knows how the people stand it. I couldn't. . . ."

Three of the dogs had now crossed the room to join him. He

stood staring out at the tarn, and the moonlight turned his hair to bright silver. I literally saw a gust of wind ripple along the surface of the lake and heard its moan about the building.

"Mr. Tolson called it the Spanish Woman's room. Why is that?"

Askew fidgeted for a while without attempting a reply. He checked the closet again, as if he were counting the hangers, lighted the candle on the mantel and carried it to the oak chest. "The Spanish Woman . . ." He took a deep breath. "The Spanish Woman was the second countess of Askew. It was a kind of derogatory term given to her in this household where anyone both Catholic and Spanish was not welcome. Her husband, the second earl, was also Catholic—many of the landowners still were Catholic or were changing from Catholic to Protestant and back again according to who was on the throne. But this was Elizabeth's reign, and so the Protestants were in power. The second earl was accused of plotting to put Mary, Queen of Scots, on the throne, and he lost his head on Tower Hill. He was a relic of the old faith, rather a fanatic, I'd judge. Before he inherited the title he spent some years in Spain—at the court of Philip the Second—where he married a Spanish bride. It may have been love, but more likely it was politics. She was a noblewoman, distantly related to Philip, and, of course, Philip hoped to bring England back to Catholicism. He was already preparing to send the Armada. It would be a great help to have a Catholic nobleman and ally here in Cumberland. And if Philip should successfully invade—or if Elizabeth should die and leave Mary the throne—the earl would have become one of the premier earls of England, instead of a minor border lord. Then, too, his Spanish bride came with a dowry and a promise of large wealth to follow. She joined her husband here just before he was arrested and taken off for trial. In the little time they had spent together she had become pregnant with a possible Catholic heir. Her husband's brother, who would have succeeded if the marriage had been without issue, was Protestant.

"Stories were spun about her over the years, how many true, one doesn't know. It seems that her brother-in-law sent her own servants away, and she was left entirely alone—no friend but a young English serving boy who had been with her husband on his travels and who spoke a little Spanish. There must have been precious little comfort or kindness for her. One imagines—I've imagined—how frightened she must have been, wondering if Elizabeth's commissioners were riding north to question her or if the next mouthful of food was poisoned. They say that for distraction she took to walking high and far on the Brantwick road."

Suddenly he turned and motioned to me. "Look at the tarn down there—innocent, isn't it? Well, she drowned in the tarn. Some were prepared to swear that she had been murdered by her brother-in-law. Poor, lost, lonely little Spanish Woman."

It was the first time I really liked him. As he spoke I knew that the Spanish Woman was a real person to him, not a dry family legend. He pictured her growing heavy with child, a political pawn, longing for the sound of her own language, the dry heat of the Spanish plains. She must have written her sad letters at the table here, sat in that chair by the fire—the chair with the footstool that suggested she had been a small woman. Then I shook my head; I was falling into the earl's mood. It was impossible that no one had disturbed the arrangement of this room in all these years, that that had really been her chair.

Beside me Askew stirred, as if waking from a dream. "You'll be all right here? Perhaps I shouldn't have told you—"

"I'm glad you did. She has to have some friends, doesn't she—the Spanish Woman?"

His smile thanked me for sharing his dream, and I was lost to that smile, as I was sure many women had been. I began to understand very well the presence of his own Spanish woman, the modern beauty who had followed him to this remote, cold world. It would be easy enough to follow Robert Birkett if he asked it.

"Come, dogs." They rose as one and went with him.

TOLSON hadn't become so much the butler that he attempted to unpack for guests. I sorted my clothes between the two closets. One had a wooden rod on which padded hangers rested, and at the back were stout oak pegs which served as hooks, probably there from the time the room and the closets had been paneled.

I wasn't without a sense of clothes—no daughter of Vanessa's could have been. I even had a touch of her flamboyance in that respect, which Harry Peers always found amusing and unexpected. The long skirt I put on was of brilliant orange quilted cotton, and I wore it with a yellow high-necked sweater. Tied about my waist was a long black sash I had bought for a few pounds in one of Hardy's auctions of Victorian costumes. I also wore the amber brooch which had been in Vanessa's handbag on the day of the plane crash. I wore it for her, and with love—the gold and amber had seemed so much a part of Vanessa's personality. "It shall be yours one day, my pet," she had promised.

The gong sounded for dinner, and I combed my hair quickly and added a little more pale lipstick. It wasn't a beautiful face in the mirror, not beautiful the way Vanessa's had been or in the classic mold of that Spanish beauty downstairs at the library fire. "A twentieth-century face you've got, Jo," Harry had once said. From someone, perhaps my father, I had received the blessing of dark brows and lashes, looking odd with the light-colored eyes, neither green nor gray nor blue, and the blond hair. From Vanessa came the mouth, but wider than hers and curving—perhaps to my detriment—to every mood. I made a grimace in the mirror for bothering about what couldn't be changed, and hurried downstairs.

THE dining room was not crowded as the library had been. There was another long oak table, which could only have fitted into a house of this size—Jacobean, I guessed—with a dozen or so chairs which matched it. There were two long sideboards on which the red pilot lights of electric hot trays shone eerily, some beautiful gilt-framed mirrors, and some very ordinary Chinese vases. Once more, all the dogs were grouped about the fire.

Dinner was, unexpectedly, very good. There was onion soup, hot garlic bread, chicken in a sauce that only a serious cook could make, the sort of pastry one saw on the trays of the most expensive restaurants, and a beautiful German wine poured into engraved glasses. I hardly spoke through the whole meal; I was hungry, and the food was delicious. I said so with no trace of false politeness.

"Tolson's granddaughter does most of it," Askew said. "Jessica. She's a natural cook and brilliant, too. Won a scholarship to Cambridge. She didn't take it, though I'm not sure why. Undoubtedly she's her grandfather's pet. He says she just prefers to stay here. She's quite high-strung. . . . I suppose they're afraid of what will happen to her out in the world. Tolson said she was quite seriously ill about three years ago. A pretty little thing, she is. Must be going on twenty now."

The condesa smiled. "Roberto, she will marry someone her formidable grandfather approves of, and live very close by. Wherever one goes in this house, there she is—"

"She helps with the work," Askew interrupted. "A great deal, as far as I can see. Why shouldn't she be around?"

"Housework on the top of the peel tower? I've seen her there."

"I wish you hadn't. The peel tower isn't safe. But then a bright, imaginative child probably has romantic fantasies."

"She is not a child, Roberto," the condesa said quietly. "Highstrung, brilliant—a wonderful cook? Yes. A child? No."

He shrugged, as if to end talk of Jessica, and turned to the dogs. "Extraordinary lot, aren't they?"

"More than that," Gerald said. "I almost had Joanna turn the car around when they appeared. It's hardly . . . well, it's hardly *decent*, my dear Robert. So many of them, and so huge!"

"Don't blame me. They're Tolson's dogs, but since the instant I arrived they unaccountably attached themselves to me. There have always been Irish wolfhounds at Thirlbeck. Somehow Tolson managed to feed and keep alive one breeding pair during the war."

Gerald leaned forward. "There's something particularly important about them?"

"I don't really know." He seemed embarrassed. "Tradition has it that there have always been wolfhounds here. They're a very ancient breed, said to be the largest dog in the world, and famed in Celtic literature for bringing down enormous stags."

"Do they always stay together?" I asked. "None of them ever goes off alone?"

"Not that I've noticed. Always seem to be eight sticking by me."

Then I was aware that his look hadn't been one of embarrassment but of unease. He was gentle with the hounds and offhandedly affectionate. He wasn't afraid of them, but I had the feeling that he wished they weren't there, which was the same feeling I experienced when he had said they never went off alone. I shivered, and hoped that no one had noticed. One of these dogs, I would swear, had dashed across the road before my eyes at the birch copse that evening, nearly causing me to crash.

"I don't know why Tolson bothers with metal shutters," Gerald said. "These dogs would seem better security than armed guards."

"I would not interfere with his arrangements," Askew replied.

"Nor would I, Robert." Gerald beamed over his wineglass. He was at his best at this time of evening, with good food and drinks inside him. His pleasant well-preserved face glowed. All he needed now was a little Mozart.

The wine had brought other thoughts to the condesa. "Roberto tells me your father lives in Mexico," she said to me. "He is fortunate—always the sun. And there is quite amusing society in Acapulco. Does your father go there in the season?"

I almost laughed. "No, never. He lives in a very remote hacienda south of Taxco. He never leaves it, if he can help it."

She shuddered delicately at the thought. "Never?"

"His health's no good in damp places, and sea level in Mexico is very humid."

"I remember he didn't like damp places," Askew said slowly. "He still has that weak chest, then? It rained so much when he was here, and he was trying to paint and not succeeding at all."

"He was here? *Here*—at Thirlbeck?"

"Of course. That's when I knew him." He looked at me in puzzled surprise. "He and Vanessa rented that lodge by the gate where you came in. It wasn't a ruin at that time, though the roof did leak. I would have fixed it if they had been going to stay on. But it wasn't right for either of them—for different reasons. They left with the first snow, and I left soon after." He looked directly at me. "They never told you they were here?"

I shook my head. "All my mother said was that they had rented a cottage in the Lake District the summer the war ended."

"Odd. Well, we had all survived a war, and we were rather heady with the triumph of that simple fact. We were reckless with what remained of the wine cellar my father laid down. I was grateful to them for being here then—it was my one attempt to live at Thirlbeck, and they were good friends, though they were both quite a lot younger than I. They made my attempt bearable, even if in the end it didn't work out."

I couldn't help seeking Gerald's eyes across the table. His rosy face had become almost pallid; I hoped I hadn't betrayed the same shock while Askew was speaking. Gerald and I had thought of Thirlbeck as uncharted ground, and already we had seen treasures here. And Vanessa, whom we both believed we knew so well, had once spent a summer and autumn among these lovely things. In

321

those days, even with limited knowledge, she would have recognized the best of the pieces—who could have forgotten them? Yet she had said nothing of this place—nothing.

WE WENT to the drawing room for coffee. By now I think both Gerald and I had come almost to expect what we found—a room only a little less crowded than the library, herding together beautiful pieces without any thought of display. I ran my finger over the dusty tops of a few of them—commodes, pier tables, gilt wood and tapestry chairs with the same rough string tied across them to prevent their use. A few sofas and chairs, covered in the same faded chintz as those in the library, were there to be sat on. The rest of the contents of the room—if it ever came to auction—would make one of the most exciting sales of fine French furniture Hardy's had ever mounted. I could have cried with impatience at the elaborate game we all played—no one mentioning even the smallest of the magnificent pieces while we drank coffee from inexpensive earthenware cups.

I looked again around the room and realized what was missing from the whole house. While there were beautiful mirrors, there were no pictures, not even portraits of ancestors. Their total absence made me think that in some other room with metal shutters there would be frames and frames stacked against the walls, and among them there might be just one picture that came up to the quality of the pieces we saw about us here.

There was a restlessness in the room, as if we were all holding back from saying what we most wanted to say. Gerald and the condesa were seated on a sofa, talking of nothing that much interested them. The condesa was stitching an intricate petit point design. Askew smiled a little as he stood beside me at the coffee service, and nodded toward the condesa. "Unexpected, isn't it? I always see her as the sort who should be carrying skis or skin-diving equipment—and she is expert in both those sports. But whatever part of the world she is in, out comes the tapestry, and you can be sure that every man in the room will eventually gravitate to watch the progress of the work. But how demure she looks, doesn't she? Like a girl in a convent."

"Yes," I said lamely. I was feeling a small jealousy of her, but hoped it didn't show. Why did I suppose she was rich as well as beautiful? Because she had that carelessly elegant look that is only produced by a great deal of time and money?

Askew refilled my cup, attending to me as if he thought I had been neglected. As he poured he said, "So they teach you well at Hardy's, do they?"

"They do their best," I said carefully. Was he expecting that I would be the one to break the silence about the furniture? "They try to find out what you might be good at—if anything. You spend your time on the front counter answering questions and, when someone brings something in for a valuation, phoning for the experts to come in from the various departments. Sometimes the oddest pieces turn up. You learn what you can by handling, seeing, listening."

He nodded. "What do *you* handle mostly—pictures?"

"Ceramics. What I'd really like to do is oriental ceramics, but that's very specialist. I suppose everyone in ceramics ends up by going back to the oriental things. Oh . . . I'm sorry."

"Sorry? Why?"

"I'm talking shop. Gerald thinks it's the worst form of bad manners. Fishing, he says . . . trying to smell out if someone might be persuaded to put something up for sale."

He laughed aloud, a spontaneous sound that caused Gerald and the condesa to raise their heads, and a faint flush appeared on the condesa's pale olive skin. She didn't much like me, I thought, and it made me feel better about my own burst of jealousy of her.

"Gerald, your protégée here has just told me she's been fishing and that you wouldn't approve. Shall we make her fishing worthwhile? Do you think she'd like to see La Española?"

Gerald was trying to control his excitement. "It *is* here, then?"

"Of course. Where else would it be? It will stay here now as long as it exists or the house exists. But I can't help wondering if the curse will finally leave La Española when this house tumbles before the bulldozers or gives up to the weather."

The condesa gestured impatiently. "Roberto, you make too much of this silly superstition. If you were determined, it could be sold tomorrow." She slipped the embroidery frame into its bag. "Come, show Mr. Stanton. If it is never to leave this house, it may be his only chance." She had neatly cut me out by making this showing of what they called La Española for Gerald's pleasure, not for mine.

Askew led us to another room which opened directly off the great hall, opposite the dining room. This one was paneled in linen-fold—wood beautifully carved to resemble linen scrolls. Against one wall, shelves had been built, on most of which were thick boxes—not books—bound in red leather, with dates stamped in gold that had dulled with the years. Probably estate records, I thought. At some date in this century the binding had stopped and inexpensive box files filled the lower shelves.

"Just a minute," Askew said. He left us and went to open a green baize door under the staircase, revealing what seemed to be a service passage. "Tolson, are you there?" We heard their voices, and a minute later Askew was back with us. I had a brief glimpse of Tolson's figure in the passage, and I thought there was disapproval in the stare he gave us.

The room was long, lighted only by a single lamp on a large, carved desk. "This is really Tolson's room," Askew said. "He does most of his work here." He nodded toward another desk—a humble, rather battered rolltop. While he spoke he felt for a spot at the side of the carved mantel; then he went and touched another place in the paneling itself.

"Such elementary precautions," he said, "but Tolson insists on them. I had to have him turn the alarm system off." He had opened a small door in the paneling, and he fumbled within the cavity. A light came on, showing a velvet-lined interior behind a thick glass screen. Wordlessly the three of us moved closer.

It was a blue-white diamond, roughly octahedral in shape, about an inch and a half at its widest part. It was touched at four points by simple cage grips and strung on a gold chain of medium weight. Only its natural planes had been polished, and the stone itself was relatively uncut. Still, with only these large surfaces revealed, the refraction of light from its heart, the inner facets, was of extraordinary brilliance. It seemed too big to be a gemstone. There was something almost crude in its size, and yet it lay there so quietly, so innocently, on its black velvet cushion. Askew swung open the glass screen. He lifted the massive thing on its chain and swung it gently. The light sprang from it as from a living flame.

"La Española—the Spanish Woman," he said softly. "When the countess came to Thirlbeck from Philip's court she and the jewel she brought as part of her dowry were called the same thing. How barbaric she must have thought the manners of this household."

Gerald leaned closer. "May I . . . ?" Askew slipped the gold chain over his hand, and Gerald carried it to the desk, where the light fell directly upon it. "I wondered if I would ever see it again," he mused, turning the great stone in his fingers. "I remember when, in the thirties, your father sent it to Hardy's and there were no buyers." Gerald's eyes never left the stone.

"He was right to try to get rid of it, but it wasn't the time to sell, and the reputation of the wretched thing went before it."

"You might have had it cut into small stones and disposed of. None of the buyers would have known they were getting part of the reputation of La Española." Gerald glanced up inquiringly at Askew. "Somewhere about two hundred carats, isn't it?"

"The last jeweler who examined it gave it a few more, but he made no offer. That was after the Terpolini affair, and the publicity had been enormous. So here it lies in its primitive little cave, uninsured, because I can't afford the insurance. It would be absurdly easy to steal, except that no one wants to touch it."

"Two hundred carats," Gerald mused. "Worth . . . well, four or five thousand pounds a carat. There's a million pounds, and its value is rising every day. And no one wants to *steal* it?"

"That's about it, Gerald." Now Askew touched it, his long fingers slightly reluctant in the movement. "The Spanish Woman brought it to the Birketts, and it seems she means to keep it forever."

"How so?" I was now spellbound by the sight of the gem.

"Philip the Second wanted to send her to her English husband with something substantial as evidence of good faith. He had the stone polished just a little and mounted virtually in its rough state. That, of course, makes it more valuable now. It's ready for all that a modern cutter can take from it. Well, it might have been intended for her husband and his family, but she never let it go—the little Spanish girl. About seventeen, they think she was when she came here. Old enough for those times, I suppose. Then Elizabeth's men beheaded her husband, and she was alone. She was in mortal danger, and she must have known it."

His voice now had taken on the distant tone it had had upstairs. "The story goes that in calm weather she would have the serving boy, who had been her husband's favorite, row her on the tarn. He must have grown attached to her. They say she wore the jewel

always, a kind of talisman because it had come from Philip. She waited endlessly for word from him—instructions as to what she must do, where she must go; but I can't help thinking she hoped to be summoned back to Spain. So far as we know, Philip sent no word. She just waited—waited to know if her child would be a boy and therefore third earl of Askew, displacing her Protestant brother-in-law. The brother-in-law, another Robert Birkett by name, evidently intended that the child should never be born."

It was odd, how detached he sounded, as if he weren't speaking of his own family. "They say that when she was out on the tarn he rowed after her, taking a younger brother with him. The Spanish Woman was not to survive, but no one knows precisely what happened, of course. They must have beaten the boy first and then the Spanish Woman. They couldn't let her drown and the jewel go with her. She must have struggled fiercely, but the thing was finally taken from her neck. Afterward someone whispered that he had heard the Spanish Woman's voice shouting what sounded like the motto of the Birketts—probably she reverted to Latin, the only language she had in common with anyone here. It's as wild and aggressive a motto as any untamed border lord would wish—"

"The motto?" I asked.

"*Caveat raptor*—roughly, 'Who seizes, beware.' Did she mean the jewel, her life, the life of her child? Did she even say it? Her body was never recovered, and the new earl had the jewel. He simply said she had not worn it that day. No one believed that part of it, and they began to believe that the boy had survived, a witness and perhaps the origin of the stories that began to fly about."

Askew shrugged. "The story fattened, and a curse became attached to the jewel, especially when the earl broke his neck after a drunken tumble on the stairs. He had been, they said, displaying the jewel to one of Elizabeth's council members."

Askew leaned back against the desk. "His brother, the fourth earl, died peacefully in his bed, but not before the jewel, along with anything else portable, had been taken from the house by border raiders. The odd thing was that the leader of the raid never got beyond this valley. His horse stumbled, and rolled on him. There seemed no reason for it. He was left there to die, and none of his party would touch the jewel. There was blood from his pierced lungs on La Española when it came back to Thirlbeck."

Now I could make myself touch it. Somehow I had expected it
to feel warm, as if it had just left the throat of the Spanish Woman.
"Could they really have abandoned something like this with a
dying man?"

"So they say. They must have begun to believe the motto and
the curse. The Spanish Woman, whom they wanted to forget, was
a permanent legend. A stone monument was placed near the tarn
by someone who wished her passage to be marked. But as many
times as the earl removed it, it reappeared—or another like it. He
began to see that he could not lay the ghost, and so he left her
monument alone to let the grass grow up around it.

"And La Española stayed on. There were several attempts on it
over the years—none successful. There was a serious attempt in the
twenties, but the thieves took the way out of the valley that you
came in by today. At the worst bend, where the road cuts through
the birch copse, they went out of control. Their car crashed and
burned, and they with it. The diamond, of course, survived. After
that my father lodged it in a safe-deposit vault in Manchester. It
was there three years before there was an attempt, by tunneling,
on the vaults. The thieves' tunnel collapsed, killing them all. La
Española came out covered with dirt, and shining just as ever.
We brought it back to Thirlbeck then. The Manchester bank
wasn't anxious to have it again. I made only one effort to sell
it after that. And that was when the Terpolini affair burst on
the world."

"Terpolini?" I said. "The opera singer? Isn't she dead?"

Askew looked at me. "I keep forgetting you're so much younger.
No, not dead, but she might as well be. She was at the height of
a very sensational career, and everything she did was news. She
was the mistress of the oilman, Georgiadas. He was—still is—
strongly superstitious, but he believed then that the gods looked
with particular favor on him. Until he encountered La Española.
I had sold it to him subject to expert examination, and Tolson
brought it to Milan. It was everything they had hoped for. It was
to be cut, but Constanzia Terpolini asked to wear it just as it is,
uncut, when she opened the season at La Scala. The papers were
full of the story; she was photographed, in costume, wearing it.
But the next day papers were full of the story of her fall down that
long flight of stairs in the last act of *Turandot*. They had to

bring down the curtain. She never saw another curtain go up. A fractured spine, which paralyzed her from the neck down. On the same day, Georgiadas's only son was lost in a sailing accident off Crete. That was the day the gods really turned their backs on Georgiadas. Soon after, he had La Española returned to me, and Tolson brought it back to Thirlbeck."

The lines in Askew's face appeared sharper now. "What's the capital gains tax now, Gerald?" he asked. "Thirty percent? I could live quite a long time on what was left if I could sell it—if La Española were not drenched in superstition and greed. And so my unfortunate heir will have to scratch about for the death duties on something *he* won't be able to sell or insure either."

Carlota spoke. "If you had only the will, Roberto, to find someone to cut it in Amsterdam, it could be sold. The Birketts would be rid of La Española at last, with no auction, no publicity."

Askew gathered up the gem and ended one of La Española's few moments of exposure to light and admiration. "And will you fly with me to Amsterdam, Carlota? Will you find the cutter who will touch it?" He snapped the panel shut. "I think we might just leave La Española in peace." He turned back to us. "I do, however, have one other thing that could stand beside La Española in importance and value. What would you say to a Rembrandt, Gerald?"

"A Rembrandt?" Gerald looked across at me, warning me to stay quiet, as a charge of excitement ran between us. I felt my mouth go dry. And I wondered again if Vanessa had known of this also.

"A legacy which has come to us in a perfectly ordinary fashion, Gerald. Did you know that my grandfather was only a cousin to the fifteenth earl? He never expected to inherit, but the Birketts seem to be unfortunate in losing their direct descendants. My grandfather had been a prosperous farmer, with an interest in some small mines, and he ran a few coasters out of Whitehaven. He liked to travel with them himself and often went over to the Continent— even more after he had met Margeretha van Huygens, the only child of a rich burgomaster in Rotterdam. They married. And naturally, on the death of her parents, she inherited everything. All the French furniture that the van Huygenses had picked up after the French Revolution, when fleeing émigrés had to sell good pieces cheaply. With the furniture came a collection of Dutch pictures—most of them pretty dull scenes of cows and windmills. We don't know how the van Huygenses acquired the Rembrandt. But in my grandmother's day Rembrandt wasn't in fashion, and it must have hung at Thirlbeck in a dark passage. . . . It *is* possible, isn't it, Gerald, that a Rembrandt could exist that has never been catalogued?" Askew asked.

"It's entirely possible, Robert. There is no central registry of works of art, no record of when they are sold or to whom. Even the museums don't have to tell us what they buy and sell or what they pay. It's a state of chaos which would send the normal businessman mad. Yet we live with it, because there is a general unwillingness to admit that art is big business."

Askew said, "I've had Tolson bring it out of the room where he stored all the pictures at the beginning of the war." He began to lead us across the long room. In its darkness we could see the dull outlines of a picture that hung on the farthest wall.

I thought Gerald walked with a kind of stiffness, as if the same cramping excitement I was feeling had gripped him also. If what Askew said was true, this remote house would suddenly witness the coming and going of experts to authenticate the picture, photos of it would appear on the desks of museum directors, and it would arrive at last in the special high-security rooms on the top floor of Hardy's. Television lights would go on in the great saleroom, and the world's press would gather. If the buyer was foreign, there would be the usual appeal for a fund to save it for the nation, and Robert Birkett would be condemned for selling away a national treasure. No wonder Gerald walked warily.

He stopped. "I can't see it, Robert. Aren't there lights?"

Askew pressed a switch, but that only activated the modern extension-arm lamp perched on the rolltop desk. The sconces on the wall remained dark. "Damn!" he said. "I was stupid to let Tolson hang it there—I forgot about light. Well, perhaps we can tilt this one?"

"No, don't," Gerald said. "I don't want my first sight of it spoiled. We'll look at it tomorrow morning." His tone was curiously flat.

Suddenly the excitement was gone. I was more than ever conscious that I was tired and chilled. We said good night to the condesa and Askew, and I could feel them staring after us as we went up the stairs. When we reached the gallery Askew said something, and the condesa's voice rose in sharp protest. As I glanced down she had already started up, but at the landing she turned to take the other arm of the staircase leading to the opposite wing of the house. By the time we reached Gerald's door she had vanished into the shadows.

"Can I come in for a moment, Gerald?"

He nodded, as if he had known I would say that.

"IT's NO use asking, Jo. I *don't know* why Vanessa never said anything. She must have had a very good reason, but we'll never know what it was—not now." He pulled on his cigarette wearily, but I had to talk.

"Perhaps he *asked* her not to. Yes, that would be it. From what I've been hearing, the Birketts all seem a bit touched to me—at least *he* is. Their secrecy about the house, keeping a Rembrandt hidden away. Do you suppose it really is a Rembrandt?"

"My dear Jo, I haven't seen it. There's no reason why it shouldn't be—the van Huygenses could have been of the same family as Constantijn Huygens, who wrote about Rembrandt in his autobiography. Pictures and furniture do get passed on, just taken for granted by the family."

He sat, half hidden behind the haze of cigarette smoke. "A Rembrandt . . . I wonder . . ."

"I don't much like Lord Askew, Gerald—or at least I keep changing my opinion of him. He hates this place, doesn't he? He doesn't care if it falls down. I almost felt he could sell his own grandmother—after all, it was her furniture and pictures."

"And now they're his, to do with as he will. Never forget it, Jo. It's his property. It doesn't matter if we like our clients."

I shrugged. "Of course it doesn't matter. So what if the house does fall down? It is just one of England's least known architectural treasures, stuffed with wonderful furniture—and it *would* cost the price of a Rembrandt to preserve. Who *would* want it, after all?" I wondered why I was arguing with myself, and moved toward the door. "Good night, Gerald. I hope you sleep well."

"Nothing, dear Jo, would keep me awake tonight."

I suddenly thought that I had never seen Gerald look old before. The idea frightened me. I couldn't lose him now—not just after losing Vanessa. I think I would have kissed him then, but for the fact that he might have guessed what was in my mind.

I WAS BACK IN the Spanish Woman's room after bathing in a marble tub of Edwardian proportions when I realized that my handbag and my only cigarettes were downstairs. I had managed to cut down to ten cigarettes a day, but the last and best of them was something I looked forward to. It was after midnight by now—too late to disturb Gerald to ask for his. I went downstairs, hesitating just a little at the thought of the dogs, but there was no sign of them. The lights in the drawing room were still on, and I found my handbag.

I was halfway across the hall when I saw her. She stood in the shadow thrown by the stairs, a girl of perhaps eighteen or nineteen, with a shower of silvery-blond hair framing a face of childlike delicacy. She seemed very tiny in her short skirt and plain blouse, and she had the porcelain look of a figurine—a complexion which glowed even in the shadows, and red lips that curved upward in an almost fixed half smile. She regarded me calmly, with neither curiosity nor surprise. I knew then this was Jessica, Tolson's granddaughter. I moved toward her, meaning to speak some greeting and wondering why it was I, and not this slender girl, who should feel discomforted. I just caught myself on the verge of explaining my presence here at that hour.

It was then that the door to the room which housed La Española was flung open and a sharp, angry voice reached me.

"—had enough of it! Askew, if I see one of those dogs on my land again—whether it's the land I rent from you or my own—I'll shoot it. I'm a farmer. I need my lambs. I'm damned if I'll have them slaughtered as playthings for your bloody dogs."

"Nat, you haven't a shred of proof that these dogs are responsible for your dead lambs. In any case, I think it's a matter to be taken up with Tolson. They are not *my* dogs."

"They stopped being Tolson's the minute you set foot here—by what magic I'll never fathom. So it's you I'm warning."

"What of those eagles of yours, Nat? Don't they—"

Askew was cut short. "Shows what you know about golden eagles! They almost never kill lambs."

After a pause Askew spoke again. "I accept your warning, Nat. Now won't you stay and have a drink with me? There are things we should talk about."

He was cut off again. "Some other time. I've things to see to now.

When you feel like it, come to *my* house. It'll be a long day before I sit comfortably in this hellish house."

The door closed in almost a slam, and I saw the angry face under the tow-colored hair. He was wearing the same clothes as when he opened the gates for us. But if he remembered me, he gave no sign of it. His glance swept past me and on to the girl.

"Nat," she said, also ignoring my presence, "you've a right here as much as he has. This house is yours—"

"Oh, hush, Jess," he said impatiently. They turned and started down the passage that opened under the stairs. I caught the last of his words as the green baize door swung closed. "Be a good girl and make me a cup of tea. I've got to go look at some ewes. . . ." There was a homely acceptance between them that excluded the world of run-down grandeur on this side of the door. They would drink their tea in the kitchen, and his voice would probably lose its anger as he sat with this porcelain creature, who seemed to know him so well. Unreasonably, I felt troubled by the exclusion.

"Oh . . . there you are." I turned and looked at Askew. He stood gripping the doorframe, his lips trying to force a smile but producing something that barely covered a grimace of pain. He didn't seem to think it strange that I was there, in my dressing gown. "Do me a favor, please? Go into the dining room and bring me a brandy? It should be in one of the sideboards. A large one."

I found the brandy easily enough and carried it back to him. It didn't seem possible that the exchange I had overheard could have produced such a reaction. He was stretched in a chair behind the large desk, as if trying to straighten his body from cramp. But then, almost at once, he doubled over, clutching his stomach, his eyes closed.

"Lord Askew, are you ill? Shall I call . . . ?" Whom would I call?

He opened his eyes and reached for the brandy. While he took the first long swallow, my fingers held the glass also; his hand felt terribly cold on mine, but his palm was sweating. He straightened and leaned back in the chair. I withdrew my hand.

"Not supposed to do this. Terribly bad for me, the doctors say. I've got some tablets upstairs, but it's a long way to go."

"If you tell me where, I'll get them."

He shook his head. "No, I'll get there eventually. And in the meantime the brandy gives me relief. They tell me I'm burning

333

out what's left of my stomach, but what's the choice? To live and enjoy—or not to live at all?" Then suddenly he seemed to focus fully on my face. "Oh, don't look so stricken! It's an ulcer. It kicks up from time to time. Tonight is one of the times."

"I'm sorry. Sorry that you are ill. That the man who just left is in trouble about his lambs. That you're in trouble about your dogs. I'm sorry for both of you."

He took a large gulp of brandy and made a grimace. "Do you know who he was—the righteous farmer with the dead lambs?"

"No, but he let us in at the other end of the valley."

"He is a cousin very many times removed. Nat Birkett by name. He is also my heir!"

"Your heir? But you really don't know him. I heard you—"

"I know, I know. But he's next in line. This last week is the first time we've met. And it hasn't been a happy occasion. The title and the entailed part of the estate—the nucleus of the land here in the valley, the Tolson farms, the house—they go to Nat Birkett, whatever we both might wish otherwise. Of course, he doesn't want them. A pretty sorry inheritance. But I thought he'd come here tonight as a friendly gesture, and now I find it's about his stupid lambs." He gave a half laugh which ended in a gasp of pain.

"You shouldn't be talking to me like this. What's between you and Nat Birkett is your business. It can't possibly be mine—"

"You are right, Miss Roswell. It isn't your business." At the same instant she spoke I became aware of her presence in the doorway. I didn't know how long she had been there.

I smelled her perfume, watched the graceful sway of her body in a robe of amber silk as she went to Askew. "Roberto!" Her voice shook a little, a mixture of anguish and anger. "Why do you do it?" She took the brandy glass from him, then felt for the pulse at his wrist. "Why?" she repeated. "You'll kill yourself with this madness."

His face was white, and beaded with sweat. He made a weary gesture. "Carlota—don't!"

She turned and looked at me. "Go," she said very simply. And I went.

I HAD my cigarette by one of the dying fires, thinking of what I had seen and learned that day. But I was very tired, and when I got into bed I felt the warmth of the hot-water bottles gratefully, and I was asleep almost at once. I hadn't drawn the curtains, so I awoke, startled, to the sense of a changed atmosphere. The straight, cold, direct rays of the moon were gone, and I heard the wind moan in the chimneys. What else did I hear? What did I think I saw? Was it the sound of stiff petticoats moving, or was it simply mice behind the paneling? Did I actually see a small dark shape seated in her chair, hear the sigh of loneliness? No—both fires had died now to a bed of embers, giving little light. I saw nothing, I heard nothing. It was no more than a dream imperfectly remembered. If the little Spanish Woman was there, I did not feel she resented my presence. Perhaps she only wanted recognition. I slept again, easily and deeply.

CHAPTER THREE

SHE WAS in the room before I was properly awake; there was the faintest rattle of the spoon on the saucer as she put the tray on the long table in the window bay, and I opened my eyes to the sight of that tiny figure silhouetted against the blaze of morning light. She turned to me at once.

"Hello. I'm Jessica Tolson. I expect Lord Askew told you I live here and help my grandparents." She spoke with cheerful familiarity; not for her the reserve of her grandfather, though her voice was light and whispery, almost on the edge of excitement. "I've put the tea tray over here. It's never very comfortable having things to eat in bed, is it? At least I don't think so. I hope you like the bread—I bake it myself. Do you like this room?"

I wasn't fully awake, but I struggled to answer—to find something to stem this rush of words. "Yes, I do. Very much."

"This is my favorite room at Thirlbeck." She was bending now and scooping the faded rose petals from the big delft bowl, smelling them, and letting them flutter down again. "I often come up here to read or study. I like to sit in the window, where I can see the tarn. I've written poems about it—how it looks in each season. It's not very good poetry, but it will get better."

I knew then whose hand had kept this room so immaculate, who had gathered the rose petals of last summer and let their scent linger on here. "I build up the fires in the winter and sit here and imagine how it must have been when she had this room."

335

"She—the Spanish Woman?"

"Oh, of course. They say that after the Spanish Woman died no one wanted to use it, and it was shut up for a long time. I expect they wanted to forget about her." She seemed to take it for granted that I knew the whole story.

"I've slept here just to see what it was like. But, then, I've tried most of the rooms in the house. This is the best."

She spoke of the place as if it were her own, and I suppose it often must have seemed that way. No one had lived here but her grandparents since she was born. She had never set eyes on the present earl until this past week. She was moving around the room now, touching things with loving familiarity. Her eyes quickly skipped over my toilet things lying on the big chest, alien things to her, and possibly resented. She was like a piece of quicksilver, whispery, her eyes large and dresden blue, her cheeks touched with the faint pink flush of a painted doll. And the color was her own—nothing artificial. She was just slightly fey, I thought, for she couldn't resist this chance of an audience. Brilliant, too, Askew had said, but she hadn't accepted the scholarship at Cambridge. It seemed to me that she walked the delicate line of nervous tension, which threatened to spill over on the wrong side.

And then she was around near the bed and on her way to the door. "Well, do drink your tea before it gets cold."

"Mr. Stanton—"

"Oh, I've taken tea to Mr. Stanton. What a sweet man!" Her air of sophisticated judgment infuriated me. What business had she making comment on Gerald? And then I felt like laughing, because I recognized the jealousy in my reaction.

"Breakfast will be ready when you come down. Just help yourself. . . ." She bestowed an enchanting, unreal smile upon me and closed the door very softly.

I lay back on my pillow, forgetting for the moment how badly I wanted the tea and reaching for a cigarette instead, something I rarely did at this time of the day. I could laugh a bit, but it really wasn't funny to be trapped for some days between the two opposites of ideal beauty—this tiny, perfect English rose and the haunting, dynamic presence of the Spanish aristocrat.

I flung back the bedclothes. Better try this maddening little girl's tea and bread; the tray gave me no reassurance that she ever made mistakes. The teapot was kept hot by a knitted cosy, and the wafer-thin slices of bread tasted like something everyone had forgotten how to make fifty years ago. And this girl-child wrote poetry as well. I scowled at the morning-blue surface of the tarn—not the best beginning to the day.

GERALD greeted me in a rather subdued way when I entered the dining room; he was eating a piece of toast with a very thin scraping of butter on it.

"Would you like anything else?" I said as I lifted the lids off the silver dishes. "You can have bacon, kidney, sausage—three kinds of eggs."

"Thank you, this is enough." His tone was unusually remote.

I turned to him swiftly. "Didn't you sleep well?"

"Well enough, I suppose. Yesterday was a long day. Perhaps we were overambitious. Should have taken two days to come up."

I sat opposite him. "You're missing something in this sausage."

"Cumberland sausage. They make a thing of it up here."

"I suppose you were awake enough to see the fairy child who brought the tea?"

He brightened a little. "Yes, lovely little creature."

"She's spoiled and is certainly her grandfather's pet. Likes to think *she* owns Thirlbeck, too."

For the first time that morning he smiled fully. "Jo, you sound rather like the condesa. Little Jess hasn't many friends among the women here."

"All right," I answered, "so I'm jealous."

"That's better. Always better when you face the truth."

"The truth is she could put on a drawstring bodice and a Bopeep hat and she'd be the ideal model for a porcelain shepherdess. Not really my taste in china."

"She drew my bath for me. I think she's charming."

"That leaves the condesa and me to our own opinions. And where," I said, "are Lord Askew and the condesa? Do you know?"

"Robert's been and gone. The condesa, being a Spaniard, probably doesn't like to rise before eleven." He snapped a piece of toast in two. "And I've finally remembered about the condesa. She's the daughter of a Spanish nobleman and was involved in some scandal. She took up with another man, and there was no prospect for a divorce from her Spanish husband. And when *that* relationship fell through she was on the international circuit, with barely enough money to keep her afloat, I imagine. Cut off from her family, to whom, naturally, she is a disgrace. She must be about thirty-five to thirty-seven." He was giving her the benefit of a few years, I thought, but I did not object. "Her relationship with Robert can't be of very long standing. She wasn't with him when I met him in Venice last spring. She can't like it here. It's not her sort of place."

"Perhaps she loves him," I said. "It may be that simple."

"It may be that she is forty," he answered with unusual ruthlessness. "Or more. And perhaps she is growing a little afraid. She would have come here with Robert to prevent losing him. Naturally, she can never marry again, not so long as her husband is alive."

"Now that she's seen what is here—will she ever let him go?"

"Will it be her choice? I think that since the death of his wife and son he hasn't allowed himself to become completely committed to anyone or anything. But, well, there comes a time. Perhaps he might be willing to settle with the condesa for the rest of his life. A man grows tired of endless pursuit. In fact, a man just grows tired."

He stopped. Tolson stood at the door. "Miss Roswell. There's a telephone call for you—a Mr. Peers."

I smiled, not able to help myself. Harry did that to me.

"If you will take it in Lord Askew's study, Miss Roswell—I'll show you."

"Yes. Yes, I know. We were there last night," and I hurried across the hall ahead of him.

I waited for his steps to fade away before I picked up the phone and spoke. "Harry?"

"Fine one you are! Leaving me stranded—alone—all weekend. Didn't you know I'd be rushing back to hold your hand?"

"Liar! You never rushed anywhere to hold my hand. You just happened to come back. Had a good time?"

"A good time? It was business, luv, not a good time."

"Since when has business ever stopped your good time?"

He laughed, and made no more protests. "Well, it was profitable. I'll be able to afford to take you to dinner a few more times. What

338

I'd like to know is when that will be. You're up there in those damned lakes. I once knew a chap—he went up there and never came back. Dangerous, I call it. My old mum would never let me go up there."

"Harry, you fool. If only I could believe you sometimes."

"Honest, luv, cross my heart and hope—and all the rest of it. So when are you coming back from Lord Whatsit's?"

"Perhaps tomorrow. How did you know I was here?"

"Listen, luv, when Harry Peers wants to know something there's always a way. Found out you were with Gerald Stanton. So then I found out where he was headed."

"But it's the weekend. Hardy's isn't open."

"I roused a director from his bed to inquire about Mr. Stanton." I sucked in my breath. "I wish you hadn't."

"Cool it, Jo. I didn't mention your name. And the same director thinks I may buy something quite big in a sale that's coming up. Which I might. He didn't mind talking—not at all."

"Harry, you're dreadful."

"You mean it?"

"No. You're wonderful!"

"*That's* my girl. And how is that madman, the noble Lord Askew? What's he trying to sell—that bloody great diamond? Does he still have it?"

"It's right here in this room."

For once he had no immediate reply. Then slowly, "You mean *there*—in the room with you? Did you see it? What's it look like?"

"Fabulous, Harry. It's like a—a mountain of light."

"Two hundred-odd carats. Always wanted something like that."

"You wouldn't want this one." All at once I felt a coldness about me, and I knew that I believed the stories about La Española.

"Who says I wouldn't? I'll bet I could make a tidy profit by the time it was cut into a few decent-sized hunks. Is he selling? Is that why you and Stanton are there?"

"I don't know how you know so much about La Española, but *you* ought to know that I can't discuss business with you. So far as I know, Gerald is paying a social call, and I am driving him."

"Luv, I don't believe you. But I like a girl who can keep her trap shut." His tone changed. "Are you all right, Jo?" I knew he was talking about Vanessa's death. "I just missed you in Switzerland,

and I didn't like to bust in, in Mexico—not when you were just getting to know your dad. It went all right with him, did it?"

"Yes, Harry. It was—it was very good."

"Glad to hear it. Nice to find a dad at your age, and one that won't breathe down your neck either. I'll miss your mother, though, Jo. She was my sort, Vanessa was. Smashing girl."

"I know." There was a tightness in my throat.

"All right then, luv. Take care. Try to stay dry up there, and don't fall down a mountain. See you."

"When?" I couldn't help saying it even though he hated to be pinned down.

"Oh—soon. By, Jo." I heard the dull buzzing of the disengaged line, and I felt more lonely than at any other time since Vanessa died. Harry had slipped away from me once more. And with this emptiness upon me I believed I loved him. But I didn't think he loved me. Love had been beaten out of him as he had pushed and shoved his way to the top. His women were the decorations of his success; no particular woman, it seemed, was essential to him. He was offhandedly fond of me and in these last weeks unusually attentive and kind.

I replaced the receiver slowly, hearing Harry's flirtatious mockery, seeing his half-ugly face with its strong eyebrows crooked in amusement, his brown eyes quick and knowing.

I was remembering, as I too often did, the first time I had felt those eyes fastened on mine. It had been my first exposure, too, to his cocky good humor. I had been walking from the bus stop in Piccadilly to Hardy's, noting the changes in the windows of the art dealers which lined the street. This day there had been a new pair of Chinese vases of an early dynasty, and I looked much closer. I was rooted, entranced by the pale green color, the long, tapering necks, their perfect proportion to the flare of the base. And then, behind me, Harry's voice, unknown until that moment.

"What a beautiful pair"—I turned, and his grown-up urchin's face was grinning at me, his eyes just a little above the level of mine—"of legs," he finished.

And then he walked on with me, talking about the Chinese vases with a certain degree of expertise. I made some stumbling replies, and then, to my great shock, he mounted the steps of Hardy's with me. Wondering what to do with him, I paused at the front counter to say something to Mr. Arrowsmith, the man who had presided there for more than twenty years. Meanwhile the young man—not really so young, in his thirties—continued up the great staircase to the salerooms, saluting me with an impudent wave of his hand. It was a gesture that for all the world reminded me of Vanessa.

Mr. Arrowsmith acknowledged him with a smile.

"Mr. Arrowsmith, who's that?"

"Who's that? But you came in with him, Jo."

"I'm still asking who he is."

"That, my dear, is Mr. Harry Peers. Clever young devil. Jumped up from nothing, and now he's a millionaire, they say. His hobby is spotting good buys at Hardy's. I'm surprised you haven't seen him in here before."

I was remembering all this now, as I began to move slowly away from the telephone, pausing about the middle of the room. Lord Askew's study looked so different as the morning light poured in the long windows on each side of the painting. With the same cold excitement I'd felt the night before, I stayed on to look at the picture. I stared, and a face came more and more to life—the painted face of a man with an ugly, bulbous nose, careless hair, and eyes that registered suffering. He had painted his own face so many times in his life, in great adornment. Now here he was in his old age, revealing himself in the splendid beauty of his plainness. Rembrandt van Rijn, son of a miller, painter of Leiden and Amsterdam, thrown from poverty to riches to bankruptcy—all of it looked from the portrait without self-pity or compassion. It was painted in the dark tones of his later years, but it also wore the dirt of the years since it was painted. The signature was there, almost obscured, and the date 1669.

"Ah, you're here before us, Jo." I turned to see Gerald and Askew coming into the room.

"It's almost as hard to see as last night," I said. "It happens to be in the shadow between these two windows."

Askew sighed. "Tolson seems to have picked the worst place in the house to hang it. But he insisted because of security."

"Move it onto a chair facing the light," Gerald said.

It wasn't a large canvas—about three feet by two. I propped it against the back of the chair directly facing one of the windows, and Gerald went around to look at it.

I glanced at Askew. At this moment, for all his sophistication, he was eagerly watching Gerald's face. When the waiting became too much he said, "Well, what do you think?"

Gerald spoke slowly. "Remarkable—very remarkable. An unrecorded self-portrait, but signed and dated. Would there be any provenance—any record of its being bought or when it was bought?"

Askew gestured helplessly to the wall stacked with the filing boxes. "That's full of family papers—several hundred years of them. There may be something relating to Grandmother van Huygens' possessions. Dutch bourgeois families are pretty careful about such things. Perhaps Jo wouldn't mind looking, but is it really needed? It's signed and dated."

"Yes," Gerald said. "Any scrap of provenance would be very significant—"

"Excuse me, my lord."

Startled, we all looked up. None of us had been aware of Tolson's appearance at the open door of the study, but I sensed that he had been standing there for some time, listening as keenly as Askew to what Gerald was saying.

"What is it, Tolson?"

"It's Mr. Nat Birkett, my lord. He would like to have a word with you. I've put him in the library."

"Damn! I'm busy now, Tolson. Ask him if he can come back."

"I should see him, if you can, my lord. It's about the dogs."

"Not again! We've been through all that."

"It isn't about *our* dogs, my lord. He's found the one who's been after the sheep. I think he's come to apologize. Not easy to ask a man to come back again to do that, my lord."

I was astonished to hear the tone of pleading in Tolson's voice. Evidently Askew recognized it also. He shrugged. "Very well, I'll come. Can't have Nat Birkett forced to grovel."

Askew strode from the room, and we waited for Tolson to close the door after him, but the great round-shouldered figure stayed where it was. "Is there anything I can do, Mr. Stanton?"

"Do?" Gerald looked bewildered. "Why—I don't believe so."

"Well, sir, perhaps you would like the picture hung up again."

"No, not for the moment, thank you. I'll just look at it a little longer. If you don't mind."

"Very well, Mr. Stanton." The door closed gently.

I turned at once to Gerald. "What's the matter? The picture's all right, isn't it? I mean . . ."

He didn't even glance at me. His eyes were fixed on the painting, and his face was as grave as I had ever seen it.

"Remarkable," he said again. "A wonderful piece of work. But I don't think it was painted by Rembrandt."

"Oh. . . ." I felt the excitement leave me and a dull disappointment take its place—a sense of outrage, too, that I had been so completely taken in by the picture. "But it's *signed*."

"Yes, Jo, but I have a feeling that I'm looking at a photograph of Rembrandt. Everything is here, and yet it isn't the real thing. I hope to heaven our people will come up here and tell me that I'm wrong. But if I'm right, then we're looking at the best piece of forgery I've ever seen." He shook his head, a gesture of sadness and wonder. "Yes—remarkable. Very remarkable indeed."

We stayed looking at the painting for some time, Gerald's face unhappy and pensive. Finally he shrugged. "It's no use, Jo. We'll have to bring Lutterworth up here to examine it. In the meantime what am I going to say to Robert? He believes it's the painting his grandmother brought from Holland, I'm sure of that. But I just don't think that at the time it came here anyone would have been bothering to forge Rembrandts. As recently as the 1820s and '30s, Rembrandts sold for as little as twenty pounds. But I don't need to remind you of what has happened in the last ten years. When the Metropolitan Museum bought *Aristotle Contemplating the Bust of Homer* for over two million dollars the rush was really on. Anyone who owned a Rembrandt was rich."

"Then if this is a forgery, you think it's a recent forgery?"

"Has to be." He shook his head. "I'd love to know who's good enough to have done it. Remember van Meegeren? He painted Vermeers that Vermeer had never thought of. It would have to have been someone of his quality."

"But *how*, Gerald? And when? Has someone stolen the original and replaced it with this?"

He shook his head. "I don't want to know. And it could be that I'm wrong. Perhaps you could try looking through some of those papers anyway."

"Gerald, that's a lifework."

343

"Oh, just make a game of it. Anything, so I won't have to tell Robert here and now what I think. Time enough to break his heart later, when we're sure. We'll leave tomorrow, and I'll tell him I'm sending Lutterworth for an opinion. And, Jo, you had better forget you've ever seen Thirlbeck." He stiffened suddenly. "Yes?"

It wasn't to me he spoke, but Tolson, again standing by the door, which we had not heard open. "Mr. Stanton, Lord Askew would like you and Miss Roswell to join him in the library. Shall I replace the picture?"

I wondered if he was so possessive of everything at Thirlbeck, and then again wondered why he should not be. After all, he had tended it alone for so many years that we—and I included Askew in this—were interlopers in *his* treasure house. Gerald and I must seem to him even worse—the appraisers who descended on his kingdom to put a price on everything, a price that valued beauty but not the devotion which had preserved it.

He was beside us already, lifting the picture and rehanging it on its hook. "There," he muttered. "Out of harm's way now."

THE sound of the condesa's laughter greeted us in the library. She hardly turned at our entrance, calling a good-morning and then giving her attention once more to Nat Birkett. He stood in front of the fire, wearing the desperate air of a man who finds himself with a glass of champagne in his hand at eleven o'clock in the morning and wonders why he is where he is.

Askew gestured to us with a bottle. "Champagne? Carlota's tastes run to it at this time every morning. When Vanessa and Jonathan were here we drank all there was in the cellars." He was now holding a glass toward me. "Jonathan said it reminded him of the sun. . . . Is that what you feel, Carlota?"

"I do feel gayer," she admitted. "But poor Mr. Birkett here thinks all this is a waste of time, I'm afraid. He'd really rather be getting on with his farming." The words had no sense of sarcasm.

"It's a good thing to remind farmers that they should take a few minutes for . . . well, for this." He gestured to include the room, the champagne bottle, and even, I thought, the condesa herself. She looked this morning exactly like someone one saw in a glossy magazine; her pale cream slacks and cashmere sweater, her shoes and needlework bag were the badges of understated wealth and

taste; if she was, as Gerald said, short of money, I wouldn't have minded being short of money in the same way. Nat Birkett's eyes were on her appreciatively, and she was enjoying that.

Then he looked at me. "You managed to find your way last night, then? Perhaps I shouldn't have sent you over the Brantwick road."

"Managed perfectly," Gerald said quickly. "We were grateful to you for saving us so many miles." Again I felt my skin creeping as I thought of the dog I had seen and Gerald had not. . . .

"It was a great help," I said. "And spectacular views. Formidable country, though. I wouldn't like to be lost up there."

He looked at me more closely. "You'd be surprised how many experienced walkers do just that. The trails lead them up near the top of the fells, and sometimes the temptation to see what the private land of our valley looks like is too great. A few times we've had searchers out for days looking for walkers. People won't believe how quickly the weather changes. They panic, take any way down they can, to where the paths aren't marked. There are signs along the wall telling people it's dangerous and to keep out. But one or two will always ignore a sign. This year we're getting volunteers from the district to see that no one does stray across to this side."

"Do you really need to have volunteers?" Askew asked.

For the first time Nat Birkett's face relaxed. "We've got that pair of golden eagles nesting up there on a crag of Brantwick—this is only the second pair to nest in the Lake District for more than two hundred years—and if they're scared off the nest, the young won't hatch. Then perhaps they'll not continue to return to this valley to breed. If it kills me, I'll see that no one gets near that nest—either for the eggs or just out of curiosity."

His voice grew louder. "I'm so damn sick of what's happened to this country—overrun with people and their cars and their infernal plastic picnic litter. Places where heather and ling used to grow are nothing but impacted subsoil now. . . . If I have to use a gun, I'll keep them away from that nest until the young can fly!" I wondered what there was in the life of this young man which made him both attractive and yet too blunt, angry almost.

He had stopped, aware of the silence about him. "Well, I'm assuming too much. It isn't my valley, but with your permission, Lord

Askew, I'll organize these watches. And now I think I'd better go—"

"Wait awhile, Nat," Askew said. "Have another drink. There is rather a lot I'd like to talk to you about—certain legal matters. But as to the rest—of course, you must do as you wish. The Tolsons, I imagine, will cooperate. Anything for golden eagles, Nat." Askew's air of faint amusement changed suddenly, his features twisted with a kind of distress. "Yes, I wish you *would* do it! There isn't much left in England to protect from the developers, and I'm for doing whatever can be done."

Nat Birkett was already at the door. "I'll fix it with Tolson, then. Good-by."

In a few moments the motor of a Land-Rover parked in the gravel circle was started. From where I stood I could see Jessica come running from the house as the vehicle began to move. It stopped, and she leaned her arms along the open window, talking. I could see Nat Birkett nodding, his face settled into a look of determined patience. She held him there perhaps three minutes and then stepped back. At once the Land-Rover roared into life, sending the gravel flying from under the wheels. But there was a smile on Jessica's face as she turned back toward the house.

We were silent until the condesa spoke. "That is a rather handsome young man, Roberto. What a pity he is so gauche."

"Gauche? In his own world he functions very efficiently. He's a hardworking farmer, and it must seem unbelievably frivolous to him to drink champagne at this time of day. He has no particular reason to like me, since I'm saddling him with an unwelcome inheritance—"

"He doesn't want to be Lord Askew?" She smiled at the simplicity of a person who didn't want a useful social title.

"Why should he? There's no money with it. Just this house, out of which I'll probably have sold anything of value, and this valley. The mines and quarries are worked out. Some land was sold at the time my father died, for death duties. And then, after the war, when the income from the land wouldn't support my idle, roving life, I instructed Tolson to sell what he had to. I didn't want any of the details—just the money. For that I don't doubt Nat despises me." Askew took a long drink from his glass of champagne.

"He comes of quite a different breed. He lives in a house, carefully preserved, which has been handed down for several hundred years. Not a grand house, but I'd bet it's a damn sight pleasanter to live in than this pile. He's in debt a bit—what farmer isn't? But he owns far more than his indebtedness. That will all change, though, when he has to find the death duties for Thirlbeck."

"And the estate is entailed," Gerald ventured.

"The *original* estate is entailed. What was added after the creation of the earldom is not. It's complicated, Gerald. All I know is that I can't sell certain farms the Tolsons rent, land in this valley, or some land lying toward Kesmere. The rest Tolson has been selling piecemeal as I've asked for more money. So Nat Birkett will inherit a very shrunken estate. And who in his right mind would want this house?"

Without thinking I spoke. "I would." I recognized the statement as the exact opposite of what I had said to Gerald last night.

Askew smiled at me, disregarding Gerald's frown, and went to refill his glass. "We weren't meant to be here—my grandfather, my father, and myself. Remember, my grandfather was a farmer and a merchant landed suddenly with an unexpected title. He was a reformer in his day—all kinds of new ideas about land drainage and reclamation. When he took his seat in the House of Lords he thought it was going to be a platform for his ideas—a better deal for the farmer, rather than the landowner. But he never finished his maiden speech; he was howled down. Whenever he walked the corridors of the House after that, some wit or other would set up the cry of *Baa aa* after him. Not a noble lord at all. Just a farmer. So his son never went near the House. Neither have I. Of course, if Nat Birkett chooses to go, there'll be more respect for him. These days the man who really knows what farming is about is listened to." He moved toward us. "Well, let's fill up the glasses again."

The condesa delicately tossed a cigarette into the fire. "And Nat Birkett has a wife?" she said. "The future countess of Askew? And children?"

"He has two thriving, beautiful sons, Tolson tells me. He had a sweet, charming wife. The ideal wife for a good farmer who was going to become an earl. Only she died. And do you know where? Right here in this house. She had a heart condition—serious, but not so serious, they thought, as to cause her death except in rather extraordinary circumstances. But she died in one of the upstairs rooms here. No one even knew she was in the house. And this place being what it is, they didn't find her until she'd been dead for almost a day, they think."

Now I heard his voice as it had sounded when he had looked over the wind-riffled tarn and talked of the Spanish Woman. "Poor little lost girl," he said.

LUNCH was an awkward meal during which Gerald uneasily skirted the subject of the Rembrandt, but Askew seemed so sure it was a Rembrandt that he felt no need to talk about it either. Only when Gerald mentioned leaving the next afternoon did Askew take any real notice.

"So soon, Gerald? Why not stay on a few days? You're looking far too much like a city gent."

Gerald set down his coffee cup. "I'd better ask it now, Robert. Do you want to sell the contents of this house?"

"Well, I thought just the picture . . ."

"There is some very valuable furniture here, Robert." He hoped, I thought, to turn Askew's mind away from the painting, to show him that there were other things of value, so that the disappointment, if it came, would be tempered. "It's worth more than you can afford to pay in insurance on it," Gerald said bluntly. Then, as complete silence answered him, he looked around, shaking his head a little. "It seems so wasted, somehow. Almost lonely." This was totally unlike Gerald, who loved beautiful things but was not sentimental about them.

It was a long time before Askew responded. "Lonely . . . It's always been lonely." He wasn't talking about the furniture. "This place has always felt like some enormous hotel with no guests. If I could sell it—house and all—I'd gladly do it. As it is, yes, I suppose I'd better sell what I can. *You* tell me."

Gerald's face colored slightly. "Well, I thought that was what you had in mind—to liquidate what you can and enjoy the proceeds. After all, it will lessen the death duties on Nat Birkett. No one can tax him on what's been spent."

"So what will you do, Gerald?" Askew said it almost as if he were grateful to Gerald for thrusting the decision on him. Perhaps mostly for this kind of help he had invited Gerald to Thirlbeck.

"Jo and I will leave tomorrow after lunch. I'd like to look at the

349

rest of the paintings before I go. There could be others of interest among them. And then I'll arrange for some of our people to come up here. They will have to take an inventory of every item, and you, Robert, must stay here at least long enough to tell us exactly what it is you want us to handle." He glanced apologetically at the condesa. "We must have your absolute authority for each article."

We sat for a while over coffee, and Gerald went on about his plans to set in motion what would be a great auction. "You're aware of our scale of commissions for selling, Robert?"

"Commissions? Oh, yes, there has to be commission, of course!"

"I'd just like to be sure you know it," Gerald said. "On lots up to five hundred pounds it's fifteen percent; from five hundred to ten thousand pounds it's twelve and a half percent. Over ten thousand pounds it drops to ten percent." He glanced around him. "There are a great many items here which will, in my opinion, bring far more than ten thousand pounds. You may set a reserve price, and if, at auction, the item does not reach that price, we, the house, buy it back in for you."

He was reciting this almost by rote; this scale of charges was printed in every catalogue Hardy's issued. It was one way the great auction houses were more attractive than the private dealers in modern paintings. A dealer's commission on living artists and on those who, dead or alive, were bound to him by contract was often forty, and sometimes fifty, percent.

Askew twisted his cigarette into the saucer of the coffee cup. "Whatever your arrangements, Gerald, I might as well let it all go. There aren't many fond memories attached to this place." He looked across at the condesa. "We'll have some days in the sun, won't we, Carlota?"

His answer was her hand extended to him. "Let us go for a walk, Roberto. Yes, there will be days in the sun. . . ."

They were gone, and Gerald produced his notebook and was writing quickly, muttering to himself. In my imagination I saw the place stripped of what was preserved here, of all but what was too massive to move. The beauty of the house would shine through then, but it would be a house deprived of most of its history. For the first time in my life I felt a disloyalty to Hardy's. I began to understand the jealous possessiveness of Tolson and Jessica. And then, at that moment, I thought I began to understand Vanessa. If she had seen all this and said nothing, her reasons and feelings might have been what I was now experiencing. Once again I switched to dislike of that man, Robert Birkett, earl of Askew, walking in the fitful spring sunshine with his mistress, planning their lives in a place where the sun always shone.

FINALLY Gerald had finished with his notes. "I'm going up for a nap, Jo. You'll make some sort of start on that load of papers in the study, will you? Not that you'll discover anything in a few hours, but it will, at least for now, keep Robert quiet about the painting." I watched him go up the stairs, moving quite heavily. It was unlike Gerald to retire in the afternoon, but then this day had been unusually trying.

Before I took the circular ladder from the library to begin my task in the study, I climbed up and inspected the prunus jar that I had seen last night on the top of the bookcases. But when I held it in my hand I saw that it was the sort of jar turned out by the thousand in Hong Kong. I shrugged and put it back in its place. Well, what family didn't collect junk along with treasures? As I climbed down the ladder I looked again into the bookcases and noted the volumes—many titles in Latin, some in Greek, books on botany and anthropology, and there, in faded green leather, a set of the works of Darwin, possibly a valuable first edition. This family had had its scholars, as well as its farmers. What a mixed, odd lot they were. Suddenly I felt more enthusiasm for the task Gerald had set me.

The enormity of it, though, struck me again when I wheeled the ladder into place under the wall of filing boxes in the study. I didn't even glance at the picture in its dark place at the other end of the room; that was for Gerald and the experts to worry about. I climbed the ladder and began staring at the dates on the boxes. When would Askew's Dutch grandmother have come to Thirlbeck? I allowed for Askew's age, and then gave fifty to sixty years earlier for the birth of his grandfather. When would he have married? At about the age of thirty—in 1880 or 1882? I took down a box marked 1880 and pulled on its red strings to open it, the dust tickling my nose. I noticed with annoyance that the first few papers were for the year 1883. They were brittle to the touch and brown at the edges—sheets with accounts, then a surveyor's drawing of

351

some acreage. Then something written in Dutch, I thought, something that looked like a recipe, with one absurd word at the bottom in English—gooseberries. The prudent Dutch housewife putting down the store of jams for the winter? There might have been two hundred separate sheets of paper in that box. I looked despairingly at the boxes reaching over my head to the ceiling. I sighed, and sneezed loudly.

"God bless. . . ." It was Jessica, standing in the doorway. "Can I help you?" She seemed even smaller than before and like a bright butterfly in this dim room, wearing a rather childish yellow sweater that looked as if it had been left over from school.

"Well, I don't know." I wondered why she made me so uncomfortable, as if I had been caught prying. "Lord Askew and Mr. Stanton thought I might find some references to the picture. But the papers don't seem to follow the dates on the boxes."

"No, they don't," she replied cheerfully. "You'll never get through them all this afternoon, will you?" So she already knew that Gerald and I would be leaving tomorrow. "What sort of paper are you looking for? I've been through a lot of the boxes myself—just for fun."

"Well, anything that might relate to the pictures the earl's grandmother brought over from Holland. There might have been a list of some kind . . . anything about when the family might have acquired them."

She was already shaking her head. "Is it important?"

"Quite important. When something is to be sold it helps if there are details of its history. We call it provenance."

Her face grew blank. "I don't remember seeing anything of the sort." She took a few steps toward me. "Lord Askew shouldn't sell what's here. It doesn't really belong to him—it has to be kept." The blankness was suddenly gone, replaced by a passion which made her soft voice shrill.

"Jessica!" Tolson had heard her voice and had come to the door. Then he saw me perched on the ladder. His eyes seemed to darken behind the heavy glasses. "Is there something I can do for you, Miss Roswell?"

I found myself explaining once again why I was there. His face remained impassive, and Jessica broke in before he could speak. "I've told her there's nothing. I would have found it, wouldn't I,

Grandfather? I've been through almost every box that's there."

"Hush, Jess, hush. Don't excite yourself." His tone was deliberately calm. "I expect none of us ever paid much attention to what's in those boxes. But it's far too big a task to be done in a few hours. Perhaps after tomorrow you and I, Jess, could start to look. Now I think your grandmother would like some help preparing tea. Lord Askew and the condesa have driven into Kesmere." He looked up at me. "Jessica will bring a tray to the library in about twenty minutes. Perhaps you might be good enough to inform Mr. Stanton?"

I climbed down the ladder as he turned back to Jessica. "Go, now, there's a good girl." The tone was gentle, more full of emotion than I could have believed possible. There was the sound of her light running steps in the hall and the unoiled squeaking of the service door.

"I'll carry the tray to Mr. Stanton," I said. "If that's all right. He's a little tired and might like to rest until dinner."

"Of course, whatever you say, Miss Roswell." His voice was indifferent, utterly changed from a few seconds ago. He was about to turn when I halted him. I had to ask him.

"Wait, please, Mr. Tolson. You—well, you probably remember my mother."

"Your mother?" He repeated the words as if I were a fool.

"Yes, my mother, Vanessa Roswell. She and my father, Jonathan Roswell, were here for some months just after the war. They had the lodge at the other end of the valley, across Brantwick." I was using the name as if I had known it all my life.

"Yes, I do recall. What about it?"

"Oh, just . . ." He made it impossibly difficult. "Well, I wondered how much you remembered of them. Lord Askew said they were often here with him. It was before I was born—I never knew they were on the Birkett estate."

"What do you expect me to tell you?" he demanded. "I don't remember every little thing. It was the end of the war, and things were very difficult—rations hard to get. Mr. Roswell used to drive the Bentley that Nat Birkett has now, and it used too much petrol. Lord Askew used to give him, *our* coupons. And then they had cream and eggs and even meat—from the lambs and bullocks we slaughtered. I had a terrible time accounting for it all with the

Ministry of Food. The earl didn't seem to understand about such things."

I sighed. "I'm sorry to have revived unpleasant memories. You didn't much care to have my mother and father here, did you?"

"They just came here and asked to rent the North Lodge because they saw it was empty. Out of the blue, like a couple of gypsies. Lord Askew was present at the time, and he said that they could rent it. It wasn't strictly legal. The Ministry of Defence had requisitioned the whole house and the North Lodge during the war, but they never came to use it. They hadn't derequisitioned it at that time, but Lord Askew insisted that we could go ahead without permission. . . . Then, when the cold weather came, the Roswells went off without paying the electricity bill. Lord Askew had even wanted to give them the Bentley, but Mr. Roswell said he couldn't afford to run it. They just went off the way they came— like gypsies."

Yes, it sounded like Vanessa—not to pay the electricity bill. It sounded like my father, too, who had a passion for old cars, a passion that he could now afford to indulge. The Bentley would have been a joy he must have hated to leave behind. And he had said nothing about that, either.

Tolson stood there frowning, remembering, no doubt, the electricity bill and all the wine and champagne that had been drunk that summer and autumn. Gypsies . . . And Tolson's values were so deeply rooted in loyalty to place and family. In his fashion Askew had turned into a gypsy, too. Did Tolson blame Vanessa and my father for that? Well, he surely would never say so.

"Was the house like this when my mother was here?"

"Like this? Like what?"

"All the furniture about? All the good pieces?"

"Why don't you ask her, Miss Roswell?"

I drew in my breath. Hard to believe the whole world didn't know that Vanessa Roswell was dead. "She died a few weeks ago," I said.

"I'm sorry." It was not an offer of sympathy, just barely polite. "But was it like this?"

"I really don't remember. It was a long time ago. I had put most of the furniture into one room when the requisition order came from the ministry. Who knows what strangers will do; some peo-

354

ple get a few drinks and start putting holes in things. Your mother might have seen the pieces that were too big to move. She spent a good deal of time here. She didn't like the lodge very much. Mr. Roswell was . . . artistic, wasn't he? He painted. Terrible daubs, I seem to remember. He actually gave Lord Askew one—as if he thought he would hang it."

"Were the other paintings hung then, Mr. Tolson?"

"Others? What others?"

"There were more than the—the Rembrandt. Lord Askew said his grandmother brought over a lot of Dutch pictures. Perhaps I should look at them. My father's picture might be among them. I would like to see it."

"I don't remember seeing it after Lord Askew left. Perhaps he got rid of it. But the other pictures are—are put away. In safety. And I can't remember whether your mother saw them. Why should I? She came and went. It wasn't important."

Without another word he turned and walked out. Unbelievingly I listened to the sighing squeal of the green baize door. It didn't seem possible that anyone could be so deliberately rude. Tolson was a law unto himself. He cared for nothing beyond Thirlbeck. And he had been one of the few people my mother had not charmed. I wondered if she had cared—or even noticed. She appeared not to have thought anything at Thirlbeck important enough to speak of later.

And that was what was wrong.

It was while I was having tea with Gerald in his room that the next shock came. I had just reported on the muddle of the papers in the study and seen Gerald's shrug of acceptance. "Well, I didn't think you'd turn up anything in a few minutes. I continue to hope, though, that somewhere there exists an inventory of Margeretha van Huygens' dowry. If she was the sort of house-wife I imagine her to be, there would even be a list of linen."

I had been wandering around as he talked, looking at the things that Robert Birkett's father had gathered into this, the room to which, Robert had told us, he had retreated in the last years of his life. There were a few photographs in faded brown tints. I moved on.

And then I saw it. "What's *this* . . . ?"

"I wondered when you'd come to it," Gerald said. "Aren't they charming? Almost certainly by Nicholas Hilliard, I'd say, and most likely he made the frames also, since he was a goldsmith as well as a miniaturist."

Four tiny oval portraits had been gathered into a group, the loops above them pinned to a background of faded crimson velvet. Each miniature, not more than two inches high, encircled by an intricately worked gold frame surmounted by a golden bow studded with small diamonds, was obviously meant to be worn with a chain or pinned to a gown. A man and three fair children, two girls and a boy. They all wore the ruffs of the Tudor period, and the quality of each portrait was extraordinarily high. Gerald's guess of Hilliard as the artist could very well be right. "Who are they?"

"I asked Jessica. They're the third earl of Askew—I suppose that makes him the villain of the ill-fated Spanish Woman's story— and his children."

"One miniature's missing." There was space for a fifth, and it was possible to see a faint oval of slightly darker red on the exposed velvet.

"The countess, I suppose. Jessica didn't know what had become of it. It has been that way as long as she can remember."

"Yes. . . ." I was suddenly impatient. "If you've finished, I think I'd better take the tea things down. Are you going to rest a little longer, or would you like to take a walk?"

He shook his head, his eyebrows raised questioningly, indicating with a glance the rain that pelted against the window. The spring day had changed again. "Not now."

"All right. See you before dinner."

I left the tray on the long table in the hall—I didn't quite possess the courage to penetrate into Tolson's domain behind the baize door—and hurried back to the Spanish Woman's room. I went to the closet, and I took from my handbag another of the things, along with the amber brooch, that had been in Vanessa's handbag, found among the scattered wreckage on that mountainside. I had carried it with me to Mexico and looked at it often. There was something about the tiny, perfectly painted face that had reminded me of Vanessa, and this Tudor lady had the same rather wild red-gold hair. I had imagined that Vanessa discovered the miniature during her stay in Switzerland, but I had not shown it to anyone. The contents of her handbag had been too evocative of pain to discuss. I had simply kept it with me, thankful that these few things had survived.

I sat down at the table and studied the miniature. The bag had been thrown from the plane with sufficient force to tear the leather on one side. Inside, zipped in an inner compartment, the miniature had had the protection of its soft surroundings and a little leather pouch which must have been made for it. But still, the impact had broken off one side of the delicate filigree of the gold frame, and the glass had cracked diagonally across its face. I put the fragment of the frame where it belonged and stared at it. I knew now that Vanessa had not bought it on her trip to Switzerland or anywhere else. In every respect it was the companion piece to the miniatures in Gerald's room. If I were to carry it there, it would fit perfectly into the vacant space in the grouping. Attached to the little diamond-studded loop was a small white tag, held there by a piece of fine red string, identical to the price tags Vanessa used for small items in her shop. And a number—the price, I had supposed—scrawled in Vanessa's writing on the tag.

Had she taken it from here? Had she really stolen this, and even Tolson had not dared to accuse her to me? "Gypsies," he had said. Had he been implying that she had been light-fingered as well? And had she, after all these years, been hoping to sell it out of England, where there was less chance of its identity and its real owner being discovered? I didn't believe what I was now thinking, and yet what else was I to believe?

The wind moaned softly in the chimneys, and an icy draft from the ill-fitting windows found me. I shivered in the last light of the April day. And then a sudden uproar among the pack of wolf-hounds somewhere below told me that Robert Birkett had returned to Thirlbeck.

I put the miniature back in its pouch, wishing I had a more secure hiding place than my own handbag for it. From that moment I knew I didn't quite trust the little golden-haired girl who slipped through these rooms on soft feet. If I stayed at Thirlbeck much longer, I was certain that Jessica would find it, and I couldn't bear that Vanessa's long-held secret should now, at this time, be violated.

IT IS STRANGE HOW quickly one becomes used to the unusual. Gerald and I went through the ritual of drinks in the library before dinner, dinner itself, and coffee in the drawing room, and our eyes hardly ever strayed to what was exhibited before us. Gerald's afternoon rest had seemed to restore him. He referred to the auction only in general terms; the painting was never mentioned. It was a quiet evening, even a dull one; the condesa stitched at her needlework, we listened to the news on the radio, and went up to bed much earlier than the night before. At his door Gerald said, "Good night, dear Jo. Sleep well."

"Sleep well. . . ." And once again I felt the urge to kiss him, to offer some thanks for what he had been to me. But I was not Vanessa, who would have done it spontaneously, so I moved on.

After my bath I sat by the fire for some time, savoring the last of the day's ten cigarettes. I was drowsy from wine, well fed, and comfortable in this room that at first had overwhelmed by its size. In this mellow mood even the Hilliard miniature in Vanessa's handbag had an innocent explanation. She had discovered it somewhere and known where it truly belonged. If she had ever completed that flight to London, she would have been in touch with Askew, and the miniature would have been returned to its proper place. I stubbed out the butt of the cigarette and went to stand by the windows. Once more the scene had changed. The rain was gone, the wind had died. Everything was still. Just the caps of Brantwick and Great Birkeld were now mist-shrouded; even as I watched, the mist moved higher on those two great shapes that dominated this enclosed world. In any other part of England I would have guessed that the morning would be fair and clear, but I had learned not to predict such a thing for this country. I turned back to bed, leaving the curtains undrawn, liking what the moonlight did to the room.

And if in the chair I thought I saw the same shadow as the night before—the small, quiet shadow, perhaps of a young woman heavy with child—then it disturbed me no more than it had before. If Thirlbeck had a ghost, she had no malice for those who wished her well. Soon I was easily and deeply asleep.

It was all the more of a shock, then, to wake as if an arm had tugged me rudely from sleep. I lay for a second frozen with fright. A look around the room revealed nothing unusual, but the sense of urgency persisted. I could never describe the force that impelled me from the bed. There was no sound in all the great house. But something was wrong.

I flung on my robe and, by instinct, groped my way to Gerald's door. Without knocking I went in.

The bedside light was on, and Gerald lay against the headboard as if he had struggled to prop himself up. The pallor of his face was shocking, and the sound of his heavy breathing reached me across the room.

"Gerald, what is it?" I was bending over him, feeling inexpertly for his pulse.

An expression of relief and hope flooded his eyes. "Pain, Jo. Rather bad, I'm afraid. Chest—and down the left arm. Very tight."

I had by now placed pillows behind his head. "If I help, do you think you can push yourself up a bit? It would be easier to breathe." His weight was more than I thought, but I got him almost upright and wedged the pillows so that he wouldn't slip. "Gerald, you must have a doctor at once." I looked at the clock on the mantel. It was two twenty. "I'll have to go and rouse someone. Don't try to move."

"Jo . . . ?" The whisper reached me as I neared the door. I turned back. "How did you know . . . ?"

I shook my head. "I don't know. Some—something wakened me." I had almost said "someone." "Stay quiet, please, Gerald."

Outside I paused on the gallery, wondering what to do, where to go first. Tolson or Jessica would be the best—they would know which doctor to call; but where, beyond that baize door, would I find them? Then suddenly I saw in the moonlight a sight which almost froze my blood. Onto the gallery across the hall from me, their huge white shapes well defined against the dark paneling, had come the whole pack of wolfhounds. They lined up against the railing, in near silence, and stood there, watching, waiting.

For a moment I couldn't make myself move, and then the urgency of Gerald's situation reasserted itself. I *had* to go for help. Would the dogs let me do that? I tried to remember the names Askew had called them. Strange names, names that belonged to the Viking ancestors of these dogs. "Thor—Ulf—Eldir—Odin." My whisper sounded loud in the stillness. I began to walk slowly along the gallery to the head of the stairs. The hounds moved also.

We started down each arm of the stairs at about the same time, but then they went quickly and were waiting on the landing for me. I felt my mouth go dry with fright as I made a very slow and deliberate descent toward that waiting pack.

And then I was among them. There was no growl. Why? No sign of threat. I realized that if they were to bark, Gerald might interpret their ear-splitting chorus as an attack on me, and the shock might be more than he could bear.

"Shush . . . Thor, Ulf. Come now. . . . Come now."

They were all moving with me down the stairs, some ahead, some behind, their big paws and nails making scratching sounds on the wood. We reached the bottom of the stairs, and I made to turn for the baize door. Still there was no sound from them. Then I thought there might be a quicker way to summon help. The telephone by Tolson's desk had a small push-button system on it; I could probably reach Tolson easily using it. I turned slowly and made my way, surrounded by the dogs, to the study door.

As I touched the knob Tolson's alarm system was triggered. Bells sounded everywhere. I stood petrified, the sweat trickling down my arms. Lights began to come on, from the gallery above, from the passage when Tolson swung open the door. But in that time the strangest of all the strange things which had happened since we had entered Thirlbeck occurred. Instead of adding their own chorus to the ringing of the alarm, the dogs, as if moved by one reflex, squatted down around me, those odd whiskery faces almost smiling at me and their long tails beating the floor with pleasure. None of their heads turned as Askew appeared on the gallery or as Tolson paused, rooted in the doorway.

Though the dogs were like a loving circle of protection about me I thought once more of the great white hound who had been seen by me—and only by me—on the slope of Brantwick, and I was sick with fear and bewilderment.

CHAPTER FOUR

WE FOLLOWED the flashing blue light of the ambulance along the road that led to Kesmere, I seated beside Askew in his sports Mercedes, my teeth clamped together to keep them from chattering with cold and tension. I kept watching the blue light, somehow

believing that as long as it kept flashing, Gerald would still live.
At the South Lodge a man stood by to open the gates for us. About
a mile farther along the valley, we passed a house set back on a
slope, where lights burned at a lower window.

"Nat Birkett's up," Askew said. "Either going to bed late or
getting up early. It might be a calf being born. . . ."

We didn't speak again until we reached Kesmere Hospital. We
saw Gerald only briefly as he was wheeled to a room, but I was
cheered by the smile he managed to give us. He was attended by a
man of about Askew's own age, Dr. Alan Murray. "He's a very
good doctor," Askew said reassuringly. "He looks after the Tolson
family."

We sat together in the waiting room, and I broke my rule and
smoked one after another of Askew's cigarettes. A nurse came in
and gave us some tea; she stayed to arrange magazines on the
table and offer remarks about the weather. She stared at Askew,
watched her color when he spoke to her; in his sixties he was
handsome enough to cause a woman to do that.

Then Dr. Murray came back. I jumped to my feet. "How—"

He gestured me to sit again. "Well, now, things aren't at all bad.
We've got a good little cardiac unit here. Quite new. Mr. Stanton
is all right. You're not his daughter, are you?"

"No, he's a very old friend. We work together."

"He's doing well. It was quite a mild attack—or at least that's
what the cardiogram is saying now. We'll keep him here awhile—
do a workup on him, and it's imperative that he rest."

"Would there be better treatment in London, Alan?" Askew
asked. "I don't mean to be offensive, but a lot of us regard him
as rather important. And a lot of us"—now he was looking at me—
"love him."

"He'll get everything he needs here, and fresh air as well. Probably better nursing. The journey back to London by ambulance
wouldn't help him one bit—not screaming down that motorway,
breathing diesel fumes. I'll let you know if he needs a specialist
from London. I promise you I won't hesitate about that. But until
he's completely fit to travel, he's better here."

"Can I see him?"

He shook his head. "He's dozed off. We've sedated him."

"I'll wait, then. I want him to know I'm here."

"It may be hours before he wakes. You aren't going to keep Robert waiting with you? We old men need our sleep."

"No, of course not. There's just the question of how I'll get back."

Askew got to his feet. "Here are the keys to my Mercedes. Dr. Murray'll run me back. Won't you, Alan? Not too far out of your way." He smiled down at me. "Tell Gerald that Thirlbeck is his home for as long as he cares to use it. And I will gladly stay on to keep him company. I hope you will, too. You're good for him. Oh, here . . ." He put his cigarette case in my hand. "You'll be needing these."

For the first time I was grateful to Askew. He had understood that I could not have left before Gerald woke; the time was still too close to Vanessa's death. I would wait.

One of the nurses let me sit near the windowed area of the Intensive Care Unit. From there I could see Gerald's every movement. I was watching the second that his eyes flickered open. I went and touched the arm of the nurse on duty. "Can I . . . ?" I said.

She nodded. "Be very quiet. Don't excite him."

And then I did what I should have done before. I bent by the bed and kissed him. He smiled faintly. "Knew you'd fix it, Jo."

It was beyond all the canons of my time, my generation, but I no longer wanted to play it cool. I pushed back a lank piece of hair from his forehead. "I love you, Gerald," I whispered.

And then, obeying the beckoning of the nurse, I left.

I went out into the air, to Askew's car. Against all that I had thought about the changeability of the weather here, the morning had dawned as calm and fair as the radiant night had promised.

THE gates at the South Lodge were firmly locked, and no one came to open them when I sounded the horn. Smoke rose from the chimney of the lodge, a building very much like the derelict one over beyond Brantwick, except that this one was in immaculate condition. Here the wrought-iron gates with the Birkett crest had been preserved—no doubt by the same Tolson son who was so skillful at making metal shutters. They were formidably high, beautifully worked, and painted a glossy black. The face that Thirlbeck showed to those who ventured on this dead-end road was prosperous enough, and hostile. On the wall beside the gates was another starkly painted notice.

THIRLBECK
STRICTLY PRIVATE
BEWARE OF THE DOGS

Here was an enticing, beckoning fairy-tale world to which admission was forbidden. I rattled those closed gates in frustration and returned to the car to wait until one of the Tolsons turned up. It was Sunday morning, but in a farmer's life the chores were there to be done as always.

The thought of farming brought to mind Nat Birkett. His house was there, visible on the slope about a mile back; if he had a key to the North Lodge gates, then he surely had one to these. I turned the car; better to do something than sit and wait.

Nat Birkett lived in a rather beautiful house, I thought. It was called Southdales and made of the stone and slate of the Lake Country—blues, purples, dull greens, and grays. It was two-storied, quite low, with dormer windows on the upper floor. The vines and climbing roses that twisted about its length were just beginning to put out leaf, and they gave it the homeliness of a house that had never aspired to grandeur. I began to understand Nat Birkett a little more—he, in his independence, possessing this and good farming acres as well, what would he want of Thirlbeck?

He came out quickly to meet me. "Is there trouble? Can I help?"

For the first time since I had discovered Gerald ill I could have wept with relief. It seemed that Nat Birkett would shoulder all my worries. "Yes, there was some trouble. You can help, possibly. I'm locked out of Thirlbeck. I thought you would probably have a key to this gate."

"Yes, of course." Then he looked at me closely. "What's happened? You look awful. . . . Come in."

I found myself in a kitchen which felt as if it had been inhabited for a thousand years and that all the domestic life of the house flowed from it. There was a beautiful dark oak hutch displaying blue china; red striped curtains at the windows, and two rocking chairs before a brick chimneypiece. There was an electric stove and a big refrigerator and a new sink surrounded by old oak cupboards. In the middle stood a table which was worthy of Thirlbeck itself and a set of beautiful Windsor chairs. I had rarely been in a room of such charm and warmth. I found myself seated in one of the rocking chairs, nursing a steaming hot mug of coffee into which Nat Birkett had splashed some brandy. He was rapidly making slices of toast as he listened to me talk.

"Bad shock," he said. He placed the buttered toast on an oak table stool between us and dropped into the opposite chair. "You'd better eat. You must be famished. I'll be cooking some bacon and eggs for the boys in a few minutes, and you can have some of that."

After a night of cigarette smoking I had thought I couldn't eat, but because of the atmosphere of this house, and Nat Birkett himself, I felt it was now safe to lay down the night's burdens. I ate like a hungry child, licking the dripping butter from my fingers and holding out the mug for more coffee and brandy.

"You don't have brandy for breakfast every day, do you?"

"No," he said. "But I don't have champagne at eleven either." We laughed at the memory of it; it seemed much farther away than yesterday. "I felt a right fool, I'll tell you. That elegant pair, Askew and his beautiful condesa, really put me off. I've handled champagne glasses before—I'm not quite an oaf—but I suddenly felt as if the damn thing was going to break in my hand. And then you and Stanton came in, and I felt even worse. The experts up from London—art dealers. You looked as cool as the condesa, only a bit more useful. And I must still have faintly smelled of the cow byre."

I gulped the coffee. "I don't look like that now, though?"

He shook his head. "No, you don't. You look . . . well, human. As if something got out of you that had been locked up."

Without meaning to I found myself talking about Vanessa, about the way the wreckage had looked in the snow. "It's all been so unreal. Then last night I was terrified I was going to lose Gerald. . . ." To this man, a stranger, the words were spilling out as if they had thawed from some frozen place at my center—the jumbled mosaic of Vanessa's life; the acquaintance with my father, which had quickly become a friendship; even a little of my peregrinations all over Europe to look at works of art, but somehow missing myself on the way. I think I even talked about Harry Peers —wondering if Harry saw me as the cool creature of Nat Birkett's description. All this spilled out in the half hour or so that I sat with Nat Birkett, and the sun grew stronger at the windows and a collie scratched at the door to be admitted, taking his place without question near the hearth.

"You know," he said at last, "you need a couple of weeks walking on the fells. Get yourself a pair of decent walking boots—not fancy gear—and a parka, and get up on the fells and walk. Walk until you want to drop. You'll be too tired to think. Just don't get too high, and stay on the trails."

"You think I'm going to remain here?"

"You should. Stanton needs you with him."

"Yes, I suppose you're right. But someone at Hardy's has to know at once what's happened to Gerald. I should telephone . . ."

"Time enough," he said. "No one's out of bed at this hour on a Sunday morning. Might as well have breakfast while you're here. Judging from the elephant noises above, the boys will be down in a few minutes."

"You were up early yourself—or to bed late." I told him about seeing the lights on the way to the hospital.

He grinned. "I'd like to pretend I had a roaring night out. But I didn't. A heifer had a hard time calving—" He was interrupted by a rumbling noise on the stairs. The kitchen door was flung open, and two young boys stopped dead as their eyes fell on me.

"Strawberry had her calf," Nat said. "And this is Miss Roswell. She's staying at Thirlbeck and got locked out."

"Jo is my name," I said. "What are yours?"

The older one straightened himself. "I'm Thomas. He's Richard." And then he added with complete seriousness, "We thought there might be a Harry, but Mother died."

"Shall we call the new calf Harry?" the younger one asked.

"You'd have to call her Henrietta," Nat replied. "No, I don't think you should call her Henrietta. We might sell her one day. And then Harry would be gone. You wouldn't like that."

"No, that's right." Thomas looked expectantly toward the stove. "Shall we start breakfast? It's almost time for church. Richard's lost his Sunday tie. . . . I gave him one of my old ones." The talk flowed on, and I was accepted. They were beautiful, these boys, as Askew had said. The older was about ten years, the younger about eight, and they had that soft, rosy bloom that healthy children wear. Their badly combed, still-damp hair was a wheat-colored blond. They looked like their father, but I knew that their mother must have had intensely blue eyes and a spiky fringe of lashes. Each knew his appointed tasks as Nat got out the frying pan. The eggs and sausages and bacon came out of the refrigerator, the table was set, the bread ready for the toaster.

At last the younger came close to me, patting the collie as he spoke, a gesture that protected his shy eagerness. "You're staying for breakfast, aren't you, Jo? I've laid your place."

We all sat down, and I ate as much as the boys did, and more than Nat. I watched him as he moved from stove to table, and the eggs were dished straight from the pan. "Sorry about all this," he said. "But breakfast is done to a tight schedule. . . . Thomas, elbows off the table."

"Dad, here's Mr. Tolson, coming up the drive."

"Then you're late. Put your jackets on." Nat gave a last-minute twitch to Richard's tie and straightened his socks. "There—out you get."

"Dad, you're not going to come?" Thomas said.

"Thomas, being up half the night to bring a calf into the world is as much the Lord's work as going to church."

"Can I *not* go sometimes?"

"When you're older you can decide that yourself. Until then you'll go with Mr. Tolson—and me, when I decide to go."

The door opened and Tolson stood there, clad in a severe gray suit that looked out of place on his big body. His hair had been greased in an attempt to tame it, without much success. He just stared at me. Jessica came to the door behind him.

"Miss Roswell . . ." His tone was a rumble of displeasure. "I was surprised to see Lord Askew's car here."

"You'd locked her out, Tolson," Nat said.

"There's a phone, isn't there?" Jessica observed. She looked like a spun-sugar fairy, in a pink suit which she managed to make look elegant even though it wasn't expensive. Sensibly, she wore no ornament; she knew enough not to gild the lily.

"Yes, there's a phone. But I invited Jo to breakfast." Nat cut off Jessica, as if to tell her to mind her own business. "Well," he said to Tolson, "you've had quite a night over at Thirlbeck."

"Very unfortunate. But Lord Askew says Mr. Stanton is doing well. Will you be leaving today, Miss Roswell, as planned?"

"I don't know. Lord Askew thinks it would be better if I stayed."

As Tolson's dark eyes bore in on me through the pebble lenses my resentment grew. This man dominated too much at Thirlbeck;

he was its guardian, not its owner. If I couldn't outface this man, for Gerald's sake and my own, then I might as well crawl back into my niche at Hardy's. "I will make that decision when I have consulted Mr. Stanton's colleagues," I said crisply. "But I think you may take it that I won't be leaving at once."

"Well, *that's* nice," Jessica said sharply. "Grandfather, we'll be late. Thomas, Richard." Tolson stood looking at me for a moment longer, and for the first time I sensed a sort of helplessness in him. Something in his carefully planned world had been upset. In that moment his strength seemed diminished and my own grew.

"I shall need to get into Thirlbeck, Mr. Tolson," I said. "Would you be good enough to lend me a key?"

"A key?" His head went up like that of an old lion whose territory had been challenged. "That won't be necessary, Miss Roswell. My daughter-in-law, Jessica's mother, is now back at the South Lodge. All you have to do is sound your horn. Good morning, Nat. I'll see you when I bring the boys back from church."

"You might not," Nat replied. "I'll probably be in bed. But I'll be over in the afternoon to discuss putting up some new fencing."

"In that case," Tolson said as he turned to go, "Thomas and Richard can have their lunch with us. My wife will have cold food ready for you to bring back for supper." Then he was gone.

I waited until the sound of Tolson's car had died away. "They seem to have arranged things very nicely. Do you always let them run your affairs like that?"

"I suppose it does look that way." He shrugged. "It's difficult to see how *not* to do it. And it works. Things were in a pretty bad state after Patsy died. The Tolsons have provided a continuity for Thomas and Richard that no outsider could have given them. In every crisis that's arisen one or another of them has been here to help. Jessica's mother comes up every day and does some cooking and cleaning. As the Tolsons see it, they're simply beginning a little early a service that they'd normally be giving to the earl of Askew. The boys have friends in the younger Tolson grandchildren, mothers of a sort in the Tolson wives. Things could be worse. I go along because they've made it easy for me."

"And that includes taking your sons to church every Sunday?"

"It includes about everything. Tolson has strong ideas about how my sons should be brought up. Church is one of them. School is another. Tolson doesn't think the Kesmere grammar school is fitting for the sons of the future earl of Askew. He's offered to finance sending them to prep school, using income from the Birkett estate, with Askew's permission, of course. I gave him a flat no. He really can't believe how much I loathe the idea of moving into the niche that's all carved out for me."

I was standing by the window while he talked, staying very quiet because I did not want the flow of words to stop. There was the anguish of a lonely man in them, a man who had surrendered a part of a cherished independence so that his children would have a family. I saw the two rosy faces of those children, and I couldn't blame him. And then, coldly, I wondered if Tolson had already selected the woman that Nat Birkett should marry.

"I didn't realize how well you could see Thirlbeck from up here. That peel tower, and the tarn." The sunlight had made the lake a shimmering cloth of gold behind the buildings—the England of storybooks it seemed now to be, and no one could have guessed the dark spots of its history. "Will you go and live there, Nat?"

"Live there! Never."

"Then what will happen to it?"

"I'll worry about that when I have to." He paused, and poured himself more coffee, banging the pot angrily on the table. "I suppose all women are soft about things like that. They see a great pile of stones, and just because it's got a bit of history they think it's got to go on forever. Tolson got to Patsy that way. He began to get her over there ... any excuse at all. He wanted her to think of it as her home. It was insidious, the way he planted things in her mind. He meant it for the best, of course, but it turned out for the worst. She actually died there, my Patsy, in that wretched place."

He rose to pour two glasses of brandy and carried both to the window where I stood.

"Here, drink this, and then go back and get some sleep. And try to forget all this nonsense I've talked. It gets too much at times— when I'm tired and I realize the boys are growing up. I've seen her stand there where you've been standing—she didn't look like you, though. And she didn't act like you. She was unsophisticated and given to dreaming. I suppose most people would have said she was sweet, and let it go at that. But she was generous as well. Oh, hell, what's the use of trying to describe someone you've loved?"

He moved away from me and poured more brandy. "I wonder if I'm getting drunk? Well, I'll be sober enough when I go to pick up the boys. Setting a good example, Tolson always calls it. You're right! I *do* let them run my affairs, simply because I haven't the strength to think for myself." He cupped the glass between both hands. "I'm smothering under it. They cook my food, do my laundry, clean my house—try to make it seem as if Patsy hadn't died. But they can't give her back to me. And there's Jessica. . . . My, I *am* drunk. . . ."

I put down my glass. "I'd better go now."

He didn't hear me. I had grown cold at the mention of Jessica's name, as if the sun and the brandy hadn't touched me. For a moment I stood and looked at him, and remembered some of the things that had spilled from me earlier. And now he had talked of his loneliness and the pressing sense of the future being shaped in a way he didn't want. Would we be able to forgive each other for the things we had spoken? Or would we despise each other for the weaknesses confessed?

"Good-by, Nat." I don't think he even looked up as I went. Outside, the first cloud had appeared at the ridge of Great Birkeld.

CHAPTER FIVE

I FELL into the routine of the next days and weeks with a strange ease, as if I had somehow been waiting for this pause in my life.

Later that same day phone calls were made to Hardy's; the managing director, Anthony Gower, asked me to stay on at Thirlbeck. He had already been contacted by Lord Askew, who wanted me to stay. I was to telephone daily reports to Hardy's and make certain Gerald had every attention he needed. My time, he implied, was of far less importance than Gerald's comfort.

Then, from a public telephone box in Kesmere, I talked again with Mr. Gower. This time his correct, pleasant voice had a faint note of excitement. I told him what Gerald and I had seen in the few rooms of Thirlbeck which were open to us and that it was Askew's intention that it should all go to auction at Hardy's. But nothing was to be done until Gerald was completely recovered, lest he become involved and overstrain himself. I said nothing for the moment about the Rembrandt.

I also telephoned Gerald's manservant, Jeffries. I had a difficult five minutes calming his first panic. Jeffries had been with Gerald more than thirty years; he and his wife entered Gerald's service when Gerald's wife had been living. With the deaths of those two women they had grown closer, the remains of what had once been a family unit. "Mr. Stanton really *is* all right, Jeffries, and he would like you to come up here. I'd be grateful if you could drive my car up. Then you could take over the Daimler. Lord Askew would like you to stay on here until Mr. Stanton is able to leave, so you should pack suitable clothes for you both."

I asked him to go to my flat and bring some extra clothes for me also; I would telephone the owner of the ground-floor flat, who had a key. Jeffries was the one man I could have asked this favor of; he was the sort who could buy an entire wardrobe for a woman, once given her size. I told him I would telephone the garage about my car. "You remember it, Jeffries? It's a Mini."

"A *Mini?*" He cleared his throat. "I do seem to recall it, Miss Roswell." He didn't recall it with any pleasure.

"I'll expect you late tomorrow, then?"

"First thing in the morning, Miss Roswell." It would have been useless trying to dissuade him; he wouldn't rest until he saw Gerald.

I went then to the hospital, but I was only allowed to see Gerald for a few minutes the first day. Dr. Murray said that he would probably be out of the Intensive Care Unit within forty-eight hours. The condesa came with Askew and blew Gerald an airy kiss through the glass which separated them, and I realized I was jealous because Gerald looked so pleased. He was washed and shaved, and the color of life had returned to his face. I was suddenly able to laugh at my jealousy and exult in the feeling of something won back from death.

I had arranged to meet Jeffries in Kesmere the next morning. As he pulled his long, gray-suited figure from my red Mini he was already registering disapproval of everything he saw. He couldn't see anything of merit outside London.

"How is Mr. Stanton?" was his greeting.

"I've telephoned the hospital. Doing very well, they say."

"We'll go at once, then."

"Jeffries, I don't think you should. You look tired yourself, and you probably need breakfast. It won't," I added as he started to shake his head, "do any good for Mr. Stanton to see you looking tired after such a long drive. He'll start to worry about *you*."

He submitted reluctantly, and we went and ordered bacon and eggs in a café that did a large trade with fell walkers. Jeffries was supremely out of place and seemed happy that he so obviously was. He had a highly developed snobbism from long service to a rich man, and yet he had remained kind. He asked if the Daimler was running well. I thought of his long night on the motorway in my poor Mini and laughed. "Beautifully. Not a rattle in her."

He relaxed a little after he had eaten. "What sort of people are they—who take care of Lord Askew?"

"The Tolsons—good people, Jeffries. But not . . ." I didn't know how to express it. "Well, Mr. Tolson has been a kind of steward for the estate, and all his family work for it as well as for themselves. They're not actually help. It's more *their* home than Lord Askew's."

"Most irregular," he said.

"I don't think you'll find it irregular when you meet them."

Nor did he; he made a point of driving round to the stable yard, which now housed only farm machinery, and entering through the back door. I went along with him. Before unloading Gerald's and his own bags, he carried in the large red suitcase he had packed for me. Tolson and Jeffries confronted each other in the kitchen. Mrs. Tolson was seated at the table, mixing a batter, and Jessica, wearing a neat skirt and blouse, came in from an adjoining pantry. Jeffries took one swift look at the family, the spotless, old-fashioned kitchen, and his approval was instant.

"My name is Jeffries," he announced. "I am Mr. Stanton's man. I expect to take care of him while he's here and, of course, to take over any of the extra duties which Mr. Stanton's and Miss Roswell's presence may involve. I am used to cooking, polishing and dusting, cleaning silver, and valeting. I also drive Mr. Stanton and clean his car. Anything I can do for Lord Askew in that direction I shall be happy to do. I'll take up Miss Roswell's bag first, and then, if you'd be good enough to show me where my quarters are, and if I might locate an ironing board . . . I understand Lord Askew doesn't travel with a valet. . . ."

There was a tradition of service—of how the world should be ordered—which made these people instantly recognizable to each other, as disparate as they were. I knew what was going on between them, but I was not part of it. So I turned away and walked back to the stable yard, where the Mini and the Daimler were parked. Then, for the first time since Gerald became ill, I found I was brushing tears away from my eyes. The Mini, which I remembered as perpetually dirty, was transformed. It had been washed and polished, the ashtrays emptied; the shelf which usually held half a year's accumulated rubbish had been tidied. It was the innate reaction of an extremely tidy man to a car which he would drive, for however short a time. I felt somehow shamed as I looked at it.

THERE was Harry Peers on the phone from London. "Why didn't you tell me, you idiot? I'd have come up. Listen, do those hicks up there know how to take care of him?"

"He's all *right*, Harry. He really is all right."

"Don't trust that lot myself. They know how to look after animals better than people."

"He's being very well looked after, Harry." I was beginning to grow tired of making that statement.

"Are *you* being well looked after, luv?"

"How well is that supposed to be?"

"As well as your Harry would look after you. I'm waiting for you to come back, Jo. Don't make it too long."

And then there was the vacant dial tone on the telephone after he had hung up. I suppose it was part of Harry—that habit of never letting anyone else finish a conversation.

I thought of Harry and how he would have disapproved as I took Nat Birkett's advice the next day about fitting myself out with walking boots and a parka. I had been to see Gerald quite early, and although he had made a marked improvement I knew that it would be weeks, not days, that I would stay at Thirlbeck. I felt self-conscious in the shop, not really knowing what to ask for. I was looking through the racks when Nat touched me on the shoulder. "Saw you through the window. You're in the wrong place, you know."

"But they said this was the best shop."

"I meant you're looking at the wrong stuff. Those things might look all right in Bond Street, but they don't keep the cold out up on the fells. You need a padded parka with hood and zips like this, with plenty of pockets. Here—this your size?" He jerked down a

373

yellowish one from a hanger. "Yes, that'll do." Then I found myself, under his supervision, trying walking boots that laced firmly about the ankles, worn over two pairs of heavy socks.

"Am I supposed to *walk* in these?"

"You will, once you hit the right stride. They could save you breaking an ankle." We were outside, Nat carrying the boots, and I wearing the new, stiff parka rather self-consciously.

"We'll break it in, shall we?" Nat said.

"How?"

"Take some wine and sandwiches and go to the coast. That'll get some mustard on it and put some sand in the pockets." We were walking toward the small town square and our cars. "I'll just telephone the farm. Suddenly, I feel like a holiday."

I sat in the high passenger seat of the Bentley and stared down those who stared at me. I was glad when Nat came back, his arms loaded with paper packages. "I've been causing some gossip, I think," I said to him. "People have been wondering what Nat Birkett picked up in a spanking new parka."

"Let them. Do them good. Everyone here wants to know your business." The ancient Bentley made a lot of noise as Nat maneuvered it out of the parking space. "Needs a bit of work," he shouted. "Damn thing takes more time than she's worth. . . . Don't know why I bother." The top was full of holes, he said, and so it was kept down permanently. I found myself zipping up the parka as we passed the outskirts of the town. Nat roared at me, "Cold?"

"No." But I was. I was also exhilarated, riding so high in the world, feeling the stream of air flowing about my face.

We headed west over a series of passes through the mountains. After an hour the scent of the salt wind came to us, and we turned in to a dirt track leading toward the dunes and stopped at an empty shed, almost roofless.

"This is far enough. I know the man who owns the place. He never uses it—the land isn't much good for farming. A little sheep grazing, but really only for summer. I've often thought I'd like to buy this bit so that the boys and I could fix up the byre as a kind of beach hut. But somehow there's always something else to spend the money on." He looked at the place more speculatively. "Really ought to, though. It's necessary for me to spend time alone with the boys. I can't let them grow up completely with the Tolsons."

He led us through the dunes at a place where a brook trickled down to the Irish Sea. Then we walked about a mile to a small beach that glistened between two headlands. We sat and ate hunks of bread with pieces of cheese and ham, and tried to smear on butter and mustard with plastic knives. I got both butter and mustard on the new parka, and Nat said it looked better. With our backs against a boulder we drank very good red wine, passing the bottle back and forth to each other because the paper cups spoiled the taste. Afterward we walked along the beach, and Nat showed me how to make my way up a small cliff face, using the new boots.

As we climbed he gathered the little flowers and plants that grew in the crannies of the rocks, giving them their names—thrift, scurvy grass, bloody cranesbill. Marvelous names, I thought, and tried to remember them. I tried to memorize, too, the birds he named—the terns, guillemots, kittiwakes—but only the gulls and their haunting, piercing cry were familiar. Then suddenly Nat said, "We'll have to move, or we'll be stranded here. The tide's coming in." We went back down the rock face with careful ease. But there was a sense of haste as we packed together the remains of the picnic, for drops of rain had begun to fall. By the time we reached the car it was a downpour.

He showed me how to adjust the hood of the parka so that it covered almost everything but my eyes, and then he took an old cloth cap and loose oilskin from under the seat. As he climbed in he said, "This is one of the times when I know what a fool I am to be bothering with a kid's toy like this Bentley. The Land-Rover is a damn sight more efficient and comfortable. But after Patsy's death Tolson sort of thrust it on me, as if I needed something to play with. Well, keep your head tucked down. It's going to be a long, wet, cold drive."

It was all of that. And it was worse, because Nat's mood seemed to have changed as quickly as the rain had come down. He didn't talk during the drive, and he said a perfunctory good-by in Kesmere, stopped beside my Mini. He had probably taken me to a place where he and Patsy had often picnicked, and with me it hadn't been worth the journey. As I got into the Mini he suddenly said, "Here—take these." In my hand were the little rock plants he had gathered, and the feathers of dune grasses. I didn't know whether he gave them to me as a gift or because he simply didn't want them himself. That night in the Spanish Woman's room I laid them carefully in a newspaper and put them away in my big suitcase. Then I shook the sand out of the pockets of the parka.

IN THE next few days I eased myself into the stiffness of the new walking boots. In spite of the heavy layers of socks they raised blisters in a few miles' hike. Tenderfoot, I told myself, as I soaked in a mustard bath that Jeffries had insisted on my taking. Jeffries knew all about such things as mustard baths and when to have brandy after a long walk. He'd have it poured and waiting for me in the Spanish Woman's room. Jeffries loved the Spanish Woman's room as, by this time, he loved every part of Thirlbeck. "It's a marvelous house, isn't it, Miss Roswell? And those pieces downstairs— they'd make you want to weep to see them all bundled together like that. But still, I suppose Mr. Tolson's right. He has to look after them in the only way he can. Actually his security is quite good, considering it's a homemade job." Jeffries didn't, however, like the dogs, and he was puzzled, as I was, that they had begun to hover around me whenever Askew was away. "Ugly-looking brutes, aren't they, Miss Roswell? When I saw you setting off for a walk yesterday and all eight of them trailing you I wondered if you'd be safe."

"I think I couldn't be safer."

He had looked doubtful, but then brightened as another thought came. "Well, Mr. Stanton will be out in less than a week if all goes well. Remarkable recovery. He'll live to be ninety." I had the feeling that if Gerald did do that, Jeffries would feel obliged to live long enough to take care of him. "Wonderful people, the Tolsons. There aren't many like them now. Perhaps there's something to be said for living in the country and keeping your roots. That little Jessica—very clever, she is. Can turn her hand to almost anything. It'll be a lucky man who marries her."

The ragged edges of life at Thirlbeck became smoother with Jeffries' presence. In his total devotion to Gerald he wanted to serve Gerald's friends. If he was not at the hospital, he took on any task at Thirlbeck. "I like to be busy," he said when Askew demurred about him doing too much. Then he added quietly, "One likes to be needed, my lord." And so he waited on table, pressed clothes, vied with Jessica in producing beautiful food; he baked and iced a triumphant birthday cake for a Tolson grandchild.

The condesa had an ability to amuse and charm Gerald, and she used it unsparingly. She had a knack for finding books and magazines which would interest him. She would even read aloud to him sometimes, making wry comments on English manners, which delighted Gerald. The flowers that arrived from friends in London were handed over to her for arranging, and she brought vases from Thirlbeck to replace the hospital vases, which Gerald loathed. When she sensed he was tiring she would sit quietly in the room, busy at her needlework. Jeffries openly adored her. "A really elegant lady," was his comment. "What a pity she can't marry Lord Askew."

I found my own rather solitary place in the world of Thirlbeck in those days. There was the daily visit to Gerald and a report to Hardy's. After that, at first, I drove far afield of Thirlbeck, doing the obvious things—Wordsworth's tiny cottage at Grasmere, the haunting ruins of ancient castles, the druidic circles of stones that had stood, their purpose unrecorded, from prehistory. At Askew's insistence Tolson had given me keys to the two gates of the Thirlbeck valley, so I could come and go as I pleased. But as the days passed I found myself turning back to Thirlbeck after the morning visit to Gerald. I walked the road over Brantwick, through the larch grove, to the ruin of the lodge where Vanessa and Jonathan had lived that summer and autumn. I stood often in the copse of birches where the first evening the great white hound had appeared, but I never saw it again.

I found the stone marker that Askew had talked about. Half hidden by the tall, reedy grass, it was set in the marshy area that ran down toward the lake. It was a rough-hewn stone, about three feet high, tapered slightly, giving it the air of an obelisk. I brushed the grass aside and deciphered the clumsily chiseled letters, almost obliterated by weather. JUANA. And then, beneath this, THE SPANISHE WOMAN. I traced the lettering with my fingers, wondering if this had been made by the boy who had been with her when she died. Juana . . . I wondered if Vanessa had ever seen this.

The ruined chapel and the burial ground of the Birketts was totally unexpected. It lay to the east of the house. I found it by following a path to a copse of beeches, elms, and oaks planted more closely than through the rest of the park. The walls of the roofless chapel had almost disappeared under ivy and briars; little sapling trees were gaining height among the graves, and one, a slender young birch, had even raised itself within the chapel. There were enough headstones here to account for many generations of Birketts. A stone wall kept the sheep out; the little iron gate sagged, but still held its place. It looked as if some work had recently been done on the hinges; Tolson, no doubt, had qualms about letting the sheep graze the graves of the Birkett family.

IN THE brilliant sunshine of one early afternoon I followed a sheep trod that wound steeply upward on the rough, heathery slopes of Great Birkeld and experienced the shock of seeing clouds quickly rolling down from the top, the mist descending rapidly, the trail ahead and below blotted out, the tarn obliterated, the sheep wall I had taken as my landmark gone. I understood at last the danger Nat Birkett had warned me about, and I remembered, too, that I had told no one what direction I was taking.

Now that I could no longer see the trail, every step was in question. Had it gone up here, down there? Was this a fork or some blind turning that might take me toward the dangerous rocky slope? Sounds came to me out of the mist—the faint bleat of sheep in the distance, the rasping sound of my own breathing—all thrown back and distorted by the white wall of vapor. I had definitely lost the sheep trod. This was spongy moor grass, hollows filled with dark peat and little pools of water. In the next hour I'd not found the trail again, and I was exhausted. I stepped beyond the shelter of a boulder, and my foot touched the edge of the rockfall; a few pebbles were dislodged, and I listened to them rattle and bounce on their terrible journey to the bottom. I froze then, edged back a little, holding on to the boulder as if to save my life. I sat down on the wet ground, prepared to wait for the mist to lift. After a time I grew light-headed with cold, with hunger; and sleep—that deadly sleep—began to seem a pleasant alternative. How cold did it become up here before dawn? I wondered. A kind of dreadful calm settled on me; I could begin to acknowledge that what I might be waiting for was not the mist to lift or for the rescuers to come, but for death itself.

I first heard it as a kind of far-off howl, unbelievably eerie and desolate. Was it near, or something coming from the floor of the valley and thrown back by the mist? It seemed to come from every direction. Then, very suddenly, I knew it was quite close, the sound of small rocks disturbed, the sound of feet on grass. I screamed as something wetter than the mist touched my face, and then, at once, they were all around me. Sobbing, I put out my hand and touched the whiskery faces. "Thor . . . Ulf . . . Odin . . ." I found myself clinging about the neck of one of them. Several of those rough tongues licked my face. One of the pack thrust his great head under my arm, as if to urge me back on my feet. I got up slowly; one stayed beside me, the others went off into the mist— they might have been only feet away, but I could no longer see them. Their voices called to each other and to me at intervals, indicating the direction. With my hand firmly on the collar of the dog who had stayed with me, I started down.

I don't know how long that journey lasted. I was nudged and pushed and pulled—up a little here, down at another point. I never knew if we got back on the sheep trod. They were smelling and sniffing their ways, hoarse barks of encouragement and guidance coming from the invisible leaders.

At a place where the land began to level out, the bottomland soil of the dale, the mist grew thinner. I saw the sheen of water, and the dogs led me to the trail that circled the tarn. They all clustered about me then, the whole pack, as if to convey that their task was over. Then they strung out again, the leader ahead, the last one at my side all the way back to Thirlbeck.

When we reached the house the dogs left me at once to search for Askew. As I leaned over the balustrade of the gallery I saw him open the library door to admit them in reply to Thor's insistent scratching. I could hear his voice. "Well . . . where have you been? I've never known you lot to wander off before." I was glad they could not answer; I myself could never speak of how they had come to find me on the mountain that afternoon.

Nat Birkett noticed the cuts and scratches on my hands. He found me, after my visit to Gerald, about to look for lunch in the same café where Jeffries and I had eaten breakfast. I felt his hand on my wrist. "Well, then—I don't ever see you," he said, turning my palm upward. "Were you stuck somewhere and couldn't get down?"

"More or less."

"Come and tell me. I know a rather cozier place than this café." He led me across the town square to a very small pub called The Drover's Rest. Inside, there was an instant greeting from the landlord. "Morning, Nat, what'll it be?"

Nat looked at me. "Would you like beer? It's local. Very good."

We sat over beer and a cheese salad, and great slabs of bread almost as good as Jessica's. "Gerald's coming out of the hospital tomorrow," I said. "I expect I'll be going back to London soon. With Jeffries here, I'm really not needed. I've been doing just a bit of paper sorting at Thirlbeck and driving around. . . ."

"And walking," he said. "And getting into trouble, by the looks of it."

I told him a little of what had happened, but nothing about the dogs. I simply said I had found my way down by a sheep wall.

"I never imagined you'd go off the valley floor, or I'd have insisted you have a compass." He thrust out his legs and looked as if he were trying to keep his patience. "Damn it, Jo! You could have broken your neck."

"I would have been a lot of trouble, wouldn't I?"

"You should stay in the city where you belong."

"I'll see that I do in future."

He took a drink of his beer. "All right—all right. But I've every reason to be annoyed. You've been a fool, and you must know it. Now, if you've got any time to spare, we can put you to work watching the crag where the eagles are nesting. I've put up a sort of shelter—just enough to keep the rain off. The thing is that no one, not even the watchers, must go near the nest."

"What do you do if someone tries?"

"Well, if they've come over from the other side of Brantwick, you would drive back and rouse any of the Tolsons. They'd telephone me. But if people have climbed in by the estate wall, you could easily stop and challenge them. It *is* private property."

We sat over our beer, and ordered some more, and Nat's talk drifted to his farm. He went on and on about his flocks and herds until finally he put down his beer and took my hand in his, tracing the scratches and deeper cuts. "You know, I'm awfully glad you didn't tumble down Great Birkeld and break your silly neck. And I've been talking like an idiot—about things that you probably don't care a damn for. I can't talk about old silver and paintings, Jo. It's hard for me even to imagine the world you live in. I thought, when you left Southdales that morning, that I had bored you to death with my stupid rambling—and here I am doing it again."

"And here I am listening. You listened to me, too, Nat."

"Yes, I remember. But afterward I wondered if you really had been there or if it was some drunken dream. You really don't belong at Southdales. Thirlbeck is your sort of place." He shrugged and dropped my hand. "I imagine the hay is sticking out all over me." Then he laughed suddenly at his own gloomy words. "Well, I'll walk you to your car, and then I have to come back here to see a man with a couple of good calves. He wants too much for them, but if I get enough whisky into him, he might drop his price." He was helping me on with my parka. "Farmer's talk, Jo."

"We talk shop, too. It's different shop, that's all. Don't bother to come with me. When shall I take my turn eagle-watching?"

"Would two to five in the afternoons be all right?"

I said it would, and left him. It was true. I didn't belong here, and he didn't belong anywhere else. There was a kind of amazing innocence in him that wouldn't have survived long beyond this world of his. Then I began to imagine him meeting my father and how very well Nat would have understood and respected my father's need for the lost, remote world of his hacienda.

GERALD came back to Thirlbeck, and life took up yet another rhythm. The days were mostly sunny, and garden furniture of a bygone age—teak benches and chairs, a handsome teak table—appeared in an open space which gave a view along the length of the tarn. Drinks were set out there on days when the weather permitted. Gerald's conversation was brisk and sharp, but he still returned to his room after lunch and didn't reappear until before dinner. Askew and the condesa looked forward to his coming; Thirlbeck oppressed her, I thought, and she wanted talk of other places, something Gerald could well supply.

I began to take my turn, as I had promised Nat, at the shelter below the crag where the eagles nested. My eyes ached sometimes from looking through the binoculars, but the hours never seemed long. I was supposed to watch on every side of the crag for the approach of strangers, but often I found myself just watching the flight of the eagles. I learned to anticipate, to love, that heart-stopping moment when one or the other soared above the crag and then swooped in a dive to earth. The eagles became for me a manifestation of all that was free, free to soar, to mate, and to nest—wild things that needed a territory as big as this valley and peace to nurture their fledglings. I grew to feel about those two birds as I felt about the house itself—that once it vanished something quite irreplaceable would have gone.

I was now spending several hours a day working on the boxes in the study, looking for any paper relating to the Rembrandt. Perched on the ladder, my hands smeared with dust and cobwebs, I scanned the brittle brown papers, but despaired of finding what Gerald hoped for. Indeed, there was almost a malevolent disarray about the contents of the boxes. Some would begin with the date stamped on the cover and then skip ten years. Others would bear no relation to the date on the box at all. It seemed utterly useless, but I persisted because Gerald had asked it.

Curiously, Gerald was in no particular hurry to return to London, nor was Askew impatient to leave. Both of them seemed to have fallen into their own pattern at Thirlbeck. Perhaps Gerald was more tired than he had known. Perhaps Askew was beginning to face without fear his own past in this house; he even took his turn at the eagle watch and became almost as zealous as Nat Birkett. Only the condesa chafed under the restrictions of life at Thirlbeck. She did not openly complain, but at times I sensed a growing desperation in her. I thought that she feared Askew's seeming contentment in his surroundings; it might be difficult to pry him loose. Yet she sat at her needlework with the quiet grace of a woman who has schooled herself in the art of waiting.

The telephone calls from Harry continued, but they were brief and less frequent. And then there came one during which he said he was going to Australia. "Just for a day or two, luv."

"Don't be ridiculous, Harry. No one goes to Australia for a day or two. What are you going to do there?"

"Mind your own business, luv. That way I'll never be able to blame you for talking out of school and letting some other bloke in on what Harry's already got his eye on. Back in a week. See you—that is, unless you've decided to retire up there."

"No, we'll be leaving in a few days."

"That's good. Someone else might slip into your spot."

"What spot?"

"Your spot at Hardy's, stupid. Well, keep your eye on Gerald. Worth having around, he is. By, luv."

"Harry . . . ?" But he was gone, already a world away from me.

Tolson had long ago, at Askew's insistence, produced the keys to the bookcases in the library. I searched there, too—for a diary, anything that might list the possessions of Margeretha van Huygens. In the mornings the sun came into that room—with the metal shutters thrown back it was a cheerful place, the jumble of furniture even making it seem cozy. I enjoyed sitting on the ladder, taking down books. There were a few that I began to suspect could be of more than usual interest—books in manuscript, with stately Latin phrases, illuminated, some of them. I had a sense, as I touched them, that they had been handled fairly recently. They were dusty, but the dust had not been undisturbed for years. Perhaps Jessica had also enjoyed these treasures, trying out her Latin on them. As I carefully turned the pages I wondered if I should talk to Gerald about them, or to Askew. Something held me back. I was beginning to think that, while all seemed right on the surface, much at Thirlbeck could be very wrong.

I found the Book of Hours on the top shelf of a case whose lock yielded only after I had eased its stiffness with fine sewing-machine oil. The dust inside this case was heavy and undisturbed. The Book of Hours had fallen, or been pushed, behind taller volumes. It was tiny and exquisite, this *Horae*, illuminating with those curiously medieval figures the seven canonical offices of the day. My memory spelled them out as I turned the beautiful hand-wrought pages—matins, prime, terce, sext, none, vespers, compline. So beautifully executed, this book could have been made for a princess. I could not, from my very small knowledge of such things, know for what historic personage such a book had been designed. But it once had been given, and the name of the giver, or the receiver, was written in a faded but readable script: Juana Fernández de Córdoba, Mendoza, Soto y Alvarez.

And then an ancient, brittle sheet slipped out and, along with it, a page which held Vanessa's writing.

I don't remember how long I sat on top of that ladder. I do remember staring out at the lake and back at the two sheets of paper. Finally, carefully closing the bookcase, I climbed down the ladder and left the study. When I reached the Spanish Woman's room it was more than ever a sanctuary to me.

I sat at the long table in the window alcove and spread out the two pages. One was fine parchment, yellowed, with a flowing script in Spanish. The other was ordinary modern notepaper on which, in her scrawling hand, Vanessa had copied the Spanish words. Someone had written a translation beneath:

> And this do we send unto you, beloved cousin, our likeness, by the hand of Domenico Theotokopoulos, a mirror of conscience, to keep close, in faith and in trust, until the day of the final victory and the eternal union in Christ and our Holy Mother Church.
>
> I, the King,
Felipe

I looked in awe at the signature on the yellowed parchment—that of Philip II, using the majestic title, "I, the King," as all sovereigns of Spain had done in the days of her power and glory. I knew quite surely that this scrap of parchment had been sent to the Spanish Woman to hold her loyalty to the political mission on which she had been sent, a pawn in Philip's hand.

But the vital importance of the message was in that other name, the name of an ordinary painter known not to have been greatly favored by the king, but obviously used by him for this special commission. The portrait must have been quite small or it never could have reached the Spanish Woman in secret. Domenico Theotokopoulos—the name he had been called in official documents. To the world, who would now pay almost unimaginable sums for one of his pictures, he was known simply as El Greco.

I grew weak at the thought that one of *his* canvases might exist in this house and that Vanessa *had* come across this slip of parchment in the Spanish Woman's cherished book. Vanessa had found it, copied it, and had it translated. And told no one.

I looked wildly around the room and wondered about all the rooms in this great house in which I had never set foot. I thought of the locked door which guarded the pictures of Margeretha van Huygens. Was it possible that among them, alien to those Dutch landscapes and still lifes, there existed a small portrait of a Spanish

Hapsburg face, the face of Philip, archenemy of Elizabethan England? I doubted it. *If* the portrait existed, it would be in the place where the Spanish Woman had hidden it.

I looked out on the calm, golden mirror of the tarn. The Spanish Woman had taken to her death in that tarn the knowledge of a greater treasure than the enormous jewel she wore at her neck.

THAT was the day at Thirlbeck when I opened doors I never had opened before. Until now good manners—perhaps misplaced, considering the job I held—had kept me from prying. Now I drew back curtains, lifted dust sheets. I opened chests and met only the softness of old curtains or bedcovers. There were no pictures and few mirrors. In some rooms I saw fingerprints in the dust, a trail of footprints on the oak floors. I seemed to follow a trail that someone laid before me. It could have been Jessica, who walked the rooms of this house with loving familiarity; it could have been someone whose curiosity had been greater than mine.

But when I opened the door of a room in the wing opposite the one I slept in, I realized that wherever I had gone in that house the perfume that was so strong in this room had been with me—this flowery scent the condesa used. On the room she inhabited she had indelibly stamped her personality. Her amber silk gown lay across a chair, a table with a swinging mirror was strewn with silver-topped bottles and jars. There were flowers and foliage in a big vase, arranged with the careless grace that the condesa had made into high art. And the perfume. I began to think that the perfume wasn't in each room because the condesa had been there before me. She could not have been everywhere, nor so recently. It was the strength of her personality, not her perfume, that was so pervasive. It had impregnated these walls as if she had been here forever, not just a few weeks.

But now I was realizing I had no business looking in her room or in the one Askew used, and I didn't linger.

The house, which from the front appeared to be two stories, grew to three at the center. There was a cluster of low-ceilinged attic rooms with half windows that looked over the roofs of Thirlbeck. Here was the litter of generations—old trunks, bedsteads, a croquet set. The narrow corridors all came back to a steep stair, which must have led down to the wing on the rear of the house which the Tolsons inhabited. I turned back. This, too, was territory I could not invade, and there nagged the thought that somewhere in their rooms might be the portrait of Philip II of Spain.

That night my sleep was fitful. The sense of the closeness of the Spanish Woman pressed on me; I woke to the faint noises that the room always held and to the familiar shadow that had no substance. It was not fear I felt, but something tugged at me with overriding urgency.

Unable to sleep, I lit a candle and took it to the long table. Then I brought the Book of Hours and turned its pages, feeling the faith of a young Spanish girl, who must have held this among her dearest possessions. But where had she hidden the portrait of the man whose words must have been almost as sacred to her as the text in this hauntingly beautiful book? Juana Fernández de Córdoba, Mendoza, Soto y Alvarez, the name written in her careful script. They had taken her life and the life of her child; they had tried to take away her identity, but they had not succeeded. She had lived in legend as none of the Birketts had lived; her presence now seemed a cogent reality. I turned to something she had written at the back of her book, words I couldn't understand but which must have been important to her to have written them here. Was it a message she meant to leave? The condesa could possibly have translated them, but I had no intention of showing this to her.

I slept there in the chair, and woke to the sound of a vehicle on the road that led up the valley to Brantwick. The eastern light was glowing over the top of the mountain, and that had been Nat Birkett's Land-Rover taking him to his watch at the shelter.

It was chill in the dawn when I walked to find him. But it was a morning of great radiance, the trees, the grass beaded with moisture. Yet I was weary of this place; I longed to be free of the thoughts of Vanessa's odd connection with it; I wanted to talk to Gerald about Vanessa. But he could not be worried now by such things. So I walked out in the dawn to talk to Nat Birkett, still almost a stranger.

The shelter was a kind of three-sided hut, with the open side facing away from the crag where the eagles nested; the crag was watched through a long cut in the opposite side, with a shelf where the watcher rested his elbows during the long session holding the binoculars. A little Sterno stove was for making tea, and a few biscuit tins stored the provisions.

Nat, followed by his collie, came to meet me. "I've been missing you, Jo. Have you done any more stupid things like climbing Great Birkeld? There's water for coffee on."

He had put his arm around my shoulders in a way that was warmly companionable, and I was instantly conscious that this was not enough. All at once I wanted much more than absent-minded affection from Nat Birkett. "I followed you," I said. "I heard the Land-Rover and knew it was you coming up here."

I shivered even with the warmth of his body close to me. "You're cold," he said. "I'll make the coffee."

The night had been long. I could feel my eyes swollen from lack of sleep; the worries of Thirlbeck and Vanessa's connection were back with me, and now this added new dimension of being acutely, painfully aware of Nat Birkett. "Any brandy?" I said.

"Just so happens . . ." He brought out a flask. "Do you make a habit of vigils? You always seem to be wandering in the dawn."

I ignored the question. The mug of coffee laced with brandy was comforting between my hands. "Anything to eat?" He passed over a meat pasty. And then I was talking about my disquieting thoughts. "Nat, do you believe that the Spanish Woman really brought bad luck to the Birketts?"

"The Birketts aren't unlucky. It's the earls of Askew who are unlucky. You take an ordinary but clever man of business like Askew's grandfather. He becomes earl of Askew, and everything goes wrong. He has only one son who survives, and *he's* a bit off his head—enough to make him retreat into Thirlbeck and never see a soul. Then he quarrels with *his* only child. That child dashes off to the Spanish Civil War, marries a Spanish girl—and a Catholic—and they all begin to think that the Spanish Woman is returning to take Thirlbeck back again."

I sucked in my breath. "I never thought of that!"

"*They* did. You'd think almost four hundred years hadn't passed since the Armada. Then she has a son, and, of course, the earldom would go to a Catholic. But it never did. That unlucky Askew manages to kill them both just before they ever reach Thirlbeck, when they were almost in sight of it. There's something that hangs on in that place. No wonder he's stayed away."

"Nat, sooner or later *you* will be the earl of Askew. What will you do with Thirlbeck?"

"Tear it down if I have the money."

"Nat—*no!*"

"Why not? Who wants it?"

"Who—who? I can't say who. But people want it, Nat. They *need* it. They pour out from the cities, from concrete housing developments. They drive hellish distances to *see* something different. They would come to Thirlbeck to see something built four hundred years ago, something that no one could afford to build today. It's a dream, Nat, and they want it preserved."

"Why? They don't even know what they're looking at."

"Nat!" I was pleading desperately. "Thirlbeck is as unique as golden eagles. If you lose this pair of eagles, perhaps in a hundred years or so another pair may come back to nest—there's always the hope. Once you tear down Thirlbeck, it's gone forever."

Suddenly his mug of coffee turned over and the liquid ran onto the ground. He went and gazed out the long viewing space in the wall. In time, after minutes, he came back, sitting on the ground close to me. "Jo, you ask me to preserve Thirlbeck. I owe it nothing. Do you know how Patsy died?"

"They said—yes, they said she died at Thirlbeck. Oh, Nat, I'm sorry. I shouldn't—" His face was in torment.

"But do you know where and how she was found? I'll bet no one told you that. It was agreed between the Tolsons and me that it was an inexplicable accident. When the person you love most dearly in the world is gone you don't have feelings of revenge—not against people like the Tolsons. And nothing will bring Patsy back. So we just let it go."

He picked up the mug and placed it among the biscuit tins, as if he were trying to decide whether he should say more. Then he sighed. "She just simply disappeared. Her car was still at Southdales; she couldn't have gone too far. We didn't even know she was gone until she failed to meet the school bus. It was Richard's first year at school, and she always met him. I telephoned around, but no one had seen her. Every farmer around here searched—anyplace it was possible for her to be. I thought I'd go out of my mind that night. It was November and bitterly cold. If she were out, I just knew she couldn't survive. We organized a search for

388

the next morning. It was a hellish day, so long, and yet it got dark so quickly. When the light was gone Tolson suggested a search of Thirlbeck itself. We had no reason to suppose she was there— Jessica was at the house all the day Patsy disappeared, and she said no one had come. But she also said she'd been in the vegetable garden for a while. The thing that made Tolson suggest it, really, was that La Española was gone from its safe, though the alarm system was still connected and working."

"Nat, I'm sorry. Please, no more. I shouldn't have said anything."

"Be quiet and let me talk, will you?" He was hunched on the ground beside me, his arms wrapped about his knees, his chin thrust down toward them. "She had a heart condition from having had rheumatic fever in childhood. She was often breathless; small things made her tired. We went to London to a consultant, and he said they could operate in about six to eight weeks. You have to wait for the really good guys unless it's an outright emergency. So we came home, and we were waiting for her to be called back to London. . . .

"We found her, Jo, eventually, in the Spanish Woman's room. She was lying against the door as if she had exhausted herself utterly by banging and calling. Those old fastenings on the windows are very stiff, so she broke some of the diamond panes of glass. But she wasn't seen or heard. Tolson and I had to break the lock of the door to get in. Ted Tolson said afterward that the whole mechanism had jammed; it was the lock put in when the place was built. Patsy had made it worse, he thought, by trying to turn the key to free it. It was jammed tighter. Well, those things didn't concern me at the time. All I knew was that Patsy had died there, cold and alone and frightened. She just couldn't take the state of panic she must have gone into. Dr. Murray said she died that first night. She lay there, my little Patsy. And she had La Española in her hand."

"Nat! La Española . . . *why?*"

"Why? We'll never know. She'd been encouraged to go to that house, to get familiar with it, as if it were already hers. Tolson encouraged it. The way he encouraged her to come and look at La Española, to take it, handle it. He thought she should not be afraid of it—of those stupid stories they tell about it."

"Did he teach her how the alarm system worked?"

Nat shrugged. "He *said* he did. Oh, what the hell! Who knows about the why of it? Patsy must have walked to Thirlbeck, used the duplicate key to the South Lodge gate I always left in the house. I blame myself for not checking at once to see if the key was still at Southdales. But there she was at Thirlbeck—dead. Even before I lifted her, Tolson and I had agreed that we would say nothing about La Española. I just couldn't have Patsy's death surrounded by the horrible publicity it would have brought. And then there was the question I never really asked, but it was there, all the same. How *could* Patsy have been in the house and no one know it?"

"Nat, why on earth didn't she switch on the light? Why didn't she light a candle or the fire? There's always a basket of wood."

He shook his head. "There *was* no light. That was something Ted put in afterward. The way he fixed the lock—afterward. Yes, there was a candle and a basket of wood. But she had no matches." This explained his rather fanatical preaching about always being careful, about the need for proper clothes and compasses. I felt the anguish of his thousand regrets.

"The dogs. Didn't they try to suggest that she was there?"

"The police had brought their own tracker dogs, and they told Tolson to keep the wolfhounds shut up because they might start fights. So we put them in the stable, where they howled their heads off. Another mistake, I suppose.

"After that," Nat continued, "the Tolsons sort of closed ranks around me. But when Tolson and I look at each other the question is still there. Why did we let it happen? We never speak about it. I can't talk about Patsy."

"You're talking now. About Patsy and the Tolsons. Do you understand what that means, Nat?"

"I think I do, Jo. Finally I'm talking. To you. For three years I've felt like an old man. I've acted like one. Then one morning you appeared at my door, sat in the chair that Patsy used to sit in, and I didn't mind seeing that. In fact, I liked it so much I got drunk in astonishment. I felt like a kid, and I was trying to cover it up. Well, I'm not going to cover it up anymore. Kiss me, Jo."

At first I wasn't sure I liked the way he kissed me. It was hungry, almost greedy and hurting. For Nat Birkett there had been nothing for more than three years.

"Jo . . ." he said. "I'll stop in a minute."

"Don't . . ." I moved closer to him.

"You're crazy and so am I. You're going back to London and your fancy young tycoon, and that will be that. What's all that stuff about gathering rosebuds while you may? You're not a rosebud, Jo. On both of us the thorns stand out an inch each side. But we are what we are. Jo, I wish you weren't going."

"I know I must go. I'm all wrong for your sort of life, Nat. As wrong as you'd be for mine. But kiss me again—with all the thorns. Or are they nettles? They say they don't sting if you have the courage to grab them hard enough."

But this time it was easier, gentler, his lips dwelling on mine. And then to my shock I felt my own deep hunger, which I had not recognized as being there unsatisfied. I heard my own voice. "Yes, I wish . . . I wish, too, Nat."

There are many places to make love. A forest of larches and birches a little after dawn is one of them. Not so different or unique. Lovers have done such things for centuries. But for me it felt as if it were the first time.

It wasn't that we heard anything. There was no sound, no movement. There was just the sense of another presence, and Nat's collie standing alert, ears up. Then he was gone like a flash through the wood, and we saw a figure among the trees, a slight, fairylike figure with spun-gold hair, like a wraith of the mist. She and the collie were running together, back toward Thirlbeck.

Nat crashed his fist down. "Will they never let me alone? That Jessica under my feet every time I turn around. Don't they understand I loathe the sight of her? Tolson still tries to pretend none of it happened. I suppose he's terrified she may say too much one day, or something may happen again."

"Again? Nat, what are you talking about?"

He took his time about lighting cigarettes for us both. I noticed his hands trembled a little. Then he rolled over and rested on his elbows, looking into my face. "I'm talking, Jo, as I shouldn't talk. But now that I've begun I can't stop.

"Jessica—who really knows what happened between her and Patsy? Did Jessica find her looking at La Española and resent it? Or did they take it out together? We still don't know the answers.

All we know is that when I carried Patsy's body down that night, Jessica went completely to pieces, screaming hysterically that she had nothing to do with it, that she hadn't *touched* Patsy. I heard it, and I'll never forget it. That brilliant, half-cracked kid, who'd had a nervous breakdown that summer after whizzing through all her exams, screaming and screaming that she hadn't seen Patsy the afternoon before. Patsy hadn't been in the house. She *shouldn't* have been in the house. On and on it went. And all the things she was denying, we knew had happened. She had known all along Patsy was in the house, but said nothing until she saw the body. Then her nerves cracked. The things she said about Patsy. I wouldn't have believed Jessica even knew words like that, vile words. Tolson got her to her room, but the screaming went on. When Dr. Murray came he gave her an injection. He had treated Jessica when she'd cracked up that summer; he'd no doubt have said she was still in a period of diminished responsibility. So we just told the police and all the searchers that Patsy had been found, and it was all over. . . .

"Later, as Jessica grew better, it was less possible to believe that she really had screamed those things. She couldn't, of course, ever admit it herself. Not that perfect little ice maiden!"

"Nat, what do you honestly think did happen?"

"I *suppose* either Jessica found Patsy up there with La Española or they went there together. Some row blew up, Jessica flew out in a rage, slammed the door, and that was enough to jam the lock."

"So she might not have touched her, just as she said."

He shook his head. "Probably didn't. What she didn't do was *tell* us that Patsy was there. And she reconnected the alarm system so that her grandfather wouldn't think Patsy was in Thirlbeck."

"But why? She couldn't have known Patsy would die. And she'd be in terrible trouble when Patsy did get out."

"You've seen kids do something wrong, haven't you, and try to cover it up as long as possible, even when they know it'll be discovered in the end? When all the searchers started combing the Thirlbeck valley she must have been scared stiff. She might honestly have had a mental blackout. Dr. Murray told me that same night, that he was referring Jessica to a psychiatrist in London. She went away for a while. Had shock treatment I think. Then she went to a man in Carlisle a couple of times a week for two years. And all the time since that night she's been the good little girl she is now. Intelligent, willing, very competent. I almost think she's forgotten what happened, because she doesn't seem to realize I have any reason to hate her."

He carefully squashed his cigarette butt into a rusty tobacco tin. "So, you see, it was for Jessica's sake as well as mine that the Tolsons closed in so tight, making things easier for me, plastering over the cracks in my existence. I've kept quiet, so they probably think I've accepted it. But I haven't forgotten that night, nor do I know how to wipe it all away. I feel, sometimes, I haven't breathed clean air for more than three years."

He sat up then, and I felt his hand hard on my shoulder. "For just these minutes with you I felt I was actually breathing again, Jo, coming out from under. But now I've come to my senses. You don't belong in this world, and I know you're going."

When I left him, there in the shelter, gazing after me, a special warmth still lived in me, a sense of having tasted something for which I would forever after be hungry. I felt, even, that while it might be easier to go away from Thirlbeck, it might not be better.

When I reached the tarn the mist had lifted from the tops of Brantwick and Great Birkeld. Above the crag an eagle soared across the valley and was lost to sight against the bald mountain.

I HAD thought I would find Jessica in the kitchen, and there she was. It was still very early, and she was alone, as I had expected, surrounded by pans and bowls, starting the day's cooking.

She looked up when I came in through the back passage. She was completely calm, not at all disconcerted by the fact that she knew Nat and I had seen her from the shelter. Coffee perked gently on one of the stoves. She jerked her head toward the pot. "It's ready now. Would you like some?"

"Yes, I would." In silence I poured and passed her a cup.

"Thanks." She took a sip and went on measuring ingredients. "It's Bavarian cream for lunch," she said. "Can you cook?"

"Not much."

"No, I didn't think so. I don't know what you do at Hardy's, but you're not terribly useful anywhere else. In a few years, if I keep reading, I'll know as much as you do—much more, probably. And I'll be able to run a house as well."

I drew out a chair and sat facing her across the big table. "What's that supposed to mean, Jessica? And why did you hang around the shelter this morning? What were you looking for?"

"Why did *you* go there? Nat Birkett's not the sort for smart London types to amuse themselves with."

"Who does he go for, Jessica? Your type?"

"Why not? Quite soon he'll wake up and know I'm not a child anymore."

While she was talking I had begun fingering a cream-colored bowl which stood with her mixing basins and measuring cups. It was slightly fluted at the edges, with a thin brown rim, and carved in the center and sides was a delicate line drawing of flowers and leaves—possibly peony and lotus. A very plain bowl, very beautiful. Jessica probably meant to chill the dessert in it.

"Doesn't Nat already *know* how clever and good you are?"

"Once I'm twenty he'll realize." Her voice was very soft, like a whisper. "He's been too used to thinking of me as a child."

Both of us spoke as if this were an entirely ordinary conversation, our tones level and calm. But I had seen the color come more strongly to her cheeks, and her china-blue eyes were stony and hard, staring at me with a strange fanatical glow of which I would never have believed her capable. What had Nat accused her of—hate; jealousy; a blind, a possibly murderous rage? I took the bowl in my hands and turned it over, looking at the faint marks, tracing the line carving with my finger. I looked back at Jessica, and I couldn't have told if it was she, so transformed, or the bowl I held that caused the tightening in my throat.

Her voice again, whispery, silky. "Why don't you leave, and we'll have everything back as it used to be."

"Nothing will ever be as it used to be, Jessica. Lord Askew has come home, and *that* has changed things."

"He'll go again. It doesn't really belong to him."

"Who does it belong to, Jessica?"

"To us. To my family and Nat Birkett. Why do old men stay around, making other people wait for what should be theirs?"

I thought she had the blank look of obsession now, the fixed eyes, the voice completely without emotion. I turned and turned the bowl in my hands because she seemed mesmerized by the movement.

I spoke very softly to her. "Did Patsy Birkett make you wait too long for what is really yours, Jessica? There was going to be an operation, and she might have gotten well and lived for a long time, mightn't she? She used to come and see La Española. Did *you* take the jewel out that day? Did she find you in the Spanish Woman's room with it? Or was it the other way around? Did you leave her there—alone, frightened? And when she didn't come down you didn't go back to find out what had happened. Not then, nor all the next day, when they were searching."

Incredibly, there was the faintest trace of a smile on her lips. "I did nothing to her. *Caveat raptor:* Who seizes, beware. Patsy held La Española as if it were hers, and she walked around this house as if she already lived here. These rooms—*my* rooms."

"Jessica! No more! You're imagining things again!" Tolson spoke from the doorway. His monumental frame stooped, his shoulders rounded more than before.

And at the sight of him the bowl fell from my suddenly nerveless fingers and smashed in many pieces on the flagstone floor.

CHAPTER SIX

THEN I was driving down the motorway toward London, the pieces of the bowl wrapped in a silk scarf and packed among my clothes in a suitcase. I kept pushing the Mini near seventy, getting frantic and antagonistic blasts from the horns of other cars when I did something especially stupid. It began to rain, and the driving grew harder, but I didn't relax the speed. When, hours later, I was enmeshed in the heavy evening traffic, there was nothing I could do but sit and stare at the lines of cars ahead. It was then I let my thoughts dwell on what had happened at Thirlbeck.

Askew hadn't even wanted to delay his breakfast when I told him. "You don't seem to understand, Lord Askew. It *may* be very valuable, and I've broken it."

Unbelievably he had shrugged. "It's broken. Plenty of things get broken. As well as people."

"But you *do* understand I must go tell my director at Hardy's. I've been unimaginably clumsy. He expects better of me."

"Look," he said, "just sit down and have your breakfast, and let me have mine. There's a good girl." He poured coffee. "I really

396

think you're overdoing this. After all, what need to tell Hardy's if something in my house gets broken?"

"You did say you were considering offering the contents of this house for auction. What I've just done could seriously prejudice that. Whether or not the bowl turns out to be what I suspect it might be, or quite worthless, is hardly the case."

"You *do* take yourself seriously. If it was used in the kitchen, no one had any idea it might be valuable. You could just have kept your mouth shut. Looks like a perfectly ordinary bowl to me."

"Well, not to me. And you'd imagine I'd say nothing?"

He looked at me hard. Then he laughed. "Well, no wonder Gerald sets such store by you. Scout's honor and all the rest of it. But suppose I just say forget it. There was an accident. It was my property. I overlook it. Now do you still have to rush off and confess all to your director?"

"I want to. And I *will*, Lord Askew."

I had left Thirlbeck immediately, and it was after six thirty when I reached Hardy's. I rang the night bell and was routinely examined through a viewer by the security man. "It's you, Jo," he said as he opened up. "Mr. Hudson said you were to go straight to him. Here, want to leave the bag?"

I rummaged around and found the scarf with the pieces in it.

I paused at the top of the stairs, which led on to the salerooms. How long I seemed to have been away, and yet I had left only a few weeks before. Until then I could almost have believed that my whole life had been lived here, would go on being lived here. It wasn't to be quite the same again, ever.

William Hudson rose from his desk when I entered. "Ah, there you are." He paused. "My dear girl, you look terrible! Here—" He went to a beautifully inlaid cabinet and produced a bottle and glasses. "A Scotch, Jo? I expect you've been on the road most of the day. Nasty weather for it, too."

I sipped the Scotch cautiously but gratefully. "Mr. Hudson, I don't think you'll be half as nice when you know what's happened."

His gaze went fondly, as it often did during interviews, to the beautiful glazed pottery figure of a mounted drummer of the Tang dynasty, which stood on top of the writing bureau.

"Jo, I've had a telephone call from Lord Askew. I must confess it made me most curious. He said I was to take notice of absolutely

397

nothing you said. He said he thought you were . . . well, a little *unsettled* still, after your mother's death. Jo, what has happened?"

I brought out the fragments of the bowl. "This is what has happened, Mr. Hudson. I broke it."

He drew the silk scarf toward him gently and examined the pieces. He put a few together, getting an idea of the shape of the bowl, fingering the glaze. His face grew long in concentration, and I saw the dawning of regret.

"Well . . . it looks terribly like that Ting ware basin we had last year. Sung dynasty. Beautiful piece, this—if it were in one piece."

"That's it. I dropped it this morning."

He looked across at me. "And Lord Askew wants me to pay no attention to anything you say. Did you tell him about this?"

"I didn't say what I *thought* it was. I just said I suspected it might be very valuable."

He regarded me bleakly. "He absolved you of any responsibility. Absolutely. But, of course, he didn't know that we sold that other one for forty-nine thousand pounds. That's an awful lot of money to drop, Jo, isn't it?" Again he gently touched the fragments. "And a very beautiful bowl."

"That's why I'm here. I told him I had to come and see you. He didn't understand. He said no one need ever have known."

He sipped his Scotch and seemed to be giving all his attention to the Tang horseman. "*You* would have known. And that, in my mind, is what makes the difference between a person who does a job for what's in it for him, and someone who does it for . . . love, almost. I have to deplore your carelessness and congratulate you on having a good eye for a piece that really is pretty rare. You could go a long way, Jo. I must see if there isn't a place for you in oriental ceramics." He took care not to look at my face, so that I had time to compose it again. "And as for this . . . well, it can be mended, of course, but it can never be the perfect piece it was. I assume Lord Askew was thinking of disposing of it?"

"He didn't know he had it! It's all in such a crazy state up there. He was ready to have us come up and go through the whole house. And then Mr. Stanton got ill! Now Lord Askew seems to have settled in a bit, and he doesn't want to talk business."

We launched into the talk that was close to both of us. For a time, as I described Thirlbeck, the barrier of age and status between us vanished. I told William Hudson about the rooms crammed with furniture, the books, the metal shutters. And, of course, the beauty of La Española. But I found there were things I could not say. I did not talk about the Rembrandt, which gave Gerald so much worry; certainly I said nothing about the Book of Hours, the possibility of an El Greco, or the miniature in my handbag. I didn't even mention Vanessa's ever having been at Thirlbeck; if that part of the story was ever told, it would have to come from Gerald.

I DROVE up a block to an Italian restaurant where I often ate. I was on my way through the bar to the dining section when the voice called to me. "Jo, we hear you've been living it up with the jet set somewhere. How's life? Have a drink."

In the darkened area I recognized two young men from Hardy's, though at the moment it was difficult to put a name to either of them. They were flanked by two young women, neither of whom seemed much enthused by my presence. I didn't think, after all those hours on the motorway, that my appearance posed much threat to their fresh London elegance. I dropped down into a seat beside them, and then my mind began sorting the men out.

"Peter, you speak Spanish, don't you?"

"Yes, a bit. But don't send me to take any exams right now."

"Just hold on—please. I'll be back." A Scotch had been put in front of me. "And don't let them take my drink away."

I returned quickly, bringing from my suitcase what I wanted. I unwrapped it, and Peter Warner examined it closely, a minor variation of William Hudson's behavior over the Sung bowl. "Jo, where on earth did you come across this?"

"It doesn't matter, Peter. All you have to look at is what's written in the back. Can you make out any of it?"

"Well, the Latin and Spanish is all mixed up, and the spelling is, I'd guess, sixteenth century."

"What does it say?"

"Give me a chance." He sipped his drink. One of the girls at the table looked at the other and gave an exaggerated shrug. I realized then I hadn't even waited to be introduced to them.

"*What*, Peter?"

He fingered the parchment pages. "It says, 'When I am dead, of your charity, offer nine masses for my soul.'" He looked up. "That's typical enough. The Spanish are always brooding about death."

"Thanks, Peter." I finished my drink quickly and fended off questions about Thirlbeck. Then I went and sat alone and ate cannelloni and had a half bottle of wine. Juana Fernández de Córdoba's Book of Hours lay on the banquette beside me, wrapped again. I had no more right to it than to the miniature in my handbag, and I would return it to Thirlbeck. But as I ate, the words of the little exiled Spanish girl came echoing through the centuries. "When I am dead, of your charity, offer nine masses for my soul." No one knew where she was buried or if she had a grave at all. And no one, I thought, had offered nine masses for her soul.

IT WAS probably madness to do what I was doing in this state of fatigue, but it was something I could never manage in the cool calm of an early morning. I needed the feeling of languor as insulation against the shock of visiting Vanessa's flat for the first time since her death.

I drove to Church Street and parked the car. I stared up at her window, the blackness speaking of a terrible emptiness within. My heart ached, and the puzzle of Vanessa's unrevealed presence at Thirlbeck all those years ago nagged and tugged. I suddenly knew why I had come. Somewhere in the labyrinth of Vanessa's personal possessions there might be disclosed the reason for her silence. And now the urgency of that unanswered question became a need to reestablish contact with Vanessa herself, the glowing spirit of the woman, which had not died with her body.

Gerald, who was executor of Vanessa's will, had given me keys to the flat. There was now the absence about the place of the smell of flowers, one of Vanessa's great loves and great extravagances. It was a small flat—just one long room off a hall on the ground floor, which was a combination sitting and dining room with a partly screened-off kitchen at the end, and above it two small bedrooms. One of the bedrooms had been mine when I was growing up; later it was used as an overflow office for the shop, crammed with papers, catalogues of sales—the whole paraphernalia of Vanessa's jumbled existence. It would be there, if anywhere, that I would find some reference to the summer and autumn she had spent at Thirlbeck. But up there was also Vanessa's bedroom, stamped indelibly with her character, her charm, her sensuous nature. I wasn't ready for that yet.

I went into the sitting room. When I closed the curtains on the street side it became the warm and charming room it had been in Vanessa's time—the favorite antiques, the orange carpet, the gold curtains all expressing her vibrant nature.

It was dusted and tidy. I wondered if Gerald had arranged for the cleaning woman to come still. I went into the kitchen and brewed some coffee. I hardly let myself think; it was enough that I had been able to come here. When the coffee was ready I poured a cup and carried it to the chair beside the telephone.

It was a shock to hear Harry answer almost at once. I was so used to the voice of the manservant, telling me that Mr. Peers was elsewhere. "Hello, luv," he said. "Back in London, aren't you?"

"Yes. How did you know?"

"Difference in your voice. Up there you always sounded as if you were off somewhere in cloud-cuckoo-land. A bit absent."

"It's a long way, Harry."

"Sweetheart, you don't know what a long way means. A long way is Australia—or the moon."

"What have you been doing, Harry?"

"This and that. I bought a house, for one thing."

"A house? I thought you were always buying houses."

"Luv, you don't know anything. I buy properties, I don't buy houses. But yesterday I bought a house. A house for *me*."

"You're giving up the flat, then?"

"Well, what do you think? What would I need both for? I'm good at throwing money around, luv, but not absolutely crazy."

"Where is it, Harry? And when are you moving in?"

"When you do."

I was silent a moment. "But Harry, I have a flat."

"Crazy, girl—crazy. Do you expect us to bring up our kids in that two-by-four place? Our kids are going to have nurseries and nannies and the whole razzmatazz. They're going to be wheeled in their prams in St. James's Park and wave at the Palace Guard."

"*Our* kids, Harry?"

"Who else's? The house is in St. James's Place. Nice and convenient for us both. You can get to Hardy's in two minutes—no, three, allowing for the crossing. And I can nip along to St. James's

Square and kiss you good-by on the steps of Hardy's on the way. You can keep on working right up until each kid is born, almost, and then be back again before they've missed you. And you'll end up being a director of Hardy's."

I spoke very deliberately. "I think I need to come and talk to you, Harry."

"What's there to talk about? We're going to get married. And I promise you our honeymoon can be any place in the world you want to go to look at bits and pieces of china. I'll even get you a visa into China itself. All we have to do is arrange to get together in person instead of by telephone. So . . . when will it be?"

"I'll come tonight, Harry. I'm at Vanessa's flat now."

"Not tonight. Tonight—in fact, right this minute—I'm due at a meeting. It's at my office. These guys have come over from New York. It'll be a late session."

"Harry—"

"Sorry, luv. No business meeting, no trip to China. It's that simple. Go and take a look at the house. The one tucked back beside Dukes Hotel. I'll call you. By, luv."

I sipped the coffee and noticed my hands shook a little, but a strange calmness was upon me. I had just been handed the world. I could have my job at Hardy's and kids, too—Harry's kids. I could even have China. I was being given the chance to become what I had dreamed of, the one whose name could authenticate almost any piece of ceramic that came to hand. Yet I wasn't feeling the pleasure I should have felt.

I didn't notice how long I sat there, in the quiet room, with just the one lamp lighted on the table beside me. Outside, the traffic took on its late-evening sound, and still I sat, thinking about Harry —about Harry and Vanessa. Strangely I was taking out once more the Hilliard miniature, turning it between my fingers, watching the light play on the tiny features of the woman who suddenly seemed even more to resemble Vanessa.

I don't know when I first became aware of the sound—the slight scraping from the hall. Then there was the murmur of a man's voice. I reached up and switched out the light. I remained in the chair; I couldn't have moved even if I'd known what to do. The door opened, and the light switch beside the door was found. The chandelier over the dining table sprang to life.

"Good evening, Mr. Tolson."

He looked in my direction uncertainly, peering through the pebble glasses, not quite sure of what he saw.

"Dad . . . ?"

"All right, Ted. Just close the door. Miss Roswell and I know each other well enough." Now I recognized one of the Tolson sons.

It was as if something I had been expecting for a long time was beginning to happen. "You seem to know your way, Mr. Tolson."

"Yes, it took a bit of finding, though. I've only been here once before. London's changed since then."

"But you didn't expect to find me here?"

"If I'd known, I'd have waited till you were gone," he answered calmly. "I knew you haven't lived here for a long time."

"I notice you didn't have any difficulty getting in."

He shrugged. "Ordinary locks aren't difficult for Ted."

"Convenient for you to have a son like Ted."

He moved farther into the room. For the first time his movements seemed those of an older man, stiff and cramped.

"I think you'd better sit down, Mr. Tolson. You must be tired. *I* am." I waited in silence while they settled in chairs.

"Why are you here, Mr. Tolson? I shouldn't need to ask, but you don't seem ready to volunteer any information. Does it have anything to do with Jessica this morning? Or the bowl?"

"Nothing directly. But it brought matters to a head, let us say. I've been putting off making this visit. Lord Askew's presence at Thirlbeck compelled me to be there constantly. But your breaking the bowl this morning, and the way you took the pieces to London, made me realize that soon you and others would start asking questions. It is very unfortunate Mrs. Roswell was killed—"

"*Unfortunate!* Mrs. Roswell was my mother. It was more than unfortunate!"

"I beg your pardon. Very clumsy of me. For my wife and me it was a blow as well. We grew quite fond of her over the years."

"Over the years? My mother hadn't been there since 1945."

He sighed. "That isn't quite true. In the last sixteen or seventeen years we'd seen her at Thirlbeck quite frequently. Scouting expeditions, she used to call them."

"Scouting for what—for *what*, Mr. Tolson?"

He took off his glasses and rubbed his eyes. The strength that was implied by the bulk of his body was reinforced by the sight of his eyes, a gray so deep they seemed almost black. He replaced the glasses and answered slowly. "It will be easier if I tell you the whole thing. Any questions you have to ask, I'll answer. Perhaps you will be able to answer one or two for me."

"Try me. I expect I *will* have some questions."

"I sought out your mother when the difficulties first arose at Thirlbeck. Until then—almost seventeen years ago—it is true she had not been back, but in trying to solve my problem I thought of her because I felt I could trust her—"

"*Trust* her! You were the one who called her a gypsy."

"Miss Roswell, when you asked me about her I realized that you must be wondering why your mother had never spoken of Thirlbeck. So I emphasized her—her more raffish qualities, hoping to stop your questions. At that time I hadn't quite given up hope that Lord Askew would grow bored at Thirlbeck and simply go away. It wouldn't have ended my problems, but it might have delayed the exposure of what I had been doing."

"What exactly are your problems, Mr. Tolson? Have you been stealing from Lord Askew?" I felt a kind of deadly cold anger which helped to keep my voice very even. "Are you going to tell me that my mother had been stealing with you?"

"Not that, Miss Roswell. If there's been stealing, I have done it. Your mother was only the means to dispose of items from the estate. It started in a rather small way, but as Lord Askew's demands for money have grown we have had to increase the robbing Peter to pay Paul, so to speak."

"So to speak *nothing*, Mr. Tolson. You were stealing, and you somehow induced my mother to be party to it. And all the time you despised her!"

"I'll try to tell you again, Miss Roswell. I came to your mother seventeen years ago because I *did* trust her. And I trusted her because she loved Thirlbeck—the house, everything that was in it, the valley, the wholeness of it. The summer and autumn she spent there I saw her often enough to know that. The earls of Askew were powerful because of the land they held, land amassed through gifts of the sovereigns they served—Henry the Eighth, Elizabeth. Judicious marriages brought other properties—farms, all the rest of it. I judged, I think rightly, that the land was more important to the future of the Birketts than their other possessions. And I thought, from what I knew of her, that your mother felt the same way. She was a romantic, your mother. She felt strongly about the story of the Spanish Woman, whose death was the price the Birketts had to pay to keep Thirlbeck. The loss of its strength—its land—would have made her death forfeit."

Unbelievably he paused to smile at me. "People like your mother understand such things. So when I had my first important decision to make I traced her in London and asked for her help."

"What sort of help? What could she do for you, Mr. Tolson?"

"I wasn't sure she could or would do anything. I thought she might even get in touch with Lord Askew. But she didn't. She came up to Thirlbeck with a man, a foreigner. They spent the best part of a week there, and when they left they took one small picture with them. Its sale satisfied the earl's requirements for a time. That's how it started, and it went on like that."

"Like *what?* What were you doing?"

He ignored my question. "When the rents from the tenancies failed to reach Lord Askew's demands, he wrote and told me I should start selling off the farms. I was to sell land that was not specifically included in the entail, preferably to those who were already the tenants, and on fair terms. He didn't at all mind the breakup of the estate. He always had some guilt about people being his tenants. He said the time for all that sort of thing was over. He'd become a kind of socialist, but one who could never suppress his own taste for luxury."

He went on calmly. "I chose to disobey Lord Askew's instructions, Miss Roswell. I borrowed money to buy time, and I sought out your mother. I had some idea that the house contained valuable things, but I was no expert. Oh, yes, a list *does* exist of what the earl's grandmother brought to Thirlbeck. And you would have searched till kingdom come before you found it. But I had no idea which of the paintings might be of value, except, of course, the Rembrandt. It was my effort to persuade the earl to sell *that,* instead of the land, which finally made up my mind. I judged it my duty to turn over to the next earl the estate as nearly intact as I could. If it were bits of art which had to go, then that was how it would be. I still think I made the right decision for the Birketts, though I may well end up in jail because of it."

405

"And suppose my mother ended up in jail with you?"

"That was a risk she seemed prepared to take. And for nothing more than her expenses. I was willing to give her a percentage of whatever we realized, but she refused. It seemed I had judged her feelings well. She had a dedication to Thirlbeck."

"The things—the things she handled—they must have gone to private dealers or clients. They couldn't have passed through Hardy's or anyone who'd demand to know whose property it was. And she couldn't sell the things through her own shop; she was only in the minor league of antique dealers. She would have been suspected almost at once of handling stolen property."

"She pointed this out to me. And since there was not the sort of money we needed among English private buyers, she said she would have to take the items abroad. She had contacts—"

"*Abroad* . . . without an export license? You mean she smuggled art out of this country?"

"She said she had to. Once it was in Switzerland, it could be taken without a license to America. She said that was where the money was. Museum directors and private collectors asked few questions so long as they were convinced of authenticity."

"How many times did she do this?"

He shrugged helplessly. "I've lost count. The items had to be smallish. There were the Chinese bowls and vases. And the snuffboxes. She said those were easy."

"What about the pictures?" My voice was very faint. "Did she take more than one?"

"Over the years—I expect she took about twenty."

"Can you remember any of the artists?" I had to ask it, but I was afraid to hear the answer.

"Most I'd never heard of before. There was a van Ruisdael—or was it two? A Seghers, a—a Steen? Would that be right?" I nodded, unable to speak. "There were several small panels by Rubens—"

I gestured to make him stop. "Those are quite enough, Mr. Tolson. It was more than a fine collection. I find it difficult to believe that Lord Askew does not know that they were in his possession."

"He doesn't know, Miss Roswell. He wasn't interested. None of the family had been."

"But my mother would have recognized those pictures and told him, that time she was there."

"She never saw them. Neither did your father. I told you I had made one safe room for them all when the ministry requisitioned the house. They're still there. It was one place I could keep a fairly even temperature—enough heat to keep the damp from getting to them, but not so much that they might crack. I went to the museum in Glasgow to find out about proper care for them—just mentioned that I had charge of a small collection, gave them a false name, and invented a house that didn't exist."

I sat, my stomach churning in a queasy turmoil as I thought of what Vanessa had involved herself with. "What happens when Lord Askew asks for that room to be opened, Mr. Tolson? Even he has to notice that frames are missing."

"The frames are still there, Miss Roswell. What they contain is quite different. We—your mother and I—felt it should appear as if nothing had been changed. They wouldn't deceive an expert, your mother said, but they were very good."

"You mean very good *copies*. Like the Rembrandt?"

He raised his eyebrows. "So Mr. Stanton wasn't deceived? I didn't think he was. We were only planning for the unlikely eventuality that Lord Askew might return. We wanted very good copies of anything *he* might remember."

"The forger, Mr. Tolson. Who was he?"

"I don't know. I think he was a Dutchman. But I never met him, and I wasn't really interested. Mrs. Roswell would carry out a canvas which would fit into her suitcase, and in time back would come a canvas which, to me, looked exactly the same."

"The Rembrandt deceived me, too. But fortunately, to people like Mr. Stanton, it lacks a certain quality. No expert would authenticate that picture, Mr. Tolson."

For a second or two he bowed his head as if in acknowledgment. "We really didn't expect that, Miss Roswell. Your mother warned me often enough. We knew. And I was determined that, if anything was ever called into question, your mother's name should never be connected with it."

"Were you really so naïve, Mr. Tolson? There would have been ways to trace her, the handling of money . . . and so on. If you went to jail, she would have gone with you."

Once more his head went down. There was a restive stirring from behind him. But Ted took his father's silence as a command.

I finally spoke. "So . . . she took out the Rembrandt and many others. You left an awful lot to trust, Mr. Tolson. You couldn't very well verify the price Vanessa got on stolen artworks. How did you know she wasn't taking a cut for herself?"

In my hurt I was deliberately striking out at him, forcing him to recall those things he had said to me about Vanessa when he had virtually denied any knowledge of her.

"In the beginning . . . well, naturally the question was raised by my brother. He didn't know your mother and insisted on checking up on her. There are ways of finding out if someone has more money than they should. We found that she seemed perpetually on the edge of bankruptcy—always big overdrafts and never a sign of money that couldn't be accounted for. No, she wasn't stealing— not from us, not from Thirlbeck. I thought I'd made that quite clear." His tone was not apologetic; he faced my anger and did not turn away from it.

"Thank you—for *that*. She wasn't stealing. But she was taking risks for you. Can you imagine what it would feel like to walk past a customs officer with a Rembrandt in your suitcase?"

"In an odd way it appealed to her. Your mother had quite a lot of daring. And, at any rate, the Rembrandt was to be the last thing we'd take. She had spent almost a year arranging the sale. The painting was lodged in a bank vault in Zurich. The purchaser was going there with two experts for authentication. Your mother never told me his name. She said it was safer not to know. The Dutchman who did the copying went to Zurich, too. He wanted to deposit his fee in a Swiss bank. The buyer was going to pay a million two hundred thousand pounds if the experts agreed the picture was genuine."

"A million two," I repeated. "It could have gone for twice that at public auction. Had you thought of what Lord Askew would have said to selling his property at knockdown prices?"

He gestured to indicate to me that it was a useless question. "I made my decision long ago. This last sale would be big enough to keep pace with Lord Askew's needs for the rest of his life."

While he was talking I wondered about my mother—a stranger who moved quietly, keeping her secret. How often had Gerald or I believed she was spending her weekend with a man, the latest flirtation, when, in fact, she had been at Thirlbeck or had flown to Switzerland? I felt baffled, hurt, as though I'd been shut out. Tolson continued with his story. "It all blew up, of course, the day I got the cable from Lord Askew asking me to get the house ready for him and the condesa. It came while your mother was in Zurich, and I telephoned her hotel immediately. She had already checked out, so I knew the sale had gone through. And of all the pictures at Thirlbeck, the Rembrandt was the one I needed. I needed it more than I needed the million-odd pounds in a Swiss bank. Now I have neither."

My head jerked up. "You haven't the money? Where is it?"

"I would dearly like to know, Miss Roswell. But it was in a numbered account, opened by your mother especially for this sale. She was to call and give me the name of the bank and the number as soon as she knew it. The account wouldn't be used except to transfer money to Lord Askew. We had done this before, but this time there was a mix-up, and I missed her call. I assumed she would get in touch with me when she returned to London. Then we heard about the plane crash."

"Why have you come *here*? What did you expect to find?"

"I'd the faint hope that she might have left some indication of which bank she intended to use. She might have made notes. A forlorn hope, I know. I have been nearly desperate these last weeks. The whole of my stewardship of Thirlbeck has gone for nothing. Oh, yes, I have the land intact. But now I have defaulted by a million pounds and more." He sighed. "The affairs of the Birketts have never been small. That jewel to guard . . . the estate to hold together. A collection of pictures and furniture, which your mother thought was almost matchless in this country—"

"Stop it! *Stop it, do you hear?* Do you expect me to weep for you? My mother is dead because of you and your insane ideas about the Birketts being something special. I still don't know how you managed to drag her into all this and to keep her in it for almost seventeen years. . . . *Why* did she do it—*why?*"

He breathed deeply before replying. "I thought I hardly needed to explain to you. I can see you going about Thirlbeck almost exactly as she did, falling in love with it."

"Oh, no! Don't try to drag me in, too. Haven't you done enough?"

"I was trying nothing, Miss Roswell. What has happened to you happened of its own accord. But we won't discuss that. I take it that you will not give us permission to look among your mother's belongings. There just may be the faintest chance—"

"No! You'll not touch anything. When someone looks it will be myself. And I'm not going to look now."

He sighed, and struggled heavily to rise. "Then we must be on our way back. I will have to speak to Lord Askew. I can't delay any longer. I'll try to see that your mother gets no blame."

"How good of you—*now*, when she's dead. What a miserable lot you all are up there, hugging your great estate to yourselves. It's really all been for you, hasn't it, Mr. Tolson? You've had steward-ship for so long it really belongs to you—that's what you think. If you can't inherit legally—you or your sons—then you'll have Nat Birkett so brainwashed he'll do exactly as you tell him. And really, didn't you indirectly contribute to the death of his wife? You re-mained silent, Mr. Tolson. There was no real blame placed on Jessica, although she neglected to tell you where Patsy Birkett was that night she died. Jessica hadn't been well; a lapse like that might be forgiven. She's been a good, quiet, well-behaved girl these past years—cured of all her problems. And so beautiful. You really see no reason why she shouldn't eventually marry Nat Bir-kett. If you press him hard enough, your stewardship would be justified then, wouldn't it? Nat has two sons, but if the Birkett luck runs its usual course, it's just possible that *your* descendants will inherit the earldom of Askew. You couldn't have been so evil as to plan it that way. But now, as things are, it's possible, isn't it, Mr. Tolson?"

He was at the door, Ted moving with him. "You're very tired, Miss Roswell. So am I. Those are harsh words you have used. I think we had better forget them. Perhaps we won't meet again. It would be better if we didn't. But . . . if you should find anything that might help . . ." He shrugged and half turned away. "Well, you could communicate with me through Ted. Good-by."

He was in the hall before I called him back. It was something that my years of training at Hardy's had given to me, and it could not be stopped.

He returned, betraying just a shade of eagerness. "Yes?"

"Those pictures—the ones that are left. And the ones my mother took away. Do you remember anything about an El Greco?"

His disappointment was plain. "El Greco?" He shook his head.

"No. Strange, though . . . your mother once had some such notion. She searched the whole of Thirlbeck, but she never found it."

He waited a while longer, perhaps with hope. But I simply stared at him, my anger giving me a hardness I had never possessed before. They slipped out, and soon I heard a car start. If I measured Tolson rightly, they would drive all night, and he would be there at Thirlbeck by the morning to tell his tale to Robert Birkett.

Vanessa's little Louis XIV clock on the mantel showed a quarter to one. I sat in the chair, and I thought of the smashed and burned wreckage on that mountain slope in Switzerland, the baggage lying broken in the dirty snow. There had been no suitcase I had been able to identify as Vanessa's among those assembled for inspection, no object or article of clothing other than her handbag. And that had contained nothing that would have helped Tolson. I wondered what would happen if Vanessa's true mission in Switzerland came out. There were enough people to say she had been capable of what she had done and much more. Vanessa had had only friends or enemies—hardly anyone in between. Tears of anger and fatigue rolled down my cheeks. They brought, in time, their own sort of relief, temporary but welcome; I felt myself slip toward sleep. When I woke, the clock was striking two.

I drove the Mini the short distance to the streets around St. James's Square; it was silent and almost totally deserted, except for a police car on a slow patrol. Over on one side of the square I stopped my car. The top floor of a modern building was still brightly lighted, and Harry's sports car was parked at the curb. He was still there, on that lighted top floor. I sat and looked up at it for a few minutes. I could sense a restless power which disturbed the quietness of the great square. I started the Mini and drove down into Pall Mall.

When I turned into St. James's Place it was totally deserted, too. I pulled into the tiny yard where Dukes Hotel was, and there stood the house Harry had bought—tall, narrow, elegant, with bay trees in tubs at each side of the door. Hard to think what he must have paid for it. And he was right; even with traffic at its thickest, it was barely a three-minute walk from Hardy's and only a few minutes beyond that to his office in St. James's Square. Harry had made his plans swiftly and with great precision. Yet somehow I knew that, whatever it was he planned for himself and me, I would be waiting, always waiting, for a telephone call from Harry.

It was then that I remembered the last time I had been conscious of lights burning in the early hours of the morning. It had been as we had followed the ambulance to Kesmere, and the lights had shone on Nat Birkett's hill.

I was at Hardy's early the next morning, but I didn't go directly down to the ceramics department. I really didn't know if I should be there at all. Probably Gerald was expecting me to return to Thirlbeck, but I was conscious of the need to break with that world, to return to what was familiar and understood. And yet hadn't Tolson's story shaken the foundations of this familiar world? If it became known that Vanessa had smuggled works of art out of this country, would it be possible for me to remain here? The Roswell name might become notorious in the art world, instead of mildly famous, as my father had made it. I stood for a moment at the bottom of the stairs gazing through the inner double glass doors to the street, watching a few people hurry up the steps carrying catalogues of what was on view that day.

Mr. Hudson, my director, had not told me last night whether I should return to Thirlbeck. It was my duty to ask Lord Askew if he wished the Sung bowl mended and offered for auction. Until this was clear and the paper signed, Hardy's insurance did not begin to operate. I was floundering in a state of fatigue and bewilderment, and nothing seemed to sort itself into a decision.

At last I went upstairs to the salerooms. In the central area was a display of English pictures. In two of the side rooms the morning sales of silver and Chinese ceramics had just begun. It was early in the season, and the really important auctions were weeks away; the public attending were mostly dealers and a few interested collectors. I watched the silver sale for a while and listened to the auctioneer make his expert way through the catalogue, knowing most of the dealers by name, recording price and buyer in the daybook, and always moving at a deliberate pace, never sounding pleased or disappointed. Some lots were bought back into the house, others went for prices well beyond expectation. Whichever way it went, the little hammer fell at the end of each sale, and the next lot was brought out for display. I went on to the sale of Chinese ceramics.

Here Mr. Hudson was taking the auction. I would have to wait until it was over before I could talk with him. Mr. Arrowsmith, from the front counter, appeared beside the rostrum; he had a bid commissioned for a certain lot, but the price went beyond what he had been authorized to pay, and he made his way from the room, smiling at me as he left. I turned back to look at the rostrum.

I suppose it was fatigue. The night had been too long, and there had been too much to absorb—Harry, Vanessa, Tolson. For a few seconds the room seemed to swim in a blur of faces and voices. A new lot was brought out—a jade carving too small for me to see from my place. The bidding went on—rising, rising as the auctioneer judged his audience and paced the rise to meet the competition. "Against you on the left . . . I'm offered four thousand pounds . . . four thousand five hundred . . . against you . . ." The hammer fell, the record went into the daybook. The next lot produced a K'ang Hsi vase. But as I watched, the vase seemed to become the fantasy shape of a great eagle. I saw it—majestic, awesome, fierce, with neck and crown of gold, perched on the ledge of the rostrum. And the auctioneer's voice saying quietly, "What am I bid . . . ?"

Frightened, I turned to leave, but I did look back. Everything was as it should be, the bids being placed for the K'ang Hsi vase. And no golden eagle surveyed the scene. I went then, almost running down the stairs and out into the street.

A YOUNG man in a habit showed me into a reception room with a bare polished floor, four straight-backed chairs, a small table rigidly in the center of the room. There was a single crucifix on the wall. I had come here because it was the only place I could think of quickly. Sometimes Gerald and I had come to the church to listen to one of the more famous Jesuits preach. Gerald had an intellectual interest in such things, though he wasn't a Catholic.

I stood up when a young priest entered. He held out his hand. "I'm Father Kavanagh. Please sit down." I told him my name, and then I couldn't seem to say anything else.

"Is there some way I can help you?"

They must be used to all kinds, I thought, all sorts of requests, every kind of story. "I'm not a Catholic," I said.

He smiled then. "It's still very possible you'll get into heaven."

"Well, I wondered if it's possible to offer masses for someone who's been dead a long time?"

"Of course. Is this person some relation—some friend? Would you like to talk about it?"

"She's been dead a very long time. Almost four hundred years."

"I see." He didn't show any wonder. "No prayer is offered too late, if the intention is right. You would like a mass offered for the repose of the soul of this person, I take it?"

"Yes, that's it," I said eagerly. That was what she had written: "Offer nine masses for my soul." And I added, "But I would like nine masses. Can you do that?"

"We'll offer a novena of masses. Was this person a Catholic? Not that it matters. One can still pray."

"Oh, yes. She probably died because she was a Catholic."

He raised his eyebrows. "A martyr?"

"No, not officially. Just a young girl who died a long time ago." I spelled out the name for him, surprised at how easily it came off my lips without referring to her book. "Juana Fernández de Córdoba, Mendoza, Soto y Alvarez."

He wrote it all down, and then he said, "I expect the Lord will know whom I mean if I just say 'Juana.'"

I didn't know how much money to offer him. "Anything is acceptable," he said. And he smiled again. "I'll say the masses myself. The soul of your young Spanish girl will be comforted by the fact that someone remembered her after nearly four hundred years."

I went and sat in the church, seeking its quietness to still my own racing mind. The little peace I had bought with the request for masses ebbed away. I was back with the bewildering, frightening thoughts of Vanessa and George Tolson. By now he had probably told Lord Askew. I wondered if Gerald knew yet; would he be disappointed that I had not returned? And what would Nat think of someone who had left him so swiftly, almost in flight?

I had the miniature out, and played with it between my fingers. More than ever I saw Vanessa in the features of the third countess. Again I placed the broken piece of the frame where it belonged, making it whole. But I saw something else then, something I had never seen before. Excitement caught in my stomach. I almost didn't want to reason it out; reason might destroy the hope that

415

had so quickly built. Yes . . . yes, it was possible. It could be tried, at any rate.

At my flat I repacked the big red suitcase, putting the pieces of the Sung bowl and the Book of Hours where they would be best protected by my clothes. I was going back to Thirlbeck. Just as I was leaving, the telephone began to ring. It could be Harry, it could be Gerald or Tolson. I let it ring.

I STOPPED the Mini just before I entered the birch copse on the Thirlbeck estate. I had not thought it would feel so familiar, as if I were returning to a place I had known all my life. I looked up, tracing the outline of Great Birkeld against the sky. I might have lost my life on that mountain if the dogs had not led me down, and yet the sight of it now brought no shiver of fear. It was something known, respected, and loved.

I drove slowly through the birch copse, half expecting to see the white shape of the great hound that had confronted me on that first journey. The valley widened out, the house now was visible. There were no lights anywhere. It was past two, and the valley was utterly still; not a wind stirred the mirror surface of the lake. A silent, enchanted world, frozen in the moonlight.

I drove around to the back of the house. I knew that the dogs had heard the car and come downstairs. I could hear the scrape of their paws against the door leading to the kitchen passage. And yet they did not bark. I felt a prickle of gooseflesh as I pushed the bell at the back door, hoping it would not wake Gerald or Lord Askew. The morning would be time enough for them.

Tolson came very soon, wearing a heavy woolen dressing gown; I guessed he had been sleepless, perhaps sitting before the warmth of the kitchen stove. "You should have told me you were coming," he said. "I could have had a meal ready." For the first time I heard no implied hostility in his tone. He motioned me inside. "I'll make some tea and toast."

I sat at the kitchen table and shoveled the toast into my mouth and gulped the tea. Around me the dogs sat, two circles of them, fanning out like some exotic adornment. Finally the hunger was gone, and the tea had warmed me. I leaned back in the big chair, and my hands went naturally to the heads of the dogs nearest me. I wondered how I had ever lived without dogs before.

I turned then to the waiting Tolson. "I have something to show you. I *hope* . . ." I brought the miniature from my handbag. Tolson bent over it as I explained. Then he drew back, but in that large body I sensed a quiet relief, a release of pain and despair.

"Could be," he offered.

"You've already told Lord Askew?"

"Yes, I have. He acted as you would expect a gentleman to act."

"I'll see him in the morning, then," I said.

"Yes, if it suits you. If that's what you want."

"That's the way it should be."

We sat silently for some time. A strange companionship existed between us, where before there had only been unease. A bridge of compromise had been walked in these two nights.

He spoke at last. "It's late. You'll need some sleep."

The dogs moved ahead of us up the stairs and on to the Spanish Woman's room, as if I had lived there always.

"I didn't have the bed stripped," he said as we entered. He switched on the only electric light. "I had a feeling you'd be back." He put a match under the freshly laid fires in the two fireplaces. "It'll warm up in a bit," he said. "You'll have a good sleep."

I halted him as he was about to leave. "We'll see Lord Askew together in the morning," I said. He nodded. We had entered into some unlikely compact, the two of us.

After I had undressed and washed quietly in Gerald's bathroom I sat in bed watching the light of the two fires thrown up to the ceiling. I had my cigarettes close by, but I realized that I did not really need one now. It hardly even seemed strange that two of the wolfhounds had stayed, their great lengths stretched on the rug before one fire. I thought I could even distinguish them from the rest—two males, the leaders of the pack. "Thor . . . Ulf," I whispered. The big heads raised, and a flicker ran along each tail. After a while I slid between the sheets and slept.

CHAPTER SEVEN

I HAD not thought it possible he could seem so changed. Askew faced me across the desk in the study, Gerald at his side, Tolson, who refused a chair, standing slightly behind him. Askew seemed much older, or perhaps merely his age. The boyish nonchalance was gone. I did not see him now as the natural companion of a much younger woman, but as a rather worn man made suddenly aware of his years and a responsibility he could no longer put aside.

I had told him of Vanessa's part in taking the paintings from Thirlbeck. Then Tolson had produced a notebook, and in Vanessa's hand there were lists and descriptions, rather vague, but good enough to give us an idea of the hundreds of treasures this house once held, which were dispersed forever to nameless buyers.

"The prices Mrs. Roswell got seemed very high to me," Tolson concluded.

Gerald sighed. "They would be much higher now. Most of these were sold quite some time ago." He stabbed the list with his pen. "Oh, heavens! 'Fourteenth-century wine jar. Yüan dynasty, 13½ inches, applied molded flowering chrysanthemum, tree peony, pomegranate, camellia.' If this is accurate, we might have sold almost a twin of that for two hundred and ten thousand guineas. Robert, do you hear? *Two hundred and ten thousand!* But Vanessa did very, very well for you, considering it had to have been a very private transaction."

Gerald looked at Tolson as if he were going to try to explain the enormity of what had been done, but decided against it. He merely asked, "This list was just for you, so that you could identify the pieces as you remembered them?"

"It was for her own guidance, too. There were so many pieces—saucers, bowls, snuffboxes. Mrs. Roswell didn't pretend to know all about them. She tried to replace some with modern copies, so there shouldn't be too many blank spaces."

Miserably I was remembering the prunus jar in the library. Gerald looked at Askew, who had remained silent and seemingly not very interested. "Did you know about the collection of snuff-boxes, Robert?"

He seemed to drag himself out of a daze. "Of course I knew. We never took any of it seriously. Snuffboxes seemed an odd thing to collect. They came to the family through the marriage of the—I suppose it must have been the thirteenth earl. There's a picture of him somewhere, holding a snuffbox. Snuffbox Johnny, I used to call him. Well, the boxes were all displayed in a glass case—the sort of thing you see in museums. It used to be in the library. One day, when I was about eight, I was practicing cricket strokes and the damn bat sailed clean out of my hands and smashed the case. My mother was upset and got it moved out of the library at once, before my father saw it. I don't think he ever missed it. I don't know what happened to the boxes."

"Nor do we, now," Gerald said. "Vanessa did a good job on selling this lot, and why not? They must have been very fine. 'Louis XV gold and enamel rectangular snuffbox—Jean-Marie Tiron. English chased gold snuffbox by George Michael Moser.' The best names of the finest period. Twenty-four in all. At public auction they might have gone at better than two hundred thousand pounds. Vanessa didn't achieve anything like that, but she didn't do badly, considering—"

He stopped as Askew's hand slammed down on the desk. Askew turned a troubled, angry face to each of us. "Can't we stop this?" he said. "Remember, we're talking about someone who didn't steal these things but who ran considerable risks to sell them quietly. We're talking about Vanessa Roswell. Remember that!"

Gerald answered him slowly. "I *am* remembering it, Robert." His voice was firm, and he showed no trace of his recent invalidism. It was as if this news of Vanessa's involvement in the plunder of Thirlbeck had shaken him back to life. Now his tone was thoughtful. "I knew Vanessa as a woman who enjoyed city life, who functioned best surrounded by people and talk, who thrived on the infighting in her business. She had a very quick eye. When she saw the best she always recognized it. If it was doubtful, she also was doubtful. What is taking time to adjust to is the Vanessa I didn't know—the person who recognized the best in ideals, as well as objects, for obviously she believed passionately in what she and Tolson were doing. Well, that's a dimension I have to get used to. In the meantime I must just try to evaluate what exactly was taken from here."

"To what purpose?" Askew said. "It's gone, isn't it? And none of us will ever understand Vanessa's motives. Smuggling must have been so difficult for her."

Gerald tapped the desk with his pen. "Well, we all know that smuggling goes on constantly. There are always buyers ready for what they know must be smuggled and probably has been stolen. And there's always some old family prepared to swear that a work of art has been with them hundreds of years. I would guess that for every painting Vanessa took, her contact in Switzerland had a Hungarian prince or a Prussian count in exile who was willing to give it some sort of provenance. If the article itself is genuine, there's no problem in selling."

He turned sharply to look up at Tolson. "That was why she dared the Rembrandt, wasn't it? You had run out of all the other things small enough to leave this country in a suitcase."

Tolson nodded. "She said we had taken all the really top-class things that could be taken. There was only the Rembrandt left. We hesitated for a long time about that. The man—the one who did the copying—didn't want to take it on. He had doubts about his ability to reproduce such a painting. Mrs. Roswell persuaded him. It was the money, I suppose. He was getting old, he'd been in prison for forgery, and the only employment he'd had after that was with a firm of picture restorers."

"This forger," Gerald said. "Was his name van Hoyt? He's the only copyist I'm aware of good enough to have done that." He nodded toward the shadowed picture on the wall.

Tolson shook his head. "No. I've been trying to remember a name ever since Miss Roswell asked me. I seem to remember something like . . . Lastman. It seemed a sort of made-up name to me."

"Lastman . . ." We all turned. Gerald was staring at us, his brow creased. "I remember encountering that name very recently. I stayed on there in Switzerland for a day after you left with your father, Jo. By that time only one man among the dead had not been claimed. He had a passport, though, and they said his name was Lastman. Taking that name would be just the sort of bitter jest that a man who had been in prison for forging Dutch masters might make. You perhaps remember that one of Rembrandt's early teachers was an artist named Pieter Lastman. It could have been a supreme irony for van—for Lastman to have made his final copy a self-portrait of Rembrandt—" He stopped abruptly. "Are you all right, Robert?"

Askew's face was ashen, but he waved his hand impatiently. "Perfectly all right, Gerald. As well as anyone can be who finds out what other people have been doing for him, at risk."

"My lord—" Tolson began.

Askew cut him off. "Tolson, just one more favor, please. Would you mind bringing me some brandy? Thank you."

Tolson left the room. Askew nodded after him. "It is pretty shameful to come back and find that his stewardship has been so much better than my treatment of him and this place merited. Strange . . . strange to think that he and Vanessa were some kind of superpatriots, in their fashion, determined to keep this little bit of England intact. I agree with you, Gerald. One doesn't see Vanessa that way. Tolson, one understands better. What shames me most is that he had to do it as he did because I was not here where I should have been."

I licked dry lips. "You don't intend to prosecute?"

"Prosecute? Of course not! The man hasn't stolen anything! It's all here, isn't it? Everything is accounted for. As it happens, I think he made the right choice." He shook his head. "And Vanessa's dead now. Directly or indirectly, it happened because of me."

"Don't dwell on it, Robert," Gerald said. "It does no good. What might have been, whose fault it was. You've got to live with the here and now."

Tolson had returned with a tray, three glasses, and a bottle of brandy. Askew's hand trembled as he poised the bottle over the glass, looking at me. I shook my head; then he turned to Gerald, who also declined. He poured a large amount for himself and drank quickly. After he put the glass down he said to Tolson, "For heaven's sake, do sit down! And have some brandy."

Gingerly, Tolson drew up a chair and sat down. He paid no attention to the invitation to pour himself a brandy.

Askew motioned to me. "Like the gentleman he is, Tolson refused to tell me who had managed to dispose of all the things— only that they were gone. I still don't understand why *you* had to come back here and tell us these things about your mother."

"I didn't intend to. Then something happened to change my mind. Mr. Tolson said that the payment for the Rembrandt was lodged in a Swiss bank in a numbered account—which bank and which number, only Vanessa knew."

Gerald leaned forward anxiously. "Have you found something, Jo?" he demanded. "Have you?"

"I think so—I hope so."

I took the miniature from my handbag and passed it to Askew. He tensed visibly as he saw it and seemed reluctant to take it. It was actually Gerald who took it from me. He placed it immediately as the miniature missing from the set of five upstairs. "It was in the handbag Vanessa was carrying when the plane crashed," I said to Askew. "I had never seen it before."

There was heartbreak now in talking. I had not thought it would be easy, but the agony of sifting through the pathetic possessions of the victims in that mountain village was back in full force. As I spoke I saw Askew's hand go slowly toward the little portrait of the red-haired lady now lying between himself and Gerald. He turned it between his fingers, as I had done so often, and I saw some reflection of my pain on his face. Then he laid the miniature down. "With her, you said? In her handbag?"

"Yes. I assumed she had bought it in Zurich, for there was still what appeared to be a price tag on it." I turned to Gerald. "I haven't really *looked* at it all these weeks. To me it was just the price she had paid in Swiss francs. But it suddenly came to me that it couldn't be. It's all wrong, isn't it?"

Gerald turned the tiny piece of white cardboard on its thin red string. "SF thirteen thousand seven hundred and five," he read. He looked at me inquiringly.

"In Vanessa's handwriting—I don't know why I never wondered about *that* before. It couldn't have been the price marked on it in some shop. And in Swiss francs that price doesn't make sense for a Hilliard miniature."

Askew shook his head. "Vanessa didn't buy it. I gave it to her."

I nodded. "I never could believe that she had stolen it." I reached into the miniature's little leather pouch. "This bit of frame must have broken in the crash." I had almost forgotten what I meant to say as I watched Askew place the broken piece against the whole. Gerald's voice recalled me.

"Jo, what *is* it you're saying?"

I took a deep breath. "It wouldn't have been like Vanessa to trust her own memory on figures. I searched everything in that handbag for some number. And I checked the mail that had arrived in her flat during these past weeks, in case she had sent the number to herself in London. There was nothing."

"It's possible, Jo. It's possible." Gerald's voice was shot with excitement. "The Suisse-Française bank. Almost the largest there is. Hardy's often uses it. The bank—and the number, one three seven oh five." Then his excitement died. "It's possible, but not good enough. What branch? I wonder. It has hundreds of them."

I turned to Tolson. "Where in Zurich did she stay?"

"The St. Gotthard."

"On the Bahnhofstrasse," Gerald said. "And so is the largest branch of the Banque Suisse-Française. It's a starting point. We could produce a death certificate and the passport."

Tolson cleared his throat. "If you really think that is the number, Mr. Stanton, then I might be of help."

"What do you mean?" Gerald said.

"Mrs. Roswell would designate me as the person who had access to the account—on production of the number. She handled the deposits, but wanted nothing to do with the withdrawals or transfers. While my brother was alive his name was also included in the account, and, in fact, it was he who arranged the transfers to Lord Askew's bank. It's been more difficult since he died. I was glad this was going to be the last time. Mrs. Roswell would telephone as soon as the account was opened and tell me the bank, the branch, and the number. But this time it didn't work. This time . . . well, we missed each other."

"Missed each other?" Gerald questioned.

"You see, I'd been trying all day to reach Mrs. Roswell at her hotel, but she wasn't in. I'd just received the cable from Lord Askew that he was returning, and I guessed that the question of the Rembrandt would come up. I was desperate to stop the sale. So I had left an urgent message for Mrs. Roswell to telephone here. I was up in the attic, wondering if Lord Askew would notice the absence of so many items, when I heard the telephone ring, and hurried down. But by then Jessica had answered, and said I wasn't here. The child didn't know where I was. I rang back to her hotel immediately, but they said she had just left for the airport. It must all have been done—the picture sold, the money deposited—more quickly than we judged."

Tolson turned and looked at me, knowing the pain the words must bring. "She must have wanted to get to London quickly to have taken a plane that had a stopover in Paris. My own belief is that she was a standby for that flight. When they reported the crash, there had been no vacant seats."

Askew's face crinkled into a mask of lines. This time, when he motioned to me with the brandy bottle, I nodded. Then I said something that had nothing to do with the chance flight that Vanessa had caught, in a hurry, from Zurich. I was thinking of that telephone call. "Does Jessica know—about all this?"

Tolson sought his words with caution. "Yes, I have to say she knew. I never discussed the details with anyone, but Jessica's so familiar with the house, she knew almost at once when some of the items were taken. And she knew about Mrs. Roswell's visits. She must have guessed a great deal about what we were doing."

It seemed to me that Jessica, with some kind of unhappy genius, had spun a glittering and terrible web between the last two tragedies of Thirlbeck. I thought of Patsy Birkett, dying alone, and of the telephone call that would have given Tolson the information he needed to prove his good faith. And Jessica had hung up before he could reach the phone, probably because she had disliked Vanessa and feared her influence at Thirlbeck. Tolson had paid a cruel price for his love of his granddaughter.

I looked at the three men about me; only Gerald seemed free of anguish, competent to manage what new developments my suggestion had thrust on them. In a fashion, he now took over.

"Well, we have somewhere to begin. Tolson, you must assemble any piece of proof the bank may need."

Gerald was managing, almost enjoying himself.

"As for the rest . . . well, I shall see we don't have any of Hardy's geniuses near the place until it has been gone through thoroughly. I have already looked at the pictures that remain. There's a man I can trust to be discreet, who will come and verify my opinion. And after that, if Robert wishes, Hardy's can do a complete assessment. No need to worry about the bad copies of the ceramics; every family has some of those. But we do have to make sure that not a single copy by van—by Lastman remains. To some people it would be the most delicious scandal of the decade if modern copies, all by the same hand, should turn up among the legitimate treasures. Imagine the anxious calls of collectors to their dealers asking them to verify that what they have is genuine. I must say, Lastman did a splendid job—"

I broke in. "Gerald, you know what you're saying? I mean, you're involving yourself—"

"My dear Jo, there's no need to tell me what I'm doing. A criminal act, an act of smuggling on a grand scale, has taken place. I

424

am assisting in covering it up." He sighed. "Well, what else can I do? Robert is a capable man, but in the art world, an absolute innocent. If I walk away, he'll betray himself and the whole situation. And then someone other than Hardy's will handle the sale. I have a duty to Hardy's, I have a duty to Vanessa, I have a duty to Robert and you, Jo. To discharge those duties I have to step on the other side of the law. Now . . ."

Quickly he began to discuss what we would do. Then to Tolson he added, "I hope all is in order with the tax people as far as Lord Askew is concerned?"

"I believe so, Mr. Stanton. My brother was very careful that all the income and expenditures of the estate were recorded and the usual taxes paid. But the extras paid to Lord Askew from the Swiss accounts—they're another matter. My brother handled all these things."

Gerald frowned. "Pity we don't have him to work on this. But still we must manage. Robert, are you all right?"

"Yes . . . yes." Askew sipped his brandy. "It's so damn complicated, isn't it? I've paid personal taxes, I know, but only when Edward Tolson told me to. Since he died, two years ago, I've not answered an official letter." His eyes took on a glazed, faraway expression; I caught a glimpse of the man who had fled from Thirlbeck and its responsibilities, who, until this morning, had seemed to retain much of the spirit and outlook of a boy.

Gerald looked at him with faintly disguised impatience. "I'll go ahead with all this, Robert?" It was hardly a question at all. "After we've been through the Swiss tangle we'll give our attention up here. We must catalogue the furniture very carefully and see that the right people know about it. And the pictures should be held until the next important old masters' sale."

I looked at Gerald. "Important? But I thought Vanessa had taken all the good ones."

Now a smile of real pleasure broke on Gerald's face. "She only took what was portable, Jo. It's rather difficult to take a Cuyp measuring about three-and-a-half feet by five feet out in a suitcase. You'll love it, Jo. It's a beautiful thing. There are others of very fine quality. The van Huygenses must have acquired all their pictures in the seventeenth century—almost hot off the artists' easels—during that one great period of Dutch painting. I haven't any doubt that this is . . . well, what everyone like myself dreams of—a major art discovery."

"When did you see them? I would have liked—"

"Jo, you weren't here. It was after Tolson told his story yesterday. I must say Tolson was very determined to guard every single picture the house held. We've been through everything—"

I interrupted him. "You said we. Was the condesa there? Does she know?"

"Well, it became quite impossible to conceal from her that the Rembrandt is a copy. She is an intelligent woman; she guessed that if there was this one copy, there were probably others. She understands, and she will not betray what happened here."

"And Jessica," I demanded. "Was she also with you?"

"I thought it was unwise to involve Jessica any further," Tolson said. "So I sent her home to the South Lodge. She must suspect something is stirring, but she doesn't know exactly what."

Gerald and Tolson were two men infinitely capable in their own spheres. Yes, one could leave it to them. But I made one final effort in my daze of fatigue. "You went through all the paintings—*all* of them?"

"Yes, all of them."

I turned to Tolson. "You did say you had gathered up every picture in the house? Every one? There aren't any others—not on staircases or in out-of-the-way places?"

"What is it, Jo?" Gerald asked.

"Just some odd idea I had. I don't suppose you came across anything that looked remotely like an El Greco?"

"Remotely? Jo, you know as well as I do that there is no such thing as a painting that is remotely like an El Greco. It either is El Greco or it isn't. He had no imitators."

"I'm sorry. I know it sounded stupid. So much has happened." I got to my feet. "Do you need me here, Gerald? I thought I'd take a walk. My head feels as if it's packed with cotton wool."

"No, not right now, Jo."

Askew rose, too, and rather unexpectedly addressed himself to me. "Mind if I go with you? My own head could stand a bit of clearing. Things to think over. All right?" His was the face of a desperately lonely man.

"Yes . . . yes, of course. I'll just go upstairs and get my jacket."

I was conscious of a sense of disappointment. I hadn't realized until Askew made his undeniable request that I had been intending to walk to Nat Birkett's house. I had told myself all through the drive up here that I would merely say what I had come to say, offer the miniature, and then go home. I had meant to leave Nat Birkett free of any sense that I was reaching out to hold him, to bind him in the Tolsons' fashion. We would have our memories of that radiant dawn in the shelter by the woods. But now I had to acknowledge that independence had no place in what I remembered of that morning.

Upstairs, in Gerald's bathroom, I splashed cold water into my stinging eyes. Strangely, the face I saw in the mirror seemed to have altered. I looked older. There was a twist to the mouth I never noticed—if it had been there. I did not look at all like Vanessa, maybe never had, although I'd tried to. It almost seemed as if I had stepped out finally from behind her shadow and declared myself. Perhaps it had happened when I stood at the door of my flat and refused to answer the insistent ringing of the telephone, when before I would have flown to it in the hope that it was Harry. Or perhaps when I entered Thirlbeck once again and was greeted by the hounds as if I had been known to them all my life. Or perhaps later, as the sun had risen over Brantwick and the young priest in London had robed himself to say the first of those nine masses. It could have been all of those things, or one.

But when I went back to the Spanish Woman's room to get my parka I was at once aware of an alien presence—something distant, almost warning. I looked around, but everything seemed in its place. My clothes were hanging as I had left them; the suitcase with the pieces of the Sung bowl, and the Book of Hours seemed undisturbed. I turned at the doorway and looked back. I had expected to see her, there in the chair by the fireplace or in the shadow thrown on the floor by the sunlight. But she was my friend, and whatever, whoever had recently entered here, was not. I thought of the spun-sugar fairy who had danced about on that morning I had first wakened at Thirlbeck. No. Jessica had been sent home. But home was only a mile down the valley, and Jessica had inhabited Thirlbeck all her life. No prohibition by her grandfather could keep her out.

EITHER ASKEW HAD NOT intended to take a walk or his resolution had faltered. He was there, where I had seen him before with the condesa and Gerald, on that patch of grass with the long view of the tarn. A bottle of champagne, embedded in an ice bucket, stood ready on the wooden table.

"Thought we might enjoy the sun," he greeted me. "Sheltered here. You'll have a drink?" The words and sentences were cut short, as if he had no strength for unneeded effort.

I thought of the brandy we both had drunk, and now the champagne. It hardly seemed to matter. It was the sort of day I would never live again. "Yes, thank you."

He poured for us and eased himself into the deck chair close to me. We made a slight inclination to each other with our glasses, but exchanged no salutation. As with each situation here, I was beginning to believe that I had been doing it for a long time. I believed it also as Tolson approached, walking purposefully but not hurrying. Always a Tolson come to serve a Birkett.

But it was to me he spoke. "There's a telephone call for you, Miss Roswell. It's Mr. Peers. He said he'd wait."

I started to rise; then I dropped back in the seat. "Thank you, Mr. Tolson. Would you mind telling Mr. Peers that you can't find me but you'll deliver the message?"

He nodded. "Of course, Miss Roswell."

When Tolson had left, Askew said, "You could have gone. I don't mind."

"No. For once, Harry will have to wait. He won't wait very long," I added. "After a while he won't call anymore."

"Isn't that a rather unfair way of getting rid . . . well, I'm sorry, it isn't my business, and it may not be what I think."

"Unfair? Oh, I won't just let him go by default. But I'm too tired now to talk to him. I have to wait until I'll sound as if I'm sure. Harry is used to a rather different person—someone ready to be told what to do." I looked across at Askew. "No, you really don't know much of what it's about. But for the first time I know that I don't want to drift into something just because it's easier than other decisions. It's only fair to tell Harry that I'm not the sort of person I was. Have you got a cigarette?"

He gave me one from the gold case and lighted it before taking one for himself. We sat in silence. The wind from the tarn was gentle and sun-warmed. I sipped the champagne and smoked, and wished that, for some time, life could stay just like this. I needed a little time—time to get used to the creature who had broken from the chrysalis, the wings yet feeble and uncertain. I had just handed back the world on a golden plate that Harry had offered me. I would have been safe with Harry—safe and empty, as over the years I waited for him to come back from his trips. I would have been, like my china figurines, relegated to a shelf until wanted for use or inspection.

What I would have in place of Harry I didn't know. What was important was that the person who had broken out of the mold must stay out. Suddenly I could face anyone now—anyone at all.

I turned to Askew. "What will you do now? Will you let Gerald take over arrangements for the sale? If we recover the million pounds, will you just go off and spend it?"

"I don't see how I can go off, do you? Too many people have paid too high a price because I have refused my responsibilities here. I'm thinking now . . . that I shall stay. Maybe I shall try to make some sort of arrangement for Nat Birkett, to ease the burden of death duties. There are a lot of things I could do . . . should do. I don't know how to live this sort of life, but at least I can try."

I sat silent for a while, thinking about what he had said. "But does it all have to be sold—all the furniture and pictures and books? You could open it to the public. You were born in this house. But when I first saw it I thought it had grown out of a fairy tale. It's very beautiful—all of this valley. England is a very crowded little island, Lord Askew. I wonder if it's right that people like you—and Tolson, I suppose—should be allowed to keep quite so much to themselves. This whole region is one of the few national parks we have. And you own a slice in its very heart."

"You're talking about my going into the stately-homes business. I could never do it—set up souvenir stands, have strangers walking through my house. No, but when Nat Birkett's time comes he can make his own decisions."

"By that time," I said, "the best of the furniture and the pictures will be gone—all the things that help draw people."

"Look," he said wearily, "there has to be a choice. I have to put several hundred thousand pounds into Tolson's hands to do what needs doing about this place. You can see for yourself that it needs a new roof. Tolson and his sons need new farm equipment—yes, even if they're tenants they've a right to some help. There could be a sort of cooperative for tractors and machinery. It's got to be paid for with something. What will Nat Birkett thank me for most? A flourishing estate or a few antiques?"

"Have you suddenly become a farmer yourself?"

He shook his head. "If I stay here, it will be to relieve Tolson of the financial problem of supporting me elsewhere. And he seems to think there's some symbolic value in my actually residing here."

"When did he say this?"

"Last night. After our day of revelations about the pictures and things, he and I had a long talk. I wondered what he would do with the money if he had it. He has a lot of plans. Breeding better beef cattle for the Common Market—but it takes years to do that. We should have a completely automated milking parlor for the dairy herd—and that stock needs improving, too. And he says he could get good, qualified workers if he could build decent cottages for them and pay more than the minimum rate. A model farm, Tolson paints it as—with me, belatedly, as the model landlord."

"Gerald once described you as antiestablishment. And now you'll be living an almost feudal life."

He stubbed out the cigarette and reached for another. "I had some half-baked ideas on socialism. I dashed off to Spain to fight for the common man and his rights. I thought when I told Tolson to sell the farms at fair prices to the tenants I was doing my bit for land reform. It never occurred to me that he would see it all in larger terms—that the Birkett estate should be one big cooperative. He has schemes so grand, I can't even imagine how he'll work them. But then, all he wants of me is that I be here, and let him run the show."

Why should my heart ache for Lord Askew? And yet it did. In these last few hours we had grown rapidly closer. He was a stranger in his own land and struggling, in his sixties, to make it less strange. He would try to stick it out, but I thought he would very often be making the headlong flight down the motorway to London, and then, restless and bored there, would head back north to the strangeness at Thirlbeck.

"I hope you and Gerald will come sometimes," he said. "I'd be glad if you would."

"We'll come, of course."

"Good! It will be very bad indeed once Carlota goes."

"Are you sure she will go?"

He nodded. "Yes, in time. She's a rare and exotic bird. I couldn't expect her to settle down like a little broody hen."

It was hardly a shock to see the miniature come out of his pocket. Often, as we had talked, I had noticed that his hand went there and he touched something, as if for reassurance.

"I didn't think it mattered if I took it. Gerald has the number. He doesn't need this."

"Do you?"

"Perhaps." He sat and looked at it for a moment. "It really belongs to you, but do you mind if I keep it? Just for a while?"

I had the sense that, of all the treasures Thirlbeck possessed, this was perhaps the only thing he really wanted. "Keep it as long as you want. Vanessa might have liked that best, having it go back to you. She must have thought it very special. It was in the zippered compartment of her handbag, as if she rarely were parted from it. And yet I'd never seen it before."

"I wish she had taken much more from me, but she never would. It looks like her, doesn't it? That's why I gave it to her. Red-haired and beautiful, Vanessa was—and a little bit wild. Just the way I imagined the woman in this portrait was. When I was a boy I used to look at this quite often and wish I had known her. When Vanessa came it was like seeing the portrait come to life."

Now it was I who rose and poured the champagne. Was the sensation of being totally relaxed with this man merely what champagne drunk in the sun will do? "Tell me about it. What was it like then, here at Thirlbeck? The three of you—"

"Then? Well, we were all young—that's the first point. At least we *seemed* young. I was in my thirties, Jonathan about twenty-seven. Vanessa was only twenty-one. It was very isolated up here then. At times we felt as if we were the only three people left alive in the world. No doubt we were very selfish. Every fine day was an excuse for a picnic. Mrs. Tolson was a splendid cook, and a baked rabbit was a feast. Funny, how I remember the food. After the army food, I used to look forward to every meal. I used to gather the eggs from the hen run myself, and I used to shoot deer, partridge, and pheasant. Vanessa and Jonathan eventually ate most of their meals here; I wanted their company. Any reason was good enough to bring up the best wine from the cellar. It began to seem like one long party, and we gave Jonathan very little chance to work. It made him angry sometimes, and he'd keep to himself for a day or two. But he wasn't well and he wasn't working well. So he'd be back with us, and the party would go on.

"Then one day it seemed as if we'd come to the last of the wine. It was autumn, and Vanessa and Jonathan went—quite suddenly. So I went, too. Vanessa had left an address in London, but when I went to it I found out that they'd never been there. That was when I knew she didn't want to see me again."

"But you had given her the miniature, and she had taken it. That must have meant something."

"Obviously it didn't mean what I had hoped."

What had seemed difficult before, now was easy. I asked my question directly. "Did you love her? Did she love you?"

"I loved her. I really believed I did. But perhaps she didn't believe it herself. Perhaps she never loved me. She never said she did. I remember . . . she never actually said it."

We looked at each other, and there was knowledge in the look. "And now," I said, "you know that she did love you. *That* was why she was willing to do so much for Thirlbeck and kept so quiet about it. I wonder . . . I wonder if my father knew she loved you."

Askew sighed. "I don't know. I probably was blindly selfish about that, too. She and Jonathan were married during the war. He was captured soon after and was in a POW camp right until the surrender. They'd spent so little time together. Renting the lodge here was an effort to get to know each other again. They tried terribly hard, and without me they might have had a chance."

"They really didn't have much of a chance," I said. "It was a marriage that went wrong, and they both knew it. They stayed together until I was born, and then my father went to Mexico. There seemed to be no bitterness. As soon as he started selling some paintings he sent money. Later Vanessa used to show me his letters. He sounded nice. When I finally did meet him he turned out to be rather more than nice. But I couldn't picture him *married* to Vanessa. She was a bit too much for most people, except in small doses. Perhaps she knew that. Perhaps that was why she went away and never saw you again."

He sighed. "If it was, then she was wiser than I guessed. I pressed her a little before they left. She said she couldn't compete with a ghost. I suppose she meant my wife."

I didn't try to answer him. Who could tell now what ghosts, friendly or not, Vanessa had experienced at Thirlbeck? Or had she used that phrase only as an excuse, so that the independence she had fought for would remain hers? Vanessa had always been supremely her own woman; even so young, she must have known this was how it had to be for her. For this reason, probably, she and my father had parted. They both had been rare spirits, and neither could have long remained subordinate to another.

"There are all sorts of ghosts, aren't there?" I said finally. "Do you think she thought at all about the Spanish Woman? Do you think that's why she called me Joanna?"

Before he could answer, the whole pack of hounds started a joyful rush toward us. As they came close I was aware again of their formidable size and those wise, wistful eyes that seemed to look at me from my own level. They fanned out between myself and Askew, surrounding us with a sea of moving tails.

"Strange, isn't it, how they've taken to you?" Askew said. "All the hounds I remember from my childhood—the ancestors of these dogs—were a bit reserved. This lot seemed no different until you came along. I know it infuriated Tolson. He believed he had quite an invincible force of watchdogs whom no one could cajole. But I almost think for you they'd roll over like spaniels to have their tummies scratched."

"I didn't think so the first time I saw them. I was terrified. If you hadn't come, I couldn't have moved from the car. Especially after what happened at the birch woods."

"At the birch woods?" Askew leaned forward. "What happened at the birch woods?"

"Well, I feel foolish saying it, but I thought I saw one of the dogs. In fact, I was *certain* I saw him. He ran right in front of the car—seemed to spring out of nowhere. I slammed on the brakes, and we went into a bad skid. After I got the car under control I looked back and caught the last of him, just a whitish shape, going through the trees. That wouldn't have been so strange, except that Gerald didn't see him. He didn't *see* him, Lord Askew. And when we got down to the house you said all the dogs were with you at the time—and there were no other wolfhounds around."

Askew reached out and jerked my sleeve. "Are you absolutely *sure* you saw a white hound up there at the birch copse?"

"Yes, but I tell you Gerald saw nothing at all. I could have killed us that evening—"

Askew slumped back in the chair. I had to bend toward him to hear the next words. "I *did* kill my wife and my son. There, at the same place. The day before my father's funeral. That white hound, straight in front of the car. But when I pulled myself out of the wreck and ran for help, they told me that all the dogs had been in the house at that time. No one believed me, you see. I'd been drinking—yes, I'd had some drinks before I could face Thirlbeck again. But I wasn't drunk. *I wasn't!* I couldn't stand up in court and say that a phantom hound had caused the crash. I couldn't say that strange things had happened at that place so many times in the Birketts' history. There are tales that the Spanish Woman used to go to that point in her walks, waiting for news from Spain. I wonder if one of the hounds was her companion."

He brushed a trembling hand across his mouth. "Well, that's no defense in a court of law. But you—*you* saw it. It is something that happens to Birketts—and sometimes to those who threaten them in some way. 'Who seizes, beware.' But you'd never been here in your life, never knew Vanessa had." His hands gripped the arms of the chair. "Jo—you're Vanessa's child. Are you *mine?*"

We looked at each other for a long time, face examining face, eyes suddenly familiar. A terrible weakness struck me, and the beginning of joy.

"I wonder," I said softly. There would be no way to prove it, but that didn't matter. We both knew. Then, above us, there was a far-off but powerful thrust of wings. All the dogs and I raised our faces, and across the sun came the shape of an eagle—one of Nat Birkett's golden eagles in that soaring, heart-stopping flight. For an instant the shadow of the great wings seemed to cross us, but it couldn't have; the bird was far distant and growing more distant with every second. I wanted to cry out to it not to leave us; the moment of grace was precious, and soon gone.

I looked down at the man beside me. He had collapsed in the chair, and a stain of bright red blood had trickled from his mouth and already spread evilly across his shirt and jacket.

CHAPTER EIGHT

WE DIDN'T WAIT for the ambulance or for Dr. Murray. Askew had vomited blood once more before we got him stretched on the back seat of Gerald's Daimler. The condesa was driving, and I took the seat beside her, unbidden. Tolson had called the hospital to alert them; then he called Jessica's mother to tell her to open the gates at the South Lodge. Gerald stayed behind. "I might be of more use here. I'll follow in a bit. How awful . . ."

The condesa drove quickly but with great skill. At each junction she managed to get us through without stopping, although the traffic had begun to thicken with vacationing crowds. At one traffic light we waited three minutes; turning toward Askew I saw him give a convulsive shudder, and there was more blood. "What . . . ?" I whispered to the condesa. "What is happening to him?"

Her reply was almost savage. "You saw it happen before. The pain, but not the bleeding that time. He has been warned. The duodenal ulcer. Too much drink, too much smoking, the upset of these last days. And now the massive hemorrhage. Pray God he does not lose too much blood before they can help him."

We went to the emergency entrance of the hospital, and they were waiting for us. The condesa took Askew's hand as they wheeled him inside. After I parked the car I was directed to a glass corridor connected to a small wing of the main building. Here, on a long seat, was the condesa. Someone, Jeffries perhaps, had put her needlework bag into the car, and she was reaching into its depths for cigarettes. She had none, and snatched, without thanks, at the packet I offered.

"What are they doing?"

"He has lost a lot of blood. They must make a transfusion."

Her tone was sharp. "He is very ill, they say. In shock. Why can't they *do* something?" Suddenly her anger and fear seemed to transfer to me. "*You* don't have to stay. What use for the two of us to be here?" In her agitation her slight accent became stronger. Her face, too, had altered, the high cheekbones more pronounced, the warm olive skin sallow. There was something much more elemental in her now. The sheen of sophistication had slipped from her.

"Let me wait a little, please. I would like to take back some news to Gerald. I would like to know—"

435

"To know!" She flung her hands wide. "They tell you nothing. He is closed in there, and I cannot see him!"

As she spoke a young doctor came out of Askew's room with a covered kidney-shaped vessel in his hand. The condesa jumped to her feet. "Please, you will tell me—"

"Later, madam." He half ran along the corridor. A nurse came out of the room, and I had a glimpse of two other nurses. I couldn't see Askew, but I saw the sphygmomanometer being used. Then one of the nurses came out with Askew's clothing.

"Give me those." The condesa snatched the clothes, as if the bloodstained bundle were precious, not to be touched by other hands. We waited for long minutes, and then the young doctor came back and went into Askew's room. He reappeared almost at once. In the doorway he encountered an older doctor who had come down the corridor at that sort of flying march that heralds an emergency.

"Tough one, sir," the young man said. He glanced at the condesa and his voice dropped. We couldn't hear the next words. The older man disappeared into Askew's room; the young man went to an office almost opposite us, whose door stood open. At once he was on the telephone. As eagerly as the condesa I strained to hear his words. The call was to a hospital in Penrith.

" . . . done the group and cross match. Unless I've lost my mind it's . . . Yes, I know. Well, you've got a list of donors, haven't you? I'll hang on. But do hurry!" There followed a long pause. Then the doctor's voice again. "No one at all? Well, damn—to be expected, I suppose. I'll try Carlisle."

He put through another call. The first sentences were calm. Then his voice rose in frustration. "Yes . . . that's what I said. *Yes*, I know it's rare as hen's teeth! *Have you got a donor?* Well look, will you? I'll hold on." While we waited I looked down at my hands, and they were as tense as the condesa's. We heard the doctor's voice again. "Have you? Good. Just pray he's not out at the pub, or something. How long do you think? I don't think *we've* got much time unless we can control the hemorrhaging. Alert the police and they'll give you an escort. Thanks." He hung up, and for a moment his young body sagged. Then a violent rap of his pen on the blotter. "Damn!"

It was as if his expletive suddenly broke through my numbed

436

reflexes. What he had been saying translated itself into the typed symbols on a card I carried with me always. I got up and went to the doorway. I had taken my wallet out of the pocket of my parka, and I was shuffling the few credit cards in it. "My blood is the type you need. Here's my donor's card. I'm registered with St. Giles's in London."

He sprang to his feet and grabbed the card. "God Almighty!" Then he looked at me sharply. "You related to Lord Askew?"

I looked at him very directly and then shook my head. "No, just coincidence that I'm here."

"You're sure about your blood type? I mean absolutely *sure?*"

I was getting angry. "As sure as St. Giles's is. I've been called three times for emergencies. I give blood routinely a few times a year. If you doubt *them—*"

He let out a sort of whistle. "No, I don't. But I'll have to do my own test. It won't take long. I just can't chance a mistake. If you were an incompatible donor, there could be a fatal reaction. Well, let's get going."

In a room off in another wing he took the blood sample and asked me about my general health. Then he said, "Okay. Go back to where you were. I'll be along in a minute."

When I got back to the condesa her angry hand gripped my arm. "What is happening? What have you to do with him?"

I explained about the blood, but she didn't understand. "Why can't I give him *mine?* I'd give him all of it. *All!*"

"He can't take it, Condesa. There'd be a rejection—"

"*Rejection!*" She bent her head, but she did not weep.

The young doctor came back and talked briefly with the older man in Askew's room. Then he came to the door and beckoned me.

Askew's bed was surrounded by screens, but I could see the oxygen tank. "I understand that you know the procedure," the older doctor said. I nodded. I rolled up my sleeve, kicked off my shoes, and lay down on an empty bed. I automatically clenched my fist to give them the vein sharp and clear, and felt the prick of the needle. The tubing was attached to the bottle and the suction started. After that it was a matter of waiting. A half liter was taken from me. They put the next bottle in place.

I had never gone beyond this point. I didn't care. The sounds from a few feet away told me Askew continued to vomit up blood.

The bottle of my own blood was now suspended on a stand above him; I continued to pump more into the vessel next to my bed. The voices at the other bed were low. "One hundred and forty." Was that the pulse? I turned my head and saw that the blood pressure was being monitored constantly. "Sixty," the nurse said.

People came and went. For a few seconds I heard the condesa's voice in the corridor, angry, frantic. They closed the door. I didn't know time anymore. There was a blankness creeping over me. The second half-liter bottle was taken away. Someone came over—took temperature, blood pressure, pulse.

"Can you give any more?" It was a voice I knew, though in the dizziness that seized me his face was a blur. I couldn't remember the name, but it was the doctor who had taken care of Gerald.

"Go on," I said. "I'm all right."

I watched the blood mount in the third bottle they attached to me. When it was almost full they took it away, to suspend above the other bed. The needle and tube were disconnected. I was dimly aware that a blanket was pulled over me.

I tried to cry out, to beg, but my voice was only a whisper. "Go on! For God's sake, go on! I've got more blood."

A voice said gently in my ear, "You've given all you can. Go to sleep. You've done your best."

The face moved away. I heard the soft, measured tone from the other bed. "Blood pressure fifty, Doctor."

He was going to die. I wondered if, through his shock and weakness, he had been aware of my presence in the room, of its being my blood he was receiving. I realized that the real gift I had given him was not just the chance of life but the release from the guilt he had carried through those years for the death of his wife and son. *Two* Birketts, at least, had seen that phantom white hound. The release, and the shock of recognition that Vanessa's child was also his, had started the fatal hemorrhage. I hoped he had known that I had tried to give my blood back to him.

Time passed, and still I held out against sleep, somehow believing that while I kept my senses he would keep his life. They seemed to have forgotten me and moved the screens aside to work more freely. I saw his face, colorless, and very still. "Pressure forty-seven." Then the activity seemed to cease. They remembered me, saw that my eyes were still open, and replaced the screens. The last

438

thing I saw was the empty bottle being unhooked from the stand.

He was dead. My father, Robert Birkett, eighteenth earl of Askew, was dead. I closed my eyes.

I WOKE in a private room. Almost at once a nurse came, and there was the routine of temperature, pulse, and blood pressure. The shadows outside were growing longer in the late afternoon.

"How are you feeling?" It wasn't a social inquiry.

"All right. Can I go now?"

"No, of course not. You've given about as much blood as anyone can and still be alive. You've got to rest and make it up a bit. You can probably leave here tomorrow, but it'll take weeks before you're quite fit again. We've been trying to locate that donor in Carlisle, because you really should have a transfusion."

"It didn't save Lord Askew, did it? He's dead."

"I'm sorry—yes. He kept hemorrhaging as fast as we gave it to him. You mustn't fret. You did more than anyone could expect."

I didn't answer her. I just lay there and thought about my father—the father I had discovered in the last hours of his life. I knew quite surely what Askew would have wanted to do if he had learned that Vanessa was bearing his child. And she had known, with equal sureness, that it would have been a useless thing. If they had married, they would not have remained long together. She had chosen the hardest, and the best way. And I knew also that she would have told all this to Jonathan Roswell. I now read things in his attitude which I had not seen before—his gentle protectiveness, the assumption that if we were lucky we would be friends—and we had become friends.

So I had had, in the space of a few weeks, two fathers. And I thought that few people could have that experience and be so lucky as to make friends of both of them.

A DIM light flicked on in the small room. The nurse's voice. "Lord Askew is here to see you, Miss Roswell."

I struggled half upright. "Lord Askew? Lord Askew is dead!"

And then the nurse was gone, and Nat was bending over me. "I wanted to come earlier, Jo, but they said you had to rest."

He seemed different, and then I realized I hadn't seen him dressed in a suit before. "Nat, you know all about it?"

He pulled up a chair. "I know about the blood transfusion, the rare blood group. Not really a coincidence, is it, Jo? Gerald Stanton told me about your mother having been at Thirlbeck. You're part of the family now. You and I are cousins sixteen times removed, or something stupid like that." His roughened hand lay on mine. "Jo, you look so pale. Are you all right?"

"Yes, I'm all right. But I'm sorry about—about him. He wanted to live, Nat. He was going to do things for Thirlbeck, for you. We were talking about it. He had guessed about me—before the transfusion—and I think he was glad. He seemed so lonely . . . and I was in the room when he died."

"Hush, Jo, hush. You're tiring yourself."

"I'll be all right." I fingered the dark material of his jacket. "Sometime, Nat, I'll tell you everything that happened today."

He smiled. "I'd like to hear it. I don't know what sort of mess I've inherited. There have been shocks already, like the story Gerald Stanton told me about what your mother and Tolson had been doing. The strange thing was that Askew had been here all these weeks and not found out about the land still being his." He shrugged. "Well, suddenly *I've* become the landowner. And young Thomas is now Viscount Birkett. The only thing he asked me was did we *have* to go and live in Thirlbeck, and I said no, we *didn't!*"

In the stillness we heard the Kesmere church clock striking. Nat got to his feet. "I'll have to go. They're moving the body from here to the church this evening. We're keeping it all as quiet and simple as possible. We'll bring Askew back for burial in the private ground at Thirlbeck, but the service tomorrow has to be in the parish church." He was scribbling something on a paper. "This is a phone number. The telephone company's assigned a new unlisted number to Thirlbeck, but still people find a way of getting it. The newspapers have started ringing already. Questions about La Española and the wretched curse. I hope no one on the hospital staff remembers a Roswell renting the North Lodge, or if they do, that they keep their mouths shut about who the blood donor was. The papers would have a field day. Oh, hell—why *now?*"

"Why not now?"

"Because we haven't had a chance. I thought when you rushed off to London that you were running away from me. Then Stanton told me about the bowl, and all. Well, this isn't the place to talk.

Stanton says he'll come to see you when it's over, later this evening."

"No, don't let him! He mustn't come here. Nat, take care of him. I need him now. I've lost—I've lost enough."

"Yes, Jo, I'll take care of him."

As he reached the door I called to him, "Nat, come back and take me home to Thirlbeck. I don't want to stay here."

"Tomorrow, Jo. Tomorrow you'll be stronger."

He was gone. The church clock struck another quarter hour. Tears of frustration and weakness brimmed in my eyes.

THEY brought me clear soup and toast, and a boiled egg. I ate some of it and then got out of bed. I found I could walk quite steadily, with only a slight blurring of vision. I found my clothes and slowly dressed. Then I opened the door. A young nurse was at a desk, writing. She looked up in surprise.

"Oh, you're up! I don't think—"

"Please, I'd like to go. I'm perfectly well. I wonder if I can get a taxi to Thirlbeck?"

"I'm sorry, Miss Roswell. I don't think you should go, and I haven't the authority to let you. I'll have to call a doctor."

"I'd like to sign myself out. I don't need to see a doctor for that." It took some insistence, and another nurse came along and tried to persuade me to go back to bed. But in time they produced the necessary form, and I signed it. Then I asked again about a taxi.

The younger of the two nurses glanced hesitantly at the other, then spoke to me. "I'm going off duty in ten minutes. I live in that direction. It wouldn't be any trouble to take you in my car."

I thanked her, and waited. I fingered the keys to the gates of Thirlbeck, still in the pocket of my parka. I seemed to need to get within those gates, to the quiet there, and the safety.

The young nurse's car was a Mini, just a little older than mine. "I hope it's really no trouble for you," I said.

"Oh, no. The sooner you're back in bed, the better, and since you were determined to go . . . you're sure you'll take proper care? Have some hot tea as soon as you get there, and see that you keep warm."

It was all she said until we reached the South Lodge. She used the key, then drove through the gates, leaving them unlocked for her return. "I confess I've always wanted to come in here," she said as she drove on slowly. "When you're kept out of a place you always want to see what's behind the walls." It was getting dark as we neared the house. The pace became even slower. "It's all right, isn't it?" the girl said. "I mean—there will be *someone* here?" I felt an impatience rise in me. "It doesn't matter if there isn't." A single light burned above the front door. Suddenly I realized that I didn't have a key to the house itself. I didn't know what I would do. Then, unexpectedly, the door opened and the dogs streamed down the steps. I felt the girl stiffen beside me. "They're monsters!" And then, "Oh, look—who's that?"

For an instant she seemed hardly different from the first time I had seen her—the slender figure in silhouette against the lighted hall, her face shadowed as it had been then. But now she was wearing pants and a jacket, and there was no languor in her stance.

"She—she is a friend of Lord Askew's. The one who died," I remembered to add.

The condesa came down to help me out of the car, her hands surprisingly gentle after the savagery of that morning. She was almost unnaturally calm. The girl took courage from the silence and apparent friendliness of the dogs, and came around to help, too. I was grateful for support; I hadn't imagined my legs would feel like this. The girl was talking to the condesa. "She insisted on discharging herself from the hospital. I'm a nurse there. She should go to bed at once. . . ." We had reached the top of the steps and entered the hall, and the girl's voice faded as the great extent of the hall and the staircase was revealed. The girl found her voice at last. "Would you . . . would you like me to help see her to bed?"

I expected the condesa to accept, but she shook her head. "You are most kind. But I'm sure I shall manage. The others will be back soon." She addressed herself to me now. "You understand that I could not go to—to *that*."

I felt ashamed. In my own grieving I had not thought too much of hers. "I'll leave then," the girl said, disappointed; she had wanted to see more. "If you'd just see that the dogs . . . ?"

"Of course," I said. I sat on a chair, and the dogs crowded about me. The girl gave a last long look about the hall and walked slowly to the door. The condesa was there before her, the door already open, as if she were impatient for her to be gone. "Can she have brandy?" she asked the nurse.

"I'm not really sure. Giving alcohol is always chancy. Better not,

442

perhaps. Just hot tea and hot-water bottles . . ." She looked back at me. "Well, I hope you feel better soon. Good-by."

"Thank you so very much." Even as she walked down the steps the condesa had closed the doors and begun thrusting the bolts home. I had a sudden wish that the girl had not gone. The aloofness of the condesa was disconcerting, and the house was so silent.

The condesa came toward me briskly. "I'll help you up the stairs, and then I think some brandy . . ." She cut short my protest. "Ah, what do *they* know? At that hospital they are all fools."

I could feel the athletic strength of her body as she helped me rise; I wondered why I ever thought her slenderness denoted weakness. As we mounted the stairs I thought of something else. I had seen her handbag on a chair in the hall, and the jacket she was wearing was leather, as if she were dressed for travel. All at once I realized that now she was a woman very much alone.

"I tried—" I began.

She cut me short again. "I know you did. The grief for me is that I was not permitted to try." Then her calm broke. "If we had been elsewhere—in London or Paris—Roberto would have lived. I know it! There would have been better people, better treatment."

"I don't think so," I answered. "He just couldn't keep the blood." I wondered if she suspected my relationship with Askew.

"If they could have found that other donor. The fools—they did not try hard enough." Then she cried out in fury, as one of the dogs pressed too close. "I have stood these dogs for Roberto's sake, but they are ugly brutes, always in the way. I have been trying to get into the study to telephone for plane reservations, and they will not let me pass."

I realized that I felt sorry for her, a new experience. She was much more alone than I. "I think—I think there's a telephone extension in Lord Askew's room."

"Yes, so there is." Her tone was curiously flat, as if that information was not what she sought. "But still those dogs, they follow one everywhere." Her tone became harshly nervous.

So I turned on the stairs and said gently to the dogs, "Stay! Thor, Ulf, Odin. Stay!" They halted, and the pleasured wagging of their tails was stilled. I was sorry to leave them behind. But the condesa was trying to be kind, and the dogs annoyed her.

We reached the Spanish Woman's room. I slumped into the chair

443

by the fire. Someone had relaid the kindling and the wood, but it didn't seem to occur to the condesa to set a match. All her life others had been doing such things for her.

"You should get undressed and into bed," she was saying. "I shall bring brandy." She didn't offer to help me. She wasn't the kind of person to handle other people's clothing, and yet I recalled how she had snatched Askew's clothes from the nurse that morning.

"Yes . . . thank you."

She was gone, and I was alone, wishing more than ever that I had asked the nurse to stay. It was easier for the condesa to bring brandy than to fuss with tea and hot-water bottles. I wished the fire had been lighted. I saw matches on the rim of the candlestick, but it was too much of an effort to bend down to the fire. At last I went to the closet, took off my parka, and hung it up carefully. I was like a person drunk, performing each action with great concentration. I was reaching for my nightgown hanging on one of the heavy oak pegs on the back wall of the closet when my balance seemed to desert me. I grabbed at the peg and hung there, swaying, fighting off the blackness that threatened. The strain on my arms became too much. I felt myself falling, and the very back of the closet was no longer there to support my body as I slipped down. I fell into blackness and the smell of ancient dust.

I don't know how long the blackness remained; it could have been minutes, or only seconds. I could open my eyes, but the faint light from the bedside lamp did not reach into this space—a new space, I realized, not part of the closet but an extension of it. Groping, my fingers encountered rough bricks and crumbling mortar. The dust on the floor was a thick, muffling sheet. The smell of the ages was in this recess. I crawled backward out of the space and pulled myself to my feet.

I rested with both hands on the mantelshelf for a few minutes. The fall had knocked the breath out of me, and I waited for a while to recover it. My hand trembled violently as I lit the candle. Then I went inside again, kicking aside the clothes that had fallen with me. I stood there with the candle burning steadily in that draftless space, and I saw what had survived of the Spanish Woman for almost four hundred years.

That short body, now a skeleton, had been laid with reverence on a carved oak chest. It was dressed in a gown of yellow silk, which might once have been white, as might the lace of the cap that was tied about that narrow little skull. The hair held in place by the cap was black. The gloved skeletal fingers had been intertwined about an elaborately jeweled crucifix. A heavy signet ring had been placed over one finger. Cautiously, afraid that the glove might crumble to dust at my touch, I traced the initials on the ring. J.F.C. Juana Fernández de Córdoba.

I felt no horror at what I saw. That little face might once have been beautiful; she had been only seventeen, they said. Someone—some Catholic sympathizer perhaps—had recovered her body and brought it back here, dressing her tenderly in what might have been her bridal gown. The oak chest on which she lay probably held some of the possessions she had brought from Spain, other gowns and slippers, the baby clothes she would have been stitching for her unborn child. I stood and wondered why she had been brought here. Secret places such as this were no novelty in a house of this period. Had it been intended as a priest hole—to shelter hunted Catholics? Had indeed the first earl remained secretly Catholic, even heard mass in the little room which had become the Spanish Woman's tomb?

If someone had intended eventually to bury her with appropriate ceremony, the chance had never come, and the secret of the Spanish Woman's hiding place had died. But her spirit had spoken with great force over the centuries to some of the people who had inhabited this house, this room, myself among them. "When I am dead, of your charity, offer nine masses for my soul." Today the first of Juana's nine masses *had* been offered.

I raised the candle and looked around me. The rough brick my hand had encountered was probably a chimney flue, part of the huge one that led up from the fireplace in the great hall below. The chamber itself was very dry, which could have accounted for the preservation of the Spanish Woman's clothes. Just the right amount of heat had reached this space to offset the dampness that would have caused those silken and lace garments to rot.

I held the candle higher and saw the only other thing the chamber contained. It was propped against the brick wall at the back of the chest—a smallish rectangle, completely dust-covered, but with elaborate carving on its delicate frame. I reached across the little skeleton to touch this possession of hers. My hand removed some of the heavy dust. A faint reflection glowed back at me. It was a mirror, rare in the days of the Spanish Woman. I put down the candle and stretched out both hands to lift the precious thing.

It was too much for my strength. As I was about to lower it to the floor beside me it slipped and crashed down. The old Venetian glass shattered, and two large fragments fell from the frame. I sighed in agony. Why hadn't I waited until I had help? I had destroyed, once again, something very valuable. Then another thought came, the memory of the translation of that scrap of parchment. "This our likeness, a mirror of conscience." The prickling of excitement ran through my body like warm wine. Where the fragments of glass had fallen away a canvas showed. Frantically I began to pick at what remained. Reason told me to wait, but instinct and emotion overrode it. Piece by piece the glass came out. I knelt down and lifted the candle so that the light fell upon the face of Philip II of Spain, painted, in his own words, "by the hand of Domenico Theotokopoulos." It was unmistakably his unique style. I gazed at it in awe. Priceless. The greatest treasure Thirlbeck contained. A hitherto unknown painting by El Greco.

And then, my body seeming to pulse with the joy of this discovery, I began to feel cold and weak again. I didn't understand the warmth against my hand until I looked down. In picking away the fragments of the mirror, I had gashed my palm. The blood was trickling down my fingers. I grabbed one of my dresses which was lying on the closet floor and wrapped it tightly about my hand. I tried to rise, but the strength wouldn't come. Then I remembered that the condesa would return soon with the brandy. With that thought I let myself lie down beside the Spanish Woman.

I probably had moments of unconsciousness. There was no way to mark the time until I heard the footsteps, saw the shadow fall across the candlelight. For a second I thought it must be Jessica. The sense of hostility was strong. But no, not Jessica this time. Before she spoke I had the scent of her perfume.

"What . . . ?" A long silence followed. No hand attempted to raise my head. But she had picked up the candle; its light was higher. "*You* have found it!" The voice was well-known, a kind of harsh triumph in it now. "And I have searched all these weeks. Even the picture room when they believed I was having the siesta."

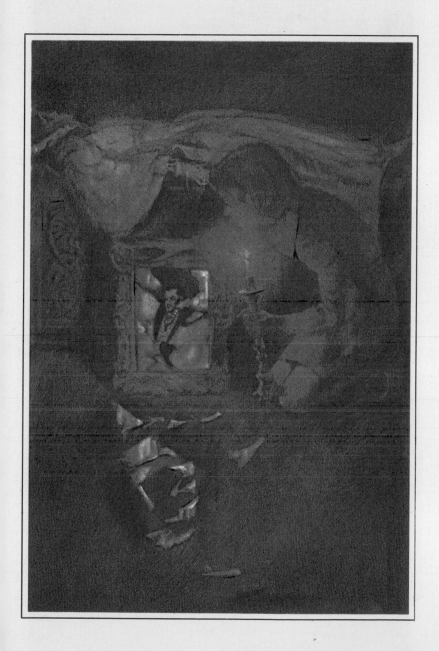

"Please," I whispered. I could feel the blood seeping through the rough bandage; I raised my hand so that she might see it.

"She is ours." Now the tone had softened, as if the condesa spoke to herself. "The Spanish lady and her possessions are ours. For many generations in our family we have known of this painting, as we have always known about the jewel. She was of our family, sent in marriage to England by Felipe. Just when I had begun to believe that it must have been destroyed *you* have found it."

I shifted my head, but nothing came into focus. "Help me!" I whispered. "I'm bleeding again. Please . . ."

If she heard me, it made no difference. Whatever anguish she might have felt at Robert Birkett's death now seemed to be submerged in the triumph of winning what she had come to Thirlbeck to seek. She was no longer a woman alone—a woman who had lost everything. "So, I take it now, since it does not belong to the Birketts but to my family. It will go to the highest bidder. Very private, and for a great deal of money."

I felt the canvas in its elaborate frame removed from my side, and then the candle itself was withdrawn. I made one last feeble attempt to stop her when she tugged at the panel which had sealed the dark little chamber. I had to pull back my fingers as the panel squeezed them. Then I could only lie there and listen to the sound of the closet door being closed. I felt tears of despair prick my eyes, but there was no energy to weep or cry out. My lips formed a word. "Please . . ." But there was no sound.

In the darkness I pulled the rough bandage tighter and clenched my fist around the cloth. Still the gentle ooze of blood continued. The stuffy chamber was suddenly as cold as death. For four hundred years this silent, dusty place had been the tomb of the Spanish Woman. And now I shared it with her.

THE sounds came from very far away; I wondered if, as a prelude to death, sounds came back that were part of life. I heard no voices, but I did hear the dogs, those strangely haunting sounds with which they had called to one another that day in the thick mist on the mountain. Strange, that in a whole lifetime of people's voices to hear and remember, the last thing I should be aware of was the cries of the great hounds of the Birketts.

Then some sense returned, and I knew the sounds were not

imagined, but real—and near. Were they beyond the door of the Spanish Woman's room, setting up that massive chorus? They kept on, insistent, almost frantic. Was there anyone in the house to hear them? Oh, God . . . I prayed for the dogs not to give up until someone should heed the demand of their clamor.

There was another period of blackness, and then the sounds were even nearer. The dogs had been let into the room, and now all eight of them must have taken their stance before the closed door of the closet. "Quickly . . . quickly," I whispered in the darkness. The closet door was open and then came the frantic scraping of claws on the other side of the panel. Whoever was there didn't waste any time. I heard the blessed splintering of wood. Something—a poker, even an axe—was tearing its way to me.

One of the dogs was through first, the great head thrusting into the hole, trying to lick life and warmth back into me. He was forcibly withdrawn, and the chopping recommenced with care. A strong beam of light was now shining on me. I felt myself being lifted with great gentleness. Nat's voice was close to my ear.

"You're going to make a rotten farmer's wife. You know that, don't you?"

THROUGH the drive to the hospital Nat's arms cradled me still. "Hang on, Jo. The hospital telephoned. The donor is on his way there. Where you should have stayed."

Tolson was driving, and I knew that Gerald was in the car with us. They had tied a tourniquet about my arm, but the dizziness persisted. I framed words, but few would come. "Gerald, the condesa . . ." It was the lightest whisper, and Nat caught it.

"Yes, Jo. We know she's gone. Don't try to talk."

I did try again, but it was no use. When we reached the hospital I was aware of the strangeness of staring face up at the lights as I was wheeled along the corridors. The wound was stitched and bound, the tourniquet released, and the transfusion begun. As they prepared to put me to sleep, I summoned the strength to demand that Nat and Gerald return. The nurses brought them in, but once more my strength failed. "The condesa . . . she has . . ."

It was Gerald who put his fingers on my lips. "Please don't try to talk, Jo. We know all about it. The condesa has gone, and so has La Española. Everything is being done, and you are to sleep."

"La Española . . ." I whispered.

"Jo, stop it!" Nat's voice. "What are you bothering about it for? Tolson has told the police. The ports and airports have been alerted to watch for her. For myself, I hope she gets clean away with it. But I don't suppose we'll be that lucky."

"Nat, please." Gerald's voice was cautioning him. "Look, there's the nurse with an injection. You *must* rest, Jo."

I licked my dry lips. "An El Greco . . ." But the words had no form, and no one heard. I could feel my rising panic. Confused thoughts whirled within me. No one knew that the condesa had taken the El Greco as well as La Española, that by telling the police, they were placing themselves in terrible jeopardy. If she were caught now, she could claim that she was merely one more of the couriers who had left Thirlbeck with a precious canvas. And the world would know the secret Vanessa and Tolson had kept so faithfully. She would implicate Gerald, and possibly Nat. But if she did get out of the country and disposed of the jewel and the painting, the danger would recede for all of us. So I didn't try anymore to tell them. It was too difficult.

I felt the jab of the needle. In the last seconds before the blackness, I managed to touch Nat's hand. He bent toward my lips, but I didn't know how the words came out. "You have to get me in the morning. Must be there when they bury him. Promise?"

He had heard. "I promise, Jo. Go to sleep now."

I felt sure that La Española would return to Thirlbeck. What had been the Spanish Woman's would remain hers. And whatever ruin followed, we would have to bear. But still the thought persisted, until the oblivion of the drug took hold, that to me she was a friendly spirit, the Spanish Woman.

CHAPTER NINE

NAT came quite early, but I was dressed and waiting for him. He entered the room with his brows settled into a frown. "Jo, you know this is madness. You should stay at least another day."

I shook my head. "I have to be there, Nat. I'll rest, I promise. But I have to be there."

He accepted the inevitable, but insisted on using a wheelchair to take me to the car—Gerald's car. "It won't shake you around like the Land-Rover," he said. Still he drove with exaggerated care. "All I want is to see you safely back in bed. I don't care how long it takes to get to Thirlbeck."

Through the slow drive I didn't speak to him of the condesa. I had listened to the early news bulletins on the radio, and there had been no mention of her. For the moment it served no purpose to lay further burdens on Nat. We reached the South Lodge, and Jessica's mother was there to open the gate for us. As we drove on, Nat said, "You know, it was Jessica who saved your life."

"*Jessica!* How?"

"She'd seen you pass the South Lodge in a strange car last evening. When it came back again quite soon she got concerned. She knew the condesa was at the house, but doubted that she could do the right things for you—see you to bed, and so on. So she walked to Thirlbeck and was in time to see the condesa drive off in Askew's car—heading over Brantwick. In the house the dogs were kicking up an almighty fuss, trying to get into the Spanish Woman's room. The door was locked, and there was no key—at least not on the outside. She heard no sound inside the room. So she telephoned the vicarage, hoping to get a message to Tolson and me, since we'd accompanied the body to the church. She reached us and said that something seemed very wrong, and we just about burned up the road getting back here."

I was silent, thinking about it. Thirlbeck was in plain view before I spoke. "Then Jessica did the exact opposite of what she did with Patsy. When she could have spoken before, she didn't. This time she took more on herself than she need have. Nat—oh, Nat, this is a bitter sort of twist for you. She could have saved Patsy, but she saved me. I suppose she was ill then, but . . ."

His hand touched mine. "I can't weigh you and Patsy in the same scales, Jo, and don't ever think it. Patsy was sweet and lovely, and I loved her. Now I love you. I have to leave behind what Jess did or didn't do in the past. Last night I think she saved your life. For that I'm in her debt, and always will be. When Tolson realized what Jessica had done he looked like a man who'd had an intolerable burden removed from him. He can face anything now. And so can I."

I had little time to get used to this new knowledge of Jessica. It was she who opened the door at Thirlbeck. She was standing there at the top of the steps as we drove up. Involuntarily I felt myself stiffen at the sight of her. And Nat's voice came gently. "Easy, Jo. We have to give her a chance."

The first greeting was lost in the surge of the dogs, their tails waving in a frenzy of welcome. Jessica had opened the car door before Nat could get around, and stretched out her hand to help me. "I waited until you came to cook breakfast," she said.

There was a blazing fire in the dining room, and a sofa had been placed before it, heaped with cushions. Jessica motioned Nat to take me to it, and I found myself with my legs up and a rug spread over me. She brought a small table, and I watched her as she moved to the sideboard to pour two cups of coffee. She was in some way older; her body did not seem to dance through its tasks, as if they were some graceful game she played. She didn't smile, and the shining blond hair was not shaken for Nat's admiration. When she had given Nat and me the coffee she said, "There's news, Lord Askew."

"Cut the rubbish, Jess. My name is Nat."

She shook her head. "Oh, no. Not anymore. Everything's changed. No one can help it. It just has changed."

He sighed, and stirred his coffee. "What's the news, Jess?"

"This morning, very early, I went to take your watch at the shelter. I knew you wouldn't be able to go. Well, when it got light I started watching the eagles with the glasses. I looked out over the whole valley, and I saw something up by the birch copse—something I'd never seen before. I went there as quickly as I could. It was Lord Askew's car; it had run off the road, broken through a wall, and crashed down among the trees. The condesa was in it. I was much too late to help her. Dr. Murray thinks she must have died almost at once. He thinks her neck was broken."

Nat looked from Jessica to me. "Dead? She's dead!"

"There wasn't anything I could do," Jessica said softly. "I did try. Honestly, I did. It was . . . it was rather horrible. There's a lot of broken glass. She wasn't wearing a seat belt, and she was jammed against the steering wheel. She had the key of the North Lodge gates in her handbag. And La Española."

Briefly Nat's head sank. "I was hoping La Española would cease to exist for us. But she never even got it out of this valley."

I grasped the coffee cup between both my hands to force still-

452

ness upon them. "Did you find anything else, Jessica?" I asked.

"Yes . . . yes, I did find something else. So that was why . . . yes, *that* was why she shut you in that place with the Spanish Woman. You had found it in there."

"What the hell are you talking about?" Nat demanded.

Jessica turned to him. "In the back of the car I found Miss Roswell's big red suitcase. I decided I'd bring it down—and La Española. It seemed strange that the condesa should have taken that suitcase and left all her own behind. Hers were so expensive."

"But mine was tough. Cheap fiberglass, but tough. Was the painting in it, Jessica?"

She nodded. "It was all packed about with your clothes—a protection, I suppose. My grandfather had never seen it before. We woke Mr. Stanton. He was much more pleased about that being back here than La Española."

Nat interrupted. "Would you mind explaining? I'm beginning to feel even more dense than usual."

I sank back against the pillows, a sense of relief surging through me. "It was a painting by El Greco." I found myself telling him what I had not been able to say last night.

From the doorway, Gerald's voice. He had entered very quietly, had been standing behind us, listening. "How are you, Jo?" He came around to inspect me. "You shouldn't be out of the hospital at all, but I'm glad to see you, my dear. You still look like a ghost— and you nearly died there with the Spanish Woman."

I went on then with what had happened the night before. "The condesa was all ready to leave just with La Española, and I made a gift to her of the El Greco as well. I even helped her take La Española. Until I came the dogs wouldn't move away from the door of the study. I made them stay on the landing, left her free to switch off the alarm and take what she wanted."

"The dogs saved your life," Gerald said. "The dogs and Jessica. Without the dogs we wouldn't have found that little chamber. I don't pretend to know what it is those dogs have bred into them, but it is something that primarily concerns the Birketts."

"What has happened to the painting?" I asked.

"Grandfather kept the suitcase and the painting here," Jessica answered. "We returned La Española to the car. It had to be there when the police came. We're just to say—when it's time to announce it—that the painting was discovered in the little room with the Spanish Woman. No need to bring the condesa into that. . . ."

"It *is* Philip the Second, isn't it, Gerald?"

He nodded his thanks as Jessica handed him a cup of coffee. "I'd say so. El Greco has made him look more spiritual than any picture I've ever seen of him. Strange, how Philip neglected the one artist who truly caught the spirit of Spain. Well, it's a splendid portrait. Almost as moving, in its way, as that wonderful *Portrait of an Unknown Man* in the Prado." He made a little smacking noise with his lips. "What a sensation! What a sale it will make!"

Then he sighed. "That poor woman, the condesa. I wonder if she fastened onto Robert just to make him come here, so that she could search for it? Perhaps not. Perhaps she only decided to take La Española because there was nothing else left for her. With Robert dead her world was collapsing." His tone dropped lower. "I do wonder about that place at the birch copse." He shrugged. "Useless wondering about things like that. . . . Never gets you anywhere."

I shivered, and Nat was quickly beside me. "You cold, Jo?"

"No," I said. "I'm all right." I wasn't going to say, not now or ever, what it might be that the condesa had seen at the beginning of the birch copse. Perhaps she had seen nothing. An accident with no apparent cause. But the dying words of the Spanish Woman had once more proved their potency.

Gerald went to the sideboard for more coffee. "There are nice obituaries about Robert in the *Times* and *Telegraph* this morning. They talk about the Victoria Cross and the Military Cross. The other papers are just treating it as a news story—digging up all the old tales about La Española and about his being in prison."

"I get angry," Jessica said. "They're not even giving Nat—I mean Lord Askew—a chance. They're already making life miserable. It will be much worse when they find out that the condesa died at Thirlbeck, and with La Española in her possession." She turned to Gerald. "Isn't there *any* way to stop it?"

Gerald shook his head. "There's no way to bottle up the news. It's part of the freedom of the press, Jessica."

She turned back to the sideboard and began slicing bread for the toaster. Then she shrugged. "Well, perhaps the publicity won't hurt in the end."

Nat said slowly, "What do you mean, Jessica?"

"Well, I suppose in the end you'll have to open the house to the public. There really isn't any other way to pay for it. People want to see places like Thirlbeck, and *they* provide the money. You could open up the valley just to this point and make the rest of it a nature sanctuary or something. There'll be some pictures left, surely, some furniture to show off." She flung a rather frightened glance at Gerald and myself. "I mean, you won't have to sell *everything*, will you? Miss Roswell would be very good at working it all out. I'm sure Mr. Stanton would help. *I'd* help all I could. I know the history of most of the family, and I'd learn the rest."

She stopped, perhaps because the silence had become too heavy. "Oh, well, it's just an idea. You'll have to do *something*." The finished slices popped from the toaster, and she put more in. "I'll go and do the eggs now."

She paused in the doorway. "We'll just all have to stick together. I've already told the children they're not to talk to the reporters, Nat—Lord Askew. They're going to the service for the earl in Kesmere. Grandfather thought it was right. But I'll stay here with Miss Roswell, and I'll go to the burial ground when you bring the body back. Nat, shall I get the Land-Rover? You could drive Miss Roswell to the burial ground in that; it's too far for her to walk." Then the door closed behind her.

After she had gone we all exchanged glances, but it was on Nat's face that a smile first appeared. "Well, there you are," he said. "Everything laid out nicely. Everything taken care of."

"And the thing is," Gerald said, "the child could be right."

"If I didn't feel so miserable—and so damn bewildered," Nat said, still smiling, "I could almost laugh. Look at them, the Tolsons. Every last one of them, I'm certain, is already planning for Thirlbeck. How we'll all hang together. There's Jessica now, fighting to redeem herself in some way. She'll give her heart and soul to this place. We've got Jessica and the Tolsons—and Thirlbeck, for the rest of our lives. Can you bear it, Jo?" He shook his head impatiently. "Of course you can. You'll bear it because I need you and because you're his daughter. My need—and your inheritance, Jo. It's a formidable combination."

He rose and went to the window, looking up the valley. "I said you'll make a rotten farmer's wife, Jo—that's the truth. But you'll be great for Thirlbeck."

Now he looked quite deliberately between Gerald and myself, perhaps even glad that there was a witness to his next words. "I'm not really asking you, Jo. I'm telling you the way things have to be. I've got to have you with me. If you decide not to stay, then that's the end of Thirlbeck. I'll sell every damn thing that's salable, and if no one will buy the house, I'll tear it down. It's possible to give up a title, and I'll give up this one. The earldom of Askew will cease to exist. I have no heart and no guts for this job unless you are here."

I saw Gerald give a faint, almost involuntary nod. I felt incredibly weary. "Nat," I said, "you won't tear down Thirlbeck, anymore than you'll give up trying to save the golden eagles. You'll handle both in a different way from the last earl, but you'll handle them, not throw them away. Yes, I know I'll make a rotten farmer's wife. The rest—I'll do what I can."

I looked down at the bandaged hand. "You'll have to go soon and get changed. You have to be at the church and be ready to face the cameras and the questions, and keep your temper. There's an awful lot to learn. We might as well begin properly."

I STOOD at Nat Birkett's side when they brought the body of Robert Birkett, eighteenth earl of Askew, back to Thirlbeck to be buried. Nat's sons, and the Tolson families, had brought flowers picked from the gardens of the farms and from the lanes and hedgerows. I looked at the faces of those about me, gathered here to witness the end of one era and the beginning of another.

"We brought nothing into this world, and it is certain that we can carry nothing out."

That was what it had all been about, and why it was continuing. We had, all of us standing here by his grave, been concerned with the property of a gentleman known as Robert Birkett. Vanessa had unwittingly died for it; Robert Birkett had died knowing that Vanessa had been willing to serve this legacy because she had borne a child to him; Tolson had endured years of punishing doubt and worry to hold this property intact. Up there, on the mountainside last night, another woman had died because she had sought to take away that property. Gerald and I had come to cast a coldly commercial eye over it and had stayed to become as enmeshed in its saving as any of those standing about us.

And I thought also of Jonathan Roswell, the other man who had loved Vanessa once, who had given me his name. One day he also would be buried in a private family burial ground, not among the English mists and green grass, but in the hard, baked earth of Mexico, and the sun would warm his bones, even in death.

Thinking this, on that bright, rainless morning of the English spring, I was surprised to find the wetness on my face, to see George Tolson's head bowed, as if he did not know how to handle his grief, and then to see on the face of Jessica the tears that would make her whole and human. The full realization of what I must take on with Nat, the responsibility for the lives and loyalties of all these people, came fully to me then. Perhaps I wept for myself as well as for my father, Robert Birkett.

THAT same day the priest came out from the Catholic Church in Kesmere and talked with Nat and myself. "I don't know why it should not be done," he said. "Every Christian soul deserves Christian burial—and she has waited a long time."

In what remained of that day we set the Tolson grandchildren to clearing the floor of the chapel, but we left the young birch tree that had sprung up within its walls. Mrs. Tolson provided a table that could be covered with a white cloth. Jessica brought great masses of flowers in big vases to set about on the ground. At the end of the day young Thomas, Nat's son, brought me white violets wrapped in damp paper. "They're for her," he said. "Dad says it will be very early, and I should not come. He said not to think too much about her—but I do. I'm sorry she's been up there in that place alone all these years." He went off with the calm matter-of-factness of a child, this future earl of Askew.

Nat sat with me late that night as I rested in the bed of the Spanish Woman. All of the dogs were with us, lying before the two fires; they had attached themselves to Nat in the immediate way they had attached themselves to Robert Birkett and to myself. He looked at them now. "We'll have to breed some more of them, Jo, as well as some kids for ourselves."

"Yes."

He was sitting in the chair where so often I had thought I saw the shadowy figure of the Spanish Woman. A candle burned on the mantel above him, and he had been trying, in a dazed and tired fashion, to make some notes of things needing to be done. He was still not completely reconciled to the idea of opening Thirlbeck to the public.

"What can we do with it, Jo? Even if they don't find out what Tolson and your mother were doing, there's still a hell of a lot of things that will be lumped into the estate for taxes. Will we be beggars because of this?"

"The revenue people will be on to you in good time. But they won't put their hands on your shoulder tomorrow. We'll just have to talk to them about it all. But there's that million pounds sitting in a Swiss bank. That's the biggest worry. If we find it, it can be paid into Lord Askew's account. Then you inherit—and pay the tax—and the rest can be spent as it's needed. No Swiss bank is going to give out information about where it came from. I don't quite see yet how it's all to be handled. But Thirlbeck is going to be saved, Nat. If you have to grit your teeth and let the public in, then grit your teeth."

He managed a tired smile. "I've got good strong teeth."

"They'd better be. You'll grind them a lot in the next few years. We might even have to sell the El Greco to the National Gallery."

"Yes, Jo, and what else?"

"A lot of the French furniture could be sold. As beautiful as it is, it doesn't belong in this house. But we should try to keep the Dutch pictures. They're a beautiful collection. We could specialize. Oh, yes . . . and there's La Española."

"What about it? Damn, Jo, can't I just hand that over to the revenue people? Let *them* get killed trying to sell it."

I spoke softly. "It can't leave here, Nat. You know that. The first accident, the first misfortune that strikes anyone who handles it, will half kill you. You'll blame yourself. It stays here. We'll have to make a deal with the revenue people. You'll pay the tax however and whenever you can manage it. And La Española will become the jewel it was always meant to be. If legend belongs to it—if people want to think there's a curse on it—then let them come and see it. Put in the best security system and relieve Tolson finally of this hellish responsibility. Then tell the story, tell it as if the Spanish Woman were telling it. Make them weep, Nat. The little Spanish girl has been neglected too long."

He came and sat on the bed beside me. "I'll do it if you say I

458

must. What a child Robert Birkett has left behind in you! You're still as weak as a kitten, and you've already begun to fight for this place. When you first came you seemed such a quiet type. Now you suddenly seem as tough as old boots. I don't really understand *your* sort of Birkett. *He* didn't want to fight, except when they put him in a war."

"I'm also Vanessa's daughter," I said. "Stop worrying, Nat. Birketts fight when there's something to fight for."

He sighed, and slipped off his shoes, lying back on the piled-up pillows that supported me. "If only we—you and I, Jo—could have started with just my farm. Farming's all a fight, but it's things you understand—the weather, crops, sheep. And what did I get? You and Thirlbeck. . . ." His voice trailed off, and in a few minutes his deeper breathing told me he had fallen asleep. We were not like new lovers then, but people long accustomed to each other, facing our problems together.

Nat's voice came again, sleepily. He spoke with his eyes still closed. "I didn't tell you, did I? The great news. One of the eagle's eggs hatched today. And . . . and I retired the Bentley. It's not to be used again." In a very little while he was asleep again.

THE next morning we were ready very early. Tolson was waiting in the library, where the oak coffin rested—the coffin which contained all that remained of the Spanish Woman.

Nat, George Tolson, and his sons carried the coffin outside and laid it on trestles in the newly tidied chapel. Mrs. Tolson's table was covered by a starched white cloth. The priest was waiting with a young boy as acolyte, both robed for the mass. I noticed that the priest's vestments were the white of joy, not the black of mourning. I had asked him to recite the mass in Latin. "She didn't understand English," I had said.

Afterward she was buried among the Birketts, and I laid Thomas's white violets on her grave. A sense of peace, of happiness, stole across me. Now that she was at last accepted among us, accorded her due place, the Birketts themselves might know change. Perhaps her spirit would become, for all of us, the benign presence it had always seemed to me. And she was truly among us. Standing in place there above the grave, the results of Nat's labors yesterday with Ted Tolson, was the roughhewn stone, with

the uncertain hand and spelling. JUANA, THE SPANISHE WOMAN.
The priest was finished; the holy water sprinkled. *"Requiescat
in pace."* For Nat and myself there was an additional blessing,
perhaps a special grace passed on to us by the Spanish Woman,
who lay at last in a hallowed grave. "And may you live in peace."

Tiny, blue-eyed Cathy Gaskin, refreshing as a spring
zephyr from her own county Wicklow, wafted into
New York with her husband, TV consultant Sol Cornberg,
for last-minute corrections on her latest book, and took a
spare hour to tell us about herself and her writing.

She leaned back demurely in a big armchair and said,
"I'm a go-for-broke person. I had no notion there was going
to be a phantom hound in *The Property of a Gentleman*,
but when the white dog ran across the road in front of
Joanna's car I thought, If we're going to have dogs, let
there be eight of them!

"For Joanna's professional background I wanted to get

myself into Christie's in London, one of the biggest art auction houses in the world. I was wondering how to do it when my British editor told me his cousin was managing director there. So his cousin came to lunch, and I was asking questions when he said the magic words I'd hoped for. 'I guess you'll have to come and spend some time with us.'

"He turned me over for a week to the man on Christie's front counter, and it was up to me to pick up what I needed by osmosis. But if you don't know the plot of the book—as I didn't then—you don't know what questions to ask. So I would have to go back from time to time to check."

Catherine Gaskin

Cathy suddenly leaned forward, hands clasped earnestly between her knees. "I'm not what is called a serious novelist. I come from a race and class of storytellers. I *want* people to read me for sheer enjoyment. I'm not going to shoot myself because I'm not Solzhenitsyn. But I believe in giving value for money. I must feel I've done my best. I'll research even a tiny detail. Hardy's, in the book, is not Christie's, but I feel immense gratitude for their kindness in allowing me behind the scenes." Then, animation momentarily spent, she lay back—lovely, still, revealing the fragility beneath her charm.

Now that all the hard work is over, what stands out in Cathy Gaskin's mind about *The Property of a Gentleman?*

"That it turned out to be a ghost story," she replied promptly. "I never expected that. In the beginning I had thought of the Spanish Woman only as decoration for the jewel. Then she began to be a real person. In the little Book of Hours, after I'd put down her name, her ghost quietly took over, and almost as if I didn't write it I put down her prayer."

Cathy Gaskin paused, and then, with the gentle lilt of an Irish minstrel, recited Juana's plea: " 'When I am dead, of your charity, offer nine masses for my soul.' " —M.D.

HIS MAJESTY'S U-BOAT

A CONDENSATION OF THE BOOK BY

Douglas Reeman

ILLUSTRATED BY Schaare

British Lieutenant Commander Steven Marshall, weary and tense after months of sea duty, is given his new command—a captured German submarine—and ordered to sail her into dangerous waters on a top secret mission. In British hands, sailing under the guise of a German warship, *U-192* could create havoc—she could destroy German supply ships, sink their floating docks, enter seas which no British submarine could penetrate. But she would be open to attack from both friend and foe. Further complications develop when Marshall encounters Chantal, a beautiful French spy. Somehow her calm acceptance of danger gives him the strength to carry out his perilous assignment. In a truly exciting story a German submarine becomes a proud member of His Majesty's fleet.

Douglas Reeman is a "gifted novelist who spins a jolly good sea yarn, knows his World War II naval warfare background, and uses it well."   *—Publishers Weekly*

Chapter 1

IT WAS nine o'clock on a February morning in 1943 when His Majesty's Submarine *Tristram* edged against the greasy piles at Fort Blockhouse, Portsmouth, and her lines were taken by the waiting shore party.

In the forepart of her conning tower Lieutenant Commander Steven Marshall watched the cables being dragged to the bollards along the pier. In the early morning, while they had idled outside the harbor until the tide was right to enter the submarine base, he had searched his thoughts for some sensation of achievement. Now, as he glanced briefly at the curious faces below on the pier, he could sense little but anticlimax.

For fourteen months he and his men had lived together in their own confined world within this hull, going from one end of the Mediterranean to the other, with each day bringing some fresh threat to their existence. These men, his company of fifty officers and enlisted men, would soon be scattered to the corners of the British Isles to share their leave with wives and girl friends, parents and children, merging for just a few weeks in that other side of World War II, the world of rationing and shortages.

When the leave was over they would be sent to other boats to form a hard core among men like the recruits being trained at this base. They would crew new boats which were being built to replace those strewn across the beds of a dozen disputed seas.

He shivered, feeling the wind cold and clammy across his face. The year was now a month old. What, when his own leave was over, would it have for him?

"All secure aft, sir."

Marshall turned and glanced at his first lieutenant, Robert Gerrard, tall and thin, with the slight stoop brought about by service in this and other boats. He seemed strangely alien in his blue uniform reefer and best cap. For months they had seen each other in almost anything but regulation dress. Old flannel trousers and discarded cricket shirts. Shorts and sandals on mild days.

"Thank you, Bob. Ring off main motors."

From the periscope standards above his head flew their Skull and Crossbones, which the coxswain had cared for so proudly. Sewn around the grinning death's-head were their recorded battle honors —bars for vessels sunk, crossed guns for those hair-raising attacks on ships and coastal installations.

The deck gave a quick shudder and lay still. They had officially arri ed. Soon the boat would be stripped and refitted from bow to stern. He sighed. She needed it. There was hardly a square yard without a dent or a scar of some sort. Splinters from shellbursts, buckled plates below from depth charges. The deep furrow across the bridge was from Italian cannon fire outside Taranto.

A wooden gangway had been hauled out from the pier. He saw the captain of the base and some other officers coming aboard to go through the formalities. He did not recognize many of them. He climbed out of the bridge and down the casing.

The base captain was genuinely welcoming, his handshake hearty. "Good to see you, Marshall," he said. "It's a tonic to read what you've done out there. Let's go to my office."

Marshall was tired, and despite a clean shirt and his best uniform he felt dirty and unkempt. You did not shake off submarines merely by the prospect of walking ashore. The smells, diesel and wet metal, seemed to get right inside you. But he was not too weary to notice a sense of urgency.

The captain returned the sentry's salute and led the officers who had come with him to greet Marshall back to the dock. Marshall walked through the familiar gates, allowing the conversation to flow around him. He saw young officers marching to instruction, others sitting in classrooms where he had once sat. Fort

466

Blockhouse seemed to have altered little. Only he felt different. They came to a large office, where a fire burned invitingly. A steward was busying himself with glasses, and the captain said cheerfully, "Early in the morning, I know. But *this* is special."

Glasses filled, everyone turned toward him as the captain said, "Welcome home. You and your people have done a fine job." His eyes dropped to the breast of Marshall's reefer. "A Distinguished Service Cross and bar, and damn well earned."

They all raised their glasses, and it was then that Marshall caught sight of himself in a wall mirror. No wonder he felt different. He *was* different. His dark hair, unruly at the best of times, had grown too long over his ears, and he noticed tiny flecks of gray in it. And he was twenty-eight years old.

Marshall could feel the whisky searing his throat, stirring his insides. *Tristram*'s return was special, all right. Five other boats of the same class had left Portsmouth for the Mediterranean. They now littered the seabed, their companies sealed inside them.

The captain said, "I was sorry to hear about young Wade."

"Yes, sir, he was due to come home the week after it happened." The others fell silent as he continued. "We did our commanding-officers' course together, and when I got *Tristram* he was given *Tryphon*. We were always running into each other."

A new voice asked, "How did it happen?"

"We were taking food and ammunition to Malta," Marshall replied. He gestured vaguely. "Nothing but a sub could get in. *Tryphon* left Malta before dawn that particular day. She was never heard of again." He nodded slowly. "A mine, I expect. There were enough of them about!"

As he spoke he recalled his last meeting with Wade. Bill Wade with his black beard and huge grin. The drinks and the ancient Maltese playing a piano in the next room. Almost his last words had been, "Never thought we'd make it, old man. I guess we were just meant to survive." Poor Bill. He had been mistaken about that.

The base captain glanced at his watch. "I think we'd better get things moving. I'll just put Lieutenant Commander Marshall in the picture." The other officers filed out of the room, each pausing to murmur a word of congratulation or welcome.

"Sit down." The captain moved to his desk and leaned comfortably on one corner. "Did you have any plans for leave?"

"Not really, sir." No plans. His mother had died before the war. His father had been commodore of a westbound Atlantic convoy. His ship and several others were sunk by a U-boat pack.

The captain seemed to be hesitating over something. "Fact is, there's a job waiting for you, if you'll take it. I'd not be so blunt about it, if there were more time. But there isn't. It could be dangerous, but you're no stranger to that. The appointment demands every ounce of the experience and skill you have."

Marshall watched him gravely as he went on.

"Ever heard of Captain Giles Browning? Buster Browning they called him in the last war. Got the Victoria Cross for taking his submarine into the Dardanelles during the Gallipoli fiasco."

Marshall nodded. "I read about him somewhere."

"He was out of the service soon after the war. Now he's come back to do various jobs, and has a special appointment in Combined Ops. It's all very vague, but it has to be." The captain was studying Marshall intently. "If you accept, I'll have you whistled up to Scotland tomorrow morning, where you'll meet Captain Browning." He grinned. "*Buster.*"

Outside the thick walls a tug hooted mournfully. Why not? thought Marshall. There was no point in spending a whole leave going from one hotel to another. He stood up. His limbs felt strangely light. He nodded. "I'll have a go at it, sir."

"Thank you. I know what you've been through. So do all those concerned. But you are what we need."

A staff officer peered around the door. "Sir?"

"Lieutenant Commander Marshall has agreed." The captain added, "You'd better send for Lieutenant Gerrard and brief him."

The door closed again.

Marshall turned sharply. "What has my first lieutenant got to do with this?"

"He will be *asked* to volunteer to go with you. We must have a perfect team at the top."

Marshall said, "He can't be pitchforked straight into another boat after fourteen months in the Med. He's married, sir. And he's due for a commanding-officers' course at the end of his leave."

"I'll let him have a couple of days at home before he follows you up north." The captain smiled sadly. "Can't be helped. This is important."

Marshall thought of Gerrard's face that morning as they had docked. Like a child seeing a Christmas tree for the first time.

A telephone started to ring. "Take yourself off and relax for a bit," said the captain. "I'll see you before you go tomorrow."

Marshall picked up his cap and left.

AT FIRST light Marshall was taken in a staff car to a naval air station a few miles inland. Once strapped into a seat aboard a noisy transport plane, he considered his experiences of the previous day. For the most part they had been disappointing. Embarrassment at showing true feelings had marred his farewells to *Tristram*'s company. It was often so in the service.

Marshall was still not sure what Gerrard had thought about the sudden change of plans. He had seemed more worried about what his wife would think than anything. Of his proposed command course he had said nothing.

When the last of his men had hurried off, Marshall had gone ashore. A taxi had carried him to the house on the outskirts of Southampton, and over each mile of the journey he had wondered what he was going to say to Bill's widow, the girl his best friend had married just two months before they had sailed for the Med. He remembered her well. And so he should! Small and dark, with the vitality and wildness of a young colt.

But his trip was fruitless. She had moved away. No, the present occupants of the house did not know where.

He had returned to the base feeling tired and depressed. He had bought a bottle of gin, and now that was not helping him face the bumpy flight to Scotland. He was grateful for the coffee and sandwiches brought by one of the aircraft's crew.

They flew to Cape Wrath, the northwesterly tip of the British Isles. He could not imagine what they could have up there. The landing field proved to be little more than a strip of blacktop surrounded by mud. Some oilskinned figures emerged reluctantly from a prefabricated hut and ran toward the plane, their bodies bowed to a steady drizzle.

As they gathered up Marshall's luggage a burly marine sergeant squelched across to meet him, gave a stiff salute and gestured toward a dripping car. Marshall climbed in and held to a strap as the car churned noisily across the furrowed ground.

The sergeant squinted through the windshield and said, "Loch Cairnbawn, sir. That's where we're 'eading." He swore as a sheep ambled across the narrow track. "If we're spared!"

It was all but dark by the time they reached the loch. There were barbed wire and armed sentries, and Marshall's identity card was scrutinized. A lieutenant said apologetically, "I'm sorry about all this, sir. Security's pretty tight here."

Marshall nodded. He could see no sign of any ship.

The lieutenant waved toward a small motorboat. "The old *Guernsey* is moored out in the loch, sir. This launch will take you out."

The *Guernsey* was not unknown to Marshall. An old depot ship, coal-fired and extremely uncomfortable, she rarely appeared anywhere these days, except as a temporary accommodation vessel.

It did not take long to reach the moored ship. As the boat plunged and dipped around her outdated stern Marshall saw two submarines tethered alongside.

At the entry port the officer of the day saluted smartly and said, "Nice to have you aboard, sir. Captain Browning is expecting you."

Like much of the ship, the captain's office had an air of shabby opulence. When Marshall entered, Captain Giles Browning stood and thrust out a large hand. "Glad to have you, Marshall." His voice was thick and resonant, his grasp hard. He gestured to a chair. Browning's face was interesting, crumpled and uneven; Marshall guessed he had once been a boxer or rugby player.

The captain's blue, very clear eyes fixed on Marshall's. "I know a lot about you," he said. He seated himself carefully in a big chair. "You've been damn good to achieve your record. But it doesn't follow that you're any use for what I want!"

Marshall came up in the chair with a jerk.

But Browning held up one of his massive hands. "Keep calm. I speak my mind. And as I'm far senior to you, I can speak mine first, right?" A grin spread slowly across his battered features.

Like sunlight on some old ruin, Marshall thought. But he found himself smiling. *Buster!* "Right, sir."

"Good. This job is very hush-hush. Has to be. You've been a long time in the Med. You know the picture out there. It's been a hard struggle, but now the Germans in North Africa are on the run. The next thing will be an Allied invasion of Europe." Browning spoke with such calm assurance that it was fascinating. He asked sharply, "Do you know what a milch cow is?"

Marshall started. "Yes, sir. A German submarine that supplies other U-boats. Well over two thousand tons each, or so I hear."

"You probably know that the average U-boat can cover seven thousand miles on an operational cruise. They lose four thousand miles just getting out to mid-Atlantic and back home again. That only leaves three thousand miles to do any damage, right?"

Marshall nodded. He could find no connection between events in North Africa and U-boat operations in the Atlantic.

"So these milch cows can meet their U-boats at prearranged billets. Supply 'em with food and fuel, torpedoes, almost anything they need. They can treble the time that each boat can stay at sea and attack our convoys, and so far we've not been able to track down any of 'em." He took a deep breath. "In the next month or so we can expect huge troop convoys from the States, if we are to exploit the North African successes. If we could bag a couple of their milch cows, or even one, it would make all the difference. It might take weeks for the Germans to realize what happened. Valuable weeks when half of their U-boats are creeping home or running out of fuel and supplies before more aid can be sent to them."

Marshall understood. His new command was to try to run a milch cow to earth. He said, "How can we hope to find one, sir?"

Browning smiled. He was enjoying himself. "Last month a U-boat outward bound from Kiel to the Atlantic developed trouble in her motors. She was not new, but her crew were. Green as grass. The weather was foul at the time, blowing a whole gale, and the U-boat's skipper decided to run for shelter. He chose a fjord on the east coast of Iceland. He took a risk but it probably seemed a good idea—the Icelanders have no love for us and the Americans since we occupied their country." He studied Marshall for several seconds. "Fortunately, the skipper of one of our sonar-equipped trawlers had had the same idea. They met eye to eye, so to speak!"

Marshall stared at him. "And you've captured the codes showing where she'll rendezvous with her supply submarine?"

"Better'n that, boy. We've got the bloody U-boat! She's out there now." Browning's eyes were dancing. "And now we've got a captain for her, right?"

Marshall forced a smile. "*Right*, sir."

Browning beamed. "Thought you'd like the idea." He seized a decanter. "Have some port, *Herr Kapitän!*"

MARSHALL stayed with Browning long into the night, listening to the other man. Capturing the U-boat had been a series of lucky incidents. Once faced by the armed trawler, the German commander had tried to scuttle his boat, only to discover that the strong gale had driven him farther into the fjord than he had intended. The U-boat had come to rest on a hard shoulder, her periscope standards still awash. Caught in the trawler's searchlight, and with a few warning cannon shells whining dangerously overhead, the submarine's crew decided to surrender without further trouble.

The news had been flashed to the Admiralty in London, and within hours an expert salvage team was on its way by air to Reykjavik. At the isolated fjord they raised the U-boat and at the first easing of the weather had her in tow, en route for Scotland.

Browning kept a ceaseless radio and intelligence watch, trying to ascertain if the U-boat had been able to signal her predicament before capture. But as the days wore on he gained confidence that no message had, in fact, been sent.

AFTER a hasty breakfast the next morning Marshall hurried on deck, where he found Captain Browning and two of the ship's officers in conversation by the guardrail.

Browning turned to Marshall and grinned. "Morning!" Then he introduced his two companions. Both were commanders who had been responsible for preparing the U-boat for sea.

One, a bearded man, said cheerfully, "We've had a lot of the gear relabeled. Meters into feet and so on, but most of the technical equipment is as before, so don't forget the fact if you go into a crash dive." Then he added gravely, "Naturally we're not in the habit of stocking spare parts for German subs. You'll have to make do with what you've got. In the meantime I'll get my people to rummage discreetly around. We may need the parts later."

During their long discussion Browning had hinted as much. If Marshall was successful, they might be able to use the U-boat in another unorthodox operation—the kind Combined Operations was set up for.

Marshall leaned over the guardrail and stared down at the boats tethered alongside. The inner one was a small submarine—H-class. Browning murmured, "We use her for training and as a guinea pig. She also helps to make inquisitive eyes ashore think we're just doing normal instruction."

Marshall did not hear him. He ran his gaze slowly along the outer craft, feeling a strange sensation in his stomach, a mixture of excitement and uncertainty. Although her conning tower was crudely masked by painted canvas as an additional precaution against prying eyes, there was no mistaking the U-boat's outline and design.

Browning said, "Vicious-looking beast, eh? Her skipper got the Iron Cross after his last cruise." He added bitterly, "Put down twenty-two ships."

Marshall followed Browning and the two commanders down a steep catwalk and across the H-boat to the deck of the U-boat. He looked up at its conning tower, where a seaman was putting finishing touches to a newly painted insignia, a prancing black bull with steam shooting from flared nostrils. The bearded commander said, "Thought it best to invent a new badge for the boat. Just in case Jerry knows he's lost her."

Browning turned. "Your new company has been training for two weeks. It was all the time we could afford. But you can rub off the rough edges while you're on passage to the rendezvous area. After all, I'm not expecting you to start looking for trouble. Just the target we talked about." The blue eyes hardened. "No heroics beyond the job."

Marshall nodded. His teeth were chattering so badly he imagined the others must have noticed. Cold, nerves, or just the apprehension of going straight back into the fire without a break.

They climbed up the straight ladder to the U-boat's bridge. It was narrower and longer than *Tristram*'s bridge, and mounted on a bandstand just behind the conning tower he saw a deadly-looking Vierling gun. Four-barreled, eighty-eight millimeter cannon with a tremendous rate of fire. He knew that much already.

Then they climbed down into the well-lit control room, which was more spacious than he had expected. Marshall saw the printed instructions that had been pasted over German wording on many of the gauges and dials. One brass plate remained on the bulkhead:

U-192. KRUPP—GERMANIA, KIEL—1941. Despite his excitement he felt a chill on his spine.

He asked, "Can we have the main periscope raised?" As he stooped to seize the handles, watching the great periscope as it hissed from its well, he had a sudden picture of those who had gone before him. He could imagine the scream of the klaxon, the commander's eye glittering in the periscope lens as it broke surface. All the world of attack and target being drawn through the small aperture for translation into action, and death. But now, when he swung the periscope slowly in a small arc, he saw only a cluster of houses across the choppy waters of the loch.

Browning said, "She mounts four tubes forward and one aft. She carries fourteen spare torpedoes in pressure-tight compartments. A total of nineteen tin fish! Excellent diesels. Will give you eighteen knots on the surface. The electric motors can do eight submerged."

Marshall looked at him gravely. It was all there on the captain's battered face. Pleasure, pride. But most of all, envy.

Poor old Buster, he thought. He's been left behind.

Browning continued. "You will have one officer who speaks fluent German. Two of your telegraphists are also handpicked for their work with enemy codes and transmissions."

Occasionally men squeezed past them as they carried on with their inspection. Marshall saw their glances. The word would soon get around. The new CO was aboard. What's he like? Wait and see. You never know with officers. And so on.

And here was the wardroom, where he would meet his officers, then the petty officers' mess and, beyond that, the refrigerator compartment, where a supply officer was checking his lists. Forward into the torpedo stowage compartment, the long gleaming fish in their racks. A glance above to the forward escape hatch, a quick look down into the sonar compartment and through the watertight door to the torpedo tubes, four gleaming breeches.

Once or twice Marshall made quick notes on his pad, allowing the submarine's shape and area to form in his mind. Finally he said, "I think that does it."

When they went back aboard the depot ship *Guernsey*, Browning asked, "D'you know a chap called Roger Simeon, by the way?"

Marshall frowned. "Slightly. He was first lieutenant of a sub last time I saw him." He got a brief mental picture of a square, reckless face, short fair hair. A man who would excite any woman's attention.

"He's promoted to commander now, of course."

Marshall waited. *Of course?* What did that mean?

"Bright lad. He's heavily involved in Combined Operations, too. First-class brain, and a real goer. You'll be meeting him shortly."

Marshall darted a quick glance at him, thinking, You hate his guts, don't you? Aloud he said, "I never knew him other than casually at Fort Blockhouse."

"Er, yes." Browning waited for the other officers to move away. "Lieutenant Commander Wade was a good friend of yours, I believe? Damn bad luck about his being lost."

Marshall watched him warily. "We were pretty close."

"You'd better hear it from me then," the captain said. "Wade's widow married Commander Simeon last month."

Marshall turned to stare through a nearby scuttle. He tried to recall exactly what Bill had said in those last days. Had he just discovered about his wife? It was bad in any sense to con a submarine out of Malta through those minefields. If Bill had had that on his mind, it would have been more than enough. It needed only seconds, a few precious moments, for a lack of vigilance to bring oblivion.

He controlled himself with an effort, but when he spoke his voice was flat. "Thank you, sir. I'm glad you told me."

For the next three days Marshall thought of little but the job in hand. He absorbed himself completely in putting his command through every test and trial he could envisage.

During the forenoon of the fourth day he was sitting in his cabin aboard the U-boat, rereading his notes. Gerrard was due to arrive that afternoon, and he would need to have every last detail at his fingertips when he began briefing him.

He found himself thinking about his officers. Apart from himself and Gerrard, there were four of them. A mixed bunch, and still hard to see as a team.

Lieutenant Adrian Devereaux, the navigator, was handsome and well-bred, with the easy drawling tone of one who could be slightly contemptuous of those around him. Lieutenant Victor Frenzel, the chief engineer, was the complete opposite. He had worked his way from lowly junior stoker to commissioned rank by the hardest route. He had dark curly hair, a broad grin, and seemed totally unimpressed by the job he had been given.

Lieutenant Colin Buck, the torpedo officer, had been a garage manager and used-car dealer. Sharp-featured, cold-eyed, he would be a difficult man to know. Unless he wanted you to, Marshall thought. The wardroom's junior member was Sublieutenant David Warwick. He was fresh-faced and outwardly had the innocence of a child. He was gunnery officer and the one picked to deal with German translations. He had passed his submarine and gunnery courses at the top of the list. So there had to be more to him than met the eye.

There was a tap at the door, and Lieutenant Devereaux, officer of the day, announced, "Captain Browning is coming aboard, sir, and Lieutenant Gerrard has landed at the field."

"Thank you, Pilot." Marshall stretched his arms and stood up. "Your department all buttoned up?"

Devereaux shrugged elegantly. "Quite, sir."

Together they climbed to the bridge and met Browning as he heaved himself over the rim of the conning tower.

He looked at Devereaux. "Are you OOD?"

"Yes, sir."

"Good. Go aboard *Guernsey* and get all your people back here. I want 'em mustered within the hour."

As Devereaux hurried down the ladder Browning murmured, "Pompous prig. Still, he has a good record." Once in Marshall's cabin he shut the door and said, "You'll be sailing sooner than we expected." He shook his head gravely. "I *know* what you're about to say, and I agree. But something's happened. I've had a signal from Iceland. One of this boat's original crew has escaped from prison camp. He may be dead, frozen stiff, or he could be hiding out or searching for a neutral ship to carry him off the island. But we have to assume that he might be able to blow our secret to the winds."

"I see, sir."

Marshall went to his cupboard and took out a bottle. It would be pointless to mention that Gerrard would arrive shortly with no knowledge of this boat in which he would be first lieutenant—

Number One. Browning watched as he poured two full glasses of Scotch. Then he said, "I sure wish you were taking me with you!"

"So do I." Marshall was surprised to find that he meant it.

Feet clattered on the casing, and Browning said abruptly, "You can slip at sixteen thirty. It'll be all but dark then. I've laid on the armed yacht *Lima* to guide you out. She'll stand by for your test dive." He sounded tired. "After that, you'll be on your own."

There was a tap at the door, and Lieutenant Frenzel poked his head inside the cabin. "We were wondering if you would join us in the wardroom before we get busy, sir?" He grinned at Browning. "And you, of course, sir."

Marshall nodded. "Thanks, Chief. That would be fine."

Surprisingly, Browning stood up and said, "Sorry. Lot to do. But I'll watch you leave, and I wish you all the luck in the world."

Frenzel nodded. "I'll pass it on, sir." He vanished.

As the door closed Browning said harshly, "I couldn't sit there drinking with Frenzel as if nothing had happened." He thrust one hand into his pocket and pulled out a crumpled telegram. "Came an hour ago. His wife and kid were killed in an air raid last night. If I told him now, it could do no good and might put the whole mission in jeopardy."

Marshall watched his despair. "It *is* the only way."

They shook hands gravely, and Browning said, "I'll tell him when you get back. My responsibility."

They walked up to the bridge, and Marshall watched until Browning had disappeared aboard the depot ship.

It was all his now.

Chapter 2

AFTER the tension brought about by last-minute preparations the actual moment of getting under way was a relief. The weather had worsened, and a stiff wind lashed the waters of the loch into short, vicious whitecaps. Close by, the armed yacht *Lima* lay hove to to guide them out to the open sea.

Lieutenant Buck climbed up through the hatch to the bridge and groped his way forward to the steel gratings where Marshall stood. "All ready, sir." He had a faint South London accent.

Marshall waved his hand. "Let go forward!" He felt the deck lift slightly as the submarine's bows edged away from the H-boat. "Let go aft! Steer two nine zero." He added, "Tell the first lieutenant to con the boat on *Lima's* stern light."

He watched the rakish armed yacht turning steeply to lead them clear. She was beautiful. A millionaire's plaything in happier times. Probably kept in the Med. Warm nights, tanned bodies, soft wine.

Warwick's boyish face appeared above the bridge screen, shining with spray. "All cables secured and stowed, sir!"

Marshall smiled. Perhaps he had been like Warwick once. It hardly seemed possible. "Right. You can go below."

Warwick asked shyly, "Can I stay here, sir?"

"Of course." Marshall watched the yacht stagger across the first of the inshore swells. "But hold tight."

Somewhere above, an aircraft droned faintly. Marshall thought suddenly of Frenzel. Over the engineer's bunk Marshall had seen a picture of his wife and small son. That had been a bad moment.

Warwick asked, "Do you think we'll get close to them, sir?"

"The Jerries, you mean?" He shrugged. "Could be. You'll have to be all about, if that happens."

Warwick murmured, "I'll try, sir."

Colin Buck said, "He'll look a right little Kraut when he gets his gear on!"

Marshall nodded. They had a selection of German uniforms on board. If they got close enough to need them, the gunnery officer would have to be good indeed.

Buck added, suddenly changing his attitude, "You'll be okay, David, don't you sweat!"

Warwick relaxed slightly. "It's all right for you. Torpedoes don't need to speak German or *any* language."

The bridge lurched steeply and brought a curtain of spray dousing over the periscope standards. It was getting wilder.

"Able Seaman Churchill requests permission to come to the bridge, sir." The lookout could not restrain a grin.

Churchill was a torpedoman who also acted as wardroom steward. His was a difficult name to have in this particular war.

He squeezed through the hatch carrying a jug and mugs against his chest. He poured thick cocoa into a mug and squinted outboard at the tossing whitecaps. Marshall held the hot mug against his face and watched Churchill slither back into the open hatchway.

A lookout whispered, "Give our love to the war cabinet!"

Churchill's head quivered in the hatchway. "Get lost!"

Buck said, "I hope the torpedoes won't let us down. I hear Jerry has a fair share of duds." He added, "I'll go forward now, with your permission, sir."

When he had gone, Warwick asked, "Was that right, sir?"

"We have our share of duds, too. Nothing you can explain. It just happens sometimes." He called over the speaking tube to Gerrard. "Watch your revolutions. The yacht is making hard going of it. We'll overtake her, if we're not careful."

As the submarine pushed farther and farther from the land the motion increased in steep, dizzy plunges. It would be better once they could clap on more speed. A U-boat was designed to run faster on the surface than they were now going. To chase her quarry and overreach it. Then dive for the kill. Marshall could feel his stomach tightening and guessed that many of the new hands would be in real torment.

At long last they arrived at the arranged position, and as the *Lima* rolled drunkenly in the steep troughs Marshall said, "This is it." He spoke into the tube. "Signal the *Lima*. 'Am about to carry out trim dive.'" To the lookouts he added, "Clear the bridge." He felt strangely calm.

The others hurried to the hatch as Marshall snapped shut the cocks on the two speaking tubes and took a last glance around. Then he lowered himself through the hatch and spun the locking wheel into place. He went down the polished ladder, where a seaman waited to close the lower hatch.

After the stinging wind and spray his cheeks felt flushed in the ordered world of the control room. He ran his gaze over the men around him. Starkie, the coxswain, small and intent at his wheel. The two planesmen, heads tilted to watch their dials. Gerrard, arms folded, standing just behind the coxswain. Devereaux by the chart table. Frenzel leaning on his control panel.

"All set, Number One?" Marshall asked the first lieutenant.

Gerrard turned toward him. "Ready, sir."

Marshall crossed to the forward periscope and swung it gently until he had found the *Lima*'s vague outline about two hundred yards away.

"Test fore and aft planes, Number One."

He watched the hydroplanes moving from rise to dive positions, before returning to their horizontal trim. Beyond the periscope he caught a glimpse of a young stoker watching him like a mesmerized rabbit. He gave him a brief smile, but the youth showed no change of expression.

"Hydroplanes tested and found correct, sir."

"Ready, Chief?" He saw Frenzel nod.

He turned back to the periscope. The moment had come. How quiet it was now that the diesels had given way to the electric motors. "Group up. Slow ahead together," he ordered. "Open main vents. Take her down to fourteen meters!"

He depressed the periscope lens and concentrated his gaze on the foreplanes as they tilted downward like fins. It was a sight that never failed to excite him. The bow dropping, the sea surging up toward him while the deck tilted below his feet. He saw spray leaping at him, and as always he was tempted to hold his breath as if to avoid drowning. "Down periscope."

He stood back, bracing his body as he looked quickly over the depth gauges and hydroplane telltales. Gerrard was doing well. Nice and smooth. He watched the big needle edging around, steadying.

"Fourteen meters, sir. Periscope depth." Gerrard sounded hoarse.

"Up periscope."

Again a quick circling inspection. No sign of *Lima*, but he could hear her ragged engine beat without difficulty.

"Down periscope." He clapped home the handles. "Twenty meters." He waited.

Gerrard said, "Twenty meters, sir." They maintained that depth and the same speed for the prescribed half hour. The hull felt as steady as a barrack square.

"She seems fine," Gerrard said.

Marshall looked at the men around him. "Well then, *U-192* is in business." He smiled gravely. "Under entirely new management!"

MARSHALL opened his eyes and stared at the curved deckhead above his bunk. He knew by the silence that the submarine was still dived, that breakfast had not yet begun. He looked at his watch. It was six in the morning. Since leaving the loch eight days ago they had spent most days submerged and most nights running on the surface, charging batteries and checking the inflow of signals. He licked his lips, tasting the diesel in his throat. It was a pity they had been made to dive overnight, but safety came first. They had driven westward into the Atlantic, avoiding the main convoy routes, avoiding friend and foe alike. The submarine was now about a thousand miles south of Cape Farewell, Greenland, and a similar distance east of Newfoundland. Out here the enemy was not only made up of men. There could be ice, and it was best to run deep.

He twisted his head to look at the German cap which hung behind his door. The one he might have to wear, if every other ruse failed. It had a white top, the mark of a U-boat commander. He had tried it on just once. The effect had been startling.

The passage to the rendezvous area where the milch cows were known to meet the U-boats they tended had been busy with all the usual teething troubles. Faulty valves and inexplicable failures in wiring which had to be traced with the aid of Warwick's translation from the German handbooks.

They had also done their first deep practice dive. It was always a tense moment in any boat, let alone this one. As they had sunk deeper and deeper, to three hundred and fifty feet, with Frenzel and his engine room hands creeping about the hull in search of faults and leaks, several men must have considered the fact that the boat's skin was less than an inch thick.

Gerrard had been busy with his slide rule and calculations before the actual moment of taking her down. The boat's trim had to be constantly watched and checked. As fuel was consumed the weight had to be compensated. Food and fresh water, even the movement of numbers of men at any one time, such as going to diving stations, had to be allowed for. A bad first lieutenant had been known to let his submarine's bows flounder above the surface at the moment of firing torpedoes, merely because he had not compensated for the sudden loss of their weight.

Every so often there had been a sharp squeak or groan, with gasps from the inexperienced men aboard. For even at one hundred feet there was a weight of twenty-five tons of water on every square yard of the hull. Marshall had listened calmly to the reports coming through the intercom. The Kiel dockyard workers had done a good job.

But everyone had to trust him and the boat. "Three hundred and eighty feet, Number One," he had snapped.

Gerrard had nodded. "Very good, sir."

More groans, and a few flakes of paint which had drifted down like snow as the hull had taken the increasing strain. As she had leveled off, the surface was the height of St. Paul's Cathedral above their heads. But nothing happened, and Frenzel was quite satisfied with both hull and machinery. The dive had given them all more confidence.

Now feet padded past Marshall's cabin and he heard the clink of breakfast cups. He sighed and stretched. Encased in heavy jersey and seaboots, he would have given anything for a hot bath, a shave and a change of clothes. But outward bound it was too wasteful.

"ALL right, make yourselves comfortable," Marshall said as he entered the wardroom. He waited for Gerrard, Devereaux and Frenzel to seat themselves and for Warwick to lay the chart on the table. Beneath the solitary deckhead lamp their faces looked strained and tense. They had now had twenty-nine days of being completely severed from the rest of the world, shut off from reality.

For the past three days they had remained submerged, watching and listening in vain for the milch cow's brief signal as they made their way across the rendezvous area. They had heard only the constant flow of distress calls from merchant ships under attack, instructions from German submarine headquarters, and garbled snatches from warships and aircraft. Marshall found himself wondering if the Germans had changed their plans for refueling U-boats at sea, or had discovered that there was an enemy in their midst. There might even now be U-boats hunting them, changing their role to that of victim.

He looked down at the chart. The submarine's present position was some two hundred miles south of Bermuda, a thousand miles east of the Florida coast. An hour earlier, when they had gone up to periscope depth, he had seen a glistening panorama of pale green sea, catching the sunlight like a million bright diamonds. But Marshall didn't dare risk surfacing anywhere in the rendezvous area until he was sure of a contact with the milch cow.

Reports had been picked up of a heavy enemy attack on a convoy to the east, and Marshall had guessed that the milch cow had taken herself to the position where she would be most greatly needed—to *this* area. Now he was no longer so optimistic.

He said, "I've called this conference to hear your views."

Frenzel leaned forward. "I'm not happy about this enforced diving, sir. We need to ventilate the boat and charge batteries. Later, if we run into trouble, we'll need all the power we can get." He looked bleakly at the solitary lamp. "I've shut down all the heaters, lights and fans I can without driving our lads berserk."

Marshall straightened his back. He said, "We'll surface tonight, Chief. It's the best I can do. I know we're pretty safe from Allied patrols out here, but—"

Buck's voice through the intercom cut him off. "Captain in the control room!"

With the others close on his heels Marshall ran for the brightly lit compartment. Buck said crisply, "Sonar reports HE at two five zero, sir." Hydrophone effect was reported whenever the listening devices picked up sounds, possibly propeller noises or the like.

Marshall strode to the shielded compartment where Speke, the senior sonar operator, was crouching over his controls. "Well?"

The seaman shrugged but kept his eyes on the dial. "Very faint, sir. Single screw. Diesel."

Marshall said, "Keep listening." He tried to hide his disappointment. Whatever it was, it was certainly not the big supply submarine.

He heard Warwick say, "I'll bet it's a damaged U-boat. Coming to another for help."

Marshall swung around and touched Warwick's arm. "You could just be right, Sub!" He looked at Buck. "Bring her around to intercept. Then sound the alarm. Complete silence throughout the boat after that." He held up one hand. "But remember, if this is a damaged U-boat making a rendezvous, we will have to act fast. The attack team must be perfect."

"Steady on two five zero, sir."

"Very well. Klaxon, please."

As the men came running Marshall could feel his weariness falling away. "Periscope depth, Number One," he said, and crouched beside the periscope well.

"Fourteen meters, sir."

"Up periscope." He glanced at the stoker. "Slowly."

He bent double, his forehead pressed against the rubber pad, watching the swirl of silver bubbles, the sudden blinding flash as the lens broke surface. "Hold it there!"

He edged around the well, watching the misty sunlight playing across a long green swell. He could almost feel the warmth across his face, taste the clean salt air. His eye still on the lens, he said, "How is the bearing now?"

"As before, sir, but still very faint," said Speke.

"Full extent." He straightened his body as the periscope slid smoothly from its well. He brought it to full power, but the haze, like steam, was too thick.

"Down periscope." He stood back. "Increase to seven knots, Chief. We'll miss this chap, if we're not careful."

As the periscope hissed into its well Warwick shouted, "Radio operator reports milch cow's signal, sir!" He had his handset to his ear. "Bearing approximately the same as the other boat."

Marshall crossed to the chart. We must make more speed, he thought. The milch cow was probably lying directly ahead of their own course, with the damaged boat somewhere in between.

He snapped, "Group up. Full ahead together. Twenty meters." He was thinking aloud. "We'll get as close as we can to the first boat. Then we'll surface. The supply boat would be suspicious of any of her brood approaching submerged. She'd dive and be away, no matter how much trouble the other chap's in."

Speke said, "The range must be about six thousand yards, sir. It's hard to tell. The one diesel sounds pretty dicey."

Only three miles. But he must not think of this one, limping target. One salvo would send her to the bottom. The other submarine was something else entirely. They must be sure.

"Diesel's stopped, sir."

"*Blast!*"

The damaged boat probably had the milch cow in sight. He could picture it in his mind. The weary lookouts numb with relief as the massive hull heaved in sight. And aboard the supply boat all the busy preparations to pipe fuel across to the battered survivor of some attack. Food and fresh clothing; there would even be a surgeon aboard to care for the sick and wounded.

He said, "Stand by to surface. Continue on batteries, but be ready to switch to main engines as soon as we're spotted."

He looked around at their intent faces. "Sub, you can muster your gun crew. See that they're rigged out in German caps and life jackets." He saw Churchill hovering by the attack table. "Fetch my cap." He knew his words had sunk in. That it was going to be close and quick.

As Churchill scurried away he added quietly to Gerrard, "If we catch it on the surface, Bob, take her deep. Don't try and save the deck party. Just get the hell out of it."

Gerrard nodded, his eyes grave. "Right."

Marshall took the white cap from Churchill, touching the salt-stained eagle, the swastika in its claws. "We'll do a surface attack with four tubes. Gun action as a last resort."

Feet clattered below the conning-tower hatch and he saw Warwick and his gun crew, some of them grinning sheepishly as they adjusted their German caps and slipped into the bright orange life jackets which were always worn by U-boat deck parties.

"Prepare your gun as soon as we surface," Marshall told Warwick. "After that keep your people hanging around. Casual, but ready to move like quicksilver."

They were all staring at him, suddenly molded together, the strain showing on each unshaven face.

He said, "Periscope depth again," and waited as the deck tilted slightly, the compressed air pulsing into the ballast tanks.

"Fourteen meters, sir."

He licked his lips. Thank God the Germans had perfected the fan method of firing. A British boat had to be aimed at her target or swung at the moment of releasing each of her torpedoes. Every German boat was fitted with a device which allowed each shot to be fired on varying bearings while the boat's course remained constant.

"Up periscope."

He let his breath exhale very slowly. There she was.

He heard Buck intone, "Range four thousand yards, sir."

Marshall ignored him, watching the other U-boat's conning tower as it lifted in the drifting haze. Smaller than this one. Dirty gray in the filtered sunlight. He could see a length of broken guard-rail, evidence of her earlier encounters.

"Down periscope." He strode to the ladder. "Open the lower hatch." He started up the smooth rungs, the gun crew crowding

485

up behind him. Someone had hold of his feet. It was not unknown for a captain to be plucked out of the hatch before the buildup of pressure adjusted itself.

He took a deep breath. *"Surface!"* It had started.

Seconds later he heard Gerrard's voice far below, and with all his strength he swung the locking wheel, feeling the ice-cold water dash into his face as he opened the hatch and dragged himself onto the bridge. The gratings were only just free of water as, with her hydroplanes at full elevation, the boat lurched into the sunlight. He ran to the forepart of the bridge, and saw the other U-boat almost broadside on to their approach.

He trained his glasses on the conning tower and saw a flash of sunlight as someone leveled binoculars on them. He could imagine the Germans' panic at their rapid surfacing, then fear giving way to relief at the realization it was one of their own.

The damaged U-boat was rolling heavily in the swell, her after-casing awash where some seamen gathered below the conning tower. She had not stopped merely because she was awaiting help. Her last diesel must have packed up.

Marshall moved his glasses very slowly. The supply boat might be visible to the damaged one, but not to him. He snapped, "Tell the chief to switch to main engines. Slow ahead together." They were rapidly closing with the other boat, but they must hold back until the milch cow showed herself. The diesels would help make conversation with the damaged boat difficult and ease any remaining suspicion of their arrival.

A light stabbed across the water and Petty Officer Blythe, the yeoman of signals, acknowledged it with his hand lamp. At Marshall's side one of the telegraphists translated breathlessly. "He's asking your number, sir."

"Reply, Yeoman. 'One nine two.'" He added, "Make the coded challenge."

He gripped the screen. Down below Gerrard would be peering through the small attack periscope, ready to dive the instant things went wrong. The wrong code, a false acknowledgment, and . . .

Blythe murmured, "Reply, sir. 'U-one five four.' Requests that we take her in tow, sir. Has too much drift to—"

He broke off as a lookout said sharply, "There she is! Fine on the port bow!"

486

Almost simultaneously Marshall heard Gerrard on the speaking tube. "Target in sight, sir. Bearing red one five. Range five thousand yards. Closing."

At first Marshall could see nothing, and he cursed as he wiped moisture from his glasses. Then he saw the great supply boat edging out of the haze like some vast nightmare creation. She bore little resemblance to a normal submarine and her upper hull was like that of a partially completed surface craft.

Blythe hissed, "Blimey, she's a big un!"

Warwick, leaning on the guardrail, was waving his cap toward the damaged boat while some of his men pointed and gestured like old comrades.

Gerrard's voice again. "All tubes ready, sir."

Marshall replied slowly, "You must carry out the attack from the control room. If they see me using the bridge sights—"

"What shall I reply, sir?"

Marshall glanced at the yeoman. He had almost forgotten the Germans' request for aid.

"Make to them that we are going to cross their port bow. Stand by on the forecasing with heaving lines." He shouted to Warwick, "Make it look as if we're trying, Sub!" He saw Warwick wave, and Petty Officer Cain dragging a spare cable and fastening it to a heaving line.

"Range now four thousand five hundred yards, sir." Gerrard sounded very cool. "Tubes one to four ready."

Marshall bit his lip. The damaged boat was barely four hundred yards away now. It would have to be soon. At any moment the Germans might notice something.

Gerrard called, "We can't torpedo the damaged boat, sir. The explosion would finish us, too."

"Yes." He beckoned to a lookout. "Pass the word to the gun crews. Rapid fire on the damaged boat when I give the word."

The other lookout said, "The Jerry's got a megaphone, sir! He's gettin' ready to chat when we gets a bit closer!"

Marshall's eyes were again on the milch cow. She was moving very slowly, like some great slab of gray pier, her upper deck alive with tiny figures.

A voice echoed tinnily across the heaving water, almost drowned by the mutter of diesels and the hiss of spray.

Slowly he removed his cap and waved it toward the damaged U-boat. It seemed to do the trick. The other captain spread his arms and pretended to hurl the megaphone overboard in disgust.

"Sir!" The lookout's voice made him freeze. "Smoke! On the starboard quarter."

"Control room! This is the captain. Smoke on the starboard quarter. Check it with the main periscope."

An agonizing pause, and then a voice called, "One ship, sir. On the horizon."

He barked, "Start the attack!"

The speaking tube went dead; then he heard Buck's orders being passed across the intercom. "Fire one!"

Marshall felt the steel screen kick gently against his chest. Pictured the first torpedo as it shot toward the milch cow.

"Fire two!"

On the forecasing one of the seamen was whirling a heaving line around his head, playing out the long, dragging seconds.

"Fire three!"

Marshall snapped, "Get *ready!*" Again the little kick. Like a conspiratorial nudge.

"Torpedoes running, sir!" The last one was to have been for the damaged boat, but she was too near now.

The lookout called, "Ship on the starboard quarter is closing, sir. One funnel. American destroyer, probably."

Marshall nodded, unable to drag his eyes from the outline of his target. He pictured the torpedoes streaking through the water.

The first explosion was like a thunderclap. In a split second Marshall saw the forward portion of the enemy's hull burst open and upward in one great searing orange ball of fire. The remaining torpedoes' detonations were all but lost in the devastation.

On the damaged U-boat the first stricken horror had changed to a wild scramble of running figures, some of whom had already reached the deck gun, where an officer was firing his pistol blindly across the narrow strip of water. Marshall ducked as a bullet clanged into the tower and shrieked away over the sea. He could see nothing of the milch cow. Just a huge pall of drifting smoke against the sky, a spreading pattern of oil and bobbing flotsam to mark her last dive.

He yelled, "Full ahead together. Port ten!"

He watched as Warwick's crew brought the Vierling's long muzzle around across the rail, following the other boat as it appeared to career drunkenly on their mounting bow wave.

"*Shoot!*" The gun bucked back on its springs, and a savage glare lit up the bridge. Marshall saw the other boat's periscope standards and radio antennae reel apart as Warwick's gunners found their mark. Another shell slammed into the exposed ballast tank, and it was possible to hear the surge of inrushing water. Some of the German gunners were running aft toward the tower. It was futile, for without engine power the U-boat was helpless.

The Vierling crackled viciously, the four barrels cutting down these same running men with the ease of a reaper in a field. The officer, isolated and alone, was reloading his pistol when a shell smashed him into oblivion.

U-192's conning tower shook violently, and a waterspout rocketed skyward a hundred yards from her side. Marshall knew the answer even as the lookout yelled, "Destroyer has opened fire, sir!"

Marshall spoke steadily into the speaking tube. "Secure the gun! Clear the bridge!"

Men tumbled into the hatch, dragging with them the machine guns, one still smoking as it vanished. Wild eyes and breathless voices, until only Marshall remained. The destroyer was approaching, her skipper probably imagining he had caught two U-boats in the act of sinking an unidentified ship.

Marshall crouched over the speaking tube as a shell screamed low overhead, the shock wave hitting his shoulders. "Dive! Dive! Dive! Ninety meters! Shut off for depth-charging!"

He closed the cock and paused to peer abeam. The stern of the stricken U-boat was just poking out of the seething bubbles and escaping oil.

Then he jumped into the hatch, feeling the hull falling steeply as Gerrard took her into a crash dive. He slammed the hatch and locked the wheel. Down into the control room. The lower hatch banged shut and he turned to meet Gerrard's gaze. "Done it, sir."

Marshall clung to the ladder, his chest heaving. He managed to nod. Then he replied, "Not too much time in hand." He felt completely spent and sick. Two submarines and some hundred and fifty men. Wiped out just like that. He swallowed hard. He hoped that Browning would be satisfied. Mission accomplished.

Overhead he heard the thrumming beat of the destroyer's racing screws, and then a depth charge exploded some distance away, like a muffled drum in a tunnel. The destroyer's detection gear had probably homed onto the sinking submarine.

He glanced at the men all around him as they listened and then understood. They were safe.

Chapter 3

Two days after her successful attack *U-192* had received a brief signal in her own top secret code. "Return to base forthwith."

The first part of the return passage had gathered something like a holiday atmosphere, as the boat had headed northeast, avoiding shipping lanes and spending most of the time on the surface. The men took turns on deck, sunning, and once even swimming.

When they had drawn nearer to the convoy routes and into the range of patrolling aircraft they had twice been faced with disaster. The first occasion had been while they were surfaced, charging batteries. A fat Sunderland flying boat had plunged out of low clouds, machine guns hammering, depth charges dropping from either wing, as the U-boat dived frantically for safety. Off the coast of Ireland they had been caught again, this time by a twin-engined fighter streaking out of the mist barely feet above the water. The bullets had clanged across casing and bridge.

For two days they had idled back and forth west of the Outer Hebrides, awaiting the right moment to meet their guide, the armed yacht *Lima*. During those last days Marshall had had plenty of time to watch his companions. Daily he had found it harder to meet Frenzel's eye or to join him in casual conversation. Soon Browning would break the news about his wife and child. And Gerrard seemed to grow more restless as hour by hour they crawled back and forth.

Marshall had spent less time than he would have liked with young Warwick. In the two months they had been at sea he had altered from a boy to a hollow-eyed stranger. Marshall was fully aware of the reason. He had seen him in the control room when they had heard the damaged submarine breaking up as she plunged to the seabed. Warwick had been shaking uncontrollably, his face like chalk. Marshall had heard Buck saying quietly to Gerrard one

491

night, "What can you expect, Number One? He's just a kid, seen nothing, knows nothing but what he's got from books. Then it all became real. And nasty."

It was to be hoped that some shore leave would make a difference. Otherwise, he would have to recommend that Warwick be transferred out of submarines. Too much depended on each of them. They needed one another's strength.

At the arranged time, as dusk was falling, they had turned toward the land. The sound of a small charge detonated underwater had told them their guide had arrived, and they had gone to periscope depth again, and followed *Lima*'s blue stern light in to the shore. When they surfaced, Loch Cairnbawn seemed exactly as before. It was April now, but the air was as keen as a knife, the choppy water just as dark as when they had left the place.

When he saw the tall side of the depot ship Marshall touched his face, thinking of a bath and change of clothes. He saw the lines snaking across a beam of light, heard the shouts from the waiting seaman, the grate of mooring cables.

"Stop together." He felt the bridge begin to roll as the loch's uneasy waters took charge.

He lowered his face to the speaking tube. "Ring off main motors. Send some extra hands up to help rig the awnings around the conning tower, just in case we're still on the secret list."

Feet clattered on the casing and a head appeared over the rim of the bridge. It was one of Browning's aides. He thrust out his hand and said, "Glad to see you! Captain Browning is waiting for you, but he wants to see your engineer officer first. What a rotten welcome for him."

Summoned, Frenzel thrust himself through the hatch. "What's all this, sir? I've a lot to do."

Marshall said quietly, "Get along over to Captain Browning. Your chief petty officer will watch things for you."

After a pause Frenzel replied, "Very well." He looked at the commander but did not seem to see him.

He knows, Marshall thought. He's guessed already.

WHEN Marshall walked into the big cabin below the *Guernsey*'s bridge, Browning strode across the carpet, both hands outstretched. "I can't say what it means to see you back safely."

490

Browning moved to the decanter and glasses, saying, "I saw Lieutenant Frenzel. He didn't say much. I think he knew why I'd sent for him." He handed a glass to Marshall and raised his own. "Well, here's to you, anyway. You've done damn well. I'm bloody proud of you." It was whisky, neat and fiery. After two months without any, Marshall could feel it going to his head.

They sat down opposite each other. Browning swallowed some whisky. "You bagged the milch cow, which the enemy'll be relying on still. We've heard nothing to suggest they know you sunk her." He shook his head. "And you caught another U-boat for good measure. Marvelous."

Marshall listened to the wind sighing against the hull. Despite the cabin's steamy heat he felt cold. He needed to bathe and change. Adjust his mind to an absence of danger.

Browning said suddenly, "The Admiralty has required us to hand over the captured codes. Escort group commanders, hunter-killer frigates and the rest will use 'em to full advantage. They insist that it will do far more good than individual operations like yours."

Marshall let the whisky burn across his tongue. "I expected that, sir. But of course it will mean that the enemy will realize what's happened just that much sooner. The codes will be changed. And what of us? Do we become His Majesty's U-boat and take a conventional place in things?"

Browning did not smile. "Well, not exactly. It is felt that you can do a lot to help in the same unorthodox way as before."

The door opened and a crisp voice asked, "All right to join the party, sir?" He did not wait for permission but strode in, a briefcase under one arm.

Marshall made to rise, but the newcomer waved him down. "Not to bother. You look bushed." He smiled, but without warmth.

"This is Commander Simeon." Browning sounded unusually formal. "He's been running our liaison with Intelligence."

Marshall eyed Simeon thoughtfully. Well-pressed and impeccable. The man who had married Gail, Bill's widow.

Simeon turned to Browning. "I'll take a glass, if there's one going, sir."

Marshall darted a quick glance at the elderly captain. It was sickening to see the way he shambled over to get a drink for his subordinate.

Simeon removed a pink file from his briefcase and opened it, one hand outstretched for the whisky. "Cheers," he said.

Marshall watched him coldly. No wonder Browning was in awe of him. This man was going somewhere, no matter who got in his way.

Simeon frowned and ran a finger down the file. "Strange how luck comes into even the best-laid plans. That Jerry who escaped from the Icelandic camp, for instance. He was found half-dead with cold less than a quarter of a mile from the place. But the fear of his escape was enough to get things *moving*, to send you off to sea double-quick. Without that, you'd have been rotting here in the loch for weeks." He looked at Browning. "By the way, sir, Operations has *U-192*'s report. I think they'd like your opinion." He walked to the table and picked up the decanter. "About now, I think, sir."

Browning walked to Marshall's chair. "I'll see you later." He did not turn toward Simeon as he added hotly, "Damn good to see a real submariner again." He slammed the door behind him.

Simeon shook his head. "Pathetic. Four years of war and we're still bogged down with old-age pensioners like him."

Marshall replied evenly, "Not too many pensioners about with Victoria Crosses, I'd have thought?" He smiled. "Sir."

"Possibly, but I'm not here to discuss him. The important thing is that I, that is *we*, have another job lined up." He leaned on the desk, his eyes very bright. "The Atlantic battle is on the turn. More U-boats sunk, more convoys getting through. In North Africa the Germans will be forced to surrender or get out. After that the Allies will have to mount an invasion in Europe." He lowered his voice slightly. "The top secret label is on this, of course, but we're going into Sicily and up through Italy. Our people will try to make a secret pact with the Eyeties, so that as we advance they will come over to our side."

Marshall watched Simeon. He could not see what Gail had found in him, what had made her turn her back on Bill.

"For years we've had agents in every occupied country, supplying anyone who can pull a trigger or place a dagger in Jerry's ribs. These partisans, patriots or bloody bandits, call them what you will, are the ones who can help us."

Marshall asked, "Where do I come in?"

"Where you have the best chances of continuing to use deception. In the Med. You know the stamping ground well. You will operate whenever and wherever you can do the most good. Cloak-and-dagger operations. Later, landing raiding parties. That sort of thing."

Marshall eyed him coolly. How much time had Simeon put in at sea? he wondered. "I can see the possibilities," he said. "But this last job taught me that it's no fun being hunted by your own ships and aircraft. It's a double strain on my crew to be an enemy of both sides. And what about leave?"

"Leave? You have to be joking. It's asking a helluva lot from you. I know it. But we simply can't afford to allow the grass to grow under our feet."

Marshall stood up, seeing himself in the bulkhead mirror, tousled hair and oil-stained sweater against Simeon's sleek image. "I'd like to tell my officers in my own way, sir."

"Certainly. Might be able to wangle a couple of days' leave for a few special cases." He was groping vaguely through his briefcase when he asked, "I believe you knew my wife at one time?"

Marshall watched him. "Yes."

"Splendid." He was being very casual. "I've got a commandeered house a few miles from the loch. You must drop in and have a bite to eat." He swung around. "How about it?"

"Thanks." Marshall paused. "It was bad luck about Bill Wade."

"Wade?" Simeon smiled distantly. "Oh, yes, it was. Hardly any of the old crowd left now. Frightful waste." He snapped the briefcase shut quickly. "See you tomorrow." He strode to the door.

For a few quick seconds Marshall had seen through Simeon's façade of efficiency and self-control. It could have been resentment harbored because he had known Gail even before Bill.

He picked up his cap and left the cabin. When he reached U-192 he found his engineer officer alone in the wardroom, staring at the glass between his fingers.

"All right, Chief?" Marshall's voice was soft.

Frenzel stared up at him. "You *knew*, didn't you, sir?"

Marshall nodded. "Yes. I'm sorry. I had to agree."

Frenzel pulled another glass from a locker. "I'd have done the same in your shoes." His hand shook as he slopped gin into the glass. "Join me?"

Marshall sat down slowly. "I think I can arrange leave for you, Chief. Before we shove off again."

Frenzel drained his glass, some of the gin running down his chin like tears. "Leave? Thanks, but no. What I like about the sea. You get lost in it. You forget."

He stood up and carefully removed two photographs from his bunk. As he laid them in his wallet something dropped across them. This time it was not gin. He said quietly, "Don't worry about me. I'll be all right."

Marshall moved toward the door. "I never doubted it."

WITHIN two days of her return to Loch Cairnbawn things had started to move rapidly for *U-192*. Almost hourly, or so it appeared to Marshall, mysterious experts arrived to whisk the submariners away to some new instruction. Shooting with pistols and automatic weapons. Hauling each other up and down gullies and cliffs. After the first grumbles they had settled down to their training with enthusiasm. It was different, and they had soon become hardened to the exercises and the Scottish weather. They discovered, too, that they had drawn closer together as a unit.

On the last full day of training Browning had come to Marshall and said, "Thought you ought to know. The Germans will learn today that we have the crew of *U-192* as prisoners of war. We couldn't keep it secret forever. It's not humane."

"They'll know about us then, sir."

Browning had shaken his head. "Not as far as I can discover. The German crewmen were taken away before our people got to the fjord. As far as they know, their boat is lying on the bottom where they left her. But when you go on your next mission you'll be without your cover. *U-192* has ceased to exist. Your guise for each operation will be as you think fit. Visual, rather than having false papers, so to speak."

Browning had had a bit of good news, too. Some leave had been granted. Local liberty for the bulk of the company. Forty-eight hours' home leave for a handful of others. Gerrard had gone south to see his wife. But most of the men remained on the *Guernsey* while *U-192* got a going over. They restricted their runs ashore to the naval canteen and nearby pubs.

A twenty-year-old stoker named John Willard went ashore on

local leave with no intention of returning at all. His desertion cast a pall of gloom over the rest of the company, spoiling their well-justified pride in what they had achieved.

Simeon said of the deserter, "He must be caught and brought back. I don't care if some MP blows his stupid brains out!"

It was never healthy to keep a man aboard a submarine who tried to desert. There was too much scope for willful damage when a man hung under a cloud like that. But it was equally unsafe to let the man pass through court-martial and punishment, where he might blurt out the secret of *U-192*.

The young stoker was picked up within fifty miles of the loch and brought back to the *Guernsey*. As Marshall sat that afternoon in his borrowed cabin wondering what he should say to the man, Simeon stepped in and slid the door shut behind him.

"You going to see this chap now?" He threw his oak-leaved cap onto a chair. Marshall nodded. "By the way," Simeon said, "you'll be shoving off in about two days' time. Your orders will be arriving later this afternoon. I'll fill you in on details."

Marshall was about to answer when there was a tap at the door and Devereaux stepped over the coaming, his features urbane as he reported, "Prisoner and escort, sir."

The stoker was duly marched in and stood between his escort and Starkie, the coxswain. Willard was small and round-faced, looking even younger than his years. In his best uniform, he presented the perfect picture of innocence and vulnerability.

"What do you want to tell me, Willard?" Marshall kept his voice calm.

"Say, sir?" Willard looked about to crack. He shuffled his feet.

Devereaux said, "Tell the captain why you tried to desert."

"I dunno what to say, sir." Willard's chin trembled slightly as he added, "It's me mother, sir."

Marshall dropped his gaze to the desk. "If your mother is sick, you should have come to one of your officers."

Willard spoke very quietly. "Me dad's a prisoner of war, sir. Only heard last year. We all thought he was dead. When I was on me last long leave I went home." He swallowed hard. "She was—" He tried again. "She was with this bloke."

Marshall said, "All right, Cox'n, you and the escort can fall out." He looked at Devereaux. "You, too."

The door closed behind them. Marshall wished Simeon had gone with the others. He asked, "Is that why you headed for home?"

The stoker nodded jerkily. "She wrote to me, sir. This bloke had been knocking her about. Threatened to carve her. He's been living off her, you see. *Put her on the street.*"

Marshall looked up, seeing the agony on Willard's face. He asked gently, "What did you hope to do?"

"All this training we've had, sir. I've never been no good in a scrap, but those commando blokes taught me *how*, sir. How to fight dirty, to win."

The telephone jangled on the desk, and Marshall snatched it up. "I said no calls!"

It was Browning. He was speaking very quietly. "Sorry about this. Is Simeon still with you?"

Marshall said, "Yes, sir."

Browning coughed. "Bit awkward. I've got a call on the ship's line from the base. Personal. For you." A pause. "Can you take it? I'm afraid she says it must be now."

The phone crackled as Browning transferred the call. Then a woman's voice said, "Lieutenant Commander Marshall, please."

"This is Marshall." He heard her quick intake of breath.

"Steven, this is Gail."

"Well?"

"Roger's going to ask you to come over to the house." She spoke quickly, as if afraid he would hang up. "I knew you'd make some excuse not to come, so I thought if I—if I said I *wanted* you to . . ."

Marshall cleared his throat. "Right." What the hell was he saying? "That will be fine." He put down the phone.

Simeon said sourly, "Browning? Couldn't it wait?"

Marshall looked at the stoker. "You've been a fool, do you know that? You were going to pick a fight with some tough and probably cut his throat into the bargain. What good would that do for your mother?"

Willard said in a whisper, "Had to do something, sir."

"Right now I'm depending on you, Willard. Your place is among your friends, people who rely on you."

He was only half listening to his own words. Why had she called him like that? Taking the risk of rousing Simeon's suspicion.

He continued. "I'll get the welfare people to check up on your story. If it's true, I'll do what I can. If not, I'll see you stand trial. But either way, I want you *here*, under my command."

"Yes, sir. Thank you very much, sir."

"Fall out." The stoker turned and almost tripped over the coaming as he stumbled through the doorway.

Simeon opened his cigarette case. "Hell, his mother's on the street and he wants to save her!"

Marshall stood up, suddenly sick of Simeon. "What would *you* have felt?" he said.

Simeon raised his hands. "Keep your hair on!" Then he said in a matter-of-fact tone, "Come to dinner tonight."

Marshall's answer came out firmly. "Thanks, sir. I will."

MARSHALL studied himself in the mirror for several seconds. Despite a steward's efforts, his best uniform still showed a few creases in the wrong places.

"All set?" Simeon appeared swinging his cap. "Now you look a proper hero, or as Buster would have it, a *real* submariner!"

Marshall smiled dryly. "Two a penny around here, I imagine."

Together they made their way to the upper deck and then into a waiting motorboat. Their shoes rang hollowly as they walked to a well-polished car, and a seaman stepped out, holding the door for Simeon to enter the driver's seat. Simeon waited for Marshall to get in and then called to the seaman, "Give her a good polish again tomorrow." He spoke as if the man were a personal servant.

Once past the gates Simeon pressed on speed with a practiced recklessness. Marshall wondered if the importance he attached to his driving skill meant he secretly envied a man who had seen close combat. The car was a good one. Expensive.

In about half an hour they shot through a wide gateway and slithered to a halt. Simeon glanced quickly at Marshall. "It's not much of a house. But I got the admiral to lend me one of his chefs, so the food's palatable."

It was a very pleasant house, comfortably furnished. A log fire burned cheerfully in an open grate, and the room to which Simeon guided Marshall gave off an air of rural prosperity.

"A few others for dinner, I'm afraid. Can't be helped." He gestured to a cabinet. "Mix yourself something. I'm going to wash." He

499

added, "Not like you. Didn't get time before I left the *Guernsey*."

Marshall smiled. Simeon always had to prove that he was the busy one. A man in constant demand.

He opened the cabinet and regarded the bottles with surprise. No shortages here. He selected some malt whisky and half filled a glass. It could turn out to be a tense evening. A door opened behind him and he turned, the words ready on his lips. But it was not Gail.

The young woman was dressed in a tweed skirt and plain black jersey. In the soft lamplight Marshall thought she looked tired.

He said, "I'm Steven Marshall."

He watched her as she moved to a chair. Very easily and lightly. Like a cat. She had short dark hair, and her eyes, which were large and partly in shadow, seemed very steady.

She said with a faint French accent, "Chantal Travis." Then she smiled. "My home was in Nantes."

"Are you staying here?"

She smiled again, but she did not answer his question. "I see you have many decorations. More than I expected."

Simeon must have told her about him. "There's a war on."

"So I believe." She sounded distant. "A war."

He said quietly, "That was a damn stupid thing to say. I was forgetting. Is your family still in France?"

She nodded slowly. "My father and mother are in Nantes."

Marshall remembered her name. Travis. "You're married?"

Again the slow nod. "An Englishman." She looked at the glass in his hand. "If I may have a choice, I would rather have a drink than any more questions." She smiled at his confusion. "Pardon me. That was unforgivable."

Marshall held up some sherry and she nodded. As he poured it she said, "Commander Simeon's wife told me about what you did in the Mediterranean."

He handed her the glass. "Have you known her long?" He groaned. "God, I'm doing it again."

She laughed. "It is all right. No, I met her recently."

Marshall sat down opposite her. It was like some invisible force between them. Holding him back. If only he had more time, he would like to stay with her. Just to hear her voice, watch the stillness in her.

Voices murmured outside and Simeon strode in with two army officers. One Marshall recognized as a medical corps major. They shook hands all around and the conversation became general.

Marshall tensed as a voice said, "Hello, Steven. After all this time." Gail was wearing a flowered dress which left her arms bare. She was exactly as he remembered her.

He rose. "You look marvelous."

Her hand felt ice-cold despite the blazing fire, and he thought it was trembling slightly.

Simeon called, "New dress? Bit bare, old girl, what?"

The major murmured approvingly. "You make a sight to remember. Don't listen to him."

The dinner was excellent—plentiful food and ample wine. As the steward poured the brandy he bent down and whispered in Simeon's ear. Simeon stood up. "Dispatch rider outside. Better go and see what's he's brought." He looked around the table. "Make yourselves comfortable."

The two army officers escorted the French girl to the adjoining room. Marshall looked at Gail. They were alone.

She said quickly, "I had to see you. To tell you about Bill."

"I *know* about Bill." He could not hide his bitterness. "Saw him before he was killed."

"You don't understand," she said. "How can you?"

"Perhaps I don't. All I know is that while Bill was in the Med you decided to leave him to marry Simeon. What else is there?"

She stood up and walked to the fireplace.

"Why did you ever marry Bill?"

"You know why." She met his eyes steadily. "I wanted you, but you were so sure you were going to be killed, remember? So damned sure."

Marshall stared at her. "D'you know what you're saying?"

She nodded. "I've had plenty of time to think about those days we had together. I've never regretted one of them." She swallowed. "Not one. But I wanted to marry, to have a home."

He said, "I'm sorry. I was very fond of Bill."

She moved toward him, her eyes searching his face. "Be honest, won't you! When I married him you felt guilt, too, didn't you? Because you remembered how it was before."

She was almost touching him. "Oh, Steven, you've changed so

much." She reached out and took his hands. "The war has turned you into a machine!"

He looked down at her, his defenses crumbling. Then his arms were around her and her face was against his chest. The words burst out like a flood. "I *have* to be the way I am. You don't know what it's like. Always telling others to keep going, to remember the ship, the fight, the target, *anything* to hold the whole show together! I couldn't have let you share that sort of life."

She said, "I would have. Willingly."

His hands were on her bare shoulders. "What about Simeon?"

She did not lower her eyes. "He gives me assurance. In his own strange way he needs me." She shook her head. "But *we* had something else again."

The door creaked and Marshall saw her eyes fill with alarm. He turned quickly. But it was Chantal Travis.

She stood very still, looking at them. Then she said, "Sorry. The wrong room, I think."

When the door closed behind her Gail said, "One day, Steven. If we could meet somewhere. No recriminations. No comparisons." She was pleading.

Perhaps his anger at her marrying Simeon had been caused by his own loss, as well as by Bill's. Whatever the true reason, it was too late now. "It's no use," he said. "It's over."

"Only if you want it to be, Steven."

The door swung open again. Simeon looked at them blandly. Then he strode over and put his arm around her shoulder. "Old confidences, eh? Ah well, the party's over, children."

Marshall nodded. In more ways than one, he thought.

Chapter 4

THE day after Simeon's dinner party Marshall received a sudden change of orders. The time had been brought forward twenty-four hours. He would slip from the depot ship at 2000 that evening.

As the sides of the loch dipped into shadow he sat in his cabin making a last-minute check. Gerrard, who had arrived back that forenoon, waited in the doorway as Marshall signed his readiness report. Marshall said, "Can't think of anything else. Have you inspected the new gear?"

Gerrard nodded. He looked tired. "Yes, sir." He smiled sadly. "Back to the Med. Would you believe it."

Buck peered in. "Commander Simeon is coming aboard, sir."

"Very well. We'll be slipping in about thirty minutes."

Gerrard moved away as Simeon appeared in the doorway. He said crisply, "Buttoned up. Ready for business. Last mail ashore and censored. Twice. I don't think we've forgotten anything."

"Why was the sailing time brought forward, sir?"

"There's a westbound convoy gathering at Greenock. Don't want you to get bogged under with that lot. *Or* with this boat's previous masters, if they're hanging around after that convoy."

"Captain Browning's not back from London yet?"

"What's that got to do with it?" Simeon frowned.

Edgy. It was as Marshall had suspected. Simeon had brought the time forward so that Browning, called to a meeting at the Admiralty, would not be here to see them go. It would be *his* show.

Simeon said, "You will be picking up three agents from one of our launches. I've already had their gear sent aboard, but their presence must be kept secret to the last minute."

Marshall stood up and they walked into the passageway and on to the control room, where Frenzel was leaning over his panel in close conversation with his chief petty officer. If it were possible, Frenzel had given even more energy and time to his engines since Browning had told him about his family.

Marshall led the way up the ladder, and they stood on the bridge watching the men slacking off cables. A voice rattled up one of the tubes. "Captain, sir. Radio operator reports ten minutes to go. *Lima* is on station to lead us out."

"Acknowledge."

Simeon said, "I'd better get over to *Guernsey*'s radio department, in case anything goes wrong at the last minute and I have to make new decisions." He held out his hand. "Good luck, then." He swung over the side of the bridge and dropped to the deck below.

Marshall moved to the speaking tube. "Control room. This is the captain. Prepare to get under way. Main motors ready."

Yeoman Blythe said, "There's *Lima*, sir. Just coming around *Guernsey*'s bows."

"Good."

He thought suddenly of Gail. The feel of her skin. The smell of her hair. "The war's turned you into a machine," she'd said. Damn her. What could he do about it?

A light stabbed from the *Guernsey*'s bridge, and Blythe shuttered his acknowledgment with the hand lamp.

" 'Proceed when ready,' sir."

"Very good. Inform the control room." He hesitated, knowing Blythe was waiting. It was expected. The thing to do. "Make to *Guernsey*, Yeoman. 'Thanks for your help.'" He doubted they would ever tie up alongside her again.

"Let go aft!" He waited. "Slow astern together." He waved to Buck. "Let go forward!"

Stern first, they edged clear of the towering depot ship, the water sluicing along the saddle tanks.

"*Lima*'s gathered way, sir."

"Very well." He crossed to the speaking tube. "Stop together." He watched the pale blue stern light. "Slow ahead together. Port twenty."

"First lieutenant here, sir. Follow the light again?"

"Yes." He heard the periscope shift in its sleeve. "We will be taking on passengers in an hour's time."

He felt the hull steady as the rudder came around, and knew that Gerrard had her under control. "Fall out casing party."

The seamen came swarming onto the bridge and down through the open hatch. Then Warwick, dragging his feet, his head toward the dark slab of land.

"Keep a good lookout." Marshall glanced at Blythe's outline. "The launch will signal. But check the code." He turned to Warwick. "Not like our other departure, Sub."

"It seems no time since we got back, sir. And now—" He did not finish it.

"I know. Can't be helped." Marshall watched the last of the light fading above some hills. "I wasn't expecting to go back to the Med." The words just seemed to come out. "Not after fourteen bloody months of it." He clenched his fists. Saying it was enough. Fourteen months. How long would it be this time?

Warwick asked, "Was it that bad, sir?"

"No." He felt the sweat under his cap. Ice-cold. "Nothing we couldn't handle." Liar. Liar. Why don't you tell him?

He added harshly, "Tell the helmsman he's too far on *Lima*'s port quarter! And, Sub, you're supposed to be able to stand a watch, so *do* it!"

"Yes, sir. I'm sorry." Warwick groped for the speaking tube.

Blythe watched them and sucked his teeth. Warwick was a good kid but wet behind the ears. Thank the Lord it wasn't one of the other officers on the bridge, he thought. That tough egg, Buck, or old "Snooty" Devereaux. They would have recognized the skipper's trouble in a flash. Poor bastard. He's got to carry the whole lot of us. But it's him who needs help.

On and on down the loch, following the light, with only a gentle swish of water to break the stillness.

Then, "Control room to captain." It was Gerrard. "Should be making the pickup at any minute now, sir."

"Very good, Number One. Tell Petty Officer Cain to get his cable-handling party on deck at the double."

Blythe called, "Signal from *Lima*, sir. 'Boat to starboard.'"

There it was. On the button. A black blob across the loch.

"Stop together." He climbed onto the starboard gratings to watch the little launch as it chugged toward the idling submarine. Then the jolting groan of timber against steel, and scrambling figures were hauled onto the casing. He heard the seamen and their passengers groping and stumbling through the hatch, and wondered what sort of men volunteered for such dangerous missions.

He said to Warwick, "Tell Lieutenant Buck to come up and relieve me. I'd better greet our visitors."

Warwick said quietly, "I can do it, sir."

Marshall could feel the intensity of Warwick's eagerness. He said, "Of course, Sub. She's all yours."

He hurried down to the wardroom and almost cannoned into Churchill, who was carrying a coffeepot. The three passengers were unbuttoning their hooded windproof jackets. One, sharp-featured and tall, turned and thrust out his hand. "I'm Carter. We'll try to keep out of your way, Captain."

Marshall smiled. "Good to have you aboard."

The man added, "This is Toby Moss, and I think you know our third member. Mrs. Travis." She was watching his face with an expression of tired gravity.

"Yes. We have met," he said quietly. He added, "We've two spare bunks in here for the men. Mrs. Travis will have my cabin."

505

Carter removed his jacket and sat down. He said, "I expect Commander Simeon has told you your part in things."

Marshall nodded slowly, his eyes on the girl. She was sipping coffee, holding the thick mug with both hands. "Yes, he did. Your equipment is stowed forward."

She looked up and saw him watching her. "I hope you enjoyed the party last night, Captain?" Her eyes were mocking or accusing, it was hard to tell.

He replied flatly, "Some of it." He left the wardroom and when he reached the bridge he took several deep breaths. He wondered about this girl. Perhaps she was a friend of Simeon's. And now she was here, penned up with the rest of them until . . . He thought suddenly of her tenseness. Her way of watching and listening. She was, like him, going back to something and hating it.

DURING the first two days of the passage south toward the Bay of Biscay, Marshall saw the girl only a few times. Each time it seemed as if she had not moved. Always sitting in the cabin chair, wide-awake.

On the third day he sat in the wardroom drowsing over a cup of coffee. The motion was sickening, for the boat was running on the surface, and the sea was rough. When he looked up he saw her standing in the doorway, clutching the swaying curtains. He got up and piloted her to one of the bench seats.

She said, "It's terrible. I've just been sick."

Marshall said, "I'm sorry. The bay is often like this, I'm afraid."

She stared at him. "Biscay? Are we there already?"

"We're about two hundred miles southwest of Brest. We're pretty safe out here, if we keep our guard up."

"Brest. I've been there several times."

He asked carefully, "Your husband? Is he in France?"

She shook her head. "Italy. We were working together. But I cannot talk about it."

"I hope my lads are looking after you?"

"Thank you, yes. It is like being with friends." She shivered. "I will miss this security."

He said gently, "They'll miss you, too. As I will."

The girl stood up, her features alert again. "I imagine that you will have much to fill your daily lives, Captain."

He watched her as she moved unsteadily around the table. "You were wrong about Gail and me, you know. It was something which happened a long while ago. It's over now."

"It's not my concern!" She swung around and looked at him with something like anger. "I don't care what you do!"

In the doorway she encountered Gerrard. "Would it be possible to go on deck?" she asked him. "The air might help."

Gerrard looked at Marshall, his eyes questioning.

Marshall nodded. "Very well. Tell the bridge. Warwick's on watch now. Ask him to fit her with a harness."

"Thank you, Captain. I appreciate it."

After they had left, Marshall went to the control room. He swung the forward periscope in a full circle, watching the spray bursting over the hull and lifting high above the bridge in long tattered streamers. Visibility was very poor. He could picture Warwick and the lookouts with the girl, standing just below the periscope standards. Warwick would hear the periscope moving and joke that the captain was trying to watch them. He swung the lens toward the sky, then froze. There was a brief flash between the clouds. He stared, mesmerized. There it was again.

"Klaxon! Aircraft on the port bow!" He clawed his way up the ladder, his mind blank to everything but that menacing shadow. It might not have seen the submarine in such turbulent waters, but one thing was certain, nobody on the bridge had seen it.

As the klaxon screamed out from below, Marshall hauled himself through the hatch, yelling, "Aircraft! Port bow!" The girl was holding on to the screen, and he tore at her harness. "Clear the bridge! Diving stations!"

As the diesels cut out, Marshall heard the plane's approaching roar. He pulled the girl toward the hatch. A lookout guided her down. A great wave burst over the conning tower, and he heard the sharp rattle of machine guns, the clang and whine of metal on metal all around them. A huge shadow swept across the bridge. The plane was barely a hundred feet overhead.

Despite the urge to get below, Marshall could only stare at the seaman on the edge of the hatch. His hands were like claws as they dug at his chest, his blood mingling with the spray. Someone pulled the man below, and Warwick almost fell after him.

Marshall jumped onto the ladder, the sea spurting up over the

screen even as he slammed the hatch and spun the locking wheel. He had to shut his ears to the man's terrible cries, to everything but the need to get the boat away.

"One hundred meters! Group up, full ahead together! Shut off for depth-charging!" He saw Gerrard watching him. "Liberator. Must have extra fuel tanks."

They looked at the depth gauges and then at the telltales as the planesmen fought to pull her out of the dive.

"Hundred meters, sir," Gerrard reported.

Something creaked violently as the hull took the pressure. A seaman jerked with alarm, as if it were a depth charge. But none came. The airmen had been as surprised as they had been with the sudden encounter.

It was very quiet when Buck said, "He's dead, Captain."

Marshall turned and stared at the little group below the conning-tower hatch. The dead lookout flat on his back, Buck and the girl on their knees beside him. Warwick was standing slightly apart.

The girl said huskily, "It was my fault. I shouldn't have gone up there." She reached out and touched Warwick's hand. "You couldn't help it." There were bright tears in her eyes.

Marshall's voice was flat. "You must always anticipate enemy bombers." What was he saying? It had been a Liberator. One of their own. Probably winging back to base now to report they had jumped a U-boat and gunned down some of the deck party.

He continued, "Take the body to the torpedo space. We'll bury him tonight." He heard the girl sobbing quietly and took her arm. "Come on. We need some coffee."

IT WAS a week after their nerve-jarring confrontation with the patrolling bomber that they had again had a most testing moment, this time while getting through the Strait of Gibraltar. Two British destroyers had been sweeping back and forth, carrying out a patrol. Fortunately an ancient, rusty Turkish freighter had come to their rescue, albeit unknowingly. She had steamed toward the destroyers with careless indifference.

Submerged, the submarine had followed her past the destroyers, keeping so close that any sign on the British sonar would be attributed to the freighter.

Unseen past Gibraltar and along the Spanish coast, past the

Balearic Islands and Corsica. Several times they had been made to run deep, as fast-moving vessels had pounded overhead, or some suspicious ship had been sighted. Now they were in enemy territory, patrolled by aircraft from Italy and Sardinia.

Marshall stood by the chart table watching as Devereaux skillfully managed parallel rulers and dividers. Devereaux straightened up. "That's it, sir. We will be at the rendezvous point in thirty minutes."

"Captain, sir?" A messenger hovered by his elbow. "Major Carter asked if you'd mind joining him in the wardroom."

He had hardly seen any of the passengers since the bay. They had been getting all the rest they could and going over their plans for their mission. For *now*.

He strode to the wardroom and paused in the doorway studying the three. The girl was wearing a black coat and sat on one of the bench seats, a suitcase on her lap. Moss had changed into a leather jacket and wore a jaunty beret. As for Major Carter, he could have been any European businessman.

Carter asked, "What d'you think, Captain? Good enough for first night at the Duchess Theatre?" He grinned. "Take care of my army clothes, won't you? Or I'll have it docked from my pay."

Marshall nodded. "I've told Petty Officer Cain to have your gear taken to the forehatch."

Carter said, "Come on, Moss. We'd better check it before we leave." They strolled out of the wardroom.

Marshall said quietly, "I hope everything goes well for you."

She stood up. "Thank you. So we are at the proper place?"

He watched the shadows below her eyes, wanting to touch her. "Yes. Midway between Corsica and the island of Elba." He hesitated. "Will it be difficult?"

"Once we have left you we will be taken to Elba. When the time is right we shall cross to the mainland." She made it sound so simple. Yet it was over ten miles from Elba to the Italian coast. She continued quietly, "We will pick up the train and make our way south. To Naples. Then we shall see."

"The major seems a pretty competent chap."

"Yes, he's good. We will travel together, but separately, if you understand me. If one gets—" She looked away. "You know what I mean. If that happens, the others keep going."

He moved closer and took her hand in his. "I wish to God you were staying here."

"So you said earlier, Captain." But she did not remove her hand.

"Or that I were coming with you."

She smiled. "They would sniff you out in five minutes! But thank you all the same." She gave a small shrug. "I am sorry for some of the things I said."

He said, "I hope we can meet again."

"You'll soon forget about me. That is good." Then she said quickly, "But maybe we *will* meet someday." She picked up her suitcase and he followed her into the control room.

Gerrard said, "All ready, sir."

He glanced at the clock. It was two o'clock in the morning. "Very well. Pass the word. Silent routine in the boat."

He hung on the moment, watching the girl as she waited for a seaman to guide her toward the rest of her party. She turned as if to watch the transformation. From a man who wanted, needed her to stay. To being a captain again.

He said, "Slow ahead together. Group down." A look through the periscope showed the lights of a small fishing fleet some miles away. "Stand by to surface."

It was surprisingly warm on the open bridge. Marshall heard a swishing sound as the rubber dinghy was hauled through the big forehatch. It was always a bad time. With the hull surfaced and the hatch open. Unable to dive if the worst happened.

He held his breath and then steadied his glasses on a small shadow moving on the water.

A lookout confirmed it. "Boat, sir. Starboard beam."

He snapped, "Stop together. Make the signal!"

Buck flashed a shaded flashlight toward the shadow and Marshall waited. He could almost feel the tracer bullets which could come shrieking out of the darkness. Instead he saw a brief stab of light. He let out his breath and called, "Cast off the dinghy!"

A splash and then spurts of phosphorescence from the paddles. The dinghy was merging with the night and with the fishing boat, which had slued around to meet them. He thought of the girl who would be going south to Naples, over two hundred miles, and of the many checkpoints, examinations of passes, questions to which she must have the perfect answers.

"Dinghy's returned and secured, sir!"

"Very well. Close the forehatch." He moved to the speaking tube. "Slow ahead together." He was still thinking about her, the immensity of her loneliness. Of his own.

For six days they continued on a southerly course, skirting the Sicilian coast before turning northeast toward the heel of Italy. It was maddening to see the dazzling sunlight whenever they crept up to periscope depth, then to turn and see the men with their worn faces, their bodies starved of fresh air and the sun's warmth.

Marshall sat at his small desk, which was strewn with papers. "We're going into the Adriatic," he said to Gerrard. "It looks as if the enemy will throw in the towel in North Africa anytime now. The Allies will be getting ready to invade their territory for a change, and Captain Browning seems confident that the Germans have been fooled into believing we're going to invade through Greece and up into the Balkans. Our job is to add to that impression. Intelligence reports that a floating dock is being moved down the Adriatic to Bari. So it looks as if they're sold on the idea."

"The dock would be ready to repair any of their large units which might get damaged in our invasion, eh?"

"Right. We're going to blow up the dock with a big bang. Make it look as if we're desperately doing everything we can to make it easier for our side when the big day dawns."

"I see," Gerrard said. "If we have to show ourselves, our future prospects are a bit grim. But it's not a bad scheme. The Jerries will probably move more naval units to the area, and might even send more troops to Yugoslavia and Greece on the strength of it."

"That's the idea." Marshall thrust his hands into his pockets. "Well, like it or not, we're going through the Otranto Strait tonight. After that we'll find the dock."

Thirty-six hours later they were creeping around the Monte Gargano peninsula, one hundred and twenty miles up the Adriatic, keeping close to the Italian shore. It had been easier than Marshall had dared hope to slip through the Otranto Strait, between Italy's heel and the coast of Albania. They had sighted one patrolling destroyer, and had picked up some fast-moving hydrophone effect on the sonar, which had suggested the enemy had some torpedo boats in the area.

Marshall stood by the conning-tower ladder as Devereaux worked on his chart. They had moved past Bari the previous day, but there had been no sign of the floating dock. If they did not meet it in the next few hours, what would he do? Keep going all the way to Trieste, where it was supposed to have started from?

Speke, the senior sonar operator, said sharply, "HE bearing three one zero." A pause. "Slow reciprocating, sir. Still very faint."

Marshall said, "Periscope depth." It did not sound like the target, but they might have to alter course.

"Fourteen meters, sir."

Marshall waited for the periscope to hiss smoothly from its well. A quick look around and overhead, and then on to the bearing, where he saw the other vessel. He said, "A gray motor yacht." It was just possible to see the tiny flag on her mast. "Italian. Antisubmarine patrol."

Behind him he heard somebody murmur, "Thought it was the old *Lima* coming to look for us!" Someone laughed.

Speke called, "Getting more HE, sir, same bearing. Heavier but very faint. Too slow for a warship."

Gerrard said quietly, "One of the dock's tugs—"

The sonar operator interrupted. "Getting jumbled HE now, sir. Might be another ship."

Marshall brought the periscope lens to full power, and he felt his heart thump against his ribs. The dock loomed through the mist, half-shrouded in haze and the smoke from a tug. It was like looking at a giant building which had somehow got swept out to sea.

"Action stations, Number One." He straightened his back. "Down periscope." He shut his ears to the grating klaxon as he said, "Tell Warwick to get ready. We're going in surfaced."

AFTER the cool damp of the enclosed hull the heat on the bridge was fierce. Marshall lifted the glasses and held them on the yacht. She was zigzagging slowly, her raked stem making a show of spray in the bright sunlight. He said, "The escort's skipper's not even seen us yet. When he does, be ready."

Beside him Buck was adjusting the torpedo sights. In his German cap and leather coat he was like a stranger. Marshall shifted his gaze to the casing below. There, too, it seemed as if the boat had been returned to her original owners. Warwick in his cap and shorts, a Luger hanging prominently from one hip, and beside him the gun crew attired in their bright life jackets.

When he looked again at the yacht he saw the towering shape of the dock looming astern of her, its outline still hazy. Heavy smoke beyond the slow-moving huddle betrayed the presence of another tug.

Buck glanced at Marshall. "What d'you think, sir? Shall we fire a full salvo right away?"

Marshall shook his head. "No. If we fire now, we might only hit the yacht. We'll need minimum depth settings on all torpedoes. Otherwise they might pass right under the dock."

He heard the yeoman snap, "They've seen us, sir!" as a light blinked from the yacht's bridge.

Blythe lifted his hand lamp. "Reply?"

"Not yet. Let 'em sweat for a bit."

Marshall tried to picture his boat as she would look to the oncoming vessels. The U-boat's number had been replaced by a large Iron Cross. It had been badly scored by sea and slime, but should appear authentic enough.

"There it is again, sir."

"Very well. Make the reply."

Through a speaking tube he heard one of Buck's team intone, "All tubes standing by, sir."

Marshall licked his lips. "Depth setting of three meters. But we must close the range still farther."

The yacht's course was bringing her slowly toward the submarine's starboard bow. He could see a few figures in white uniforms on her deck and more grouped around a businesslike-looking gun just forward of the bridge.

Blythe asked, "Shall I hoist the colors, sir?"

Marshall nodded. "Yes. We'll go the whole way." He heard the squeak of halyards and saw the big scarlet flag with its black cross and swastika rise to the periscope standards.

Blythe said, "Damn! They've got some lighters tied to the side of the dock, sir." It seemed likely that the enemy had lashed the lighters to the dock's sides as protection. A single torpedo, even a pair, might explode against the lighters without real damage to the dock itself.

Marshall leaned over the bridge screen. "Sub! Get ready to do your stuff in German if they draw closer!" When he looked again he saw the dock fully for the first time. It rode above its reflection like a pale cliff, with a spidery upperworks of derricks and gantries. He saw the lighters, long low craft, four of them. The towing tug was a great brute of a thing. The second one was still hidden astern.

The armed yacht was less than a thousand yards away now and would soon lead the slow procession across the submarine's starboard quarter. The range of the target would be just right.

"Get ready." He lowered his eyes to the sights and held his breath as first the yacht, then the towing tug and then the mass of dock moved ponderously into the sights. "Stand by one to four." He could feel tension all around him. Now or never.

"Fire one!" He felt the hull buck.

"Torpedo running, sir!" Buck held his stopwatch, his sharp features contorted against the glare.

"Fire two!"

Marshall heard the sudden shriek of a siren and knew they had been discovered. He snapped, "Gun crews get ready. *Open fire!*"

The Vierling settled its four muzzles on the yacht. Four lines of tracer ripped across the water with the sound of a band saw. Pieces of wood, steel and rigging were hurled in all directions.

Marshall moved toward the speaking tube and then felt himself hurled backward as a deafening explosion shook the bridge, followed instantly by a blinding blue flash directly below the bows.

Buck was yelling, "Bloody fish must have nose-dived and hit the bottom!" He ducked wildly as a stream of red tracer ripped over the bridge and hammered against the steel.

Marshall was almost unable to speak. If that faulty torpedo had damaged their hull, they might as well surrender right now. But he dragged himself to the speaking tube. "Carry on with the torpedo attack!" The yacht was swinging across their line of advance, with two machine guns firing from the bridge while the deck gun groped steadily toward them.

A dull boom echoed across the water. He swung his glasses on the dock and saw smoke drifting above the lighters, or where two of them had been. Another explosion slammed over the calm water, marking the arrival of their second torpedo.

"All torpedoes fired, sir!"

Marshall cowered against the steel plates as more bullets whined viciously nearby, striking sparks from the metal.

"Bloody hell! We're not hurting it." Buck wiped his eyes and peered at the dock's smoky silhouette.

Blythe called, "Two men wounded on the casing, sir!" Without waiting he bellowed, "Stretcher party to the bridge!"

The yacht was in a bad way. Her slender hull was a pitted shambles, with smoke and darting flames showing from scores of holes. An internal explosion flung a complete length of the deck into the air, and the yacht started to roll over.

"Aircraft, sir!" the lookout was yelling. "Port beam!"

Marshall tried to control his reeling mind. The aircraft was far away, probably over the land which was now hidden by smoke.

Buck yelled, "Another hit!" He was waving his cap in the air.

The torpedo had struck the dock some two-thirds along its tall side. A column of smoke stood frozen against the sky.

A figure blundered through the bridge, carrying a bag with a red cross on it. It was the young stoker, Willard, the one whose mother was "on the street." The boy looked at him and grinned, then leaped over the side and down the ladder to the casing.

The last torpedo hit the dock within yards of the previous one. Another tall column of smoke, but no flames. Marshall stared at the dock's square outline, unable to believe that anything could survive such a battering.

"Aircraft's turning, sir!"

Marshall swung the glasses abeam, seeing it alter its course toward the battle far below.

Buck was shouting, "Shall I clear the bridge?"

Marshall gripped his arm. "No! We must make sure of the dock! Tell the Vierling gunners to stand by to repel aircraft!"

"Aircraft closing, sir!"

He turned as a low, sullen rumble came across the water from the dock. It went on and on like some piece of massive undersea machinery.

Buck gasped. "We got her! She's done for!"

The dock was tilting toward them, very slowly. A tall derrick fell outboard and hung downward above the sea like a dead stork, and other fragments could be seen splashing along the full length of the side. The towing tug was burning fiercely.

Marshall snapped, "That's it! Clear the casing! Prepare to dive!"

He heard the klaxon screaming as the guns fell silent. Men clambered over the bridge, some dragging wounded with them.

The aircraft burst into view just four hundred yards abeam. Marshall saw the stabbing flashes from its guns, the hail of bullets plowing across the water, over the casing and away to the opposite beam. The Vierling followed around, the sharp explosions and darting tracer making some of the running seamen falter.

Buck shouted, "Get below! Move your bloody selves!"

More bangs, and the attendant clang of steel on steel, before the plane streaked out of range to begin another turn. One more attack like that and they might be crippled and unable to dive.

Marshall thrust his mouth against the speaking tube. "Hard astarboard! Full ahead, group up!"

Buck hung over the screen calling, "There's the last of 'em!" It was the stoker, Willard, his round face as white as a sheet. Trying to save a wounded gunner. Trying as he stood alone on the casing to show Marshall what he could do. What it meant to him.

Buck swore savagely and then croaked, "Get below, you fool!"

The plane had turned and now burst out of the smoke, the machine guns firing as before, some whipping through the German flag overhead, some straddling the casing. Marshall saw the stoker, who had reached the wounded man, stagger sideways and then jerk violently through the safety rail to roll over the side.

Marshall shouted, "Take her *down*, Number One!" He saw the stoker's body being washed along the saddle tank, arms and legs moving languidly. The deck was tilting and the air full of noise. The sea was surging up and over the casing. Somehow Marshall's feet were on the ladder. Then he was in the control room as the boat glided down as deep as she dared. He watched the depth gauges, listened to the regular reports from the echo sounder. He knew exactly what was happening, yet felt no part of it.

A deep echo rumbled against the hull. The dock coming to rest on the bottom.

Gerrard crossed to his side. "I've seen to the damage, sir."

He removed his cap and stared at it. The German eagle clutching the swastika in its claws. He walked up and down. Finally he said, "You can fall out diving stations. And tell the cook to prepare a meal." It was as if he had to keep giving instructions.

517

As he walked to the door, Gerrard walked with him. "I'll call you if anything happens, sir." He tried to smile. "You get some rest."

Marshall did not fight back. He replied quietly, "That was a bad one. It seems to get worse every time."

Chapter 5

FOR over a week after sending the great floating dock and its escort to the bottom they had endured the frustration of uncertainty, while Frenzel's fuel levels had dropped and food supplies had become exhausted. It was like being forgotten by that other world to which they listened on the busy radio waves. Then at last the signal had come. When it had been decoded and the references marked on Devereaux's charts, Marshall had headed toward the North African coastline. Someone at last had remembered them and with any sort of luck would have the fuel and supplies waiting to be loaded. And there would be a chance to rest.

They had been on the surface for nearly half an hour, but everything was wet and icy to the touch. Marshall steadied his glasses across the bridge screen.

Gerrard's voice echoed up the tube. "Should have made a sighting by now, sir. We're ten minutes overdue."

"Yes." He moved his glasses slightly to starboard again. Nothing. Nor was there a sound above their own stealthy approach. "Maybe something's gone wrong."

Buck said, "I was thinking. Suppose the Jerries have made a comeback? We might run smack into one of their patrols."

Marshall smiled. "I'm getting so that I can't remember which side I'm really on."

How could he chat, when every second dragged at his nerves and even the placid sea appeared to be full of menacing outlines?

"Sir!" Buck was leaning over the screen. "Boat! Port bow!"

Marshall pushed past him, his heart beating urgently. The boat was little more than a darker blob against the sea. He said harshly, "No wonder we couldn't hear them. They're drifting." He saw the quick stab of a lamp. "Reply, Yeoman."

Blythe shuttered off their recognition code. Instantly a boat's engine coughed into life and a dark shadow edged closer to the submarine's hull. It was a very old boat with the high bow and stern posts of a Portuguese fisherman. But the voice which boomed through a megaphone was British enough. "Just follow me, Captain! The Jerries were thoughtful enough to make a bit of a breakwater with some sunken ships when they were last here."

A bobbing stern light presented itself beyond the U-boat's bows, and they set off toward the invisible shore. Marshall saw something loom past the starboard side. A ship, or part of one, like a buckled, rusting reef, man-made, and left by men to rot. When the war ended, would they ever be able to clean up the debris?

A bright beam of light probed from the darkness and moved slowly along the submarine's hull. Marshall saw a heaving line snaking into the lights, and figures hurrying with fenders to ease the first contact. The hull lurched and the deck party secured the boat against a motionless wreck. A figure was helped over the saddle tank, and even as Marshall ordered Frenzel to ring off the motors a head rose above the bridge screen and said calmly, "So you made it, old son. Good show." It was Simeon.

To Marshall it was unreal and vaguely absurd. Two men meeting out here in the black wilderness. Simeon said, "Let's go below, eh? It's a bit snappy. I'm not dressed for it."

Down in the brightly lit control room Marshall made comparisons. His own men, tired-eyed and in filthy sweaters as they hurried about their business. Simeon, on the other hand, was perfect, wearing pale khaki drill. He followed Marshall into the wardroom and stared around at the untidy interior with ill-disguised amusement. "Really, you chaps have been roughing it!"

Marshall took out a bottle and two glasses. He said shortly, "We sank the dock. Cost us two men—" He faltered, remembering Willard. "I'm still not sure about our damage. A faulty torpedo—" He broke off, seeing the emptiness in Simeon's eyes. He didn't care.

Simeon took his glass and replied, "We heard about the dock from other sources. Good show. The enemy still doesn't seem to know about *you* though." He lifted the glass. "Cheers."

Marshall swallowed the whisky in one mouthful.

Simeon said, "Now don't you worry about a thing. I'll give you your full capacity of diesel fuel before daylight. Water, too, and almost anything else you want."

"Thanks." Marshall could not help feeling admiration.

Gerrard appeared in the doorway. "Could I let some of our hands ashore, sir? They can start taking our gear to wherever Commander Simeon has earmarked for us while we're here."

Simeon eyed him coolly. "Look after the lads first, eh?" He smiled. "But it's not on, I'm afraid. This boat will be out of here by dawn, or I'll want to know why."

Gerrard stared at Marshall. "Is this true, sir?"

Simeon snapped, "Look, I don't intend to discuss my arrangement with everyone. I will tell your captain. He will tell you." He eyed Gerrard for several seconds. "If he feels like it."

Marshall stood up slowly. "Carry on, Number One." He waited until Gerrard had left and then said, "Didn't you see my people when you came aboard, sir? Some of them have been on their bloody feet for days and nights on end!" He could feel his limbs shaking. "What the hell are you asking of them now?"

"*Do* sit down and I'll explain." Simeon regarded him calmly. "The war out here has reached a climax. The Germans are almost gone from North Africa. Everything's geared for an invasion through Sicily. It's a vital time. I don't feel inclined to order a halt while you and your company sit on your backsides!"

Marshall stared at his empty glass. "What is it you want?"

"That's more like it, old son." Simeon took out a fat notebook and flicked through the pages. "The Intelligence people have got word that the Germans have invented a new weapon. A radio-controlled bomb. Once dropped from an aircraft it can be homed by radio onto any large target. No big ships would be safe or capable of maintaining a bombardment for the invasion. The army would have to hit the beaches on their own."

Marshall asked, "Where do we come in?"

"I want you to lift off some agents," Simeon said. "They'll know, if anyone does, what the Germans are up to. If this invasion is to work, we must know for sure what we've got against us."

"A sea pickup?" Marshall looked away.

"No. You must lift them off the Italian mainland. There's an alert out for them. Even now, we might be too late."

Marshall stood quite still, listening to a motor chugging busily as fuel was pumped into the U-boat. Fill her up and get her away by dawn. That was all that mattered to the men onshore. It was unfair. More than that, it was dangerous to push the boat and her crew beyond their limits.

He heard Simeon say quietly, "One of the agents is that French girl. You brought her out here, remember?"

Marshall swung around. "Of course I remember."

"I could ask for a conventional submarine, of course. But under the circumstances, I think this is best."

"Yes. I understand."

"I knew you'd see it my way." Simeon stood up. "There'll be a few Intelligence chaps coming with you."

Marshall followed him out of the wardroom and saw Warwick standing by the conning-tower hatch. "Officers' conference in the wardroom in one hour, Sub." He watched Simeon vanish up the ladder and walked to his cabin. He stared at the bunk, fighting back the urge to lie down and let darkness sweep over him. Then he remembered that she was somewhere on the enemy coast. Waiting for help. For him.

An hour later the assembled officers listened to him in silence. Buck lolled against the bulkhead, his eyes red-rimmed and almost closed. Devereaux was little better, and young Warwick could not stop himself from yawning repeatedly. Frenzel stared at his logbook, his eyes blank and unseeing. Only Gerrard seemed to be holding on.

When Marshall had finished, Buck lurched to his feet. "I'm going to get the spare torpedoes shifted from their containers on the aftercasing while we're still tied up to something steady."

Frenzel also stood up. He looked at Marshall and smiled. "Pity Commander Simeon's not coming along for the ride." He followed Buck through the door.

Devereaux rubbed his eyes and murmured, "Just tell me where, sir. I'll find the right chart for it."

Gerrard said simply, "Good bunch, sir."

Marshall touched his arm, unable to face him. "Best yet, Bob."

"Captain in the control room!"

Marshall threw himself out of the bunk and hurried from his cabin. He could not recall whether he had been asleep. One second he was lying on his blankets, the next he was at Gerrard's elbow.

Gerrard grimaced. "Just picked up some fast-moving HE at two six zero, sir. Might mean we're getting near trouble."

Marshall nodded and walked to the chart. It had been three

days since they had left their makeshift harbor. Three days of unnatural quiet, as if the whole Mediterranean were taking a brief rest after the months of battle. The strain had been all the greater because of it, he thought. Impossible to relax.

They were now heading toward the well-known bottleneck between Sicily and Cape Bon on the Tunisian shore. Eighty-odd miles over which the struggle for mastery had swayed back and forth without letup, where submarines of both sides hunted ceaselessly. They did not want any trouble now. Not from either side. It would take another two days to reach the pickup point on Italy's west coast and more valuable time to get into position.

He thought of the three Intelligence men in the wardroom, no doubt sleeping while they still had the time. The senior one was a Major Mark Cowan. Slightly built, with a matter-of-fact manner, he looked anything but a regular soldier. From the little he had said, he did not seem too hopeful for the success of the mission.

A radio message had been sent to the agents to tell them the pickup time and rendezvous point. But no acknowledgment was expected. Cowan had said that the Germans had discovered the agents' hiding place, and any radio message from them would certainly kill their last chance of rescue.

"We'll take a look," Marshall said to Gerrard. "Up periscope." He crouched down, his fingers on the twin handles, locking the periscope on to the last bearing, then edging it around. Hold it. Even at full power the ship was indistinct. Probably a destroyer.

"Down periscope." He looked at Gerrard. "Steer three two zero. Take her down to thirty meters."

He turned and saw Major Cowan by the bulkhead door. "A destroyer on patrol," he said. "Well away from us."

Cowan replied, "Not what I imagined. Thought there'd be bells ringing, men dashing about. That sort of thing."

Marshall smiled. Stick around a bit longer, my friend. Aloud he said, "I'm just going to have some coffee. Join me?"

In the wardroom he said, "Will you fill me in on some details?"

Cowan smiled. "What exactly do you want to know?"

"Mrs. Travis. What is her part in all this?"

Cowan sighed. "I was against her getting involved again. She worked in Paris the last time. Being French, her services were invaluable. But her cover broke and she was caught."

Marshall thought of the way she moved. Like a hunted animal.

"Our people managed to get her out of it just in time. A close thing." Cowan shrugged. "But when she was asked to do this job, she agreed without hesitation. Her husband's in Italy."

"I see. So he's working for you, too?"

Cowan watched him sadly. "Actually, no. He's working for the other side. A collaborator. An engineer. Doing the same sort of construction job he was doing in France."

Marshall felt dazed. "And she agreed to see him?"

The major put down his cup. "Did she mention her parents? Well, her father works for the Resistance. He's with the French railways. Very useful contact. And we heard that Travis is getting cold feet. Wants to change sides again. Come home and be forgiven. She is the only one he might listen to. She despises him, but he trusts her."

Marshall looked at his cup, suddenly sick. "And your people let her go back to him. Knowing the Germans might suspect her."

Cowan said, "It is a risk of course, but she is his wife, she has the right papers, and she knows her job." He added quietly, "Travis knows about those new bombs. If we can get him out alive, we might save countless of our own people later on."

"And if she's failed to convince him?"

"Then we'll just have to get what we can from the other agents. We can't know for sure until—"

The rest of his words were lost as the deck gave a sudden lurch, and from the control room came a cry of alarm.

Marshall staggered and almost fell as the hull jerked violently, and he heard a new sound, like a saw on metal, screeching along the submarine's casing. He ran to the control room. Gerrard was clinging to the periscopes, his face like chalk as he yelled, "Blow all main ballast! *Surface!*"

Marshall gripped his arm. "Belay that order! Klaxon!" He could hardly think because of the screeching around him. "What happened?" He had to shake Gerrard's wrist to make him react.

Gerrard stared at him. "The hull plunged. Then that noise!" He looked around as the sound stopped. "I thought we'd hit a wreck."

Marshall said, "Check the trim." To Frenzel he added, "Report damage to hull."

One of the planesmen said hoarsely, "Can't hold her, sir! The afterplanes are jamming. We must have picked up something."

Marshall nodded, seeing Cowan and his two companions in the bulkhead doorway, yet not seeing them.

Frenzel reported, "No hull damage, sir."

Marshall made himself wait for several agonizing seconds. When he spoke he expected to hear a break in his voice. "Take her up slowly, Number One. Periscope depth. If she starts to dive, blow everything."

The sound came suddenly as before, like a jarring whine, ending just as abruptly with a violent clang across the casing.

"Fourteen meters, sir." Gerrard sounded very tense.

"Up periscope." Marshall brought the lens toward the stern and depressed it slightly. There, bobbing close astern, was a mine.

It was covered with green slime, and had probably broken adrift from a field months ago. But it was as deadly as the day it had left Germany. Or England.

To the control room at large Marshall said, "It's a mine. We are towing it about fifty feet astern of us." He saw their stunned expressions. He crossed to the chart. "How about it, Pilot?"

Devereaux wiped his mouth with the back of his hand. "It's a bad place to surface, sir."

"I didn't choose it." He leaned over the table. "Smack in the middle of the strait. Alter course and steer due north." He warned them sharply. "Take your time. The cable is caught around the afterplanes. I don't want that mine veering into the screws!"

Cowan asked quietly, "Couldn't we wait until dark, Captain? If you surface, you might be spotted."

"If we tried it in the dark, we would most likely get blown up, Major." Marshall thrust his hands into his pockets. "Chief, get your men and all the gear you need. As few hands on deck as possible."

Buck said, "I'll take charge, if I may, sir." He forced a grin. "I reckon I've cut up more bloody cars in my garage than the chief's had hot dinners. This is right up my street."

Marshall nodded. "That makes sense." He sought out Warwick. "Automatic-weapon crews stand by."

Tools clanked in the background, and then he heard Buck say, "I'll want that, and that big cutter over there." He sounded satisfied. "Ready when you are, sir."

Gerrard said, "I'm sorry, sir. I should have kept my head."

Marshall eyed him thoughtfully. "Not to worry," he said.

Men pushed toward the ladder. Deck party in life jackets and carrying Buck's tools. Gun crews with their ammunition belts.

Marshall said to Gerrard, "Shut off the boat once we're on the surface. If this thing explodes, do your best to get our lads out the escape hatches." He paused. "If you get clear and we don't, Major Cowan will tell you where to go and what to do. It'll be up to you to get those people off." He gripped his arm. "All right, Bob?"

"Yes." Gerrard nodded jerkily. "But watch out."

The lower hatch clanged open and Marshall began to pull himself up the ladder. His voice rang hollowly in the tower. "Surface!"

LIEUTENANT Colin Buck tugged his cap down over his eyes and stared at the mine, a slime-covered sphere with bobbing horns. He watched a petty officer, naked but for a pair of shorts, crawl along the edge of the casing above the hydroplanes. Despite the dangers of being on the surface in sunlight, Buck felt quite calm.

"Well, Rigby, what d'you make of it?"

The petty officer leaned over the edge and pointed into the U-boat's gentle wake. "The cable seems to be wrapped tightly around the port hydroplane." He squinted up at Buck.

"I see." Buck turned and looked at Marshall's silhouette on the bridge. "Cable's fouled around the plane, sir," he shouted. "It will have to be cut underwater."

Rigby muttered, "Don't fancy that job. Not with a bloody screw spinning around me."

Buck shouted, "If you stop the motors, sir, the weight of the cable will pull the mine into our stern."

Marshall called, "Any ideas?"

Buck looked at his small group of helpers. "My lads will shove that mine clear if it comes any closer." He was stripping off his shirt. "I'll do the cutting."

Rigby grimaced. "Watch out for the undertow, sir. There's always a nasty tug under these boats."

Buck nodded. He fixed some goggles over his eyes and eased himself outboard over the slimy casing, a bowline tied around his waist. The sea was like ice. A shock after the sun's warmth.

He ducked under the water, peering at the cable. It was jagged and coated with rust and growth. He dragged himself into the

warm air again. "Never do it with this wire cutter. Tell the chief to rig a power cutter and be bloody quick about it."

Buck heard Marshall questioning the man who had gone forward with his message. He was a good bloke, this Marshall. Not a bit like some of the stuck-up sods he had encountered when he had enlisted. Men like Marshall made it all worthwhile.

Buck leaned out to watch the screw. One slip. Just one, and it would be his lot.

Rigby said, "Here comes the cutter, sir."

Two seamen were dragging the electric cable aft, the powerful cutter between them. It was a useful piece of gear. Most U-boats carried one, so that a diver could hack through antisubmarine nets and harbor booms while the hull was submerged.

From their position on the bridge Marshall and Warwick saw Buck vanish below the surface with the cutter. Warwick asked Marshall, "How long will it take, sir?"

Marshall shrugged. "Half an hour. Hard to tell."

He swung around as Warwick said, "From control room, sir. Fast-moving HE at one five zero. Closing."

Marshall ran to the rear of the bridge and leveled his glasses. Haze masked the dark line of the horizon. "Keep a good lookout. Maybe it'll go away."

Warwick said, "Lieutenant Buck, sir. Shall I tell him?"

"Negative. I don't want him to get flustered."

Minutes later he saw Buck emerge gasping beside the hull.

This unknown ship was almost certain to be British or American. But he could not dive with the mine still in tow. It would hamper their movements, and even a badly aimed depth charge would explode it and rip off their stern.

"HE steady on same bearing, sir. Range approximately twelve thousand yards." Warwick added quietly, "*Two* ships, sir. Speke thinks they may be destroyers."

A lookout said, "Lieutenant Buck's gone under again, sir. That's five times."

Marshall peered up at the main periscope. It was raised to full extent. Soon now, it had to be.

Another lookout yelled, "Ship's in sight, sir!"

Warwick said between his teeth, "Coming out of the sun. We'll be sitting ducks!"

Marshall knew that Rigby was staring at him from right aft. It did not take a genius to know something was happening. He said to Warwick, "Go and find out how Buck's managing."

"They've opened fire, sir!"

Marshall heard the crash of gunfire and saw twin waterspouts burst skyward directly in line with the hull, but well clear.

"Out of range, but not for long." He pictured the other captains as the reports started to come in. A U-boat on the surface. Hasn't dived, therefore damaged. The chance of a lifetime.

Two more columns shot up from the blue water, hanging in the sunlight like glittering crystal curtains before dropping reluctantly. Closer—a bare half mile clear. The destroyers would be charging through the sea like the thoroughbreds they were.

Warwick came back. "Nearly through, sir. Just a few strands more." Two more shells burst. Wider apart. Getting the range.

A lookout muttered, "To think they're our own blokes out there!" Another pair of shells exploded. This time the hull gave a sharp jerk. The destroyers were clearly visible now, the leader almost dead astern. There were more flashes and abbreviated whistles as her shells smashed down into the sea.

"Aircraft, sir! Starboard bow! German. Dornier 17Z. Turning toward us."

Marshall watched as the twin-engined bomber roared overhead, its bomb doors open. The pilot had weighed the situation. A German submarine pinned down by two destroyers. He would do what he could. But even now, as he started to climb, the air around the plane erupted in several blobs of dirty brown smoke. Any destroyer which hoped to survive in the Mediterranean was a floating gun platform. The plane wouldn't have a chance, Marshall thought grimly. But it could give him valuable time.

There was a hoarse cry from aft. "Cable's cut, sir!"

Marshall saw the mine spiraling away and Buck being hauled aboard, his slime-covered hands and body running blood. Cuts from the rough wire and plating.

"Diving stations!" Men tumbled down the ladder hurling tools and equipment through the hatch.

The bomber was rocking dangerously, and Marshall imagined it had been hit by shell fragments. The German pilot *had* given them time to get rid of the mine, but the destroyers would still close in for a depth-charge attack. He stared as a bomb detached itself from the Dornier's belly and plummeted into the sunlight.

"Clear the bridge! *Dive, dive, dive!*"

But Warwick clutched at him, yelling, "That bomb, sir! It can't be! It's *tracking* the destroyer, *following her around!*"

Even as he found the bomb with his glasses, Marshall saw it hit the destroyer just abaft her bridge. There was a tremendous flash, followed by a mounting pall of smoke, and with stunned surprise he saw the destroyer begin to turn turtle, the impetus of her speed thrusting the raked stem into the sea like a plowshare.

Then he was dragging the hatch over his head, as he heard the sea surge hungrily over the conning tower.

He said sharply, "Hold her at periscope depth, Number One!"

He blinked to accustom his eyes to the control room, and saw Major Cowan by the chart table. "It was a British ship, Major." He let the words drop like stones. "Sunk by one of those radio-controlled bombs that were *supposed* to be secret!"

He turned to the periscope and took a long look astern. One ship where there had been a pair, and it had stopped to lower boats. No sign of the bomber that had saved them.

"Down periscope. Resume course and depth." He nodded to Gerrard and walked quickly to the wardroom. Buck was slumped on a seat, eyes closed, as Churchill dabbed at dozens of grazes and cuts with a wad of dressing. Marshall opened the cabinet and said, "Whisky for the torpedo officer." He held up the all-but-filled glass. "I'll see you get recognition for what you did back there."

Buck gaped at him. "Whisky will do for me," he said.

Marshall said, "Stay with him, Churchill." Then he left the wardroom and walked to Devereaux's table. As he studied the Italian coastline he kept seeing the destroyer as she had staggered brokenly onto her side. Simeon had stressed the importance of the mission, but he did not know the half of it. The enemy not only had invented a new weapon, he was already using it.

Chapter 6

THE air in the wardroom was clammy and unmoving as they crowded around Marshall's chart. He tapped it with his dividers. "This is where we are. Naples is about sixty miles to the southeast of our position. We are about three miles south of this cape."

Major Cowan nodded. "Seems all right to me." He jabbed the chart with his finger. "Our people will be here. All being well."

Marshall asked, "Anything we ought to know?"

"Nearest place of any size is Terracina, about ten miles east of where we'll be." He shrugged. "Mostly Italian guardposts in the past. But now . . . we'll just have to see."

Marshall straightened. Just have to see. It sounded so easy. He said to the major, "Number One will give you your landing instructions." Then he glanced at Gerrard. "We will surface in fifteen minutes. If it all seems quiet, I shall get close inshore and watch for the signal. Then we'll open the forehatch and launch the boat. Questions?"

Cowan shook his head. "None from me."

Buck stood up. "I'll get forward and check the dinghy."

Marshall turned to the three passengers. "Good luck. I hope you get them safely."

They followed him to the control room. Marshall looked at the bulkhead clock. "Ready, Number One?"

Gerrard's eyes glittered in the dimmed lights. "Yes, sir."

Marshall nodded gravely. "If we get a hot welcome, we'll head out to sea. Fast." He walked to the ladder. "Surface!"

As usual, the noise seemed deafening, and as Marshall, Warwick and the two lookouts clambered out onto the bridge he found it hard to believe that nobody heard. Yet he knew that a submarine breaking surface was barely audible a hundred yards away.

He moved his glasses very slowly to port. It was very dark. But the air was like wine. Cool and sweet.

Warwick whispered, "Control room says five minutes, sir."

How quiet it was. Just the easy murmur along the saddle tanks, the gentle pulsing of the motors. He could distinguish the land now. It was an uneven edge below the stars.

A lookout said, "*There*, sir! Starboard bow!"

In the pitch-darkness the signal seemed incredibly bright. Marshall relaxed as the light went out. "Open forehatch. Gun crews close up."

Warwick said, "Pilot says we're about one thousand yards offshore, sir." He hesitated. "Suggests you start your turn now."

"No. Must get closer. We have to give them a chance, Sub.

Imagine paddling that damn dinghy there and back." He tensed. "There's the signal again!" He touched Warwick's arm. "Get down to your gun and train it on the light. Be ready for anything."

There was a brief clank of steel, and Marshall saw figures hauling the dinghy onto the casing.

"Ten fathoms, sir."

"Stop both motors. Slip the dinghy." Marshall watched the little boat bobbing clear. He looked at his luminous watch. Wait for the major's own signal and then get under way. By the time they had made a full circle and arrived here again, the dinghy should be back and waiting. He found he was clenching his fists with sudden desperation. Chantal had to be safe.

"Signal, sir," the lookout reported. "The major's made contact."

Marshall lowered his mouth to the speaking tube. "Slow ahead both motors. Take her around again, Pilot."

"Aye, aye, sir." The submarine swung toward open sea, the gun pivoting to cover the land until it was masked by the conning tower.

"There's the dinghy, sir!" Blythe pointed over the screen, his voice hoarse with excitement.

Marshall held his glasses very steady while the submarine lifted and plunged. He could just make it out. "Are they all there?"

The yeoman did not reply immediately. "Hard to be sure."

"Stop both motors."

Marshall saw the dinghy slue around as the first line was made fast, heard Warwick shouting to a seaman to assist the passengers aboard. A figure was lifted onto the casing. He felt his heart thumping against his ribs. Dead or injured? It was impossible to say.

Then Major Cowan came running aft. He said tersely, "They've had a bit of bother, Captain." He gestured toward the shore. "Been running and hiding for days. The whole place is swarming with patrols." He sucked in long gulps of air. "But we've got Travis."

"What about the others?"

"We lifted off some of our chaps. A paratroop lieutenant who has been working with an Italian sabotage group. And Moss, the only one of the original party."

"And the rest?"

"Major Carter and Mrs. Travis went inland. It was the only way

531

they could draw off the search party. Moss was shot in the thigh, so he couldn't help."

Marshall said, "Do you think they've been caught, Major?"

Cowan nodded. "They intended to be. Nothing else would have convinced the enemy and given us the chance to get Travis off."

Marshall said to a seaman, "Get the first lieutenant up here immediately. I'm going forward." He flung himself over the side of the bridge and hurried along the wet casing, Warwick and the major close behind him. The dinghy was still in the water.

Marshall sought out the paratroop officer, whose name was Smith. "Do you know this area well?"

"Fairly well. I wasn't involved with *this* affair." Smith added bitterly, "I'm afraid I'd have shot that Travis character."

Marshall's thoughts raced. "I'm going ashore." He continued sharply, "Do you think we could find them? Get them away?"

Smith shrugged. "Not much chance. But . . ." He nodded slowly. "I'll come with you." He turned. "How about it, Major?"

Cowan replied, "I'm sorry. My orders are to start the investigation on Travis."

Gerrard appeared on the casing, groping along the guardrail.

Marshall said, "I'm going ashore, Number One. You will assume command. Stand well offshore and rendezvous here in four hours."

Gerrard exclaimed, "It's madness! You'll never stand a chance."

Petty Officer Cain called, "Five volunteers be enough, sir?"

Marshall looked at him. "Thank you. Submachine guns and grenades. Just like they taught us in Scotland."

He and Smith followed Cain and his men into the dinghy. "Shove off." He gripped a paddle. "Let's see how fast we can move this thing!" When he turned his head he saw the submarine looming above him, and felt a sharp sense of loneliness.

Smith said, "I know the only likely place where the Eyeties would hold prisoners until the Gestapo arrives. But if I'm wrong, we can forget it. It'll be dawn in four hours."

As the shoreline took on a more definite shape nobody spoke, and Marshall was conscious of their tension. Cain said suddenly, "'Ere's a bit of beach, sir. We'll 'ave to wade the last part."

They scrambled into the water, and Marshall felt the undertow pulling at his feet. He said, "Two stay with the dinghy. If we don't come back, you will rendezvous with Lieutenant Gerrard."

Smith held a wrist compass to his eyes. "Follow me. Keep quiet, and freeze when I do. If you have to fight, then fight. No fancy stuff, just kill." He turned on his heel and strode up a steep bank.

Only once did he pause, and that was to whisper in Marshall's ear, "You know, Captain, it might just come off. After all, nobody but a raving lunatic would attempt this sort of caper."

SMITH guided them inland through rough and deserted countryside. They had been on the move for over an hour when suddenly he rolled onto his side and they all dived into the grass, hearing the rumble of vehicles growing and then fading into the stillness.

Smith said calmly, "Probably troops called off from the hunt." He stood up. "About two miles farther on there's a police post on the road junction. Used to belong to the carabinieri. Now they have a permanent squad of soldiers."

They moved forward cautiously, each man holding himself low, as if to avoid a sudden burst of gunfire. Finally Cain whispered, "There's a light, sir." He sounded excited.

Smith nodded. "That's it." The police post was very easy to see, white-walled, with double gates. He gestured to Marshall. "One sentry. Just inside. See his cigarette? The guardroom is directly opposite the gates. Usually about ten men and a lieutenant."

"Car coming, sir!"

"*Down!*"

They flopped into the long, coarse grass as the engine grew louder along the road. Marshall saw headlights sweeping across the white wall, heard a string of angry German words.

Smith murmured, "Bad. The Krauts are here now."

Doors slammed. The solitary cigarette reappeared by the gates.

Smith snapped at the men nearest him, "One of you at each end of the wall, but this side of the road. That'll give good cross fire." He handed something to the third seaman. "Up that telephone pole and cut the cable."

Cain whispered uneasily, "That leaves us then, sir."

"Right." Smith was examining his grenades. "We just go in and let rip." He reached down to pull a commando dagger from his boot and vanished across the road. His figure was etched against the wall. There was not even the slightest sound. But the glowing cigarette was moving very slowly to the ground.

With Cain beside him Marshall ran across the road. Smith wiped his knife on the dead sentry's coat and stood up. They followed him toward the main building.

Smith's head showed briefly against a lighted slit in a shutter. Then he whispered, "A good dozen in there. Swilling vino." He reached up and gently tested a corner of the shutter. "Careless." He added, "Two grenades each. Pull out the pins, release the levers, count two and then pop them into the window."

Marshall and Cain pulled the pins from their grenades as Smith dragged back the shutter with all his strength. "Ready? *Now!*"

They barely had time to throw themselves down before the front of the building erupted in one great burst of fire and noise. Glass, woodwork and stones flew across the yard, and from above came a deluge of tiles and plaster.

Smith yelled, "Inside!"

He kicked open the sagging door and dashed into the room. In a dark corner someone was screaming and choking. He aimed a short burst of automatic fire, and the screaming stopped.

Smith ran into the passageway, his gun cutting down a terrified man in a cook's apron who had come careering around the corner. Smith reached another door and threw his weight against it, falling almost flat as the catch collapsed.

A single shot came from the room, cutting plaster from the wall by Marshall's shoulder. He saw an Italian officer staring at him wildly, an automatic in his hand. Smith screamed, *"Get him!"*

Marshall felt his gun jump, and saw the officer spin around like a puppet, the wall beyond him splashed with scarlet.

Cain shouted, "'Ere's the major's body, sir!" Carter had been shot several times, and his face was barely recognizable.

The door at the other side of the room, narrow and heavily studded, opened very slowly and a hand appeared, holding a white handkerchief. Marshall could feel himself gritting his teeth and panting like a wild animal.

Smith yelled, "Come out with your hands up!" There were two Gestapo men. Smith gestured to the floor. "Down! Hands behind your heads!"

Then he said quietly, "Watch 'em, Cain." Very gently he pushed the door wide open.

Marshall followed, the gun almost slipping from his fingers as he saw the girl. She was lying naked on a heavy table, her arms and legs tied to its corners. She looked like a small broken statue.

Smith snapped, "Don't touch her!"

He moved swiftly to the table, while Marshall stood motionless. There were wires connected to the girl's breasts and thighs; they in turn were attached to a humming metal box.

Smith ran his fingers over a line of controls. The humming stopped, and he said quietly, "Now give me a hand."

Marshall took her head in his hands, his eyes smarting as he saw the raw marks on her body, the blood on her mouth. Smith unclipped the wires one by one. Only then did she open her eyes, her stomach contracting as if to resist some new torture. Marshall whispered, "It's all right. *It's all right.*"

Smith took off his long leather coat. "Here. Get her into this."

Marshall eased the girl from the table. Just one movement made her cry out, and then she fell limply against him.

"Let's move." Smith jammed a fresh magazine into his gun.

As Marshall carried the girl through the adjoining room, Smith called, "You two. In here. *Schnell!*"

The two Gestapo men scrambled to their feet. As Smith backed from the cell he threw his last grenade at their feet, then leaped outside and dragged the heavy door shut. He heard their screams, their frantic fists against the door before the grenade exploded. "Sleep well, you bastards!" he said.

Outside on the road he snapped to the sailors, "Give your captain a hand."

Cain stumbled after them, the gun dangling at his side. It was not real. He thought of Major Carter, all bloody and broken. And that poor girl, what they had been doing to her. He thought of the way Marshall had carried her. No sign of weariness. He had marched as if he were carrying the most precious thing in the whole world.

Chapter 7

"IF YOU'LL wait in here, sir." The orderly held open a door. "The captain will see you in just a moment."

Marshall walked slowly to the one wide window which overlooked the harbor of Alexandria. Outside it was blazing hot, the glare throwing up shimmering reflections from the many anchored ships and the broad expanse of blue water.

The room's fine mosaic floor and domed ceiling gave it an air of calm, and after the passage from the depot ship where the U-boat had secured just an hour earlier it felt as cool as a tomb.

Marshall looked at the huge murals of voluptuous dancing girls and turned away, recalling with sickening clarity the girl strapped to the table a week ago. He remembered her twisting in his arms, fighting him without strength or purpose.

Once on board, with the submarine heading into open waters, he had made sure she was comfortable in his cabin.

Major Cowan had protested. "But I'm trying to interrogate Travis in there!"

Marshall had snapped, "Do it somewhere else. Stick him in a torpedo tube, for all I care!"

For by then he had discovered that Travis had not come willingly to help his own country. The Paris office of the Gestapo had sent details of his wife's suspected connections with the Resistance to the Italians at the site where Travis worked. Her arrival had sprung the odds against him, and with moments to spare, he had been smuggled through a tightening cordon. As the small party had moved through "safe" houses in the countryside, Travis had seen his wife as the main cause of his own destruction. But for her he would have been working safely for the Germans.

Over and over again Marshall had tried to imagine the sort of man who would knowingly let his wife go straight into the hands of the Gestapo. Just to give him time to get away.

On board, Marshall had done all he could to make her feel safe. He recalled the first time she had spoken to him. He had been standing just inside the cabin, watching Churchill hold a cup of soup to her lips. How small she had looked. Lost in a submarine sweater and somebody's best bell-bottom trousers. She had suddenly pushed the cup away and had said huskily, "Where *were* you? You didn't come!" Then she had fallen back on the pillows.

Churchill had said, "She ain't makin' sense yet, sir."

Once in Alexandria, alongside the depot ship, things had moved swiftly. Grim-faced officers had come for Travis and the three agents. Medical staff had looked after the girl and the wounded agent, Moss. Smith had been the last to leave. "I wish you well,

Captain. You are a brave man." He had tapped his heart. "But too much of this, I think."

The door opened silently. "The captain will see you now, sir."

Marshall followed the orderly to a room where Captain Browning was silhouetted against the window. He turned and said, "Marshall, you never fail to astound me!" He gripped his hand. "You look well, despite what you've been doing."

Marshall placed his cap on a table and sat down.

"I've read your report, of course. About the destroyer being sunk by a guided bomb." He shook his massive head. "Terrible."

"Which ship was she, sir?"

"The *Dundee*." Browning turned to look out of the window, his swivel chair creaking. "My son David was midshipman in her."

Marshall stared at him. "Were there any survivors, sir?"

Browning took a deep breath. "A few. He wasn't one of them."

"I'm very sorry, sir," Marshall said.

Browning cleared his throat and turned over some papers on his desk. "I'm afraid there'll be no leave for your people. I've told the depot ship to make 'em comfortable. Baths, a few film shows, that sort of thing. I'm sorry I can't do more. Security."

"I was wondering about the girl, sir." Marshall watched for some reaction. "What will become of her now?"

"Back home, I imagine. Her department will deal with it. Brave girl. I'd like to have met her." A smile puckered his mouth. "That was a fine thing you did. Some people take a different view." He shrugged.

The door opened. "Commander Simeon is here, sir."

Simeon strode into the room and threw his cap onto a chair. "Damn it, Marshall, I've had just about all I can take from you!"

Browning said, "Sit down. I'm not having a row in my room!"

Simeon sat down and continued in a quieter tone. "When I heard how you jeopardized the mission, the submarine, *everything*, for your own amusement, I could hardly credit it."

Marshall replied, "The submarine stayed to the precise moment laid down in your instructions." He studied him calmly. "Sir."

"I didn't tell you to go off like a madman on your own!" Simeon's face was flushed. "Mrs. Travis had her job to do. We all have."

Marshall was on his feet. "She was being tortured. Not sitting behind a desk. She and Major Carter went inland alone, knowing

537

they would be caught. Just to save that gutless traitor you've been talking to." His eyes were cold.

Browning stood up and said, "Now I'll have my say, gentlemen. I've been with the chiefs of staff for the last few days."

Simeon momentarily forgot Marshall. "What's this, sir? I've not been told."

Browning eyed him blandly. "I'm telling you now, aren't I? We're going into Sicily in the first two weeks of July."

"Oh that, sir. I know about *that*."

"Good." Browning smiled. "But before then, there is something more we in this section must do."

Simeon sat bolt upright but said nothing.

Browning continued. "These radio-controlled bombs are assembled at the site where Travis was employed. From there they go by rail and road to the various airfields. Mostly to the east and the Adriatic coast. A good supply is in Sicily, though nowhere near the amount there would be if the enemy knew our real intentions. The storage point there is under the command of a certain Italian general. I knew him well during the last war. But for the present circumstances we would still be firm friends."

"Well, I shouldn't talk too much about *that*, sir!" Simeon laughed.

"Oh, but I did. To the chiefs of staff, as a matter of fact. They all agree that we will get the Italians on our side once we invade. The general I spoke of is shrewd enough to know that if he cooperates *before* the invasion, his future will be secure."

Simeon half rose. "*Before* the invasion, sir?"

"That is what I said. Given a solemn promise, he would be able to take over all the bunkers where the bombs are stored and seal 'em off. By the time the Jerries got more supplies of bombs brought from elsewhere—" He swept a beefy hand across the desk. "Bang! John Bull and Yankee Doodle will be there!"

Simeon exploded. "And who would be entrusted to make him such a promise, if I might be told *that*, sir?"

Browning smiled. "Me."

"But, but—" Simeon looked around the room wildly. "You have no experience in this sort of work, sir!"

"No? Too old, eh?" Browning sighed contentedly. "Well, some think otherwise. If you hop over to the commander in chief's office, you'll be filled in on details. Because you'll be coming, too."

Simeon stood up very stiffly. "Very well, sir. If it's all settled, then—"

"It is." He smiled again. "Definitely."

As the door closed, Browning hurried to a cupboard and produced a bottle. "I've waited a long while for this. Just to see his face, damn his impertinence!"

"You'll be needing my boat, sir?"

He nodded. "I'm fond of you. You're very like David might have become. Or so I like to think."

Marshall said, "Thank you. I appreciate that, sir."

Browning said, "I'm glad. After this I think we can give this boat a proper name and allow her more conventional work to do."

"What about you, sir?"

"Well, I am getting on a bit." He sounded very casual. "There has been talk, just talk, that I will be made a rear admiral and put in charge of a submarine base somewhere."

"I'm pleased for you, sir. You've more than earned it."

"I'll need a good chap to run the base for me until it's just as I want it. An *operational* man, not some stuffed shirt from the Admiralty. Think about it."

Marshall felt dazed. "I will, sir."

"It'll be a while yet before I can get my little scheme moving, so I've arranged for you and your first lieutenant to be quartered ashore. How is he, by the way?"

Marshall wrenched his mind back to Gerrard. "He's fine."

"Good. He did a fine job in getting you off. I've put him in for a decoration." He grinned. "Too." Before Marshall could speak he added, "Now be off with you. I'm going to have another drink and bask in my petty victory."

The army truck jerked to a halt. The driver, a bronzed youngster, gestured toward a white-walled building at the roadside. "That's the place you want, sir."

Marshall climbed down and the truck roared away.

At the gateway an army sentry saluted. "Can I help, sir?"

Marshall held out a pass. "I have permission to visit a patient in the hospital."

It was no ordinary hospital. It was for those who had been hurt, physically or mentally, in espionage work. Inside, a messenger ex-

539

amined Marshall's pass. He picked up a telephone. "The room at the far end. Number twenty."

Marshall walked to the end of the corridor, but as he hesitated outside the door it was opened by a nurse.

"I'm Lieutenant Commander Marshall," he began.

She nodded. "We've been informed." She looked at her watch. "Don't stay long. She may want you to go immediately. They do sometimes." She stood aside and closed the door behind him.

Chantal was lying on a white cot, her head and shoulders propped up on pillows. She turned slowly toward him, her eyes completely hidden by dark sunglasses. "It's you." One hand moved upward, pulling the sheet closer to her throat. "They told me you had come." There was no emotion in her voice.

Marshall moved to the bedside and sat down on a chair.

"I wish I'd had time to buy something for you." He wanted to reach out and hold her hand. "How are you?"

"I can watch the window from here." She lapsed into silence.

He leaned forward slightly and saw her flinch.

He said, "You look marvelous. Even in service pajamas." But she did not smile. "It's like an oven outside." He felt the despair crowding through him. He was useless. Clumsy and useless.

She turned toward him. "How is that nice sailor? From London."

"Churchill?" He forced a smile. "Fine. He misses having you to look after." Then he said quickly, "I wish I could take you out of here. Right now."

She shrugged. "And where would you take me?"

"Where you could be free of war. We could see the pyramids at Giza. Have dinner by the Nile. You could ride on a camel. Be like tourists." He laid his hand on hers. "It might help. . . ."

She pulled her hand away and thrust it under the sheet. "The pyramids." She seemed very drowsy. "You have seen them?"

"Only in the films."

Fascinated, he watched her hand emerge from the sheet. Like an animal coming from its hiding place.

She whispered, "But they would never allow it." Her hand lay beside his. "Regulations."

"I could try." Her wedding ring was gone. "I know I'm not much in the way of company, Chantal, but—"

She fastened her fingers on his hand, gripping it hard. "Do not say that! You are a fine person. When I think how I once treated you. What you did for me—"

Two tears ran from beneath the sunglasses and she said, "No, it is all right! I find I cry a lot here." She did not draw back as he dabbed her cheeks with his handkerchief.

He said, "I'll speak with the doctor." He stood up.

"You called me by my name just then." Her lip quivered.

"Of course." He smiled. "It's a beautiful name."

"And you are Steven." She nodded. "Nice."

"Is SHE going to be all right?" Marshall asked Dr. Williams.

"To be frank, I don't know. She might rally. Or she could slip right under."

After he listened in silence to Marshall's request, he said, "How long have you got?"

"I'm not certain. A few days."

"It might work. I don't see too much against it. Unless . . ."

"Unless what?"

"If you try to force a recovery, she might crack up completely. Any real human contact is a risk at the moment. But a worthwhile one. Fix it at your end. Leave the rest to us."

CAPTAIN Browning dabbed the back of his neck with his handkerchief. "Bloody hot." He gestured vaguely at the litter of folders and telegrams. "I'm just waiting to tie up a few loose ends. After that, I'll expect you to give me a ride." He grinned. "A meeting with my Italian friend has been arranged."

Marshall nodded. He was thinking of his visit to the hospital yesterday. He had spoken to Browning about his idea, but the captain obviously had a lot on his mind.

"I can get you four days. If that's what you want?" Browning said suddenly.

Marshall stared at him. "Four days, sir?"

Browning beamed. "Dr. Williams has fixed it from his end. He has a house in Cairo. He and his wife started off with Mrs. Travis about an hour ago." He rose and propelled Marshall to the door. "I've wangled the chief of staff's driver for you. If he gets a move on, you'll be in Cairo before dusk." He cocked his head to one side. "Four days. Make the most of 'em!"

IT WAS A SMALL BUT VERY pleasant-looking house on the outskirts of Cairo, close enough to the Nile to see the crowded masts of the local craft. Dr. Williams came down some steps to greet him.

"Here, let my houseboy take your bag. He'll get a bath ready, but first, a drink." He led the way to a cool, book-lined room. "Gin suit you?"

Marshall nodded and sat down, feeling strangely relaxed.

Williams gave him a glass and said, "Cheers. Fact is, I want to put you in the picture, as you naval chaps say. She's upstairs, by the way, with Megan, my wife."

He seemed to be assembling his thoughts. Then he said, "Chantal met her husband in England just before the war. She was a student, and he, too, was at the university. He's a first-rate engineer. I can imagine he would seem very attractive to any girl. Anyway, they got married and went straight to France. He was working there when the collapse came. Chantal had by that time gone home to Nantes, to her family."

Marshall started. "Left him?"

"Yes. She had discovered he was not the man she thought he was. He acted like a dyed-in-the-wool Nazi, and the German military authorities were damn glad to get him."

Marshall asked, "Then why did she go back to him in Paris?"

"Partly because she was afraid for her father. He is a Resistance chief in Nantes. I think she thought Travis would get at her through him. Give his name to the Germans." He sighed. "She started to work for Intelligence herself when Travis betrayed ten Frenchmen to the Gestapo. They were tortured, and the lucky ones were shot. From that moment Chantal was determined to find out what she could and warn the Resistance, or inform them if any chance of sabotage was likely.

"She was smuggled to England when the Gestapo were almost on her neck. Travis thought she was visiting her parents. When the department heard of these new radio-controlled bombs, and that Travis was in charge of the construction work in Italy, she was an obvious choice for making contact. A terrible risk to her, of course." Williams stood up. "I hear them coming."

The two women entered the room, and Marshall caught his breath. The girl was in a plain white dress which made her skin seem gold by comparison. She was wearing the same sunglasses.

The doctor's wife beamed at Marshall. The girl held out her hand. "I'm glad you could come. I expect you can do with some leave after—" Then she stiffened. "I am sorry. No *shoptalk*."

He replied, "Just four days, I'm afraid. But far better than I'd dared to hope."

She smiled for the first time. "You sound as if you mean that."

"He does." Williams strode to his cabinet. "Now we'll have a couple of drinks while *he* hops off to a bath and some dust-free clothes."

As Marshall followed the houseboy toward the stairs, the doctor's wife said, "What a nice fellow, but he looks so tired."

He heard the girl say simply, "We must try to make his leave a happy one."

He made his way up the stairs. We must try. For *his* sake. It was a beginning.

THE first two days were crammed with incident and color, with cheerful companionship and only a few moments of tension. Williams took them to Giza and the pyramids. Panting after a nimble-footed guide, they climbed the Great Pyramid of Cheops, all four hundred and fifty feet of it. Williams and his wife had stopped halfway, protesting it was too much at their time of life.

Once at the summit they looked at the spectacular view with pleasure and awe. She said, "I feel free up here. I really do." She added, "Are you happy?"

He touched her arm. "Very."

She did not draw away, but looked down at his hand, as if to test her own reactions.

At the foot of the pyramid Marshall had a camel ride. He could appreciate why they were called ships of the desert. When the beast rose to its feet in four separate lurches, it was all he could do to hold on. Chantal stood watching him, clapping her hands like a delighted schoolgirl.

On the third day Williams and his wife went into the city, and as Marshall sat opposite the girl at lunch he could feel an uncertainty growing between them.

She looked at him searchingly. "What will you do next?"

"Another job." He found he could hardly bear to face it. He hesitated. "I want to see you again. Very much."

543

"You hardly know me."

He watched her gravely. Was she pleased? "I want to know you, Chantal. I need to."

She stood up and walked to the window. "I might bring you unhappiness, as I have done to others."

He moved quickly to her side. "You must not say that. Any man would give his life for you. I know I would."

His hand was on her shoulder, but she pushed herself away. "But don't you understand, Steven?" Her voice was shaking. "I might hurt you! Perhaps I will never be able to—to *feel* anything."

"I can wait as long as you like."

She relaxed slightly. "I know that, too." She touched his mouth with her fingers. "But it would be cruel. I would never hurt you willingly."

"Well, then." He forced a smile. "Trust me."

He pulled her very gently against his chest. He could feel his heart pounding, matching hers. "I mustn't lose you, Chantal. I don't think I could go on."

She whispered, "Oh, Steven, I never thought this would happen."

Williams's car rattled past the window and then the doctor came into the room.

Marshall said, "It's all right, Doc. We've not been up to anything." He and the girl laughed like two conspirators.

Williams bit his lip. Marshall saw the paper in his hand and asked dully, "Recall?"

"I'm afraid so. They're sending a car for you." He added, "I'll go and tell Megan."

Alone again, they looked at each other. She said quietly, "Oh, Steven, your face. I hadn't realized. I am so full of my own troubles." She shook her head. "You have to go back. And I cannot even begin to share it with you." She dropped her forehead against his chest. "It's not fair. One more day would not have hurt them!"

He lifted her chin with his fingers. "I'll be back. There will be more than one day then."

She was studying him, the tears pouring down her face quite unheeded. "I will remember everything—the Great Pyramid, how you looked on that camel, *everything*."

Marshall heard a car outside. He stooped and kissed her gently on the forehead. Then he turned and walked out into the sunlight.

FRENZEL WAITED IN the cabin doorway until Marshall finished signing some papers and looked up. "All ready to go, Chief?" he asked.

"The depot ship's engineers have just gone, sir," Frenzel said. "They made a pretty fair job, considering the lack of time."

It was seven in the evening. Sailing time had been set for nine. Browning had informed Marshall that the Italian general had been given Browning's personal message by British Intelligence agents. Phase two would be this rendezvous at sea.

Gerrard edged around the door and said, "I've made arrangements for our passengers, sir. Captain Browning would like to bunk in the wardroom."

"Yes." Marshall smiled. "I offered him this cabin, but he'd rather get the full treatment, apparently."

Frenzel chuckled. "He'll be one of the boys again."

A boatswain's mate peered over Gerrard's shoulder. "Beg pardon, sir, but Commander Simeon's comin' aboard."

Marshall said, "I'd better go and meet him." He found Simeon in the wardroom, staring at a cup of coffee. "Has your gear been stowed, sir?" He was careful to be formal.

Simeon looked at him calmly. "Yes. Captain Browning will be aboard in about an hour with the others."

"Who will they be?"

Simeon eyed him without expression. "An Intelligence chap from HQ, and of course, er, Travis."

"Travis." Marshall stared at him. "What the hell for?"

"Browning got his way over meeting this Italian *friend* of his. But apart from the old-comrades association, we need something else to bargain with. Insurance. If this wavering Eyetie brass hat is to understand what might happen if he goes against us on *the day,* Travis is the man to tell him. With his knowledge of the bombs' potential and how the Jerries intend to use 'em, who better?"

"I see." It made Marshall feel sick that Travis was to be aboard his ship again. "Will he be under guard, sir?"

Simeon smiled. "*Watched.*" He gestured vaguely. "But he will mess with us. Give him a sense of belonging again."

Marshall regarded him gravely. You know. About Chantal. You're enjoying it. Getting your own back. Aloud he said, "As far as I'm concerned, he can go to hell."

Simeon nodded, his face very serious. "Of course, old chap. You run the boat, and leave the diplomacy to us, eh?"

Marshall walked past him. By the time he had reached the bridge he was feeling calmer. A seaman climbed up the ladder from the casing and saluted. "The mail, sir." He held out an envelope. "For you. By hand, from a Dr. Williams."

Marshall almost tore it from the man's fingers. There was a photograph inside and a short note: "Got it developed as fast as I could. Thought it might help."

She looked just as she had when they were alone together. Sad, happy, wistful. He stared at it fixedly, remembering her voice when she had said, "I would never hurt you. . . ." He put the picture carefully in his wallet. The doctor had done far more than he knew.

Warwick called, "Prisoner and escort coming aboard, sir!"

Marshall shook his head. "Not a prisoner, Sub. Mr. Travis is to be treated as a passenger."

Warwick stared at him with astonishment. "Aye, aye, sir."

Travis climbed up the ladder and greeted Marshall with a curt nod. "We meet again," he said.

The army captain who accompanied him said, "I'm not much of a one for ships, sir."

Marshall replied, "It should be calm enough."

He turned his back on them as Captain Browning arrived, obviously excited by the prospect of his trip in a submarine.

Marshall saluted. "You're very welcome, sir."

Browning beamed. "I have a feeling we're going to be lucky on this mission."

Soon the deck picked up the steady quiver of Frenzel's motors. Marshall saw the blink of a light from the depot ship, heard Blythe say, "Proceed, sir."

"Let go forward."

He could feel Browning just behind him, hear his heavy breathing as he lived each separate function and movement. Marshall saluted and said, "She's all yours, sir. If you'd like to take her out." Browning stared at him. Then he stepped up onto the foregratings and tugged his cap firmly over his eyes.

Marshall stood aside, and was glad he had made the offer.

A voice called, "Control room to bridge."

The massive head moved very slightly. "Bridge."

The other voice sounded surprised. "Commander Simeon requests permission to come up, sir."

Browning glanced at Marshall. Then he bent over the speaking tube. "Denied," was all he said.

Chapter 8

It HAD taken six days to reach their present position off the northwest coast of Sicily. A careful, steady run, surfacing only briefly to charge batteries at night.

All day they had prowled back and forth, well clear of the land, but as evening had drawn near Marshall had ordered a change of course, one which would take the submarine directly south to the rendezvous. General Cappello was to meet them in a launch, then come aboard the U-boat.

Marshall and Browning entered the wardroom and found Simeon making notes on his personal chart. Captain Hart of Intelligence, who had moaned and retched through most of the passage, was drooped at the table, his face the color of cheese. Travis was slumped in a corner, staring fixedly at nothing.

Simeon asked, "Satisfied, sir?"

"Quite, thanks." Browning sat down. "Tonight, God willing."

Travis remarked, "Not too soon for me."

Simeon looked at him. "What'll you do after the war?"

"Go back to work, I expect," Travis replied. "Why?"

"Just wondered."

Travis said curtly, "I know what you think. I couldn't care less. Your bosses appear to know my real value."

Simeon smiled. "What about your *wife?*"

"None of your damned business." Travis's composure was fading. There was something frightening and unbalanced about him.

Simeon glanced at Marshall. "How was she when you saw her in Cairo? Pretty fit?"

Browning interrupted. "That'll do."

Simeon held up both hands apologetically. "Sorry, sir, if I put my big foot in something." He looked at Marshall. "Didn't realize it was like that, old boy."

Marshall felt anger rising inside him like a flood. "Well, now you know, don't you, sir?"

So Simeon was using Travis to get at him. To needle him into saying or doing something stupid. It was Gail. Simeon was brooding over the fact that long ago he and Gail had been lovers. It hurt his pride.

MARSHALL waited beside the periscope well and watched the busy preparations around him. According to all the reports they did not have too much to fear. There was no regular antisubmarine patrol in the rendezvous area, and though by day there were plenty of aircraft on the lookout for intruders, the Italians seemed loath to do anything at night. He looked at the clock. Nearly midnight.

Browning came in dressed in fresh khaki drill. He grinned and said, "Mustn't let the side down. Want to look my best, eh?"

The seamen by the ladder smiled broadly. They all seemed to like Browning.

"Ready when you are, sir," Marshall said.

Browning said, "Let's get it over with."

Marshall nodded. "Take her up, Number One. Periscope depth."

Through the periscope he was pleased to see the sky clouded over. He said, "Surface," and then, "Try not to let the general fall in the drink. It would be a bad start."

The responding laughter was lost in the roar of air into the tanks, and Marshall was up the ladder and spinning the locking wheel. The night air struck him in the face like a wet towel, and he had to grip the streaming metal to stop himself from falling.

Blythe struggled up beside him, opening the speaking tubes.

Marshall moved his night glasses across the screen, wondering how good the agents' report had been about this Italian general. Then he saw a small stab of light, almost lost in spray.

Blythe called, "It's the right signal."

"Good. Acknowledge. And get Captain Hart up here to interpret for me."

Hart appeared on the pitching bridge. "You all right?" Marshall asked.

The soldier nodded. "I feel better in the open."

The other craft was lifting and rolling on a cautious diagonal approach. Someone was shouting through a megaphone, and Hart said angrily, "The general won't come over to us, sir. He wants us to go aboard the launch."

549

"Ask him why the change of plan."

"He says there have been two fast patrol boats from the mainland poking about to the north of this area, sir."

Marshall could hardly blame the general for not wanting to be caught in an enemy submarine. He said to Blythe, "Yeoman, tell Captain Browning what's happening."

A line was thrown across, and as the launch surged and groaned into the fenders that had been rigged, Marshall saw the helmsman glowing faintly in a compass light. There were several other figures, but not many. The general was taking no chances.

Browning reached the bridge, panting fiercely. "Seems I'll have to go over. I'm taking Travis and Hart with me."

Marshall said, "I'll send an armed party with you, sir."

"You won't," Browning said. "I'm not even taking Simeon. It takes long enough to get out of trouble without having half the bloody navy in the launch!"

Marshall guided him to the ladder. It made sense of course. And in any case the launch was now firmly lashed alongside. It was just that he disliked the idea of Browning going with only Hart and Travis for company.

Browning lifted his leg over the coaming and muttered, "In any case, I've got my revolver with me. And thanks, my boy. You know what for." Then he was gone.

Marshall held his breath as the three men made their way across the treacherous pattern of spray between the hulls.

On the speaking tube he heard, "Control room to bridge. Fast HE to the north of us, sir. But it's very faint. Nothing to worry about yet."

Blythe, who had returned to the bridge, said, "Probably those patrol boats, sir."

Gerrard's voice came again. "Control room to bridge. Torpedo officer wants to come up, sir."

"Trouble?"

Gerrard hesitated. "I'd rather he told you, sir."

"Very well."

Buck pounded up the ladder. "The Very pistol, sir. Missing from the wardroom." He was breathing fast.

A lookout yelled, "Sir! They're fighting aboard the launch!"

Marshall climbed up to the screen. He saw several figures reeling about in the wheelhouse, and then a man burst out and ran aft waving his arm in the air. There was a dull crack, and seconds later a flare burst.

"It's Travis!" Marshall yelled. "Shoot him down, Cain!"

Marshall saw Browning's bald head shining in the glare as he groped his way toward Travis, who was bent double, reloading the flare pistol, his hair blowing wildly in the wind.

Cain yelled, "Can't shoot, sir! The others are in the way!"

Browning steadied himself against a ventilator, dragging the revolver from his pocket. Travis raised the pistol once more, his teeth bared as if he were laughing or screaming.

"Control room to bridge! HE at zero one zero. Closing!"

Blythe said desperately, "They'd be blind to miss that flare!"

Travis pulled his trigger even as Browning dropped on one knee and fired. Then, as Browning's bullet smashed the other man down, the second flare exploded into the rear of the small wheelhouse in a searing ball of fire.

In the next instant the whole of the launch's deck seemed to be on fire. Blazing petrol ran down the scuppers, and Marshall saw two men leap screaming into the sea.

Gerrard was yelling, "HE closing fast, sir! *We must get out of it!*"

Marshall watched the launch helplessly as more petrol burst into flames, the fire licking toward the submarine until the mooring lines parted like cotton.

Blythe gasped, "The cap'n's had it, sir!" Browning had lurched to his feet, hesitated, and then toppled backward into the flames.

The wind and sea were carrying the burning launch clear. Then with a great spluttering sound it sank under the surface.

Marshall heard himself say, "Casing party below. Clear the bridge." As soon as he heard the distant roar of engines he shouted into the speaking tube, "Dive, dive, dive!"

Men dashed past him, then he himself ran to the hatch. As his boots thudded onto the control-room deck he said, "One hundred and eighty meters."

The hull gave a sharp creak as the boat went into her dive. Down, down, the depth needles crept around remorselessly.

"One hundred and eighty meters, sir."

Marshall clenched his fists, thinking of Browning, fighting back the sense of loss and the anger. He swung around as Simeon shouted in his ear, "Why did Travis do it?" He was almost screaming. "Why?"

Marshall brushed him aside. "Probably because you triggered him off. *Sir!*"

THREE minutes later the first charges exploded. Several seamen exchanged quick glances, but Marshall kept his eyes on the depth needles. She was going down, deeper than she ever had in his hands, and metal groaned as the pressure mounted.

"HE closing from astern, sir. Two vessels."

The first attack had been made by one vessel. The second had no doubt stopped, to keep her sonar unimpaired by the attacker's propeller noises, but would join the attack any moment.

Marshall tightened his grip on the support, picturing the depth charges rolling off their little rails, falling slowly, ten feet a second.

The charges exploded, the echoing detonation booming against the hull. The boat rocked to one side, shook herself and came back again. Flakes of paint drifted through the lamplight.

Marshall listened to the subdued roar of engines as the attacking vessel tore away to prepare another sortie. He snapped, "Group up. Full ahead."

Simeon asked harshly, "What are you doing? Wouldn't it be better to lie low until they give up?"

Marshall replied, "I think not, sir. The real job of these patrol boats is to pin us down until dawn. By then they'll have plenty of help." He looked at Simeon impassively. "I'm not waiting."

Blythe murmured, "Here we go again."

The engine noises grew louder, rattled high overhead and then faded again. The charges exploded much nearer, making the hull tilt and yaw. Marshall said, "Take her up to ninety meters. Slow ahead."

Gerrard glanced at him quickly. "Take her *up*, sir?"

"Yes. They're getting us fixed." He waited, listening to the compressed air as it drowned out the enemy's engines.

"Ninety meters, sir."

"Hold her so."

The deck rocked gently as a charge exploded. It seemed a long way off, and somebody gave a disbelieving whistle.

Marshall looked at the chart. "Starboard twenty. Steer three zero zero. Must get more sea room." He turned to Gerrard. "What d'you think, Number One? How many charges do they carry?"

"They've not room for more than a dozen each, sir." He swung around at a scratching sound, the echo from the patrol boats' sonar.

Marshall said, "One hundred and eighty meters again!"

A pattern of six charges exploded in a long and ragged bombardment. The last pair burst with such a roar that the hull tilted its stern too steeply for Gerrard's men to restrain the dive. On every side the boat seemed to be jerking and groaning in agony. More paint flaked down, and when a signalman grasped the conningtower ladder for support he shouted, "It's *bending!*"

When the telltales flickered into line, the depth gauges read two hundred meters. Even the air felt different, as if it were being squeezed solid by the tremendous pressure around the hull. Marshall smiled at Gerrard. "Makes our first deep dive seem a bit trivial, eh?" It was all he could do to speak so lightly.

Devereaux cleared his throat. "We are in six hundred fathoms, sir. As far as I can see, we've plenty of sea room now."

Marshall looked at Simeon, and was surprised to see him sitting on the deck, his back against the main bulkhead. He was staring at a space between his feet, like a man under a spell.

"HE closing from astern, sir." The monotonous *thrum-thrum-thrum* seemed endless.

They all looked at the deckhead, visualizing the great depth of water above, the crushing darkness below.

"HE's speeding up, sir!"

Marshall glanced quickly around the control room. His men would all know why the engines were increasing speed. The charges were coming down . . . *now*. The enemy was haring away to avoid having his own tail blown off.

There were three, and to those who crouched and clung to the wildly bucking hull it was like an avalanche crashing about their ears. Lights shattered, glass flew in all directions and pieces of loose equipment rained down on the sobbing, gasping men.

"Emergency lights!"

Marshall skidded on broken glass and heard someone calling for help. He watched, fascinated, as the depth gauges took another

553

slow turn. They were over seven hundred feet beneath the surface. It was incredible that they had withstood the pressures of both sea and explosions. He peered at the clock. After three in the morning. The attack had gone on for over two hours.

Gerrard croaked, "She's steady, sir."

"Hold her." Marshall touched his arm. "You can do it, Bob!"

Gerrard nodded dumbly, and turned back to his gauges as Marshall added, "Check all departments now."

No damage or casualties were reported. But they heard the distant revolutions again as the enemy began another slow sweep somewhere to starboard.

Simeon crossed to Marshall's side. In a fierce whisper he said, "Get us out of this! Increase speed, do what you like, but get me out of it!"

Marshall regarded him coldly. "You said *us* the first time, sir."

"HE still closing from starboard, sir."

Marshall did not turn. "I'm going to increase speed very soon now. When I surface, not before."

"HE's stopped, sir."

Even the operator turned in his seat as Simeon exclaimed, "*Surface?* Are you bloody mad? You'll kill the lot of us!"

Marshall replied quietly, "The enemy's stopped. They're probably looking for flotsam and oil slicks, or bodies maybe. So we'll stay down here. Silent routine until they go away."

Simeon was shouting. "And if they don't go?"

"Then we'll have to stick it out till tomorrow night."

Simeon gaped. "Tomorrow night. Another day of this?"

Frenzel said flatly, "By then they'll have whistled up the heavy mob." He was watching Simeon with disgust. "We'll have plenty of company."

Marshall said to Simeon, "Get a grip on yourself and I'll—"

Gerrard shouted, "They've started up their engines!"

The even thrumming beat grew and then began to fade until it was lost completely. Marshall breathed out very slowly. "Ten minutes and then we'll go up for a look."

The ten minutes seemed twenty times as long as the attack. Nobody spoke, and apart from the motors' purring hum and the occasional creak of protesting steel, they stuck it out in silence.

Marshall thought of Browning's face above the screen before

he had gone aboard the launch. "Thanks, my boy. You know what for." What had he meant? For replacing his dead son perhaps. Marshall hoped it was that.

He said, "Stand by to take her up, Number One. But first warn all departments. In case we're jumped as we pop up."

But when they rose to periscope depth Marshall found the sea devoid of movement. He told Buck to take over the periscope and then walked to the intercom beside the wheel. He paused, not knowing what to say.

"This is the captain. It's been a noisy night." That would make someone smile. "Some of you still don't know about Captain Browning." He bit his lip. "Well, he died back there. Doing something he thought was worthwhile, as I did, and still do." He turned to hide his face from the others. "If he could, I'm sure he'd be the first to compliment you on the way you've behaved. I'm trying to do it for him. Thank you all." He tried again. "Very much."

He released the button and said quietly, "Open the lower hatch. We'll switch over to the diesels and begin charging as soon as I've had another look around."

He saw Frenzel blocking his way to the ladder. "What's wrong, Chief?"

Frenzel faced him gravely. "I just wanted to say thanks to you, sir. From us."

Chapter 9

THE room in Alexandria looked just the same, yet without Browning behind his big desk it seemed totally different. Marshall tried to relax in a cane chair, surprised that he felt no tiredness. He had berthed his submarine alongside the depot ship in the early morning. Now it was evening.

There were four others in the room. The chief of staff, two lieutenants and Rear Admiral Dundas, the top liaison officer with British and American Intelligence. In a lightweight gray suit he looked rather like a retired schoolmaster. The rear admiral pressed his fingertips together and regarded Marshall through heavy-framed glasses. "We've had a lot more information since the last time you were here. The Germans are building up stocks of radio-controlled bombs, some even larger and better than the one you saw at work." He added, "If our invasion of Sicily is to have a chance of succeeding, we *must* minimize the use of this weapon."

Marshall replied, "Captain Browning believed that, sir!"

Dundas went on. "The invasion is timed to take place three weeks and four days from tomorrow. We can forget about the bombs already in Sicily. The first wave of commandos will have to neutralize them. The dump on the mainland is the real headache. It's a port called Nestore in the Gulf of Policastro. It has good rail and road links to carry the bombs to different military sectors."

Marshall stood up and walked to the nearest wall chart. Nestore. It was shown as a small fishing village.

The chief of staff crossed to his side. "The Jerries have made the place into a strongbox. They have an antisubmarine net across the harbor and several observation towers, and the Italians are supplying an around-the-clock antisubmarine patrol."

"What about a bombing attack, sir?"

"Out of the question, I'm afraid. It would be too difficult to make a real impression. And it would tell the enemy what we were really afraid of, and why. Just as if we'd given him the time and place of the invasion."

Marshall said, "I think we could do it, sir." He had spoken almost without realizing it.

Dundas regarded him gravely. "Do you really know what you're saying?"

Marshall did not reply directly. "We've had my submarine for months now, and yet perhaps none of us has properly understood how to use her to full advantage." He began to move restlessly back and forth in front of the desk. Browning's desk. "This one last job would prove our worth."

Dundas added, "And prove Browning's faith was justified from the beginning."

"Yes, sir. Something like that. But I'd want a free hand. Once we reach the place. My decision whether we go in, or turn and pull out if the situation's hopeless."

The chief of staff's eyebrows rose very slightly, but dropped again as Dundas snapped, "Agreed. It's quite an idea! You'll carry a landing party, Marshall, about thirty Royal Marine commandos. You'll have to cram 'em in where you can." He rose and held out his hand. "I thought I'd seen every sort of bravery. Yours is a new kind.

557

I'm proud to have met you." Then he turned to the chief of staff. "I'll want maximum effort, Charles!"

"Yes, sir." The chief of staff looked at Marshall. "My men will get on with running repairs. I understand from your engineer that the starboard screw is a bit damaged after that last attack?"

"A flaw in one of the blades, sir. Could be awkward."

The admiral waved his hand. "Do what you can, Charles." To Marshall he said, "I want you right out of it. I can't give you more than three days, I'm afraid. But if I let you remain here, you'll be poking around the boat, and I want you *fresh* when you put to sea again."

"Thank you, sir." Marshall felt confused. She would know by now about her husband. Would she blame him?

"One other thing." The admiral was smiling broadly. "Your promotion to commander has come through. Congratulations. So be off with you. I'm grateful. As many others will be when you've pulled this one off."

At least he had not said "if."

Marshall picked up his cap and walked out the door.

In the room a lieutenant said, "Surely, sir, it's not possible, is it?"

Dundas said, "An hour ago I'd have said it was completely *impossible*. But after meeting that young man, I'm not certain." His eyes sharpened. "If anyone can make a go of it, *he* will!"

IT WAS one in the morning when Marshall reached Dr. Williams's house beside the river. All the way from Alexandria in the chief of staff's car he had been thinking about this moment. How she would accept him. What she might say.

The door swung open as he reached for it. It was Chantal. His heart beat painfully just to see her. With the light behind her she looked very slim. He could smell the scent of her hair and wanted to hold her and not let go for a long time. Instead he said quietly, "You shouldn't have waited up."

She took his arm. Her eyes looked very bright. "The others have gone to bed." She smiled. "Tact, I think."

There were cold meat and salad on a small table. A bottle of wine stood in a bucket of ice beside it. She said, "I will pour you some wine now, yes?"

He sat down. "About your husband, Chantal. I . . ."

He saw her fingers tighten on the bottle. "They explained. I was so afraid this might happen. Right from the moment I heard, I began to worry."

He replied, "I'm sorry. I thought you might feel like this."

She turned very quickly. "No!" The bottle fell back into the bucket and she ran across the room. "I was afraid for *you!*" She dropped on her knees beside him, her eyes searching his face. "When I learned they had sent him with you . . . " She touched his hand. "But you are back. I have been praying for that."

Marshall felt the strain giving way to a peace he had never known. He said quietly, "To hear you say that. To know . . . "

She tried to smile. "Do not look so sad, *please*. You are back. It is all I care about. When Dr. Williams told me it was over, I . . . " Her hand gripped his wrist. "Steven, it *is* over? Tell me!"

He replied dully, "It didn't work, Chantal."

Then she said very softly, "You're going to do another mission? Is that what you are telling me?"

He nodded. "Yes."

"But why must it be *you?* You have done enough. Let someone else take over."

He ran his fingers through her hair. "I must do it, my darling. You, of all people, must know that I have to."

"Yes, Steven, I do. That only makes it worse."

"I've got three days. They want me out from under their feet."

"Three days. Why do the British always think three days is just the right amount?" She smiled, tears running down her cheeks.

She went to the table and poured wine, and they drank in silence until Marshall said suddenly, "When I get back will you please marry me?"

She stared at him for several moments. As if she had misheard. He said, "You must know how I feel."

"You do not have to ask, Steven." She touched his hair. "If *you* are sure. I am so worried that—"

The rest was lost as he pulled her against him. It was all he wanted. To know she felt as he did.

They walked up the stairs and she left him by his door, saying, "I am glad I waited up for you. Perhaps you would have changed your mind otherwise?" She moved away before he could answer.

Later, as he lay in bed half listening to a breeze against the shutters, he stiffened, hearing the door open and close very softly. The girl stood motionless beside the bed, her figure a pale ghost.

She said, "Please. I had to come." She sounded as if she were shaking. "But do not touch me, my darling. Try to understand."

He lay beside her, hardly daring to breathe. He could sense her desperate uncertainty, and he wanted more than anything to help her. He listened to her breathing until it became steadier.

She reached out impulsively and took his hand. She slowly laid it on her breast. "Steven." She kept repeating his name. Then she said, "Love me, Steven. *Love me.*"

In the depot ship's operations room Marshall followed Rear Admiral Dundas to the chart table and nodded to his own officers.

There were others, too. The Royal Marine commando officers, the senior operations officer, Intelligence experts, the chief of staff and, he was surprised to see, the paratroop lieutenant called Smith, who had so recently led them to find Chantal.

Dundas stood looking down at the chart and then said, "You have been given details of the mission. To enter the port of Nestore and destroy the enemy's bombing capability. This job is the big one. The grand slam. Captain Lambert is in charge of a detachment of thirty marines and their equipment. Including their canoes"—he shot the captain a quick smile—"or cockles, as I understand they are known. Lieutenant Smith will be in charge of demolition and act as general adviser on local matters. The submarine's fuel and fresh water will be reduced to a minimum to help compensate for the extra load." He looked at Marshall. "You want to add anything?"

Marshall shook his head.

Dundas consulted his watch. "You slip from the depot ship in approximately eight hours. You will embark the marines as soon as it is dark." He looked at Frenzel. "You want something?"

"The damaged screw, sir. Can't it be repaired?"

"The base engineer said it would take too long." He smiled thinly. "The Allies will invade Sicily three weeks from tomorrow. If you fail to destroy the enemy's supply of radio bombs, there may be no invasion . . . period." Dundas was closing his briefcase. He said suddenly, "I should add that Commander Simeon will be accompanying this mission, to take overall control of land operations."

Marshall remained impassive. He already knew about this. He also knew why Simeon was absent from the briefing.

He had been unpacking his grip in a borrowed cabin aboard the depot ship when Simeon strode in, his face cold with anger. "So you're the admiral's bright boy at last!" he had said.

Marshall had stayed silent.

Simeon had gone on, "Well, I've had your number for some time. I knew what you'd been up to with my wife—"

Marshall had interrupted. "Before you knew her."

Simeon's face had been pink with rage. "And now you've stepped into Travis's shoes, and no doubt his bed as well!"

Marshall said quietly. "Oh, I forgot to mention my promotion. Now, *old chap*, I can't be accused of striking a superior officer!"

The pain had lanced up his arm, and he had seen Simeon sprawled on the bunk, blood running down his chin and over his impeccable white shirt.

MARSHALL stepped over a sleeping marine and walked into the control room. The boat was crammed with marines and seamen, struggling to sleep, eat and work in some semblance of order. They had had over a full week of it.

Frenzel was standing by his control panel. "Still bothered, Chief?" Marshall asked.

"A bit." Frenzel cocked his head. "That flaw in the screw. We can't do more than six knots submerged without making a bad vibration. Any good sonar would pick us up in no time."

"Then six knots it must be, Chief." He smiled. "If there's a real emergency, we'll have to take to the cockles!"

He entered the packed wardroom and waited while the others eased into position to see his large-scale plan. With all but essential fans and machinery shut down, the air was greasy and humid, and everyone was showing signs of wear. But their eyes were lit by that old excitement. Anxiety, tension, fear, the need to get it over with. He said, "Most of you know that the weather report is bad. Strong winds from the southwest and a rough sea."

He looked at them slowly. The marine officers and Smith, his own small team, except for Gerrard and Frenzel, who were on watch. And Simeon, sitting at the opposite end of the table, arms folded, his face devoid of expression.

He continued. "So this is how we'll handle it."

They all craned forward. On the chart the port of Nestore looked like a large pouch, with the entrance barely a quarter of a mile across. Marshall said, "We know there's an antisubmarine boom here"—he reached out with some brass dividers—"controlled by a single vessel which pulls it open and closed as required. The left side of the port is an almost sheer cliff, and to the right, where the main fishing village once stood, the land has been cleared and pillboxes have been constructed to give a good field of fire." He tapped the small colored circles.

Devereaux asked, "What about the coastal patrols, sir?"

"Yesterday we were able to time one of the boats. They are regular and precise, and therefore predictable." He added sharply, "However, we shall take nothing for granted when we surface and lower the cockles."

They had had a brief run-through of the method of unloading the cockles two days earlier, and one unpleasant fact had come to light. On their own the cockles were very light and easy to handle. But loaded with weapons and demolition gear they would break up, if an attempt to slide them outboard was made in bad weather. Buck had come up with a simple solution. The submarine's deck gun would be used as a derrick to sway them over the side.

Marshall looked at Simeon. "Over to you."

Simeon took the dividers. "Here is a railway which runs from the port. Captain Lambert will lead half the landing force and carry out demolition. I will take the other party, and with Lieutenant Smith will do our bit above the village itself." His eyes flickered toward Marshall. "And our commander here will carry out a torpedo attack on the main loading jetty at the top of the harbor. It is a concrete bunker which enables the bombs to be loaded aboard ship without appearing aboveground." He added, "The engineer, Travis, stated that the construction is formidable, but once brought down, it would block the whole installation for weeks."

Lambert said, "Should be interesting."

Marshall said, "It's mostly a matter of timing. The nearest German garrison of any size is sixteen miles northeast of the port. So, bearing that in mind, we have three vital points." He ticked them off on his fingers. "First, the coastal patrols. Second, the boom and the inner harbor patrol. Finally, how soon or late the port defenders will be alerted and thereby call for inland support." He smiled at their strained faces. "Any comments?"

Warwick asked, "Couldn't we cut the boom and slip through undetected, sir?"

"Afraid not, Sub. The port is only about six fathoms deep. It was dredged for coasters and medium-sized ships. We will approach the boom at the arranged time. Fire our fish into the top of the harbor, and then lift off the landing parties, who with luck will have created their own sort of pandemonium by then." He looked at his watch. "We'll go to action stations in four hours. German uniforms and equipment will then be issued, but first I want everyone to have a good meal."

MARSHALL wedged his elbows painfully against the bridge screen and leveled his glasses toward the land while the conning tower swayed dizzily through a steep arc. The weather was bad, and with a following sea it felt as if the boat were out of control.

Blythe shouted above the tumult of spray and wind, "All clear on sonar, sir!" He spluttered as a wave exploded over the bridge. "*Hell*, what a night!"

Marshall said, "Open the main hatch."

They had been surfaced for ten minutes. It seemed like an hour. He peered across the bows. If they could get the cockles in the water without mishap, the wind might help them reach shore. He made up his mind. "First landing party prepare to move off."

The forward hatch scraped noisily, and the first of the little boats was hauled toward the makeshift crane. Marshall watched as Warwick's crew swung the gun slowly over the side, one small cockle, complete with occupants and weapons, dangling from the tackle like an overloaded basket.

Buck yelled, "Lower away, lads!" and the cockle touched the tossing water almost shyly. In a second it was free and away, its paddles glinting.

"Next!" Buck was clinging to the guardrail. "Lower away!"

Finally all five canoes were off, and Blythe gave a great sigh. "There they go, paddles flying like bottles in the fleet canteen."

"Good. Close the forehatch. Gun crew below." Marshall wiped his streaming face. "Clear the bridge."

He groped for the speaking tube. "Bring her around onto the

new course. Then take her down. Ninety meters." He scrambled down the ladder with Blythe.

It was a relief to run in deeper water again. The motion steadied, and he felt his cheeks tingling from wind and sea.

Simeon was watching from the chart space, his eyes in shadow as he asked, "How long now?"

Marshall moved to the chart. "It'll take Lambert's party all of three hours to get ashore." He could picture the tiny cockles bobbing over the waves, Lambert and his men peering through the darkness for a first glimpse of land. And then . . .

He walked over to join Lieutenant Smith. "I will get close to the boom and drop your party. You shouldn't have too much bother."

Smith grinned. "I've briefed 'em, sir. I know this part of the coast from way back, when the good people of Nestore caught fish."

Marshall smiled and said, "Just remember the arrangements for pickup, even if you forget everything else."

The hands on the control-room clock moved slowly. One hour. Then two.

"Getting close, sir." Devereaux's fingers were twisting a pencil over and over in short nervous jerks.

"*Sir!*" It was Speke, the senior sonar operator. "I'm getting some strange echoes at green four five."

Marshall put a hydrophone headset to his ear and heard it, like water tinkling in a fountain or someone tapping a delicate glass at regular intervals. He thrust his hands into his pockets to stop their shaking. Then he said quietly, "They must have laid a complete detection grid on the seabed. As much as two miles out."

To reach any sort of position for attacking the harbor installations they would have to be right up to the boom. He felt anger and despair squeezing his brain like a vise. He looked at the clock. "What time is first light?"

Devereaux said dully, "Couple of hours' time, sir."

Marshall said, "We will go in *on the surface.* We will retain Lieutenant Smith's landing party until we are inside the harbor."

It seemed an age before anyone spoke. Then Devereaux said, "But they'll never open the boom for us, sir!"

"You'll talk your way inside, eh?" Simeon could not hide his amusement. "I think you're deluding yourself!"

"Perhaps. But that is how we will do it, so pass the word to all sections." He looked at Gerrard. "The enemy will most likely keep the boom shut while they send a boat to investigate."

In his mind he could see it. The submarine lying surfaced and naked under the eyes of a coastal battery. The boom vessel's skipper being called to his bridge. It would all take time. He said in an expressionless tone, "It's too late to execute another raid, even if we had the means. It's this boat and our lives balanced against what is at stake in ten days' time." He paused, watching their faces. "We have to succeed. That's my decision."

Smith whistled. "Right up to the front door!"

Simeon came forward and stood almost touching Marshall, his face tense and pale. "If you wreck this one, my friend, I'll see that you never even command a ferryboat for the *rest of your life!*"

Marshall met his stare. "If *we* wreck this one, I don't imagine anyone will be left, do you?"

As MARSHALL, with the lookouts and Blythe at his heels, burst through the hatch and climbed to the bridge, he realized that the weather had eased. Warwick climbed up beside him and adjusted his binoculars against the small patch of paling sky.

"Control room, sir. Commander Simeon wants to come up."

"Granted." Marshall looked at Warwick and Blythe. "We have intelligence reports that *U-178* is one of several U-boats working with the Italian navy. She's not supposed to be in this area, but when we're challenged to identify ourselves we'll claim her number and hope for the best."

Simeon's voice came through the gloom. "My, we are getting cunning."

"If you wish to remain on the bridge, just remember, one more crack like that and down you go."

"Five thousand yards to the detection grid, sir." The muzzles of the Vierling were shining in the first faint daylight.

The machine gunners were standing by their weapons, their heads encased in German coal-scuttle helmets. Warwick, too, was in his enemy uniform.

Marshall consulted his watch. Getting close.

"Tell the chief to switch to main engines. No friendly boat would come sneaking inshore using battery power."

He jumped as the clutches brought the heavy diesels into use, the exhaust spluttering and coughing throatily. Out there, dozing over his radio set in some shore bunker, the enemy operator would hear it soon enough. Probably long before the detector on the seabed made any direct contact. The uneven swish of their damaged screw. The fault might yet be used to their advantage.

He snapped, "Run up the German ensign, Yeoman."

Simeon was crouched almost double, fumbling with a submachine gun. He said irritably, "I hope this thing works!"

The scarlet flag flapped in the wind above their heads. Marshall glanced at it. Hating it. Depending on it.

"Sonar reports echoes from dead ahead, sir."

Marshall sucked in a long breath. "Tell your deck gunners to prepare, Sub."

"Your cap, sir."

Marshall took it and pulled it over his unruly hair. He said, "Any second now, I should think."

The light seemed to grow with each turn of the screws, laying them bare and vulnerable. Across the sharp stem he saw the first blunt outline of land. In half an hour there would be no room to maneuver, if the plan misfired.

Suddenly a piercing blue light blinked over the undulating water. "The challenge, sir." Blythe licked his lips. "I'd better get ready." He seemed unable to hold his lamp firmly.

Marshall turned deliberately. "Now don't get jumpy. We've had a bad time of it and we're trying to get into the first available *friendly* port, right?"

All but Simeon nodded in time to his quiet voice.

He touched Warwick's hand. "You've got the signal ready. Read it to the yeoman." He hoped Warwick had made a proper translation. The signal read, "We require assistance." Nothing more. What any submarine commander might send, if he were at last within sight of safety.

The blue light blinked again. Warwick said, "They're asking our number, sir."

"Then make it. *U-178.*"

This was the vital moment. He bit his lip. Someone out there was trying to make a decision.

When he raised his glasses again he saw the full breadth of the harbor mouth and, poised just to starboard, the boom vessel, her bridge windows glinting faintly. He moved the glasses slowly, noting the lines of dots, the buoys which held the antisubmarine boom in position.

"Tell Lieutenant Buck to stand by. Tubes one to five."

Gerrard's voice came up the tube. "There's a freighter moored in the harbor, sir. I just saw it on the main periscope." He was almost shouting. "We won't be able to hit the installations!"

Simeon crossed the bridge in three strides. He spoke in a savage whisper. "Well, you can't fire now, can you? That ship will take the salvo, and the Jerries will have the wreck moved within a week!"

"Signal, sir." Warwick was listening to Blythe. "They want us to heave to. They're sending someone out."

"Slow ahead both engines. But retain course."

Soon a small harbor boat could be seen crossing the boom.

Simeon said fiercely, "Let's get out while we still can!"

Warwick said, "Captain Lambert's party will be coming back by now, sir, if they've not been caught. We can't leave them."

Marshall said to Simeon, "He's right." He looked at Warwick and added, "Thanks, Sub." He turned away. "Tell Smith I want him on the forecasing."

Blythe had glasses trained on the approaching boat. He said, "Eyetie launch, sir. But there's a Jerry officer in charge!"

Some of the seamen on the casing were waving at the launch, and Marshall saw an unfamiliar sailor just below the bridge. It was Smith, who had stripped to his shorts and wore a German forage cap rakishly over one ear. He, too, was waving, and he shouted something in German.

Clinging to the launch's small wheelhouse was a white-clad lieutenant, a megaphone in one hand. "*Was ist los, Herr Kapitän?*"

Marshall took Warwick's arm. "Tell him we've got engine trouble." He licked his lips as Smith climbed down to the saddle tank. "And ask him aboard for a drink. He'll like that."

Simeon muttered, "It'll never work."

But it did.

As hands took the launch's lines, the German lieutenant clambered up the slippery bulge of the tank. He was met by Smith, who wrapped his arms around the surprised German and drove a knife into his stomach. Other figures scrambled down into the launch, and in minutes it was over.

Marshall said, "Quickly now. Smith's landing party in the launch. Make the Italian seamen understand that they'll live only if they do as we say."

Simeon stared at him and then said, "I will take the launch. We'll move that moored freighter and get clear as best we can."

Their eyes held.

"I'll pick you up when the job's done." Without conscious thought Marshall thrust out his hand. "Good luck."

Simeon stared at his hand but made no effort to take it. Instead he said, *"Go to hell!"*

As the launch idled clear Marshall had to shake himself. The boom vessel lay unmoving as before. The launch, with two or three Italian seamen on deck, was steering toward the harbor. He waited, hardly daring to blink, as the boom vessel slowly began to winch open the antisubmarine net.

"Half ahead together. Follow the guard boat."

Nearer and nearer, until all at once the boom vessel was gliding abeam, an officer coming out to the bridge to salute as the U-boat entered harbor.

"He's closing the boom behind us, sir."

But Marshall was watching the little launch as it increased speed and dashed toward the moored freighter.

"Launch is alongside the freighter, sir."

"Slow ahead together."

Marshall tried not to think about the pillboxes on the hillside. He watched Cain and the casing party making a great pretense of preparing lines for mooring, and on the little jetty he saw a handful of yawning Italians.

Warwick was saying hoarsely, "Come on! Come on!"

Marshall snapped, "Watch the freighter. As soon as Simeon's party casts off we've got to move fast." He looked at his watch. Surely something would break soon.

Warwick gripped his arm. "The freighter's moving, sir!"

Marshall sprang to the speaking tube. "Full ahead! Port ten." He felt the hull lurch forward, the bow sluicing past the jetty and the mesmerized Italians.

"We've got to take the freighter's tow rope and warp her clear," he shouted. He conned the submarine around in one huge arc, while high in the freighter's bows he saw the marines lowering a hawser. Others held their submachine guns trained on the shore.

Somewhere in the distance a klaxon blared, and within seconds tracer ripped above the harbor, although it was obvious the garrison had been caught completely unprepared.

"Stop the port engine!"

He gritted his teeth as the freighter loomed over the conning tower. There was no time to rig fenders. No more time for anything. A bullet smashed into the tower and whimpered away over the water.

More machine-gun fire probed into the harbor, and Warwick yelled, "Open fire, sir?"

"Yes," he replied. "Stop starboard!"

The submarine's starboard bow shuddered and lurched below the freighter's great anchor, metal screaming in protest as both hulls ground together. Hands hauled on lines, dragging the hawser down onto the casing and to the forward mooring bollards.

The air seemed to split apart as Warwick's gun crews fired long bursts of cannon shells and tracer toward the nearest pillboxes. From one came an answering volley, and someone fell thrashing wildly in a pattern of blood. Against the dull steel it looked like black paint.

"Hawser secured, sir!"

"Tell the boarding party to get back here on the double!"

He winced as the deck gun crashed out. The shell exploded beside a pillbox and the firing stopped instantly.

There was a short whistle and a violent explosion. Devereaux was shouting, "Mortar! Above the bunker!"

Blythe yelled, "Chief reports he's ready to tow, sir!"

Marshall shouted, "Slow astern together!"

He saw the hawser tauten, felt the towering hull alongside shudder violently as a mortar shell exploded on the upper deck. But she was answering. Slowly and painfully, as the U-boat pulled astern, the freighter began to swing away from her original moorings. Another mortar shell shrieked down and burst on the ship, hurling splinters and fragments of steel in all directions.

Farther around and still farther, with gunfire blasting from every side, although there was so much smoke it was hard to tell friend from enemy.

"She's sinking!" Warwick was waving his cap like a madman. "Simeon has opened her cocks!"

It was true, and with the damage caused by the mortar, it would not take long before she settled on the bottom. A rope ladder had been thrown over, and Marshall saw some of the marines clambering down and being dragged bodily onto the casing.

A savage burst of bullets swept from the land, and when Marshall looked again he saw several of his men sprawled on the deck and others dragging themselves toward the conning tower.

A dull boom echoed and reechoed around the hills, and Blythe yelled, "Captain Lambert's charges have blown, sir!"

"That'll get 'em out of bed!" The lookout who had spoken clutched his chest and toppled with an amazed gasp. He was dead before he hit the deck.

Marshall snapped, "Prepare to cast off. Stop both motors." He could not wait another second.

Blythe shouted, "Here comes Lambert's mob!"

The returning raiding party were scampering behind the pill-boxes, and the air shook and crashed to their grenades. It must have been a nightmare for the Germans in the pillboxes. The grenades, the lethal clatter of submachine guns. Oblivion.

Cain cupped his hands and shouted, "Two more men to come from the freighter, sir!" Marshall ducked as more tracer slashed overhead. One of them had to be Simeon. He shaded his eyes and peered at the listing ship.

Then he saw them, Smith clambering down the ladder, with Simeon clutching his body like a drowning man.

Warwick gasped, "Simeon's bought it, sir."

Marshall shouted, "Open the forehatch." To Cain, "Help those two across!"

But just as they reached the casing a groan went up. A bullet had found Smith. He lost his hold and fell to the water, the foam around him turning crimson.

Marshall saw Simeon being dragged toward the hatch and shouted, *"Cast off!"*

When he looked again the forecasing was almost empty but for a cluster of dead sailors. Devereaux was struggling to get the heavy eye of the hawser off the bollard, while Cain tried to help him, one arm bloody and useless at his side.

Simeon was halfway through the hatch, his shoulder shining where a splinter had cut him down on the freighter's deck. He pushed someone away who was trying to aid him and lurched back onto the casing. Devereaux turned and saw him; then he, too, was down, his life splashed across the buckled plating. Simeon pushed Cain toward the hatch and then threw himself on the heavy hawser. Once, twice, and then it was free, splashing into the harbor.

He turned and stared toward the bridge, and seemed to grin. Or perhaps it was a grimace, for even as Simeon made to follow Cain he dropped to his knees and toppled slowly over the side.

Marshall said hoarsely, "Full astern. We'll pick up Lambert's party *now*."

The submarine hardly paused as she slid stern first past the small jetty where they had first seen the waiting Italians. It did not take long for the breathless marines to leap aboard. Lambert was with them, but he had less than half his men intact.

"Help those men below," Marshall shouted. "Then clear the deck. We must finish what we came for."

The stern was edging out into the harbor again. "Stern tube *ready*." He rested his forehead on the sights, watching the boom vessel through the crosswires. "Fire." He winced as more metal crashed into the hull, and saw Warwick pulling a wounded marine through the hatch like a sack.

The hull kicked very slightly as the torpedo burst from its tube. When the spray and fragments began to fall he saw the boom vessel toppling onto her side in a welter of smoke and flames. She would soon sink, and with her the boom.

He staggered to the forepart of the bridge again and saw what they had come all this way to destroy. With the freighter leaning at a steep angle on the opposite side of the harbor, the towering wall of concrete and the cavernous mouth of the bunker stood out as they had on Travis's neat diagrams.

"Standing by, one to four, sir."

Marshall shouted a reply. "Fire one. Carry on firing. Three-second intervals."

He concentrated on the pier at the entrance of the bunker. A powerful mobile derrick, and some big metal cases beyond. Bombs which would have been in the freighter tomorrow morning, en route to some German airfield.

The fourth torpedo had left the tube when the first exploded against the pier. After that it was impossible to tell one from the next, or night from day.

The torpedoes must have touched off some of the stacked bombs, and in an instant a massive explosion rocked the harbor, sending a small tidal wave creaming wildly toward the submarine. The noise went on and on, fading and then mounting again as the piled explosives detonated far inside the bunker, into the hillside itself.

Marshall coughed in the smoke which had almost blotted out the harbor. "Full ahead starboard. Wheel hard astarboard!"

Metal cracked into the bridge, and he found himself on the gratings, a terrible pain in his side. He felt Blythe pulling him toward the hatch, but managed to haul himself back to the speaking tube.

"Full ahead port. Wheel amidships." He moaned with pain.

Then he heard Gerrard's voice and saw him clinging to the screen at his side. "It's all right, sir. I've got her now."

Marshall stared at him. "Clear the boom area, Bob. Then get her down and run for it."

Gerrard said, "I can cope. You get below and have that gash cleaned." Blythe half carried Marshall to the hatch.

Then Gerrard crouched over the tube and snapped, "Steer one five zero. Maximum revolutions!" He glanced astern, but there was only smoke and the intermittent sound of underground explosions.

He thought of Marshall and what he had seen him do. What he had done for all of them. The victors.

THREE days later, surfaced, and with both diesels damaged almost beyond repair, the U-boat was steering west for Gibraltar. Marshall stood on the battered bridge, watching the sea.

They had done all they set out to do, and now there was nothing left but to reach Gibraltar before some new failure left them at the mercy of an enemy attack.

Two destroyers found them on the morning of the third day, and as they plowed toward the crawling submarine Blythe muttered, "I hope they've been *told*, that's all, sir."

They had. As the lights stammered back and forth Blythe asked thickly, "Their senior officer wants to know, sir. Do you wish to abandon or shall he take you in tow?"

Marshall turned and looked up at the flag overhead. The proper one, for once. Then at the full length of his ship. "We've come this far," he said. "I'll not leave her now." He touched the ache in his side. "Tell him neither. Tell him His Majesty's U-boat is rejoining the fleet."

"Signal from escort, sir. 'Congratulations.'"

Marshall smiled. "Thanks. I think we've earned them!"

Douglas Reeman lives in Bolitho Cottage, in a fashionable London suburb, surrounded by trophies of his lifelong love of the sea. In the hall—a watercolor of the motor torpedo boat on which he served in the North Sea during World War II. On the drawing-room wall—his own ceremonial Royal Navy sword and a painting depicting a dozen of the heroines of his modern sea stories—ships, every one. Guarding the front door of the cottage, but not at all out of place, is a nineteenth-century naval swivel gun, for under the pseudonym Alexander Kent, Reeman also writes historical romances about Horatio Bolitho, fictional nineteenth-century sailor.

His Majesty's U-Boat is his fifteenth "Reeman," and much of the background is authentic. A German submarine, *U-570*, was in fact captured by the British, rechristened the HMS *Graph* and then used against her previous owners. In 1943 the Germans did have a secret weapon in the form of a radio-controlled bomb which could be launched and directed by one of their aircraft. After the Italian invasion the Allied navies often took part in the kind of cloak-and-dagger operation that "Buster" Browning attempted with the Italian general. In real life one of the Allied officers to undertake such a mission was American General Mark Clark.

Douglas Reeman

Reeman, who served in all the major theaters of war, learned about much of this background firsthand.

"I firmly believe that an author should have some experiences to offer his readers," Reeman says. "In my case the experience of war at sea came swiftly. I entered the navy straight from school, and my mind was bare, like an unused canvas. I took part in seaborne invasions, sailed in convoys and learned what it was like to feel a ship sinking under me and to see others destroyed in a dozen different ways. Good friends lost, sights too awesome to understand—they all left their mark on me."

When peacetime came, Reeman became a policeman and then a welfare worker. Eventually he bought a twenty-five-ton yacht, aboard which he and his wife cruised for seven years, and on which he decided to write his first books.

That was sixteen years ago and he has never had to search for a subject. For Douglas Reeman it has always been fighting men and the sea.   —N.D.B., London

ACKNOWLEDGMENTS

Page 3: *Fall Plowing,* an oil painting (1931) by Grant Wood, is used by permission of Deere & Company, Moline, Illinois.

Page 207, lines 6-10 and lines 22-25: from *Journal of a Soul* by Pope John XXIII, translated by Dorothy White, © 1965, are quoted by permission of Geoffrey Chapman Ltd. and McGraw-Hill Book Company.